ALIGNED

The Complete Series

ELLA MILES

EllaMiles.com

ella@ellamiles.com

Editing: Jenny Sims, Editing4Indies

Books in Aligned Series

Aligned: Volume 1
Aligned: Volume 2
Aligned: Volume 3
Aligned: Volume 4
Aligned: The Complete Series Boxset

ALIGNED: VOLUME 1

Chapter One

ALEXA

I feel my hand slipping from his, but I'm not ready to let go. I reach out, desperately trying to grab hold of anything to keep him with me. I feel silk beneath my fingers. I pull hard. He has to come back to me, but all I'm left with is a torn piece of green silk fabric.

THE TIRES SQUEAL as the cab jolts to a halt in front of my condo building, slamming me into the back of the passenger seat. I slowly unstick myself from the seat before trying to catch my breath. My heart is fluttering faster than a hummingbird's wings. I attempt to breathe but only manage a wheezing sound. I wave at the cab driver to try to get his attention, to alert him that I can't breathe, but he is engrossed in his phone, not paying any attention to me.

I feel my anxiety increasing. Hot and dizzy. My chest is tightening around my heart — squeezing it to death, and not letting it beat. I'm going to die right here in the backseat of a cab that smells like sweat and smoke, next to an old fast food wrapper. My skin is burning hotter. In a matter of seconds, I expect to be engulfed in flames. I'm going to *die*. I claw at the door to let in the air so I can breathe. But it doesn't budge. Trapped without air, my lungs burn with each breath. Just let death be quick. "Miss," a voice says barely audible over my pounding heart. I wait for the voice to come back. "Miss Blakely," it says this time calmly. "You are having a panic attack. You are not going to die. Take a deep breath," says the voice I now recognize as my therapist. I take a deep breath wincing at the deep burn as I fill my lungs with air again. I take another deep breath and listen to the rhythm of the waves I faintly hear in the distance. Each breath is calmer than the previous one. Each breath expands my lungs and the space around my heart to release it from its cage and let it beat.

"Miss, the ride's thirty-four fifty." I open my eyes to look at the cab driver, not my therapist, sitting in front of me. He wears an annoyed expression as he waits for me to hand him his money. I'm still visibly shaking from my attack, but at least I'm breathing. I dig a shaky, sweaty hand into my purse and pull out two twenties. I awkwardly climb out of the cab with my two plastic bags of groceries, purse, and crutches in hand. The cab speeds off the second I close the door; the driver doesn't bother to help me into the building.

"Asshole," I mumble under my breath.

I look up at the towering building in front of me. Afternoon light bounces off its shiny, modern surface making me squint. Floor-to-ceiling windows cover every surface and make it look more like an office building. If it weren't for the balconies protruding from the sides, nobody would know that people live behind its icy façade. I sigh at the daunting task before me. I have to make it through the lobby, to the elevator, and up to my eighth-floor condo before I can collapse on my bed.

I take a deep breath of calm, salty, ocean air before I move my crutches forward, swing my body through, and land on my left leg. I repeat the process several times before I make it to the doors of my condo building. Each step I take is agony. I'm already sweating profusely from just the first five steps. I'd prefer to just pass out on the cold marble floor in the lobby, rather than take the next hundred steps to my unit. I open the door and move through as quickly as possible, but the door swings shut and catches my right crutch. I tumble onto my ass for the fifth time this week.

Shit! When will I learn? I lie on the cool floor for several seconds, not moving. At least I got my wish. If it weren't for the large windows surrounding me, the light almost blinding as it bounces off the large chandelier above me, taunting me with its beauty that I no longer possess, it would be so easy to just fall asleep right here on the cold floor. I look to my left. Most of my groceries have rolled and tumbled well out of my reach toward the sleek white couches lining the wall of windows that look out over the beach. It's not worth my effort to gather them all. I'll just order pizza again. Eating healthy is not worth the trouble. I glance to my right where a large white desk sits vacant. Thank god, no one witnessed my embarrassing fall. I close my eyes, contemplating my next move.

"Ma'am, are you okay?" a deep voice says to me.

"I'm not a ma'am," I say, not bothering to open my eyes or move. He's confirmed that I'm not dead, so I expect him to leave me alone. I have learned after living in LA for the past three months that the people here aren't any more considerate than the people in NYC are. I exhale when I hear the lobby door swing shut again.

"I'm such a disaster," I mumble to myself.

The same deep voice laughs. "A beautiful disaster." I open my eyes and see golden brown eyes peering curiously at me. I slowly sit up and gulp at the sight in front of me. He grins and my cheeks burn a bright shade of red. His dark brown hair is tousled; it doesn't look like he's ever combed it. Dark stubble covers his strong chin and neck. He's not wearing a shirt - just shorts and running shoes, which allow me to see every perfect muscle glistening from the sweat covering his body. Tattoos cover his torso and arms. Beautiful. I realize I'm staring, but I couldn't tear my eyes away from him if I wanted. He's too beautiful. I feel my heart racing again, my breath quickening and the sweat forming have nothing to do with my earlier panic attack.

He gently places one finger under my chin, raising it to close my gaping mouth. I flush a shade redder, but I don't stop staring. He has a gleam in his eyes as he looks intently from my mouth to my eyes and then my forehead.

"Shit, you're bleeding," he says, breaking the spell that has come over me.

"I'm sure I'm fine. I just need to get back to my condo," I say as I begin to stand. He offers his hand to me, and I take it as he easily pulls me into a standing position. He holds onto my sweaty hand for much longer than what is necessary for me to regain my balance. I stare up at him now as he towers over me before he quickly jogs around the lobby picking up every apple, orange, and tube of Pringles that rolled out of my bags when I fell. My mouth gapes open again, but no words come out. I just stand frozen.

"Breathe," he says, smiling. My face heats up again as I release a breath I didn't know I had been holding. *Get it together.* You can't be into him. It's too soon. I reach into my pocket to feel the warm green fabric there. It reminds me of what I've lost and what I am not willing to lose again. I take a pained breath as I let the guilt wash away.

"Come on. Let me help you to your condo."

My mouth moves to form the word 'no,' but it would be so much easier with his help. So instead, I follow him to the bank of elevators at the far end of the lobby. He presses the button and the doors open immediately. We enter in silence.

"What floor?" he asks, as the doors begin closing.

"Eighth," I respond, trying not to look at him and embarrass myself again.

But I still see the crooked grin he flashes me out of the corner of my eye. This time I see a hint of dimples I didn't see before. "So what's your name?"

"Alex ... ah," I respond in a voice barely audible. *Dammit!* Why is it so hard for me to act like a normal human being around this man? He's good looking, sure, but he has heartbreaker written all over that smug grin.

"Alex what?"

I open my mouth to correct him but snap it shut quickly. My name is Alexa, not Alex, but coming from his mouth, Alex sounds perfect. He doesn't need to know anything else about me. As soon as we get to my condo, I plan to get rid of him and will never see him again.

"Just Alex. So who is my rescuer?"

A surprised look crosses his face, confusing me. "The name's Landon. Just Landon."

I give him a weak smile back. The elevator doors open, and he holds them to give me time to get out without crashing again. We reach my condo after winding down the long hall, and I dig through my purse to find my keys. I fumble with the key in the door before it finally unlatches. I walk past the kitchen that opens into my living room, heading straight for my couch. Collapsing on it, I let my crutches fall to the floor, finally feeling like I can breathe again. I frown at the closed drapes across from me, blocking my view of the ocean. I'll have to get up again to open them, so I can see the waves as I drift off to sleep.

"You can just set the bags on the counter in the kitchen," I say, not bothering to turn my head to him.

"Did you just move in?" he asks, striding around my condo, examining all the boxes lining most of my walls. He walks as if he owns the place. Not like a stranger should. I look around at the neatly stacked boxes that I haven't been able to bring myself to unpack. When I do, it means this is real. This is my home. And I don't know if this should be my home or not.

"Sort of," I answer.

I hear Landon digging around in one of the boxes in the kitchen, but I don't have the strength to lift myself off the couch. He can rob me for all I care, just as long as he doesn't take this couch so I can sleep. I hear him run the faucet in the kitchen and then walk toward the couch. He kneels on the floor next to my head before pressing the wet washcloth to my forehead. I shiver despite the washcloth being warm. He continues to hold the washcloth to my forehead for several minutes. Neither of us really speaks, and I just close my eyes to try to relax. I expect him to ask questions about my leg or my still bruised face, but he doesn't. I realize, as I look down at my leg, that he can't see the damage. My long skirt keeps it hidden. I've never been more thankful to be wearing a skirt in my life. If he saw my damaged leg, he wouldn't be able to get out of here fast enough. He wouldn't be wasting any time on me, even if he is just trying to be nice. The scars covering my face, arms, and chest are usually enough to scare everyone away, which allows me to spend most of my time by myself. And that's how I like it.

He removes the washcloth. "I think the bleeding has stopped. Do you need help unpacking?" It takes me longer to answer than it should, as the smell of his sweet sweat and deodorant has distracted me. I'm a little shocked at how nice he is being. It seems out of character for the model bad boy in front of me.

"No, I can manage," I say, as I move to get up to let him out.

"You stay," he commands as if I'm a dog. "I can let myself out."

I lie back down, despite how I hate when people order me around. I just really need to sleep. The afternoons are the only time I get a reprieve from the darkness that consumes me at night, giving me only a few hours to sleep before the darkness comes for me.

I watch as he moves to a box labeled pillows and blankets. He pulls a blanket out and drapes it over me. I close my eyes to hide the tear I feel escaping and falling down my face. The blanket still smells like him.

Chapter Two

LANDON

You stumbled into my life
A beautiful mess
With fighting words
Not to be messed with.

I PUT her last frozen pizza into the freezer, adding to the other dozen pizzas already there. I have finished the last of her groceries, although groceries might be too strong a word. Junk food is more like it. I don't have a clue how she can look so strong and in shape with the food she is putting into her body.

"Alex, can I get you anything before I go?" I walk into the living room where I left her.

"Alex," I try again.

She snores in response. I chuckle and take a seat on the ottoman next to the couch. I brush her auburn hair off her face. She has two healed scars on her left cheek that look like warrior paint. Another scar jets out from her right eyebrow up her forehead. The small cut that was bleeding next to it is nothing compared to these scars. Most women I know would have caked on the makeup trying to cover the scars but not Alex. She displays the scars as easily as she shows off her toned arms. They are just who she is, displaying the struggles she has gone through that she doesn't need to hide. I move my focus to her small nose that has a simple diamond stud piercing I didn't notice before.

She groans. I pause waiting for her to wake up, but she doesn't. But now I can't do anything but stare at her gorgeous plump lips. I want to taste them, but I restrain myself.

I continue looking over the rest of her body. She's wearing a tank top showing off small perky boobs with tattoos covering her chest and toned arms. A long flowing skirt covers her legs preventing me from seeing what I can only imagine are toned, delicious legs. I want those legs wrapped around my body as I drive my cock deep inside her tight pussy.

I'm practically drooling as I pant over this woman. *Shit, when is the last time I had a good fuck?* It's been a couple of weeks since Caroline, and I haven't had time to pick up any of the usuals at a bar. I look down at this snoring beauty. I want her, and I'm willing to work for her if it means I'll get to bury myself in her later. She wants me, too. Her stares and breathing earlier said enough. I get out my phone and text Drew.

Me: Meet me outside room 823.

Drew: Why?

Me: Just come.

I pocket my phone and head to the kitchen that sits less than ten feet from her couch, where I'm already somewhat familiar, and begin opening boxes. I look around her small condo that consists of a small kitchen connected to the living room with one door leading to what I assume is her bedroom. The whole place could fit in the bedroom of my condo that sits ten floors above this one. I will never understand how people can live in such small spaces without feeling suffocated by the walls. I need more room than this just to breathe. I finish putting her basic dishes away into the simple white cabinets when I hear a knock on the door. I open the door and find myself looking eye-to-eye with a frowning Drew dressed in his usual business suit.

Drew sighs. "Please tell me you are on your way to the studio."

"No, we are unpacking today. I still have writer's block anyway. Going to the studio isn't going to help."

"And unpacking is going to help?"

I ignore Drew and walk back to the kitchen. Nothing can help my writer's block. I've tried everything – from forcing myself to sit down every day and write to trying to live as many experiences as possible to find inspiration. Nothing works. My career is going to be over before it even really gets started. I'll end up being the failure my father always thought I was going to be.

"You can finish unpacking everything in the kitchen. I'll start in the bedroom," I say.

"What the fuck, Landon? I have meetings all day. And you have to get to the studio today." Drew stomps into the kitchen trying to intimidate me with his flaring nostrils and glaring eyes.

"As my manager, I pay you to do what I say. So unpack and stop your bitching." I glare back and hand him a plate.

"As your brother, I have the right to tell you to go fuck yourself. Whose condo is this, anyway?"

"My friend, Alex," I say, heading to the bedroom before Drew realizes this condo belongs to a woman and not a man. A woman who has piqued my curiosity. She might give me the escape I need from the pressures of my reality. I peek over the couch as I walk past the living room. She lies peacefully and continues to snore loudly.

I walk into her bedroom and am surprised to see only three boxes stacked in the corner. Her perfectly made bed is covered with white linens and a turquoise throw pillow, which is the only clue so far of what this woman likes. A small tan nightstand with a tag sticking off it sits perfectly aligned to the bed. I go over to the tag that reads "Jim's Rentals." I see another tag attached to the bed and realize she's rented all of her furniture. Why would someone rent furniture that other people have used? She can't be that poor if she can afford to live in this condo building, although this is a smaller unit than most in the building. She must just frequently move and doesn't want to have to take a lot of big bulky furniture with her.

I check the tiny bathroom that is connected, and there is only one small box of toothbrushes and hair supplies in there. Her closet already has some clothes hanging grouped by color and style, but I'm shocked at how few items are in there. I've been in enough women's closets to know that they are always bursting with clothes.

I begin unpacking. Going through most of her boxes, I don't find anything that reveals much about this woman. The clothes in her closet reveal nothing. Only that she doesn't have a particular favorite style. She has fancy and comfortable, trendy and classic clothes. She can't seem to make up her mind; instead, she prefers to have a little of everything. I walk to her nightstand with a handful of phone chargers. I pull on the drawer to open it and place them in, but the drawer doesn't budge. I try again when I see the small lock holding the drawer close. Weird that she locks the drawer of her nightstand. Maybe she's into kinky stuff and keeps her handcuffs and whips in there. I can wish anyway.

I pull the last item out of the box and am surprised when I see it's a framed picture of her and a guy - a guy I immediately hate. He's a slick looking guy in a suit with perfectly combed hair and no tattoos or indiscretions in sight. But he still doesn't look good enough for her. I guess I won't be fucking her after all. *I'm a dick*. I fuck women all the time without any intention of more than one night, but I'm not a big enough dick to fuck another man's woman. I put the frame on her nightstand before heading to the living room where Drew has started unpacking.

"So have you fucked your friend, Alex, or are you planning on fucking her?" Drew asks.

I glare at Drew. "None of your business."

Drew rolls his eyes. "Because if you haven't fucked her yet, I don't think throwing all of her stuff in cabinets and drawers is really considered helping her unpack."

I clench my jaw. "Just help me finish so we can get out of here and move on to more productive things."

Ten minutes later, we have finished unpacking all of the boxes, albeit not in the most organized manner. At least she won't have to deal with the boxes anymore. I glance around the condo that still has bare cream walls; no pictures or decorations sit on any of the hard surfaces other than the one frame in her bedroom. There is nothing here that shows that a woman is living here. I look back at Alex, disappointed that she didn't wake up. I would have loved to see her emerald eyes one last time. I make a phone call before I follow Drew out of her condo and out of her life.

Chapter Three

ALEXA

I feel him fighting against my grip. We will both drown if I don't let go. But I can't.

MY PHONE BUZZES on the ottoman in front of the couch, waking me from my nightmare. Tears continue to fall from my face as I stare at my phone, but I don't remember putting it there. I slowly sit up and look out the window to see that it's dark. I must have fallen asleep. I continue to stare oddly at the open window – that I don't remember opening – when I feel the salty tears burning my cheek. I wipe the tears on the back of my hand and pick up my phone. The word 'Landon' flashes on the screen. I didn't give him my number. Did I? I open the message.

Landon: I hope you got plenty of rest and like your condo. You sleep like a rock. Text if you need anything.

What does he mean by that? I get up and hobble to the kitchen before realizing I haven't tripped over any boxes. I look around my condo and don't see a single box in sight. I open drawers that are filled with silverware and cabinets filled with dishes. 'Filled' being the keyword because, as I open a cabinet, several plastic cups tumble out, thumping against the dark wood floor. I don't bother to pick them up; I just open the next cabinet that has cups, plates, and Tupperware all mixed. I open another and it's more of the same. *A giant mess.* I look around the living room and see DVDs piled next to the TV stand and my blankets thrown haphazardly over the back of the couch. I hurry into my bedroom and find clothes hanging in my closet. Summer and winter, pants and shirts, dresses and sweatshirts all mingling together. I open the drawers filled with clothes. I'm almost shocked that my underwear and socks are in different drawers, but that's the only thing he thought to separate. Holy shit! How did I not wake up when he was doing all of this? And I think I prefer the boxes to this unorganized mess. Not to mention how violated I feel right now. He went through *my* personal things. Things I haven't been able to bring myself to touch, and he did it in the course of a few hours.

My nostrils are flaring as I head back to the living room where my phone is laying. I glare at the screen, my face burning red as I type a response.

Me: What the hell? I said you could put away the groceries not put away everything in my home!

Landon: You're welcome.

Me: What the fuck were you thinking?

Landon: Just trying to help. Now you can spend time with your boyfriend instead of unpacking.

I throw the phone onto the couch too furious to respond. He must have felt sorry for me. Well, I'm not going to be his charity case. I can do things for myself.

I hobble on my crutches back to the kitchen and open the fridge to make something for dinner. I'm going to need the energy if I have to spend the rest of the night reorganizing everything in my condo. *Son of a bitch.* Sitting in my fridge is three takeout dishes from a restaurant called Antonella's Italian Bistro with baking instructions taped to them. Landon definitely thinks I'm incapable of taking care of myself. I immediately feel my attraction for him plummet. I sure as hell am not going to be hanging out with a guy like that.

Sighing, I take out the pizza dish and stick it in the oven. There is no sense in letting good food go to waste.

"Hi, this is Abby with *Inspire* magazine. May I speak with Alexa Blakely?" I hear the bubbly voice on the other end of the line. I feel my body tense. My hand shakes as I place the cup of coffee in my hand onto the small patio table in front of me; the sun is barely peeking up over the horizon providing me with little light. What in the hell could a magazine want with me? I'm damaged goods.

"Hi Abby, this is Alexa," I say in a friendly, cautious voice.

"Oh Alexa, I'm so glad I reached you. I'm sorry if I woke you. You don't know how many different numbers I have tried. We are in a bit of a jam. Our photographer backed out. I guess he has the flu or something. But are you available Thursday to do a shoot for us?"

I rub my swollen eyes that didn't rest at all last night. I don't tell her that I didn't sleep and am always up before the sun. "Um ... I don't think that's the best idea, Abby. I'm still recovering ..."

"Oh, my gosh! I'm so sorry. I completely forgot about your accident. How are you doing, sweetie?"

I smile. "Still recovering. Still on crutches."

"Good to hear. Why don't you come by our offices tomorrow and we can discuss all the details? We will make sure you have assistants and have whatever else you need. You are the best in the business, and we could really use the best for our one-year anniversary cover," she begs.

"I guess I could come by tomorrow. But I'm not promising ..."

"Wonderful!" Abby squeals interrupting me again. "I'll see you tomorrow at eight to discuss everything."

"See you tomorrow," I say before ending the call. What am I doing? I haven't done a shoot since the accident. Can you forget how to do something you've spent your whole life doing? Can you stop loving it, too? Did the accident take another thing I love away from me? I would have no purpose left in my life if it took my love of photography away from me, too.

I guess there's only one way to find out. I head back inside and put on another long skirt and tank top before throwing my hair on top of my head in a loose bun. I put my camera around my neck, along with a towel, and head down to the beach.

I MAKE it down to the beach easily as I'm feeling full of energy. The waves are crashing gently against the warm sand as the sun rises higher over the horizon behind me. Few people have gathered on the beach yet this early, so no one sees me struggle. I place my crutches into the sand, take my first step, and watch as the crutches immediately sink into the sand. They provide me no support, almost knocking me off balance. I try again with the same result. I throw down my crutches in frustration, take off my flip-flop, and hop on my good leg several feet down the beach.

Finally, I collapse onto the sand in exhaustion. But it was worth it. The feel of the warm sand is amazing. I lie on the sand for a good twenty minutes before sitting up and grabbing my camera still looped around my neck. I stare at it intently, as if it's going to jump out of my hands and start taking photos on its own. Before the accident, photography was my life, but I haven't even touched this camera since.

I hear a man and his son laughing several feet from me, holding hands as they walk along the beach. They seem to be enjoying the beautiful morning before the beach becomes crowded with tourists. I position the camera and take several pictures, but it doesn't look right. I'm almost on autopilot as I make adjustments and try again. Before looking at the second set of pictures, I take a deep breath. I grin as I look at the images. I haven't forgotten.

I continue to get lost in my own world taking photos. I feel like me again, if only for a brief moment sitting here on the beach. I have a purpose again. I make more adjustments on my camera before bringing it back up to my face to find my next muse. I lock my gaze on a fit male running along the beach. I can't take my eyes off him as he continues to run toward where I sit on the sand. I take several pictures of him running before I realize who the gorgeous man is. A man who I am no longer attracted to after our encounter yesterday. *Yeah right*, that voice inside me says. As Landon continues to run toward me glistening in sweat, I feel my breath catch in my throat only proving that little voice right.

"Crap," I whisper to myself. I try to sink into the sand, covering myself with my towel. Now would be a great time for quicksand to swallow me up so I don't have to deal with this hot asshole. But it's too late. A crooked grin forms on Landon's face and his eyes focus on me as he runs in an easygoing manner toward me.

I take several slow breaths trying to calm my breathing and erratic heartbeat, but it doesn't work. This man is sexy as hell, and I forget how mad I am at him for treating me like an invalid when I see his grin. He stretches his arms over his head casually before sitting down next to me.

"Hey, gorgeous, if I didn't know better, I would think you're the paparazzi," Landon says.

I frown finding his comment odd. "Why would anyone think I was paparazzi? Although I could probably make some good money if I sold these photos to teenage girls online."

Landon laughs causing his tight ab muscles to contract and flex drawing my attention back to his fit body. "No reason. You just looked like what I would imagine they look like. Trying to hide beneath your towel, sinking into the sand."

"I was not hiding," I say, fidgeting with my towel that is now covering my legs.

"Yes, you were," he says, laughing again.

I shove him on the shoulder to get him to stop laughing, but he just laughs harder as my shove doesn't move his hard muscles an inch.

"What the hell were you thinking going through all of the stuff in my place? That was such an invasion of my privacy! And if you are going to help someone out, at least learn how to help them. Shoving dishes into the cabinets isn't helping. I spent my entire night reorganizing your mess." I shove him again in frustration.

Landon playfully puts his hands in the air in surrender. "Whoa, calm down. I didn't invade your privacy. Honestly, I figured you would wake up at some point, and we'd get caught. And ..."

"Wait," I say, interrupting him. "What do you mean 'we'? Who else was in my condo?"

"Just my brother. It's no big deal really."

"Well, it's a fucking big deal to me!" I cannot believe that this complete stranger has the nerve to do this.

He just smiles back at me. "You swear a lot, don't you?"

"Only when I'm pissed. And you seem to piss me off a lot," I say. "Stop changing the subject."

"I'm sorry. It won't happen again," he says, smirking at me.

Dammit, now I'm smiling. "Only because it can't happen again. All my stuff is unpacked."

"What are you doing out here anyway?" he asks, with a more serious tone to his voice.

"I could ask you the same question. I would guess you were running, but you're barely breaking a sweat," I tease.

"When that leg of yours heals, you'll have to run with me. Then we will see who the real pussy is," Landon says, giving me a challenging look.

"That wouldn't be a challenge for me. But since I don't plan on seeing you again after today, we won't ever know. I don't socialize with people who think I'm an invalid."

"I think you're scared that I would beat you." Frowning, he says, "Or maybe that boyfriend of yours wouldn't like it."

"Fine. If you're up for an ass whipping, then I will gladly deliver."

He grins when he realizes he won the argument. "So what are we betting?"

I frown. What have I agreed to? There is no way I'll ever be able to run again. And I really don't want to see him again. Distance is what I need to dampen the burning desire surging through my veins. If I continue to see him, there is no telling what kind of mess I'll end up in.

"Landon!" a high-pitched voice screams, saving me from answering. I look around but can't quite figure out where the voice is coming from. From the look on Landon's face, he knows the body that goes with that voice. His nostrils flare and his face reddens, but I don't miss the look of desire growing in his eyes as he looks at the woman growing nearer.

Landon brushes a strand of my auburn hair behind my ear before leaning in close. His lips are almost touching my ear. "You can whip my ass any day. In the meantime, we will have to find other ways to meet again. I have to go."

Before I have a chance to answer, Landon jogs back to the condo building and disappears inside.

"Where did Landon go and what were you two doing together?" I hear the same screechy voice say.

I look up to see a gorgeous, tall woman with long flowy blond curls wearing a perfectly fitted sundress. The woman looks at my camera.

"Oh, you're the paparazzi. If I had gotten here just a few minutes earlier, it would have been the perfect opportunity for you," she says, before digging into her Prada purse. "Well, here's my card in case you want to get a photo later." She hands me the small card with the words 'Caroline Parker—Actress' written on it before heading inside the condo building. *Why the hell does everyone think I'm the paparazzi?* Sure, I have a camera, and she's an actress, but that doesn't automatically make me the paparazzi. These people are way too hung up on themselves.

I cross my arms allowing myself to sulk as she follows Landon. She's beautiful and is obviously with him. If Landon is attracted to that woman, there is no chance a short brunette covered in tattoos who's damaged would get his attention - not that I want his attention. Ah, hell what am I doing?! Guilt immediately overcomes me. I reach into my pocket. Feeling the worn silk between my fingers. Reminding me of him. One thing I know for sure is I need to stay the hell away from Landon.

Chapter Four

LANDON

But I kept coming back
Trying my best
To break down your walls
To find a way in

"LANDON! WAIT!" Caroline screeches.

I ignore her and head toward the stairs that are really only used as a fire escape and occasionally by maintenance. No one wants to walk up hundreds of steps in a grungy stairwell that smells like piss, but I could use another workout today, so I begin climbing the stairs two at a time.

"Landon!" I hear her screech again.

I stop on the second floor to face her.

"What do you want, Caroline?"

"You. I miss you. It's been weeks." To my surprise, she starts climbing the stairs. She's a slim girl, but not exactly in shape, so by the time she reaches me, she's panting hard.

"You should have thought about that before you banged that model," I snarl.

"Baby, this is what we do, though. We mess up and then we forgive each other. We fuck and forgive. You know we are meant to be together." Caroline presses her body against mine. My cock immediately responds to her body pressed against mine. Her fake boobs are now pushed high above her dress. She presses her lips to my ear, and I respond. I grab her waist, and she automatically wraps her legs around me as I shove her against the wall kissing her hard. I taste every drop of desperation dripping from her lips as my tongue presses into her mouth. But I don't care. It's been way too long. I need my cock buried deep in her tight cunt. Punishing her cheating pussy over and over until she screams for me to stop.

I grab her breast releasing it from the dress encasing it. She doesn't fight me as I do. Instead, she moans. She lets me control her; expose her to the world in a stairwell anyone could enter. But this dirty whore doesn't care. She just wants a good fuck and my money to buy another dress after I ruin this one. I rip the dress in half and now she's fully exposed. She's not wearing anything under the dress.

"Yes, fuck me right here, baby. I can't wait," she pants. But she's not in control here, despite how she tries to control every other aspect of my life. I flip her around pressing her hard against the brick wall. I bare my teeth and bite her shoulder; my erection grows as she screams out in pain and ecstasy. She tries to reach for my hard length, but I pin her arms behind her back. I press myself into her ass as I breathe into her neck.

"I'm going to fuck your ass." She pants as I smack her ass hard. It glistens bright red as I smack it again and again. She screams when I hit her sensitive flesh. I cover her mouth with my hand muffling her screams. "You deserve to be punished."

I move my hands to my pants. Pulling them down enough to release my cock. "Tell me you deserve to be punished."

"Punish me. I'm a dirty whore that deserves this," she pants.

I push her harder against the wall with my hand at her throat so that she's barely breathing. I move my cock to her ass when I see it. A tiny heart-shaped tattoo just above her ass.

"What's this?" I say, pointing at the tattoo.

She tries to speak, but she only manages a high-pitched wheeze. I release her throat and step back from her. "What is this?" I say again in a growl.

She glances to her back to see where I'm pointing.

"Oh, that. It's fake. But I can get it for real if you'd like. We could get something together and remember the pain every time you fuck me."

But I'm not with her anymore. My mind immediately goes to the heart-shaped tattoo covering Alex's chest, though hers is much darker. More sinister, representing a more complicated love. Not a Hallmark representation of sweet, endearing love. Alex's tattoo represents what love really is – a complicated mess of emotions and heartbreak. A mess that I want a lot more than this bitch in front of me.

"No," I say. Turning from Caroline, I tuck myself back in my pants and begin climbing the stairs again.

"What do you mean no? I'll fuck you any way you want. However dirty or painful. No one else can give it to you as I can." Caroline screeches at me, but I keep climbing.

"And what am I supposed to do now? You destroyed my clothes, you monster!"

I stop. I am a monster. A monster who doesn't give a shit about the women he fucks. I just want to live with no plans for tomorrow. I dig into my wallet and pull out a wad of twenties. I drop them. They scatter into a mess landing all over the stairwell below.

"For the dress," I say. I run up the rest of the stairs without looking back.

I SLAM the door to my condo. I feel like I can breathe again once I've entered the large open space occupied by my oversized, luxurious dark-wood furniture. No one would mistake this place for anything but what it is: a man's escape. I head to my makeshift studio on the top floor of the condo I share with Drew, passing my bedroom as I do. I slam the door to the studio, although it doesn't bring me the satisfaction for which I'm looking. I'm still red and breathing fast. Running up eighteen flights of stairs did nothing to ease my frustration. I've never before let myself get this sexually frustrated. I usually just go out and fuck the next thing that moves, but I just turned down my chance. I sit down at the piano and try to get my frustration out through the dark chords I play on repeat. Slamming the keys.

I write the chords and then pick up playing the song. I continue this process of playing then writing for a good hour before I realize what I'm doing. I crumple the paper up and toss it into the trash can. I'm not going to let her control me. I'm not going to write another song about her. I don't want to make a career singing only heartbreak songs about Caroline. She doesn't deserve any more recognition or fame.

I plop onto the couch, not caring that I'm sending papers flying as I do. I should really hire a maid although I thrive in the mess. I'll have Drew do it later maybe. I think about taking a nap or jacking off. Then I could write later. But I've been putting it off for months now. I need a new song, and fast, or the label is going to make me record a song I didn't write - a song in which I don't believe.

I sit up and look through the pile of papers that are scattered on the floor. Most are random thoughts I've had while running. Others are interesting people I have met in coffee shops, restaurants, or just randomly watching from my balcony. None of them inspires me. None of them gives me what I'm looking for.

I picture that tattoo again, the emerald eyes, and the smart mouth that goes with them. A woman I'm desperate to have. Just for a night. To fuck and own. Then I can move on. God, I'm such a dick for even considering fucking her when she's involved with another guy. But I don't care. I want her. I snatch a blank piece of paper off the pile. I write the first words I've written in three months since my single dropped.

You stumbled into my life
A ~~gorgeous~~ beautiful mess
With fighting ~~mouth~~ words

Not to be messed with.

But I kept coming ~~fighting~~ back
Trying my best
To ~~crash through~~ break down your walls
To find a way in.

Chapter Five

ALEXA

Another wave crashes over us. Pounding us over and over. Sucking our last breath away with it.

I WALK into the grand building covered from floor to ceiling in windows. I immediately walk toward the elevators at the back, not bothering to enjoy the elegant and beautiful modern architecture as most others would. I don't pay attention to the large expansive windows, the dark beams, or the plants and flowers making the entrance feel more like a garden than an office building. Instead, I move my crutches as fast as I can across the marble floor and try my best to not trip. I don't want to draw any more attention to myself.

I make it to the elevator without noticing anyone's stares. I press the button and immediately the doors open. I make my way inside the elevator and press the button to the twenty-eighth floor. A tall man in a suit enters the elevator just as the doors are about to close. He hits the thirtieth floor. I don't look at him, but I feel immediately when his eyes burn into my leg. Well, what's left of my right leg. I'm wearing an A-line skirt and jacket. Even though it's an appropriate outfit for a business meeting, I feel completely naked. I feel completely exposed by my stump of a leg that just barely protrudes from beneath the mid-thigh length skirt. The rest of today I'm going to have to deal with assholes like this staring at my leg as if I've just sprouted tentacles. I'm no longer human to them.

"What happened to you?" the man asks, wide-eyed, as he continues to stare at my leg.

"Car accident," I say, hoping this elevator will move faster so I can get off.

"I'm so sorry. That's such a horrible thing to happen to such a beautiful woman. Shouldn't you be in bed resting?"

"No," I say, as the doors open and I walk off. I have no idea if I'm on the right floor, but I can't be with that man for another second.

I move toward the receptionist's desk that, thank god, has the words 'Inspire' written in large block letters on the wall behind the floating modern desk. Sharp, crisp flowers are the only thing on the desk besides a computer screen and phone. A man and a woman both sit behind the desk. The man meets my eyes first, giving me a smile that's too bright.

"Hello. I'm Braden. Welcome to *Inspire* magazine. How may I help you?"

"Hi, I'm Alexa Blakely here for a meeting with Abby."

"Oh, wonderful." He presses a button and picks up the phone. "Miss Blakely is here. Should I send her back?" He listens intently to the response, which must have been affirmative as he gets up from his desk after hanging up.

"If you will follow me, I'll show you to Miss Novak's office. Would you like me to carry your bag for you?" he asks while staring intently at my oversized purse.

I close my eyes tightly trying to calm my growing frustration. This man would have never offered to carry any other woman's purse. Only because I'm on crutches does he assume I need help. I open my eyes back up and plaster a fake smile on my face. "No, I have it. Thanks."

The man starts heading toward Abby's office, walking no faster than a snail would. He makes sure to hold open every door for me while asking me several times if I need to rest during our lengthy walk to the far side of the floor. The only reason I would need to stop is to pummel his so-called manners out of him.

We reach the end of a long hallway filled with offices enclosed by glass windows and doors when I see a petite woman with jet black hair and blue streaks jump up from her desk, running toward us.

"Oh, my god! Are you Alexa Blakely?"

"Yes," I say, smiling and feeling a little like a rock star.

She squeals before embracing me in a hug, causing me to drop one of my crutches.

"I'm Abby Novak. I'm so excited to meet and work with you. I'm a big fan of your work. You are one of the reasons I majored in photography in college. Although, I realized quickly that I'm better at directing than actual photography."

"Thanks," I say, feeling old. Although, this woman can't be more than three or four years younger than I am.

"Well, let's get started. We have lots to discuss. I have the meeting room reserved," Abby says, walking toward a room a few doors down.

I bend down to pick up my crutch that has fallen to the floor before following her. I'm smiling brightly now that I'll be spending the rest of my morning with a woman who will treat me as an equal. Or maybe she was just in too much shock from seeing me that she didn't notice my leg. Either way, I'm now looking forward to this meeting.

I take a seat at the long wooden table that can easily seat ten people. Papers are scattered all along the tabletop, and Abby is frantically searching through them. It's giving the obsessively clean side of me a heart attack looking at this disaster of a room.

"Abby, can I help you find whatever you're looking for?" I ask.

"Oh no, I'm just looking for the shoot schedule. I'll find it here in a minute." Abby continues to dig through papers with no thought of organization or a method to the ones she has gone through or not gone through. I let out a slight giggle when she proclaims she found it to only discover moments later that it is the schedule for a different shoot.

"Abby, how long have you been doing this job?"

Abby looks up at me reluctantly as she collapses into her chair. "A week. I wasn't hired for my organizational skills, obviously."

I laugh. "I can see that. Why don't we start by just discussing the basics?"

Abby smiles. "Good idea! As you know, you will be shooting the one-year anniversary cover of our magazine. We are thrilled to have snagged such an amazing, well-known photographer. The goal of our magazine is to present inspirational people showing the world what inspires them in the most natural way possible. We don't use any Photoshopping at the magazine, and we do not alter the photos in any way."

"I'm excited. I love that message."

"Kyle Haynes, the actor in practically every romance movie lately, will be who you are shooting." Abby looks at the picture of him dreamily. I smile because he's good looking, although I have no idea who this actor is. I continue listening to Abby ramble about what inspires Kyle and ideas of how we should incorporate them into the shoot. Relief fills me as ideas of how to position my subject, where the lighting should be, and what equipment I will need flood my brain. I'm more excited about this now than I was before the meeting. I feel a glimmer of myself coming back.

THE BELLS CHIME as I enter the therapy clinic, causing me to smile like an idiot. Most people hate going to therapy because it's painful. Most people leave here aching, sweating, and cursing their therapist for making something as simple as lifting their leg hurt so much. But not me. I love feeling my muscles get harder and stronger. The blood pumping through my veins warms my body and fills the empty hole, if only temporarily.

This place feels like home. It also looks more like a home than any other clinic or hospital I have ever been to. The building is an old house turned into a clinic. I walk the few feet to the entrance. Instead of a large waiting room and receptionist, a simple table sits with a sign-in sheet. I walk further into the clinic and enter the large, open space that used to be a living and dining room combination. Now, there sits large therapy mats and machines pushed against the exposed brick and beams of the house. The kitchen still sits on the far end of the clinic. The therapists all have offices upstairs in what used to be bedrooms.

"Hey Alexa, Calvin will be right with you," Stacey says, smiling at me as I enter. I smile back and nod. I love how the therapists all know everybody. It's like one big family here. I take a seat on the small couch, lifting my stump to rest on the couch and give it a break before the pounding begins. My crutches lean against the wall. That's probably the other reason I like coming to therapy - I don't have to use my crutches as much here.

"Hey, good lookin'," Calvin says as he walks over to the couch where I'm sitting.

I look up at him smiling. "Hey, you."

"Ready to go to work?"

"Yep," I say as I get off the couch and grab my crutches, loving that Calvin doesn't offer his hand to help me up. He never offers to help me while I'm here. In order to become stronger, I need to learn to do things for myself, and I need to learn to ask for help when I need it. I feel like a person here, not like half a human with part of me ripped away.

I follow Calvin over to one of the high mats where I take a seat before letting my crutches drop to the floor. Calvin starts massaging my stump. I wince as his hands go over an incredibly sensitive spot. What should feel good to have a hot man rub his hands all over my leg feels like torture as shooting pain runs through my body at his touch. Although it's gotten better since we started therapy almost three months ago, it's still more sensitive than I would like.

"Anything new with you?" Calvin asks. I welcome the distraction.

"I'm doing a photo shoot for *Inspire* magazine later this week."

Calvin's eyebrows rise just slightly. "Really? I didn't think you would be ready to get back into photography so soon."

I let out a low growl when Calvin taps my leg harder than usual. Calvin gives me an 'I'm sorry but not really that sorry' smile. "I don't think I am ready. But I need to do more with my life than just go to doctor and therapy appointments."

Calvin glances down at his watch. "Stretches." He starts stretching my leg. His hands get close to intimate areas, but after coming here three times a week for the past two months, it doesn't faze me. I glance over at the young woman Stacey is working on. Her eyes are glued to Calvin, and her mouth has dropped open. I roll my eyes at her before returning my attention to Calvin. He's attractive. Tall, muscular, blond. His blue eyes seem to sparkle a little when he looks at you. He's also one of the nicest and most caring men I've ever met. I can see the attraction. Yet I don't feel anything when he touches me. No butterflies when I feel him nearby. Not even a tingling.

"Just don't push yourself too hard," Calvin says, as he finishes the stretches. He walks over to get some bands and weights. He hands them to me, and I start lifting the weights with my arms.

"I never do."

Calvin laughs. "You always do. That's why I worry."

I frown but don't argue as I do fifteen reps instead of the ten Calvin has requested. There is nothing wrong with pushing yourself. It's the only way to get strong again. The rest of the session is much the same. Calvin asks me to do ten reps, so I do twenty. Calvin asks me to hold a stretch for twenty seconds, so I hold it for thirty.

Calvin hands me a towel and cup of water to help me cool down when I have completed all the exercises he has planned for me today.

"So I have good news for you," Calvin says.

"You finally hired a stylist and you're burning all of your horrendous clothes," I tease, although Calvin's clothes are anything but horrendous. He's wearing tight fitting dark jeans that most men couldn't pull off. But somehow on Calvin they accentuate every perfect muscle. His striped coral and yellow shirt should look ridiculous, but instead, it makes his blond hair and blue eyes pop.

Calvin laughs. "No. Your prosthesis should be in next week. You'll be able to start walking again."

I freeze. I don't know what to say or how to respond. This is what I've been waiting for since the accident four months ago. I hate these damn crutches. But they have been a bit of a security blanket. Now that I am almost free of them, I feel oddly nervous. Will I even be able to walk using a prosthesis? It's still painful when Calvin touches my leg. I can't imagine every step I take being that painful.

"Earth to Alexa," Calvin says waving his hand in front of my face and bringing me back to the present. "I thought you would be jumping up and down with excitement. You can get rid of those damn crutches you hate so much soon."

"I am excited." I pull Calvin into a hug. I feel his arms tighten around me, and I welcome the touch. I can't remember the last time anyone has hugged me like this. But when I go to move away, I feel him pull me tighter for a few more seconds. When he pulls away, his face is tense and his eyes looked pained.

"I'm sorry. I'm just worried about you. Have you been talking to anyone?"

I plaster a fake smile on my face. Calvin doesn't need to worry about me. I'm fine. "Yes, I see a psychologist once a week."

"Anyone else?" Calvin looks at me with concern.

"I'm fine. I should go."

Calvin nods somberly. "Talk to someone real. I'm here, but if not me, someone else."

I just nod my head before heading to the waiting cab outside. I don't want to promise Calvin anything. I'm not ready to talk to anyone.

Chapter Six

LANDON

But I can't help it
When I see you
My heart skips

"LANDON, ARE YOU LISTENING TO ME?" Drew says.

I look up from my phone over to where he sits across from me in the limo. I hate riding in this fucking thing. I like the control and freedom my car represents. But the stupid music label wouldn't hear of me driving to my own meeting today. "Do I ever listen to you?"

"No, not even when we were kids. Listen to me. I'm trying to talk with you about your meeting with the music executives later today. If you're not prepared, they are going to walk all over us. You need to listen."

I look back at my phone scrolling through the endless names of women. Women I fucked and never called again though I'm confident any of them would easily take me back for a round two. All it would take is one text. But my fingers keep scrolling back to Alex's name, not letting me settle on anyone else's name. She would make a good fuck.

But shit, she has a boyfriend. *That's never stopped you before.* But fucking a woman who has a boyfriend is bad news. They become attached, and I don't do attached. One night is all they get. Caroline is the only woman I've fucked more than one night. She doesn't get attached. I hit the delete button. Still staring at my phone, a message pops up 'Are you sure you want to delete this contact?' I hesitate over the confirmation button. No, I don't want to delete. But I hit delete anyway. I should have just taken Caroline up on her offer. Maybe then I wouldn't be in such a foul mood.

"Landon!" Drew yells at me. But I just keep scrolling. I pay him enough to handle everything for me. He'll handle the meeting just fine by himself.

That's when I feel the force of an angry bull crashing down on top of me. I drop my phone turning my full attention to Drew as he pummels me in the ribs. Drew is a muscular guy and tall to most people. But not to me. We are the same height but I still have at least twenty pounds of muscle advantage on him so, no matter how angry Drew is, he's not going to win this fight. Drew only gets one more swing in before I pin him to the floor of the limo.

"What the hell, Drew?"

"Get your head out of all the boobs on your phone. Your mind needs to be clear. We need to pick out backup dancers for your show next month and then we have a meeting to get you more time to finish writing songs for your album."

"Relax, Drew. When have I ever been anything but professional?"

Drew just shakes his head at me. "Why did I think it was a good idea to tie my paycheck and happiness to whether or not you can remain professional?"

I grin and climb off him. "Because I'm amazing and you'd miss out on all of this awesomeness if you had turned down the job." Drew just rolls his eyes at me as he dusts off his suit jacket before climbing back into the seat across from me. "Fine. It's because I'm your twin and you love me."

I ruffle his perfect hair before climbing out of the stopped limo.

Drew climbs out after me. "Consider this my two weeks' notice," Drew says, scowling at me.

I just laugh at his joke as we enter the studio.

"I'M GOING to have the finalists dance with you now so we can make sure it's a good fit," Darren, my choreographer, says. This is one of the best parts of this job. I get to watch hot women dance all over me while I judge their bodies and dancing ability. I get up from my seat in the auditorium, making my way on the stage to take my spot in the center of the dance floor. Darren hands me a microphone before taking my seat next to Drew and John, one of my music executives.

"Numbers 5, 29, 145, and 263, you're up," Darren says to his assistant who gathers the women who have been waiting in the hallway. The women quickly take their places around me. I haven't learned this choreography yet, but I've been sitting here for almost three hours now watching Darren do the routine as the women dance around him, so I could do this routine in my sleep. I'm a better dancer than I am a singer, but singing is my passion. And it helps that I can make a lot more money as a singer than as a dancer. Instead of being a lowly backup dancer, I can control my own destiny and all that shit as a singer.

The audio guy starts the music, and I hear Darren count out, "Five ... six ... seven ... eight." I automatically start moving to the music as I lip sync the words to my song. I spin the first woman before flipping the second right on cue. More hips gyrate before I spin and have their hands all over me as the choreography ends.

"That was great, ladies. We'll call you. Next, I need 15, 56, 179, and 190," Darren says.

I walk over to the side of the stage where cups of water fill a table. I slug two cups down. "That was impressive," number 145 says.

I look down at where the number 145 covers her large, likely fake breasts protruding from her barely there bra. "You're quite impressive," I say, still looking at her boobs.

"I'm Jennifer," she says as she reaches her hand forward. I assume she wants to shake my hand, so I extend mine. Instead of shaking my hand, she places her hand into my front jeans pocket.

I raise my eyebrows at her action but don't say a word. When her hand comes back out, she's holding my phone. She quickly types into the device before handing it to me.

"Call me," she says, handing back my phone. I smile. I plan to. I slug down one more cup of water before heading back to do the same thing all over again with the next group of women.

I WALK into the large meeting room with Drew. It could easily hold twenty people around the large oak table. There are no windows; dark walls contain us, making me feel a bit claustrophobic as I enter. Even though sweat drips off me, I don't bother changing. I shake each of their hands before taking a seat next to Drew at the long table. I don't listen to any of their names or job titles as I shake each of their hands. Instead, I think of them as big nose, hairy arms, and woman with too much lipstick. Hairy arms visibly grimaces after shaking my sweaty hand. Although, I should be the one grimacing after having to shake Sasquatch's hand.

"We are here to discuss when we are releasing your album and what songs are going on it," big nose says.

Drew nods politely, but I continue just sitting here staring at the men and woman who wouldn't even have a job if it weren't for people like me signing with them. But these people want more than just money; they want complete control of my creative abilities. I should be grateful. These people make it possible to pay my extravagant bills every month, but that doesn't stop me from wanting full control.

"We have set a release date for next month and will start doing press early next week," big nose continues.

"When would the songs on the album need to be finished for that timetable?" Drew asks calmly.

"Two weeks," hairy arms says.

I scowl at hairy arms. "No fucking way!"

"It's not enough time for Landon to put out the quality of album that he would like to produce," Drew says diplomatically. "Extend the release by a month. That will give Landon another month to write the songs for the album."

Lipstick woman looks at me sympathetically. Maybe if I sleep with her, they will give us more time.

"I'm sorry, but Landon's initial single is going to start falling down the charts in a matter of weeks. We need a follow-up single, and we need to release the album. The songs we have given you are perfectly fine. Record them and then we will release them," big nose says.

"The songs you gave me are shit, and you know it!"

"Then write something better. You have two weeks. Write something better that we can use as a single then we'll give you more time to complete the album, or we release the album as it is in a month," big nose says before standing to leave. His minions follow him.

"Fuck," I say, pushing back from the table and sending my chair falling backward.

Drew stands calmly from his chair. He knew this was how the meeting was going to go. He knew I was out of time. Some brother he is.

"Just write a song, Landon." He gathers his things and walks out. If only it were that fucking simple. I walk out of the building dialing number 145's number as I do.

Chapter Seven

ALEXA

A roar surrounds me. I must be hallucinating or dead. Dead would be nice. But I still feel the pain in my leg. A louder roar vibrates through my body as the road tumbles into the water. I reach my hand out grabbing the only thing next to me. Him.

I GLANCE at my watch as I walk into the warehouse. 4:12 am. Early by anybody's standards. The dark sky still blankets the city that's barely awake. I welcome today, though. I welcome the freedom to have a purpose for being up this early. I hardly sleep so, for once, I have a reason to be up.

I move my crutches confidently through the large, open warehouse filled with people moving around heavy equipment. I don't bother to notice the stares I'm sure I'm getting. Today, I'm in my element. I'm wearing a simple button-down white shirt with a short A-line black skirt making my stump very visible. Makeup distracts from my scars but doesn't fully cover them along with the tattoos shining brightly on my arms and chest. I must look like a freak. But today, I'm here to show the world that even though a part of me is irreparably damaged, I can still do this.

"Alexa!" I hear Abby shout. I turn around and see Abby running toward me with a cheerful smile plastered on her gorgeous face.

"I'm so excited to be working with you and Mr. Davis today!" Abby squeals. "Follow me. I have a lot to show you before he gets here."

"Wait. Who is Mr. Davis? I thought we were shooting ...?"

"Oh, I'm sorry, I completely forgot to tell you. Mr. Haynes canceled due to a scheduling conflict, but you will never believe who we got to replace him. We are so excited to have him. He is the biggest thing right now. He has a number one song, and he has the potential to become bigger than Justin Timberlake. And he is hot! You know not in the babyface teenybopper kind of way, but in the dreamy, sexy, bad boy kind of way that make your panties wet with just one look." Abby is now completely lost in her own fantasies about this guy, making me laugh.

"So who is this dream guy?"

"Are you Abby?" a tall man interrupts.

Abby turns to face him. "Yes, it's nice to meet you, Drew. I've heard a lot about you." Abby extends her hand and shakes his. "Let me introduce you to the photographer today. This is Alexa Blakely. Alexa this is Drew, Landon Davis' manager."

I fake a smile and shake his hand quickly. I'm too frozen to do anything more. It has to just be a coincidence. Landon is a fairly popular name, after all, isn't it? But the man standing in front of me looks like an almost exact copy of Landon. A more tamed, professional looking version.

"Great! We are working with a newbie and a cripple. I knew we shouldn't have done this contract. So you two listen. We are going to do this shoot my way. Landon's career is new, and we don't want anyone screwing it up," he says, glaring at us.

"Drew, we are both professionals and are more than capable of handling this. Landon is in good hands," Abby says, giving him a sweet smile.

"Nice try, sweetheart, but if you want us to do this photo shoot, you'll listen to me. I will approve of the outfits, the set, and the models he will be working with. All of it," he says.

This is not going well. If Abby keeps trying to keep things sweet and professional, Drew is going to walk all over us today.

"Excuse me. I don't think you heard Abby correctly. My name is Alexa Blakely - one of the most sought after fashion and entertainment photographers in the world. I have made careers with just one photograph. I also know how to ruin careers with one photograph," I say glaring at Drew.

"Abby has earned her career at one of the top entertainment magazines in the industry while you probably became a manager because you are Landon's brother. So while we are open to hearing suggestions from you, we will both do an amazing job without you. If your client would like to grace the cover of *Inspire*, then he is going to have to learn to work with us. Considering I have never even heard of your client, I think he needs this magazine a whole lot more than the magazine needs him. Now, we need to get back to setting up the first set. You make sure your client is ready in fifteen minutes or we can find somebody else to do the shoot," I say, walking away.

My face is still red and my nostrils still flared from talking to Drew when Abby rushes over to me.

"I'm so sorry, Alexa. You shouldn't have had to intervene," Abby says weakly.

I glare at her. "It's your job to handle Drew! If you can't handle that, then why are you even here?"

"I'm sorry," Abby says. Her cheeks flush pink in embarrassment.

I take a deep breath trying to calm myself. "No, I'm sorry. I shouldn't have yelled at you. I'm just anxious about the shoot today and want it to go perfectly."

"I needed to be yelled at. I don't deserve this job anyway."

"What do you mean? You didn't earn this job?"

"My father owns the magazine. He gave me the job."

"That doesn't mean you didn't earn it and that you don't deserve it. You had some fantastic ideas at our meeting. You just need to learn to stand up for yourself. Then others will start believing you deserve this job too."

"Maybe," she says smiling.

"So the first set is still on a motorcycle?"

"Yes, then we will move to the beach."

Great – the beach. The worst obstacle for a girl on crutches.

"Let me introduce you to your assistants. We couldn't get any of your usuals due to such short notice, but all of them have come highly recommended," Abby says.

The butterflies fluttering in my stomach are not swarming when I hear my usual assistants won't be with me today. The confidence I walked in with is dwindling by the second. I don't feel ready for this.

"This is Nora and Nathan," Abby says. I shake each of their hands.

"We have everything set up for the first shot, but let us know if we need to make any adjustments before we get started," Nora says.

I smile. *Thank god!* I don't even know where to start. But as I look around, I see complete organization and order. No chaos. "Thanks, Nora. I'll let you know," I say.

I start to work on adjusting the camera and taking test shots of Abby while waiting for Mr. Davis to get here. I don't let myself think about him until I hear the murmuring and see the stares of the crew around me.

I turn to see what they are looking at just in time to see Landon walking over to the set, surrounded by an entourage of stylists and makeup artists. My jaw drops. It's Landon from the beach. Landon, 'I like to invade your personal space and treat you like an invalid,' Landon. Landon, whose crooked grin and dimples are beginning to invade my thoughts, Landon. And he is walking toward me with sexy dark jeans hanging off his hips along with a tight blue V-neck and black leather jacket. He still has dark stubble, but his hair is more perfectly tousled than the last time I saw him.

He hasn't seen me yet because he's talking to Abby. I feel like making a run for it. I'm going to be too distracted to do a good job with this shoot. Every step he moves closer, my heart beats faster and faster until I'm sure it's going to explode from of my chest. I start to feel lightheaded and realize that I'm barely breathing. I automatically go into the breathing exercises I have been taught to help with my panic attacks. Slow breath in, count one ... two ... three ... slowly exhale.

They walk closer before Abby turns him toward me. “Landon, this is Alexa Blakely. She is your photographer today.”

Landon’s eyes dilate when he sees me, but otherwise he keeps his composure.

“Nice to meet you, Alexa Blakely,” Landon says, emphasizing the -a- on Alexa. He’s grinning at me as if he knows a secret that I don’t. He extends his hand, and I shake it. My body is much too warm as I take his cooler hand in mine. I barely mumble something that I hope sounds like ‘nice to meet you too’ back. But I’m still in a bit of a shock that he is a pop star. Suddenly, I feel incredibly stupid. It all makes sense now – his remark about me being paparazzi and his shock that I didn’t know his name.

Abby saves me from further awkwardness. “We are going to do several different shots and looks today. The theme of the shoot is things that inspire you. We have talked with Drew about what inspires you, but please let us know if you have any additional ideas that we can incorporate into the shoot. We are going to start off outside with your motorcycle, and then we will move to the beach ...” Abby continues to chat him up as she leads him to the motorcycle giving me time to regain my composure. He’s just like any other client I have shot before. He’s just a hot body I need to make look even hotter so that women will melt every time they see the cover and have to buy the magazine. I look up at Landon, who is now mounting the motorcycle. *If I don’t melt first.*

I take my place behind the camera balancing on my good leg. I let the crutches fall to the floor as I hold the camera in my hands. *Just don’t fall.* I don’t want to break the expensive camera and look like an idiot.

“Just sit naturally and don’t look at me. Pretend you’re riding,” I say to Landon. He turns his face from me, and I begin rattling off several initial shots. The first few shots are a little blurry and the lighting could be better. But that isn’t the worst part of the shots. Even after I adjust the camera and lighting, Landon is still going to look like a statue - rigid and unnatural.

"Try to relax," I shout to Landon. Landon's shoulders slump, but he doesn't look badass. He looks out of place despite his tattooed body and motorcycle apparel. I take several more shots after adjusting the focus and lighting. I feel as if I've found my groove and connection with the camera because the shots of the sunrise and Landon are perfect.

But unfortunately, Landon hasn't. "What do you think, Abby?"

Abby looks up from the computer screen where she is viewing the photos. "These suck," Abby says without thinking and then her face goes white.

Chuckling, I say, "Thanks for the honesty. I agree."

"The photos look amazing with the sunrise in the background. It's just that Landon ..." she trails off.

"Let's try an action shot," I say.

"You read my mind." Abby hops up from her chair and goes to tell Landon the new plan.

"We are going to try a moving shot. Can you change the lighting for me?" I say to Nathan.

"Already on it," Nathan says. He begins barking orders to Nora to start moving equipment. I work on adjusting the focus and settings on the camera.

"Ready!" I shout to them when all the adjustments have been made. Abby leaves Landon's side and jogs back over to me despite her spike high heels. I grimace just watching her walk in them.

"I just told him to ride up and down the street a few times and then we would direct him from there."

"Perfect," I say as one of his assistants throws Landon the keys. I start snapping shots again, but Landon bobbles the keys before starting the ignition. I trade a nervous look with Abby as we both watch the train wreck that is so out of character for Landon. Gone is the smooth talking, cocky bastard that I know.

Landon starts revving the engine and I relax. I start taking more photos and I catch every moment as he kicks the kickstand up, starts moving about three feet forward, stalls, and falls over on his side. I can't help it. I laugh uncontrollably to the point where I'm snorting. I don't even remember ever snorting before. Everyone around me is laughing, including Drew, until Landon scowls at him. Drew immediately stops laughing, and now, he's wearing his own scowl and heading right toward Abby and me.

"You talk to Drew. Just be the badass I know is in there somewhere. I'll handle Landon," I say to Abby before grabbing my crutches and heading over to where makeup artists and wardrobe people now surround Landon. Everyone is trying to pretend as if nothing happened.

"Can you excuse us just a minute?" I say. The crew immediately scatters.

I smile at Landon, who looks so cool sitting there in his leather jacket. Why couldn't he act like this before?

"I don't ride motorcycles," Landon says matter-of-factly without a hint of shame.

"You could have fooled me," I say, laughing at my own little joke.

Landon laughs too, causing me to snort again. "Attractive," he says sarcastically.

I try to stop snorting as I point at the motorcycle and back to him. "That was totally attractive."

"Nice comeback," Landon says, still laughing at me snorting.

I let the snorting go until it turns into a giggle and then stops. "Well, why did you tell us you can ride motorcycles if you can't?"

"I didn't. People assume."

I look at him sitting there covered in tats wearing the leather jacket and jeans perfectly. He looks like he can ride a motorcycle. I look around trying to get some sort of inspiration on how to salvage this. The sun is rising, and we are going to lose the perfect lighting if we don't hurry.

"You play guitar?"

"You did not just ask me that." He looks at me angrily. "Of course, I do."

"Did you bring it?"

"I think so."

"Can someone get Landon's guitar?" I shout to the crew nearby. One of the assistants runs into the warehouse and comes back out quickly carrying his guitar. He hands it to Landon.

"Well, prove it. Go lean against the motorcycle and play me a song," I say, doing my best to provoke him before heading back to my camera. I nod at Landon to start when I'm back behind the camera. He casually leans against the motorcycle and starts playing. As soon as he does, the room goes silent. He's in his element. He looks exactly like he sounds. Heavenly.

I'm not really listening to the words he is singing. I am getting exactly the shots that I was looking for. He flashes me another sexy grin with a twinkle in his eyes, and I know then that was the perfect shot. I re-adjust the camera, and that's when I hear him sing, "She's a green-eyed beauty with auburn hair."

I freeze. His girlfriend has blond hair, and if I remember correctly, brown eyes. He is probably just making up a stupid song to get under my skin. I'm not going to let him.

"We got it!" I shout.

Landon stops playing, but his eyes never leave mine. His crooked grin remains plastered on his face. I can't move either. I just stare back. Needing his eyes on me. Needing him. I'm not free until his assistants whisk him off to wardrobe.

"That was great! That last shot was incredible," Abby says.

I just smile. This day is going to be torture. I can't fall for him. He has a girlfriend. And I have ... I shake my head. I can't go there. Not today. And even if I fall for him, it's not like he's going to return the sentiment. He's not the type to settle down with a woman missing half her leg covered in ugly scars. I'm not sure if anybody would be willing to fall for a monster like me.

"I'll have them pull the car around to take us to the next location," Abby says. She pauses, searching my vacant eyes before she leaves. But she doesn't ask me about it, and I'm grateful.

Chapter Eight

LANDON

I can't wait to see you
See what more we could be

I CONTINUE STARING into her emerald eyes until I'm whisked back to wardrobe. Outfits to try on and model are thrown at me until they find the perfect one. It doesn't stop me from thinking about her. The song I made up on the spot was part of what I had already written and part completely new. Just looking at her standing confidently behind the camera, barking out orders to everyone, was sexy as hell. I couldn't help but flirt a little.

I should keep my distance. But I can't because I need to finish the song. It would keep my music label from breathing down my neck and give me more time to finish the album. I just need to find a way to spend more time with her. Find more inspiration.

Another pair of jeans is thrust into my hands, and I remain on autopilot as I try them on, not caring that I'm half-naked standing in front of a large crew of mostly women. I don't think I've ever been in more shock when I saw her standing there. I thought I'd never see her again after deleting her number. But there she was. As beautiful as ever, standing next to the bubbly art director. The art director who introduced her as Alexa, not Alex. That's going to take some getting used to. Why the hell did she tell me her name was Alex? I think Alex suits her better.

And her leg. What the hell happened to her? Her scarred face is less visible with the makeup, and from what I can tell peeking out of her clothing, her arms and chest aren't much better. They are just less visible due to the tattoos hiding the scars. But her leg is so much worse than I thought. How did I not notice half of it was missing before? Am I that oblivious or is she just that good at hiding it?

"God, those women are so annoying," Drew says busting into my dressing room. An attractive blonde starts rubbing oil all over my chest. Drew continues, "They have no idea what they are doing. This shoot needs to be amazing. We need it to keep people interested in you before your album is released."

But I don't pay either of them much attention. All I can think about are her supple lips. How it would feel to taste them. Or better yet, to have them wrapped around my cock. Shit, I can't fuck her, though! But that won't stop me from having a little fun flirting with her. I grin. I think it's going to be fun getting under her skin.

"All done," the blonde says.

I smile at her but don't bother to look at her boobs that are overflowing from her shirt. I look over at Drew, who is looking back and forth between me and the blonde. He scrunches his brow in a confused look. I don't know if it's a twin thing or if Drew is just much more observant than I am, but he always knows what's going on. When he sees me not flirting with blonde boobs, he knows.

"The photographer is Alex," he says connecting the dots. I don't answer. Instead, I just leave the dressing room and head toward my car to drive to the next location. Drew climbs into the seat next to me.

Sighing, Drew says, "Just fuck her already. I'm tired of dealing with moody Landon."

Chapter Nine

ALEXA

Fire swirls around me. Burning the limo and my flesh. I cough but don't scream. I won't breathe much longer. The smoke will end the pain.

WE GET to the cliff overlooking the ocean where all of the equipment is already set up. Thank god for assistants. A chair sits behind the camera. Although I appreciate the chair, it's only there because my assistants feel sorry for me. Right now, I don't care. I'm tired of balancing on one leg.

I move over to the chair and relax.

Nora walks over to me. "Everything set up how you like it, boss?"

I smile at her. "Yes, this should be an easy shot. It's so beautiful up here. All Landon will have to do is work out on top of this gorgeous cliff and let the scenery do the rest."

She just nods her head and walks back to the other assistants. I've realized that Nora is a woman of few words. I lean back in my chair almost falling asleep waiting for Landon and his entourage to show up.

"What's taking him so long?" I mouth to Abby sitting at a

computer under a small tent hiding from the intense heat that is now pounding down on us.

"Diva," Abby mouths back as she laughs.

Twenty minutes later, Landon finally shows up. Abby rushes over to him to give him instructions while I make sure my lighting and focus are still good. That's when I feel him standing behind me.

"What do you want, Landon?" I say as I look up at him. That was a mistake. All he is wearing is athletic shorts. Oils rubbed all over his body cause it to glisten. He looks better than he does when he actually works out and sweat is covering his body.

"I wanted a close up of the drool coming from your gaping mouth when you saw my body again," he says. A smug grin covers his face.

I close my mouth, wiping the drool off on the back of my hand. "I fell asleep waiting for you to get your diva ass here. I tend to drool when I sleep. Just get your ass up there and lift those fake weights. We wouldn't want to assume that you can lift a lot of weight just from the look of you."

Landon glares. "Just take the pictures." He jogs easily up the hill and into spot. I should be taking pictures as every perfect muscle contracts on the way up. But I'm mesmerized by every drop of fake sweat glistening on his body instead of doing my job. I close my mouth. I'm not going to let Landon have any more fuel to harass me.

Abby yells, "We're ready!" to divert my attention to the job at hand.

Landon starts lifting the fake weights at the top of the cliff. He looks perfect. *Inspire* isn't going to be able to keep up with the demand they are going to have for this magazine issue. I've never seen a more perfectly sculpted body. His tattoos seem to blend perfectly with his body and muscles. Almost like they have always been there since birth instead of slowly etched all over.

Abby looks at me from behind the computer screen and indicates that we have enough photos, but that's when Landon takes it up a notch. He climbs onto a large rock on the edge of the cliff. Just standing on top of the rock, Landon looks gorgeous. He doesn't need to do anything else. But of course, it's not in his nature to be safe or fake.

Next thing I know, he is balancing on the rock on one hand. His arm dips and I think he's going to lose his balance and tumble over the cliff. I let go of the camera searching for my crutches laying on the ground. But when I look back up, he has pushed his body back up until his arm is extended again. He's doing a one-handed push-up on a rock over a cliff. Every woman within a mile must be panting in heat right now. And he knows it from the smug grin on his face.

I quickly take the pictures that I know are going to end up in the magazine. The pictures represent Landon perfectly. Dangerous, wild.

"We got it!" I shout before Landon comes up with another ridiculous idea.

Landon jogs back down the cliff, and I mouth, "Show off."

He grins back. "You like it."

And I don't refute him because I did. My stomach growls, and I head over to the spread of food laid out in one of the tents. I need my strength for the last shot of the day. Subs, fruit, chips, and pizza are laid out on a table. I head straight for the pizza. Taking a pepperoni slice, I scarf it down.

I STAND on the beach wearing a simple one-piece suit with swim shorts. Camera in hand, I stare out at the vast ocean that haunts my dreams – the water that changed me forever – and I feel completely exposed.

"You okay?" Abby asks. I didn't even hear her walk up next to me.

"Yes." I drop my crutches next to the tent before hopping down toward the ocean. The assistants have begun moving the now waterproofed lighting, reflective papers, and camera equipment into the water.

I take several hops into the water, almost falling with each step, as the tide tries again and again to knock me over until I'm waist deep and can just float. I let myself float. I let myself just be.

"You can ask for help you know. It doesn't make you look weak," Landon says. I don't open my eyes. I know he will look just as amazing as before, and I don't want to feel the urge to jump him right now.

"Thanks but you would be helping me a lot right now if you could go pose with that model and start bawling your eyes out so that I can get out of this ridiculous position," I say.

He laughs, but I don't hear him moving. So I open my eyes to glare at him.

"Oh, you were serious. Sorry, I'll go. But you look sexy as hell. And I am still waiting to hear when that ass kicking is going to happen."

I stare at him incredulously. "It's not going to happen."

"Sure, it is," he says winking.

He drifts back into the ocean toward the actual sexy model in a barely there bikini, showing off her perfect body. Not a scarred one like mine. Despite the one-piece swimsuit, I know the scars are still visible. Nothing can hide them. Not to mention the scary looking tattoos that make me almost unapproachable to most people.

Landon and the model position themselves right at the edge of the rocks. The sun is starting to set in the background. My assistant, Nathan, hands me the camera. I'm surprised that I have the strength to keep the camera and myself afloat since I can barely touch the ocean floor.

I start taking pictures moving closer as I do. Trying to capture any emotion Landon is showing his sexy model. He looks sexy and confident and not even a little bit heartbroken.

"Landon, you need to look heartbroken. This is going on the cover and is supposed to tie into your song about heartbreak. You need to look less confident," I say.

He slumps his shoulders but otherwise his body language doesn't change. The female model is doing a good job. She pulls herself away from him, drifting off into the ocean. Landon is supposed to be struggling to pull her back. I have to get this soon or the sun is going to set and we are going to be screwed.

I feel the images flooding my own brain. I try to push them back, but they keep coming. So I let them. Every painful memory I let out.

"You feel yourself sinking, drowning in the water. Chaos is all around you. You can't breathe."

Landon looks at me confused, but I keep talking. I keep snapping pictures. That's all I can do.

"You can't move as another wave crashes down on both of you.

Trapping you. But you hold onto her still. You don't let her go. You can't let her go. You try to swim to the shore, but the current is pulling you away. This woman is the love of your life. Your everything. Your reason to exist. Your reason to fight."

Landon finally seems to understand as he starts feeling my words. Enacting my words. I continue to speak entwining truth with lies. Filling in missing blanks in my own head.

"She fights against your grip. Needing you to release her. You're drowning both of you. But you fight her. You need her."

I take more pictures as I see Landon's body begin to break. The tears forming. The female model struggles in Landon's grasp. Then I feel the rain drizzling down on top of us.

"Another wave crashes over you sucking your last breath away. Your only chance to breathe again is to let her go. But you can't. You hold her tighter. You'd give your last breath to not be apart from her."

Landon's tears are falling hard now. His breathing uneven. His grip on her hard as she pretends to be pulled out to sea. The rain pours harder, but the sunset glows bright orange from behind them.

"But you can't let her drown. You won't let her drown. She has to survive. She has to live. You let her go." As I say the words, Landon lets go - it's a perfect shot.

As soon as I get it, the rain stops. I hand the camera to my assistant, Nathan, and swim hard for shore. I need to get out of here. I dunk my head under the waves to wash my own tears from my face. By the time I reach the sand, there is no way to distinguish my tears from the salty ocean water. I crawl up the sand, not bothering to stand or think about how ridiculous I must look. I make it to the tent where someone immediately gives me a towel and my crutches. I shiver despite the heat.

I can't plaster a fake smile on my face as I talk to Abby. "I need to go. You have everything you need," I say as more of a statement than a question.

She nods. "Take one of the cars that brought us here."

"That's okay. I'll take a cab. You guys will need the cars to get the equipment back."

She just nods again. "I'll call you. You were fantastic."

I don't respond. I just dig my phone out of my purse and call a cab before I hobble toward the street soaking wet and cold.

Chapter Ten

LANDON

I lose my breath
Trying to drink in your scent

I HAVE to know what the fuck just happened back there. Those words were straight out of someone's worst nightmare. But were they Alex's nightmare? I run toward the beach and people immediately swarm me. Trying to hand me towels. Telling me how great I am. But none of them are her. I search the tents lining the beach. She is nowhere in sight. There is no way she can be that far ahead of me. I spot Abby barking orders at people. I wipe the water dripping from my chest with a towel as I make my way toward her.

"That was wonderful, Landon. The cover is going to look amazing," Abby says bubbly.

"Where's Alex?" I ask.

"Alexa took a cab back home." Abby smiles weakly at me.

"Thanks," I say, curtly. I start walking toward the parking lot. I spot Drew as I walk.

"Keys," I say. Drew tosses them to me without another word. He knows me too well. He knows I'll end up in her bed tonight. He doesn't question me or try to stop me.

I hang the towel around my neck as I approach the parking lot. I scan the parking lot quickly when I see her leaning on her crutches. I walk as calmly as I can over to her.

"Need a ride?" I ask, although I want to order her to get in my car - not ask for permission like a pussy.

She doesn't look at me. "No, a cab is coming."

Look at me, dammit! I need to see her face. Maybe then, I'll understand what the hell just happened back there. Now, what do I do? I can't throw her over my shoulder and force her to take me up on my offer, as much as I want to. I feel a raindrop hit my face. I look up to see it's sprinkling again. Thunder roars in the distance. She shakes as it does.

"Wait here. I'm giving you a ride." I jog over to my Porsche, throwing the door open and sending the engine roaring to life. I pull it over in front of her. I hop out expecting a fight, but she already has the passenger door open and is climbing in. She hands me her crutches, which she finagles between our seats.

"Thanks," is all she says. Her eyes examine the interior of my Porsche 911 Turbo. She runs her hands over the leather interior in appreciation, trying to distract herself. She closes her eyes and sinks into the leather seat.

"No problem. We live in the same building. It's not exactly out of my way." She nods before looking out the window, shivering slightly. I turn the heat on despite how warm it is outside. I watch her as she settles into the warm seat, letting it surround her. I sit in silence just watching her out of the corner of my eye until I can't stand it anymore. "Was that what happened to you? That story you told. Is it yours?"

She turns her head, finally looking at me. When she does, I see the devastation and the damage she is trying to hide. But I see it. It's like my own reflection when I look in the mirror.

"No. It's a story of someone close to me. Neither one of them made it. They both died in that water."

"I'm sorry. I didn't mean to bring up those memories for you. You must have been close to them." I want to ask what happened to her leg. But I've already brought up enough disturbing memories for now.

"So I guess I need to listen to the radio more. I can't believe you're this famous rockstar. You must think I'm an idiot or a recluse or something," she says, startling me with her change in topic.

"It's the or something. I need to pay more attention to the photography world because you're this famous photographer."

"Today was a bit of a struggle for me. I haven't done a professional photo shoot in months," she admits.

"You didn't look like you were struggling much to me back there. Especially since your muse was less than cooperative." I stare at her incredulously. There is no way she didn't feel confident back there.

"Thanks. The photos will turn out well. That's all that matters," she says.

I disagree. A lot more matters than how the photos turn out. We get closer to our condo, and I know I'm about out of time. I may not have another chance with this woman.

"Why didn't your boyfriend pick you up today?"

She stifles a giggle as her eyes open wide. "You're not nosy at all."

I grin guiltily and bat my eyes. She laughs. "I don't have a boyfriend. Why isn't your girlfriend hanging all over you at the shoot today?" she fires back. The differences between Caroline and Alex are tremendous. Caroline is tall, fit, and girly. I'm supposed to be with that type of girl. Alex is rough, fit, and anything but girly. I've always thought eventually when I was done fucking every woman I could, I'd settle down. Caroline ruined any chance of that ever happening because she's the only steady woman in my life. But right now, I couldn't care less about Caroline. I want to fuck Alex. One night is all I need to get her out of my system, and then I can focus again on writing songs. But she's not the type I can just buy a drink for at a bar and then have her. No, Alex is a woman I will have to work much harder for.

"I don't have a girlfriend."

"That's not what Caroline told me," Alex accuses me. I feel the heat rising in my body. I'll have to talk with Caroline again. She knows her place. She is not to interfere with my relationships, or I'll have to end our arrangement. I grip the steering wheel a little tighter and speed through a red light turning a corner sharply.

"Caroline is my ex."

I wait for another snarky response, but she doesn't say anything. I look over at her, and panic is covering her face. She's breathing fast and uneven. Her face is scarlet red, and sweat pours down it. I can't move. I have no idea what's happening or what to do, but I have to do something. I pull the car over, and it takes me less than a second to run around to her side. I throw open the door and unbuckle her seat belt.

That's when I notice the panic in her eyes. I blow gently in her face trying to get her air. Get her to calm down so she can tell me how to help her.

"Breathe, Alex. Slow down and breathe." I blow on her face again. What I would give right now to have some bottles of water. "Focus on me, Alex. You're going to be fine. Just focus on me."

Her breathing slows a little, so I keep talking to her.

"Breathe, Alex. Keep breathing. I'm right here." I take deep, slow breaths trying to show her how to breathe. She starts mimicking my breaths until we are breathing in unison. When her breathing is calm, I pull her toward me onto my lap on the side of the street, hugging her gently. I hold her for several minutes, hoping she feels safe in my arms. I feel her sink into my chest, fitting so perfectly with my body. I don't want to let her go. I know when I do she will leave a gaping hole that I didn't even know needed to be filled.

"Do you need to go to a hospital?" I ask.

"No, I just had a panic attack. I have them frequently still."

I nod and wait, hoping she will tell me more. She doesn't.

"Is there anything else I can do for you?"

"Just take me home." She moves to get up, and I let her go. I miss her warmth the second that she moves away.

I nod and help her back into the Porsche. I drive her home in nervous silence. I don't understand how she keeps pulling me back to her. I look at her sitting anxiously in her seat fidgeting with some piece of fabric sticking out of her purse. To any person, she would look like an anxious mess, but there is more there. She's hiding something, not letting it break free. I pull in front of our building. I don't want her to have to walk further than she has to.

"Thanks for the ride and for calming me down," she says, before turning to climb out of the Porsche.

"Wait. I want to see you again." My voice is more desperate than I want to let on.

Her eyes dilate the tiniest bit, giving away the tinge of excitement she tries to hide. I smirk.

"I don't think that's a good idea. We are both busy people anyway. All I have time for right now is therapy appointments, work, and trying to heal," she says.

"Then let me take you to a therapy appointment. You know you want another chance to get to ride in my Porsche again." I wink at her before realizing my mistake. I'm so used to the Porsche being a woman magnet. But with Alex the ability to go fast may be a deterrent.

She shakes her head. "Landon, I don't think ..."

"It's decided. When is your next appointment?"

"Thursday."

"Perfect. Text me the time and details and I'll take you."

She doesn't protest. I don't think she has the energy. She just climbs out. I hand her the crutches through the open window and watch as she disappears inside the building. I want to chase after her. I want to make sure she makes it to her condo. But I am not some eager, desperate prick. I don't play that game. I'll have to find another way to get my one night with her.

Chapter Eleven

ALEXA

I bite my lip trying to stifle my scream as the pain radiates through my body. Burning and encasing me as it goes. The pain hits me again, and I can't hold it back. I scream.

MIRRORS. I hate them. Despise them. They tell the truth that I try to hide from myself. They show me how broken I really am. How fragile. This full-length mirror standing in my bedroom, in particular, taunts me with all of my imperfections. My missing leg. The ugly stump that barely protrudes from beneath my running shorts. Shorts that I don't need because why would a girl missing her leg be able to run again. Burns and scars cover the rest of my body, showing the physical pain I went through that night.

Most days I have hope. Hope that I can fight through this. Become stronger. Find myself again. But all it takes is one look in this mirror to lose that hope. Because even when every scar heals, when the burning in my lungs subsides, when I walk again - the pain won't go away. I will still feel empty. I will still be missing a huge part of me that I will never get back. Stupid mirror. I slam the mirror to the floor. It shatters it into a million broken pieces, matching my own brokenness.

I should make an appointment with my psychiatrist. The darkness is consuming me again. Ever since the photo shoot, when I let the images flood my brain, I haven't been able to escape it. The images don't just control my nightmares, but also my every thought during the day as well. Instead, I walk to the bathroom and pop two pain pills, washing them down with a swig of whiskey. I have to push the pain out today. I have to be strong today. Even when I can't.

I SIGH BEFORE SIPPING the sangria the waiter just brought me. It's twelve-thirty, and Laura still isn't here, despite agreeing to meet at twelve. The painkillers have helped keep the darkness away, for now, but not the boredom. I take out my phone and Google Landon Davis. I immediately get hundreds of hits. He already has a Wikipedia page, so I click on it. I skim the article and find out basic information about him. He's twenty-eight years old. A year older than me. He has one twin brother, Drew, who is also his manager. He has a Bachelor of Arts degree in music from Texas A&M. He met Caroline his sophomore year in college. They had dated for almost four years before they broke up. Caroline was his inspiration for his number one song 'I Don't Need Your Love.' Rumors speculate they are back together.

The page is fairly short, and I don't get much information from it that I didn't already know. I click on several other tabloid articles about him. There are pictures of him and Caroline as recently as a few weeks ago. There are also several pictures of him leaving bars with other girls. I find a link to his music video for 'I Don't Need Your Love' and watch it.

Morning pretty girl lying in my bed
With your long blond curls
Loving you was more than I ever dreamed
I would have given you that ring and

Made you my everything

I should have known that you were never really mine
That all this time you called him mine
Sleeping in his bed
Fucking him instead

Now I'm left to pick up the broken pieces of me
Shattered by the love you claimed to have for me
It should have destroyed me
Instead, you set me free

I don't need your love
I don't need to call you mine
I don't need your heart
Or to fuck at night
I don't need your love

I treated you like a queen
But even that wasn't enough for you
I should have been destroyed
When I found you in his bed
But you set me free instead

I don't need your lies
I don't need your fake smiles
I don't need your schemes
Or your fake dreams
I don't need your love

A TEAR HAS FALLEN down my cheek from watching the video. Throughout the song, Landon chased a blond woman with an uncanny resemblance to Caroline through all the old places they went on dates. Each time, the woman is with another man. In each scene, I saw more and more of Landon's heartbreak until he was completely shattered. He sung about not needing her love when he clearly did. And when he didn't get it, he was left broken. Landon poured his heart into the song and the video. I wonder how he was able to show that much emotion and why it was so hard for him to do the same during the photo shoot. It also makes me mad that Caroline did this to him. However, I'm not convinced that they are really broken up.

But most of all, I hate myself for falling for him. His heart is obviously taken whether he wants to admit it or not. And my heart is gone. I spin the large diamond on my finger feeling so out of place, but I would never meet Laura without it. I tuck my hand in my pocket feeling the warm silk instantly relaxing me.

I take my third piece of bread from the basket and smear a healthy portion of butter onto it. I'm starving and am about to just order my lunch.

"You shouldn't be eating that. It will go straight to your hips," Laura says from behind me in her annoyingly sweet voice.

I stand from my chair and give her a hug and quick kiss on the cheek. "So glad you made it," I say, giving her the best smile I can muster.

Laura takes a seat across from me. She orders a sparkling water before eyeing my sangria in disgust. "Don't you think it's a little early to be drinking, dear?"

I take a deep breath before I speak. I know it's not worth arguing with Laura. And I wouldn't put up with her if she wasn't the only family I have left. She's the only link I have to my past.

"How has organizing the charity ball been going?" I ask changing the subject to something that I know will keep Laura talking.

"It will be amazing. I won't let it be anything less than amazing, even though I have to do all the planning and organizing by myself."

I've offered to help Laura plan several times, but she doesn't want my help. She just wants me to tell her how amazing she is. "No one else could do a better job than you."

The waiter interrupts us asking for our order. Laura orders a salad with vinaigrette dressing. I order a pizza, and I don't feel guilty about it. "You really should be watching your figure. Especially since you can't exercise much right now."

"I go to physical therapy three times a week and exercise every day. I think I can handle a slice of pizza."

"Well, maybe you should increase your therapy because I would have really thought by now that you would be walking. You can't be doing that at the charity ball. It will embarrass the entire family. And you need to learn how to dress to cover that leg." Laura glances down at my outfit and my stump poking out from beneath my khaki shorts. Compared to Laura, I look like a frazzled mess. Laura is wearing a beautiful blue dress matching her eyes, setting off her long blond locks and making her look much younger than mid-fifties. I meet with Laura at least once a week, and every week it is a mix of torture and hope. Hope that she will finally accept me into her family, but instead, she criticizes my every move.

"I'll set you up an appointment with my stylist. Maybe she will be able to do something with you."

"Thank you," I say sighing. I don't want to meet with her stylist, but I'm tired of looking like a complete mess. Maybe after I meet with the stylist, Laura will finally accept me. I watch as Laura pulls out her phone, flips through her contacts, and dials a number.

"Hello Elisabetta, this is Laura Wolfe. Do you have time next week to take Alexa shopping for a dress for the charity ball? She will also need a full makeover. You should see the state her hair is in," Laura says before patiently waiting for Elisabetta to answer her. I take a long drink of my sangria, trying not to let her words affect me, but they always do.

"Wonderful, Tuesday at 8:00am would work perfectly," Laura says while eyeing me. I nod in agreement before Laura hangs up the phone. Tuesdays are one of the days that I usually have therapy, but Calvin will be fine with me changing it this once.

I try to change the subject before I have to hear more about the charity ball and how I will embarrass her. "I did a photo shoot for *Inspire* yesterday. It felt good to be back behind the camera," I blurt out.

"You shouldn't be doing a photo shoot. It's not proper for someone who has been through what you have to be doing that," Laura says in disgust.

Shit. I should have known that Laura would react that way. I rack my brain trying to come up with something else to talk about that won't get me into trouble.

"I'm sorry," I say feeling like a five-year-old scolded by her mother.

"We need to discuss the speech you will be giving at the ball. What have you written so far?"

I spin the ring nervously on my finger. "Um ... I haven't started yet." I look up to see Laura's eyes burning a hole through my heart at my words. "It's just too painful for me to write it. Every time I start, I end up crying myself into a puddle. I need to be strong though, for him. I'll write it this weekend," I say trying to save myself.

"No need. I figured this would happen. It's already written. I'll just send it to your email so you can practice beforehand."

I smile at Laura although a fire is raging inside. I can write my own speech for ...

"Oh, my god! I can't believe I keep running into you. Did you bring your camera?"

I look up to see Caroline standing, with what I assume is a girlfriend, over our table. She is a picture of perfect. Beautifully styled long hair, a sundress, and makeup that makes her skin glow. She looks like she could be Laura's daughter.

"Sorry, no. I'm a professional photographer, not the paparazzi."

I look over at Laura who is beaming at Caroline. "Introduce us, Alexandra," Laura says. I wince as she says her nickname for me. Alexa is my real name, but Laura always thinks I should adopt the longer, prettier name.

"This is Caroline Parker, aspiring actress. Caroline, meet Laura Wolfe ..." I stutter on what to call Laura, but of course, Laura is always there to rescue me.

"Her mother-in-law," Laura says smiling.

Caroline's eyes widen slightly before her mouth goes into a sly smile. I fidget with the large ring covering my left finger. "Oh, how wonderful." Caroline grabs my hand examining the large diamond that feels out of place on my finger. "That's gorgeous! Landon and I will have to double date with you and your husband, Alexandra. But I really need to go now. I have a business meeting."

"Of course, sweetie. But first let me give you an invitation to a charity ball I am hosting in a few weeks."

Laura pulls a fancy invitation out of her purse and hands it to Caroline. Caroline's smile brightens as she looks at the invitation to one of the biggest events of the year. "I'll definitely be there. It was wonderful to meet you, Mrs. Wolfe. Alexandra, I'll see you later."

Caroline leaves us to the rest of our lunch. And after Caroline blabs her mouth, Landon won't want anything to do with me again.

Chapter Twelve

LANDON

It
Could be the rain
Could be the stars
Could be the way your auburn hair
Falls down your face
Could be the cause of my speeding heart

I LEAN against the wall in the lobby waiting for her. She told me she didn't want to leave for another hour. But I know her. I know she's going to try to come up with any excuse not to go with me. She doesn't trust herself with me. And she shouldn't. My intentions are not very pure.

Ten minutes after getting down here, I spot her coming out of the elevator.

"You're early." I grin at her. I know I've won. She didn't escape before I had a chance to take her. "You ready to go?"

She bites her lip trying to hold back a grin. She's happy today though I don't know why. Going to physical therapy can't be the highlight of her day.

"I can take a cab. You don't need to take me."

"I'm taking you. Even if I have to throw you over my shoulder and carry you there, I'm taking you."

She doesn't hold back her grin. "I think some people would consider that kidnapping."

I smirk at her. "But I think you would like it."

She blushes but doesn't answer.

"Come on. Let's get you to your appointment."

We both climb into my silver Porsche, and I start heading in the direction of the clinic. I drive as carefully and cautiously as I can. I don't want her to have another panic attack. She never did tell me why she had the panic attack, but I know enough to know that something traumatic happened in a car. And if I had to guess, it's what led to the loss of her leg.

"Landon, you're driving like a nervous grandma. I know we left early, but your Porsche is embarrassed to be going this slow."

I laugh and increase my speed a little but am still well below the speed limit.

"You can do better," she says.

I laugh. "My Porsche doesn't want you to have a nervous breakdown again for going too fast."

"I know that this is going to shock you, but the going too fast part is not the problem. It's more the lack of control."

I look down at her missing right leg. "Sorry, beautiful, but you aren't going to be driving her anytime soon. I don't trust her with able-bodied people."

She laughs paying no attention to my insult. "You called the car a 'she.' I'm assuming you have a name for her, too. So let's hear it."

I shake my head. "I don't have a name for her."

"Uh-huh. And as soon as I get used to a prosthetic leg, you should let me drive *her.*"

"No way. You have no idea how to handle her."

A devious look appears on her face. "Try me. I'll let you drive mine if I can take *her* out for a spin," she says as she challenges me with her eyes.

I look at her incredulously. "You don't drive anything anywhere as nice as *her*," I say petting the steering wheel.

She just laughs. "No, I drive something better." She reaches out her hand to mine. "Do we have a deal?" she asks, smirking.

I shake my head but take her hand in mine shaking it. I've known this woman less than a month, and I've already agreed to two bets. This may be the day that I let my arrogance get the best of me.

I lean into the dash. "I'm sorry, Silvia," I whisper to my Porsche. I'm afraid I just let her into the hands of a crazy woman who doesn't know a thing about cars.

Alex looks at me curiously. "Did you just talk to your car?"

"No," I say rolling my eyes.

"You did! You called your car Silvia. It's because it's silver, isn't it! Silvia the silver Porsche." She starts laughing uncontrollably again until she's snorting. I just frown at her lack of appreciation for my car. She doesn't understand the beauty that she is riding in.

When she finally stops her snorting for a second, I ask her, "Why are you in such a good mood today? I would have thought going to therapy would make you grumpy."

She just smiles shyly. "You'll see."

I FOLLOW Alex into the building that looks more like a house than a clinic. It's an inviting place. I can see now why Alex seems happy to be here. And then I see him and my blood is boiling. He immediately comes over and hugs her. I don't know if I've ever seen her smile so bright. If she tells me this is her boyfriend, I'm going to lose it.

"Calvin, this is my friend, Landon. Landon, this is Calvin, my physical therapist."

I shake the bastard's hand. I don't like or trust him.

"Come on back, Alexa. I know you're excited. Landon, you are welcome to wait for us in the lounge area at the front," Calvin says. Alex turns to follow Calvin, but I'm not going anywhere.

"I'll stay," I say following them back. Alex doesn't argue and so Calvin allows me to come back with them. The score is one Landon and zero Calvin, although somehow I feel like I've already lost as Alex continues to light up with each step we take.

"Have a seat on the mat," Calvin says, and Alex obliges practically throwing her crutches down on the floor.

Calvin takes a seat on a rolling stool. I take a seat on a small chair next to the mat Alex is sitting on. Calvin spins around behind him pulling something metal off the table. When I finally see what it is, I can't contain my own smile.

Alex squeals when he hands her the prosthetic leg. Her prosthetic leg. I relax a little now that I know why she is so happy today. But it doesn't mean I like Calvin any more.

"Hold on, you can't run away yet. Let me show you how to put it on," Calvin says. He immediately begins explaining all the parts and how to put it on. He puts it on for her the first time, touching her leg as he does. My body tenses when he caresses her toned thigh as he slips it into the prosthesis. When his hand reaches up higher, disappearing between her thighs, it takes all of my strength to stay glued to my chair. I try to focus on Alex, but her face is still glowing brightly from her excitement. She is completely at ease with Calvin. I know my feelings aren't valid, but I hate it. I want to punch this guy.

"All right, I'm going to have you try standing at the parallel bars. Use your crutches to get over there and don't put any weight on your leg," Calvin says. Alex hobbles over to the parallel bars, and Calvin and I follow her.

He has Alex stand between the parallel bars, and he stands behind her with his hands on her hips. I have a hard time watching, but I want to see her walk again for the first time. I want to be there to support her.

"I'm going to help you shift your weight onto your right leg now," Calvin says.

Alex smiles brightly, but it immediately turns into a grimace as she shifts weight onto her leg that hasn't bore her bodyweight in months. She shifts her weight back to her strong leg.

"How did that feel?" Calvin asks.

"Painful but in a good way."

"We are going to do that a couple of more times and then we will work on taking steps."

Alex shifts her weight back and forth several more times. Each time she does, the pained look on her face becomes more and more relaxed.

"Let's practice taking a step now. I'll help you get the feel of how to swing your leg forward."

Calvin moves his hand to help her take a step forward. They continue walking the length of the parallel bars until she is walking without his assistance.

"You're amazing!" Calvin and I say at the same time as she walks back along the parallel bars by herself.

She giggles. "Thanks."

I watch in amazement as she continues to walk back and forth for the next forty-five minutes. Each time, she uses less and less support until she is walking confidently by herself. That's not possible. The first time she is walking with a prosthesis, and she can do it without difficulty or help. Her strength is amazing. She pushes herself beyond normal limits. Beyond what Calvin asks her to do. I can't stop staring at her. Her strength draws me in, and with each step she takes, I fall further and further under her spell. I don't notice anyone else in the room. Only her. I want to tell her more. Find words to express how amazing she really is. But no words come out. I feel my own brokenness bubbling under my skin, reminding me of my own weaknesses. But when I see the strength before me, I have hope.

"Okay, time to stop and take the prosthesis off," Calvin says.

Alex's lip curves into a pout, but she obliges. She sits down and takes the prosthesis off her swollen, red leg.

"Landon, can you pull *Silvia* around? I don't want to walk further than I have to," Alex says teasing me.

I stand from my chair intending to go get the car, but I can't leave without touching her first. I lean down and embrace her in a tight hug, drinking in her scent of raspberries mixed with sweat. I let go giving her a gentle kiss on her cheek before standing up. Her eyes widen at my kiss. "Amazing ... I'll meet you out front."

I tear my eyes from hers and walk to my Porsche. Pulling it to the front, I think about how many ways I'm going to fuck her when I get the chance. Fuck, I can't wait much longer. I'm going crazy waiting. I see her come out of the clinic and I let her climb in on her own. I know better than to try to help her at this point. After she climbs in, I'm surprised to see that her smile is clearly gone from her face.

"You okay?"

She nods.

"I don't trust Calvin," I say not able to keep quiet about it.

She smiles. "Funny, he said the same thing about you." She leans back in the chair, yawning as she closes her eyes. "Take me home. I'm exhausted."

And so I do, overwhelming her with compliments all the way.

Chapter Thirteen

ALEXA

A sharp jab pierces my neck. I scream, but it comes out silent. This is it.

God, I'm exhausted. I almost took Landon up on his offer to carry me up although I know he was just kidding.

I drop my crutches and bag holding my prosthesis on the floor before collapsing on the couch. You would think putting on a prosthesis would make me feel whole again. A feeling of completeness after finding the missing puzzle piece. But it didn't. Instead, I feel just as empty as before. I'm grateful to have the chance to walk again. I want to run and jump and be myself again. I was hoping that getting the prosthesis would be an instant antidote to my depression. *Just give it time*, that voice says again. Maybe, but I don't want to wait.

But that wasn't the only disappointing part of my session. As soon as Landon left, Calvin asked me on a date. He's such a nice guy, and I'm so thankful for everything he has done for me, but I'm just not interested. He said he would find me a new therapist because he couldn't wait any longer to ask me. But I told him no. I wanted him to remain my physical therapist and to keep our friendship. I don't know why it was so easy for me to tell Calvin no when I keep saying yes to Landon.

Calvin's words haunt me, though. "You will never heal until you talk to someone." He's probably right. I should find a friend to talk to, but I'm not ready. I don't know if I ever will be.

My phone vibrates, and it startles me. It's not a number I recognize, but I answer anyway.

"Hey, Alexa, this is Abby with *Inspire*."

I smile weakly. "Hey, Abby."

"The magazine is finished. It looks amazing! You did a fantastic job."

"That's great. I can't wait to see it."

"I know your life is crazy busy right now, but we'd love to work with you again. We have a shoot next month, and you would be our first choice."

"I'd love to!" I need as much distraction as I can get. And photography is the only thing I have left.

"Awesome! What are you doing tonight?"

"Relaxing after my therapy appointment today. I got my prosthesis, but it's exhausting learning to walk again."

"Perfect! I'll be over around seven. I'm taking you out to celebrate the magazine and how awesome you are going to rock that prosthesis soon."

"Abby, I don't really go out and party anymore. I don't think that's the best ..."

"No buts. I'll be over at seven to help you get ready." She ends the call without giving me a chance to respond. I move from the couch to my bed. I'm going to need the energy to deal with Abby later.

I HEAR two loud knocks on my door. I answer as quickly as I can on crutches. My body is still completely exhausted from my therapy.

"Come on in," I say to Abby. She bounds through the door with a large bag slung over her shoulders, her hair now a bright shade of red instead of the black with blue highlights from before.

"Oh, my god! This place is amazing," she says, looking at my view of the ocean.

"Thanks. It's pretty awesome, isn't it? I love being on the beach," I say.

Abby quickly makes herself at home on my couch. She starts digging through her bag and knocks over a frame on the end table. "Oh, sorry," she says picking up the fallen frame with a photo of him and me. "Who's the hottie? Your boyfriend?"

"No, not anymore," I say.

Placing the frame back on the end table she says, "Oh, then why do you still have his picture?"

"It's complicated. I don't really want to talk about it," I say.

She reaches into one of her bags and pulls out tequila and margarita mix. "No worries. Let's get this party started."

"I'm not really supposed to drink with the medications I'm on," I say even though that has never stopped me before.

"Is it going to kill you to have a drink?" she asks.

"Well, no," I say.

"Good. I'm fixing some drinks then," she says heading to the kitchen to find glasses. I follow her slowly.

"I think you found your inner bossiness," I say as I take a sip of the margarita she hands me.

"Sorry. You can blame yourself for pushing me to find it. I needed it. So thanks. I thought I could show you a fun time in return. I know how hard it is to find actual friends in LA," she says.

"Cheers to making new friends," I say lifting my glass to hers.

"And finding some hotties tonight," she says clinking her glass with mine.

She stands awkwardly in the kitchen before she finally asks, "Car accident or are you a klutz who falls down stairs?" while staring at my leg.

"Car accident," I say giggling, while waiting for more probing questions.

"Want to talk about it?" she asks.

"Nope," I say taking another sip of margarita and relaxing a little as I do.

"Good. I'm ordering. Pizza or Chinese? I'm starving," she says.

"Pizza."

We spend the next couple of hours eating, laughing, and trying on outfits, makeup, and fixing hair. Abby laughs as she watches me attempt to put on makeup, which I've never had the desire to learn how to do properly, so she ends up doing my hair and makeup for me. She also can't believe I don't own any club outfits or high heels. I look in the mirror when she is finished. A beautiful woman is staring back at me, but it isn't me. The woman in the mirror is flawless, so she can't be me. I have too many imperfections to cover up with a little makeup. I continue to stare at the beautiful woman in the mirror as Abby rummages through her bag.

"This is the one," she says holding up a tiny piece of black fabric that looks like it will fit around my arm.

"What is it?" I ask holding the piece of clothing up awkwardly.

"Are you serious? It's a dress! It's my roommate's. She is a stick like you, so it should fit. Just put it on," she says.

I give her an incredulous look before going to the bathroom to put it on. When I come back out and look in the mirror, I'm in shock. There is no way I can wear this in public. The black dress hugs every curve of my body and stops just under my ass. It has small straps barely holding it up and the back is a large swoop, completely exposing my back to my ass.

"I can't wear this. I look like a hooker!" I shout at Abby.

"You absolutely can wear this. You look hot, and nobody is going to be paying any attention to your leg or crutches in this outfit," Abby says.

She is right. All of the attention will be on my ass. But then I look at Abby's outfit, and I realize mine is tame in comparison. She is wearing a silver sparkly dress that has a large V-neck in the front just past her belly button; a tiny strap under her boobs is the only thing preventing them from popping out. I don't believe anyone can walk in the sky-high black heels that she's wearing. She tries to convince me to try high heels, but agrees to let me wear some strappy silver flat sandals since I'm on crutches.

"Now, let's go find us some hot ass to bang before all the good ones are snatched up," Abby says. Rolling my eyes at her, I follow her out of my condo at a leisurely pace. I don't know if it's the alcohol or what, but I'm really enjoying my night. Surprisingly, I am not dreading going to the club. Abby chats nonstop as we get out of the elevator. I exit without looking where I'm going and run smack into Landon.

"Shit. I'm sorry," I say before moving around him to catch up with Abby. But Landon doesn't let me go. He just keeps staring at me wide-eyed, "Alex, is that you?"

"Hi, Landon. We were just on our way out. See you around," I say trying to end this conversation.

But Landon doesn't let me go that easily. "That's a new look for you. I'm assuming you are going to a club?"

"You're quite the detective, Landon," I say sarcastically.

Abby gives me a sly look before jumping in. "You should join us, Landon. We are going to Fire and Ice."

"And how are you going to get in? It's one of the most exclusive clubs in town," he says turning his incredulous look to Abby.

"Oh, we will get in," Abby says.

Drew slams the door to the lobby yelling something into his cell phone before motioning to Landon to join him. "Enjoy your night, ladies," he says regretfully before following Drew.

Abby and I climb into the cab that is waiting for us and take off toward the club without looking back.

"You didn't tell me that Landon lives in the same building as you. You are so lucky. Did you see the way he was looking at you tonight? His eyes were devouring you," Abby says.

"You're crazy. It was more a look of disgust with what I was wearing," I say. *And disgust with how I look in general.* He only sees me as a friend who needs help, nothing more.

"And why did he call you Alex?" she asks.

"Because the first time we met, he thought I said Alex instead of Alexa," I say.

"He totally has a thing for you. He even has a cute nickname for you," she says teasingly.

"I don't think so. He's still hung up on Caroline," I say.

"He is not. He broke up with Caroline months ago. It was all over the tabloids," Abby says.

"Well, I think they rekindled their relationship. I've seen several recent photos of them cozy together," I say. Plus, Caroline said they were together. *And after she talks to him, there will be no chance for me, if there was even a chance to begin with.*

"Maybe to make you jealous. But he totally has eyes for you. You should go for it. You know a guy like that has got to know how to handle a woman in bed," Abby says as she reapplies her lip-gloss.

"No more talk of Landon. I just want to have fun," I say.

Chapter Fourteen

LANDON

Could be I'm fallin' for you

I TAKE a sip of my drink. My head is pounding from the music and lack of sleep, but it's worth it to see her again. I know I shouldn't have followed her, but after running into her in that slinky dress that hugs her every curve, I couldn't help myself. I couldn't think straight, so I just followed. And here I am. A stalker perched high in a club looking down at her. Any minute now I'll be spotted and the whispering will start, spreading throughout this club like wildfire. And she'll catch me.

Until then, I'll enjoy the view of her enjoying her own drink with her bubbly friend. Fire and Ice is my favorite club. Large beautiful chandeliers sculpted to look like fire or ice falling from the ceiling dangle above the club. Several private balconies, like the one I'm in, allow me to enjoy the atmosphere and club without anyone noticing. People fill the dance floor and smaller booths tucked into every corner, but my eyes never leave hers. I see her laugh, and I can't help but let my lips curve into a slight grin. I think about earlier today. Seeing Alex walk for the first time was amazing. But right now I'm fuming. Tonight would have been the perfect night to seduce her in this club. Get the one night we both deserve. But I can't fuck her. To distract myself, I let my mind drift back to earlier today.

———

"LET'S try putting the lyrics of 'Could Be' with the music and see what you think, Landon," Jackson, my lead guitarist, says.

The band starts playing, and I jump in with the first verse "You stumbled into my life ..."

"Wait, stop. Landon, you're late. Let's try it again."

The band starts again, but again, I miss my entrance.

"Come on, man. You got this." He looks at me confused. I have never had an issue like this with a song I wrote. This time, he signals for me to come in, and I sing the lyrics:

You stumbled into my life
A beautiful mess
With fighting words
Not to be messed with.

But I kept coming back
Trying my best
To break down your walls
To find a way in

But I can't help it
When I see you
My heart skips
I lose my breath
Trying to drink in your scent

It
Could be the rain
Could be the stars

Could be the way your auburn hair
Falls down your face
Could be the cause of my speeding heart

We stop where my lyrics stop because I haven't finished the song. I know what I need to write next, but that's the problem when you write a personal song about your personal life. You know what the song needs even if you aren't ready to admit those feelings to yourself yet.

"It sounds good, man. We can work more on finishing the song for you since you have rehearsal."

"No. I'll finish it. I'll have the song finished tonight."

I head across the street to the dance studio to practice for my upcoming performance. We are going over the dance portion today with the dancers. I haven't learned the choreography yet while my backup dancers have, but I'm not concerned. I always pick it up the first time.

"Hey, Darren. Is everybody ready?"

"Yep. I'll show you the choreography with the dancers then I'll have you perform it a few times and we will get out of here."

I watch him perform the complicated movements to my song. When it's my turn to perform it, I'm a disaster. I don't think I do one right move. And I threw one of the dancers who was supposed to do a flip off me so far that she almost hit the wall.

"Stop the music!" Darren shouts. I walk off to the side to drink some water, and Darren follows me. "What's wrong with you, man?"

"I just need a minute. Keep rehearsing without me."

I grab some water and storm out of the building. I take several deep breaths trying to get my shit together. But all I can think about is her. How her eyes lit up when she took her first steps. How I want to taste those lips that grin so brightly. If I could just have her for one night — own every inch of her body — then maybe I could get her out of my head.

"I think you could use a good fuck," Caroline says from behind me. I turn around to face her.

"Maybe I do. You offering?"

"Always, but that's not why I'm here."

"What do you want, Caroline?"

"I'm here to tell you about Alexa Blakely. Or should I say Alexa Wolfe. That little photographer you are so infatuated with. I met her mother-in-law the other day. They were having lunch."

"What do you mean?"

"She's married to an Ethan Wolfe." She throws me newspaper article from a few months earlier with a picture of their wedding announcement. She is in a poofy white dress. All of her tattoos are hidden behind makeup. Her piercing is gone; a small hole in her nose no larger than a dot in the picture is all that remains. Scars aren't covering her body. And it looks like her leg is still intact. The man next to her is dressed in an expensive suit. He's the same man from the picture in her condo. Shit, I knew better than to fall for her. I knew there was more she wasn't telling me. I don't do married chicks. It's way too damning for my career, and they are always after one thing: to get me to propose so they can leave their husband and their horrible little life. I slam my water down on the floor. God, I need to punch something.

"Now, you can forget about her," she says smirking at me. She couldn't have planned this better if she had planned it herself. I slam my hand against the door, needing to get some of my frustration out. I knew better than to fall for her.

"One more thing. Are you available to go to a charity ball with me on the twenty-fourth?"

"Talk to Drew about my schedule. If I'm free, I'll go with you."

Caroline puts her arms around me, even though I'm still steaming, and kisses me hard on the lips. "Call me tonight. I've missed you."

AFTER A DAY LIKE THAT, I have no idea why I'm sitting here sipping my drink watching her. I want to find out how many other guys she's cheating with. Or maybe that husband of hers will show up. But still I sit here. Hiding in the shadows. Waiting.

Chapter Fifteen

ALEXA

Tires screech. We must be spinning, sliding across the icy road. But I don't feel anything. All I see is darkness when chaos must surround me. I don't panic. I just let it happen.

We arrive at the club, and just as Landon predicted, there is a line around the building. How the hell are we going to get in? A hot babe and a cripple. I think we should just give up now and go find a more low-key bar, but Abby is determined. She skips the line and goes right to the bouncer. "We are meeting Landon Davis here. He will be arriving soon, but he wanted us to get his usual table ready - table three overlooking the dance floor."

"Name?" the bouncer says.

"Lindsey Evans and Sara Bryan," Abby says.

"Right this way," the bouncer says leading us to a table overlooking the dance floor.

When the bouncer leaves, I say, "How did you just do that?"

"I'm in the entertainment business. I know where all the celebrities like to hang out and what their preferences are. I was here a couple of weeks ago, and Landon was sitting at this table. He usually comes here after tour rehearsals with a couple of his dancers. I asked around and found out their names. I figured they would be on his list of approved people," she says.

A waitress stops by our table to take our order. Abby orders a cosmopolitan, and I order a whiskey. We both sit quietly in the booth and watch people on the dance floor until the waitress returns with our drinks.

I take a sip, and it goes down easy. "I can't believe you can drink that straight," Abby says.

"Years of experience. I don't want any fruity shit in my alcohol," I say.

Abby digs into her purse to grab something.

"Now that we have drinks and are ready to celebrate, are you ready for this?" Abby says.

I just look at her confused. "Ready for what?"

"This," she says plopping a copy of *Inspire* magazine on the table.

I gasp looking at the cover picture. Landon is completely heartbroken. Tears drip down his face as he lets go of the woman he loves. The sunset in the background reflects the ending that is happening between two people who love each other. The waves crashing off his perfectly sculpted body show how strong he is despite how broken he feels. My fingers automatically start tracing this outline. Every perfect muscle and tattoo. I study them all. I can't tear my eyes from him.

"It's something else, isn't it?" Abby asks.

"Uh-huh," I say, still infatuated with the picture I took. Looking at this picture, it feels like the first time. Every other time I have looked at him, I only saw the cocky, smug bad boy. But this picture shows more.

Abby laughs at me. "You definitely don't have a thing for him."

I blush slightly, but I don't care that she sees my attraction for him.

"Let me show you the others so you can drool over them too," Abby says, flipping the magazine to the rest of the spread.

I grin and relax when I see the rest of the pictures. These show the rough, cocky bad boy I know. I raise my glass. "To a successful shoot."

Abby raises her glass clinking it with mine. "To strutting your stuff without crutches soon."

After two more drinks, Abby is completely wasted and I have a nice buzz starting. We have spotted at least five celebrities and pointed out every hot guy in the club.

"I want to dance. Let's go," Abby says getting up from our comfy booth.

"You go ahead. I don't think I can really dance with crutches," I say.

Abby pulls two guys who have been dancing close to our booth over. "We want to dance, but my friend is on crutches. Do you think you can help us out?" she asks them.

"Hell yeah," one of the guys says lifting me out of the booth. I don't even think he notices my missing leg. Abby and the other guy follow behind us as he carries me out to the dance floor. The guy almost drops me several times as we walk the few feet toward the center before he clumsily puts me down on my good leg. We both start moving to the music. He's not a great dancer, but he at least keeps rhythm well. I move my upper body trying to match his movements, and occasionally, I have to grab hold of him to keep my balance.

I scan the dance floor looking for Abby, but I can't see her anywhere in the crowd of people covering the dance floor. My dance partner decides it's time for a change of pace; he turns me around and presses my ass against his crotch holding me close as he grinds to the music.

I try to move out of his grasp, but he just pulls me closer. "Relax, babe. We're just dancing."

I try to relax. I don't really have any other good options at the moment. Everyone else is dancing this way. We continue dancing for half of the song when he starts running his hand up my body grabbing my breast while he slobbers onto my neck. "Let go of me," I say firmly. When he doesn't, I elbow him hard in the nose. He pushes me forward as blood starts pouring down his face.

I try to grab hold of anyone to keep from falling but there is no stopping me - I'm going down, hard. I groan loudly as I land on my right shoulder. I have no idea how I'm going to manage to get up and back to the booth. That's when I feel strong arms picking me up like air. Slowly, I open my eyes and see Landon.

"What are you doing here?" I ask.

"Well, I was planning on punching that guy in the face, but I think he's suffered enough," he muses.

I look over Landon's shoulder and see the guy I was dancing with running off toward the bathroom with blood still dripping on the floor behind me. He continues to carry me back to the booth I had been sharing with Abby. I can't help myself and take a deep breath of him. He smells like fresh deodorant, a hint of cologne, and something that is all male. He places me gently into the booth before climbing in across from me. I immediately miss the feel of heat from his arms holding me, and I shiver. Without missing a beat, Landon pulls off his jacket and drapes it around my shoulders. "Better?" he asks.

"Yes." I raise my eyebrows at him, always shocked at how much of a gentleman he can be. I feel much better sitting with him now that I'm more covered up.

"Do you need ice for that elbow?" Landon asks.

"No, I'm fine. I did more damage to him than he did to me," I say.

Landon shifts in his seat before staring up at me again. "Lindsey, is it? Or are you supposed to be Sara?" A hint of his dimples appears as he says it.

"I definitely look more like an Sara, I think," I say trying not to smile.

"So Sara, when do you think you will be able to dance again? I noticed your broken leg, and I don't think you will be able to keep up with the choreography," Landon says maintaining my rogue.

"Would you like your usual, Landon?" the waitress interrupts us.

"Yes, and Sara will have another whiskey," Landon says looking at me for confirmation.

I nod my head at the waitress, and she leaves. "How did you know what I wanted to drink?" I ask.

"It's just a gift I have. I can tell what drinks people are going to order," Landon says in a deep sexy voice.

"Bullshit," I say.

Landon laughs. "It's the truth."

"Bullshit. How did you know?" I say eyeing him.

"Fine. I'll tell you if you tell me the story of how you snuck in here," he says.

"First of all, there was no sneaking in. We just told the bouncer that we were with you and wanted table three - your usual table. He asked for our names, and we gave him two of your dancers' names. That's how Abby got us in. The perks of working in entertainment magazines allows her to know all the stars' secrets. Your turn," I say.

"I have been here for about an hour watching you and Abby from upstairs," he says.

I smile. He's been watching me. Did he come here just to spy on me? No, Abby said he comes here all the time. My heart sinks. He's only sitting here because he felt some need to save me again.

Landon looks at me curiously seeming to notice a change in my mood. But the waitress comes back with our drinks before he gets a chance to ask me what's wrong. I take a sip of mine before I see what Landon has ordered.

"There better be vodka in that water," I say looking at his drink.

"Nope, it's just water," he says casually.

"You don't drink?" I ask.

"I drink water, coffee, tea, energy drinks, an occasional soda ..." he says.

"That's not what I mean," I say interrupting him. "Do you drink alcohol?"

"No, not usually," he says.

"Why?" I ask genuinely curious. I have never met someone who didn't drink.

He shrugs. "I like to remember when I have a good time. And I don't want it to mess up my vocals."

"So you're a goody two-shoes. You don't drink. I bet you don't smoke or do drugs either. Your girlfriend is your college sweetheart. You go around saving others. You sing about heartbreak. I bet you've never done a bad thing in your life despite your tattoo-ridden body suggesting otherwise," I say teasingly.

Landon grabs my hand and pulls me around the booth so that I'm sitting right next to him. "You obviously haven't read too many tabloid magazines if you think I'm on the straight and narrow. Sexual pursuits are more where my bad boy reputation factors in." He leans in closer, his hot breath warming my neck. "Let me take you home and I'll show you."

I feel my heart racing in my chest. I open my mouth to give a smartass comment back but nothing comes out. He had to have been joking. There is no way he wants anything more than just silly banter. Is there? I'm saved from responding when Abby comes running back to the table with the guy she was dancing with earlier trailing behind her.

"This is Brian," Abby yells over the loud music not bothering to tell him our names. "We're getting out of here. Are you guys going to be all right getting home?" She winks at me as she says it.

"Call me later," I say.

She pulls the magazine out of her purse and tosses it at me. "Show him the cover," she says before she leaves with her new boy toy.

I place the magazine down on the table so Landon can see. This time instead of drooling over the cover, I watch Landon's expression as he studies the image in front of him. He does a double take. "This is me?" he asks.

I laugh. "Yes, that's you."

His eyes scan the image more thoroughly, looking over every ounce of his vulnerability. He looks so human in this picture. I look at his eyes studying the picture, and I swear I see a tear fall. I touch his tense arm, and he jumps slightly. He recovers quickly and smiles brightly at me.

"Looks good. The photographer did a great job." His voice catches slightly as he says the words. "Where are the rest of the pictures?"

I flip the magazine open to the inside spread. His body visibly relaxes as he sees the more carefree Landon.

"I think we can safely say you are going to have women flocking all over you after this issue is released."

"Good thing I'm single then," Landon says staring into my eyes.

I stare back. "Yeah, good thing." I can't handle the intensity any longer and begin fidgeting in my seat. I take the magazine and place it in my purse.

"You ready to go too?" Landon asks.

"Sure," I say.

"There is a back exit where they won't get a photo of us," Landon says getting up. He hands me my crutches and waits until I'm ready to follow him. As we walk toward the exit, I see a tall man following us. It takes me a minute to realize he's probably security.

We exit the club and his Porsche is sitting right at the curb. Landon opens the passenger door for me before climbing in the driver's side. It takes all my strength to pull myself into the seat.

"How did they know we were leaving and that you would want your car?" I ask.

"The club makes it their business to know. That's why you see so many celebrities here. It's easy to get in and out without being noticed," he says.

We sit for a while in silence as Landon drives us back to our condo building. My leg is bouncing up and down to deal with the anxiety of riding in a car, but the awkwardness of the silence is starting to amp up my anxiety. I turn on the radio to get rid of the silence.

A catchy song comes on the radio, and I try tapping my foot to the beat instead of shaking. I start singing along to the chorus the second time through and glance over at Landon, who has that damn grin on his face again.

"What are you smiling about?" I ask.

Landon continues to look at the road and grin. "Just glad you like the song, but your voice is pretty terrible."

"Well, we can't all be ..." I start to say before I realize what he was smiling about. "Oh, my god! That's not nice. You should have told me it was your song!" I say embarrassed.

"I liked seeing your reaction to the song. You didn't just say you liked the song because you were being nice. Everyone is always bull-shitting me and saying my songs are amazing when they don't actually feel that way," he says.

"I can't believe I didn't recognize one of your songs," I say feeling embarrassed and hiding my face in my hands. But I'm grateful to be feeling something other than anxiety. "I haven't really had time to listen to music since my accident."

Landon glances over at me waiting for me to say more, but when I don't, he just exhales loudly.

"Why did you decide to become a musician?" I ask to change the subject.

Landon looks at me seriously. "You want to go for a walk on the beach with me?" I hadn't noticed until now that we are parked at our condo building.

"How about a sit on the beach?" I say.

Chapter Sixteen

LANDON

Just give us a chance
Give me a reason to exist

I SMILE and get out of the Porsche to help her out. We walk from the parking garage out to the beach. I take her crutches and lay them on the sand. She drapes her arm around my shoulder as we walk toward the water. We take a seat on the sand where our toes barely touch the water. She pulls my jacket tighter around her shoulders before lying back to look up at the stars. I do the same. We lie like this for several minutes before either of us speaks.

"My mom died during childbirth. I don't really know anything about her. My dad was a mess. He wasn't exactly abusive, but I wouldn't give him a father of the year award. It was mainly just Drew and me trying to raise each other. When I was six, I found an old guitar in the basement. I intuitively knew that it had belonged to my mom. I taught myself to play and sing as an outlet. Drew tried to learn too, but he was too impatient for it. Music has always been a part of my life. I went to college and majored in music. Drew majored in business. We slowly started getting more and more gigs. And then about six months ago, we signed our first record deal. I don't know if that old guitar was my mom's or not, but I feel she was the one who pushed me into music. It's my only connection to her. Music is just who I am," I say.

She just lies there looking up at the stars. Not sure what to say back to me, but I don't want her to say anything. We just share the moment together staring at the stars. "So tell me something about you," I say as I roll onto my side to look at her.

"My life is pretty boring." She giggles nervously, not making eye contact.

I chuckle. "You are anything but boring." I reach out needing to touch her. I lazily lay my hand on her wrist. I hear her suck in a small breath as I do. I turn her left wrist over and trace the black lines inked there. Lines so similar to those covering my own body. I want so much to know what every tattoo means. How she got every scar. How she lost her leg. She's not used to being pushed, and I decide I don't want ruin the night by pushing her. "Why did you decide to become a photographer?"

"My mom was a painter. I used to love watching her paint. She painted everything from sunsets to portraits. My favorites were the sunsets. I spent hours trying to copy her paintings. But I just couldn't. My mom realized quickly that I couldn't make my hands move in the same way that hers did. One day, she came home with a camera and handed it to me. That night at sunset, I was able to capture it just like my mother. She died when I was seven. Ovarian cancer."

"I guess we have more in common than just the tattoos that cover our bodies," I say.

This time her eyes meet mine, reflecting my own brokenness and heartache. I move closer to her, needing her. She doesn't move, and I can't hold back any longer. I don't fucking care if she's married. I don't care if she's just after my money. I have to have her. She moistens her lips before opening her mouth, but I don't let the words escape. I crash my mouth onto hers, finally getting to taste her soft lips that taste like whiskey and need.

Her body goes still at first as I kiss her softly. I continue holding the soft, sweet kiss until she is groaning softly into my lips. But I need more. God, I've waited too long to taste this amazing creature. I pull her to me running my hand through her hair that's softer than I imagined. Her tongue darts further into my mouth begging for more, and her hands hold me tight to her. I roll her on top of me feeling every inch of her hard body pressed against mine.

I release her mouth and start to nibble on her neck. She screams as I do. So sensitive to my every touch. I trail my kisses down her neck to the peaks poking out of her dress. She moans again as I massage her breasts. I grin as I pull her lips back into my mouth. "I love screamers."

She breathes heavily. "I ..." I kiss her neck again letting another scream escape her lips. "... am not ..." But she grins as she groans loudly when I tease her nipple beneath the thin fabric of her dress.

I see the wicked gleam in her eyes when she gets an idea. She grabs my hard cock beneath my jeans, massaging it roughly. I groan loudly from the unexpected touch. God, I want to take her right here on the beach. She pushes my shirt up needing to feel my skin against hers. She kisses up my abs to my chest as I moan at her warm kisses. I growl into a loud scream when she bites down on my shoulder, tasting me. "Good thing I love screamers too," she teases back.

I toss her onto her back pressing my own body hard on top of her, ready to retaliate the pain she just caused me. She squeals again as I squeeze her nipple hard. "You don't play fair," she moans.

"Playing by the rules is never fun."

I take her breasts in my hand springing them from her dress, intending to see how far she will take the pain mixed with pleasure. A much higher pitched scream escapes her lips. I stop, afraid I've scared her by going too fast and exposing her here on the beach. My eyes widen in shock when I hear her squeal in laughter before snorting. I stare at her in confusion as she starts trying to push me off her.

"Hurry, get off of me!" she says, still giggling.

"Why?" As I say it, the tide washes up, drenching her and half of my body. In the heat of the moment, we had rolled down the beach toward the ocean, instead of just sitting on the ocean's edge as we were before. I start laughing, too.

She starts hitting me again playfully. “Get off me before it comes back.” I stand up, pulling her up with me. We both just stand awkwardly for a minute until the giggles subside.

When we both have the same gleam return to our eyes, I pull her to me, kissing her again. A salty taste combines with the whiskey now, making her taste even more amazing. I grab her around the waist, and she wraps her leg around me. I need her. We stay like this, locked together with our lips never leaving the other’s as I head toward her condo.

Chapter Seventeen

ALEXA

"Ladies and gentlemen, let me introduce for the first time in public - Mr. and Mrs. Ethan Wolfe!" I smile at my new husband and take his hand in mine. 'Til death do us part.

LANDON CARRIES me into the lobby, and neither of us comes up for air. We just have a pure need to feel close to each other. Our stories are so similar with our mothers being the reason we started our crafts. I think about the article in my dresser drawer. It is the last interview I gave, telling the same story I told Landon about my mom. But I lied. Unlike Landon, I don't miss my mom. I should stop this. I should tell Landon about the article and all the other newspaper clippings that lay in my drawer locked away. But I don't. He palms my breast again, something I haven't felt in months, causing another loud moan to escape my throat.

He stops when we approach my door and reaches into my purse that I didn't notice he was carrying. He finds my keys and then his breath slows. "I can wait," he says. A shocked look appears on his face as if he didn't mean to say that. It's clear he doesn't want to stop.

"I can't," I say, as he unlocks the door pushing it open with my body. Landon walks straight to my bedroom and lays me on the bed, soaking it with our wet bodies before climbing on top of me again. My brain is screaming at me, *He's an arrogant bastard* ... But I don't care as he trails kisses down my body all the way to my ankle removing my shoe. *You're no different from the rest of them.* He kisses back up my leg, and I feel my heartbeat speed up again. *He'll fuck you then leave you all alone.* I feel hot and sweaty. *I don't care. All I want is one night to make me forget everything.* I pull my soaking dress off revealing my black bra and panties. Landon isn't looking at them, though; he's soaking in every inch of my body with appreciation in his eyes. They soak up my tattoos covering my torso and arms, hiding most of the scars hidden beneath them. He glances at my damaged leg with a gleam in his eyes.

"I can't wait to see what positions we can get you into. Missing one leg could have its advantages," he says devouring my body with his eyes. He pulls his own shirt off and kicks off his own shoes before covering my small body again with his large body. I feel tiny beneath him. I tug at his jeans needing those off as he kisses the newly exposed skin on my stomach and chest. He obliges by pulling his jeans off. I see the large strain beneath his boxers. *What have I gotten myself into? He's huge!* And I haven't even seen it all yet.

I let him take control as he pins me to the bed. He stretches my arms over my head and traps my wrists beneath one of his hands as I feel his hot breath on my neck. Teasing my neck, he bites down softly to test my pain tolerance. I moan softly as he does, enjoying the pain. He moves down my body, pulling my bra down with his teeth. He takes my nipple into his mouth making me squirm beneath him. I feel his grip tighten on my arms as I squirm harder, my panting fast. He rests more of his weight onto my body, crushing me. I try to breathe, but I feel trapped beneath him as his large body squashes me further and his hips move against mine. I feel the darkness overcoming me, the light around me barely visible. I close my eyes trying to keep the darkness at bay.

When I open my eyes again and look back up at Landon, he's gone - replaced by Ethan. His perfect black hair replaces Landon's messy dark brown. Dark brown eyes replace Landon's golden. A suit replaces

Landon's bare chest and legs. I try to breathe, but I can't. He tries to kiss me again when I punch him in the face. Just needing him to stop. Needing the nightmare to stop. It's not real.

I take several deep breaths before I open my eyes. Ethan is gone. Landon is sitting on the edge of the bed, blood trickling down his face. He wipes the blood on the back of his hand staring at it. His gaze drifts to me. A mix of shock and anger.

"Why should I stop, Alexa?"

I wince when he uses my name. He's never called me anything other than Alex. I don't understand the anger displayed on his face.

"Why should I stop, Alexa Wolfe? Because you're fucking married?!"

"No, I was married!" I feel tears welling behind my eyes as I realize that Caroline told him, but I don't let them come. I hate that I have fallen for Landon so easily. The guilt is overwhelming me. I need to tell him.

"What the fuck happened?"

"He's dead!" is all I can get out before the sobbing tears form. I let them flow before I continue. "My husband's dead," I say again, trembling a little.

Landon takes me in his arms, but I can't collapse yet. I have more I have to tell him. "I can't do this. It only happened four months ago. I shouldn't be able to move on so easily. But I..."

His lips suffocate me, stealing my air, and I let him. And I steal his breath right back. My body responds to him. Needing more and more of him as the heat and desire grows deep in my belly. I should stop this. There is more to tell him, and I'm not ready to take this any further. The images and panic will come flooding back in a matter of minutes. But I can't stop this. When he stops and I can finally come up for air, I'll tell him the rest.

I was married to a man who I don't even know.

ALIGNED: VOLUME 2

Chapter One

ALEXA

"Get off me," I scream. He doesn't budge. Instead, he slobbers over my neck and down to my breasts. I look up at the man on top of me, but I don't know who he is. All I see are two dark eyes suffocating me.

I LOSE myself in his kiss letting thoughts of Ethan drift away as his body consumes mine. I devour him back. I know I only have precious minutes, maybe only seconds left, until my world comes crashing down on top of us. The panic will return, as will the guilt, and I'll put a stop to this. We shouldn't be doing this. We *can't* do this. It will destroy me if I go through with this, but it doesn't stop me from enjoying this moment wrapped in his arms.

I open my eyes with his next hungry kiss trying to take him in. Every tattoo and ripped muscle of his tanned body. With each kiss, I take more of him in so I will have this memory when I tell him we can't be together. We can never be together. I can never be with anyone ever again.

Landon tries to move back to kiss me somewhere other than my lips, but I don't let him. If he moves his lips, the panic will return faster, and I just want this to last as long as possible. I grab his thick, wavy hair and keep his lips pressed to mine; I barely let either of us come up for air between panting kisses.

I can't stop his hands from wandering all over my body and making me moan. He grabs my ass and pulls me closer to him; he's begging my body for more, but I can't give him more. He pulls his lips away from mine just enough to speak against my lips.

"God, Alex. I want you so bad." He runs his tongue over my lips, and I feel myself melting into his arms as he holds me up, not letting me fall. "I'm such a monster for wanting this after what you just told me, but I don't care. I know you need this too," he says.

He pulls me on top of him on the bed giving me control to do what I want. He's giving me the chance to walk away if I want to stop this, but I can't.

"I'm the monster," I whisper before I nibble on his ear. I move my hips against him, feeling him beneath my panties as I grow wetter. *If we do it quickly, we could be done before the panic even starts.* I unhook my bra and throw it to the floor. I bite my lip when Landon takes in my naked chest with an appreciative groan. His hands immediately go to me, and I know I won't last; the second he plunges into me, I'll come.

I move to release his cock from his boxers when the darkness comes for me.

"You little slut," Ethan says. "I haven't even been gone four months and you've already moved on."

I'm shaking at the voice of Ethan haunting me. I squeeze my eyes shut trying to escape, but his voice is still there.

"You never loved me," Ethan says.

"No," I mouth but nothing more comes out.

"You're a slut, a whore," Ethan says again as his hands go around me, trapping me. I can't escape. I'm never going to escape the past even if I don't remember it.

"You never loved me. You were just after the fame, the money. You never loved me," Ethan says again squeezing me harder as I gasp for air, trembling in his arms, as the panic rises in my throat.

"No!" I scream as I rip myself from his arms. I'm shocked at how easy it was to get free. I hop to the bathroom and lock the door, hoping to keep him at bay. I pant hard, my heart fluttering fast as I collapse against the door. I pull my thighs to my chest holding myself to try to stop my legs from shaking.

When my breathing has returned to slow pants, I stand from the cold tile floor. My legs tremble slightly as I walk to the mirror and look in horror at the sight before me. My hair is a tangled mess, and my makeup is running down my face in ugly black smears. I begin wiping the smudges from my face with a towel, but what I really want is a shower. I turn the shower as hot as it will go while I strip off my panties, the only clothing I'm still wearing.

I hop into the shower, and after five minutes of standing under the hot water, I start to feel relaxed and realize what just happened. Another panic attack. I need to go back out and tell Landon what happened if he hasn't already ran from the crazy psycho that I feel like. The images of Ethan are still fresh in my mind making him feel more real than ever. *Ethan is gone. He's not coming back.* I reluctantly turn the water off, grab the white towel hanging outside the shower door, and dry myself off. I could just stay in the shower forever and not have to deal with my past. I find an oversized shirt and shorts that I had laid out before I left for the club. I put them on and comb my wet hair, stalling as long as I can before facing Landon again. When I can't think of anything else to keep me in the bathroom, I open the door and stumble out, expecting Landon to have already made a run for it back to his condo - *wishing* is more like it.

I hop back when I see Landon sitting on my bed; I'm shocked that he is still here. He's put his jeans back on, but his shirt is still in a crumpled mess on the floor. He looks downward staring at the hard floor lost in his own thoughts. He glances up when I hop into the room. He makes no other movement. It's almost as if he's frozen; he doesn't know what else to do, so he just watches me. I see my crutches on the floor by the bed, but I decide instead to hop the few feet and sit on the bed next to him.

I look over at him as I sit next to him, his eyes looking vacant and sad.

"I'm sorry. I shouldn't have let it get that far when I knew I would have another panic attack," I say looking at his empty expression. I search his face for a hint of life behind his blank stare and find nothing. I sigh before I continue speaking. This conversation is going to be harder than I thought.

"I don't remember who I am," I say before falling back on the bed. I stare up at the ceiling waiting for him to move. I wait for him to respond, to give some indication he heard me. I wait a long time as he just sits there. I watch his chest rise and fall as he takes a deep breath before he leans back on the bed next to me, careful not to let any part of his body touch mine.

"What do you mean you don't remember who you are? You're Alexa Blakely, famous photographer," he says with a nervous laugh.

"The car accident took more than just my ability to walk and run for a few months. It took more than my husband. It took something much more devastating," I say.

His eyes read of confusion; his mouth opens to ask a question, but he doesn't ask it. I feel the fluttering in my stomach begging me to stop. I need to keep talking, though. I need to tell him, for my own sanity as much as his.

"It took my memories," I say in a trembling voice.

Landon's eyes grow wide. "What do you mean?"

"Brain damage ... the car accident caused severe brain damage. The car went into the water sucking the oxygen from me, filling my lungs with water. When they found me, I was unconscious and not breathing. They rushed me to the hospital where I was in a coma fighting for my life for two weeks." I feel the tears falling, rushing down my face as I remember the few memories I have. The nightmare as the limo spun out of control before bursting into flames. I thought the worst was over when that happened. The pain was unbearable, but Ethan and I had both survived the initial crash. Until the bridge collapsed over the river, sucking us under. Taking Ethan with it.

"When I awoke, they told me that Ethan had drowned. What made it so much worse was that I had no memory of who Ethan was. I have no memories before that night. And my memories of that night are fuzzy." The tears fall faster until I'm sobbing. I feel Landon's gentle arms around me, and I lean into him. He holds me gently in his arms for what seems like hours, not saying a word or judging me until my sobbing stops and turns into annoying hiccups. I think about showing Landon the torn green pocket square, the ring, the newspaper clippings, and the few photos of my mother – the few actual possessions I have locked in the drawer of my nightstand – to make it more real for him. To show him all I have lost and will never remember, but they are too precious to show him.

"I'm sorry. I knew I shouldn't have pushed you. You probably hate me for pushing you beyond your limits." He pauses and turns my chin so I'm looking at his golden eyes. They shine brightly at me and hope still lingers for more.

"I've just never wanted anyone more in my life than I want you. I let myself get caught up in the moment, but I can be patient. I told you earlier tonight I can wait for you and that still holds true. I'll wait for you."

I sink into him as his words sound like music to my ears. How easy it would be to take him up on his offer. I could have a friend to talk about my struggles for now, and in a few months, I could have a lover waiting for me when I'm ready to move on. I can't move on, though. I untangle myself from his arms, needing space to get through the rest.

"You can't wait for me. I'll never be ready for a relationship again. The pain I've experienced after losing Ethan is unbearable. I can never experience losing someone I love again. I won't do it. I'm not supposed to be with anyone else. I just want to move on by myself."

"You can't live life without love, without pain. You need both to live. Otherwise, you merely exist," he says. He tries to pull me back to him, but I push him away.

"Then I just want to exist!" I say. I drop my eyes from him, staring instead at my hands. I want so much to be holding the piece of green fabric; that always calms me. "I don't deserve anything more after forgetting someone I loved," I say.

"You can't blame yourself for not remembering him. I'm sure you loved him, and he knows that."

"Maybe, but how do I mourn someone I don't remember? How do I live with that guilt?" I say looking back up at him.

"By living when he can't," he says as he wipes the tear from my eye that I hadn't even noticed.

I shake my head. "I don't know how to live anymore," I say weakly.

"Then let me show you how as your friend," he says.

"I don't think I can. You'll always want more, and I can't give you more. I don't even know who I am really. I just need to focus on healing and finding out about my past."

"Let me help you," he says.

"You can't." I turn away from Landon. If I keep looking at him, I'll give in and destroy both of our lives. I can't do that. I just need him gone, out of my life, so I can live my life — alone.

"Just go," I say still not looking at him. I can feel his eyes on me; he wants to say more, but he doesn't move.

I close my eyes tight to keep the tears at bay. How can I still need to cry after all the tears that have already fallen tonight? "Please," I beg.

I hear Landon get up from the bed, but I don't dare open my eyes and reveal my pain. I don't dare look at Landon to see his pain. I just keep them closed trying not to think about how lonely I'm going to feel a few minutes from now. I feel his wet lips brush against my cheek.

"Good-bye, Alexa," he says. I wince at the words. When I hear the door close, I open my eyes. He's gone. Just like everyone else I have ever loved, but I don't love Landon. I didn't fall for him yet, so really, I'm preventing the pain before it starts. This pain is bearable. This pain I will get over. I let the tears come as I use the crutches Landon leaned against the bed next to me to find my purse on the counter in the kitchen. I ruffle through it until I find the little piece of green fabric. The only comfort I will have tonight. I carry it back to bed with me, taking deep breaths, trying to find his scent that still lingers on the silk. No matter how long I lie here breathing in his scent, it doesn't bring back any new memories. Just the same painful memories of the accident I'm never going to escape.

Chapter Two

LANDON

It could be the raindrops pouring down your face.

"Twenty minutes to showtime," the spunky assistant, Samantha, says as she pokes her head into my dressing room and leaves just as quickly. Just like Alex, she entered my life, turned it upside down, and then was gone before I even knew what was happening. *Why does everything always fucking remind me of her?* I have to get her out of my head. She doesn't want anything to do with me. At least, I won't have to worry about being jealous when I see her with another guy because there won't be another guy.

I'm fucked up. I know it. I don't want to settle down and be someone's knight in shining armor. Unlike her, though, I at least have friends. Well, Drew. At least, I have Drew, and I have women to keep me company at night. Although I haven't had that in weeks. The appeal is just gone, along with her.

I should be thankful. Alex is messed up; I was right about that. I should have just left her alone and found someone else to fuck. Staying in her life would only cause more drama in mine, which I don't need right now. I should just be thankful her presence got my creative juices flowing again. I've basically finished the song she inspired, which has gotten the label off my back. I'll release the single in a week, and they'll give me more time to finish the rest of the album now that I've proven I've overcome my writer's block. I just need to let her go. It hasn't been difficult to do that these last two weeks since I've been on the road appearing on several talk shows and opening for other musicians. Today is my last show, my last appearance, and then I'll be back in LA. Back to the same condo building with only ten floors separating us. It will be hard to keep my distance then.

The door to the dressing room opens. "You ready?" Drew says as he steps in wearing his usual business suit. I will never understand him. He doesn't need to wear a suit when he is going to spend his entire night backstage making sure everything runs smoothly. Everyone else is dressed casually in jeans and t-shirts but not Drew. He always looks professional and snooty.

I look at myself in the mirror. My hair has been tousled perfectly, and I'm wearing powdered shit all over my face to make my skin look flawless. I have on tight, dark jeans, and a black t-shirt reveals my tattoos on my arms. I've warmed up my voice and stretched. I'm ready. I stand from my seat and follow Drew out of the dressing room without saying a word. I don't have to. Neither of us ever does, we just know. Some people say they feel the same after falling in love. They don't have to tell their partner anything; a connection exists that speaks louder than words. I'll never know. Drew is all I'll ever have.

We walk down the long, dark hallway that leads to the side of the stage. My band and dancers have gathered just off stage, and they are ready to run on stage to do our short set. I hear the crowd just beyond the stage. I forget what town we are in. Seattle? Or was it Portland? Everything mixes. It will be much worse when I do my own tour. I've only been on the road two weeks; a tour will last months.

Energy is flowing through my veins as I hear the crowd in the distance. Each step I take increases the adrenaline. I was meant to do this with my life. I approach my band and dancers, listening as one of the guys starts shouting and tries to get everyone pumped up for the show. I don't need to be pumped up because I already am. The band runs on stage on cue and starts playing the first chords to 'I Don't Need Your Love.' I wait in the wings with my dancers, a wide grin forming on my face and my eyes sparkling with excitement. Most performers will tell you no matter how many shows they do, they still get nervous — but not me. I live off this excitement. I'm calm, relaxed as I hear my cue to run on stage and take my place in the center.

The crowd cheers loudly as I sing the first verse. Most openers perform to half a crowd merely warming up the crowd as they take their seats before the main act. As I look out over the crowd, I see a full house. These people came to see me, not just the act to follow. My grin widens as I continue to sing and perform the song they all came to hear.

I COLLAPSE on the bed in my hotel room. I hate hotel rooms. I've lived in enough motel and hotel rooms as a kid to make me value having my own space. Even this luxurious hotel with its bellhops, thousand-count sheets, and mini bar doesn't entice me to want to stay here. It's only one night, though, and then I'll be back in my own bed tomorrow. How I'm going to survive living on a tour bus and in and out of hotels for months on end while on tour, I'm not sure. Maybe that's why most musicians turn to drugs or alcohol to cope.

I glance over at the alarm clock sitting on the dark wood night-stand next to the glass lamp. It's 1:35 am. Not late by my normal standards. Usually, after the concert is over, we party the night away until we pass out sometime around sunrise, but tonight, my heart just isn't in it. Two weeks of partying is enough for me. Especially when I'm not getting laid. Sex is my drug of choice, and I'm afraid I'm going through withdrawals. I'm irritable, depressed, and anxious. I swear I'm even having tremors at night from the lack of human contact. There is no reason I shouldn't be getting laid every night. The band and dancers sure aren't having any trouble finding someone to keep them comfortable at night.

It's not as if I haven't tried. I have. I've found some of the hottest women on the face of the earth swarming me in the VIP sections of the clubs where we party. We dance. We make out. She tries to take me back to her hotel, and my body doesn't move. Sometimes, she just tries to find the nearest bathroom or closet. My body still doesn't cooperate. *Damn Alex!* All I can think about when I'm with them is *her*. The smell of fresh raspberries along with some other fruity shit she always smells like. I didn't even know a woman could smell like that. Somehow, she always does; even when she's drenched in salty water, she still smells like raspberries. I not only ache from that smell, but I also miss her snarky banter. How hard she tries to hide her affection for me. No one else tries to hide anything; instead, they throw themselves at me. I miss the chase, the excitement of making a woman fall for me. It's too easy now that I'm a superstar. They just want their one night to say they banged Landon Davis and hope to be the one who makes the bad boy settle down. That will never happen.

I hear a loud knock at the door. I groan not wanting to move from the bed. I thought I was going to be able to get to sleep early today even though sleep hasn't come easy lately. I pull myself from the bed.

"Dammit, Drew!" I shout as I stumble to the door. "When are you going to remember your key?"

I throw the door open ready to pummel Drew to the ground; instead, Caroline stands in a skin-tight leopard dress. Or maybe it's giraffe? I don't know my animal prints. I'm about to slam the door in her face, but I can see the tears welling in her eyes. I've known Caroline since we were kids. We didn't meet in college as the tabloids had reported. We've known each other since we were five. We were the three musketeers – Caroline, Drew, and I. We never left each other's side. Her family has put her through a lot of shit. Almost as much shit as Drew and I have been through. In all of our years together, I have never seen Caroline cry. She's never shed one single tear – at least, not in front of me. I know it's something big from the look on her face.

I hold the door open. "Come in."

Caroline walks in never faltering as she moves in her spiked heels.

"I need a drink," she says taking a seat on my bed and removing her heels. I walk over to the mini bar and find her favorite — vodka soda. I hand her the drink, and she gulps it down. I take the glass from her heading back to the mini bar and pour her another. I don't bother to pour myself anything. Alcohol does nothing for me. She takes the drink from my hand sipping a little slower this time.

"I hate them," she says before taking another long drink.

I sit down on the bed next to her. "Who?"

She pulls her phone out of her purse and scrolls to a page on her browser. "Them!"

I look at the article. Shit, the horror movie she is starring in opened in theaters yesterday. It's just a small indie film, but I should have remembered. I know she'd directing half of her anger at me, as much as she's directing it at the film critics giving her a horrible review. *Some friend I am.* She had asked me a while ago to attend the premier with her, but I couldn't go due to my schedule. I'm an asshole. I could have at least sent her flowers or something. Our relationship is complicated at best, but at the core, we will always be friends. Always be there for each other no matter how many times we have hurt each other. Shit, tonight is about to get a lot more expensive.

I stand from the bed and extend my hand to her. "Come on. Forget those guys. We are going out to celebrate."

She smiles brightly, downs the rest of the vodka, slips on her heels, and follows me out of the hotel.

Chapter Three

ALEXA

I punch him in the face with my free hand. Instead of releasing me, he flips me onto my stomach and grabs my arms tying them together behind my back. I continue to scream and kick trying to get him off me.

It's been two weeks. Two long fucking weeks without any contact. He hasn't texted me, called me, run into me in the lobby — nothing. It's as if he's disappeared off the face of the earth. I've even spent time lingering in the lobby and on the beach on the mornings he usually runs. Nothing. He's giving me the space I wanted; now, I just need to figure out how to get him out of my head. It doesn't help that I only have a few months of memories to reflect on while he has a lifetime of women to replay in his head.

I never thought he would actually leave me alone without a fight. I thought I had weeks of dealing with his stalker tendencies before I was rid of him, but just like that, he's gone.

"Alexa ... Alexa," Calvin says.

I shake my head turning to face him. "Sorry, what did you say?"

"You're hopping again instead of walking smoothly."

"Sorry." I try to change my gait as Calvin asks, walking more smoothly. We have been doing therapy every day for the last two weeks. I want to perfect my walk by the charity ball, which only leaves me another week. I'm still a little awkward and trip frequently, but I'll be ready in a week. I don't have a choice not to be.

"That's better," Calvin says as he watches my gait. More like watches my ass as I walk. Ever since he professed his love and requested to take me out on a date, I have felt awkward around Calvin. He, on the other hand, doesn't seem to be bothered at all. He glances at his watch and his face falls slightly, the only indication that he still has feelings for me.

"Time's up, but I'll see you tomorrow, right?"

"Yep. Till tomorrow." I grab my small purse and walk out of the clinic. Without my crutches, I should feel more free, but I don't. I still feel trapped and confined by the prosthesis that won't let me run and jump or do anything right now other than an awkward walk. I walk toward the parking lot with a large grin on my face as I see my silver Tesla Roadster sparkling in the bright morning sunlight. She had been sitting in NYC for the longest time until I decided I wanted her shipped here, but after driving her once with my left leg, I realized it would be more comfortable to have the accelerator moved to the left side. I just got her back from the shop yesterday.

I climb into my shiny car, my pulse running faster than usual. I put the car in drive and speed back to my condo. I roll the windows down as I drive, loving the fresh air on my face. This is the only time I feel free. The only time I feel normal. I contemplate turning the radio on, but I'm afraid I'll hear Landon's voice. I decide to try a country station and bounce excitedly to the crooning guy singing about corn and flyover states instead.

"I CAN'T BELIEVE you are walking so well so soon," Abby says looking at me with awe in her face.

"Well, when you have a mother-in-law like mine with high expectations, it's good motivation," I say. I adjust the camera again trying to capture a less condescending look from the actress I'm shooting, but I don't think that's possible.

"Ex-mother-in-law," Abby corrects me. Smiling, she turns her attention back to the actress, her grin immediately turning to a frown. "Try a smile!" she shouts at the actress, but it's more of an evil grin than a smile.

I capture the look wishing, for once, the magazine would allow a little Photoshop. I have spent a lot of time with Abby over the last few weeks working on ideas for this photo shoot. I felt comfortable with Abby, and I ended up telling her everything. After rambling about Landon for the last two weeks, she insisted on hearing the whole story. So I told her. It was easy after telling Landon.

"If only Landon was here. Then we could get the jaw-dropping, sexy look we want from her. One look at him and she would be melting in front of the camera," I say before realizing my mistake, but I can't help it. Landon is always on my mind, always the solution to every problem.

"You have to get over that boy. He's moved on, so you should too, but that does give me an idea." She turns to Nathan. "Go find me a male model in his underwear and parade him around, please." Nathan scurries off to meet Abby's request.

"Wait ... what do you mean he's moved on," I say staring at her instead of my muse.

Abby ignores me. "Try sexy! Think about your boyfriend and pretend you are trying to get him into bed with you."

I stop taking pictures and walk over to Abby sitting behind the monitor five feet away from me. I glare at her and grab her by the arm pulling her into a standing position. "Ow," she screeches as she reluctantly stands up.

"What do you mean he's moved on?" I snarl.

Her eyes won't meet my gaze. She moves her hands to the keyboard and types in a few things.

"Look for yourself," she says pointing at the screen. I haven't looked at a magazine article in weeks. I was afraid I'd see Landon, but I'm shocked at the sight in front of me. Caroline draped all over him as they stroll through downtown Seattle. They look good together.

Landon even looks like he is enjoying himself. I feel my face growing red to the point I'm afraid a vein is going to burst. I shouldn't be angry. I have no reason to be. I told him to move on and leave me alone, and he did. I just hoped it would have been someone else – someone better – then it wouldn't be so hard. Who am I kidding? Seeing him with anybody else would have been torture. I just need to focus on my career, on healing, and on remembering my past. Not be hung up on a guy. Landon Davis is an arrogant asshole. I will not let him control my thoughts ...

DAY two of not letting Landon control my thoughts is not going well. I have spent the entire day shopping with Elisabetta and Laura, and nothing I try on is good enough for them. I'm just not elegant enough, classy enough, or beautiful enough. I'm just not enough, and no dress or hairstyle is going to change that.

I come out of the dressing room wearing another large black ball gown that swallows my tiny figure. I have to wear black to show I'm still mourning the husband I lost while also making sure to cover my prosthetic leg. Otherwise, people would think I'm trying to pull focus from the loss of Ethan by displaying the loss of my leg. I also have to look elegant and beautiful with a hint of sex appeal so the attendees will find me attractive and care that I lost Ethan, but not so attractive that I look like I'm a slut and ready to move on to the next guy. It's exhausting. Elisabetta and Laura both agree the best way to do that is with a ball gown. I disagree.

I stumble into the room almost tripping over the large gown.

"Shoulders back. Stop slouching, Alexandra," Laura barks at me.

I hold my tongue trying my best to smile instead of ripping Laura into tiny pieces. *Oh Ethan, why did you leave me?* I don't know if I can handle dealing with his mother for much longer, even if she is the only connection to my past. It's not as if she shares anything about my past with me except how wonderful Ethan was and how I was never good enough for him.

"No, this won't do," Elisabetta says as she studies me. She looks at Laura, and they both sigh as if I'm a lost cause. Like they would have better luck dressing up a dog in a dress to parade around the ball.

"I'll go change," I say heading back to the dressing room, making sure to keep my shoulders back and holding my dress up to ensure I don't trip again. I close the door to the dressing room and let out the growl I've been holding back as I rip another dress off and crumple it on the floor. I sigh looking at the crumpled silk and chiffon; it's not fair to the dressing room attendants to leave it that way. I pick up the dress, smoothing the wrinkled fabric before putting it on a hanger. I look at the pile of dresses I have yet to try on. Each black ball gown will suffocate me in its tent-like fabric. I hate dresses and would prefer never to have to wear one, but I know if I have to wear one, these aren't going to be it.

I dig through the hangers hoping to find a gem beneath the horrendous pile of poofy fabric when I spot it. Its black, long fabric lies flat against the wall as if the larger, heavier dresses have smothered it. It doesn't look exciting, but to me, it's the glimmer of hope I've been looking for. I quickly put on the dress to find that its simple strapless top fit nicely to my chest and the fabric hugs my curves without exposing too much. A large slit on the left side allows my toned left leg to be seen without showing my hideous right leg. This is the dress. Now, I just need to convince Elisabetta and Laura.

I walk confidently out of the dressing room toward them chatting away, most likely complaining about something else I have done. Complaining about how Ethan didn't marry a more sophisticated woman. I make sure my shoulders are back as I move to the center of the room standing as tall as I can when I look at myself in the mirror. I even wear a bright smile, and I swear I see a twinkle in my eye when I gaze at myself in the mirror.

"What do you think?" I ask.

Silence is the response I get, which makes me smile brighter. Elisabetta finally gets up from her seat circling me as a vulture would, searching for a flaw she can point out, but none can be found.

"I think this will work. We will have to find some nice jewelry to go with this. A bold necklace and earrings. And we are going to have to deal with your hair, but I think we can make this work. Do you agree, Laura?"

Laura stands, scrunching her eyes at me as she studies me. "It will have to work. We have a salon appointment in an hour to make."

Thank god! I think silently. One bit of torture is finally over, but there are still plenty of hours in the day to experience the rest. I turn back when I see black eyes staring at me in the mirror, reminding me of the eyes I keep seeing in my dreams. I turn from the mirror to find the man, but he is gone. I want to ask Laura about it. She could tell me if the dreams I have are true or not, but every time I've ever brought anything up, she shoots me down. She will only ever tell me about Ethan's past. She doesn't seem to care if I have forgotten everything else and never go back to the past. She just wants me to remember him as the god he was. I resolve to forget about the dreams and just live my life for now. And today, my focus is on surviving the salon.

Chapter Four

LANDON

Could be the stars sparkling in outer space

I SIT on the white leather couches in the lobby, occasionally glancing out the windows to watch the ocean. Mostly, I just sit and wait for her to come through the doors. I know she isn't in her condo. I spent enough time knocking on her door to know. I think I pissed off all of her neighbors with the noise I was making. Two weeks is all I could go. I'm all out of self-control, and I'm not above begging today just to spend some time with her.

I hear the door to the lobby open, and I sit up straighter trying to get a glimpse of the woman walking through the door. The woman walking through the door is beautiful, blonde, but not Alex. More like Caroline than Alex. Caroline and I had a good time last night. *Too* good of a time if you base our night on what the tabloids are publishing today. I didn't feel anything for her, though. Caroline didn't turn me on the way she used to. I didn't feel the excitement, the adrenaline, the rush I would expect from going out with a woman. Right now, the only woman I have a chance of experiencing that with again doesn't want to see me and doesn't want to talk to me. So I'll sit and wait. Wait. I hate that word. I'm not a patient man, but I find myself wasting half a day away just sitting and waiting for her.

I hear the door to the lobby open again, and I don't even bother to look up. It won't be her. I fidget with my phone trying to look busy, and after a reasonable amount of time has passed, I look up at the passerby. Alex. She's walking toward me, a sly grin on her face. *She's walking*, without crutches, or a cane, or anything. She walks with her prosthetic leg as if she has been doing it all of her life. Amazing. I hold back my own smile as she walks toward me, trying to look indifferent so she can't see how she affects me, but I can't keep the smolder out of my eyes or my heartbeat from speeding up.

She stops walking when she realizes what she is doing, that she isn't supposed to be walking toward me. We aren't friends anymore; we aren't anything. I get up from my seat and move the few feet to her, not letting her escape into the elevator without talking to me. Maybe if I just hear her voice it will be enough for me to get through the next few weeks without her.

"Hello, Alex. You look amazing," I say. I pull her into a gentle embrace, breathing in her scent of raspberries and fresh flowers as I do. The only girly thing about her. Otherwise, she looks like a tomboy in her running shorts, tank, and tennis shoes. I don't think she's bothered with makeup, and she's pulled her hair back into a ponytail. She fits perfectly into my chest, though, when I embrace her. She just fits. When I reluctantly let her go, I see the flicker of disappointment flash across her face before she plasters a fake smile in its place.

"You look good too, Landon," she says, taking in my full appearance. Her eyes linger over my chest before making their way up to my face. She moistens her lips with her tongue and my mouth goes dry imagining her tongue on my lips. I clear my throat to try to remain normal, but that's impossible when I'm around her. I'm drawn to her in a way I don't even understand.

She notices my reaction and frowns as her eyes drift to the ground. She folds her arms across her chest and retreats from me, shifting her weight backward. "I should go," she says motioning to the elevators behind her.

"Wait ..." I say putting my hand on her shoulder to stop her. Her emerald eyes meet mine, and sadness emulates from them. She stares at me waiting, but I don't know what to say. *God, what is wrong with me?* I always know what to say. I'm turning into a pussy every time I'm around this woman.

"What about the bets? The agreements we made," I say, and my shoulders relax as I speak. This is the way. This will be how I get back into her life at least as a friend.

"What bets?" A confused expression scrunches her face.

"We agreed that when your leg healed, we would go running and see who the real pussy was. We also agreed if I let you drive my car, then I would get to drive yours. I would like to take you up on one of those offers today." I grin smugly waiting for her to argue with me, but she won't win. I never go back on an agreement.

To my surprise, her eyes light up just a little, and she grins smugly back at me. "Fine. My car is right outside. Let's go, old man."

I follow her outside, not sure what to expect. She has a small condo, and while she has a well-established photography career, I have no idea how much money she makes or what her dead husband used to make. But I am definitely not expecting what I'm looking at when we walk out the door.

"This is not your car. You're kidding me, right?" I stare in disbelief as I look at the silver Tesla Roadster. She shrugs and tosses me the keys. I catch them with one hand. She climbs into the passenger seat as I continue to stare in disbelief.

"Are you coming or not?"

"Definitely coming." I run to the driver's side and climb in. The inside is just as sweet as the outside. I look down and notice the three pedals instead of just two and assume the car is a manual transmission. It's been a while since I drove a manual car, but it's nothing I can't handle. I look at the stick shift, but it isn't there. I glance up at Alex in confusion.

"Just use the two on the right like you are used to. The pedal on the far left is for me since I drive with my left foot."

I nod and put the car in drive. I take it slowly as we drive down the highway next to the beach. I don't want to cause a panic attack in her car.

"So do you have a name for this baby?" I ask motioning to the Tesla.

She laughs softly seemingly relaxed in the seat next to me. "No, I was going to name her Silvia, but that name was already taken."

I laugh and keep driving. "I'll have to help you come up with a name then. How 'bout Gabriella?"

She shakes her head.

"Valentina?"

She shakes her head more fervently sticking her tongue out in disgust.

"Isabella?"

She laughs this time as she shakes her head. "Do you only know Italian supermodel names? I think you've been with a few too many if that's all you are thinking about."

I frown. "Well, then you name her."

She sits for a minute thinking deeply as if this is the biggest decision she is going to have to make. Her lips curl up into a slight smile. "Tessie!"

I shake my head and stick out my tongue in disgust. "That's not a beautiful enough name for a beautiful car like this."

"Nope, it's my car. I get to name it, and I like Tessie!"

"Fine." I shake my head laughing. "Tessie, it is. How long have you had this car, anyway? I can't believe a girl would pick out this nice of a car."

She hits me on the shoulder for the last comment but then frowns slumping back into her seat. "I don't know how long I've had this car. I don't even know if I picked it out or if Ethan did. Although, it feels like a car I would pick out." *Dammit!* I have to work on filtering myself before I ask her questions about her past that she obviously doesn't know the answers to. She opens the glove compartment searching through the papers until she finds what she's looking for.

"Last year. It's just in my name so I would assume I picked it out." She thinks for a moment. "This is the only car I found. We lived in downtown NYC before the accident, and if Ethan were anything like his mother, he would have preferred to hire a driver to drive us around."

"But not you?"

"I don't know what I was like back then. I've been told that after a brain injury like what I experienced, personalities can change. I might not be the same person I was before, but the now me likes driving my own car."

I smile at her, the excitement in her eyes as she talks about the car. If I had to make any bets, I would guess she liked cars before, too, if she spent the money to buy this one.

I look over at her a minute later to see her fidgeting nervously in her seat.

"What's wrong?"

"Nothing. Just thinking."

"What are you thinking about?"

"These last couple of weeks. I saw the pictures. It looks like you and Caroline had a good time in Seattle." She tries to hide it, the jealousy behind her sad eyes and too bright smile, but she doesn't fool me. She's jealous, or she wouldn't have brought it up.

I can't help it; it makes me happy to know she's jealous of Caroline. "We were just celebrating her movie premier as friends."

"It looked like more to me."

"Caroline is a friend who used to be more."

"How did Caroline break your heart?" she asks. My hands tense on the steering wheel.

"I don't want to talk about her."

"That's not really fair. I told you all of my secrets," she pleads sticking out her pouting lip.

"I'm not talking any more about her." If I told her the truth about Caroline and me, I'd never see her again. She doesn't need to know.

"Fine, then I want to go home." She looks out the window not looking at me as we drive for several minutes. My heart races as I try to decide what to do. I don't want to take her back to the condo yet. I want more time, but I don't want to share my past, and I don't want to lie. I reluctantly go for the lie I've told the media many times before.

"I met Caroline my senior year of college. She was a sweet

Southern girl. Smart. She was a finance major. I wasn't looking for a relationship. I needed to finish college, needed to keep writing music, but I didn't have a chance. I fell in love with her hard and fast. We were inseparable. We moved in together the next semester. She loved my music, which made me love her even more."

I glance over at her, and she nods for me to continue.

"When I got signed to a music label three years later, she wanted me to pay her for the work she did. I paid her. I would have done anything for her. I loved her. A couple of months later, she wanted more. She wanted to get married, so I proposed."

I watch as she gasps. She hadn't realized that I had been engaged or possibly even married. Her chest stops moving before she asks, "Did you want to propose?"

"Yes, at the time. I loved her. It was her idea, but I would have eventually come to the same conclusion myself and asked her anyway."

She frowns in her adorable way. I want to laugh at how cute she is, but I try to hold back. A small chuckle escapes making her frown deeper, her face growing red with jealousy.

"Did you get married?"

I raise an eyebrow at her jealousy before continuing. "Caroline started planning a big, fancy wedding. Drew convinced me to have a prenup, but Caroline didn't want the prenup. When she realized Drew wasn't going to let me budge on the prenup, she blackmailed me to keep a negative story out of the tabloids. When I wouldn't pay her, she went public with this story about how I was abusive. How I had cheated on her."

"That lying fucking bit-" She looks up at me with embarrassment covering her burning cheeks. "How awful, I mean."

I smirk. "But what she didn't count on is that Drew had hired a private investigator to follow her. He had pictures of her cheating on me. She retracted her story, but the damage to my heart was already done. It completely shattered me. It took me a while to realize she was in it for the money. That's all she wanted."

"Well, you don't have to worry about that with me. I have more money than I need," she says, covering her mouth with her hands in horror as she insinuates that we could have more.

Desires spring to life inside me at her words, at even the possibility. "I'm not sure how I feel about the girl I'm seeing making as much money as me in a hypothetical way."

"I think technically I'm worth more than you," she teases.

I growl. "You're worth a lot more than how much is in your bank account."

Her legs start bouncing nervously as I continue driving. "All right, turn back. It's my turn."

I turn back.

Chapter Five

ALEXA

He stands up; I think he's going to leave me alone, but he kicks me hard in the side. I let out a gasp as I try to catch my breath. He kicks me over and over, continuously knocking the breath out of me. All I can feel is the pain.

HE PULLS my car into my parking spot, and I jump out needing some air, some space. *What in the hell am I doing?* I'm supposed to be keeping my distance and getting over him, not getting closer to him. But I can't help myself.

I watch as he reluctantly climbs out of my car. "My turn!" I say.

His lips curl downward. "I don't think that's a good idea. You had your car modified so you could drive it. My car has no such modifications."

"Nope, a deal is a deal. I let you drive mine, and now, it's my turn to drive yours."

He chuckles. "Man, you are dirty when you want to be."

I laugh too. "Keys."

He reaches into his pocket pulling out the keys to his Porsche. I grin, ready to feel the adrenaline and excitement of driving a fast car.

The freedom it brings is like nothing else. We walk through the parking lot until we find his car. I climb in and watch Landon as he settles in the passenger seat next to me; I swear he's sweating more, and if I look closely, his hands are trembling. I begin to remove my prosthetic leg so it won't get in the way of the pedals. I try not to let Landon's stares bother me as I take off my prosthetic leg and hand it to him, but I'm still not comfortable with my deformed body. He doesn't seem bothered, though, as he places it next to his feet.

I adjust the seat and mirrors so I can see, feeling small in the large car. I test the foot pedals with my left leg; it will do. I look over at Landon. "You ready for this?"

He closes his eyes, gripping the armrests tightly and bracing himself. "Yes."

I put the car in drive and zip out of the parking garage, making the tires squeal as I do. I glance over at Landon and see the panic rising in his eyes; it brings me joy to see the cool, confident bad boy in such a panicked state.

"Slow down," he says. Instead, I speed up as we zoom down the highway. I roll my window down to let the wind blow on my face, feeling the fresh, salty air and feeling alive.

"Silvia drives really well." I look over at Landon still stuck to his seat, his eyes only peeking open slightly.

"Silvia is about to have a heart attack. Keep your eyes on the road."

I laugh and turn my attention back to the road. I love driving this car, but as I drive, my thoughts go back to Landon. After I drop him back off, what are we going to do? Are we going to go back to ignoring each other? Are we going to try being friends? I can't handle more ... can I? Maybe if it was just sex. Landon is the kind of guy who is used to just sex, but would my panic attacks get in the way of even trying that?

"What are we going to do when we get back? What is this between us?" I blurt out before I realize I'm speaking.

"No talking," Landon barks. "Just focus on driving."

I sigh and return my attention to driving the car back in silence.

When I pull the car back into the garage parking spot, I hear Landon take a deep, relaxing breath. He barely breathed the whole time I was driving, but I don't give him time to breathe for long before I start my questioning.

"What are we doing?" I stare down at the floor not wanting to meet his eyes; I know my eyes would give away too much — deeper feelings for him that I can't have.

"I think we are friends with more. Whether we stay away from each other or hang out every day, I don't think anything will change that."

"Friends with more what? Like friends with benefits?"

"Friends with more possibilities. You need help getting over your panic attacks. I need inspiration to write more music. We could help each other. It wouldn't just be about the sex. It would be about helping each other. After we do, we can go back to just being friends who have a deeper understanding of each other." I stare at him still confused, but the confusion doesn't stop me. All I could do while he was talking was stare at his moist, inviting lips. And remember how amazing it felt when they touched mine. My lips meet his almost of their own accord. Almost in unison, his hand grabs the back of my neck to pull me toward him as my hands go to his thick messy hair. I pull him against me, showing him that I want him just as much as he wants me.

His tongue explores every inch of my mouth as I moan in ecstasy, but his hands don't stay on my neck, they travel down my body feeling my breasts. I moan loudly as he pinches my nipple so hard I'm afraid he's going to leave a mark, but I don't care as I feel warm liquid escape me. I can't believe how fast he is turning me on.

When his hands drift between my panties, I scream. He moves his lips to my neck nibbling his way up and down trying to quiet me.

"Baby, you're going to have to be quiet. I don't feel like getting arrested today."

"Mmm," I moan quieter this time as he touches my hot slit. He rubs slowly at first, getting me used to the sensation before he starts moving his finger faster against my bud. I groan louder, and his hand goes to cover my mouth, muffling my scream. I take his fingers into my mouth, sucking roughly, as his other hand builds me faster and faster. I bite down on his fingers when he slips one inside me unable to hold back my scream. He slides another finger in, moving faster and building me until I'm almost there when suddenly his fingers stop.

"Don't stop. I want more," I say.

Landon smiles and kisses me sweetly on the lips. "Not today, baby. I need you to get so heavy with heat and need that when I do take you, there is no way any image or thought will cross your mind except how much you need me." He removes his hand from my dripping pussy, and I pout because I need more of him. I need to come, but I understand he doesn't want me to have another panic attack. I melt a little as he licks his fingers tasting my mixture of salty and sweet.

"Are you available Friday?" he asks, although he says it more like a command. I frown even more. Friday is three days away. Three days until I can feel his hands on me again. I'm going to spend the next few days with a vibrator in my hand.

"Yes, as friends with the possibility for ..." I let my sentence trail off, not wanting to say a possibility for sex, but Landon is on the same page as me.

"More," Landon says winking at me. He hands me my prosthetic leg. I put it on quickly, and we both get out. He walks me back to my condo. My leg's a little shaky from my almost earth-shattering orgasm a few minutes earlier. He never takes my hand in his, though, as we walk back; he only occasionally touches the small of my back when I seem to be off balance. He doesn't do anything to make it seem like we are more than friends. Friends who would like to bang each other. I open my door and walk in; he pauses at the door as I take a seat on my couch.

"Oh, and Alex, don't touch yourself before Friday." Then he leaves grinning like the bastard he is and leaves me aching for more.

Chapter Six

LANDON

Could be your emerald eyes

"So are we just going to head up to your condo?" Alexa asks as soon as she walks off the elevator and over to where I'm waiting for her on the couch. I chuckle at her yearning, flushed look. I guess I would be excited too if I hadn't had sex in almost five months, and if I didn't have my last sexual experience to replay in my head over and over again when needed. In no way am I going to rush this. I only get one night of everything with her, and I'm going to make sure that one night is memorable, not full of the demons obviously still haunting her.

"No, we are going to go have dinner first."

Her face falls into a pout, her appreciative gaze turning to a brutal one filled with disappointment.

"That sounds like a date."

"Not a date. Just two friends getting dinner and relaxing. We will get to the sex part of the night later, but you're not ready for that yet."

"Yes, I am."

I laugh. "No, come."

Her brow furrows as she looks at me confused but follows. "Where are we going?"

"To a restaurant three blocks down that sits on the beach. Are you good to walk?" I hate to ask. I know she is going to give me crap for asking if I need to help her, but to my surprise, she doesn't chastise me.

"Yes, and if not, you can always carry me." A hint of a smile returns to her lips. She doesn't bother to hide her gaze as she stares at my muscles bulging from my t-shirt.

"Good, come on." I take her hand in mine rubbing my thumb gently in circles over her palm. I watch as her lips part the slightest at my touch letting me know a small ache is growing between her legs. That is what tonight is about: driving her wild as she thinks about me and nothing else except how good it feels to be touched. I know she doesn't want a romantic relationship again. She doesn't want to get hurt again, which I can understand. I'm the same way, but I won't allow her to go the rest of her life without feeling the touch of a man bringing her to orgasm. She shouldn't deny herself that.

She moves with me as we walk down the sidewalk toward the restaurant. Usually, I would have taken her to the beach, but I'm not sure how she would be able to handle the sand just yet with her prosthesis. She walks confidently on hard surfaces, but I've never seen her try more. I try to come up with things to ask her without bringing up her past, but I come up empty. So many questions and topics lead back to her past and she doesn't have an answer. I need to do something about that.

She seems content just to hold my hand as we walk. Instead of bringing up senseless topics that neither of us really cares to talk about, I focus on making that ache stronger. I lean in close and nuzzle her ear with my lips. "You look beautiful." I kiss her softly on her neck, breathing heat before I pull myself away. A slow flush burns her cheeks, and her eyes dilate. "Thanks, but I don't think ..."

"Shh." I press my fingers to her lips stopping her from disagreeing with me. She may only be dressed in a plain shirt and jeans, her hair may not be styled perfectly, and other than mascara, I don't think she is wearing any makeup, but that doesn't change the fact she looks beautiful. Alex is confident in her own skin, with who she is, even if she can't see it. Yes, her leg is gone and showing, but that doesn't stop her from living, which is the most beautiful thing about her. She may feel like she's given up her life, but she hasn't - she's still living.

"Come on, beautiful. We're here," I say motioning to the Italian restaurant as she blushes brightly. I will have to say it more if I get that kind of reaction each time.

The staff immediately seats us at a private table in the back as I requested. I'm thankful nobody seems to recognize me as we walk quickly through the restaurant to a room with a window overlooking the ocean.

"Now, this really seems like a date," Alex says as she glances around the small room. The table has a white tablecloth and simple candle, but the rest of the room is what creates the ambiance. The candlelight on our table and the few candles on the tables around the room that sit empty provide the only lighting. Red flower arrangements and rose petals are scattered throughout the room.

"Stop thinking. This is not a date. This is just a way to get you to relax and get in the mood. So stop thinking and just let things happen."

She nods but still looks unsure as the waiter hands us the menus.

"What can I get you to drink?" the waiter asks.

I look at Alex, who has a contemplating look on her face. I suspect she's trying to decide whether to order alcohol since she knows I won't drink.

"Bring us a bottle of your best chardonnay," I say to the waiter. Alex nods and smiles in agreement.

"I won't drink a whole bottle by myself," she says eyeing me, suggesting I should join her, but she can't tempt me. I never break that rule. I can't let myself go there again.

"What looks good?" I ask ignoring her statement.

She glances back at the menu looking overwhelmed at the choices, but I already know what she's going to order. The question is why?

"I was thinking of trying one of the pizzas."

A grin immediately spreads over my face. She notices my reaction. "What?"

"You just proved my theory correct."

"What theory?"

"That you only order pizza."

"I do not." But as she says it, she realizes there is no point arguing. "How do you know that? We haven't ever shared a meal together."

"I stocked your fridge full of pizzas. I saw you at the shoot and all you ate was pizza. It was just a guess, but that's why I brought you here. What I want to know is why?"

Her eyes drop to the table as she fidgets in her seat. I wait, though, not pushing her until she's ready. "It's the only food I know I like. I don't remember what foods or drinks or anything I like, so I play it safe."

I smile at the beautiful woman sitting in front of me, embarrassed by something that doesn't matter, that she can't change, and that she has no control over. The waiter returns, pouring a glass of wine for Alex, but I decline.

"We will have one of everything."

"Yes, sir," he says, leaving. I turn to her and her eyes grow wide in disbelief.

"What ... why would you order that much food?"

"You need to try more than just pizza. You need to find what you like now."

"But that's too much."

"We are splitting the bill anyway. Since this isn't a date, I know you won't let me pay. And I know after seeing that car of yours ..."

"Tessie."

"Yes, Tessie," I say chuckling. "That you have more than enough money to go around."

She gets the excited gleam back in her eyes, but it's not enough. I need her begging for me to take her to a closet, a bathroom, or just take her right here because she can't wait any longer.

I reach across the table, take her hand in mine, and begin the slow torture of rubbing my thumb against her palm in slow, agonizing circles. She takes a sip of her wine to distract herself from my touch, but it doesn't do anything to cover the slow flush growing over her cheeks.

"How did you remember how to be a photographer? You didn't seem to have any trouble at the shoot."

She moistens her lips before answering. "Physical things I have done before seem to just automatically come back. I don't even really think about it. It's as if my body is on autopilot. So things I have done a million times before like using a camera, my phone, writing ... it all comes back to me rather easily. I just don't remember how I know how to do these things. I just do them."

"Hmm." I smirk at her deviously, not letting her eyes leave mine. "So sexual things your body remembers."

She fidgets uncomfortably in her seat as she tries to pull her hand away, but I don't let her. I hold her hand and her gaze. "Probably ..." she says.

"But you don't remember any specific sexual experience?"

"No," she says blushing again.

My eyes smolder with her words, showing how much I appreciate I'll be the only guy she remembers. Her first again. The waiter starts bringing hordes of food out to our table piling the first round of appetizers until it's covering the table. Her eyes go wide looking at all of the food, with no idea where to start. I take my chair and slide it closer to her; she eyes me nervously as I do.

"So I can point out what everything is." Also, so I can touch more than just her hand. As much as I need to drive up her desire and ache for me, I can't bear to be across the table from her when my own desire is growing intolerable.

"Try the calamari." I slide my hand around her shoulders, stroking her neck gently with my thumb. Her lips part and her eyes grow softer as I stroke her neck. I take her fork and stab a piece of calamari before brushing it over her lips. She opens, and I feed her the bite. She moans as she chews, but I don't know if it's from my touch or the taste of something other than pizza on her tongue.

"You like it?"

"Yes," she says not telling me if it's the food or my touch that she likes. I don't move my hand from her neck as we continue to eat the array of appetizers in front of us. She tries everything, and every time, she groans as she chews. Each time her body grows warmer, and by the time the main courses appear, I think I could take her up against the wall right here, but I don't.

Instead, I move my hand to her thigh. I wait as she initially pulls away from me, shocked by my touch, but within a few minutes, her legs have parted for me. I start slow just stroking her thigh as we continue to try the food, neither of us saying anything. Our sensory overdrive prevents us from needing that form of communication when our bodies are saying so much more.

As she takes a bite of pizza, I let my hand drift to her core. Her breath catches as I move my hand in slow, firm circles against her jeans. I can see the tingling move in every nerve ending in her body as she chews the pizza. When she stops chewing, I stop too. When she takes another bite, I start moving my hand again, begging for her juices to soak my hand against her jeans. The waiter returns as my hand stays in place rubbing harder, faster, with more urgency. She glares at me imploring me to stop in the waiter's presence, but that just encourages me to push her further.

"Can I get you anything else? Dessert perhaps?" the waiter asks Alex.

She bites her lip to hold back a moan. She elbows me discreetly and hard in the gut. I answer the waiter. "We'll take the check. We will get dessert at home." I wink at Alex as I say it, but I don't let up my sweet torture against her clit. Her body goes still, just as she did before she was ready to explode in my Porsche. I stop my hand, needing her to feel absolute torture and to ache as we make our way back to her condo.

The waiter leaves, and Alex slaps me across the cheek.

"Don't ever do that to me again," she says, smiling as she says it.

"Yes, ma'am." I grin wildly, loving her feisty spirit. She will be fun to control when I get her in bed. *But I don't think she can handle being controlled.* The last time I tried to control her in the bedroom she panicked. I may have to give up control to this woman. Can I really do that?

"How do you feel about giving up control?"

Her eyes meet mine with terror at the thought. "Not good."

I hate giving up control. I already feel like a puppet controlled by my music label, Drew, Caroline, and even Alex. Alex giving up control isn't just to satisfy me, though. She needs to learn to find pleasure again, that she can experience freedom in giving up control.

"I think it would be good for you. You need to learn you can't always control life. Sometimes, you just need to enjoy the chaos."

She smiles shaking her head. "And you like control too? It benefits you if I give in."

I smirk. "Maybe, but this is not about me. You already control me in ways you will never understand."

She looks intensely at me trying to break through my walls.

"I'll think about it," she finally concedes.

The waiter returns with the check. I throw my credit card on the bill without glancing at the number, and she does the same. I smile as she does, enjoying the stark contrast between sharing a dinner with Alex and sharing a dinner with Caroline. Money just being a minor difference.

Chapter Seven

ALEXA

He's back on top of me pulling my clothes off. He pulls his clothes off too. I can't get away ...

My body is tingling all over as Landon strokes my hand and leads me out of the gorgeous restaurant. The ache between my legs makes it difficult for me to move without exploding from the friction of my jeans with every step. It wouldn't take much, just another touch of Landon's hand to bring me there. Or maybe just a look, one glance of those smoldering golden eyes and I would explode. My heart is beating fast at the thought, and I try to slow it, but it doesn't surrender.

"Beach or sidewalk?" Landon asks.

"Beach," I say feeling adventurous. As much as I just want to get back to our condo as fast as possible, I'm afraid. Afraid that as soon as we go back, I'll have another panic attack and ruin the night. Or worse, I won't, and after we have mind-blowing sex, he'll be gone. The 'friendship' he claims he wants will be nothing but a memory. Just a lie he told me to get into my pants, but that's what I want. A man to fill my needs at night and then be gone by daybreak. No complications. No attachment. I'll be left alone, empty, like I always wanted.

We reach the sand, and I feel Landon's hand tighten on mine as I take my first hesitant step onto the sand with my prosthetic leg. I feel my leg give too much and am prepared to tumble into the sand, but Landon's hand holds me firm, keeping me from falling. We take several steps down the beach, but I'm too exhausted and focused on every step to enjoy the beach or my time with Landon.

"Maybe we should head back to the sidewalk," I say.

Instead, Landon squats down in front of me. "Climb on," he commands me. I oblige him and climb on his back, wrapping my arms around his neck. He holds onto both of my legs as if it's normal when, in reality, he is holding a piece of hard metal in one hand as it jabs into his side every time he takes a step. He doesn't seem to care. I take a deep breath, breathing in a fresh, clean scent that's all man. He isn't doing anything sexual right now, but the ache grows stronger just feeling my body pressed against his.

I look at the beach and out over the dark ocean, trying to distract myself from the growing ache.

"Look!" I point toward a cliff jutting over the ocean as a man jumps off before plunging into the ocean. The crowd gathered on the beach cheers as he does.

Landon moves us closer to the cliff so we have a better view. "Amazing," I sigh resting my head against his shoulder. But Landon doesn't stop at the base of the cliff; he keeps climbing higher until we reach the top. Overlooking the ocean and lights on the beach, it is an incredible view.

"Beautiful," I say.

Landon turns his head toward me, trying his best to look at me still dangling on his back.

"You up for jumping?"

"What? No way!"

"Oh, come on. It will be fun."

"I don't think so. It's not safe."

"Life's not safe, but you have to jump anyway." I try to think back to our earlier conversation about giving up control and enjoying the chaos, but I don't know if I can do that. I've already given up so much control of my life. I like order, predictability. He places me on the ground, tucking my fallen strands of hair behind my ears and sending chills throughout my body making me shiver. I watch as he pulls his t-shirt off, followed by his shoes and jeans until he is just standing in his boxers. The moonlight shines on his muscles, making him look invincible at this moment, but he's not invincible — nobody is.

He leans into my ear. "Trust me. You need this. The adrenaline you will feel, the freedom, will awaken more senses than my hands on your body ever could." He pulls away giving me space to decide what to do. I hesitate for only a second before I begin pulling my shirt off followed by my shoes and jeans until I'm standing exposed in my black underwear and bra, giving up complete control. I stare at my prosthetic leg, deciding it will be best to take it off. So I do, piling everything on a rock on top of the cliff. Landon will have to come back and get our things after we jump.

I feel Landon's eyes on me, but I don't look at him. I'm afraid I'll lose my nerve if I do. He takes my hand and helps me to the edge of the cliff where everyone has been jumping. I feel my heart beating faster and faster until I'm afraid it's going to leap out of my chest. My breath quickens to the point that a panic attack is only seconds away, and Landon seems to realize this. He doesn't count to three or give me any warning of when to jump. He just says, "Go." So I jump, hand in hand with him.

I feel a scream escape my lips, but it's not a scream of fear. It's a scream of excitement, adrenaline, and a little fear. But mostly letting go. As I fall, I feel my whole body awaken. I feel the wind flowing through my hair, I taste the salt water before we even land, I hear the crowd cheering, I hear the silence of the ocean, and I feel Landon's rough, firm hand holding mine. I feel every nerve in my body come alive as we fall. I feel everything. We hit the water, and it comes too fast and too slow at the same time. Almost as if time had stopped as we were falling.

I hold my breath when my head goes under the cool water, and

Landon's hand falls from my grip. I feel the darkness tingle at my skin trying to break through the walls, pushing its way into my subconscious. Instead of Landon's hand, Ethan's springs to my mind. Ethan's hand was much smoother. Landon's hand is rough full of calluses and experiences while Ethan's was smooth, pampered, taken care of.

I try to kick my way to the surface to break the memory. I'm afraid I won't be able to reach the surface just like in my nightmares, but when I move my left leg and kick with my right, my body propels itself toward the surface easily. I keep kicking until I feel the warm night air on my face. I open my eyes to find Landon watching me with a look of yearning on his face.

He pulls me to him, hugging me. It feels incredibly intimate to be holding each other in the water with only our underwear as a barrier. He moves us toward shore until our bodies are barely in the water anymore.

"Wait here." He releases me and runs back up the cliff to get our things. I stay at the edge of the water waiting, feeling alive for the first time in months.

LANDON COMES BACK QUICKLY with our things. I put my prosthetic leg back on as Landon hands me his t-shirt. I slip that over my body to cover enough to feel decent again. He pulls on his jeans over his wet boxers.

"Come on," he says holding his hand out to mine. I take his and we walk up the beach, neither of us bothering to put on the rest of our clothes. He pulls me into the nearest building.

"Where are we going?" I ask, confused that we aren't headed back to our condo building.

"To warm up," he says, but that still doesn't answer my question. He pulls me into the lobby of the building and up to the desk of a hotel.

The man behind the desk eyes us suspiciously but doesn't question our drenched barely clothed bodies. "How may I help you?"

"We need a room. The best you have available."

"Name sir?"

"Drew Davis," Landon says. I look at him wide-eyed, confused as to why he gave this man his brother's name. I try to get Landon's attention to tell him I can really wait until we make it the few blocks back to our condo, but Landon doesn't pay any attention. Except for the slow stroking of his fingers on my neck again, which lights every nerve in my body on fire. I can't wait.

The man hands Landon a key, and we walk quickly toward the elevator, as fast as I can on my prosthetic leg. Dammit, I need to learn to run on it for times like this. Landon presses the button, and to my relief, the doors open immediately. He presses the top floor button, but I don't notice which floor exactly because I attack him by pressing my lips hard against his, needing to taste him, needing his body intertwined with mine.

He hungrily kisses me back pressing my body hard against the elevator walls. It brings a slight pain and thrill to my body as he does, but the movement just makes me grow wetter with want for him. I claw my hand against his chest leaving marks. In retaliation, he grabs my hands pinning them above my head to just the point where it hurts to be up so high. I growl loving the sweet mixture of pain and pleasure.

Landon kisses me hard biting my lip and causing a trickle of blood before sucking my wound clean. I move my hips against him, trying to feel our bodies pressed together, needing his body to feel my ache growing stronger. When the doors to the elevator open, I expect more of the same — more rough, primal need to carry us from the elevator to our room. Instead, the sound of the doors opening seemed to have reminded Landon of something because he immediately releases my body holding my hand much too softly as he takes me to our room.

He unlocks the door and immediately releases my hand as he enters the room. He walks past the living room into a door I assume is the bedroom, but he doesn't ask me to follow, so I don't. I catch my breath before exploring the living room that is larger than my whole condo is. Gold and white fill the hotel room, and it screams of elegance and money. I take a seat on the cream couch trying to figure out what set Landon off. Why did he change so quickly?

I look up to see Landon standing in the door. "Come, beautiful, let's warm you up." I stand smiling brightly expecting him to warm me up with urgent, brutal sex. Instead, I follow him past the large bedroom with an oversized king bed to the elegant white bathroom accented with gold trim.

I look over at the large tub filling with water and bubbles. I sigh. I don't think I can handle any more foreplay.

"I want you, though," I say to Landon.

"Not yet, baby. I can't control myself in that way, and that's not what you need. I'm not going to cause you any more pain."

I sigh. Maybe he's right. I need more control and more relaxation to keep my demons at bay, but that's not what I want. I want bossy, controlling, brutal Landon, not sweet, caring Landon.

"You have to stay with me. If it gets too much, you tell me to stop," he says, not breaking eye contact with me.

I nod my head, but apparently, that's not good enough. "I need to hear you say you'll tell me to stop."

I swallow hard, "I'll ... I'll tell you to stop."

"Good. Now, undress," he says.

I take the t-shirt off that has stuck itself to my wet body. I quickly undo my bra exposing my hard nipples hiding beneath the black lace. "Holy fuck," he lets out as his eyes worship every curve on my body. I pause as I run my thumbs under my underwear and slowly slide it down my legs. I've never been fully naked in front of him before. I thought it would feel uncomfortable, awkward. Instead, I feel ... "Beautiful," he says as he lets out the breath that he was holding while watching my body.

He begins to unbutton his jeans. He pulls off his jeans and boxer briefs in one motion, his cock springing free. He watches me; my eyes widen as I take in the sight of him, and he grins. "Like what you see?"

I blush slightly. A few tattoos cover his torso and ribs. His stomach stronger and chest even broader than I imagined making my pussy drip with want. I want to feel his large cock inside me. He walks toward me until our bodies are just inches apart. He lets his lips brush against mine just enough to feel the electricity flow between us before pulling away.

"You're driving me crazy," I say.

He just smiles and extends his hand. I take it and sit on the edge of the tub taking my prosthetic leg off before I sink into the warm water. I close my eyes as my muscles melt. He locks his eyes with mine as I scoot up, allowing him to climb in behind me. He climbs in carefully, not letting us touch.

The warm water mixed with the jets is relaxing, and we both sit quietly in the tub barely touching. I feel relaxed leaning back against his chest causing him to take a sharp intake of air.

"I'm okay," I promise as I realize the tension he is holding in his chest.

"I know, but I'm not sure I am. I'm trying to go slow, but you make that hard," he says.

"Speaking of hard." I begin gyrating my hips and pushing my ass against his hard cock. He rewards me with a groan in my ear as he nibbles softly. He continues with heated breath, kissing my neck and ear as he had done before, but he keeps his hands firmly on the side of the tub, not touching me no matter how desperate I am.

"Touch me," I groan, but his hands don't move. It seems to be taking all of his willpower to continue to grip the tub and not attack me like a lion attacks its prey.

"Not yet," he breathes as he moves his kisses to my shoulder. I can't wait any longer; I grab his hand and pull it toward me. I take his finger and slowly move my mouth over it swirling my tongue from the base to the tip. "Fuck," he breathes, growing harder as his control loosens.

I move his hand down my body until he is massaging my breast. His finger ever so slightly rubs my hard nipple causing my breathing to become erratic. He stops every time until my breathing steadies again, building me up until I'm ready for more and then stopping just short of bringing me there.

He slowly moves to my other nipple rubbing gently at first. I hold my breath willing him to rub harder, faster, to taste them. "Fuck," I moan when he pinches my nipple hard between his fingers.

His hand drifts down my smooth belly causing my toes to curl. He keeps one hand firmly on my breast as the other trails between my thighs. My breath quickens faster and faster in anticipation, but as my breathing quickens, he stops.

"Are you still with me?" he whispers.

I take several deep calming breaths, focusing on his touch, trying to prove I'm still fine. "Yes," I groan. When my breathing is calm again, he shifts my hips pulling one leg half out of the tub turning my body gently. "Jesus," I groan as the jet hits my clit. He mouths my nipple again flicking his tongue back and forth in slow, cruel motions. His other hand moves back to my slit. He slowly slides one finger inside me and moves it slowly in and out of my entrance. My body melts into his, feeling all of the slow sensations moving over my body.

"Stay with me," he whispers.

The heat of the water mixed with Landon's hands makes me warmer and warmer until I'm burning from the heat. The blood rushes fast throughout my body, making it hard to breathe in the warm heat. That's when the darkness finds a way to sneak back in.

The warm water burns my skin as he thrusts inside me. The shower raining hard pellets on my head. I can't stop it from happening. I don't even try. I just let him do what he wants with me without fighting back. I have no fight left. He rips into me again, but I don't even scream. The pain does nothing to me anymore ...

"Alex!" I feel myself being pulled by the arms, the warm water leaving me. But I don't register what's happening.

"Alex!" the man says again smacking me gently on the cheeks.

"Open your eyes! Look at me!" he screams, but I'm not sure why he's screaming.

I reluctantly open my eyes to stare at the bright light overhead peering into my eyes. When I see Landon, I feel relieved. He grabs a towel wrapping me in it and carries me to the bed.

"I'm sorry ... I went too fast ... I pushed you too far again." Landon keeps talking, but I barely hear him. It takes me several minutes to remember the tub, Landon's hands touching me, and then the nightmare. This time, Ethan wasn't the one who haunted me. The man was different with two dark black eyes, a man who has begun sneaking into more and more dreams lately.

“Stop. It’s not your fault. I wanted this. I still want this. I just need to find a way to put the demons behind me first.”

Landon pulls me into his arms holding me on the bed. Neither of us says anything. There is nothing to say. Neither of us has any answers. All I know is I want this man whose arms hold me as I drift off to sleep. I want him for a lot longer than one night.

Chapter Eight

LANDON

Could be your stubborn cries

I AWAKE to the faint smell of coffee and bacon in the distance. I roll over and stare at the large numbers on the clock on the nightstand. It reads 5:25 am. That's sleeping in by my standards. I head to the bathroom to relieve myself before realizing what's wrong. I return quickly to the bedroom and stare at the large empty bed of the hotel. No Alex.

I search the room for my clothes spotting my boxer briefs wadded in a pile on the floor next to my jeans. I pull them on, thankful they are at least semi-dry and most of the sand has fallen to the floor instead of sticking to the cloth. I storm into the adjacent living room expecting to have to run back to the condo to find her, but the food tray stops me in my tracks. Why is there a large table filled with covered dishes in the living room? I'll worry about that later. I head to the door; reaching for the handle, I throw it open with frustration. No one walks out on Landon Davis.

"Good morning," Alex says from behind me with a heavenly voice.

I turn to face her. She's wearing a hotel robe wrapped around her body, but enough skin is showing to make my erection twitch at the sight of her.

"What are you doing awake?" I ask grumpily.

"Well, you're pleasant this morning." She grabs a cup of coffee and hands it to me before slumping onto the couch with her own cup in hand. I make my way over to the couch and take a seat across from her. I sip my coffee staring at how awake she seems this early in the morning.

"I thought you had left."

"No, I thought about it. It would have been easier to have just run out when I woke up at 1:30 in the morning in a strange place. It would have been easier to have just gone back to my condo and never spoken to you again, but that's not what I want." Her eyes meet mine trying to tell me more. I try to understand what her eyes are saying. Instead, I just get lost in her beautiful emerald eyes. I could look at them forever and still find a new shade of green reflecting from them.

"Did you have trouble sleeping because of your panic attack last night?" I ask still guilty for pushing her too far, for not recognizing the warning signs. She is smart not to give up control to me. I don't deserve it.

"No. I don't sleep much at night. I usually sleep a few hours in the afternoon, but the night is too hard for me. The nightmares overwhelm me then, so I don't usually even try to sleep at night." She takes a piece of the bagel as she is speaking and dips it into maple syrup. My lips curl into a grin, but I don't stop her from taking a bite of bagel with syrup. She chews slowly deciding if it's good or not. By the time she swallows, I still don't think she has decided. I laugh causing her to look up at me.

"Here," I say picking up a pancake and handing it to her. "Dip this into the syrup. It will taste better." She takes the pancake from me and dips it into the syrup, chewing the more familiar food in her mouth as it goes down easily.

"Thanks. I knew there was something wrong with that." She takes another bite of pancake with syrup. I lean back in the couch smirking at her. I'm amazed she is willing to try anything this world has to offer, even when she doesn't have someone guiding her.

"It's weird how your brain remembers some things like how to work a camera but not that you shouldn't dip a bagel into syrup."

She bites her lip and her eyes leave mine as she tries to decide what she's going to say. What she wants to say. "About that. There is so much I don't know about my past. I can relearn what foods I like, what songs I like, what movies are my favorite. With time, I can better understand who I am and what I want out of life. I already know that photography is a huge part of my past and will continue to be a huge part of my future because I love it. What I can't relearn, though, is my past." She stops talking, taking a deep breath as if what comes next is tearing her apart. I hold my breath as she holds hers, bracing myself for the words that come next.

"I'm going back to New York."

I stare at her frozen in my spot. I thought we would have more time together. We need more time together to get her over her panic attacks. I know I can help her, and I selfishly hope she can help heal me in return.

"What do you mean exactly? You are going back to visit for a few days, weeks, what?"

"No. I'm moving back to New York. I came here after the accident for two reasons. One was the best surgeons in the country are here. At the time, they were trying to save my leg, but there was no hope. The second reason was the only family I have left, Laura, my mother-in-law, lives here. I wanted to be close to her in hopes I would find out more about my past and remember. Both of those reasons no longer exist. I've physically healed, so there is no need to be near the doctors here anymore. I can just as easily continue my physical therapy in New York. And Laura hasn't been as helpful as I would like. My best chance at remembering my past and putting the nightmares and panic attacks behind me is to revisit my past. And my entire past, everything I know about it, is in New York."

"What about your job? What about your friends here?" I ask.

"I can fly back to do a magazine shoot, but I can just as easily get jobs in New York. And as for friends ..." She stops staring at me, biting that lip. "I just have to go."

I suck in a deep breath trying to calm myself. This news shouldn't be this upsetting to me. She's barely my friend. She's barely anything to me. She was a distraction that helped me write again. It hurts, though. Even though it shouldn't, it hurts. I know Alex needs to go, but I'm afraid the more she learns about her past, the further she will drift away from me until she's completely gone.

Her phone buzzes and she looks at the screen before back up at me. I swear I see a tear behind her eyes, and I'm afraid this is good-bye. "I need to go," she says.

I nod. She stands and hurries into the bedroom. When she comes back out a few minutes later, I'm still in the same spot and she's fully dressed. I stand on autopilot and walk past her to find my t-shirt on the floor in the bathroom. I pull it on before coming back to the living room where she stands waiting.

"Come on. I'll walk you back," I say. She nods and follows me out of the hotel. We walk in silence the five blocks back to our condos. I want so badly to take her hand in mine, to touch her in some way, but I don't. I'm ice, and I won't melt for her. I haven't fallen for her. I'll say good-bye and forget she ever existed. When she no longer lives here, I won't have to think about her again. We make it to the condo and into the empty elevator, each of us pressing the button for our individual floors. When the doors open on the eighth, she steps out without a word, glancing back just once as she rounds the corner of the hallway out of view. I should have just let her go — a clean break — but I can't. I can't not hold out hope that we will miss out on something that could be more between us.

"Wait," I say blocking the door of the elevator doors with my body. "I want to see you again before you go. Promise me we will have one more date before you leave."

I see the twinkle flicker in her eyes. The flicker of hope. "We don't do dates, remember?"

"Sure, we do." That makes her smile. "Promise me."

"I promise," she says still smiling as she walks away from me to her condo. I climb back into the elevator and let the doors close, feeling better than if she had given me a hot and heavy kiss before leaving. I have one more chance.

Chapter Nine

ALEXA

I try to kick him again, but I can't. He has all of his weight pressed down on me so I'm still pinned with my stomach to the ground.

I STARE at myself in the mirror. I usually hate mirrors, but not this one. This one makes me look like a movie star ready to walk the red carpet instead of the outcast I feel. The black dress fits me like a glove hugging every curve and making my one good leg stand out. My tattoos shine brightly on my skin. Elisabetta and Laura wanted me to cover them as they had done for my wedding, but I refused. I'm beginning to love that part of me. I love how they tell the story of my past even when I can't remember. I refuse to hide anything anymore. My hair falls perfectly in sexy loose curls. My face looks flawless. Makeup covers every scar and every flaw, making me look like a model. If it weren't for my prosthetic leg hiding beneath my skirt, I would feel every bit like the model they tried to make me appear.

"Have you memorized your speech yet? It will be on the teleprompter, but it helps if you are comfortable with it. To know when you're going to smile and when you're going to cry," Laura says.

I look down at the piece of paper sitting on the table in front of me. I have it memorized. It's a simple speech, really. I'm supposed to say how much I miss and love Ethan. How his life ended too soon due to a drunk driver. Thank everyone for the donations to fight drunk driving. To stop this from happening to someone in their family. Play the mourning wife, show that the Wolfe family is still strong and will keep fighting despite this loss, and that we are starting this foundation in Ethan's honor. Just don't show weakness; Wolfes never show weakness. It all sounds good and like a worthy cause until you realize Laura's real agenda. It's not to raise money for a foundation in Ethan's honor. It's to raise money for the Wolfe family. The more awareness she brings to the foundation, the more awareness she brings the Wolfe Corporation. She's a businesswoman at heart who has run her father's law company for years, turning it into a billion dollar company. Her son's death just gives her company more exposure. Running the foundation in addition to the company will just give her more power and money than she has ever had before. It disgusts me.

"Five minutes until the limo arrives," Elisabetta announces looking at her watch. She comes over to me and hands me the heels I agreed to wear. I had to have my prosthetic leg adjusted to be able to wear the heels. I've practiced walking in the heels before, but it still makes me nervous. We will be walking the red carpet, and I will have to walk onstage to give this speech without falling. Everyone's eyes will be on Laura and me for the entire night. The widow and mourning mother making their first appearance since Ethan's death.

I slip on the heels and practice walking, each step feeling as if I'm walking on stilts. With each step, I feel more and more off balance, but maybe it's just the whole night. I wish I could just tell the truth in my own words about what happened, and how hard it is for us to move on from this. I haven't said anything about moving back to New York to Laura yet. She expects me to stay here, stay close to her, and help run the foundation. I do not intend to run a foundation that is really just a moneymaking venture for the Wolfe family. I want no part of that.

"Time to go," Laura says. I look at the impeccably dressed woman, also in black, as her dress sparkles in the light. Her hair and makeup are flawless. And suddenly, I have turned back into an ugly stepsister instead of the gorgeous princess I felt like only seconds before. I climb into the limo and wait as Laura climbs in after me. She doesn't say a word to me the whole ride, which just makes it easier for the darkness to overwhelm me, as I fear I won't get out of here alive.

I MAKE it a whole hour without tripping or disgracing the family. A whole hour of showing off my beauty and demonstrating why I belong to the Wolfe family. A whole hour of walking elegantly on a cloud and pretending not to feel like the outcast I really am. Yet it all ended when I saw them *together*. Walking hand in hand, smiling at the photographers like a real couple should. Whispering into each other's ears and stealing sweet kisses. When I see them, I lose it. They stand at the entrance to the ballroom answering questions from a reporter. My body starts moving toward them in what I assume is a run. At least the closest thing I have done to a run since the accident. I was standing next to Laura speaking to the governor, and next thing I know, I'm face-first on the ground; my dress has come up exposing my ass and prosthetic leg while the reporters' attention is now on me snapping pictures.

My face is bright red with embarrassment and anger, but I hide my embarrassment and can't make myself move from the floor. I know I'll get an earful from Laura later. I deserve it for making a scene. Now, instead of the media publishing stories about Ethan, his broken widow will be all they talk about. I feel arms around me pulling me up into a standing position, but I don't want to look at the man who pulled me to my feet. I already know who it is, and I don't want him to see the anger on my face. The anger that is unfounded. I can't be angry with someone who was never mine. He can take whomever he wants to an event like this. He can sleep with whomever he wants. He's not mine. He'll never be mine.

"Are you okay?" the deep voice says with concern.

"Yes, just go back to your date." I rip my arm from his with a smile as I turn to the crowd gathered around us.

"I knew I should have practiced more in my heels," I say to the crowd trying to make them laugh. It works as everyone chuckles and goes back to their earlier conversations. I make my way toward the bathroom to freshen up before I go find Laura and start my apologies. I open the door to the bathroom and find it empty. *Thank god!* I head to the sink and splash water on my face before I think about what I'm doing. *Shit*! I don't know if the makeup is waterproof or not. I grab a paper towel and start dabbing the water from my face. I look back up at the mirror and the makeup still seems perfectly in place, unlike my heart. I'm a piece of shit for letting Landon bother my heart when I'm here for Ethan. To honor Ethan, I can't do that if my heart is anywhere near Landon. Maybe I should just ask him to leave. He owes me that. He made his appearance so all the papers will say how charitable Landon is for supporting his photographer friend, but now, he just needs to leave so I can get through this.

I hear the door open to the bathroom. I don't glance up. I just reapply the lip gloss I was given pretending I'm completely fine.

"He's mine," a feminine voice says.

"I'm sorry?" I turn to face the woman. Caroline is standing at the sink next to me glaring at me in her short sexy red dress that makes mine look ridiculous in comparison. She looks like a perfect model, unlike me, who is much too short even in my heels to be intimidating to this woman.

"Landon's mine. You get one taste of him but nothing more. He gets one night with you, and then he'll be gone out of your life forever. So you better make that one night memorable because your dreams will be the only way you will be with him again."

"What are you talking about? What do you mean he only gets one night? I think that's Landon's decision of how many nights he wants to be with me."

She smiles sweetly as if I don't have a clue. "No, it isn't." She turns and leaves without another word. Damn this night. *I will get through this without punching anybody*, I repeat to myself over and over. *I will get through this ...*

I WALK off the stage to thunderous applause. I did well. I only bobbled one word when I saw Landon in the crowd staring up at me, watching my every movement as if he couldn't get enough of me. As if he wants me. Like he's looked at me so many times before when he takes me with his body. I almost said Landon instead of Ethan, but I caught myself. I pretended it was too hard for me to say Ethan's name, and instead, let a tear fall down my face.

"Well done," Laura says glaring at me as if I didn't do well at all. "Now, if you could just stay on your feet the rest of the night, I think we can consider tonight a success despite your earlier mishap."

I glare back ready to fight it out right now with Laura backstage, but I don't. Instead, I let my glare fall from my face and I just nod before heading back to mingle with the crowd. The dance floor is full now, and Landon and Caroline are at the center of it dancing. Caroline looks beautiful with him. He's the dark bad boy, and she's the beautiful princess. It's a perfect mixture of dark and light blending together. I look down at my own tattooed and broken body. Landon and I together would be like dark and dark. There is nothing beautiful about complete darkness. It's magical watching them dance together as if they have been doing it their whole life. They look fantastic together. I've never seen Landon move like that. I've only seen one of his music videos, and he didn't dance in it. He moves smoother, more in control of his body than any dancer I have ever seen. I can't help but stare at him as he glides across the dance floor. I look around the ballroom, and everybody has stopped to watch him.

I grab two glasses of champagne off a tray as a waiter walks by. I haven't had a drink all night. I didn't want to stumble or look drunk on stage, but now that that part is over, I don't care. I need the drink to get through the rest of the night if I'm going to have to keep watching him with her. I down the first drink and set it back on a passing tray before I start sipping on the second. I try to pull my eyes from his body, but I can't. Even as his eyes find mine, I can't rip mine away. I see his lust grow in his eyes as he looks at me, but it does nothing to me. He's with her, not me. And as Caroline said, "I'll only get one night with him." One night would be more than enough to break my fragile heart. One night already has.

Chapter Ten

LANDON

Could be I've fallen for you

I FEEL her eyes on me. I've felt them on me the entire night. I made a mistake coming here with Caroline. I didn't even know what I had agreed to when Caroline asked me. If I had, I would have refused her, but Caroline knows how to manipulate any situation to her advantage. She knew I would destroy whatever I had with Alex by coming here with her. I'm an asshole. I dance in the middle of the room with Caroline as we have thousands of times before. I know her body, how she is going to move, how to turn her on, but as I dance with her now, I've never regretted my relationship with Caroline so much in my life.

The music stops and I dip Caroline right on cue, but my eyes are on Alex. Beautiful Alex in her perfect black dress that looks like it was made for her. Appropriate color for a widow mourning her husband, yet she still glows despite its dull color. I can't keep my eyes from her. She holds her chin high; her face is a deep red, and I can see her uneven breathing even from here. What scares me most is the cold in her eyes, like stone that is unmovable, unbreakable. She's put up more walls I'm afraid are going to be impossible to break down.

I release Caroline as I move toward Alex. She shakes her head with just the slightest movement. She doesn't want to draw attention to her. I don't listen to her, though. I keep moving toward her as her scowl turns into a fake smile as the crowd's eyes turn from me to her.

I reach her and take her smooth hand in mine. I can't help but smile at the feel of her skin, the electricity running through us. And I know she feels it too despite how hard she tries to keep it at bay. It's there, running through her body just as easily as it runs through mine.

"May I have this dance?"

She nods; her fake smile still covers her face as the crowd looks at us. They ooh and aww as I walk hand in hand with Alex to the center of the dance floor. The crowd thinks I'm trying to cheer up the widow by letting her dance with the famous rock star. That it is out of charity, not out of longing. A slow, haunting song starts, and I take her in my arms as we float across the dance floor.

Our movements aren't as perfect as Caroline's and mine were. I have to move slower to help her maintain her balance in the heels that I'm awed at her wearing with her prosthetic leg. Her body feels perfect in my arms as if her body was made to align with mine. She's the missing puzzle piece from my body this whole time. I don't know how I'm ever going to let her go when the song ends. How am I ever going to let her go again?

"I'm sorry," I say into her hair.

She glances around the room, the same fake smile still plastered on her lips. "Fuck you, Landon," she hisses between clenched teeth so that only I can hear.

I take a deep breath before trying again. "I'm sorry. I didn't know this ball was for Ethan. I had no idea what I agreed to when Caroline asked me here. I just thought it was like any other event we occasionally attend together. It would be boring as hell, we'd make an appearance, and then I'd leave after fulfilling my duty as her friend."

"It didn't look like two friends dancing to me."

My jaw clenches. "We are just friends. Nothing more."

"Like you and I are 'friends'?"

"Yes, exactly!" I say. Her face drops the fake smile as anguish fills its place. "Wait ... no, that's not what I meant." I take her chin lifting her eyes to look at me. "We are friends, but there is so much more I want between us."

She closes her eyes, I think to avoid having to look at me, but when she opens them again, I see the moisture building there. Shit! I'm making it worse instead of better. I keep moving us across the floor. I realize the song is close to ending and I'll have to let her go, but this conversation is far from over.

"Alex, please just give me a chance to explain my feelings. Meet me in the conference room down the hall. It will say McCally conference room on the door. I'll meet you there in five minutes." I don't want to draw any attention to our relationship. Neither of us needs the bad press that would ensue to see her at her dead husband's event with another man so soon.

The song is ending, and she still hasn't answered me. "Please," I beg again. I see in her eyes the desire for more, and I know she'll be there. As the song ends, I spin her making her the center of attention as the crowd cheers loudly for her. When she stops spinning, I expect her to be wearing her fake smile again with appreciation for the crowd in her eyes. Instead, tears fall as she looks at something behind me before running from the room. I look behind me and see Caroline smirking at me, just as she no doubt did to Alex. *Fuck five minutes.* I need to find Alex now.

I RUN to the conference room and duck inside without being seen. It's dark in the small room that fits only ten or so people. I'm not sure if she's even here or if she just ran off and left me.

She shoves me hard before I realize that she's here. It just makes me smile. I'm relaxed that she still came despite how angry she is with me. Even if she only came to hit me and yell at me, I don't care. She came.

"How could you? How could you bring her here?" she says between sobs. I don't defend myself as she says it again and again. Hitting me over and over again on my shoulders and chest. Trying to get her anger out with each sob, word, and hit. When she finally stops, I pull her to me needing her against my chest. She lets go, needing me too.

When she calms and finally pulls away, I reluctantly let her, feeling empty the second she is gone from my arms. Her eyes have turned back to stone, her breathing calm as she says, "You still love her ..."

"What?" I pull away from her in shock.

"You still love Caroline."

"No, I don't. I did at one time, but that was a long time ago. We are just friends."

"You're more than friends. I saw it in the way you are together."

"We are nothing. She's nothing to me but an old friend I still try to take care of."

"Then why did she threaten me? What arrangement do you and Caroline share? She said I only get one night with you. What did she mean? Why does she know anything about our relationship?"

"She's just a friend ..." I can't tell her more. I can't tell her the truth.

"No, *I'm* just a friend. Caroline is something different."

She waits for me to say something, but I don't. There is nothing to say. I try to keep my anger at bay, try to remain rational, but it takes all of my energy to do so.

"What are you hiding?"

"I can't tell you."

"Why?"

"It will destroy you." She takes a step back at my admission, searching my eyes for the truth. When she sees I'm speaking the truth, her body grows stiff again. She's shutting me out. One by one, she is putting up every wall to keep me out.

"I need to get back," she says without a hint of sorrow or pain.

"I want you, Alex. I want more with you."

"I need to go," she says again, not looking me.

"Where does that leave us? What about our arrangement?"

"We are nothing. Consider this the good-bye I promised you."

"Alex ..." I start, but I don't know what to say. I know she won't stay without me telling her the truth, but it's not something I can tell her without pushing her further away from me.

"Good-bye Landon," she says and walks out the door.

I DON'T WALK ten feet out of the conference room before Caroline stops me.

"Let's go home. This party is boring. We can have a lot more fun in bed," Caroline says slobbering on my neck. I don't feel it. I'm too numb to feel anything.

"Not tonight, Caroline," I say. She pouts but seems to be expecting it, so she just slides her tongue down my neck again to see if I'll change my mind. I don't.

"Just leave me alone before I say something I'll regret."

"Don't get mad at me just because your plaything of the week won't put out."

I grab Caroline by the arm glaring at her. Her muscles quiver beneath my grip and fear registers on her face. "You did this. You drove her away," I growl at her before continuing. "I'm done, Caroline. It's over," I say releasing her.

She stumbles back, but her sly grin creeps back easily over her face. "We will never be done. I own you, Landon, or did you forget? I know every secret about you, and if you have more than one night with Alexa, I'll destroy you with your own secret. You get one night with her. That is our agreement, and then you better come running back to me like the good little puppy you are."

My body tenses, my jaw clenched. I want to punch something, destroy something. I don't look at Caroline; I just make my way to the valet. I hand him the ticket, and he returns quickly with my Porsche. I climb in not waiting for Caroline. She can find her own way home. I drive off fast, making the tires squeal behind me. I don't know where I'm going. I just drive. I'll drive until I find something to take away the pain.

Chapter Eleven

ALEXA

He covers my mouth with his so that I can't scream. I can barely breathe, but I wish I could stop breathing when he pushes himself deep inside me. He rips me apart over and over and over ...

I LET the ice spread over me as it slowly turns each muscle, nerve, and vein to stone. I feel nothing. I am nothing. I just exist. This is what I wanted before Landon – to feel nothing, to be nothing. I want to just exist so I would never feel pain again. And I got my wish. I walk back toward the crowded ballroom when Laura spots me. She pulls me into another conference room. This one is bigger than the one I was just in. It was weird how Landon knew that conference room was there and even knew the name. He's probably fucked countless women in that room. God, he makes me sick. My nausea spreads as I stare at Laura. She doesn't show any emotion on her face, but I know why I'm here. Nothing gets past her.

"You cannot be with him. You must break it off now."

"Don't worry. It's already done."

She nods as she looks at my rigid body void of any emotion.

What I don't expect is the slap that rings across my cheek. I don't feel it, though; it was more the shock of her hitting me than the pain.

"That was for Ethan. Don't you ever betray his memory again."

"Yes ma'am," I say.

She walks out of the room apparently having nothing else to say, or maybe she can't stand the sight of me any longer. It just reinforces my decision to move back to New York. I don't belong here. I have no family here. Nothing worth staying for.

I go back to the ballroom and make small talk like I'm supposed to. I dance with several older gentlemen and retell made-up stories about Ethan and me together. I recount the fairy tale love story. The story of when we met and how I was broke, homeless, and living on the streets. I would have had to turn to prostitution if it wasn't for Ethan. He saved me and then we fell in love. It's a beautiful story, but it's just not mine. My story starts and ends with the accident. Nothing else exists for me.

The night doesn't end until well past 2:00 am. The limo takes me home to a lonely condo that has never felt like mine. I have nothing, so it's certainly no home. I make my way into the building intending to go upstairs and start packing. I won't be able to sleep. I could maybe even catch a plane tomorrow and get out of here before anybody would think to look for me.

I pause my step when I see Landon sitting on the white couch in the lobby. I'm not ready to face him again. I've had enough. I intend to walk past him, head straight for the elevator, and pretend he isn't there. As I begin walking, though, he stands up, and that's when I realize it's not Landon sitting there. It's Drew. Landon sent his brother to try to get me back. The guy has no boundaries.

"I'm not talking to him, Drew," I say passing him quickly. He catches up to me in two steps.

"I can't find him. I'm hoping you'd know where he is."

I look at Drew my eyes wide with surprise. "Why would I know where he is?"

"Because you love him."

I move my hand to slap Drew, but he grabs my hand moving much faster than Landon did. Or maybe Landon could have moved just as fast, but he chose not to.

"You're not ready to admit that yet. And I used to think you were nothing but another gold digger out for Landon's money and fame, but I was wrong. You're good for him. Whatever happened between you two last night, you need to fix it. He's worth fighting for," Drew says.

"It doesn't matter if I love him or not when he's still in love with Caroline."

Drew laughs at that as if I'm crazy for even considering thinking that. "He's not."

"How do you know?"

"I just do."

"How original," I say sighing. This is getting us nowhere.

"He is the one who hurt me. He is the one who brought Caroline. He is the one keeping the secrets. Not me."

"You have secrets just like he does. He's been hurt before, by Caroline, by other women. He just needs you to fight for him."

"Yeah, well, I'm not interested anymore."

"Just tell me where he is, Alex, and then I'll leave you alone."

"It's Alexa, not Alex. It was never Alex, and I don't know. He left after our fight."

"Shit," Drew says pulling out his phone.

"What?" I say genuinely curious as I see the concern grow on Drew's face.

"I just need to find him before he does something stupid."

"What would he do?"

"Nothing you want to know about," Drew says before walking out the door.

Fuck my life. I follow Drew out and climb in the passenger seat of his Mercedes.

WE PULL up at Fire and Ice. The only place either of us knows to look. I climb out while Drew goes to park the car. There is no line outside, and I make my way inside easily. I feel my heart beating fast in my chest. Drew didn't tell me what happens when Landon drinks, but from the look of terror in his eyes, I know it isn't good. I search the club, but I don't see him anywhere. The bar is mostly empty for a Saturday night, but I still can't spot him anywhere. I take a seat at the bar hoping the bartender will be able to tell me where he is.

My heart immediately sinks. Just when I'm about to give up, I see a man stumble out of the bathroom. *My man,* I think before shaking my head. I try to turn my heart back to the ice it was before, but it's hard when I'm just thankful he's still alive.

He continues to stumble over to the bar and asks for another drink. I slowly make my way over, expecting him to make a run for it when he spots me. He doesn't look up at me until I take a seat on the barstool next to his.

I almost wish he hadn't looked at me. Gone is the sparkle, the look of lust and admiration. His eyes are empty except for a tinge of anger. Landon downs his glass of whiskey. He could be angry with me all he wants. I just need to keep him here until Drew arrives to help me. Landon indicates to the bartender to get him another.

"Don't you think you've had enough?" I snap at him. He's obviously had a lot to drink, and that's not good for a man who claims he doesn't drink.

He glares at me with his bloodshot eyes. "I'm fine," he says with surprising clarity.

"You're not fine. You wouldn't be here if you were fine." I turn to get the bartender's attention. "Two waters, please. And we would like to close his tab."

The bartender nods his head at me and quickly brings us the two glasses of water. "Drink," I say to Landon.

"I'm fine," he says again.

I roll my eyes at him and take a drink of my water. The bartender brings over the check and Landon's card. Landon takes the pen to sign but then just stares blankly at the check. "Are you going to sign?" I ask. Landon doesn't look up at me as he says, "I'm fine." Landon's face is starting to turn rather red, and I notice him swaying slightly. He looks like he's about to puke. Drew needs to get here fast.

I take the pen out of his hands and scribble his name quickly. No wonder he feels this way; the check has too many items to count. I turn in time to see Drew making his way over. He takes one look at Landon and says, "We need to hurry before he pukes." I nod my head in agreement. Drew tries to get Landon to stand up, but instead of standing, Landon falls to the floor. Crap.

With the help of two other men, we get Landon into the backseat of Drew's car. I took the time to grab a trash bag since I wasn't much help in moving Landon. I climb into the backseat next to Landon and hold the bag out in front of him. As soon as Drew starts moving, Landon retches. I gently rub his back. Damn, how easily my feelings of anger subside when I see him hurting. Between heaves, he speaks. "You ... came ... back ... for ... me ... I ..."

Then he passes out. I look at Drew, who is staring at me in the rearview mirror, but he doesn't say a word. God, why is this so hard for us? Why can't we just date like normal people? My heart flickers beneath the ice that was hardening around it. I have no idea how to feel anymore. I'm still mad at Landon. That won't go away, but neither will the need for him. The ache that won't subside. It just makes it even more imperative that I leave right away before I let him back in.

Chapter Twelve
LANDON

Yeah, I've fallen for you
Yeah, I might just love you

MY HEAD IS POUNDING as I stand in the hallway outside her condo waiting. My eyes are barely open, squinting at the bright light. The hallway is quiet, but that doesn't stop my pounding headache. My stomach churns ready to spill its contents at any second. *God, I just want to go back to bed!* But standing here in the hallway waiting to apologize to her is more important. I don't remember much about last night thanks to the alcohol, but I do know I was an ass. And if I don't fix this now, she'll leave and I'll never get a chance again. I know that much about life; it doesn't give second chances.

I hear a slight scream coming from her condo. *Shit, I wasn't expecting her to scream.* I bang on the door, but I can't get in. I press my ear up against her door trying to decide if I should break it down, pick the lock again, or call the police. I can't hear her over the siren going off in her room. I decide to pick the lock when the door suddenly opens. Standing in front of me is Alex. Barely awake with a shirt and shorts on. Her hair is a disgruntled mess on top of her head. Her eyes are wide staring at me while her lips have parted just barely revealing her shock.

"Good morning, sleepyhead," I say. I kiss her softly on her cheek before sneaking past her to turn off the smoke detector blaring in her kitchen. She remains frozen in her doorway as I quickly turn it off.

"What the fuck are you doing?" she says.

“Turning off the smoke detector so we can go workout,” I say flashing her a guilty smile.

"Wait ... you pulled the fire alarm to get me out of bed at 5:00 am? So you could get me to work out with you? Don't you think that's a little harsh for the other people who live in this building? And illegal?" she says.

"It's not when the alarm only went off in your room,” I say.

"How?" she says.

“I’ve picked a lock or two before.”

“I’m going back to bed,” she says, turning around in the doorway to head back inside.

“I don’t think so. I have to spend the day groveling at your feet and you owe me one ass whipping,” I say.

“Landon, it’s done. We just need to go our separate ways, and I don’t want to kick your ass.”

“Yes, you do. I believe you issued me a challenge shortly after we met that you would kick my ass when you got rid of those crutches. It’s time to do some ass kicking, baby,” I say.

I already see the fire growing in her eyes as I issue the challenge. She won’t back down. I knew it would work before I came here. Just like with the cars, she can’t back down. “Fine. Let the ass kicking begin.”

Alex follows me slowly out of our condo building and onto the dark, empty beach. I don’t care as long as she’s still following me. I’m no doctor or therapist, but I know the sand on the beach is probably not the best place to start running again. But at least it’s soft if she falls. I know she won’t let me catch her.

We both sit down on the sand. I begin to stretch and grab her running shoes to hand to her. She puts them on, moving even more slowly now. She finally ties them then looks up at me. Worry covers her face. "I don't even know if I was a good runner before my accident. I have no idea. I may have never run a day in my life."

I can't help but grin like a goofy teenager at the worry showing on her face. I scoot closer to her on the sand. "You were a runner. These shoes on your feet are quality running shoes that have been worn in. Your body is still strong and lean despite months of non-activity. You have the incredible fighting spirit of a runner. You'll remember how to do it. The only thing stopping you is your head and maybe that leg of yours."

She thinks for a minute as she starts stretching on autopilot. "You're right."

I long to kiss her softly on the lips, but I don't. I just need to find a way to stay in her life. "Let's go," I say breaking the images flooding my mind. I stand and extend my hand to her to help her up. She doesn't take it. Instead, she gets up on her own - refusing my help again.

I start walking down the beach, and she falls into stride next to me. I start with walking slowly to warm our muscles up and to ensure she gets used to the uneven surface. I laugh when she starts to move ahead of me, always a stride in front of me. I increase my walking speed until we are almost jogging. She matches my speed. Her breathing increases slightly, but otherwise, she shows no outward sign of increased difficulty.

We continue for half a mile before we start jogging. Her breathing increases to more of a pant. Every other step, she scrunches her face in a wince as her right foot hits the ground. Instead, she tries to hide it. So I push her. "Is that all you got?" I say, not at all out of breath.

"No," she says between pants. She increases her speed again. I follow. Now, she winces and a slight grunt escapes her lips at each step. We keep running. Her previous impeccable form is now sloppy. Each step takes more energy than the next. I know that look. She won't last much longer, although she's made it much farther than she should have.

"I ... have ... to ... stop," she says. Her body collapses to the ground. She lies stretched out on her back, her chest the only part of her moving as the exertion she just put her body through causes her to take deep breaths.

I lie down next to her. My breathing is back to normal in seconds. Her breathing takes longer to return to normal. I feel the sun begin to come up as we continue lying here. I know soon the beach will start to fill with other runners, but I don't rush her.

"Well, we know one thing for sure. You are a runner," I say.

She smiles. "Yeah, but I still have a long way to go to be able to kick your ass out here."

I smile back at her. "You'll get there."

I stand up and extend my hand to her. This time, she takes it, and I help her up. I don't let go of her hand as we walk back to our condo. She limps now as she walks, but the pained look has disappeared from her face. I want to scoop her up and carry her back, but I know she doesn't want that. So I just keep holding her hand hoping it somehow makes the walking easier.

We make it back to our condo building an hour later. We step into the elevator, and I press the button to the eighteenth floor. She moves to press the button for the eighth floor, but I stop her. I still haven't apologized. I haven't told her anything. I just need that chance to change her mind. I've kept the morning conversation light, just getting her used to being around me again, but now, it's time to grovel at her feet.

"Just give me five minutes. Five minutes to at least apologize so we can part on civil terms." I look at her expecting more fight, more arguing. Instead, her eyes peer up at me and a faint smile touches her lips. "Okay."

Chapter Thirteen

ALEXA

A tear trickles down my face as he flips me over and starts in again. He grabs my breasts and puts all his weight on my chest forcing the air out of my lungs. When I start to drift away, I welcome it. The escape. I don't feel anything.

WHAT IN THE hell am I doing following him to his condo? I'm going to have a hard time keeping my defenses up if I spend more time with him. As it is, I feel my icy shield melting again, wondering why I was ever mad at him in the first place. Landon opens the door to his condo and walks in. My mouth drops as I look around the large place. I know Landon has money and likes to flaunt it, but I never imagined he lived in a place like this. In comparison, my condo feels like a closet.

I glance around the large, open space that looks to be a living room, dining area, and kitchen. Hundreds of people could easily fit in the space.

"You must throw some raging parties here," I say.

He looks out at the large open space. "No, I don't like having people here."

"What? Why?"

"I just like keeping my private life private. I throw parties, sure, but not here. The only people who come here are Drew and me. That's it."

"Not even other women?"

He looks at me seriously. "Not any women. Not Caroline. Just you."

I feel my stomach fluttering as he says *just you*. He's trying to make me feel special, unique, and it's working.

"What do you do with all the empty space then?" I say lightheartedly shaking off the spell he is casting over me.

"Nothing," he says smiling. I follow him to the back and stop at the amazing view of the ocean from the floor-to-ceiling windows. A large deck wraps around the entire length of the floor. I know my mouth has dropped open and my eyes are much too wide as I stare at this amazing place.

"Come on," he says taking my hand as he pulls me up a grand staircase in the center of the open room. We reach the top and walk past a couple of doors. I assume one has to be Landon's bedroom, and I just hope he isn't taking me there now. Because if he is, I don't know if I'll be able to control myself.

We reach the end of the hallway, and I hold my breath as he opens the door. I hesitantly step inside as he holds the door open for me. It's a music studio. An incredibly messy, disgusting studio. I laugh because I feel paper and plastic crumpling beneath my feet with each step.

"So you're a slob," I say in teasing disgust.

He shrugs, not looking guilty in the least. "I have more important things to do than clean."

"You could hire someone then."

"I could, but I kind of like living in the chaos." Landon pauses while his eyes meet mine searching for something. He sighs.

"Come on," he says grabbing my hand again and leading me out the back door to another smaller balcony. This one is beautiful, tranquil. It has the perfect view of the ocean. Beautifully bright colored flowers and plants surround the balcony, making it feel like a floating garden over the ocean.

He leads me to a comfy sofa chair. I take a seat in awe of my surroundings. He holds up one finger. "Just a sec." And heads back inside. I don't care, though. I could spend the rest of my life up here and never get bored. I'd never lose sight of the beauty surrounding me. When he comes back, he is holding an old looking guitar and a bottle of water that he tosses to me. I stare at him confused as he takes a seat across from me. I notice his shaking legs, his blushed face, and his uneven breathing.

"What ..." I start, but he holds up a hand to stop me.

"I want to share a song I wrote." That's all he says before he starts playing the chords on his guitar. So I just sit back, take a long swig of water, and listen.

You stumbled into my life
A beautiful mess
With fighting words
Not to be messed with.

But I kept coming back
Trying my best
To break down your walls
To find a way in

But I can't help it
When I see you
My heart skips
I lose my breath
Trying to drink in your scent

It
Could be the rain
Could be the stars
Could be the way your hair
Falls down your face
Could be the cause of my speeding heart
Could be I'm fallin' for you

I can't wait to see you
See what more we could be
Just give us a chance
Give me a reason to exist

It
Could be the raindrops pouring down your face
Could be the stars sparkling in outer space
Could be your emerald eyes
Could be your stubborn cries
Could be I've fallen for you

When he stops playing and looks up at me, he sees the teardrop rolling slowly down my face. He rushes over, concern etched on his face. It's not a sad tear as he thinks. It's a beautiful, happy tear because even though he didn't say anything, I know he wrote that song for me. And as my heart beats wildly in my chest, I know I feel the same way back.

He kneels at my feet as he wipes the tear gently from my eye. Realizing that I'm grinning beneath the tears, he relaxes just a little. "Alex, I don't want just one night with you. I want many nights. Hundreds of nights together. I want to own your body and happiness. I want to be forever connected. I don't know how to give you more than what I am, but I want to give you more. I want to find out what we could be because this could be everything I never knew I wanted." He stops smiling up at me. The nerves erased from his face. Instead, his smirky, crooked grin replaces it. "I love you."

I let his words sink in. I know I've been told 'I love you' in the past. I'm sure Ethan said those words to me. I'm sure my mom said them. I'm sure even Laura has said them to me at some point in the past. To me right now, though, this is the first time. The first time I've ever heard those words. As much as his words scare me, I know they are true because I feel the same way. I pause for another second because I know as soon as I open my mouth that I'm deciding my destiny and my future. I'm not just deciding if I want to give Landon a chance. I'm deciding if I'm willing to live again instead of just exist.

Chapter Fourteen

LANDON

I don't want to wait anymore
I love you, you, you

God, she makes me wait for what seems like hours, days before she opens her mouth. Her face has been practically blank as I gave my speech. Even when I was playing her the song, I was having a hard time reading her. The sunlight covered most of her face making her expression unreadable to me. I don't even care if she says 'I love you' back. I just want her to give me another chance. Keep me in her life because I'm not sure I could keep breathing without that chance. I'm afraid if she says no I'll just drop dead right here. She opens her mouth, but then closes it again. Come on! I take a deep breath and move my eyes from hers. She's going to say no. She's trying to let me down easy. I prepare myself for it by taking another deep breath before I let my eyes meet hers again.

"I love you too."

Her lips immediately find mine, our tongues urgent to feel the other needing more and more. I tangle my hand in her thick hair to feel more of her as I deepen the kiss. She opens her mouth easily for me letting me push myself deeper into her mouth. I've missed her touch, her smell, how her body perfectly conforms to mine. I keep kissing her - practically attacking her with my lips. She doesn't hold back her own brutal kisses and devours my mouth, making me grow hard with need for her. This is going too fast. If I don't slow things down now, she'll end up having a panic attack. And I won't be able stop when we get to that point.

I start pulling back, easing up on the kisses. I untangle my hand from her hair leaving it to rest gently on her neck. I work on increasing the space between our bodies. She grabs my shirt desperate to hold me in place, to keep my body plastered to hers. Her kisses become firmer as her urgency increases. I hold the distance though. I'm not going to hurt her again. I feel her pull my lip into her mouth sucking ferociously. I groan letting myself enjoy one last deep kiss before I pull away from her ending this for now when I feel her bite my lip hard until I taste blood in my mouth.

I remember our first make-out session on the beach; she bit me then too. She never asked me to slow down or be gentle. She liked the rough, brutal kisses. Maybe she just needs the pain as I do in order to feel. Maybe we aren't so different. I know guilt still lingers in her heart about moving on so soon after losing Ethan, but she hasn't told me everything about her panic attacks yet. I saw the fear in her eyes the last time. I tried being gentle, being someone I wasn't, and that made the panic attack worse instead of better. She pulls me back to her, sucking my neck as she claws my back. I growl immediately and turn to retaliate by grabbing her neck and pushing her hard against the sofa as I take her neck and suck hard enough to leave a mark.

She moans as I do. I move back to her lips pulling them hard into my mouth as I hold her gaze with my eyes looking for any signs of panic or fear. Instead, I see her desire grow as I pull harder on her lip. I release her suddenly, and she lets out a large gasp from the sudden loss of my lips on hers.

I know she craves what I crave. The pain, the darkness that makes me feel alive. I just don't know if it's what's best for her. She studies my face and understanding grows on her face as the darkness grows on mine. I watch as her own desire grows in her eyes as she watches me. Both of us breathe even and calm, but my heart is beating wildly. I watch as she moistens her lips as they curl into a grin at the sight of me panting for her.

"Mark me," she says seductively as she runs her tongue across her lip.

"What?"

"Mark me, own me, make me yours. I don't want gentle. I want pain, love, desire."

I stare at this incredible woman in front of me. Confidence flows out of her veins as she speaks.

"I don't think I can stop ..."

"Fuck, don't stop. Don't stop ever."

"But ..."

"It's not going to happen. The panic left my body the moment you said I love you. I won't let it back in."

She moves her body forward, tangling her hands in my hair, brushing her lips against mine. Neither of us moves further.

"Mark me," she says again, her lips breathing on mine as the words escape her lips.

I grab her then and pull her toward me as I stand up. I unleash the monster. She wraps her left leg around me while she does her best to keep the right one from dragging behind her. I grab hold of the cold metal holding her to me as I tangle my hand in her soft hair.

We only make it to the door before I stop and press her hard against the glass door. She lets out a sound that is half moan, half growl as I hold her there while my hand finds the hem of her shirt. I push it up and off her body so I can feel her smooth stomach. My hand makes its way up to her simple black bra covering her small chest. I push that up too until her nipples harden as they feel the warm salty air.

I dip my head to taste the soft mounds of flesh. I grab one nipple with my teeth pulling them, sucking them into harder points.

"Oh fuck," Alex moans enjoying the delicious mix of pleasure and pain. When I stop long enough for her to think again, she claws at my shirt to pull it off. I feel every nail as she runs her hands down my back leaving claw marks while she runs sweet soft kisses down my chest.

"Fuck, Alex," I moan as she encourages the monster further out of its cave. He hasn't been out for a long time. Even Caroline has her limits and restrictions on how far the monster can go. But I don't think Alex is going to have any limits.

"Hold on," I say as I pull her from the door. I open it, stepping through as she continues her kisses over my body. I walk until I find my dark bed covered in black like the darkness around my heart. I throw her onto the bed, not careful how she lands.

She lands in a twist of arms and legs sprawled out on the bed. Her bra still pushed high on her chest revealing her bare breasts. I need more of her bare. I pull on her shorts as she twists and squirms in the bed until I pull her shorts and underwear off in one swoop. I pause just staring at her unique body. A body filled with tattoos and scars. I can't wait to suck her dry as I feel her between my teeth.

Her eyes watch me as I take in every beautiful ounce of her body. She squirms as I see her ache growing whenever my eyes find a new part of her body they haven't seen before. She's been naked in front of me but never like this. Alex is splayed out on my bed so I can see every sexy inch of her. My bed that no other woman has ever been in. My eyes drift to her leg covered in metal and plastic. Her eyes drift with me and her cheeks flush a nice pink as I look at her leg. She reaches for the covers to hide her beautiful leg from me. I grab her hand instead holding it tight so she can't move beneath me.

I see a tinge of fear flutter beneath her eyes. Shit! I need her focused back on me.

"Beautiful," I say as I suck on her wrist that's trapped in my hand. She moans letting the fear go. I kiss down her body in a tender moment.

I reach her prosthetic leg. "May I?" I ask as I hold her prosthesis in my hands. She nods bashfully. I begin taking the prosthesis off just as I have seen Alex do before. I keep my eyes glued to hers so she can see the desire fill my eyes as I take it off. I see a bit of surprise as I take it off. To me it's just like taking off another piece of clothing. The last piece of clothing before she will be completing naked and completely at my mercy. I place the prosthesis on the floor carefully, and then she's fully naked and I can't keep the monster at bay any longer. The look in her eyes says she doesn't want me to either.

In one movement, I pull my pants and briefs off before attacking her with my body. I grab her hair pulling hard so her lips meet mine. She groans into my mouth at my attack as she grabs my ass pulling me to her. I grind against her body letting her feel the full length of me slick against the wetness between her legs.

I flip us over so I'm beneath her as I grab her hips and pull her to my face. I need to taste her pussy. She wiggles on top of me as I pull her wet lips into my mouth. Alex tries to pull away from me as I take her clit into my mouth tugging hard.

"Fuck, Landon," she groans as her legs push away from me. "It's too much." She moans again as I let my tongue lap faster over her clit. I taste her sweet wetness as it pours out of her with each lap of my tongue against her sweet flesh. I slap her ass hard.

"Don't move." I press my tongue into her, giving her clit a break from its torture, but this just makes her writhe harder on top of me. Her hands find my hair trying to move my head back to her clit where she wants it so she can come in sweet ecstasy, but I'm not ready for her to come just yet. I grab her hands from my head and place them on the headboard behind us before coming back to torturing her body. She moans and lets her hands drop back to my body. I grab her hands again roughly putting them back to the headboard.

"Don't move your hands again. If you do, I'll stop and you won't come."

She reluctantly puts her hands back on the black headboard, her eyes full of desire and need. I move my tongue back to her clit as her reward for listening to me. I grab her nipple twisting hard as she rides my mouth.

"Fuck," she moans again. I watch as she builds closer and closer as I move my tongue faster and faster against her. I bite down, and she goes wild above me seconds away from letting her orgasm overtake her, but she lets go of the headboard, so I stop and release her clit from my mouth.

"Fuck you, Landon," she says as she's left frustrated again.

"Hands on the headboard," I say more sternly. She grabs the headboard hard, making it shake. I take her back into my mouth licking and sucking until she's seconds away again. This time, I plunge my fingers into her tight cunt as I bite her clit and I watch as she explodes around my fingers.

"Landon," she screams, her face displaying the full beauty of her orgasm.

I grab her hips again throwing her across the bed to her back as if she weighs nothing. I smirk when she gives me a dirty look for throwing her across the bed. I move on top of her body, to fuck her properly as I want when she slaps me hard across the cheek.

I growl as I look back at her. I want to tie her up so she can't slap or claw me again, but I don't have anything within reach, and I don't think I can wait any longer to be inside her. I grab her wrists holding them together with one hand as I drag her up the bed. I reach into the top drawer of the nightstand to find a condom. I rip it open and roll in on with one hand as she stares at my large cock with her big emerald eyes. I see the fear creeping back into her eyes. I take her sensitive nipples in my mouth, and within seconds of nibbling and sucking, she's mine again.

I move myself to her entrance ready to plunge inside with a mix of pleasure and pain, but I stop suddenly. This is the first time for her. Our first time together will not be about the pain. I rest myself at her entrance looking at her pleading eyes as I still have her arms locked high above her head.

"This will be all pleasure. This will not be about pain." She nods her head as she groans as she feels me pushing at her entrance, her body aching for me to fill her. But I keep my promise about this not being painful for her. My eyes never leave hers as I push myself inside her farther and farther until I completely fill her.

"Fuck, you're so tight," I moan as I move my lips to hers. I shift inside her and watch her wince, so I slow, enjoying just being inside her. When she relaxes again, she has a wicked gleam in her eyes.

"Fuck me," she says. I release her hands letting them crawl all over my body again as I move inside her. She moans with each thrust, with each movement as we both climb higher. God, she feels amazing as she wraps her leg around my body. I move my hand to her sensitive bud, and she almost explodes at the simple touch.

We each grow closer as I move faster, more brutally against her body. I move my lips to hers and kiss her softly there as my body moves hard against her pussy — bruising her, marking her, making her mine.

"You're mine," I growl against her lips.

"Yours," she groans back.

I pull her lip into my mouth and suck hard. I hold onto it with my teeth as I say, "Come for me." I thrust and squeeze her sensitive bud as I bite down hard on her lip. We both come, full of screams and moans of pleasure, pain, and feeling alive. I pull out and release her lip from mine. I gently suck on the blood forming on her lips. She reaches her hand to touch the sensitive spot on her lip.

"You marked me," she says smiling.

I smile back collapsing on the bed next to her. "You're mine now."

"I love you," she says in almost a whisper as she drifts off to sleep. I smile. Most people wouldn't think of what we just did as love, but it was the greatest expression of love we could give each other.

I pull her body to me needing to feel her against me. I kiss her hair as I say, "I love you too ... forever."

Chapter Fifteen

ALEXA

"Keep breathing," someone says in a whisper. But I don't want to. It hurts to breathe.

I WAKE up to the morning light shining brightly in Landon's bedroom. He has his arm draped over me, and he snores softly beside me. I can't believe I slept all night without a nightmare waking me. All I dreamed of was Landon. Last night was amazing. Easily the best night of my life. Or the best night I can remember. I take the time to examine Landon's room since I didn't have time to last night. The large bed we are sleeping on is a dark shade of black. Likely matching who he feels he is. A dark monster. That's not who I see, though. He's my light bringing me back from the hopelessness I felt before. With him, there is a possibility of a future, of meaning again. The rest of the large room is simple. A black nightstand sits next to the bed and another black dresser sits in the far corner. The amazing ocean view that woke me from my sleep is from the windows that surround us. They slant and curve not only covering two of the walls but also part of the ceiling.

I've never seen anything like it. I could get used to waking like this every morning – an amazing view of the ocean and naked Landon.

One night. The words creep over me. One night. That was all Landon initially wanted when he met me. Caroline said that's all I would get. I sit up quickly as the uneasiness washes over me not caring if I wake Landon up. I climb out of bed searching for something to wear. I hop over to find his t-shirt. I throw it on my body and find my shorts. I slip them on as well. I hop around the bed looking for my prosthesis. Needing it on in case I need to make a quick getaway. He said 'I love you' last night. He did amazing, incredible things to my body. I don't know how I'll get over it if it was just one night and he said those words to me to get me into bed and nothing more. I find my prosthetic leg and start putting it on when I hear him.

"Good morning, gorgeous."

I smile. I can't help it. "Good morning, Landon." He notices me pulling my prosthetic leg on and frowns.

"Come back to bed."

"Um ... no, I need to get this on."

Landon stands up, walks toward me, and throws me over his shoulder to carry me back to bed. I kick and scream the whole time trying to get him to put me down.

"You aren't running out on me. We just had an amazing night, and you aren't ruining it with your insecurities."

I huff as he throws me back on the bed. He climbs on top of me forcing me to stay.

"Why are trying to run out?" he asks as he holds me down.

"I wasn't. I was just prepared to get kicked out."

His eyes grow wide. He looks as if I just slapped him and not in the sexy way he did after I slapped him last night. He looks seriously hurt. "Why would I kick you out?"

"Because this was just a one-night thing."

He shakes his head incredulously. "Were you not listening to me yesterday? I want you. I want you in my bed every night. I want to fuck you and make love to you every night and every second I have a chance. I want to write more songs for you. I want to know everything about you. I want you to let me own you. Own your pleasure and pain."

He grabs my cheeks in his hands trying to make me believe him. "I love you, Alex. I love your crazy spirit and determination. I love your fearlessness and strength. I love that you love fast cars. I love your love for freaky, rough sex. I love how you look when you come. I love how I will probably have to fight and argue with you about everything our future holds because we are both scared about what that could mean, and we are both too scared to admit it. I love that we are two halves of a whole and that you had my heart before I even knew it was mine to give away. And I will keep telling you every fucking day until you realize that I love you."

I grin up at him. A grin that reaches my eyes and overcomes my whole face. "That was some speech."

He grins back. "Yeah, what do you think about it?"

"I love you too, Landon Davis." I kiss him softly on the lips, but the softness quickly turns to desire and roughness. I feel his cock grow hard beneath me, and I know that our time for talking is over despite the fact we haven't really resolved anything other than we love each other. He pulls my sore lip into his mouth licking it gently, his eyes turning wicked.

"How do you feel about being tied up?" He stares at me trying to look innocent as he asks me.

I smile wider. I didn't realize until last night how much I enjoy the boundaries of pleasure and pain. The pain makes me feel the pleasure more. It makes me want to be with Landon more. The thought of being tied up just amps up my excitement and desire even more.

"Tie me up," I pant in his ear as just the thought has gotten me much too excited. He smirks at me as if I don't know what I've just agreed to. He gets off me and walks through a door I assume is a closet. When he comes back, he has a rope in his hands.

I frown looking at him and then remember the condoms in the drawer. "I thought you didn't bring women up here."

He stops. "I don't. I just keep the stuff here and bring it with me when I need it." I accept his answer because after last night, I completely trust him. With my body and even my heart. He walks over to me and pulls me to him.

"Put your hands around my neck." I do, and he picks me up. My prosthesis is still lying on the floor at the foot of the bed, so I allow him to carry me, and I love every minute of his strong arms around me protecting me. I love how he can be soft, gentle, and caring one minute, and then turn into the rough monster that pulls my orgasms from me the next. I think back to last night, to the two mind-blowing orgasms I experienced. Something I couldn't even do for myself before without causing panic or guilt.

He places me down in the doorway to his bedroom. He takes each hand and ties the rope around them. Throwing the loose ends on the other side of the door, he then closes the door. My arms stretch over my head, as I stand naked on one leg leaning against the doorway. I'm completely as his mercy, which makes me grow wetter, even though he has barely touched me yet. Gone is the panic, guilt, or need for control. As soon as he said he loved me and wanted more, it was as if he broke some kind of spell holding me hostage. It just vanished.

"We need some kind of word you can say if I go too far and you need me to stop."

I stare at him. "No, we don't. I trust you. You won't go too far. I live for the pain, just as you do."

He smirks as he moves closer to me. "I know you do." He moves away from me to grab a condom from the drawer and something else. I can't see quite what it is until I feel the sting of its black threads on my breasts. He tortures my breasts over and over with the sting of the crop. I scream and moan and writhe against the ties holding my arms in place. The pain and pleasure each touch brings me is amazing. I watch his body grow harder with each strike as he enjoys watching me enjoy the touch of the crop. I know he likes to feel the pain too, and I wonder how I'm going to be able to let him feel it with my hands tied high over my head.

Suddenly, I feel his body against me, his cock pressing on my dripping pussy. Our lips meet easily but are gentle as we're both still sore from last night.

"Oh fuck," I groan as he pushes inside me in one quick movement. Expanding me to my limits. He grabs my thighs, and suddenly, I'm off the floor as he holds me in his strong arms. He releases me with one hand, and I panic a little that he's going to drop me.

"I got you," he says, pinching my nipple. I squeal and immediately relax as he works my nipple with his fingers and thrusts inside me. The mix of soreness and pleasure overwhelms my body with each thrust as we both reach higher. He moves his hand to my clit to make sure I'll come with him. When we are both close, I squeeze around him as hard as I can, giving him the pain he seeks. He growls into my shoulder as we both come in sweet agony.

He immediately unties me and brings me back to bed where he wraps me in his arms. I know if we stay like this, we will both drift off to sleep and waste away the day with fucking and sleeping.

I try to sit up on the bed, but Landon's strong arms hold me in place.

"What about Caroline?" I ask, and suddenly, we are both sitting up in bed. His eyes focused on mine trying to read me.

"What about Caroline?" he asks confused.

"Are you and Caroline going to still ... you know?"

He looks at me incredulously before laughing. "No, that's over. We haven't since I met you."

"Really?"

He nods still chuckling. "Really. I'm yours just as you are mine. There won't be anyone else as long as we are together, which I envision will be a long, long time." He pauses. "There are too many delicious positions I want to fuck you in to give you up anytime soon," he teases. I smile satisfied with his answer.

"I'm still planning to go back to New York."

He frowns at that. "Why?"

"Because I need to. I need to find out about my past. Then I can truly move on without that baggage hanging over me."

"I'm going with you," he says not asking. He never asks, and I find I don't want him to.

"Okay," I say smiling.

"Okay," he says repeating my words.

Chapter Sixteen

LANDON

I don't want to wait to make you mine
I love you, you, you

WE WALK through the airport toward security and my anxiety increases. We have been together less than forty-eight hours – forty-eight glorious hours – but Alex has yet to experience my real life. She has yet to be swarmed in public or have everything she does photographed, twisted, and then displayed on every magazine cover in America. This four-day trip to New York City could change all of that, and I'm not sure how she's going to react.

This trip makes me nervous for other reasons than just dealing with my fame. We agreed to four days. Four days to find out what we can about her past, and then we would decide after that what is best for her memory. Whether she needs to stay in New York longer or if just traveling back and forth will work better. I'm afraid once she sees New York and starts to remember her past that her future will no longer include me.

I hand the TSA agent my ID and ticket waiting for her to recognize me and blow my cover, but the older woman doesn't notice or doesn't care, even after I take off my ball cap and sunglasses covering my face.

"You're being ridiculous. Nobody is going to recognize you," Alex says next to me. She throws her bag onto the conveyor belt for security and steps through the metal detector with ease. I step forward having to take my sunglasses and hat off again. I place them in the machine and then step through quickly trying to avoid eye contact with everyone around me. She just laughs as I take her lips in mine kissing her hard while we wait for our bags to get through the X-ray machine. I figure if her face covers mine, nobody will notice who I am. As soon as my sunglasses and cap make their way through the machine, I slip them back on, grab her hand, and hurry toward our gate where we can hopefully find some privacy.

We are riding up an escalator when I see the first flash. I don't see where it's coming from, and it can't be the paparazzi; they would be stuck on the other side of security. As we step off, I see another flash and then another. Shit! I know this photographer. He was the one who got the photos of Caroline and me.

"Hey!" I shout to the man hoping to reason with him not to publish the photos of Alex and me walking hand in hand through the airport.

He waves grinning at me before shouting to a group of people. "That's Landon Davis over there."

Suddenly, people everywhere are attacking us. Asking for selfies and autographs. I just take Alex's hand, pulling hard, as we practically run through the airport. I find a small janitor's closet, and we duck inside to escape the crowd. Alex is laughing the whole time, not understanding the seriousness of what just happened back there.

"It was just some girls. Relax, Landon, they aren't going to post those photos anywhere other than their Twitter page, which isn't going to get national attention."

"No, but I know the first photographer. He was the one who took the photos of Caroline and me. I don't know how he does it, but he always finds me. Those pictures will be on every magazine cover by tomorrow morning."

"Oh, shit!" Alex says as she paces in the small closet. "I can't let Laura see us together. I can't do that to her. It would destroy her to know I moved on so quickly." I nod in understanding. It would also piss off Caroline to see us together, but I don't tell her that. I take my phone from my pocket and hit Drew's number.

He answers on the second ring. I don't bother with formalities or greeting. "Drew, I need you to do damage control."

I focus my eyes on Alex as she watches me talk to Drew about what angle he could throw to the magazines to keep them from speculating about our relationship.

"We will have to give them new photos of you and Caroline together," Drew says. I hate it. Alex will hate it, but I know it's the only way to keep Alex out of the spotlight for now.

"Do it," I say ending the call. I turn back to Alex's worried eyes. "It's taken care of," I say to Alex.

"Maybe this was a mistake."

I brush her hair out of her face and tilt her chin up to look in her gorgeous green eyes. "This. Is. Not. A. Mistake. We will do this slowly and carefully so that we don't hurt anybody, but the only way to heal our hearts is to be together."

I press my lips firmly to hers, tangling my hand in her wavy hair as I press our bodies together with urgency, letting her know how much I still need her despite taking her body over and over again in the last forty-eight hours. My erection is already hard when she deepens the kiss. I open my eyes ready to pull away after I made my point, but I see the wicked gleam in her eyes and I know this isn't ending here.

"You're insatiable," I say smirking. I flick the lock on the door hoping it will keep anybody at bay long enough to become decent again if someone tries to open the door. I don't really care about displaying our affection if someone walked in on us. I'm more worried about the pictures and press that would come with it. Then no matter what damage control Drew does, we would be fucked.

Alex attacks me first, her claws digging into my chest as she kisses her way up and down my neck. I growl loving the way she marks me as hers. She moves her hand down my body squeezing my cock hard beneath my sweatpants as I moan loudly. I grab her hand pulling her toward me needing one last taste of her lips. Our tongues move in unison tasting more and more of each other. I walk her back until her ass hits the counter behind her. I spin her around holding her breast with one hand, her hip with my other. I bend her over the counter rubbing my cock against her ass. She moans with pleasure.

"Grab onto the counter. Don't let go," I threaten.

She moans but does it anyway. I pull her pants down rubbing her ass then moving to her already dripping pussy.

"Always so wet for me," I groan as I let the wetness cover my fingers. I move my hand quickly over her clit building her quickly. She wiggles her ass with every touch from the pleasure I'm bringing her.

"Fuck me," she says growing impatient. I take my cock out, and rub it against her ass, teasing her body with my touch. She pants harder as I tease her entrance with my cock over and over but never push in.

"Please," she begs between pants.

I grab her hair pulling it hard as I thrust into her. "Fuck, Landon," she screams before realizing where she is. I move my hand to cover her mouth.

"Don't scream." I thrust inside her harder as I continue flicking her clit with my thumb. I feel her moan against my hand.

"Don't make a sound, or I'm going to punish you so hard when we get to the hotel."

I thrust again deeper, and she whimpers against my hand. I remove my hand and slap her ass hard as I move again. She whimpers louder loving the touch. Finally, I push her over the edge with a flick of her clit and a bite to her shoulder. Her soft moans send me over the edge right after her. I dispose of the condom in the trashcan and pull both of our sweats back up before turning her around to look at me. A dreamy look covers her face.

She smiles up at me.

"Come on. We have a plane to catch."

"Where we can join the mile high club?" she asks raising her eyebrows at me.

I just shake my head taking her hands in mine as we exit the closet. "You're insatiable," I mumble to myself. And you're all mine.

Chapter Seventeen

ALEXA

"Just keep breathing," I hear again.

I HATE CEMETERIES, but I need to do this today. I need to be here for closure. So I can feel at peace with my decision to be with Landon. I step out of the cab and walk until I see it. The simple gravestone marked Ethan Wolfe, beloved son. It's sad that even on his gravestone it doesn't even say beloved husband.

Landon hangs back at the cab. He's been amazing so far. Giving me space when I need it and being there for comfort when I need it. We visited my mother's grave earlier. I hoped I would feel something, break down in tears. Anything. Nothing happened, though. Not one tear welled in my eyes.

I kneel before the stone and place the flowers I brought at the base. I pause waiting to feel some emotion before I begin what I came here to say. "Hi, Ethan. I'm sorry I haven't visited before. I moved to LA for surgery and had a hard time coming back. But that's not a good excuse. I'm here to tell you I'm sorry. I'm sorry for forgetting you. But

I know that when we were married I loved you with every fiber of my being. I loved you deeply and truly. I'm so sorry our time was cut so short. We should have had forever together. I'm giving you back these rings to hold onto for me." I take my wedding and engagement rings out of my pocket before I dig a small hole at the base of his headstone. I place them in the hole, and I cover them up with the dry dirt. "I'm not sure how things work in heaven or if there is a heaven, but if there is, you might need them to give to another girl or maybe to give back to me then if that's how things work. But I need you to know I found someone else. I never intended to, and I don't know if it's fair to your memory so soon, but the heart doesn't believe in fairness. It just loves. I hope you want me to be happy and continue to feel love because I don't know how else to live. I hope you are at peace." I stand up and pause for a moment. "Good-bye, Ethan." I walk away as I let a single tear fall down my cheek.

The cab ride to the apartment is quiet. Landon just holds me. The cab pulls up in front of the apartment that used to be Ethan's and mine. We didn't stay here last night. We got a hotel instead. It didn't seem right for me to share a place that was once Ethan's and mine.

"I'm not sure I'm ready to go in," I say to Landon as we sit outside the building.

"Maybe not, but you're strong enough." I smile at his words. I am strong enough. Landon and I walk hand in hand into the building and into my apartment on the top floor. I wish I could say the memories came flooding back as soon as I step foot in someplace familiar, but it didn't. I still feel cold and empty as I walk into the large, airy space. Everything in the apartment is in shades of white and cream. It looks straight out of a magazine. Everything is clean and organized. I stepped foot in here once, right after the accident, to gather a suitcase of belongings before going to Los Angeles. I needed to go to LA for surgery, so I didn't really have time to examine everything here.

I walk around the strange place running my hand along the different textures of the furniture as I do. I take deep breaths trying to find a familiar scent, but I can't find anything other than a clean scent. I take the green pocket square from my pocket and place it to my face breathing in deeply, the manly scent that was once there is practically gone. I put it back in my pocket and then walk back to Landon, who is just standing awkwardly in the entryway. He doesn't look around the place; his focus is fully on me.

"I love you," he says as I put my arms around him needing to feel comfort.

"I love you too. Thank you for doing this with me. I don't know what I expected. To have memories jump back into my brain from just being here."

He smiles. "It will just take time to remember. And if not, we will build a new past together."

I nod. "I would like to spend the rest of the evening just looking at every picture, every everything, and then we can go back to the hotel later."

He nods. "I'll order pizza." Landon walks into the kitchen and gets on the phone to order pizza. I continue to examine everything. I see a framed picture of Ethan and me together. I look so different. I don't have the tattoos, or if I do, they are covered up. My nose piercing is gone. I look classy and elegant in a simple black dress, Ethan in a suit. I look at every picture in the living room of us, and they are all the same. I pick up the last one and I see just a hint of the tattoo on my shoulder faintly through the makeup I must be wearing. Why would I cover up something that was obviously important to me at one point?

I look down at the visible tattoos on my arms. They look beautiful to me. I'm not sure I could ever find them not beautiful. I hear a knock on the door just as my stomach grumbles. I smile. *Just in time*. I walk to the door with my wallet in hand hoping I have some cash to give the guy.

"How much do I owe you?" I ask as I open the door. My world freezes when I look up. A pizza delivery guy doesn't stand in front of me. A man dressed in a ratty tux with rips and dirt does. A man who looks completely broken and shattered with blood seeping from fresh cuts on his face, and several other more healed cuts and bruises blanket his body. His face is swollen, and his eyes are barely open. What has me entranced, though, is the other half of a green pocket square that sticks out of the jacket.

"Ethan ..." Tears fill my eyes as I look from the man standing in front of me to the man standing in the kitchen. My heart immediately rips in two ...

ALIGNED: VOLUME 3

Chapter One

ALEXA

I put the flash drive into the box. The flash drive that contains the key to everything.

My heart is torn staring at the man in front of me. The man who is supposed to be buried in the ground along with my rings. My husband. He's alive. The only fact that I knew for sure about my life was that Ethan, my husband, died in a car accident six months ago. In the same accident that took my leg, along with my memories.

I try to focus my gaze on the shattered man in front of me. Maybe this man isn't him. After all, my memory isn't reliable. My eyes run over his ripped and dirty dark black suit. Blood oozes out from large cuts along his arms and legs. I can't bring myself to meet his eyes or even look at his face. I'm sure it is just as badly beaten as the rest of his body. Instead, my eyes are transfixed on the green piece of torn fabric barely protruding from the jacket. The missing piece of fabric in my pocket would align so perfectly with it. I reach my hand inside and pull out the torn fabric. I bring it to my face breathing in the lingering manly scent as I stare at the man in front of me. Ethan is alive.

I turn to look back at Landon standing behind me in the kitchen. Less than a few seconds must pass between the time I look at Ethan and the time it takes me to meet Landon's gaze, but it feels like minutes, no hours. I don't know how to feel. All I feel is disbelief. I meet Landon's eyes. His gorgeous golden eyes that have seen me come now too many times to count. Eyes that I have told I love you to. Eyes that held promises of more. Of forever just the night before.

I'm tied naked to the large hotel bed. My arms and legs spread wide for Landon to do whatever he pleases. I never thought I would feel this comfortable giving up complete control. Not after life dealt me one painful thing after the next. I like to know what the next second, next hour, and next day brings. But with Landon, I love giving up control. I love just letting go and enjoying the pleasure mixed with the tiniest bit of pain. I love him.

Landon comes back from the bathroom, completely naked allowing me to take in his growing erection. I watch his lustful eyes soak up my bare breasts before finding my hungry eyes. He bites his bottom lip as he walks toward me, and I find myself biting my own lip wishing it were his mouth there instead of mine. I watch him light the candle sitting on the end table to set the mood, I assume. Although he's done enough to romanticize me tonight between the carriage ride in Central Park, dinner, and this incredible hotel room complete with a Jacuzzi tub that looks like a small pool. We will definitely have to try that out later.

I focus my eyes back on Landon as he leans down and kisses me on the lips. He tugs at my lip with his teeth filling me with delicious pleasure. He leaves me wanting more when his lips leave mine seconds later. I run my tongue over my sore, swollen lip as I wait to see what he will do next. I want to demand more. Make him give me what I want faster, but I don't want to beg. Not yet anyway.

"Do you trust me?" he whispers in my ear. His hot breath on my neck makes me shiver.

"Yes," I breathe.

My vision is gone in an instant, buried beneath the cotton fabric of his shirt. His manly smell engulfs my nose as I wait for more. I feel his tongue flick my nipple causing me to gasp from the unexpected touch.

"Fuck." I moan as his tongue swirls around my other nipple. His touch feels amplified a hundred times over.

"God, I can't wait to be inside you."

"Please," I beg, needing him to follow through on his promise. His tongue moves to my clit flicking over it as my toes curl. But he doesn't stay there long. His tongue moves down to my slit, lapping up my juices as his tongue thrusts inside me. I moan, but it's not enough to satisfy my need for him to fill me and stretch me until I can't take anymore.

"Please," I beg again. "Please, Landon. I need you inside me." I feel like I'm going to burst from the energy flowing through me. The energy he causes.

I feel the bed shift as me moves, but I don't feel him. I wait for what seems like an eternity. My nipples hard and my lips swollen — wanting more. Needing more. But instead, I wait. And wait. And wait.

When he does finally push inside me, I scream from the unexpected fullness. He thrusts again and again as he rubs my clit with his thumb. He builds me fast to my brink before his thumb stops suddenly.

"I want to mark you. I want to make you come. But I want you to beg for it first."

I moan as his thrusts slow, and he doesn't let me come. His actions don't bring me any relief either. Instead, he just makes me wet with need.

"Please mark me. Make me come," I beg. I'm panting hard from being brought so close and then denied. I try to slow my breathing. I try to slow my beating heart. I try to anticipate what he's going to do to me. To mark me. To make me his. But my heart doesn't let me calm down enough to think.

That's when I feel it, the burning of my flesh on my soft belly as Landon moves harder and faster inside me. He does it again, but this time, it ignites me.

"Make me yours," I say when I realize that it's hot wax arousing my body. Gently warming my skin and reminding me of this night forever. A night I will never forget. The night I realized I wanted this man forever. He is my future. I don't care about my past. I only care about my future with him.

When I looked at him that night, our eyes both held the promise of a future. Now, when I look into his eyes, all I see is pain. There is no hope of a future, only emptiness. He knows that the man standing in the hallway is Ethan. I need to tear my eyes from his, and I need to go to Ethan. He is my husband, after all. Not that I remember him, though. He's a complete stranger to me. I just don't understand how this is possible. How is Ethan alive? What the hell happened to him?

My hand grabs my chest over my heart to try to relieve the pain pounding in my chest. This is why love isn't worth it. This pain that I will never get over. My heart knows. It knows that Ethan coming back means the end of Landon and me.

I hear a loud thump behind me, which forces my eyes away from Landon. Ethan has crumpled to the floor.

"Ethan!" I scream as I run the twenty feet from the living room to where he lies completely broken. It takes me less than five seconds to reach him, but that is more than enough time for the guilt to consume me. Whatever happened to Ethan was horrible. And instead of looking for him, saving him, I moved on to Landon. How is he ever going to forgive me for that?

"Ethan!" I scream again as I kneel down beside him. He doesn't respond. His body is still limp on the floor.

"Check to make sure he is breathing," Landon says calmly standing over me.

I gently roll Ethan's body onto his back and watch as his chest rises and falls. He's still breathing.

"We need an ambulance. A man is unconscious but breathing," Landon says into his phone. I let his voice drift off as I look back at Ethan. His jet-black hair has started to grow wild and unkept. Dark stubble covers his chin and neck unevenly. Bruises cover his face. He looks just like I did after the accident. It's like for him the accident happened yesterday instead of almost six months ago.

"An ambulance is coming. The operator just said to make sure he is still breathing and not to move him," Landon says.

I nod not able to say any words. What am I supposed to say? Landon, this is my husband, Ethan, who was supposedly dead and who I can't remember. Ethan, this is Landon, the guy I've been fucking even though you've been alive this whole time. No. There are no words. No words can make any of this right.

"I love you. It's going to be okay," Landon says.

I shake my head as the tears fall. Those words are definitely not the right words. Those words don't make anything better. It's never going to be okay again.

Chapter Two

LANDON

I used to think love didn't exist
That it is purely just a myth.
Something visited in fairy tales
But never found in real life.

WATCHING Alex fall apart over Ethan's body broke me. Somehow, after everything, I'm going to lose her. I've lost enough. I can't lose anyone else I love. I won't go through that again. I won't lose Alex.

I watch as the woman I love paces back and forth in the waiting room. My strong, beautiful, passionate woman is a fucking mess, and I can't do anything to fix it. Not one fucking thing.

Ethan was immediately rushed back as soon as he arrived by ambulance to the emergency room, and they haven't told us anything. All we have is questions. Like what the fuck is her husband doing alive?

I hate him. And not just because he could ruin everything between Alex and me. I just don't trust him. What man abandons his wife for six months?

I get up from my chair and walk over to Alex, pulling her into an embrace. She melts into my arms. Her warm body fits perfectly with mine. This is how it should be. Just like this.

"It's going to be okay," I say again. Although, I have no idea how it will ever be okay again. Maybe he will have amnesia too. Maybe he won't remember who she is either. Maybe he will want to start a new life with someone new and leave Alex to me.

I tuck a loose strand of hair behind her ear trying my best to comfort her. She doesn't say anything. She just lets me hold her. Lets us be together even if these are the last few moments we will ever have together. I try to engrain this moment into my memory forever. The smell of raspberries lingers around her. Her beautiful red hair and emerald eyes. Her pale skin covered in tattoos and scars. Her flushed cheeks and bloodshot eyes. Everything about this moment, I will remember.

Her arms tighten around me, squeezing me so hard I can barely breathe, and my arms tighten around her in response. We are both hoping that our bodies will mesh as one in such a way that we can never be separated again.

Her body presses so tightly against mine that I know she can feel the ring box in my pocket. Well, she would notice if she wasn't in such a trance. I wasn't going to give it to her yet. I was going to wait. I just carry it with me in case the perfect opportunity appeared. Now, it never will.

"Mrs. Wolfe?" an older male doctor says. I wince as I hear him speak the name. Alex's real name.

Alex pulls away from me letting go so easily.

"That's me," she says walking over to him.

I follow close behind needing to be close to her. Needing to find out any information I can use against this bastard.

"Mrs. Wolfe, your husband has lost a lot of blood, which probably caused him to pass out. He suffered extensive internal bleeding and damage. He is still unconscious but is in stable condition. We are moving him to intensive care where you can see him shortly. Do you have any questions?" the doctor says.

"Do you know what happened to him?" Alex asks.

"I'm sorry, Mrs. Wolfe, but until Ethan wakes up, we won't know anything more than what you told the police in your statement," he says.

"Thank you, Doctor," Alex says before turning back to me. She immediately wraps her arms back around me as if she knows this moment is fleeting. I watch over her shoulder as the doctor leaves. I know that in a matter of minutes, someone will return to take Alex to Ethan. To her husband. To where society says she belongs. It isn't the *perfect* moment. In fact, it's the *worst* moment. But it's the *only* moment.

I untangle myself from her arms, and while still holding onto her hands, I kneel in front of her feet. I pull the box from my pocket and open it to reveal the sparkly ring to her.

"Alex, I love you. I know this is crazy, but marry me," I say.

Her large eyes stay glued to mine. She doesn't even glance down at the ring I'm presenting to her. She opens her mouth to speak.

"Mrs. Wolfe, I'll take you back to see your husband now," a young nurse says.

Alex nods to the nurse as she wiggles her hand out of my hold and begins to follow the nurse. I stand quickly and take her hand back in mine.

"Alex?"

"No," she says as she pushes through the door to the ICU leaving me empty and waiting.

Chapter Three

ETHAN

I hate these goddamn parties. There is never anyone here worth my time. I should just go, I think as I slug down another shot of tequila. It burns my throat, but I don't feel the pain. I never do. I glance at my watch. It's past midnight. I have to be up in less than five hours. I walk toward the entrance of the bar when I see her.

I OPEN MY EYES. I know the pain exists, but I don't feel it. I never feel it. I've never felt pain, not even when I was a kid. Instead of pain, I feel nothing. I look at my bruised and broken body lying in the hospital bed, but I still feel nothing. I feel nothing until I look up.

Staring back at me are the most beautiful green eyes I have ever seen. The eyes that got me into this whole mess to begin with. God, I've missed these eyes. Excitement doesn't fill her eyes as I had expected. Instead, sorrow fills them.

"Hey, beautiful. Everything is going to be okay," I say.

Alexa smiles, but it's weak and not her normal, wide smile that fills her whole face. She stands from the chair and sits on the edge of my bed.

"I'm glad you're okay. We thought you were dead. The police said you had most likely drowned and that your body was swept away. Your body was never found, so we thought you were dead," she says.

I reach my hand out to her, and she collapses into my arms on autopilot, as if she has done it thousands of times before.

"I'm sorry it took me so long to get back to you," I say into her hair as I hold her body close to me. The smell of raspberries immediately overcomes me. I smile. She hasn't changed.

Alexa gently pulls away from me to look me in the eye. Her eyes are dripping with tears that are so out of character for her. I reach up and wipe the tears away, and she winces at my touch.

"What happened? Ethan, where were you?"

I take a deep breath preparing the words to explain.

"Do you remember that case I was working on before the wedding? The Alfie King case?"

She shakes her head. I worked on that case for over a year. It was basically the only thing I had worked on since we got together. She should remember.

"He was the only case I ever lost. It cost me a lot more than just the lost case. His men came after us. It wasn't a random hit and run. Or a drunk driver that hit us the night of our wedding. It was King's men. They tried to kill us." I tighten my hands into fists as I think about the men who did this to me. They will fucking pay. My face reddens and my breathing quickens just thinking about what I plan to do to them. They'll be begging me to kill them before I am done with them. What they did to me won't even compare.

"When we didn't die in the initial crash, they dragged me away. Tortured me. Threatened to kill me every day for six months." My face softens a little as I feel tears forming behind my eyes. Alexa continues to stare at me. Waiting to hear more.

"I thought you had died. They told me you had, and after six months of torture, I finally had my chance to get free. They forgot to lock the door where they were keeping me in the basement of a building about ten blocks from our apartment. That's what killed me the most. Being so close, but not being able to get to you. As soon as I was free, I ran straight home. I just needed to see you. I needed to know if you were really dead."

I pull her to me needing her lips on mine. I kiss her hard needing to feel every inch of her mouth on mine. She doesn't kiss me back, though. She just lets me kiss her. I try deepening the kiss needing her desperation for me to match my own. When I push my tongue into her mouth, she finally kisses me back. Slowly, with less urgency, but the need to kiss me is still there.

"I've missed you so much, Alexa," I say, as my lips hover over hers. "Every day without you, I died a little more thinking I could never have this again." I grab her hand needing her touch. Needing to know she is real. Alive. I run my hand over her fingers expecting to find her engagement and wedding rings, but they aren't there.

"Where are your rings?"

Alexa pulls her hands from mine. She grabs the bottom edge of her shirt fidgeting with it. Shutting me out.

"Alexa?" I try again. She winces slightly when I say her name. I watch as her shoulders rise and fall as she takes a deep breath.

"I buried them."

"What do you mean you buried them?"

Alexa pauses to take another deep breath before continuing. "You were gone. I had to let you go. So I buried them at the gravesite to free myself from the guilt of moving on ..."

I grab the back of her neck pulling her lips to me so I can kiss them softly. "I don't care what you did while I was gone. We can get the rings back or buy new, better rings. It's about us together now, forever."

I smile brightly at her, but all I see is worry covering her face.

"What's wrong?"

"Ethan, it's not that simple." She stands up and starts pacing the room. She runs her hand through her thick, red hair before turning back to me. Her pants rise up a little and I see it. I can't believe I haven't noticed it before. I try to climb out of bed to take a closer look at it, but my IV pulls on my hand keeping me in place.

"Alexa, what ..." I can't bring myself to finish. My eyes are glued to her leg as she walks to me.

"It's amputated. Gone," she says calmly as if she has fully accepted it. "The car accident ... no the car *attack* took it, just like it took you from me."

"Come here," I say. She walks to me and sits back on the edge of the bed. She watches as I pull her amputated leg into my lap and roll her pants up so I can see the damage done. I can't hide the look of disgust from my face. I can't believe she lost her leg. I hate who did this to her. I hate him more than anyone knows. I'll kill to make this right.

I kiss her thigh letting her know that I still love her.

"I'll always love you. No matter what happens," I say. I wait for her to say 'I love you' back, but she doesn't.

"I'm sorry," Alexa says.

I tuck her loose hair behind her ears trying to comfort her. "You have nothing to be sorry for," I say.

"Yes, I do. The attack took more than you or my leg. It took my memory of you, my memory of everything."

I pull her to me and hug her tightly.

"Everything is going to be okay," I say in her ear. Although I know that's not true. Love doesn't make anything okay. It just makes it painful.

Chapter Four

ALEXA

Without the flash drive, I will never be free.

"I FEEL INCREDIBLY guilty that I don't remember you," I say, averting my gaze from Ethan. I also feel incredibly guilty for being with Landon when Ethan was still alive. Is it cheating if you think your husband is dead? I can't bring myself to tell Ethan about Landon. It would destroy Ethan if I told him about Landon. It would destroy me.

"Don't be. It could be fun making you fall in love with me again," Ethan says, winking at me.

I smile and blush, but it doesn't make the guilt go away. I just have to end everything with Landon now before I sin any further. I think back to just hours ago when Landon kneeled down on one knee. That was ridiculous. We haven't been together long enough to think of marriage. But he did. He must have, to have already gotten a ring. A ring I didn't even bother to glance at.

I try to imagine now what the ring would look like. Was it large and expensive? A princess cut maybe? Or did he choose something small and simple? I'll never know. Just as I will never know what it would have been like to say 'yes' instead of 'no.' Because if it wasn't for Ethan, I would have said 'yes,' even though he was crazy to ask so soon. Because one crooked grin springing to his face would have made me melt.

A knock sounds on the door breaking up my daydream just before a nurse enters. "How is your pain?" she asks Ethan.

"I don't have any pain," he says smiling at me.

"Uh-huh," she says. She takes out her stethoscope and starts checking his breathing.

"All your vitals are fine, but I'm going to up your pain medication so you can sleep," she says.

Ethan just nods. She starts administering the medication through his IV, and Ethan quickly drifts off to sleep. I sit on the edge of the bed watching him as he breathes. This man. This stranger is my husband. He's *my husband.* I promised to love him every day until death do us part. But my heart has changed. It betrays Ethan. I gave it to Landon, and I don't know how to get it back.

I just have to find a way to fall back in love with Ethan. That shouldn't be that hard since I loved him before. I can see he's an attractive man, even with the bruising and scars. Right now, he looks a little rough around the edges, but from all of the pictures I've seen of him, I know he likes to wear a clean-cut, professional look. As I stare at him lying in the bed, my heart doesn't speed up. It doesn't recognize him, but maybe after spending more time together, it will.

Maybe I'll remember everything. Who I am. What my wants and dreams were. Everything. And if not, Ethan knows my past. He can answer all my questions. He is the key to finding myself again.

I stare down at my own broken body. Scars that have healed over tattoos making my skin look rough instead of smooth. My leg is gone. And while I'm not ashamed of it, it's a struggle for anyone to find beautiful. My memory is gone. What does Ethan even have to love about me? What can he find attractive now that I've changed so much from the woman I was before?

"Can I get you anything before I go? A blanket and pillow maybe?" the nurse says.

"That would be great. Thanks," I say. The nurse turns to leave.

"Wait," I say, realizing I do have questions for her.

She pauses at the door.

"Can you tell me Ethan's prognosis?"

"His prognosis is good. All the tests we have run indicate that he will make a full recovery. He has some broken ribs, but the surgeons were able to control the internal bleeding. No brain damage. No long-term damage. The only thing we have to worry about now is infection and getting him strong again. He's a lucky guy. Tomorrow, we should be able to move him out of the ICU and into a normal room. You're going to get to keep him a long time."

I frown. I shouldn't be upset that Ethan is going to be fine. I should be ecstatic.

The nurse pauses and looks back at me. "It's going to be okay."

I sigh heavily. "God, I wish people would stop saying that."

She chuckles and waits until I meet her gaze. "It's all people know to say when there are no words to make it better."

I try my best to smile at the kind woman, but I'm afraid it still looks like a frown. "It doesn't make me feel any better, though."

"Maybe the young man waiting in the waiting room will," she says with a knowing look.

"It's not what you think. He's just a friend."

"Maybe. Maybe he's more. But whoever he is, go talk to him before he does something stupid like break down a door to come find you. And maybe whoever he is can make things okay."

"Okay," is all I say back as I watch the nurse leave. I want to go talk to Landon. I want to *be* with Landon. But I'm not sure I can face him. I'm not sure I'm strong enough to tell him 'no' again.

Chapter Five
LANDON

But now that I've lost you
I know it really exists.
I never thought I could feel
So empty without you in my arms
Without your strength surrounding me.

"FUCK!" I howl, throwing one of the blue plastic chairs across the waiting room. It slams into the wall with a crash that ricochets off the walls in the waiting room. I watch as it bounces off the linoleum floor before knocking another chair over. I have been in this waiting room for over eight hours. Eight long fucking hours without seeing her. Without a word from her.

The woman I want to marry. The woman I want to spend the rest of my life with just said 'no.' Not maybe. Not we will see. Just no. She didn't even hesitate when I begged her for an answer before she left to go be with her husband. She just spat it out, demolishing my heart with her words.

I know asking her to marry me wasn't a rational decision. I know even if her husband hadn't come back into the picture to ruin everything, it would have been way too early to ask her. I know that asking her to marry me, while technically still married to another man, is insane. But I thought she would have at least considered my offer. Shown me that she at least gave a shit about me.

Instead, she's left me to pace in this damn waiting room for eight hours. I've spent the time texting her. Calling her. Begging the damn nurses to let me back to see her. I don't want to see *him*. Just *her*.

"Sir, I'm going to have to ask you to leave or I'll have to call security," an older nurse says to me. I look around the room. Everything in the room is white other than the damn chairs, and I've had enough of the antiseptic smell to make me sick. The only things that seem alive in the room are the people sitting in the damn plastic blue chairs. Their eyes are transfixed on me, breaking out of their gloomy blank stares and instead, wearing a look of fear. Fear that I caused when I threw the chair. They probably think I'm a drunk throwing a tantrum. I've seen my dad drunk enough times to know that this is what I look like right now. But I'm not drunk. I'm just in unbearable pain because I know I've lost Alex.

"I'm sorry," I say to the nurse. "I'll go."

I start walking out of the waiting room watching as every person I pass hides their eyes from me as if I'm going to attack them for just looking at me. I approach the automatic doors that open slowly, almost as if they are reluctant for me to leave too, when I hear her voice.

"Landon," Alex says.

I grin. I can't help it. I've waited all day to hear those words. Any words from her. I turn and look at her. My grin immediately fades. Her face is red and blotchy. Her eyes swollen from crying. Her hair is a tangled mess. I pull her to me and wrap my arms around her. To my surprise, she lets me. She sinks back into my chest like a perfect fit. Gone though is the smell of raspberries, replaced with antiseptic and hints of him. He's already left his scent on her.

"We need to talk," she says. I wince at the dreaded words that no one ever wants to hear.

"There's a coffee shop across the street," I suggest.

She nods and forces her body away from mine. I walk next to her side by side, but I resist the urge to reach out and touch her. I resist throwing her over my shoulder, throwing her in my car, and just driving until all of this is nothing but a distant memory.

The walk is cold despite the morning light shining down on us in the middle of summer. Even Mother Nature knows this is not a pleasant morning worthy of beautiful weather. Has it really been almost twenty-four hours since I last fucked her? The last time my life felt perfect. Has it really been ten hours since Ethan knocked on the door? Ruining my life. Eight hours since I proposed? Further ruining my life. Eight hours since I last saw her? It doesn't seem real, my life.

How easily it changed in twenty-four hours. Really how much it changed in one second. Just the amount of time to knock on a door. Because one glance at Ethan and I knew my life was over.

I look up at the glass door to the small local coffee shop. Everyone inside is happily drinking their morning coffee. Some are chatting while others are engrossed in a book or their computer. Coffee shops aren't for uncomfortable conversations. They are for happy conversations between friends. This conversation is going to ruin coffee shops for me forever.

Alex walks straight to the counter and orders us both coffee. I hand the barista my card to pay. It's like paying for your last meal before your execution. That's how I feel paying for this order. It's beyond painful.

Alex takes a seat at a small table in the far corner of the shop. I wait for our drinks. I want the wait to last forever because as long as I'm standing over here, I can't be at the table listening to Alex explain why we can't be together. But the wait ends quickly. The barista hands me our coffees, and I take the short walk to the table.

I hand Alex her coffee before I sit across from her. I watch as she takes a sip from her coffee, but I don't bother touching mine. When she sets it down, she starts talking, but I don't really hear the words. I'm too focused on the plump pink lips I will never get to taste again. Her perfect green eyes that sparkle even now as tears threaten. Her hair that, despite it being a tangled mess, still flatters her. I think about the strength she embodies every day. How selfless she is to be thinking of Ethan and me instead of herself. I'll never get to experience her strength, selflessness, or her fighting spirit. All of it is going to disappear from my life after today.

Sure, I hear words like 'Ethan,' 'kidnapped,' and 'tortured,' but I don't listen to the details. I don't care what happened to that fucker. If I were married to Alex, I wouldn't let anybody stop me from being with her. Sure as hell not some damn kidnappers. All I want to know is if Alex is safe. Or is there some lunatic on the loose trying to get to her?

"Have they caught the guys yet?"

"No, but we should be safe enough for now. The hospital has security, and it will be a few days before Ethan is released."

Fuck this. I'm tired of hearing about Ethan. I want to know about us. If she is just going to pretend like these last few weeks didn't happen.

"Alex, I love ..."

"Stop, just stop." She holds up her hand and then takes a deep breath. Her hands fidget with her cup of coffee in front of her. I watch as she takes breath after breath trying to calm herself as she has done before when she was having a panic attack. Except this time she isn't suffering from a panic attack, she is suffering with dealing with real life. I watch as her hands slowly relinquish their grip on her cup and her breathing becomes even enough that she can speak.

"Landon, I want to thank you. For everything. For opening my heart again. After the accident, I tried to hide away so I couldn't feel the pain. I thought that the only way to feel love again was to go through intense, unbearable pain. I was right that loving often comes with intense pain, but I was wrong in thinking that the pain isn't worth it." She pauses making sure to catch my eyes before she continues.

"It is worth it. I wouldn't give up these last few weeks for anything. I fell in love again. I learned to open my heart. You released me from the pain I was carrying with me. But what I've realized is that our love isn't meant to be an everlasting love. Our love was always meant to be temporary so that when we both were faced with our pasts, we would be ready to love again." She reaches across the table and grabs hold of my hands, tighter than she ever has before.

"I love you, and I'll take that memory with me forever. It's what is allowing me to open my heart back up to Ethan. Thank you for setting me free from the cage I was living in." She releases my hands and stands up.

"I'm not coming back, and I won't answer your texts or calls. You're free," she says walking away from me and taking my heart with her.

I don't follow her. I'm too broken to say anything that will make her stay. She's made up her mind about her future, and it doesn't include me.

Chapter Six

ETHAN

I watch her emerald eyes scan the crowd taking in the crowded dance floor and bar. She doesn't seem to be searching for anyone, just content to get out of the cold. She's plainly dressed in jeans and wearing a bulky sweater that covers most of her body. She's perfect.

"Oh, my God, Ethan!" my mother screeches in her high-pitched voice as she bursts into my hospital room. Tears flow freely down her cheeks as she rushes to my bedside and pulls me into an unusually tight hug. She's never been one to show any emotions that could be seen as weak. I've never seen her cry. Not once. Not when her father died. Not when her husband died. Never.

But right now, she's bawling as she squeezes all of the oxygen from my lungs. My nurse and doctor are standing in the doorway smiling at the reunion of a mother and her child, not caring at the damage she is doing to my body. Mother releases her grip and kisses me on the forehead like most mothers usually do when they kiss their children good night. Except mine never has before today. This is all for show. This is all for the doctor and nurse standing in the doorway.

"I can't believe you are alive," Mother says between fake sobs. I know Mother loves me, but I've always wondered if she loved me more because of the money I bring the Wolfe company rather than as the son who she loves spending time with.

"What happened to you? Any serious injuries?" Mother asks.

"I'm fine, Mother," I say. I look at up at my nurse and doctor who have seen enough of my mother's spectacle to know that she loves me. "Will you excuse us?"

The doctor nods while my nurse smiles. "If you need anything, just press the button. I'll be back in about an hour to check on you."

I just nod not bothering to smile back as they both leave my hospital room to give us some privacy. I turn my scowl to my mother who has already turned off the tears and is powdering her face.

"What was that about?" I ask.

"Can't a mother show affection for her son?"

"No, you can't."

She smiles as she closes her compact. She hasn't changed a bit.

"Why didn't you tell me about Alexa's leg?"

"It wasn't important. The only thing you needed to know was her memory. That it's gone. Her leg doesn't matter."

"It matters to me."

"Oh, stop it. You are too close to that girl."

"She's my wife."

Mother smiles her sly smile again. "For now."

I frown. "What does that mean?"

"Never mind. You ready to talk to the police and reporters."

"Yes."

"Excellent." She walks to the door and pokes her head out. After a few words, two men follow her back into the room.

"I'm Officer Michael Nibbs, and this is Officer Chad Burner. I'm so sorry to disturb you while you are in the hospital recovering, but we would like to nail the bastards who did this to you and your wife."

"It's not a problem at all. Take a seat," I say gesturing to the folding chairs at the far side of the room. I watch as each officer pulls a chair up next to my bed.

"Can you tell us what happened? What you remember?" Officer Burner asks.

"Sure. It was New Year's Eve. Alexa and I had just gotten married that night at the Plaza hotel. A limo was driving us home. The roads were pretty icy. Next thing I remember, the car had gone over a bridge into the river. The rest of my memories from that night are vague." I close my eyes trying to remember more from that night, but nothing comes to me.

"The next thing I remember, I was tied up in the basement of a building."

"Do you know what building you were held in? Or can you describe the building in any way?" Officer Nibbs asks.

"It was a building about ten blocks from our apartment. I was able to walk straight to the apartment when I broke free. I would need a map to show you where exactly."

Officer Nibbs pulls out his phone and hands it to me. I enter in my apartment and then study the map as I retrace my steps. Down alleyways and streets that I'm pretty familiar with after living in the apartment for several months. I finally find the spot where the abandoned building stood.

"Here," I say pointing to the spot. "They kept me in the basement of the abandoned building on that lot."

"We will make sure to send a team immediately," Officer Nibbs says.

"Good."

"Do you know how many men kept you hostage?"

"Yes, there were three men."

"Can you describe them to a sketch artist?"

"Yes, but they did wear hoods. I could describe body types."

"That will have to do. We will have a sketch artist come by this afternoon."

"What did they want from you?" Officer Burner asks.

I frown before clearing my throat. "Revenge. They wanted revenge. And money."

"One last question. Do you know who did this to you?" Officer Nibbs says.

I let my lips curl into a smile. "Yes."

Officer Nibbs returns my smile. "Who do you believe did this to you?"

"Alfie King. He ended up in jail because I lost his case. Or at least that's what he thinks. He wanted revenge. His men did this."

"Thank you for your time. I think we have everything we need to start our investigation. If you think of anything else, here is my card," Officer Burner says, handing me his card before heading out the door. Officer Nibbs follows but stops short of the exit. "Don't worry. We will get King." He winks at me before leaving. I smile. I do believe he will get King.

Chapter Seven

ALEXA

I don't know who did this to me or why, but the evidence is wrong.

"MORNING, BEAUTIFUL," Ethan says sitting up in his hospital bed. I cringe at the words that remind me of Landon, not Ethan. The morning light is shining in brightly despite the thin blinds trying to keep it out. It's not a beautiful morning, though. It's day one without Landon. Day one living with a shattered heart and it's only been an hour since I said good-bye to Landon. I haven't let the pain consume me yet, but I know it's coming. It's only a matter of time, but I won't let Ethan know. He can never know.

I get up from my chair and fully open the blinds to let in more of the light. I need all the help I can get to keep from losing it today. I need to find hope for a future with Ethan. I walk over and sit on the edge of the bed next to Ethan.

"Morning," I say, trying to smile as brightly as I can, but I'm afraid it comes across as weak.

Ethan frowns at my fake smile. His eyes study every inch of my face before he speaks. "You don't have to always be strong."

"Yes, I do," I say staring at his dark brown eyes.

"No, you don't," he says tucking my hair behind my ears. "Come here." He holds his arms out to me, and I fall into his embrace. He moans when I hit his bruised ribs.

"I'm sorry," I say trying to climb off his body, but his arms hold me in place.

"Don't ... I need you right here. It's the only way I'll heal," Ethan says, his voice strong, reassuring. As I lay on his chest, I hear his heart beating fast and uneven in his chest. I look over his broken body. He is the one trying to be strong when he shouldn't. He has no reason to be. He was the one tortured for months. He was the one who didn't know if he would live or die. He was the one who actually suffered from the loss of me. He needs me to be strong right now. Not a broken mess upset that she had to break up with her boyfriend of a couple of weeks. Poor, pitiful me. While Ethan has dealt with real pain, I've been crying over spilled milk.

Ethan squeezes me tighter. "I can't believe you're mine. I can't believe I ever thought I lost you. How stupid am I to think I could keep breathing if you weren't still alive somewhere holding out hope that we would be together again? I love you so much, Alexa."

Tears fall then. Slow at first, barely visible as they roll down my cheek onto Ethan's chest. Then suddenly they flow all at once, like a faucet down my face.

"Shh, baby, it's okay. Everything is okay now. Just let it all out," Ethan says as he tries his best to rock me like a baby in his lap. The tears keep falling. I don't even know why the tears are falling.

Are they falling for Ethan? For everything he has lost.

Are they falling for Landon? For everything he has lost.

Or are they falling for me? For everything I have lost. I don't know, and I'm not sure I care. I just let them fall.

They fall until a knock at the door breaks me out of my sadness.

"Hi, Ethan, I'm Mark Lewis with physical therapy," the man in khakis and a red polo says as he enters Ethan's hospital room.

Ethan glares at the man entering. Probably for interrupting my blubbering and crying on his shoulder. But I can't stay here any longer. Ethan needs his therapy, but I can't stay. It brings back too many painful memories of lying in a hospital room alone for months. My daily therapy visits from Calvin the only thing bringing me any hope of getting out. I can't think about Calvin or the pain. I can't think about any of it. I just need to get out of here.

"I have a few errands I need to run. I'll leave you and Mark to your therapy," I say, kissing Ethan softly on the cheek. I can't bring myself to kiss him on the lips again. Despite breaking up with Landon, it still feels like a betrayal to our relationship. *God, I'm a mess!* I care about betraying Landon's and my relationship, but did I care when I was betraying my relationship with Ethan?

"Okay, but take James Proc with you," Ethan says.

"Who is James Proc?" I ask, confused that there might be more people I don't remember from my past.

"He's one of the new bodyguards Mother and I hired to keep us safe until they catch the guys that did this to us," Ethan says.

I pause staring into space trying to register his words. I never really thought we weren't safe. I guess I just assumed the police would easily be able to catch them or they would be long gone to Mexico or some other far-off place. I never imagined there was a possibility of them still being here in NYC.

"Are we not safe?" I ask looking back at Ethan.

"It's just a precaution. You are completely safe. I would never let anyone hurt you, ever," Ethan says, his eyes hardening as he says it as if he's imagining the pain he would inflict on someone if they ever laid a finger on me. Except he has let someone hurt me before. *That's not fair*, I immediately think as I shake my head. Ethan had no way of knowing that losing King's trial would cause him to come after us. He did try to save him, whether he was guilty or innocent, and King got a fair trial. It wasn't Ethan's fault.

"Okay, I'll take James," I say, trying my best to smile and feel brave. Although where I'm going, I'd prefer to go alone.

"WHERE TO, MA'AM?" James asks from the front seat of the limo he is driving. He's nicely dressed in a perfectly fitted suit to his large six-foot-six frame that is all muscle. The only thing that seems out of place is his long blond hair pulled back into a bun on top of his head.

"Just call me Alexa and the cemetery please," I say. I don't have to say which one. He already knows.

"Yes, ma'am. I mean Alexa," James says. He takes a hard left turning us in the direction of the cemetery. I watch as the tall buildings go by that will eventually turn to countryside as we get closer to the cemetery. I hate the helpless feeling I get when someone is driving me around. I want to have as much control over my life as possible, especially since my life so far has been completely out of my control.

"So can I ask why we are going to the cemetery?" James asks.

"I just left something there I need to get back," I say.

"What?" James asks.

I can't help it; I giggle just a little at James's blatant curiosity. James is a little older than I am by probably four to five years, closer to Ethan's age than mine. I never expected him, though, to want to carry on a conversation with me. I expected him to keep things professional, all business.

When I don't answer, he asks, "You don't remember me. Do you?"

I shake my head. "I didn't know I was supposed to remember you. Did we have a security team before?"

"No. We were friends. I went to high school and college with Ethan. I was Ethan's best man at your wedding. We used to be good friends, you and I. We would tease Ethan about his perfect hair and goody-two-shoes relationship with his mother," James says.

"Why didn't you come visit me in the hospital after the accident?" I ask, angry that I had a friend, someone who could have helped me heal, but he wasn't there for me.

"I tried, but Laura wouldn't let me. She wouldn't allow you any visitors. One day, I came to the hospital to at least give you flowers, to let you know I was thinking about you. They told me you'd been transferred to a different hospital. I had no idea where."

"You never tried to look for me?" I ask, practically screaming with anger.

"Of course, I did, Alexa. I looked for you every day. I finally found you when I was invited to the charity event in Ethan's honor. An oversight by Laura, I'm sure, but I realized then that you had no idea who I was. You were too hung up on that guy to notice anyone else anyway."

"I was not hung up on any guy. He was just a client I photographed."

"Yeah, sure." James sighs quietly. "Don't worry. I won't tell Ethan but just stay away from that guy. Ethan deserves someone who loves him like you used to."

"I know he does. I just don't know how to love someone who I don't remember." I look quickly up at James meeting his eyes in the rearview mirror, before glancing back out the window. I'm embarrassed that he saw me with Landon.

"You'll remember. Don't worry."

"Are there any other friends from my past that I should know about?"

"No. You didn't really have friends. Your maid of honor was one of Ethan's annoying cousins. The only people you guys hung out with other than me were at Laura's charity events."

I sigh. I have no one else to talk to about my past. All I have are Ethan and James. And somehow, I think their memories of my past are going to be skewed.

James stops the limo in front of Ethan's gravestone. He guessed where I wanted to go. Although I guess it really isn't that surprising.

"I'll wait here," he says.

"Thanks," I say as I begin to climb out of the limo. Before I shut the door, I stop and poke my head back into the limo. "James, I'm sorry I don't remember you. Thanks for being a good friend to Ethan and me. I'll try my best to remember you too."

He smiles. "I don't care if you remember me. I'm too lovable for us not to rekindle our friendship. Just do what you need to do to love Ethan."

I nod as I move back out of the limo and close the door. I walk down to Ethan's grave and kneel in front of it just as I had done a few days earlier.

I don't know what to do or say, so I just sit in silence and let the warm sun fill me. Letting it do its best to give me hope and love.

"Hello, Ethan," I finally say although I know full well that Ethan's body doesn't lie under this stone. I think it's best to tell this to this Ethan instead of the one lying back in the hospital bed.

"I'm hurting a lot, Ethan. This pain in my chest has gotten worse since you came back instead of better. I'm scared. I'm scared that I will never love you the way I used to. I'm scared that I will never be able to fully let Landon go. I'm scared for our lives." I place my hand on the headstone. "I have questions. So many questions. How did we fall in love? What was our wedding like? Why did the accident happen? How did you manage to escape? What am I supposed to do now?"

I dig my fingers in the soft dirt shifting it around. It takes a while to find them. Maybe I don't really want to find them. But eventually, I do. I grasp the hard metal and pull them from the ground. My rings are right where I left them two days ago. I dust the dirt off the two rings. I take out the green silk fabric from my pocket and consider wrapping them back in the cloth to stick in my pocket. That's where they feel right. But I can't live for myself anymore.

I am going to find a way to love Ethan again and give him the life he deserves. So instead, I slip the rings onto my left ring finger. They fit perfectly, but the large engagement diamond looks out of place on my finger. I will get used to it, though. I will love Ethan again. I take the torn green fabric and put it back in the hole the rings were just in. I bury it, along with any memories since the accident. I will forget everything and start my new life with Ethan.

Chapter Eight

LANDON

As I watch you, my heart bleeds
At the sight of you kissing him.
You were my love I know that now
But it's too late, you're his now.
I've lost my love.

A KNOCK POUNDS on the door, waking me from my drunken stupor. My head is pounding, my eyes are dry from lack of sleep, and my stomach rumbles ready to spill its contents if I move from the bed. So I don't move. I let the pounding continue. I know who it is, anyway, and I'm not answering the door. I'm never answering a door again. Not after the pain it caused me after Alex opened the door the last time.

The pounding stops. *Thank fucking God.* I begin to drift back to sleep quickly as the alcohol takes its hold on me again. A few seconds later, I hear the door rattling as a card key is inserted into the door. He won't get too far, though, because the chain is still in place over the door keeping any intruders out.

"What the fuck?" I say, as the door flies open and lights come on in my hotel room, blinding me.

"Time to get up or you'll miss your flight," Drew says, standing at the foot of my bed acting all business. He presses his phone back to his ear. "Yes, two o'clock ..." Drew says into his phone.

I ignore the rest of the conversation and pull the pillow over my head to drown out Drew and block the blinding light.

All of a sudden, I'm drenched in icy cold water, which forces me to jump out of bed to escape the cold water.

"Fuck!" I scream as I try to shake off the excess water.

Drew throws me a towel, which I immediately use to begin drying off with.

"What was that for?"

"I'm done watching you sulk. You've been sulking, and drinking, and acting like a big baby for over a week now. It's time to grow up and start acting like a man. It's no wonder Alex left you."

I throw the soaked towel at Drew, getting his perfectly tailored suit wet. "Stop acting like you're my father. You're not." I plop on the couch and grab the remote to flip on the TV. "And don't talk about Alex."

"Wow, that comment should have at least gotten me a punch to the face, a nasty glare, or something. You really are a mess, man," Drew says, grabbing the remote from me and turning the TV back off. I don't even put up a fight. I just close my eyes and let my head fall back until it's resting on the cold soft fabric.

"Get it together, man. It was just a chick. Once you go on tour next week, you will have more chicks than you know what to do with. Just like before."

I don't bother to open my eyes as I respond on autopilot. "She wasn't just some chick. She was *the chick*."

"What do you mean she was *the chick*?"

Damn! I squeeze my eyes tight hoping to make the headache go away, but it doesn't help. I haven't told Drew the whole story yet about what happened with Alex. All he knows is she broke up with me, and I'm not really in the talking mood to say anything more.

"Nothing. It doesn't matter." I move to get up from the couch to find my clothes, but Drew shoves me back.

"Nope, start talking. What the hell did you do?" His face is red, his nostrils flared, and a tiny bead of sweat has formed on his forehead indicating how angry he really is. He's pissed and has no doubt guessed what I did. Not point denying it now.

"I proposed to her, in the hospital waiting room, while she was waiting to hear if her husband was dead or alive."

"Fuck, Landon! You're a bigger idiot than I thought." I watch as Drew begins pacing the room as more beads of sweat trickle down his red face.

"Where is the ring?"

"I tell you Alex's husband is alive and you care more about the damn proposal part? What is wrong with you?"

Drew takes a deep breath and exhales slowly, trying to calm himself, but his face is just as red as before.

"I already knew that Alex's husband is alive. It's all over the news. You would know that if you joined the living during daylight hours. What did you do with the ring?"

My stomach churns when I lift my head to look at him. "I don't know. I think I threw it into a river or something."

Drew's shoulders relax; his face softens from a bright red to more of a pale pink. "Good."

"Why does it matter what I did with the fucking ring?"

"Because if you still have it on you, then you are likely to propose to anyone in your drunken state. Or worse, someone will get a picture with you and the ring, which will cause a media storm. Caroline will find out and reveal what happened last year to the media. That *can't* happen. It will ruin you. You could end up in jail."

I huff but don't protest. He's right. I can't propose to anyone. Ever. It was stupid of me to propose to Alex, for many reasons. It was stupid of me to get involved with her in the first place. Too fucking late now. My heart is already hers, and I don't want it back. But I don't know how to move on without her.

Drew walks over to the dark brown dresser, opens the drawer, and pulls out some of my clothes. He walks back to where I still sit on the couch and throws the clothes at me. "Put these on. We need to go."

I just stare at the clothes. I can't leave. If I leave New York, I have no chance of getting her back.

"Put the clothes on. You need to give her space. Last time you were apart, she came back to you. Maybe that will happen again," Drew says somberly.

I just stare at the pile of clothes in my lap because I don't believe him for a second. Alex is stubborn and loyal. She'll be loyal to her husband no matter what. Even if she never loves him, she'll never leave him.

"Just put the clothes on. You can't chase after her if you are naked."

"Sure, I can." I can't help it as my lips curl into a slight smile. My brain drifts back to an earlier memory that has nothing to do with Alex. One of the good memories I have of Caroline, Drew, and me. The memory of my twelfth birthday.

An alarm clock sounds loudly. Except it doesn't sound like a normal alarm clock. It sounds more like a foghorn blasting loudly in my room. I sit up and look around my room. All I see is shaving cream. It's all over my body. It's covering my bed. I climb out of bed but slip and fall landing in a large pile covering my floor. It's everywhere. It's going to be a bitch to clean. And if father finds it ... Well, let's just hope he stays clear of my room like usual.

I glance up and see Caroline laughing hysterically at what she did. Drew is standing behind her smiling brightly, although I know who the mastermind is behind the prank. Caroline. Drew doesn't have a fun bone in his body.

My eyes grow tight, and my face grows red as I prepare to tackle her in the shaving cream. Although I'm not as angry as my face leads her to think I am, her eyes grow wide as I hear Drew tell her to run. She gives me one more innocent glance before she takes off running through the small house. I get up and carefully maneuver through the shaving cream past Drew.

"Wait ... you can't chase after her naked!" Drew exclaims.

I smile a wicked grin. "Sure, I can."

I take off through the neighborhood. Thankful that only an older gentleman sees me running through the streets while I am only wearing underwear and covered in shaving cream. He just shakes his head with a small grin on his face at the sight of me.

I chase Caroline through the neighborhood. She is fast, but I'm faster. I see her dart down her street, and I cut through the neighbor's yard. I tackle her to the soft grass in front of a stranger's house.

"Get off me! You're getting shaving cream everywhere!" she squeals.

I laugh but don't move off her. Instead, I do what my body has been craving to do to her for months now. I kiss her.

I CLIMB into the private jet and take a seat in one of the far back chairs. It's just Drew and me on this flight, despite the four empty chairs in front of me. I'm thankful he sprung for a private jet. I don't think I could handle a commercial flight right now. I don't think I can handle any flight right now. I'm still hungover, but I'm at least dressed and have some basic food in my stomach. Drew takes a seat next to me and I pull my ball cap over my face and lean my chair back to sleep. It's the only way I'll get through this flight.

Drew immediately grabs the ball cap off my face. "I don't think so. After you being MIA for a week, we have some work to do."

I growl at Drew. "I think my time would better be spent sleeping. That's why I pay you to handle stuff, so handle it."

"I am. Just thought you might like to see the magazine article about you and Caroline coming out tomorrow."

That gets my attention. "What article?"

"The article that is doing damage control so they don't post anything about you and Alex."

Shit. I forgot about that. I put my seat back up and give Drew my full attention.

"Show me."

He grins and then pulls out his phone and begins scrolling. I wait impatiently for him to find it. In the meantime, the pilot announces that we are taking off. Drew and I both buckle our seat belts, and I glance out the window one last time. One last glance of New York. One last glance at Alex.

Good-bye, Alex, I think, and then I close the window covering, trying to block her from my mind. It's hard because my mind immediately goes back to her. How her body perfectly fits with mine. How she moans when my teeth sink into her. Her face as she comes. It is all permanently etched on my mind. I can't escape it.

"Here." Drew hands me his cell phone. I take it from him and immediately begin to read the article. I read through before looking at the picture. It's bad. Really fucking bad. It's Caroline and me kissing. Although this picture is an unreleased picture from when we were dating, it's made to seem like it recently happened. Alex is going to flip. Broken up or not, she won't tolerate this.

"What did you do?" I'm still staring at the screen. I can't tear my eyes from the incriminating picture.

"I fixed the problem."

"Alex is going to flip out!"

"Good." Drew grabs the phone out of my hands.

"Why is that good? She'll never talk to me again. I'll never have a chance of getting her back." Not that I have a chance anyway. She's completely committed to that slick looking bastard.

"No, the exact opposite. She'll call you the second this becomes news."

"To scream and yell and call me a cheater."

"Yes, but she'll talk to you for once instead of ignoring your calls like usual."

I relax a little. Maybe Drew is right. She'll call. Then I'll get a chance to change her mind, or at the very least, hear her voice again until she comes to her senses.

Drew gets up from his seat and moves to the front of the plane while I plot what I'm going to say to Alex when she calls. When he comes back, he shoves my guitar in my lap. I stare at him, my eyebrows raised in confusion as the guitar rests in my lap.

"Start writing a new song. You have three hours till we land. Make yourself useful."

"I don't have anything to write about."

Drew laughs. "Sure you do. Her."

Chapter Nine

ETHAN

I watch her take a seat at the bar before I make my move. My eyes are trained on her as I move across the crowded bar. I take a seat right next to her.

"TELL me about how we first met," Alexa says. She fidgets with her engagement and wedding rings in her lap as she sits in a folding chair next to my hospital bed. I smile remembering when she first came back from visiting my grave. She walked straight to me with the rings already shimmering on her finger. When she hugged me and kissed me, it felt, for the first time, like she meant it. Like she wanted me. She hasn't done that again since.

"We first met at a party."

She stops fidgeting with her rings and looks up at me. Alexa always looks at me intently when I'm telling her something about her past. She tries to soak up every detail of the story as if she's reliving it. But every time I finish telling her a story about her past, she gets sad, withdrawn. She hasn't remembered anything about her past. No matter how many stories I tell to refresh her memory, she never remembers. She never will.

"Who's party?" Alexa asks; she rests her elbows on the edge of the hospital bed. Her whole body leans forward so that her head is resting on her elbows. She's as close to me as she can be without climbing into my bed. Not that I would complain. I miss her body. Her touch. Anything that would make me feel warm, instead of the dead cold I currently feel inside. Coming back from the dead isn't as glamorous as one would think. I've been through more physical therapy appointments, medical exams, tests, police interviews, and news interviews than I can keep track of. It's a wonder I've gotten stronger instead of weaker with everything going on. Strong enough to go home tomorrow. Then Alexa and I can go home — together.

"Who's party?" Alexa asks again bringing me back to focus on her. She's gorgeous despite being dressed in sweats and a t-shirt. Her hair is thrown up on top of her head. Not an ounce of makeup touches her face. Mother would complain that she looks like a scoundrel being so unkempt, but she is always beautiful to me.

"You're beautiful," I say, unable to help myself.

A slow blush begins to form on her cheeks. She smiles before leaning back in her chair away from me. She does that when I make her uncomfortable. It's not anything new. Alexa's done that since day one. It's one of the things about her that intrigues me so much. She isn't easily caught. I have to fight every day to keep her mine.

"I'm a mess."

"You're beautiful."

She just shakes her head barely looking at me.

"The party, it was James' bachelor party."

"I didn't know James was married."

"He's not. He caught her cheating with the stripper the next morning and called off the whole thing."

"But why was I at James' bachelor party? I thought I met James after I met you."

"You did. You were couch surfing at the time. Sleeping on anybody's couch who would let you. Sometimes, you slept on the streets. Occasionally, you had enough money from your photography and waitressing job to rent a motel room for a night or two. But most of the time, you would reinvest any money you made into your photography business. That night you had just gotten the biggest payday of your career and had ducked into the nearest bar to celebrate with a drink."

"What job was it? How did I go from that to this amazing photographer? Why did I not have enough money to pay rent?"

I chuckle. "Whoa, calm down and let me finish the story."

"Sorry." She blushes again, embarrassed that she interrupted the story.

"I was hanging out with James and his buddies, bored out of my mind, about ready to leave when I saw you walk in. You weren't wearing a coat even though it was winter. Instead, you had on probably five layers of clothes and jeans. Your hair was pulled up just like it is now. But something about your eyes drew me to you. Your beautiful green eyes seemed so happy that night that it was contagious. I had to go talk to you. I had to meet you. So I did. I offered to buy you a drink. You agreed. You drank a whiskey straight, to my surprise."

Her eyes light up when I say that, almost as if she remembered something.

"Do you remember anything?" I ask.

Her head drops just a little. "Not really. I just ordered a whiskey on autopilot the last few times I've been to a bar. So somewhere deep inside, I must remember."

I nod and smile. As much as she tries, I don't think she's ever going to remember me. I will have to fight all over again to gain her trust, her love.

"We sat and drank at the bar for a little while. I introduced you to James at the bachelor party, not that he remembers meeting you that night. I even got you to dance. Just one fast song. You were never much of a dancer."

She laughs at that. "I'm still not much of a dancer."

"Then after the dance, you were gone. You said you were just going to the bathroom, but you disappeared out of my life for what I thought was forever. I took James to the next bar assuming I would never see you again."

"But you did see me again. How did you find me?"

I take a deep breath trying to calm my tense body. Not sure if she should hear what happens next or if I should just let it remain buried.

"I read about you a couple of days later in the newspaper."

"What do you mean?"

"That night the reason you disappeared when you went to the bathroom was because you were attacked." I swallow hard preparing to say the next words that will extinguish her fire. "Alexa, you were raped that night."

Her eyes widen. Her mouth falls open, but she doesn't speak. I'm afraid she's gone into shock.

"Alexa," I say, waving my hand in front of her face. She doesn't move.

"Alexa," I say again. Louder this time. I sit up in bed so that I can reach her and shake her body. She slowly comes to but still doesn't say anything.

"Are you okay?"

"Yes," she says immediately. She rubs her hands up and down her arms as she stares again into nothing. "How is that possible?"

"I know it's a lot for you to take in. I'm sorry." I reach out to touch her hand, but she moves it into her lap out of reach.

"Who?"

"Daniel Woods. His name is Daniel Woods. He is still in jail. He got twenty-five years although he will probably get out before that."

"I can't ..." she says standing. "I can't deal with this right now. I'm sorry." She runs from the room.

I was wrong to tell her, I realize immediately. She's dealt with too much pain. Too much loss. I just hope I can help her heal.

Chapter Ten

ALEXA

I went to see him. His eyes are blue ... not black. Not even dark brown. They are bright sparkling blue. It can't be him.

I HEAR the door slam behind me as I leave Ethan's hospital room. I don't care that the nurses look up from their stations as I run down the hallway. All I care about is air. I need air. I run down the long white hallway to the elevator. Running down the hallway faster than I ever have before. I should feel free running like this, but I don't. I feel trapped.

I try to hold my breath to prevent the antiseptic smell from burning my nose, but I can't. I let the disgusting smell in, and it burns. It always burns. I reach the elevator and press the button to get off this floor. I just need to get away. Away from here. Away from the truth.

The elevator doesn't come right away. I stare at the blank white walls. A large picture frame of pastel flowers sits on the wall next to the elevator. It is supposed to be soothing, but it's not. It's just a boring picture that doesn't distract me from my thoughts. I look down the hallway from where I just came. White walls are all I see. A few nurses are walking, but other than that, there is nothing to distract me. I turn back to the elevator and start counting ...

One.

Two.

Three. Still no elevator.

Four.

Five.

Six. I begin twisting the rings on my finger.

Seven.

Eight. The elevator dings indicating the doors are about to open. My foot begins bouncing waiting for the doors to open.

Nine.

Ten.

Eleven. The doors open. I walk into the empty elevator. A hand touches my shoulder as I enter. I jump at the unexpected touch, but I don't exit the doorway of the elevator. I won't miss my escape to freedom.

"Are you okay?" James asks.

I force a false smile on my face as I turn to look at him. "Yes, just going to get coffee."

James studies my face. I try my best to remain calm and seem at ease. The only thing I allow myself to do is to spin the rings on my finger. It's the only tiny piece of nervous energy that's visible.

James returns my smile. "I'll go with you."

"I can go by myself," I say, trying my best to seem nonchalant.

"It's my job to go with you," James says stepping into the elevator.

"What about Ethan?"

"He has his own bodyguard. My job is to protect you."

I sigh but step into the elevator. James pushes the ground floor button where the coffee is. I begin counting again. Steadying my breathing as I do.

One.

Two.

Three.

Four.

Five. I take a deep breath. Preparing myself as the elevator descends the six floors.

Six.

Seven. The doors open. I run.

I don't just run. I fly. My legs are moving so fast I'm not sure they even belong to me. I run through the lobby. Past the janitor mopping the floor. Past the kid crying while his mom holds his hand, a terrified look on her face. Past the tired nurse getting another cup of coffee to get through the day. I run past it all, and I don't look back.

I run out the front door until I can finally taste air. Real air. I take a second. Just one second to just breathe. My legs don't move for that one second. In that one second, I can taste everything. Fresh cut grass. Flowers blooming. Hope. I smell hope.

After my second is up, I immediately force my legs to start moving again. Faster and faster. I run a block before I feel any pain in my leg. The pain is nothing though compared to what I feel in my heart. So instead of slowing down, I run faster trying to block everything out.

I block out Landon and ...

Ethan and ...

James and ...

My leg and ...

My memory and ...

The rape.

I block it all out. I just run. I let myself run block after block thinking about nothing other than my breathing. All I think about is my breathing. I breathe in more wonderful flowers. I breathe in rotting trash. I breathe in the exhaust from the cars driving next to me. I don't care what I breathe in anymore. I just breathe. In and out. Over and over. That's it. That's all I do.

Until my prosthetic leg hits a piece of uneven cement on the sidewalk. Then I'm no longer running. No longer breathing. I feel my body fall to the hard cement. I catch myself with the heels of my hands and my left knee. I feel them instantly bruise. I start counting again.

One.

Two.

Three. Then I feel his hands on me. That's all it took. Three seconds. I was never really free when I was running if he was only three seconds behind me. Protecting me. Is this my life now? Always having a shadow. Living in fear. Never being alone.

"Alexa," James says, his hands on my shoulders. He wants to help me stand up. I can feel his hands encouraging me to stand. I don't want to stand. If I stand, I will have to face everything, and I'm not ready for that.

He pulls me up anyway. I immediately assess my injuries. I was right. Bruises. No broken bones, not even a scrape. Just bruises. That level of pain doesn't even register right now.

"Come on, we have a long walk back," James says, his hand on the small of my back guiding me back in the direction of the hospital. When I start walking, he removes his hand and just lets me walk. He doesn't ask questions.

My mind doesn't have anything to focus on this time on the way back. My breathing is too easy to focus on that. The minor pain my body feels isn't enough either. My mind immediately goes to my dreams. My nightmares. They are true.

"Get off me," I scream. He doesn't budge. Instead, he slobbers over my neck and down to my breasts. I look up at the man on top of me, but I don't know who he is. All I see are two dark eyes suffocating me.

I keep walking. Letting the nightmare sink in as true. That happened to me.

He stands up; I think he's going to leave me alone, but he kicks me hard in the side. I let out a gasp as I try to catch my breath. He kicks me over and over, continuously knocking the breath out of me. All I can feel is the pain.

I walk. I should be crying but no tears come.

He covers my mouth with his so that I can't scream. I can barely breathe, but I wish I could stop breathing when he pushes himself deep inside me. He rips me apart over and over and over...

I walk farther. Side by side with James. I don't show emotion. I don't need to. Because on some level, I think I already knew. The nightmares. The panic attacks. This was where they all originated. This attack started the fear.

A tear trickles down my face as he flips me over and starts in again. He grabs my breasts and puts all his weight on my chest forcing the air out of my lungs. When I start to drift away, I welcome it. The escape. I don't feel anything.

No more. I won't let the fear consume me anymore. I won't let the panic stop me from living. Landon showed me how to stop. I'm not going to let the fear back in. I'm not going to let it stop me from trying to remember. If I can remember horrible, terrifying things that happened to me, then I can remember the good too.

I stop walking. We haven't made it back to the hospital yet, but I don't feel the need to keep walking. I look up and see we are standing outside of the coffee shop that Landon and I last spoke in. Here. I just need to be here, with Landon.

"I think I want that coffee after all," I say.

James just nods and follows me into the coffee shop. The smell of coffee beans immediately overwhelms me. A smell I will forever associate with Landon. I feel my heart racing unevenly in my chest, telling me it's not ready to face the breakup with Landon. Not so soon. Not after being strong enough to handle learning that all of the horrible things from my nightmares are true.

I ignore it, though, walking up to the barista.

"Welcome, can I take your order," the woman says with a large smile plastered on her face. I wonder if she is really happy or if she has just done this job long enough that she can smile that big no matter what is going on in her personal life.

"A black coffee please."

I turn to find James to see if he wants anything. But he is standing near the entrance scanning the three tables of people who are busy looking at their phones or computers, not paying him any attention. I shake my head at him. I just need a friend right now, not protection. I don't get that, though.

I reach for my purse before realizing I didn't grab it before I left Ethan's hospital room. I dig in my sweatpants pocket but only find my phone. Crap. I can't even get a coffee.

"Here," James says, handing the barista his card.

"Thanks. I'll repay you."

"No need. I'll be over by the door. If you need anything, just holler."

"Okay."

I walk to the far end of the counter to wait for my coffee. The wait is short as there is no one else waiting for a drink in the small coffee shop. I take the coffee and immediately head to the same table Landon and I sat at.

I pull the rickety chair out from the metal table and listen as it screeches across the hard floor. I sit in the chair taking a deep breath as I do. Why did I think this was a good idea? I pull out my phone and set it beside my coffee on the table. I could call him. See if he is still in New York. *I can't.* I promised I wouldn't call him. He needs to move on. It wouldn't be fair.

I take a sip of my hot coffee. The liquid burns my tongue as it goes down. It's still much too hot to drink comfortably. I pick up my phone and begin typing his name into the search bar on my browser. Maybe just seeing a picture of him will be enough to comfort me.

The browser takes a second to pull his name up, but when it does, there are over a dozen articles about him and Caroline. *Recent articles.* Like just published in the last twenty-four hours recent.

I open the first one, expecting to see bullshit. Instead, I'm faced with a giant picture of Landon locked in a passionate kiss with Caroline. The picture is dated two weeks ago. Two fucking weeks ago! When Landon and I were together. That bitch!

I scroll through the article, reading every word.

'Landon chased Caroline across the country to tell her he loved her ...'

I read further.

'Caroline accepted his apology with a passionate kiss caught by bystanders at the LA airport ...'

The same airport I let him fuck me in.

'Drew, Landon's manager, says that yes, the rumors are true. Landon and Caroline are back together ..."

The words rip out my heart. They're true. Drew even clarified. That cheating fucking asshole! I take the coffee and pour the hot liquid down my throat, welcoming the burn with every swallow. But the pain isn't enough to cover the old pain.

I grab my phone and head to the bathroom where I will have some privacy. I don't care that I'll break my promise. I need to call him. I need to yell and scream. Then maybe my heart won't feel completely destroyed by this monster.

I open the door to the small bathroom that just includes one toilet and sink. I lock the door keeping James or anyone else out. Away from me.

I find his name at the top of my contacts, and I press send. I pace the small room back and forth while I wait for him to pick up. One ring. Then two. I pace some more trying to ignore the smell of urine clouding the room. Three ...

"Hi, Alex," Landon says. I take a deep breath, melting a little when I hear his voice. A voice I never thought I would hear again except on the radio.

"I guess you saw it," he says.

"Yeah, I fucking saw it, you pig. How could you? I thought you and Caroline were over. I thought you loved me. I thought you wanted to fucking marry me. I thought I was the one who destroyed everything. I thought I had broken your heart. I thought I was the one who caused so much pain. The one who had to live with the guilt. But it wasn't me who destroyed us, it was you."

I pause waiting for him to say something. To tell me I'm wrong. Please tell me I'm wrong. I don't know if I can live knowing he never loved me. That it was all a lie just to get me in bed with him.

"I'm sorry," he finally says, softly. Like it hurts him too much to say it.

"So it's true. It's all fucking true. The whole time, Landon. Was it all a lie?"

"I'm sorry." He pauses. "I have to go. Good-bye, Alex."

I remove the phone from my ear and glance down at the screen that shows the call has ended.

"Good-bye," I whisper before falling to the tiled floor. Now, the tears I've been holding in all day fall. They fall for that stupid fucking bastard I fell for. My body trembles as the tears keep falling. He never loved you, you fool. The only person left who loves you is Ethan, and if I'm not careful, I'll lose him too.

Chapter Eleven

LANDON

But I'll let you go if you need
Tear out my heart til I bleed.
I'll watch you love another man.
This is my prayer.
This is my plea.
Please find love.
Please ...

I LET the phone drop from my hands. The face immediately shatters making the phone unusable. I close my eyes trying to block everything out. The pain, the love, the need. I try to make it go away, but it never goes away. I don't know why I didn't defend myself. Tell her she was wrong. I never cheated on her with Caroline. I loved her. I still love her. I want to marry her, not Caroline.

I sink to my knees keeping my eyes closed. I've never felt this destroyed in my life. Even when I felt like a monster for ruining Caroline's life a year ago, I didn't feel this broken, this destroyed. She will never forgive me now. She will never trust me again.

"Hey, Landon, break's almost over, man," Steven my guitarist says.

"Get Drew," I say without opening my eyes or moving from the floor.

"Be right back, man," Steven says.

I let myself sulk on the ground while I wait for Drew. I pretend this isn't true, just like in my dreams. I imagine a world where Alex said yes instead of no. A world where Alex wears a pretty white dress. One where we spend our life traveling the world taking pictures and singing. A world that involves giving all of that away to take care of our children. A world that doesn't exist and can never exist. At least not for me. But maybe for her. Maybe she will find that with Ethan. It's time I face my own fate. A fate I chose over a year ago when I let alcohol consume me. Maybe if I accept the fate, it will finally set Alex free. Seeing her free might just keep me breathing.

"What now?" Drew says irritated to see me broken on the floor. I may be broken, but I've made up my mind. I'm going to do the right thing, the only thing for once in my life.

"I need you to call Caroline for me." I stand up as I say it, not because I don't like looking weak in front of my brother, but because I need to be strong in this moment to do what needs to be done.

"Why? What's wrong with your phone?"

"It's broken. Just give me your damn phone. And order me a new one when you get a chance. One with a different number and none of my old contacts in it."

Drew raises his eyebrows, but he does as I ask. He pulls his phone from his pocket and hands it to me.

I take it and dial her number before I change my mind. She answers after the first ring.

"Hello, Drew."

"It's Landon."

"Oh. What are you doing with Drew's phone? By the way, I loved the magazine article. The press will do wonders for my career."

"I need you to meet me at my condo tomorrow morning around eight," I say ignoring what she just said. I glance at Drew to make sure my schedule is free. He nods without me having to ask the question. Benefits of being a twin.

"I don't know, Landon. I have a really busy schedule this week with auditions. Wait ... did you say your condo? You never let anyone at your condo."

"I know. Just meet me there. I promise to make it worth your while."

I can practically feel her smirking on the other end of the phone. "I wouldn't miss it."

I hang up without a good-bye and hand the phone back to Drew.

"What did you just do?"

"Accepted my destiny." I leave Drew standing in the hallway while I walk back in the studio to keep working on a new song about Alex. My last song about Alex. I just hope she never realizes it's about her. If I know her, she'll assume the worst. That it's about Caroline.

"Ready to start again, boss," Steven says.

"Yes, let's try the chorus again this time with more bass."

"Sure thing," Steven says.

Steven indicates for the band to start playing this time with more bass. I take a seat on a small stool in front of a music stand with the typed lyrics I've already written. I take my time. Ready to sing the words that will break my heart every time I sing them. The song that only Alex should hear but, instead, I'll sing for the world. I'll sing them for everyone who has ever experienced real heartbreak.

I thought that was what my debut single was about—heartbreak—but I was wrong. "I Don't Need Your Love" was not about heartbreak, it was about revenge. "Please" is about heartbreak. It's about death. It's about living. I begin softly singing the words on the sheet in front of me as the music plays...

I don't want to wait anymore.
I love you, you, you.
I don't want to wait to make you mine.
I love you, you, you.
But I'll wait forever if you need.

I KEEP SINGING EVEN when the band stops, singing new words that just fit.

Just keep breathing
Keep your heart beating
Don't let me lose my love.

I can't lose my love.
I won't lose my love.
I'll breathe for you.
Lend my heart to you.
Just don't lose my love.

I SCRIBBLE the words down on the piece of paper as I go. Steven tries to pick up the melodies of the notes I hit with each word, matching them on his guitar.

I'm destroyed without you
Destined to a life of pain.
Please, I just can't lose you
I'll never be the same.

But I'll let you go if you need.
Tear out my heart til I bleed.
I'll watch you love another man.
This is my prayer.
This is my plea.
Please find love.
Please ...

I STOP SINGING. Unable to finish the song. I'm not ready to face it yet. I can't.

"I need a break," I say standing from the small stool I was sitting on.

"But we just had a break," Steven says.

"Keep working on putting music to the lyrics I just wrote." I grab the white piece of paper with the scribbled words off the music stand and hand it to Steven.

"I'll be back in a few. I just need a break." I walk out of the room that feels like a cage. I walk down the hallway and out of the building till I taste fresh air. I don't just need a break from writing music; I need a break from my life.

I LOOK at the clock sitting on my nightstand next to my bed. 7:45am. Fifteen minutes until the end of my life. Until I face my execution or at least what feels like my execution. My life will never be the same. I slowly get dressed, putting each leg into my dark jeans as slowly as possible without losing my balance. Maybe if I move slowly, time will move just as slowly. I glance back up. 7:47am. Nope. Time is still moving.

I walk to my closet and pull out a plain black V-neck shirt. I slip it on. I walk to the bathroom to glance at my appearance in the mirror, but when I get there, all I see is a desperate, sad man. A man I haven't seen in years. I have everything. Money, fame, a career I love. I never wanted anything more. I never wanted love, and marriage, and kids. I had music. I didn't need anything else. Now, after tasting love, I realize how hollow my life really is. How empty.

I have to find a way back to the man I was before love. The man who just wanted sex, money, and shiny toys. Caroline will help me find that man again, or she'll kill me. Either way, this man staring back at me will be gone.

I walk out of the bathroom and then out of my bedroom. I glance quickly back at the clock before leaving my bedroom. 7:51. Nine minutes left. I walk slowly down the hall and down the staircase that takes me to my living area. It feels weird to walk so slowly. I usually take the stairs two at a time but not now. Now, I take every step slowly wishing there were more.

Drew is waiting at the bottom of the stairs. A scowl covers his face, and he has a confrontational gleam in his eyes.

"You don't have to do this."

I chuckle. "Yes, I do. And why are you trying to stop me? You've wanted me to do this every day for the last year."

"Yes because it is the only way to keep your secrets buried. But I'm not sure it's worth it anymore. We can find another way to keep your secrets buried."

"Maybe, but that's not why I'm doing this." I walk past Drew and take a seat on my couch to wait out my fate.

I don't have to wait long. Maybe a minute or two. I don't have any clocks in my living room. I don't wear a watch, and I have yet to get a new phone. But I hear the knock and immediately get up to walk to the door. It takes me seventeen steps to get there. I count each one. It's the only way I can keep my body moving forward.

I open the door to see Caroline dressed in a tight black dress as her long blond curls hang in perfect spirals. She looks like she is ready to party at some fancy bar instead of the business meeting this is. She has a lustful look in her eye as her eyes travel over my body. No doubt thinking about all the dirty things we could do together.

She pushes into my condo as her hands pull my face to hers. Her lips lock with mine, and she quickly pushes her tongue into my mouth desperate to get more.

I grab her hips and gently push her away from me, trying my best not to upset her before she hears me out.

"That's not why you are here," I say as soon as I get free from her.

Her eyes narrow and her smeared red lipstick can't disguise her grimace. "Why am I here then?"

I wipe the rest of the lipstick from my own lips and walk into the kitchen.

"Do you want anything to drink?" I ask. Caroline stands on the other side of the island from me. Confusion still reads on her face.

"Um ... white wine."

I walk to the fridge and pull out a bottle of Pinot Grigio. I uncork the bottle and pour her a glass. I place it on the island in front of her before walking to the liquor cabinet on the far side of the kitchen. A liquor cabinet that only exists for Drew because I never drink from it. I pull out a bottle of whiskey. I pour a double shot into a glass and then walk past the kitchen out onto the balcony.

I notice Caroline raise her eyebrows at me as I walk past. She knows better than anybody else does why I don't drink. Why I shouldn't drink. But right now, I need the alcohol to get through the rest of this morning. Later, when we negotiate details, I'll need to be sober, but now, I need liquid courage.

I take a seat on a usually comfortable chair that overlooks the ocean. Today, it feels like I'm sitting on a hard stone. I sip from the whiskey, feeling the burn from drinking the liquor straight. I wait for Caroline to follow me out with her glass of wine. She takes a seat in a chair next to me so that we are both looking out at the ocean.

She sips her wine, patiently waiting for me to tell her why she's here. But I'm not ready yet.

"Do you believe in love?" I ask. I don't look at her. I keep my gaze glued to the ocean as I drink more whiskey waiting for her answer.

"No," she says easily. "I don't. I believe whatever people call love isn't really love. It fades too quickly to be real love. And even love between a mother and child doesn't come easily."

She stops and takes a sip of her wine.

"That's a sinister way to look at the world."

Out of the corner of my eye, I watch her roll her eyes. "It's the only truthful way to look at the world. Anybody trying to find true love is just chasing a fairy tale that doesn't exist."

I nod although I don't agree. Love isn't just a fairy tale. It exists. But I can understand Caroline's point of view. Growing up as we did, it's hard to believe that love could really exist when it doesn't exist in our world.

Caroline will be able to help me, though. I have no doubt she'll turn me back into the stone I was before Alex. I lift my glass to my lips and down every last drop of alcohol. It's now or never. I don't move from my chair to get down on one knee. Although I'm sure when I do this again in public, I will.

I just say the words that I already know the answer to. Words that hurt so much to say but have to be said. "Will you marry me?"

Chapter Twelve

ETHAN

She smiles at me when I take a seat. That's when I notice she's not wearing a bulky sweater. Instead, she is wearing layers upon layers of clothes.

"Let me buy you a drink. Wine? Cosmo? Champagne?"

Her smile doesn't falter as she says, "Whiskey."

HOME. Today, I get to go home with Alexa. I never thought that was going to be possible. All of the internal bleeding is gone. The broken bones healed. The swelling and bruising have lessened. No permanent damage has been done.

"You must be happy to be getting out of here today?" my nurse says. She's a new nurse who hasn't taken care of me before. I think her name is Melissa or Sara. Something ordinary and bland that isn't worth remembering.

I smile at the woman. "Yes. You have no idea how happy I am."

She smiles happily as she takes the IV out of my hand. The last piece of medical equipment tethering me here. She glances at the recliner where Alexa is sleeping.

"Do you want me to wake her?"

"No, let her sleep. I'll wake her right before it's time for us to go."

She nods. "I'll leave you to get dressed then." She scurries out of the room to take care of the more critical patients. I climb out of the bed that has held me hostage for over a week. I walk over to the small duffel bag Alexa brought me from home. I find that Alexa has picked out a pair of jeans, underwear, and simple t-shirt for me. I shake my head staring at these inappropriate clothes. Alexa really doesn't remember our life at all.

I begin to get dressed, happy to be getting out of the hospital gown. I look at Alexa sleeping so peacefully; the tiniest drop of drool is visible on the recliner under her lips. I'm happy she's sleeping because she hasn't been sleeping well. I probably wouldn't either if I had to sleep in that recliner every night. She'll be happy to get back to our old bed.

I frown when I look at her clothes, though. She's wearing another pair of sweatpants with a ratty t-shirt. She'll regret that choice later.

I slip on my own t-shirt, not sure how I'm going to make this look any better, when the door opens. Mother stands in the doorway with a look of disgust on her face.

"You are not wearing that."

"I don't really have a choice. It's all Alexa brought."

"Don't fret. I brought suitable clothes for the two of you to wear. I saw what Alexandra was wearing earlier and knew that wouldn't do. I honestly don't understand why you married the girl, Ethan. She's a complete disaster."

I give my mother a stern look as I take the bag from her, but I don't argue with her. It's not worth it. Not when Alexa can so easily wake up and hear us.

"Hurry up and get dressed. We can't keep everyone waiting." I watch my mother leave the room before I open the leather bag. Inside are khaki slacks, a button-down shirt, and loafers. For Alexa, a simple long green dress with nude heels.

I walk over to Alexa and kiss her softly on the cheek.

"Wake up, baby."

She smiles and stretches her arms over her head before opening her eyes. Her smile disappears when she sees me.

"It's time to get dressed and go home."

She looks down at her clothes. "I am dressed. I just need to comb my hair and I'll be ready to go."

I soften my expression at how adorable she is. "You're going to want to change."

"Why?"

"Because waiting for us outside are a slew of reporters."

"Oh, my God. Really? But I don't have anything else to wear."

"Don't worry. Mother brought clothes for both of us."

Her face reddens, but she doesn't say anything. I take her dress and heels from the bag.

"Here, put this on."

She takes them from me and stands up from the recliner. She looks more closely at the heels.

"I can't wear the heels," she says.

"Why? You aren't walking very far. I'm sure you can handle it."

"The prosthetic leg I'm wearing doesn't adjust for heels."

I run my hand through my hair as I glance down at her leg. I forgot. Forgot she is no longer perfect. I forgot that her leg is gone.

"Just put the dress on. Let me worry about finding you shoes."

She starts walking toward the bathroom, but I stop her.

"You can get dressed here. You don't need to hide in the bathroom. We are married, after all." I wink at her.

"I really need to pee," she says, hurrying past me into the bathroom.

I sigh. This is going to be harder than I thought. I change quickly and then head out to look for shoes. Mother approaches me as soon as I exit the hospital room.

"You look as handsome as ever."

"Thanks, Mother."

"I've talked with security and they assure me everyone will be safe so you can talk with the reporters like we planned," she says, refusing to call the members of our small security team by name.

"Good. Alexa is just getting ready, but she can't wear the shoes you got her."

She sighs. "And why not?"

"Because her prosthetic leg won't allow it. We have to find her something flat."

"I've seen her walk in heels before with *it* on."

"Apparently, she has to wear a certain type to wear heels," I say, shrugging.

"For heaven's sake," Mother says.

Thirty minutes later, we have finally found some simple flat tan shoes that will do after we paid a woman, waiting for her grandfather to have cataract surgery, a small fortune to give us her shoes. They are a little big on Alexa, but they will have to do for now. Nobody is going to be taking pictures of Alexa's feet anyway. Alexa finally emerges from the bathroom looking beautiful and nervous.

"Beautiful," I say. I walk to her and take her hand in mine to trying to erase the uneasiness from her face.

"Presentable," Mother says before turning to exit the room.

I press my lips to kiss her hand. "Don't worry. I'll do all the talking. Just stand next to me and smile and look like your gorgeous self."

She swallows hard and nods. I guide her out of my hospital room. The nurse stops me to sign some papers, which only takes five minutes to my surprise.

When I'm done, I take Alexa's hand back in mine. "Ready?"

"Yes."

We walk hand in hand down the hallway. We hold hands while riding down the elevator. We hold hands walking through the lobby. I feel like I have my partner back. Now, I just need my lover back.

Nick, the head of my three-person security team, meets us at the door to the exit of the hospital.

"Everyone's in place."

"Let's go then."

Alexa walks next to me as we exit the hospital. Flashes of light blind us as we walk down the sidewalk. We only make it ten feet before the microphones are shoved into our faces.

"Ethan, what does it feel like to come back from the dead?" the first male reporter shouts over the crowd.

"It feels amazing. I never thought I would see this beautiful woman again." I beam at Alexa a moment before continuing. "Wouldn't you find any way possible to keep living if you had this beautiful woman to come back to?" The reporters chuckle and nod their heads accordingly.

"How were you able to escape?" another reporter asks.

"I'm not supposed to talk about too many details until the investigation is complete and the perpetrators caught."

"Do you worry about your wife's and your safety?" the same reporter asks.

"Of course. But if they come after us, we will be waiting. I hired the best security team in the world. If they come after us, they will pay."

"Are you suffering from any long-term damage?" another reporter asks.

"No. Nothing that a nice warm bed and a beautiful wife can't fix." I wink at Alexa before kissing her passionately on the lips, giving the reporters a nice show. She keeps her eyes open initially, startled by the kiss, but she doesn't pull away. It gives me hope.

"Alexa, how does it feel to have your husband back after thinking he was dead for so many months?"

I smile at Alexa encouraging her to talk. "It's been a dream come true."

"Alexa, do you plan to return to the world of photography and entertainment?"

Alexa looks at me with a blank stare.

"I think we've had enough questions for today. We'd like to get home and enjoy our new life together."

Nick and James walk over to us and guide us past the reporters and cameras to the waiting SUV. Nick opens the door for us, and I help Alexa into the car before I climb in next to her.

I look up at Curt, the last member of my security team seated in the driver's seat.

"Take us home please."

THE DRIVE to our apartment is long, slow, and quiet. Curt is a professional who kept his eyes on the road throughout the forty-five-minute drive. Alexa spent the first five minutes in the car bouncing her legs obnoxiously up and down. I rested my hand on her right knee, trying to calm her, but immediately pulled it away when I felt the metal of her prosthetic instead of the flesh I'm used to. She didn't say anything when I did, but I know she was disappointed in me. I'm disappointed in me. It will just take some time to get used to her leg. After being together for so long and expecting her to be a certain way, it's hard to adjust.

Alexa pretended to sleep the rest of the car ride instead of talking to me. I could tell because her breathing was short and rapid instead of long and calming, and her legs still bounced slightly throughout the ride.

I spent the trip planning. Trying to come up with anything I could do to mend this relationship. To get her to trust me again. To love me again. She's barely talked to me since I told her she was raped. I don't blame her, but I need to find happy memories to share with her.

First, though, we need to get through tonight. Curt pulls up outside our apartment building. Relief fills me at the sight of our home. Everything will be better now.

"Wake up, Alexa," I say, shaking her body softly. She immediately stirs.

We both exit the SUV without a word. Curt grabs our bags and holds the door to our apartment building. We walk in and take the elevator to the top floor. To our home. When we get to the door, Curt unlocks the door and places our bags inside.

"James and Nick already searched the place to make sure it's secure. I'll stand guard outside, but you're safe," Curt says leaving us alone in the entryway.

I take a deep breath relaxing as I look around the apartment that hasn't changed since we left. I walk to the living room that still looks like it's straight out of a designer magazine. An engagement picture of Alexa and I sit next to the TV. I pick it up and look at how happy we were together. We got married a few months later, but we never got the pictures back from the wedding. The attack and kidnapping happened that night. Destroying our wedding. We never went on a honeymoon. We will have to remedy that at some point, but not now. Now, I just want to get back to our regular life.

I walk to the kitchen just past the living room. I glance out the large windows overlooking the city. It's a beautiful spring day.

I walk back to the living room to the open stairs leading to our bedroom. Alexa just stares at me from the living room.

"Come on," I shout as I jog up the stairs. It feels good to be moving instead of stuck in bed or held by a physical therapist afraid I'll fall. I reach the top floor of our apartment that holds our bedroom and bathroom, but that's not what I care about. I care about the large balcony that juts out from our bedroom. I slide the door open and immediately breathe in the pleasant summer air.

I lean against the balcony railing overlooking the city. Alexa joins me standing quietly next to me. I feel at home for the first time.

"It's beautiful out here," Alexa says.

I smile. "It is. It's our favorite place in the apartment. It's the reason we bought this apartment. For this right here."

She smiles back. "I can see why. I could easily fall in love with this spot again." Her eyes meet mine when she says the words. Her eyes say so much more. That she could easily fall in love with me again if I helped her find a way. *I will,* I promise with my eyes. I will.

Chapter Thirteen

ALEXA

I have to find my own evidence.

"LET'S GO TO BED," Ethan says getting up from the couch on the balcony overlooking the NYC skyline as lights sparkle beneath the dark sky.

I nod and get up from my chair opposite him. We haven't said much since we came out on this balcony. Instead, we opted just to enjoy the warm breeze. We ordered pizza for dinner, and other than that, we haven't left this spot. Both of us hoping that if we stayed out here long enough, this peaceful spot would bring us back together. Unfortunately, this place isn't that magical. All it brought us is a sense of peace.

Ethan heads straight to the bathroom, and I head to my bag sitting on the floor next to the bed. I dig through my bag trying to find something suitable to change into. All I brought to sleep in is corsets, lace bras, and fancy underwear. Things I was expecting Landon to see, not Ethan. I'm not ready or brave enough to wear this type of clothing in front of a complete stranger, even though I'm married to him.

I stand and walk over to the white dresser sitting on the far side of the room next to the door to the bathroom. I open the top drawer to find more fancy underwear. I immediately close it. I try the next drawer, but I find nothing but socks. I try again with the third drawer and am rewarded with shorts. Mostly running shorts, but they will do. I grab a pair and head to the closet, remembering which closet is mine from when I picked out some clothes to take with me to LA. I step inside the large closet overflowing with fancy dresses and business attire. I search through the piles of clothes hoping I didn't take all of the casual clothes with me to LA. When my hand touches soft cotton, I relax. I grab my shorts and a t-shirt and head to the bed to wait for Ethan to finish in the bathroom.

I sit down on the edge of the bed. My hands are trembling a little holding the clothes against my legs. I don't know what Ethan expects tonight. Sex is the obvious answer after not being with his wife for six months. After being held captive, tortured, and thinking he was going to die, sex would be very life affirming, but I don't know if I can do that. I stare at the large rings on my left hand. I've made a commitment to try my best to love Ethan again, to remember him. But Landon is still there in the back of my mind. He's still in my heart, even though he shouldn't be. He never loved me. It was always about sex with him. There is no reason I shouldn't have sex with Ethan tonight, but something is holding me back.

The door creaks open and Ethan emerges from the bathroom shirtless. His ripped muscles flex and bend as he walks out. His body looks much like mine. Bruised, broken, and scarred. I stand and walk to him, drawn to the scars covering his heart. I reach my hand to touch the scars on his chest before I realize what I'm doing. My hand freezes less than an inch from his chest.

"It's okay. You can touch me," he says, grinning.

I don't grin back, but I do touch his chest. Fresh bruises and scars cover his chest. I run my hands over each scar lightly with my fingertip as his breathing becomes more and more erratic. I feel his pain every time I touch a new scar. I can see on his face that he remembers how each spot was inflicted. I trace down his arms to his wrists. His wrists are the worst, showing how hard he struggled against the ropes that held him prisoner. I kiss each wrist softly. He lets out a small gasp at the unexpected touch.

It makes me feel good to see him relax just a little when I kiss him, so I keep going. I kiss my way up his arm. He rewards each kiss with a gasp or small groan. I make it to his chest and continue kissing every bruise and scar. They all seem so fresh. I haven't found any that have healed as mine have from six months ago. He must be a good healer. I kiss the large scar on his chest when he loses whatever control was holding him in place keeping him from moving.

He grabs my face and traps my lips beneath his kissing me passionately.

"God, I've missed you, Alexa," he says between kisses. My hands go to his neck almost on autopilot. My tongue responds to his, liking the pleasure filling my mouth. He grabs my ass and pushes us back until we hit the bed. He lowers my body gently onto the bed before climbing on top of me until our bodies are pressed together. His lips immediately find mine again, and I try to lose myself in the kiss as his hands start exploring my body and touching areas I'm not ready for him to touch yet.

"Moan for me, Alexa. Show me how much you are enjoying this," Ethan says.

When he kisses me again, I try my best to moan, to please him, but I'm afraid it comes out more pained than I would like.

"Fuck, I want you, Alexa," he moans as he moves his kisses to my neck.

I close my eyes trying to keep myself calm. *I can do this. I want this.* I grab the nape of his neck pulling his head back to my lips, something I enjoy and can focus on. I focus on his taste. The spearmint toothpaste fresh on his tongue. I feel him grabbing the fabric of my dress and hiking it up to touch my skin beneath it.

He rips off my clothes. I can't stop him. I try to scream, but nothing comes out as he sits on my chest preventing air from moving in or out. I'm going to die.

"Alexa, stop it! What are you doing?" Ethan says holding my wrists above my head. I open my eyes and realize the image is gone. A stranger isn't trying to rape me. Ethan is just trying to have sex with me, but my body registers it as the same thing. It *is* practically the same thing for me.

"Let go," I say a little too harsh as I try to break free from his grasp.

"Why were you hitting me and screaming? What is going on, Alexa?" he asks still holding onto my wrists firmly above my head.

"I had a panic attack. I've had them a lot since the attack. Let me go and I'll tell you the rest," I angrily spit out the words at him.

Ethan reluctantly releases my hands and sits beside me. I sit up and rub my wrists, but when I look at Ethan's wrists, I stop. His arms are shaking slightly and I realize that he probably has plenty of anxiety and emotional trauma of his own that I brought back when I started hitting him.

I soften my voice when I speak. "I have had several panic attacks since the accident. They are always of one of two events that I have some memories of. The accident or the rape. I wasn't sure if they were real, but now, I know they both are."

His arms stop shaking so badly, but he doesn't speak.

"I'm sorry if I brought up anxiety or a panic attack of your own when I started hitting you."

"You didn't." His eyes dart away from mine. "I just thought you hated me."

"I don't hate you. I just don't remember you. It will just take some time to get used to you again. When Land ..." I let my sentence trail off. I almost told Ethan about Landon and I. Shit.

"When what?" Ethan asks.

"Nothing." I stand from the bed not ready for more conversation. "I'm sure the panic attacks will get better. It will just take some time. I'm going to go change and get ready for bed." I hurry into the bathroom grabbing my clothes off the floor as I go without looking back at Ethan.

Once in the bathroom, I sigh in relief. I change out of my dress and into the shorts and t-shirt as my heartbeat slows back to normal. Shit, that was a disaster. A big fucking disaster. Are either of us ever going to get past our demons?

I move to the sink and splash some water on my face. I notice the pink toothbrush sitting next the blue one. Toothbrushes that have been untouched for six months. I touch the hard bristles. How simple was our life back then? We had everything going for us. Were we happy living a simple life? Or were we one of those couples who fought incessantly and passionately but made love in the same way? Did we want kids? Or were we happy just living as the two of us? All I have to do is find out the answer to those and so many other questions.

I open the cabinet next to the sink and find a new pink toothbrush to replace the old one in the stand. I brush my teeth quickly and then throw the old brush in the trashcan. I feel much calmer as I open the bathroom door that leads back to our bedroom. Ethan has already climbed into bed. His bare chest visible above the covers. I walk over and take a seat on the opposite side of the bed. I debate taking my prosthetic leg off or leaving it on. I'm supposed to take it off every night. It gives my skin time to breathe and it feels so much better, but I feel vulnerable without it. If I need to make a quick escape, I have to put it on first.

I begin taking it off using my body to block Ethan's view of my leg. He doesn't need to see how disgusting I look yet. I place the prosthetic next to the bed and climb in. I hope as I do that he didn't catch a glimpse of my disfigurement. If he sees, he doesn't comment on it. There are so many discussions for us to have. So many things running through my head.

"What are you thinking about?" Ethan asks as I lean back against the pillow next to him, careful that our bodies don't touch, which is easy in this king-size bed.

"There is just so much to talk about. So many questions that I need answered."

"Then ask them."

"It will take years to answer all of the questions I have."

"Then ask me one question a night for the rest of your life if you need."

I nod. "One question a night sounds good." Although it seems like torture to only ask one question a night, maybe it's for the best so I stop focusing on my past and start focusing on the future.

"So what will it be?"

I think over all of the questions floating around in my head. What happened with the rape? How did we fall in love? Where did we get engaged? Married? Why was I living on the streets? What do all my tattoos mean? Does he like them?

Instead, I end up blurting out, "What's my favorite food?"

He looks at me his eyes wide and then he laughs. A full belly laugh.

I frown. "Why is that funny?"

"Because of all the questions you could ask, that's what you ask."

I laugh a little too, but it felt like the right question to ask. It is a light-hearted question. I don't think I could handle anything too deep right now. And the question has more meaning to me than he knows. It was something Landon picked up on. Pain beats at my heart when I think of Landon, but I try my best to tune the pain out and focus on Ethan.

"Pizza. Yes, pizza was by far your favorite food."

I smile although inside my heart is bursting. "Why?" I ask barely able to get the words out let alone make them sound normal.

"You okay?" he asks staring at my pained face.

"Yes, I just hit my leg funny. It still hurts sometimes," I lie.

"Is there anything I can do?"

"Just distract me with stories about my past."

He squints his eyes together staring at me intently before continuing. "You loved pizza because that is what you could afford whenever you made a little money. You would always spring for pizza. Even after you made millions as a photographer and you could go get any type of expensive food in the world, you always wanted pizza. You used to say as long as I can afford pizza my life must be pretty good."

I smile. It doesn't sound like I've changed much since before. Maybe that's what I was getting at with my question. Just trying to find out if I have changed at all.

Ethan reaches over and kisses me softly on the lips.

"Good night, baby."

"Good night," I say. Ethan turns off the lamp next to the bed and rolls away from me. I roll the other way, thankful that he didn't try to snuggle with me tonight. I don't think it would have gone well.

My mind immediately wants to think of Landon, but I don't let it.

If I do, I'll be in tears in no time and I can't let Ethan think I'm crying because of what happened tonight. I try counting and focusing on my breathing like my therapist taught me.

I breathe in.

One.

Two.

Three.

I exhale.

Four.

Five.

Six.

I repeat over and over, but I don't fall asleep. I listen to Ethan snoring softly beside me. I'm not ready to fall asleep. If I do, the nightmares will come again, and I'm not ready to face them. I climb out of bed and find a blanket from my closet before heading back to our large balcony. I curl up on the couch and stare up at the barely visible stars. I know I spent a lot of time out here and not because Ethan said I did. I can feel it. I feel comfort here. I just want to stay right here forever. Instead, in a few hours, I'll go back inside and pretend to sleep next to Ethan, but for now, I'll stay out here where I don't have to think about a thing except the stars.

Chapter Fourteen

LANDON

Please don't leave.
Please give me back my love.
Please don't give up now.
Please come back to me, love.
But most importantly
Please be happy, love.

"YES!" Caroline squeals getting up from her chair and tackling me with her body. Her lips find mine as she assaults me with her tongue. I push her back as soon as I feel her slippery tongue on mine. I don't want a kiss. And I definitely don't want more.

She sits back on my lap, her lips immediately falling from the smile she was just wearing.

"It's not going to be that type of relationship. At least, not right now. It's a business arrangement. That's all. Isn't that what you always wanted?"

Her mouth falls open and her cheeks redden as if I just slapped her. "Well ... yes," she stutters. "But we can have a *real* marriage."

"Our marriage will be real in the legal sense. We may even occasionally have sex and enjoy parts of the marriage, but that won't come until after we have discussed the marriage and have lawyers present to draw up a contract."

"Oh really? *You* have terms now that you want in the contract. You forget I control you." A smug grin curls onto her lips.

I push her off my lap and stand up. "No. I control you. I don't care anymore if you plaster my past all over every tabloid magazine. Do it if that's what you want. But if you want to marry *me*, if you want *my money*, then you will do this *my way.*" My body is an inch from hers as I shout the words.

"You love her." Caroline's lips curl into a smirk again.

"What?"

"You love her. The slutty photographer that's married. You love her."

"It doesn't matter who I love." I run my hands through my hair trying to remain calm, desperately trying to forget about Alex, but I can't.

Her smile widens. She runs her hand up my chest. "See, that's where you're wrong, Landon. It matters a great deal who we love. I love you. Well, as much as I can love another person. I always have, but you already know that. That's why you think you can control me. But you ..." She pushes her fingers into my chest. "You love Alexa. Which means she has the ability to control you. There is a reason you want to marry me. It's to protect her."

She starts circling me as she tries to figure it out.

"Is it to protect her from your past?"

"No," I snap.

She smiles as she circles again, her eyes probing me for information.

"You think you will hurt her?"

"No," I snap again.

She circles again, her sly smile still there.

"You're protecting her image from the shit storm that would take place if you married her instead?"

"No," I snap louder grabbing her to keep her from circling again.

"I'm getting closer."

"No. Stop this now or I'll retract my offer."

She smiles brighter. "I don't think you will." She breaks from my hold. "All the same, I'll stop. For now. I'll figure it out at some point anyway." Caroline inspects her perfectly manicured hands as if this conversation isn't life changing. But it is life changing for both of us.

"So you will marry me?"

"Yes, but I have some terms of my own," she says glancing up as she narrows her eyes.

I sigh before walking back inside. She follows. I walk her all the way to my door. I'm ready for this bitch to leave. I open the door and wave her out.

She stands calmly in my doorway. She kisses me softly on the lips before turning to leave.

"Drew will be in touch to schedule a meeting with our lawyers."

"Of course, he will," she says never bothering to turn around or say a good-bye. What have I gotten myself into? This was probably the worst mistake of my life. Too bad it's a mistake that will be relived every day for the rest of my life.

I WALK with Drew into the large office building that contains my lawyer's office. Neither of us speaks. Drew doesn't try to convince me to stop. And I don't share how much this fucking hurts. We just walk side by side, as we have done for years. I know Drew will always have my back no matter how badly I fuck up. He's already proven as much. I just hope he knows the same goes for in reverse. I don't care if Drew murders someone in cold blood; I will be there to break him out of jail. It's what we do for each other. We protect each other.

I feel calm as we enter the elevator to take us to the tenth floor. A few other people enter the elevator with us, but no one talks. No one ever talks in elevators. Maybe that's why I feel at peace as we climb higher and higher. I should be nervous to sign away my life to another, but I don't. This is what I want. This is the only way to protect Alexa.

Caroline was right about that, but after today, after she signs the contract my lawyers have written, Alexa will be protected. Forever.

It will just be a matter of pomp and circumstance after today. A media storm will ensue. That will sting and cause Alexa what she thinks is unbearable pain. The same pain I brought her when I told her the tabloid article was true. But it could be so much worse if she found out the truth ...

I'm saving her unbearable pain. This is easy in comparison.

The elevator doors open and we walk out to the secretary's desk.

"Here to see Allen Mund. He's expecting us."

The young woman who barely looks out of high school smiles at us. "Just a moment. Who should I tell him is here?"

"Landon Davis and we won't be waiting." I walk past her desk and into the meeting room where we all agreed to meet. Drew follows without a word. There was no way we were waiting in a hallway where everyone could see us. Allen will understand.

I take a seat at the far end of the long table, and Drew takes a seat next to me. We sit in comfortable silence until the door opens two minutes later. Allen knows better than to make us wait long. I am one of his best-paying clients, after all.

"Landon, Drew, it's so good to see you both again," Allen says as he walks over and extends his hand to me first then Drew.

He plops a huge pile of paper on top of the table and takes a seat next to me.

"We are all set. I have everything you asked for in the contract. I'll make sure you get everything you want or she will get nothing. But I do need you to do something for me." Allen looks at me with a stern look, similar to how a father would scold his son. Not that I'm familiar with the look. Allen may be the closest thing to a father figure Drew or I have in our life right now, which is a shame since we are paying him to look out for us. The connection we have with him isn't real. He's just another paid employee who tries his best to look out of us.

I nod for Allen to continue. Not trusting words right now.

"You will say nothing when Caroline and her lawyers get here. You will say absolutely nothing unless I tell you to say something first. Do you understand me?"

"Yes," I say.

"Good. The same goes for you, Drew. Not a word unless I tell you to. We are not going to give them anything to counter our offer with. We will show them no weakness."

Drew nods. "We understand. Not a word."

I hear a gentle knock on the door as the young receptionist pokes her head through an open crack in the door.

"They are here," she says in almost a whisper.

"Well, bring them in," Allen says, shaking his head.

He turns to us. "It's so hard to find a competent receptionist nowadays. Twenty years ago, it was so much easier."

We both just nod at Allen, not caring what he says. I just want this over. I just want Caroline to sign then this can be over. Then everything will be okay.

I watch as Caroline enters the meeting room accompanied by three men in business suits. I grin, though, unexpectedly. The suits they are wearing are cheap from a department store, no doubt. Not expensive tailored suits like the ones Drew, Allen, and I are donning. They haven't won enough cases to afford better. Allen is going to walk all over these clowns.

"Landon," Caroline says smiling at me as she takes her seat from across the table.

"Caroline," I say nodding back in her direction.

Allen immediately whispers in my ear, scolding me without making it known he is doing so to everyone else in the room. "You are not to speak."

I want to roll my eyes at this man, but instead, I sit back and smile like he just whispered the best secret ever into my ear instead of scolding me like a child. I can't even greet Caroline. Fucking ridiculous.

"I take it you have had enough time to look over our contract and have agreed to its terms by now. It's more than fair," Allen says.

Caroline looks to her team of lawyers who nod their head at her. "I will agree to the contract. I just have one item that I would like to add. I want Landon to propose to me publicly with a ring of my choosing that I get to keep no matter how this ends," she says smiling wickedly at me.

Allen bends to whisper in my ear. "We need to put a top price limit on the price of the ring. And I think we should take out the part about her getting to keep it. If she breaks the terms of the contract, then she should be required to return it."

"I'll agree to her terms. The most I'll pay is one million for the ring," I whisper back to Allen.

"Are you sure? We can get better terms than that. That's why you hired me."

"I'm sure. No matter what happens, she deserves at least that." It will only give her enough money to take care of her brother for a few years if she sells the ring if the terms of our agreement aren't met. It will still ensure that she won't break the contract. She wants to be taken care of for the rest of her life. I'm giving her the exact life she has always wanted. She knows she doesn't have the talent to make any real money as an actress.

"We will agree to the terms. Just give us a few minutes to amend the agreement," Allen says.

"No need. I'll take Landon at his word," Caroline says as her eyes pierce my soul. My eyes narrow in return as I do my best to read her. She's much too confident. Although I would be too if I was going to easily make five million or more a year for the rest of my life by just signing a piece of paper.

"Excellent," Allen says, unable to contain his excitement. He must think it will be for the better if that isn't added to the contract. That he will be able to get me out of it if I need to later on. But he doesn't know me well enough if he thinks I would let him do that. I'm a man of my word.

I watch as Caroline quickly signs all the necessary documents before they are passed back to me to sign. I glance over the legal terms written all over the documents. It doesn't make a lot of sense to me, but I trust Allen and the basics of our contract:

I WILL ...

1. Pay for the treatments for Caroline's brother and living expenses for the rest of his life, which isn't hard since I already was.

2. Give Caroline twenty-five percent of my monthly income for the rest of her life.

3. Buy Caroline one house of her choosing that is equal or less than five million dollars.

4. Agree to remain faithful to her alone throughout our marriage.

5. Agree to marry her and pay for all wedding expenses up to one million in total costs.

CAROLINE WILL ...

1. Agree to turn over all video footage of the incident and forfeit any rights to pursue me in a court of law over the incident.

2. Agree never to speak of the incident publicly or in private.

3. Agree to never speak of Alexa or cause Alexa any emotional or physical harm.

4. Agree to remain faithful to me alone throughout our marriage.

5. Agree that I can end the marriage if any of the terms are not met, but that the terms of the contract do not end if we divorce.

WE BOTH HAVE to agree never to speak of the terms of this contract or even to mention that such a contract exists. If Caroline breaks any part of this agreement, she will be required to pay back all of the money I have given her and her brother will be cut off. It's my insurance that she will never break this contract. She would never be able to abandon her brother like that. And she made a promise a long time ago never to live poor and hungry again.

If I break the agreement, I will have to pay her fifty percent of my income for the rest of her life, plus she is freed from fulfilling her end of the contract. I will never allow that to happen.

It may seem like Caroline gets the better end of this arrangement, but it's pretty equal. We both get freedom. I get freedom from my secrets and from any harm to Alexa. Caroline gets money to buy her freedom from the harsh life that has always followed her.

Caroline and I have had an arrangement before, but it was never legal. I promised to pay for her brother's expenses as well as give her money when she needed it and in exchange she kept my secret. I also had to promise not to get serious with anyone, which wasn't difficult. I never wanted to go on more then one date with anyone before. Not before Alex. Now though, now I need something legal to keep my secret safe.

I watch as Allen slides the papers over the smooth wooden table. I watch until they land in front of me. Allen hands me a pen that I take and sign the papers in one fluid motion. I repeat the movement several times next to Caroline's name until I've filled all the blank lines in, and Caroline's mouth is bound forever by the signatures. The signatures will hide my secret. The signatures will keep Alexa safe from me.

"Everything will be filed and taken care of immediately. I would like to remind you both that this agreement is effective immediately, not the date you choose to marry," Allen says.

Caroline's and my eyes lock as we both nod. They stay locked as everyone else gets up.

"I'll see you outside," Drew says. He's the last person to leave after the lawyers. Caroline and I are sitting across from each other at the long table.

"Did you get everything you want?" I ask.

"You speak," Caroline says cocking her head. "I thought something had happened to your voice. I was worried you are no longer worth the millions you are reported to be worth."

"Don't worry, my voice is just fine."

"Good. Now, about that ring. You remember what I like?"

"Yes. I remember," I say, thinking back to before.

"Hello, may I help you?" the clerk asks.

"Yes, I'm looking for an engagement ring."

The old man smiles knowingly at me. "You've come to the right place. Anything you had in mind?"

"Yes, I'm looking for a ring that has a long skinny diamond that sort of forms a point at each end."

The man smiles a little brighter before going to one of the cabinets and pulling out the ring I described.

"A marquise shaped ring," the clerk says handing me the ring. I look at it. It's

a perfect size and shape and looks almost identical to her mother's engagement ring. The one she had to sell to be able to afford to live and go to college.

"I'll take this one."

"That ring is quite expensive, young man. Maybe you would prefer a little smaller size."

"No, this one is perfect. She deserves it. Whatever the cost."

I still have the ring. Drew insisted I keep it just in case. And honestly, I couldn't part with it. Even after she cheated on me, I still loved her. I still cared about her, and I wanted her to have the ring. I know it's what she wants. It's all she has ever wanted.

"I'll make sure the proposal is to your liking and that there are ample paparazzi there."

"Good. I'll see you around, future hubby," she says winking before leaving me in the meeting room alone.

The word stings, but it was worth it. I reach into my jacket pocket and pull out a small box. A box that holds Alex's ring. Another ring I will never be able to part with despite it never gracing Alex's finger. A ring I kept despite telling Drew otherwise. Today, everything went exactly how I needed it to. There is no turning back now.

Chapter Fifteen

ETHAN

My eyes widen slightly at her response, but I turn to the bartender. "Two of your finest whiskey on the rocks."

I turn back to her as James and his buddies burst into another loud fit of laughter behind us. "Sorry about my friend's Bachelor party," I say as if that explains their rude behavior.

Her eyes smile brightly as she looks at the rowdy crowd of boys behind us. "I don't mind."

TODAY IS the day I get my wife back. I make her fall in love with me again. Or, at the very least, convince her that she wants to fall in love again with me. Tonight, I'm going full on romantic. Pulling out everything I've got to get back into her heart. Or, at the very least, get her back in my bed.

I pace back and forth at the foot of the stairs as I wait for her to finish getting ready so we can go. I bought her a new dress with sparkly high-heeled shoes to wear tonight. When she opened the box containing them, she was a little in shock at the expensive items. She was worried about walking in the heels with her prosthetic leg, but I told her we wouldn't be walking much on our date tonight. And I really want to see her in heels looking more like herself again.

I hired a team of makeup artists and hair stylists tonight to do her hair and makeup so she wouldn't have to worry about a thing. I want her to feel pampered tonight. To feel special. Just like it was almost a year earlier when I proposed on the Fourth of July. Most wouldn't think that was the most romantic night to get engaged on, but I knew she would like it. She loves the sparkle and explosion of the fireworks. It's the same reason we got married on New Year's Eve almost six months later. The fireworks always got to her.

I hear rustling coming from upstairs making me pause my pacing.

"Alexa?" I shout up the stairs.

"I'm coming," she shouts back.

I stand at the bottom, waiting to see my princess descend the stairs. When I see her, my jaw drops in awe of her. Her sparkly green floor-length dress hugs every curve while still keeping her leg hidden. Just revealing the sparkles of her silver shoes beneath the dress. Her hair flows in long red curls down her back. I smile loving the hair extensions the stylist chose. Very similar to what she wore that night a year ago. The only thing that isn't quite right is her tattoos. They are very visible in this dress. That night she had hidden them beneath makeup. I'll have to work on her keeping them more hidden in the future.

Alexa doesn't look at me as she takes another step with her right leg. This time, the heel catches on a snag in the carpet, and she tumbles down the last five stairs. I do my best to catch her, but there is nothing I can do. We end up in a pile on the floor.

I laugh. "You always were a bit of a klutz. That hasn't changed."

She laughs too, although hers is a nervous laugh. "I think my leg may have made it worse."

I shake my head. "No, you would have still fallen. I should have been more prepared, but I'm a little out of practice."

"We may need to install a slide so I don't have to bother with stairs at all."

"When we buy a house one day, we will," I say in a serious tone. When we buy a house, start a family, and I find my redemption, I'll buy her whatever she fucking wants. I don't tell her all of that yet. It's too soon to scare her with talk of the future, but that's what I want. To have kids, that will absolve me of all the wrong I have put out into the world.

I help her stand up and hold onto her until she has gotten her balance back.

"James has a limo waiting outside. He will be driving and protecting us tonight. Do you think you can make it outside safely?"

"Of course. You just may have to hold me up," she says, attempting to flirt with me. It feels good to see her try.

I hold my elbow out to her, which she takes and we exit our apartment.

"Where are we going?" she asks.

"It's a surprise."

"Have we been there before?"

"Yes."

"Is it my favorite place?"

"It's definitely in your top five."

She smiles. "Good. I want to go somewhere I already love."

"THIS IS WHERE WE ARE EATING?" she asks in astonishment staring at the tall building with a great view of the Empire State Building.

"Yes, it's the best steakhouse in town. And you won't believe the view from the restaurant on the top floor."

James pulls up in front of the restaurant but remains in his seat.

"James," I hiss, hoping he will get the hint.

James looks back at us. "Oh, sorry," he says when I raise my eyebrows at him. He immediately climbs out of his seat and opens the door for Alexa.

"Sorry," he says again as he helps Alexa out of the car. "I'm used to doing security, not being a chauffeur too."

Alexa laughs. "I'd prefer to not have either, but ..." I watch as she whispers something into James' ear that makes him laugh. I feel heat surging through my body as I watch how easily James has been able to pick up a relationship with Alexa again when it's so hard for me. They spent half a day together earlier while I was at therapy, and she seemed happier that evening. Happier than I've seen her since I returned. I want James and Alexa to have a good relationship, again, just not before we have rekindled ours.

I climb out of the car and glare at James, who has his hand on the small of her back.

"I'll take it from here," I say, placing my hand on the small of her back and guiding her inside.

We walk into the lobby and up the elevator to the top floor where the restaurant sits.

"Reservations are under Wolfe," I say to the hostess.

She smiles and shows us to the best table in the restaurant. The table sits against large windows that overlook the Empire State Building.

We both sit at the table opposite from each other. Alexa's jaw drops as she looks out over the skyline. Several minutes pass as I watch her stare out the large windows. Finally, she moves her attention to the rest of the restaurant; tables covered by elegant white tablecloths with only the best roses in the center of each.

"This place is amazing," she says.

I smile. "It is one of our favorite restaurants."

She returns my smile before fidgeting with her napkin in her lap, returning her attention to the skyline out the window. The sun has just begun to set. Tonight is perfect, just like it was almost a year ago.

"Hello, I'm Silvia," a young waitress interrupts us. "I'll be your waitress for the evening. Mr. Wolfe has already arranged the meals and drinks for this evening. I'll bring your cocktails momentarily. Is there anything else I can get for you, Mr. and Mrs. Wolfe?"

I turn to face Alexa to see if there is anything else she needs, but her mouth is gaping open as she stares at our waitress. I assume because she called her Mrs. Wolfe, although technically her name is still Blakely. We will have to change that soon.

"Alexa," I say, trying to break her out of her daydream.

"Sorry." Her eyes slowly become alive again breaking the spell of her daydream. "I'm sure whatever Mr. Wolfe has ordered will be fine," she says. She takes a sip of her water before looking at me.

"So um ... at some point we will have to go back to LA to get my clothes and car and things." She pauses to clear her throat as she shifts her body uneasily in her seat. "I mean if we are planning to stay in New York," she says barely making eye contact with me.

"I agree we will have to make arrangements, but let's not focus on that right now. I just want us to focus on tonight. Not the past and not the future. Just now."

She nods as Silvia brings our cocktails, the finest whiskey they have. Most people might have champagne on a night like tonight, but not us. Whiskey has always been our favorite drink.

Alexa lifts her glass. "To focusing on tonight."

I lift mine and clink it with hers. "To the best night of our lives."

A wonderful five-course meal is served for dinner. Alexa eats every bite of everything from the oyster appetizer to the lobster and steak main course. She doesn't even leave a drop of her favorite cheesecake. We don't talk about anything except how much we are enjoying this moment.

"That was amazing," Alexa says as the waitress clears the rest of our dessert plates.

"The night's not done yet," I say winking at her. I stand from the table and pull her chair from the table to help her stand.

"Where are we going now?" she asks. Her eyes sparkle with excitement.

"To the heart of New York," I say as we leave the building. I notice James and Nick fall into step in front and behind us as we exit into the beautiful warm air. Alexa doesn't seem to notice as she holds onto my arm.

She smiles when we get to the lobby of the Empire State Building. It wasn't hard to guess where I was taking her.

She squeals just a little when we walk straight to the elevator and are the only ones on it.

"I'm so excited. I've always wanted to go to the top of the Empire State Building."

I laugh. "You already have, but it's exciting to see the same reaction for a second time."

When the doors open, I guide Alexa out into the open air. Her eyes shine brighter than I've ever seen as she steps onto the observation deck. She runs to the edge to look out at the city sparkling in the darkness around us. I let her walk, no, run around the observation deck pulling me along until she has seen every part of it.

"Wait ... why is no one else out here?" she asks. I chuckle. It took a good twenty minutes for her to realize this, just like last time.

"Because I didn't want anyone else here when I did this." I take her hand in mine and bend down on one knee.

"Alexa, I love you. I can't imagine spending the rest of my life with anybody else. I know we are already legally married, but I want to do it again. That night will forever be ingrained in our minds because of the accident. I want this wedding to be just for us." I pull the box containing her new larger engagement ring out of my pocket and open the velvet box. "Alexa Blakely, will you marry me?"

She sucks in air just like before holding it for a few seconds before exhaling slowly as she makes up her mind. "Yes."

I smile and stand before placing the large diamond on her finger. I pull her into a tight embrace and part her lips as I sweep my tongue inside. Her tongue finds mine easily like we have known each other's bodies for years. It feels like it should.

When we pull away from each other, she stares at the large ring. "Wow. That diamond is ..."

"Amazing," I say, finishing her sentence.

"Yes," she says smiling.

"Is this how you proposed before?" she asks.

I guide her to the railing so that she is facing the city and I wrap my arms around her waist holding her from behind. I kiss her softly on the cheek. "Just like last time. Except last time there were fireworks ..."

"Really?" she asks excitedly.

Right on cue, the first firework explodes in the distance as I feel her excitement pulse through her body. Everything is just like last time ...

Chapter Sixteen

ALEXA

I don't know who to trust. I can't trust the police.

THE LIGHT SHINING in through the window wakes me. I was asleep, at night, I realize as I turn over and see Ethan sleeping in bed next to me. I look down at my clothes. I'm wearing a gorgeous silk nightie. My prosthetic leg is still on, but somehow, Ethan managed to get me out of that tight dress and into this nightie. I don't remember anything after climbing back into the limo. I must have fallen asleep on the ride home.

I feel the weight of my new engagement ring hanging from my finger. I move my hand side to side and watch as the light bounces off the large rectangular shaped diamond. The ring feels even odder on my finger than the rings he bought me before. Am I still expected to wear those rings too? Or is this large ring enough? I don't know how I'm going to wear it without hitting it on something or losing it.

I sigh as I turn my attention from my ring to Ethan, who is still sound asleep and naked, I realize, in bed next to me. I study him closer while he is sleeping. He really is a sexy man. I'm attracted to his toned muscles, his flawless complexion, and even his perfect hair. I can see why I was attracted to such a man before. Such a perfect, strong, accomplished man would have felt like stability in my life after living on the streets for so long. I'm still attracted to a man who can provide my life with that. Maybe that's why when he asked me to marry him again I said yes. Not out of obligation but out of want.

Last night was amazing; easily, one of the best times that I remember. Only one other night tops it. A night of adventure followed by a night of passion. Passion I have yet to reciprocate with Ethan. Can I really do that? Can I let Ethan fuck me and own me like Landon did? No. At least, not yet. But I can give Ethan something to show I care about him and am trying.

I move my body closer to Ethan's so that my body presses against his side. I begin kissing and nibbling on his neck as my hand rests on his hard chest. I continue kissing him, watching as he slowly stirs out of sleep before I let my hand slide down his chest, past his hard abs, to his length growing harder with each kiss.

I grab hold of it firmly in my hand and begin moving up and down his thick shaft.

"Baby, what are you ... aw, that feels good," Ethan says as I pump again.

"Shh," I say as I nibble on his ear. "Don't move."

Ethan nods and closes his eyes as he groans again as I move to his balls massaging them thoroughly before moving back to his cock. I kiss down his hard body, kissing every scar and bruise. Doing my best to kiss away the pain. I reach his cock and take it in my mouth without thinking. My mind immediately begins making comparisons. Ethan's light bruised skin compared to Landon's tanned, tattooed skin. Ethan's perfect hair compared with Landon's tousled hair. Landon's large cock compared to Ethan's almost equally equipped cock.

I push both men out of my head and just focus on the task of bringing the one in my mouth pleasure. I close my eyes and move my mouth up and down swirling my tongue around the thick shaft in my mouth as I hold his balls firmly in my hand. I hear Ethan moaning as I begin moving faster, sucking harder, but I don't register the sound. Instead, all I hear is Landon's voice playing in my head. "I can't wait to see you, see what more we could be, just give us a chance, give me a reason to exist ..."

I keep moving my lips and tongue to the beat of the music that keeps playing over and over. Knowing I'm destroying any chance of those words ever coming true. *No!* Landon destroyed any chance of us ever being together. I'm just moving on. I'm bringing my husband the pleasure he deserves. I move my lips and hands over Ethan's cock faster and faster until I'm going at a furious pace.

I pump up and down with my lips and hand, taking out all my anger and frustration on the thick hardness between my lips. I can barely breathe as his cock hits the back of my throat over and over, but I enjoy the pain. *Fuck, I'm so messed up!* The only way I can enjoy any sexual act is with pain to take away the demons. It's the only way the panic stays away.

I suck again, savoring the pain deep in my throat when I feel the warm, salty release ooze down my throat. I swallow the liquid before licking him clean. I slowly move away from Ethan until I'm lying back on my side of the bed. My cheeks flush a bright red with embarrassment over what I just did. I close my eyes and calm my frantic breathing. It's over. There is no way Landon would ever forgive me for what I just did. Not even to become friends again. I open my eyes staring at the still practically complete stranger lying next to me. This man is my life now. Forever.

"That was incredible," Ethan says catching his breath. "Your turn." He reaches for my neck to pull me into a kiss.

"Soon," I say smiling as I gently keep him at arm's length. Soon, I'll be ready for more, but not today. Never today.

Ethan leans over and kisses me softly on the lips. "Yes, soon."

I watch as Ethan climbs out of bed. I watch every hard muscle as he pulls a pair of boxer shorts out of the top drawer and puts them on. He then heads to his closet and pulls out a robe and puts it on.

"I'll go make us breakfast."

"I'll meet you out on the balcony."

Ethan grins before heading downstairs.

I climb out of bed and head to my closet. My leg aches with each step after wearing my prosthetic leg all night. I have trouble keeping my balance as I walk on my toes. I make it to the closet and let my body fall to the floor so I can remove the prosthetic leg meant to wear with heels. I have three different prosthetic legs – one meant to wear every day, one to wear with heels, and one specially designed for running. I haven't tried the new prosthetic leg for running, but I have a feeling I will try it soon. I take off the leg designed for heels and put on my everyday leg. I find a fluffy white robe hanging in my closet. I run my hand up and down the soft fabric. I don't usually wear such nice things, but I put the robe on anyway. My stress immediately begins to melt away as I wrap the soft fabric around me.

I walk out to the balcony and sit on the couch. The warm sun beats down on me. I relax for a minute before I hear the door open and see Ethan step out onto the balcony. He places a small tray on the coffee table in front of me before taking a seat next to me on the couch.

"Your breakfast," Ethan says proud of the meal he has placed in front of me.

I laugh. "Cereal, fruit, and coffee. You really went all out." I grab a strawberry and take a bite of the fruit.

"Trust me, you don't want me to cook. I'd burn the whole apartment building down with my cooking skills. We usually hire a chef to cook for us or we just eat out."

I take the cup of coffee off the table and curl my legs underneath me so that I'm facing Ethan. Now seems like a good time to talk. To find more answers.

"How did I make so much money as a photographer? How did I go from nothing to having all of this?"

Ethan finishes eating a spoonful of cereal. "Me. You found me." He takes another bite of his cereal as if he didn't just shatter my world.

"What do you mean it was you?"

"When I found out you had been raped, I helped you find justice. I represented you as your lawyer and helped you win your case."

He shovels another spoonful of cereal into his mouth before continuing.

"After we started dating, you were getting more jobs photographing weddings, but it wasn't enough to be stable, so I helped support you."

Ethan stops to shovel a couple of more bites into his mouth as I try to digest what he is saying.

"You were extremely talented, and I knew that. You never went to college, but you had this immense skill. My family has connections to powerful people. I got you a job doing a swimsuit shoot for a magazine. They loved you so much that that job led to another and another and another."

He sets his empty bowl of cereal back on the coffee table.

"Eventually, I helped you get a job with the top entertainment magazine in the country. That was by far your most successful shoot. From there, you were able to charge any amount you wanted to do a shoot."

I let his words sink in. That he was the reason my career took off. My talent wasn't enough to get me a job. Without him, I would be nothing. I would have nothing. I am nothing ...

"We should talk about what we are going to do now."

"What do you mean?" I ask, trying not to think that I could have easily starved to death if it wasn't for Ethan.

"I don't think you should go back to photography. I'm not even sure if I should continue my work as a lawyer."

"Why?" I don't know what I would do if it wasn't photography.

"I want us to just spend time together. Life is too short. I just want to spend all of my time with you and with Mother. With my family. I don't want to deal with the legal system anymore. It's too dangerous."

I nod. I want him to be safe. I can't handle any more fear or death in my life.

"Mother wants us to help her run the non-profit charity she started in my honor."

"She's continuing that even though you are alive? Even though a drunk driver wasn't the cause of the accident?"

"Yes. She's realized that she needs to do something to give back to the world. I would like if we could do the same after such a tragic event. We could both move back to LA to be close to family, find a real house, and then we could start a family. We could have kids. Start over doing something better for the world. What do you think?"

"I ... I ... don't know."

"Just think about it." Ethan tucks a strand of loose hair behind my ear. "I'm going inside to get ready for the day. You coming?"

"In a minute." Ethan walks back inside our apartment while I sit outside. He wants me to move to LA. He wants me to work with his mother and give up photography. He wants to have kids. What if I can't give him any of those things?

Chapter Seventeen

LANDON

I don't want to wait anymore to make you mine.
But I'll wait forever if you need
For you to come back to me.
Don't stay his.
Find me still.
Please find my love.

I STEP out of the limo to flashes blinding my eyes. I smile at the photographers while I button my tuxedo jacket. I reach my hand back into the limo; Caroline takes my hand and climbs out after me. She's beaming as she steps out in her floor-length gold sparkly dress.

I hold my elbow out for her, and she takes it as we walk down the red carpet. We stop every once in a while to pose for the cameras as a couple, but we aren't stopped for questions until we get to the far end of the carpet.

"You guys look amazing. Who are you wearing?" asks the entertainment reporter before thrusting the microphone in Caroline's face.

I tune out as Caroline talks about her dress and jewelry. She really does look beautiful in her dress, but then she always does.

"Caroline, how does it feel to be a small part of such an epic movie franchise that has taken the world by storm?"

"It felt amazing. It really was a dream come true to be able to act in a film that is so iconic with so many great actors. I have learned a lot from this experience. You'll see me starring in a major film soon. You'll just have to keep an eye out for me," Caroline says laughing, although I know inside she is angry for the snide remark about her having a 'small role' in the film.

I wrap my arms around her waist holding her close to me, trying my best to support her. Her eyes brighten when I do and the practiced reporter notices right on cue.

"This may seem like an obvious question, but are you and Landon finally back together?"

"Yes, we rekindled our love for each other a few months ago. We have always had strong feelings for one another, but a few misunderstandings kept us apart."

"But you've gotten past those misunderstandings?"

I take Caroline into my arms planting a passionate kiss on her lips as I dip her for the cameras.

"Yes," I say when I let Caroline come up for air.

"That's wonderful. I wish you both happiness in your relationship," she says effectively dismissing us. We gave the cameras the show they wanted; now, they need to move on to the much bigger stars who will be arriving soon on the red carpet. But I'm not done giving them a show yet. Instead of moving on as they are expecting, I get down on one knee.

I hear the reporter gasp at the same time hundreds of lights flash simultaneously trying to get a picture of us.

"Caroline, you are the love of my life. Will you marry me?" I say as I take out the box containing the same ring I had used to propose before. The ring she loves that Drew kept safe for me even after I found out about the cheating and lying. I couldn't get rid of the ring.

Caroline's mouth drops open and a surprised gasp escapes, showing off her acting skills. I've never thought she was much of an actress, but seeing her now makes me reconsider. A tear rolls gently down her cheek glistening as the cameras continue to flash around us. Finally, a large smile appears as she answers, "Yes."

I smile too as I stand to place the diamond on her finger. While inside, all I feel is pain. Rotten, horrible pain. This isn't about contracts or keeping Alex safe. Today is about Caroline. Reality sinks in that this is real. I'm marrying Caroline, not Alex. Never Alex.

I place the ring on her finger and then lean in for a passionate kiss. I put everything I have into the kiss, giving the cameras a grand show as I slip my tongue into Caroline's mouth as I dip her again. I pull her back to a standing position as some of the crowd around us applauds at our little show. Maybe I should try my hand at acting as well.

"Well, that was unexpected. Was it as unexpected for you as it was us?" the reporter asks Caroline.

Caroline looks down at her ring, her smile spreading over her whole face before she looks up at the cameras.

"Yes, this was completely unexpected for me as well. But I'm so happy. This is the best day of my life," Caroline answers.

"You two have been engaged before. What makes you think this time will last?"

Both our mouths fall open slightly before turning to reddened frowns. "We were young then. We didn't know what a commitment we were making. This time, we do." I pause to glare at the woman. "Caroline, why don't you show off that gorgeous ring of yours?"

Caroline extends her hand to the camera that zooms in on her ring. More flashes go off getting a picture of the ring.

"It's the same design as my mother's engagement ring. I had to sell my mother's ring many years ago to be able to afford college and food. But Landon remembered how important that ring was to me. He really is amazing," Caroline says leaning into my arms.

"That ring is beautiful. You did a wonderful job picking it out, Landon. Any idea when or where you two will tie the knot?"

I rub my hand up and down Caroline's back slowly to prevent myself from rolling my eyes at this woman's ridiculous questions.

"We don't have any dates picked out obviously. But I think soon. We don't want to wait to start the rest of our lives together. And as far as where, you'll just have to wait and see," Caroline says.

"But we will get an invite right?"

"Of course," Caroline says winking.

We are ushered on to a couple of reporters from smaller entertainment sites who ask the same questions.

What are we wearing?

Can we see the ring?

When are you getting married?

Nobody ever asks about Caroline's talent. Nobody asks about my music career. And nobody asks about the photographer I was seen with a few weeks earlier.

We are finally ushered into the theater where we take our seats that are surprisingly close to the front despite Caroline's small role in the film. I try not to think about what just happened. That I'm really engaged. I just want to spend the rest of the night watching a crappy mainstream movie in a dark theater.

"Why did you have to drive home again? Why couldn't a limo pick us up like normal people? We are going to miss all of the parties," Caroline whines.

I roll my eyes but don't let Caroline see as we wander through the parking lot to find Silvia, my Porsche.

"Because I hate being driven around in a limo. And the good parties don't even start for another two hours."

Caroline lets out a painful groan. I'm a few feet in front of her, but I turn to see what the problem is now.

"What's wrong?"

"My feet are killing me in these heels."

I don't hold back my eye rolling this time. Alex walked in heels several times with a prosthetic leg and never complained. We are only a block away from the car, but I know if I don't do something, it will be the longest block I've ever walked.

"Wait here. I'll go get Silvia," I say. I begin to run the block to my Porsche, happy to have a few minutes away from Caroline. I get to the car quickly and climb in, happy to see that it is right where Drew said he left it. I start up the engine and stomp on the gas to get back to Caroline as quickly as possible.

I unlock the door when I pull up beside her but don't bother to get out and open the door for her. She climbs in huffing and groaning making it known that she is unhappy. Well, too fucking bad.

I step on the gas as we zip out of the parking lot and toward the first party we are supposed to make an appearance at.

"God, Landon, slow down," Caroline shouts holding onto the handle of the door.

I ease off the gas, not sure if I can handle any more of her complaining today.

Caroline holds her left hand in her right as she examines the ring closer. A ring she only wore for a couple of days last time.

"Thank you," she finally says.

"For what?"

"For giving me this ring. I wasn't even sure if you still had it ... this is the one I always wanted. In every other area of my life, I'm vain and want the best most expensive there is, but not this. This, I wanted to be about my mother." She wipes a tear and sniffles quietly. "Just thank you."

Maybe the tear from earlier was real, not fake. Maybe what I thought was her just putting on a good show for the cameras was real emotion. But I'm afraid to ask.

"You're welcome," I say instead.

An awkward pause passes over us as Caroline works to get her emotions under control.

"We should find a time to talk about when we are going to get married. Where we want to live. All of those details."

She takes out lipstick from her clutch purse and begins reapplying. "Yes, we should. I want everything to happen as soon as possible. Keep this publicity going and keep it fresh on everyone's minds. It will be the best for both of our careers, don't you agree?"

"Yes, we should get married as soon as possible." Before I change my mind and do something incredibly stupid that will ruin everything ...

Chapter Eighteen

ETHAN

We get our drinks before she speaks again. "What's your name?"

"Ethan Wolfe."

She grabs her glass and downs her whiskey. "I'm Alex."

"Short for Alexandra?"

"No," she says shaking her head in disgust. "It's short for Alexa."

"Nice to meet you, Alexa," I say extending my hand to her. She takes it but shakes her head slightly at my response. Her eyes roam over my body before meeting my gaze again.

"Dance with me? Or should I ask one of the other bachelors if they want to dance?" She eyes a young blond guy, one of James' friends.

I take her hand and drag her to the dance floor.

I UNLOCK the door to my office before opening it slowly. I don't know what I expect, but I don't expect what I see. Boxes. Several boxes are stacked on my desk with a few piled in the corner. Each with my name on them. I'm surprised my associate, Dean, hasn't taken over this much bigger office yet.

I flip the lights on before maneuvering around the boxes to take a seat in my big comfy office chair. I don't even know where to start with all of the boxes. I could unpack them all and start over again here. I could continue running the New York firm, just as I always have, although Dean has been chomping at the bit for years to run this office. And from what I can tell, he has been doing a good job while I was gone. Mother would love me to get out of law and to find a safer, easier job. Or just live off our incredible wealth in peace in LA near her. I just need to convince Alexa that LA is where we should be. We should start a family and start over with a new life. She could even help Mother run the non-profit while I help run the LA law firm. I just don't want her gallivanting all over the country doing photography. It's not safe. I want her with me.

LA should be an easy sell since she has made her home there for the past six months. I open the first box while I contemplate on how I'm going to convince Alexa it's for the best. I glance down at the picture frame with a photo of Alexa and me that sits on top of all of the other crap that is in the box. I smile. We look happy. I just want us to be that happy again.

I pull out my cell phone from my jacket pocket and dial Mother's number.

"Hello, sweetie," she answers immediately.

"Hi, Mother."

"Are you alone?"

"Yes."

"Good. Does she remember anything?"

"No. She doesn't remember anything," I say sighing. I don't want to hear my mother complain about Alexa anymore.

"Good. I still don't like the decision you've made to marry her again, but I'll accept it for now."

"I'm happy to hear that, Mother."

"Have the police caught King's guys yet?"

"No, Mother, but they will. They were close last I heard."

"Excellent."

"Have you found it yet?"

"No, but I will. I just need time. In the meantime, we're safe."

"You need to get out here soon to look for it."

"I will."

"Have you convinced her to move out here yet?"

"No, but I will."

Mother sighs. "I love you, Ethan. I'm just trying to protect you."

"I know, Mother. I love you too. We will talk again soon. Good-bye."

"Good-bye."

I end the call and glance back to the photograph lying on the top of the box. I need to do so much before the happiness that is apparent in the photo will ever return. First, I need to talk to Dean and see where his head is at. Then I can deal with convincing Alexa.

"YES, I would love the opportunity to be a partner at the firm. I would have run you off that bridge myself if I had thought it would have given me a chance to run the firm instead of ownership going to Laura," Dean says leaning back in his chair at his desk across from me.

My eyes tighten at his much-too-soon joke.

"Sorry," Dean says, realizing his mistake.

I take a deep breath. "Good. I will write up a contract that will make you a fifty-fifty partner over the company. You will run the day-to-day operations of the company when I move to LA. I'll just help out some when I can."

Dean extends his hand and I shake it. "You've got a deal." My lips curl into a smile. M first step toward happiness is complete.

Dean's office phone rings. He answers, "Yes."

I motion with my hands that I'll be going. Dean holds up a finger for me to wait. So I wait.

"Send them up to the meeting room." He hangs up the phone.

"That was the cops," he says. "I sent them up to the meeting room. They said they have good news to share with you."

My smile brightens.

"See you later, Dean," I say getting up and heading to the meeting room a few doors over. This has to be it. The news I've been waiting for.

I hear a solid knock on the door shortly after I enter the meeting room. I head to the door and open it to a waiting Officer Nibbs and Officer Burner.

"Come on in. I hear you have good news for me."

"We do," Officer Nibbs says.

"Have a seat and we can get started," Officer Burner says.

I take a seat on the opposite side of the table from them.

"We caught them. We caught Alfie King's men. There was three of them who we believe are involved in your kidnapping and torture," Officer Nibbs says.

"That's wonderful news," I say leaning back in my chair. A huge weight lifts from my chest as I take a deep, calming breath.

"So what happens now?"

"We need to take you down to do a lineup to see if you can identify them. After that, we will be questioning them to see if we can get a confession out of them, but we have enough evidence from the warehouse you led us to where you were held. We can easily go to trial with a good chance of winning," Officer Burner says.

I nod, but I don't want a 'good chance of winning.' I want to lock the bastards away for the rest of their life. I want to destroy their lives and know they have no chance of coming back after me, after Alexa. I want to know that I will win.

"We will get a confession out of one of the bastards who work for King, don't worry. When we take this to trial, we will put them away for life," Officer Nibbs says.

"I know you will."

Officer Burner shakes his head softly at Officer Nibbs, likely not happy that he said they would get a confession when they can promise no such thing. But I have faith in Officer Nibbs; we have worked together on many cases before. If he says he will get a confession, he will.

"Do you have time to head back to the station now to do a lineup?" Officer Burner asks.

"Yes, just give me a moment to lock up and I'll meet you outside."

The officers both nod before heading out. I head to my office door and make sure it's locked before letting Dean know I'm heading out.

'I'm safe' keeps repeating over and over in my head as I walk out of the office. Although that's not quite right. I'm almost safe. One step closer. Now, I just need to convince Alexa to move to LA and find it. Then I'll be safe. Then we will be safe.

Chapter Nineteen

ALEXA

I can't trust Ethan.

IT'S BEEN weeks since I've come. Weeks since I've had any sort of release. I could ask Ethan to help me. I'm sure he would gladly offer his services, but I'm not ready for that yet, though. But I need a release. I'm desperate for it.

Ethan's gone to his office for the day. I'm alone in this apartment by myself. Left with thoughts of Ethan's desire to move back to LA. Do less photography or better yet quit altogether. Work on a non-profit with Laura. Have kids. I don't think I can do any of those things. Not. One. Thing.

Not to mention that LA would be torture without Landon. Despite how mad I am at him for cheating, LA will always be ours. And photography is all I know. How could I do anything else? How could I handle working for his mother day in and day out? I can't ...

I can't think about that right now, though. Right now, I have so much pent-up sexual frustration that I'm going to explode if I don't do something about it. Landon started a fire inside me, but I can't go back to him to help me extinguish the flames. And I can't go to Ethan yet. So I will take care of it myself.

I move my body upstairs as fast as my legs will move me. Ethan said he would be gone for several hours, but who knows. He could be home faster than I think. We only live three blocks from his office. An easy distance to walk if he decides the office is too much and he needs to come home.

My gaze drifts around the bedroom, *our bedroom*, as I look for where I might hide a vibrator. The only three options are the nightstand, dresser, or closet. I start with the nightstand but find nothing. I quickly look through the dresser, nothing. I glance in the closet, but there are too many boxes. I would be in there for hours looking. Time I don't have.

Instead, I lie down on my back on the bed. I adjust the throw pillows surrounding me until I'm comfortable. I close my eyes and let my mind wander to whomever it chooses. Ethan or Landon.

It chooses Landon; despite how angry I am with him, it's easier to imagine being with him. Ethan has been amazing and he's very attractive, but it's just too hard for my brain to comprehend at the moment.

I start moving my hand over my body imagining it's Landon's touching my neck and fondling my breasts. I imagine as his rough fingers reach into my panties encouraging the warm liquid to pour out of me. I pretend it's his kiss on my neck when a cool breeze gives me chills. I move my fingers over my clit. Soft and slow at first. Giving the liquid a chance to form.

I think of Landon's hard body towering over me. I think of Landon's hard cock driving inside me when I push my fingers inside, but my fingers don't even come close to feeling the same. I try to imagine his teeth sinking into my skin as I move my hand in and out of my slit. Faster and faster.

I feel myself building. My breath coming faster. My muscles tightening, readying for release, but it doesn't come. I need more. I take my phone out of my pocket and search for pictures of Landon. Hundreds come up and I click on one of him posing practically naked with his guitar.

I move my fingers over my clit again. Twirling faster and faster. I build again. My body doing everything to get the release it needs. I pinch my clit hard like Landon has done before, hoping it will send me over the edge, but it doesn't.

I flip through the pictures, hoping to find a better one of Landon that really does his body justice. But instead of another photo of Landon, there is a picture of Landon and Caroline with an engagement ring blown up in the corner of the picture. I stare at it. Not blinking. Not moving.

"When was this photo taken?" I yell at my phone. I search, but the picture shows no indication of when this was taken.

I stop masturbating and begin frantically searching websites trying to find out what happened when I read it. 'Landon Davis proposed to Caroline Parker on the red carpet.'

I click the article and skim it. He proposed with one of the most beautiful rings I have ever seen. She said yes. They want to get married as soon as possible. A beach probably.

I open another article. 'Landon Davis taken. Heartbreak among woman everywhere. Turns out Landon Davis did need Caroline's love after all.'

The articles are wrong. Heartbreak isn't happening in women everywhere. It's happening here. Right here.

"I hate him," I scream as I grab a damn throw pillow and slam it into the ground. I grab another and punch it over and over imagining Landon's face with each punch. Funny how moments earlier, I was pretending his hands were all over me, pleasuring me. Now, I want to rip out his heart.

I hear the door slam downstairs. I freeze listening to Ethan walking around downstairs. I pick up the pillows and put them back on the bed. I walk to the bathroom and close the door as I hear Ethan climbing the stairs. I lock the door and take a deep breath as I lean against the door, trying to calm my pounding heart.

"Honey ..." Ethan shouts.

"Be out in a second," I shout back through the door. I walk to the sink and look at myself in the mirror. Tears I didn't even know I had been crying have rolled down my cheek and stained my shirt. My cheeks are flushed a bright red. My hands are shaking with adrenaline and anger.

I take a deep breath before turning the faucet on. I watch the water come out in a continuous stream. Trying to think about anything other than how sexually frustrated and angry I am. I run my hands under the water and splash some on my face. Washing the tears away. Doing my best to wash the pain away with them. I take the hand towel and dry my face.

I don't feel any calmer. The pain hasn't even begun to wash away, but I look normal as I stare at myself in front of the mirror. I head out of the bathroom and see Ethan sitting on the edge of our bed holding an enormous bouquet of roses.

I do my best to smile. "What are those for?"

"You."

"Why?"

"Because you are beautiful and you deserve to have something equally as beautiful." Ethan stands and meets me halfway between the bathroom door and the bed. He hands me the flowers and I breathe in the smell. The smell immediately relaxes me.

"Thank you," I say, genuinely thankful to be married to someone so thoughtful to bring me flowers on a day I needed them the most. Even though he didn't know I needed flowers.

"I have something else for you," Ethan says giddily.

I raise my eyebrows at him. "The flowers are more than enough. I love them."

"Well, this is even better." He pulls out two plane tickets and hands them to me.

I stare. "We are going back to LA? I thought we weren't going back until the police were done with their investigation..."

"They're done."

"What?"

"They caught the men who did this to us."

My eyes light up at his words, unable to process what he is saying.

"They are in prison."

My smile gets bigger.

"One of the guys even confessed which, along with the evidence, will put them away for life."

"We're safe," we both say simultaneously. Our eyes meet revealing every emotion we are both feeling to each other. Happiness. Joy. Anger. Revenge. And need ...

I drop the beautiful flowers on the floor and wrap my arms around Ethan's neck as my lips collide with his. I don't know if it's the fact that I haven't had sex in weeks, that I'm angry with Landon, or that I'm relieved at being safe that causes me to want more with Ethan. But whatever the reason, I don't question it.

Ethan kisses me softly, expecting me to pull away like I usually do. Instead, I sweep my tongue farther into his mouth welcoming more from him. I wrap my arms tighter around his neck, pushing my body closer to his. His tongue pushes back, testing my boundaries. I massage his tongue with mine welcoming him in but wanting more.

I shove him backward, unable to wait any longer, and we are both falling on top of our bed in a tangle of arms and legs. His mouth falls open and his eyes widen in surprise at my blatant need for him.

"Alexa?" he asks hesitantly, still not sure if he is reading my signs correctly, as I press my body on top of him.

"I want you." I run my tongue over his lower lip.

"I want all of you," I say seductively as I pull away from him.

He groans and tucks my hair behind my ear before grabbing the nape of my neck forcing my lips back on top of his.

"I want you too, but are you sure?"

I smile. He's been beyond chivalrous these last few weeks. He needs this as much as I do. He has to be losing his mind having his wife back but not being able to love her as he wants. Not being able to fuck her and own her body as he would like. Tonight, that is going to change.

"Fuck me, Ethan. Make me yours again."

That's all it takes to convince him. He flips us over so that I am underneath him. His shirt comes off immediately followed closely by mine. He presses his warm skin against mine as he kisses me hard and fast. I try to savor the kiss, but he moves too fast to fully enjoy the kiss.

He unhooks my bra exposing my hard peaks to the cold air. His hands find my nipples as he teasingly rubs them, encouraging them to form harder peaks. They respond easily to his touch as they probably have a thousand times before. He takes one in his mouth, swirling his tongue around it.

"Mmm ..." I groan at the feel of my sensitive flesh. I squirm underneath him needing attention down there as well before I explode from just his touch on my bare breasts.

He pushes his hard cock between my legs as he continues flicking my nipple with his tongue, making it hard to focus on anything but the sensation. I can feel his hard cock as he rubs it against me, sending liquid pouring out of me. Soaking my panties and begging him to enter me.

But the material between us is preventing that from happening. I grab at his pants needing them off. Now. He gets the hint and stands to pull them off as I get my own pants off. Needing to feel good. Needing the release.

Ethan's eyes travel down to my prosthetic leg. I can see his uncertainty form in his eyes. He has no idea what he needs to do with it, and I'm not ready to take it off in front of him.

"Come here," I say, wiggling my finger at him to come to me.

He obliges letting thoughts of my prosthetic leg drift from his mind as he move back on top of me. I feel his hard cock settle between my legs as he kisses me hard.

I take his bottom lip into my mouth and bite down, encouraging his blood to fill my mouth.

"Ow," he says pulling away from me.

"Sorry, I want more. I want you to be rough with me," I say.

He shakes his head. "I don't think that is a good idea. I remember how you like it. Trust me." He wipes the trickle of blood from his lip and moves to my neck. Every kiss there sends chills all over my body.

I close my eyes and just let him take over. I trust him just like he asked. His hand moves to my clit. His fingers move in slow torturous circles.

I groan at the wondrous sensation. The sensation quickly overtakes me, as I go higher and higher to where I can't take much more if he keeps this up.

His hard cock pushes at my entrance, testing to see if I'm ready for him.

"Fuck me," I groan, needing him inside me when I come.

He pushes inside in one quick motion, stretching and filling me. He doesn't move as he kisses me hard on the lips while waiting for me to adjust. It doesn't take long to adjust to his cock, not after having Land...

He thrusts back and forth, as he rubs up against my clit. It distracts me easily from my thoughts.

"Oh, Alexa. You feel so good," Ethan moans as he thrusts again, picking up a steady rhythm that is bringing us both to the brink of climax.

"Yes," is all I can say being so close.

He thrusts again as his thumb finds my clit. I moan my release as I clench around him.

Ethan thrusts again and again, plunging into me and finally coming before collapsing on top of me. Both of us stay collapsed on the bed barely moving for several minutes. My mind is too fuzzy to compute what just happened.

"That was incredible," Ethan says kissing me softly on the lips before heading to the bathroom to clean himself up.

I stay in bed. I stare at the white ceiling while I slowly process what just happened. I just had sex with Ethan, with my husband, but I feel *dirty*. I feel like a whore who just cheated on her spouse. *But I didn't.* I just had sex with my spouse. That's the way it is supposed to be.

It felt good. It felt incredibly good to finally have a release, but it was missing something. Missing roughness, fire. Missing the sweet mixture of pleasure and pain. Missing Landon.

Chapter Twenty

LANDON

Please stay with me.
Please give me back my love.
Please don't give up now.

ARMS AND LEGS tangling with mine wake me from a deep sleep. The room spins as I open my eyes revealing a hotel room I don't remember. I press my fingers to my forehead trying to stop the pounding that I know accompanies drinking too much alcohol.

I've woken up too many times this year just like this. With a pounding headache. A nauseous stomach. Sensitivity to light. All the regular symptoms swarm over my body, but one thing is different. A woman is draped over my naked body.

Shit! What the hell did I do last night? I remove the woman's arms from my body, but I can't see her face because her head is buried beneath the covers. I step out of bed and find my boxers lying on the floor. I slip them on and walk around the bed. Bracing myself for what I'll find. *Please be Caroline. Please be Caroline. Don't let it be a stripper.*

I yank the covers off the woman. Caroline. Just Caroline. I sigh. I should be happy, but I think a tiny part of me was hoping it was Alex instead of Caroline naked in my bed. It doesn't take a genius to figure out what happened. We had sex. We must have.

I walk out of the bedroom hoping to find a bottle of water somewhere in this hotel room. Once out of the bedroom, I find a small living space with a kitchenette. I walk to the fridge, open it, and find a couple of bottles of water. I open the first, chugging it quickly while I try to figure out what happened. I grab a second bottle and walk to the living room trying to figure out what time it is when I see Drew snoring on the couch.

"Hey, wake up," I say poking him with my water bottle before sitting on the chair next to the couch he is lying on.

"What?" Drew asks opening his eyes slightly. When he sees he's in a strange hotel room, he pops up. He immediately regrets the decision as he grabs his own head. He must be hungover too.

"You hungover?" I ask.

"Yeah ... you?"

"Yeah. Do you remember what happened last night? How did we end up in this hotel room?"

Drew shakes his head. "I met you guys at the second after party and then everything is fuzzy after that. I can't believe we drank ... again."

"It gets worse ..."

"What is worse than us drinking and waking up in a strange place?"

"Morning," Caroline says as she walks into the living room and sits in the only vacant chair. She has a thin sheet wrapped around her body, but it doesn't hide her hard nipples from pressing against the fabric.

"Good morning. Do you remember what happened last night? How we ended up in this hotel?" I ask, while keeping my eyes focused on hers instead of her chest.

"No," she says, but I watch her eyes meet Drew's. They exchange glances, and I watch as Drew's eyes grow wide with realization.

"What happened?" I ask directing my question to Drew.

"Nothing, I don't remember," Drew says. He stands and grabs a t-shirt from a pile on the floor. He puts it on along with his dress pants over his boxers.

"I'll order us some breakfast. It's obvious we all got drunk after the party. We were too drunk to drive home and ended up sleeping it off here. Nothing else happened," Drew says, staring intently at Caroline.

Drew walks to the hotel phone in the bedroom and begins ordering room service.

"What happened?" I try again with Caroline.

"I got you both drunk at the party. People were taking pictures of you and Drew without a drink. So you drank to stop any rumors from spreading. We came back here. We had sex. Drew slept on the couch. That was it."

"Then what was that going on between you and Drew."

"We just want to protect you. You keep getting drunk and we want to make sure nothing happened that you would regret. That's all."

Drew comes back into the living room. "Breakfast will be up shortly." We both watch as he takes a seat back on the couch, none of us saying a word.

"We should talk about when we want to have the wedding. I'm meeting with a wedding planner this afternoon," Caroline says as Drew shifts awkwardly on the couch.

"Whenever and whatever you want. I already told you that. Just check with Drew to make sure it fits in my schedule."

Caroline's eyes flicker to Drew's before connecting back with me. "But you don't care how soon? If I plan the wedding for next week, next month, or next year? You don't care if we get married in LA or Jamaica or somewhere cold like Alaska?"

"No, I don't care. Whatever you want."

"Okay," she says hesitantly. Completely out of character for her. Usually, she would be demanding complete control of the wedding plans and not asking for permission.

"I'm going to go shower," I say as I get up from my chair leaving Caroline and Drew alone. I close the bedroom door and lean up against it, listening.

"We have to tell him," Drew says in a hushed breath. "I can't keep a secret like this from him."

"No ..."

"But ... he deserves to know."

"No, he doesn't. It's my decision to make. So drop it."

The voices turn quieter, barely audible now. I have no idea what the hell they are talking about. I close my eyes trying to remember what happened last night. There was alcohol and dancing and paparazzi. But nothing registers after that. I have no memories of what happened after we left the last party. Nothing.

My thoughts go to Alex. This is how she feels every day. Not being able to remember her past no matter how desperately she tries. But instead of only forgetting one night, she can't remember a lifetime of memories.

I walk to the bathroom and turn on the shower. I undress before stepping into the lukewarm water that hasn't had a chance to warm up yet. I will probably never find out whatever happened. And I don't care as long as it doesn't hurt Alex. I already feel like I betrayed Alex by sleeping with Caroline. Although, Alex thinks I've been sleeping with Caroline the whole time. What I did last night didn't hurt Alex, it just destroyed me. I don't want to know Caroline's secret. I just want to find a way to survive without destroying any more of myself.

Chapter Twenty-One

ETHAN

We dance freely to a fast-paced song. Her dancing isn't bad, but I wouldn't call it good either. Free is what I would call it. She dances freely as if no one else is watching. I try to match her moves, but mostly, I just watch her as she draws me further under her spell.

We walk into Alexa's towering condo building. The modern building gives off a cold, uncaring vibe that is so unlike our warm, charming apartment building in NY. I don't understand why she would choose to live in a building like this.

I watch her eyes searching the lobby. They dart back toward the entrance and then focus on the small crowd of people waiting to take the elevators up. I have no idea what she is looking for. A friend maybe? A neighbor? Does she feel unsafe? I have no idea.

I try to sense what she is feeling, but I don't sense anything. Nothing is coming from her. Not excitement, anxiety, joy, fear. Nothing. I don't know what she is hiding, but it's something. Something she has locked deep inside that I need to find. I will find out what it is she is hiding. I will find it.

We enter the elevator, and I watch as she hesitates over the buttons before selecting the eighth floor. She couldn't have forgotten which floor she lived on. She hasn't been gone from here for more than a couple of weeks.

The ride up is quick giving me no time to contemplate what is going through Alexa's mind. When the doors open, Alexa leads the way to her condo a few doors down. She sucks in a breath as she unlocks the door and pushes it open. I follow her into her condo and find a tiny place full of cheap furniture. It doesn't look elegant or inviting at all. It doesn't look anything like our classically designed apartment in NY.

"What do you think?" Alexa asks as she puts her purse on the kitchen countertop.

"How did you manage to live here for six months? It's so small."

She frowns at me, but I can't do anything but stare wide-eyed at the tiny place trying to wrap my mind around the fact that Alexa chose this place to live instead of a mansion that she could have afforded. She chose *this* tiny place. It doesn't make sense to me.

"At least, it won't take us long to unpack," I say trying to bring a small smile to her face. Any brightness will do.

She nods, but her frown stays. "All of the furniture is rented. We just need to pack up my clothes and a few kitchen items."

"Good." I walk into her bedroom, hoping to see something grandeur in there that would help me understand why she chose this place. I find a small, simple bed instead. Next to the bed sits a small nightstand with a lock on the drawer. I sit down on the edge and watch her walk into the condo. She's wearing her ugly sweatpants and t-shirt again while I'm dressed in a suit. Alexa argued that we were flying private and she wanted to be comfortable. I gave in and let her wear it. There are bigger battles to fight, like buying a house in LA, convincing her to work for Mother, and convincing her to have kids. So I didn't fight, but I will.

"We will have lots of time for other things," I say winking at her standing in the doorway. I don't expect her to want to do much. She's exhausted from the flight and lack of sleep. We also haven't had sex since that one incredible night. I know she enjoyed herself, but something still holds her back from giving herself to me fully.

She laughs quietly before sitting on the bed next to me. I wrap my arms around her body and lean in to kiss her firmly on the lips. I slip my tongue in begging her for more. She quickly brushes me off, putting a stop to anything that might happen.

"Come on. Let's start packing."

I grab her hand as she leaves the bed holding her in place. "I have a better idea."

"Ethan, I'm not in the mood." She sighs as I hold her hand higher.

I shake my head. "I want to go look for a house."

She pulls away from me as she paces back and forth in the small bedroom. "Ethan, I haven't had time to think about what I really want. I don't know if want to buy a house or not. I don't know if I want to live in LA or NY. I don't know if I want to keep doing photography or help you and your mother run the charity. I don't know if I want kids yet. I just don't know what I want ..."

"But I do," I say standing. Finding her hands again, I hold them in mine. "I want us to live in LA. To start new. I want to be with family while doing something good in the world like running a non-profit charity. Most importantly, I want to have kids with you." She doesn't look at me. Instead, she focuses on our hands clasped together. I lift her chin hoping I'll win if she can see how desperate I am for her to go with me. Her eyes finally find mine. "Just go look at houses with me. I've already scoped a few out that I know you will love."

"I don't know. If we fall in love with something, then what?"

"Then we buy it and move here. Come on. I'll call to get James to take us to see the houses."

"No, I'll drive us. I had my car shipped here."

"The Tesla?"

"Yes," she says. Her grin is wide and infectious.

"But what about your leg?" I ask my grimace softening.

"I had some modifications made to the car to make it easier for me to drive."

My phone buzzes in my pocket. The screen flashes the word 'Mother.'

"Mother," I say motioning to the phone. Alexa walks back into the living room as I take the call.

"Hello, can I call you back? We were just on our way out."

"No, you've been in LA for over three hours now and haven't stopped by to see me. Come now and then you can go gallivanting around the city."

I look at my watch. It's just past two in the afternoon. Alexa could use a nap anyway before we go looking at houses. "Fine, I'll be there soon. But I'm not staying for more than an hour."

"Good," Mother says as she ends the call. I put my phone back in my pocket and find Alexa sitting on her balcony. I don't pay the view much attention. It's pretty, sure, but just not my thing.

"Slight change of plans. I'm going to go stop by Mother's for about an hour and then we can go look at houses and go out for a nice dinner. It will give you time to rest and get changed before we go."

Alexa looks down at her clothes and then back at me.

"Fine, but I get to drive."

"Agreed," I say, smiling widely. "As long as you go look at houses with me, I don't care how we get there."

I OPEN the large oak door that leads into Mother's home. A home I grew up in. A home I did my best to get away from since college. A large, beautiful home constructed with seven bedrooms and five bathrooms as well as a chef's kitchen and enough living and dining areas to host a hundred-person dinner party.

A home I would do anything to get back to now. Only now, after everything I've been through, do I fully appreciate what a wonderful home it was to grow up in.

"Mother," I shout as I head to the back of the house to her favorite room; her sitting room looks out over the garden behind it. I know she'll be there drinking tea and fussing about some gossip or another.

"Mother," I say again as I walk into the large room. I smile when I see her sitting in her light pink chair, tea in hand, phone in the other as she gossips away.

"Oh, Margaret, I have to go. Ethan is here," she says putting the phone down. I walk over to her and kiss her softly on the cheek.

"I'm so happy you are back home. You are back home for good, right? You told Alexandra you are staying here."

"Right to the point as usual, Mother," I say and take a seat in the chair opposite hers.

"Would you like Richard to get you some tea?"

"No. Who is Richard?"

"He's the butler I hired but never mind that. You never answered my question. Are you home for good?"

I lean back in my chair, hoping it will feel less like a police interrogation if I'm relaxed.

"I think so, Mother. I have some houses lined up for Alexa to see later tonight. One, in particular, I think she will fall in love with. The house is gorgeous, and the view is just what Alexa always wanted."

"Good, good. You need to find a large home where you can throw wonderful parties. I can't wait to show off your new home."

"Slow down, Mother, we haven't even looked at anything yet, and Alexa certainly isn't ready to buy anything."

"And children. When are you going to make me a grandmother?"

"You don't even like Alexa. Why do you want us to hurry and have grandchildren now?"

"Well, if you are going to stay married to her, she might as well be of use to you and bear your children."

"Mother," I say sternly.

"What? It's not as if she can hear me. We can speak freely here. Has she agreed to work for me? It really would be for the best. That way I can mold her into the type of woman suitable to be married to you."

"I'm working on it, Mother. The first step is to get her to move here."

She nods. "I agree; butter her up first and then lay down the law." She picks up her tea and sips calmly. I glance at my watch. I need to get back if I'm going to have time to take Alexa to see the houses tonight.

"I need to be going," I say. I go over to Mother, lean down, and kiss her softly on the cheek.

"I'll make sure to come by again early next week."

"Oh, wonderful." She pauses as a thought crosses her mind. "I almost forgot to ask. Have you found it yet?"

I don't have to ask what she means. I already know. It's been my focus anytime Alexa leaves me alone. "No, but I will. I think I know where it is." My mind goes to the locked drawer next to Alexa's bed. I thought it was weird to have a lock on a simple drawer. It has to be there.

Chapter Twenty-Two

ALEXA

I can't trust James.

I ZOOM through another yellow light loving the thrill and power that driving a fast car brings me. Ethan sits next to me with a terrified expression on his face. Much like Landon's was when he rode with me. I shake off the memory. I can't keep going back to Landon every time. I have to let him go. All I could think about when we walked through the lobby of my condo was Landon. I looked everywhere for him. I felt him there, but I found no trace of him.

I have to find something else to think about. What other questions do I have for Ethan? I rack my brain trying to think of all the questions that remain unanswered. The main one that keeps playing, though, is one Ethan can't answer for me. Do I want to live in LA or NY? Do I want to be a photographer or please Ethan and his mother? Do I want kids with Ethan? Do I want to be with Landon or Ethan? They are all part of the same question. One I don't know how to answer. Do I want to be Alex or Alexa? Instead, I ask Ethan the first thing I can think of. A question I basically already know the answer to.

"What happened to my parents?"

Ethan doesn't tear his eyes from the road as he answers. He's too focused on every move I make with the car.

"Your mother died of cancer when you were young. You used to tell me some stories about her, about how she was a painter. You never knew your father. He had left you and your mom before you were born. You lived most of your life in the foster care system."

I grip the steering wheel tighter. I already knew, but it still hurts. It doesn't make it better hearing Ethan confirm it.

"What about your father?"

"He died when I was young – four or five – from a heart attack."

"I'm sorry."

"It's okay. It happened a long time ago."

"Do you remember any of the stories I used to tell you about my mother?"

Ethan thinks for a moment before shaking his head. "Sorry. You didn't talk about her much. All I remember is that she was a painter."

I nod feeling emptier than ever. I want to hear stories of my past, but Ethan barely tells me anything when I ask.

"Do you happen to remember where you kept a key to our safety deposit box?"

I frown. "No, I don't remember anything. The only keys I found were for the apartment and my car. Why?"

"I had my copy with me when the accident happened. I lost them then. I called and they won't let us access it without the key. It's not a big deal. It mostly just contained things like our birth certificates and marriage license. Things we can replace. But it held a few valuables we can't replace. You kept some things of your mother's there. Things that could help you remember her. I'll do my best to find the key, but if you remember, tell me."

I nod as I stare blankly at the road in front of us. Trying to think of where I would keep a key that was important enough to guard precious treasures that belonged to my mother. Nothing comes to mind, though. I let the sadness overwhelm me at losing something else. Even if it is just a material possession, it still belonged to my mother.

Ethan flips on the radio as I continue to drive to the first house.

But the thrill of driving is gone. I try to remember my mother, but I can't. All I know about her is the story I told a reporter once. A story about how her painting inspired me to become a photographer. I can't give that up. No matter how much Ethan wants me to, I can't. I know that. I just have to find a way to tell him and to tell his mother without hurting them.

"This next song is by Landon Davis. It's called 'Could Be,' and we are guessing it is inspired by his new leading lady, Caroline Parker. Congrats on the proposal, Landon," the DJ on the radio says.

I freeze. My eyes dart over to Ethan, who still focuses on the road. Not on my reaction to a radio song. I could change the channel. I could turn the radio off, but that might draw more attention to me.

Landon's voice starts singing and fills my car with his beautiful melody. A song he supposedly wrote for me.

You stumbled into my life
A beautiful mess
With fighting words
Not to be messed with.

But I kept coming back
Trying my best
To break down your walls
To find a way in.

But I can't help it
When I see you
My heart skips.
I lose my breath
Trying to drink in your scent.

It
Could be the rain.
Could be the stars.
Could be the way your hair

Falls down your face.
Could be the cause of my speeding heart.
Could be I'm falling for you.

I can't wait to see you
See what more we could be.
Just give us a chance.
Give me a reason to exist.

It
Could be the raindrops pouring down your face.
Could be the stars sparkling in outer space.
Could be your emerald eyes.
Could be your stubborn cries.
Could be I've fallen for you.

Yeah I've fallen for you.
Yeah I might just love you.
Yeah I've fallen for you.

THE SONG IS BEAUTIFUL. A song meant to tell a beautiful love story. It's just not mine. Whether Landon wrote that song for me or for Caroline, it doesn't matter anymore. The song is hers now. I chose Ethan. Landon chose Caroline. I have to accept my new love story. But how can I let him go if everywhere I look I see Landon?

"Turn right here," Ethan says as he turns down the radio.

I turn and climb up a long hill with only a few houses bordering the street. We reach the top of the cliff when the most beautiful house I have ever seen comes into view. It's a large house. Much too large for just two people to live in. The windows and door on the front are massive.

I pull into the long, curved driveway that leads to a four-car garage on the side of the house. I park the car and climb out, not waiting for Ethan. I open the wrought-iron gate that leads from the driveway to the back of the house. I try to prepare myself for the view, but it doesn't help.

The view is amazing looking down at smaller cliffs below to the ocean. I sit on the grass, not bothering to look to see if there are chairs for me to sit on. All I care about is taking in this view.

"I want it," I say as Ethan stands behind me.

He laughs. "You haven't even seen the house yet. Plus we have two more to look at after this one."

The warm salty breeze blows through my hair welcoming me here. Welcoming me home.

"I don't care what the house looks like. I want this one. This view. This feeling."

Ethan smiles brightly. "Whatever you want, baby. It's yours."

"Sit down," I say, patting my hand on a patch of grass next to me.

"Come join me up on the patio. We can sit up there."

I shake my head. "I'll join you in a minute."

I knew Ethan would never dare to chance ruining his suit to sit on the grass with me, but right now, I don't care what he does. I just want to sit on the grass and watch the clouds roll by over the dark blue ocean. I watch a couple walking on the beach swinging a toddler between their hands. I smile trying to imagine Ethan and me doing that with our child one day. I can't quite imagine it yet, but maybe if we move here, I'll be able to.

This spot makes me happy. Something I haven't felt in weeks. I want this feeling forever. Nothing else matters right now. I want this ...

"I WANT THIS," I repeat to myself as I sip my glass of water and wait for Abby. Last night was great. We picked out a house. To buy. To have kids and a family in. To live happily ever after in. I'm just not sure I'm ready for all of that yet.

I lightly trace the tattoo on the inside of my left wrist. A tattoo in memory of my mother. A mother I will never remember. I let my thoughts drift off to last night as I sit at the table waiting for Abby ...

"I've already contacted a realtor to draw up the papers to put an offer in on the house. We will be homeowners by the end of the week," Ethan says.

I choke on my wine as he says the words. Everything is moving much too fast.

"Ethan, I love that house, but I'm not ready to make any decisions yet. I know I said I wanted it, but I'm just not ready."

"If we don't make an offer on the house, we could lose it, though. And even if we don't want to make LA our permanent home, we will want a house here for when we visit Mother. If not, we will have to stay with her every time we visit."

My lips press together in a slight grimace. "I guess you're right. And I do love that view ..." Although I feel like Ethan would say anything to get us to move here, away from NY. It doesn't make sense to me. If our entire lives were in NY before, then why would he want to move here? Why does he suddenly want to be close to his mother?

"I'll agree to buy the house on two conditions. The first is you answer a question truthfully."

"I will," Ethan says, smiling as if he won as he takes a sip of his wine.

"Why?"

"Why what?" Ethan asks unfazed as he takes a bite of bread.

"Why do you want us to move to LA?"

His smile grows larger. The glint in his eyes sparkling more confident than ever. "I already answered that. We need to start over. I don't feel safe in NY anymore. Everything horrible that happened to us happened in NY. It makes sense to move to LA. We can help Mother run the charity. We can start a family here. We can start a new life here."

"But why not any other place? We have plenty of money to start anew anywhere. We could start our own charity if that's what we decide we want. Why LA?"

Ethan narrows his eyes at me trying to read through the question to understand what I really want from him. I gaze back unflinching, hiding any meaning behind my question with it.

"I want to be near Mother ..."

"Bullshit."

Ethan's eyes stay transfixed on mine. His cheeks redden as he lets out a long, slow sigh. "Fine. I want you to be near Mother. I think she is good for you. I think she can help you remember the woman you once were."

The words sting although I don't think they were meant to. I don't think Laura is good for me. In fact, I know she will inevitably bring out the worst in me if I spend too much time with her. The only reason I've let her boss me around as much as I have is because of Ethan. I felt guilty for not loving his mother when I thought he was dead. She was my only connection to the man I lost and didn't remember. If I was anything like Laura before the accident, I don't want to go back to the woman I was before.

"What is your second condition?" Ethan asks.

"That I will continue to do photography instead of helping your mother run the non-profit ..."

The rest of the night did not go well. Ethan argued with me incessantly about how being with his mother day in and out is what was best for me. I disagreed. I think doing the one thing I love, the one thing I truly remember how to do, is what's best for me. It's the only thing that connects me to my own mother. It's the only thing that feels right in my life.

"Alexa!" Abby squeals running to engulf me in a hug.

"Hey, Abby," I say squeezing her back. "I'm so glad to see you."

"How have you been? I heard everything that happened with that husband of yours. Wild!"

"Yeah, it's been a wild ride for sure."

"You are so lucky! You got two hot, sexy guys while I can't even snag one."

"Yeah, I'm really lucky," I say even though I feel like the most unlucky woman on the planet.

"You have to tell me all the details!" Abby leans forward on the table ready to soak in every little detail about these past few weeks.

"I will, but first, I was just hoping you had a photography job for me. It looks like Ethan and I will be here for a while and I could really use the distraction."

"Absolutely!"

"Good," I say, smiling. I need just one day when I can feel normal.

Chapter Twenty-Three

LANDON

Please come back to me, love.
But most importantly
Please find your own love.

"MORNING, sleepyhead. Wake up. Today's our wedding day," Alex whispers into my ear.

I grin. "I'm not supposed to see you before the wedding. It's bad luck."

"I already got you covered. Open your eyes," Alex says seductively into my ear as she bites on the lobe.

I open and see nothing but dark fabric covering my eyes.

"Good thinking," I say.

Her lips cover mine and her tongue licks over my lips begging for entrance. I oblige and deepen the kiss tasting spearmint on her tongue. Delicious.

"No one said anything about sex before the wedding being bad luck, though," Alex says as she grabs my hard cock in her hand.

I groan. "I guess not." She strokes my cock harder making my desire for her unbearable. I reach out to grab her but come up empty.

"Uh-uh," she says. "No touching. I'm in control today."

I growl. "I need you. Now."

I can feel her smile, though I can't prove it because of the blindfold covering my eyes.

"Patience."

I feel her warm breath as it moves over my body, but her lips don't make contact anywhere. Instead, they are teasing me. Taunting me with where she is going to touch me next. I do what she asks and don't touch her despite my hands being free to do so. If she keeps this up much longer, though, I won't be able to hold my hands back from attacking her soft, smooth skin.

Her lips suddenly wrap themselves around my hard length.

"Fuck, Alex," I groan as she bares her teeth into my flesh. Her lips are amazing wrapped around me. She knows just how to move to bring me the highest level of pleasure. To push me over the brink. But I don't want to come in her mouth, as easy as it would be. Not today. Not on our wedding day. I want to feel as connected to her as possible.

I find her body with my hands and rip her from my cock. The loss of her touch immediately makes me empty, but the pleasure that is soon to come will fill the void. I flip her onto her back and thrust inside her. As soon as my cock touches her entrance, I feel at home.

"Oh, Alex. You feel amazing, my soon-to-be wife."

I thrust again as she claws on my chest trying to get me closer to her. I rub her clit starting in a slow circle and quickly picking up the pace as I thrust faster inside her. This is going to be fast, much faster than I want. But tonight, we will have all the time in the world to make love over and over.

"Landon ... I'm going to ..." Alexa screams. I can't stand it. Fuck tradition. Fuck not seeing my wife on our wedding day. I take the blindfold off. Instead of Alex lying on the bed, it's Caroline.

Fuck! I sit up in bed before realizing it was a dream. Just a dream. I'm sweating and panting hard as I try to get the image out of my head. I climb out of bed and throw open the window to look out at the beautiful Hawaiian beach that the hotel sits on. That's when I remember that it wasn't just a dream. Today, I'm getting married ... to Caroline.

I don't get to dream of Alex any more after today. I don't get to dream of what we could be. Fuck, why did I write songs about her? Every time I sing them, I will think of her. The songs will make me desperate for her until it drives me mad. This is my life now. A life of madness.

I'M DRESSED in a full tux. The only thing missing is my jacket that is slung over the hotel chair. It's still an hour until the wedding starts. An hour until the end of my life. An hour until everything changes. An hour is all I have left of me.

I don't know why the fuck Caroline wanted me here an hour early. It's not like I can do anything but wait. Wait for my life to end. I watch Drew, my only groomsman, talk on his phone in his own tux.

"Goddammit, Drew, get off your phone," I say throwing a pillow from the hotel room at him. He flips me off before walking into the hallway to finish his call. Leaving me to continue sulking on my own. Alcohol. I wish I had alcohol; that might make this easier. But I won't. I can't. Alcohol would make everything worse.

I peek out the window to look down at the beach where we will have the wedding ceremony. We are waiting until the perfect time of day to get married. Sunset, as per Caroline's wishes. How she threw this grand of a wedding together in such a short amount of time is beyond me. Chairs line the beach and a beautiful arch of flowers sits near the ocean where a beautiful sunset behind us will give the media we invited the perfect shots of our wedding to plaster all over their magazine covers. For a small fee, of course.

I don't know why so many chairs line the beach. Neither of us has any family left. Except Drew and Caroline's brother. And her brother won't come anywhere near me, not that I blame him. And neither of us has many friends. The chairs, I assume, are for media and celebrities she invited who want to say they were at the famous Landon Davis and Caroline Parker wedding. Sure to be the wedding of the year.

"Stop sulking," Drew says as he lets the door fall behind him. He throws the pillow back in my face. "You chose this. You have no one to blame but yourself for making everyone miserable."

"Who am I making miserable other than myself?"

Drew shakes his head. "No one."

"You are supposed to be giving me brotherly advice as my best man, not talking business on your phone."

"I wouldn't have to talk on that fucking phone all the time if you wouldn't do everything so last minute. Do you know how many people I have to call to make sure this wedding goes off without a hitch?"

"Isn't that Caroline's job?"

Drew sighs as he collapses into a nearby chair. He looks worse than I do today. He has dark circles under his eyes and his usually perfect hair is a little out of place. He looks like he's aged ten years overnight. I don't know what the hell is wrong with him.

"No," is all he says.

"So you have a new girl you're seeing?" I ask as I flip through my phone, trying not to make him feel pressured.

"Why do you say that?"

"You look like you haven't slept in weeks. It's either you've been fucking a girl all night or your heart is broken because of a girl. Which is it?"

"Neither. Just trying to get this fucking wedding organized."

"Uh-huh, I'm going with fucking a girl all night long. You haven't had time to fall for a girl. I expect to be introduced to this broad at the wedding."

"There is no girl," Drew says his cheeks flushed a bright shade of red.

Sure, there's not.

"IT'S TIME. LET'S GO," Drew says. I walk down the sandy aisle toward the arch at the end of the beach. I hope Caroline didn't wear heels because there is no way she will be able to walk on this sand in them. Drew stays back. He's walking Caroline down the aisle since she has no other family to do it.

As I walk, I smile, doing my best to seem happy. Flashes from the cameras blind me as I walk toward the arch, where a minister is already standing. I've never even met the man who is marrying us. I reach the end and turn to face the aisle. Flashes continue to blind me. I think Caroline hired enough photographers.

A woman stands from the front row of chairs and begins singing a beautiful song as Caroline's bridesmaid walks down the aisle. I smile at the petite woman who looks similar to Caroline except with brown hair. This woman is probably who kept Drew up last night. If not, then maybe she should be the woman who keeps him up, judging from her tight body.

The woman finishes her song and motions for the crowd to stand as the traditional bridal march begins. I look around but don't even know where the music is coming from. The crowd gasps as they get their first view of Caroline walking down the aisle.

I catch my own view of her a second later and gasp as well. She's beautiful. More natural than I expected her to look. Her dress is beautiful and hugs all of her curves. It's more simple than I thought it would be. Her smile is large and bright. She's glowing as she walks. I catch a glimpse of her bare toes poking out from underneath her dress. She's walking barefoot down the beach.

"When I get married, I want something simple where I can walk barefoot on the beach ..."

The memory from when we were kids, probably not any older than ten years old, sinks into my thoughts. My smile turns from fake to real in an instant. She got her wish. Caroline. I think about Caroline for the first time. This whole time I've focused on what's best for Alex and how horrible my life is going to be after today, but I never thought of Caroline. I just thought she should be happy to get the money and fame she's always wanted. But she's always wanted more. She deserves more. She deserves to be happy.

I can give her that. I can give her happiness. I may never be able to give her true love, but I can give her happiness.

I continue smiling brightly as she walks down the aisle until I see Drew. A scowl covers his face as he walks stoically next to her. 'Smile,' I mouth to him through clenched teeth. He ignores me.

I ignore him and lock eyes with Caroline instead. I do my best to tell her how I feel. That we can be happy together. She deserves it. Her smile gets brighter as she reaches me.

I take her hand from Drew as he takes his place beside me. She hands her bouquet to her bridesmaid before she grabs hold of my other hand so that we are holding each other with both hands.

"You look beautiful," I say meaning every word.

"Thank you. You look very handsome as well."

"We're going to be happy together," I say, not able to hold back from actually saying the words making them feel truer than ever.

"I know."

We both turn our attention to the minister who begins the typical speech made before the wedding.

"Landon," I hear Drew hiss in my ear behind me.

"Shh," I say between clenched teeth trying to keep a smile on my face. Why the hell is Drew trying to talk to me during my wedding?

"Landon, it's Alex," Drew says again.

"Shh," I say again.

"Alex is in the hospital. It's all over the news. She ..." Drew pauses not able to get the next words out. "She might not make it ..."

Chapter Twenty-Four

ETHAN

When the song ends, she mouths the word 'bathroom' to me. I nod and watch as she heads to the bathroom at the back of the large establishment. My eyes never leave her body as she walks into the bathroom.

"I'LL JUST GET the papers ready for you and Mrs. Wolfe to sign," Heather Doyle, my realtor says.

I nod my head at her as she leaves me alone upstairs in the large mansion we are about to buy. Alexa basically gave me her blessing to go ahead and buy the house the last time we talked, but she had conditions. Conditions I don't plan to honor. She doesn't remember our life before, and she doesn't know what is at stake now. We aren't as safe as she thinks we are. The only way I can protect her is if she stays here.

I open the door to one of the spare bedrooms. The door creaks slightly as I open it. We will have to have that fixed before we move into the house. The bedroom is painted a calming pale blue. I walk over to the white crib against one wall and glance inside to see blankets covered in blue clouds. A stuffed baby elephant sits in the corner. I bend over the crib to pick up the soft toy and stare at it intently. This is what I want. A baby. Something I can pass on my legacy to. Something that will tie Alexa to me forever. Something that will redeem me for all of the damage that I have done.

My back stiffens in pain from bending over the crib. I reach into my pocket and pull out the bottle of pain medication I was prescribed at the hospital. I haven't had to use much, but today is different. I open the bottle and throw back two pills before swallowing without water.

I place the stuffed elephant toy back into the crib, cringing slightly at the pain as I do before I glance around the room. Toys are scattered along the floor in an unorganized mess. Diapers are stacked high on top of a dresser. Dirty clothes are falling out of a clothes basket in the corner. The whole room looks like one big disaster.

We will definitely need to hire a nanny and a maid to keep this room from looking like this when we have a kid. I couldn't live in a house this disastrous. Especially when we fill up the five other bedrooms with kids. There is no way this level of disorganization would be tolerated.

But this is what I want. A family. A real life. A redeeming baby.

I glance down at my watch. Time to go check on Alexa. I move down the stairs quickly two at a time. I head out the large entryway and out the large door to find James sitting in the SUV he brought me here in. I climb in and wait for James to drive me back to Alexa's condo where she is back from meeting Abby.

I don't like that she had a meeting with someone from a magazine. That means she wants to get back into that world, and I can't let that happen.

My mind immediately drifts to the key that I have yet to find. I looked in the drawer she had locked, but it wasn't there. I'm out of ideas of where she could have kept it before the accident.

"I have to find it, James."

"You will," James says glancing into the rearview mirror to meet my gaze.

"No, I have to find it. My life depends on it."

"What's so important about this key?"

I drop my gaze from James' stare.

"Everything. It's everything. Without it ..." I can never be safe. I can never have a family. I can never have redemption. "I just need it."

James nods. He knows me too well to ask more.

"She hasn't said anything to you?" I prod again.

"No, she hasn't said anything about a hidden key." James laughs. "I think you have really lost it, man."

I glare at James. "Has she remembered anything?"

"No, she hasn't. It's unfortunate. I really thought she would remember me. We used to be buddies." I notice a frown forming on James' lips, but I don't have time to deal with James' sulking. I ignore his comments. I just hope he's smart enough to tell me if she starts remembering anything around him. Even the smallest detail of her past. I need to know.

I glance back down at my watch as James pulls up in front of Alexa's condo. It's three o'clock on the dot. The exact time we agreed to meet in the lobby so we could go together to get the house of our dreams. I stare into the lobby, though, as I wait in the car. I don't see her. I dial her number on her phone. I wait as it rings two, three, four times before going to voice mail.

I sigh before opening my door to climb out of the SUV.

"I'll be right back," I say to James, who just nods and pulls his phone out of his pocket. I shake my head as I slam the door shut and begin walking into the building. He really is terrible at security. If he weren't my friend, I would have already fired him.

The elevator ride up is quick. I walk to her door and knock. I wait, but I don't hear a sound inside her condo. I try the doorknob, and it opens easily. I push inside and that's when I see her. Lying on the floor. Covered in blood.

Chapter Twenty-Five

ALEXA

I can't trust Laura.

PAIN IS ALL I FEEL. I try to open my eyes, but the pain prevents me. I try to speak, or move, or breathe, but the pain compounding in my head is too much. It's unbearable. What the hell happened to me? Why is everything so painful? Why can't I open my eyes?

Everything comes back slowly.

I remember having lunch with Abby ...

I remember driving home ...

I remember opening my door to my condo ...

I step into my condo ready to go take a warm shower before facing Ethan to tell him I took another photography job. I close the door before I realize something is off. It feels cold in my condo. Like all the warmth has been sucked from the room. I rub my hands up and down my arms trying to warm my body as I step into the kitchen to grab a glass of water before I go shower. I freeze. Cups and plates are shattered all over the floor. I let my eyes trail up the cabinets. Most of the drawers are half-open, their contents all mixed. My eyes drift up to the countertops and find a couple of pieces of white jagged ceramic scattered along the top. I glance higher to the open cabinets that are now empty.

I tiptoe over the broken glass and ceramic covering the floor. I grab a piece of broken glass off the counter and hold it high in my hand ready to attack if need be. I walk slowly and as quietly as I can into the living room as another chill runs up my body. I don't pause to warm my body up this time, though.

I check the living room for any signs of life but find none. The stuffing has been ripped out of the couch. The pile of DVDs is scattered all over the floor.

I creep slowly to my bedroom door that's closed. I never close the door. My heart beats wild in my chest, my palm sweaty as I grip my weapon of broken glass so hard I feel a trickle of blood running down my shaking hand.

Whoever did this, whoever tore my condo apart looking for something, is behind that door. I can feel his cold heart beating steadily behind the thin door. I don't know what I should do. Should I call 911? Should I run? Should I burst through the door and attack? I don't have time to think.

I turn to run out of my condo as fast as my legs will take me. I don't think about the steps or being careful not to disturb the broken glass. I don't know where I'll run. I just know I have to get past the front door. I just run.

I'm not far from the door now. Maybe five feet. I'm going to make it.

"Don't move," a deep voice says.

I stop in my tracks only three large steps from the door. Three steps from freedom. A freedom that will never come. I feel something hard pressed into my back. I assume it's a gun, but I'm not sure. I feel my body trembling slightly. I'm going to die.

I've survived an entire lifetime of pain. A lifetime of one disaster after another. My dad leaving at a young age. Mother dying not long after. I survived foster care. I survived living on the streets. I survived rape. I survived a targeted car accident. I survived my own death. I'm not going to die now. Not here.

"What do you want?" I ask my voice shaky. The man doesn't respond, though.

"I have money. Lots of money," I say a little calmer. Money is the key to everything. To my survival.

"Shut your mouth, bitch, or I'll shoot you," the man says.

He grabs my arm and pulls me back. I cry out from the pain of his nails in my arm before I realize that I've made a sound.

Pain shoots across my jaw from a hit with something hard. Like the butt of a gun. I open my mouth to cry out again, but instead, only a small whimper escapes. I'm afraid to do more and end up in more pain. Or worse ... dead.

He continues to jerk me back toward the bedroom. Away from the door. Away from freedom. Landon and Ethan both flash across my mind. At least, now, I won't have to choose. I'll just be gone.

I stumble backward as he pulls me through the kitchen. I grab onto the counter to keep from tumbling to the floor when I feel the hard glass jab farther into my hand. My weapon is still in my hand. At least, I'm not going to go out without a fight.

I feel my blood pulsing fast through my veins, and I use that as fuel. In one motion, I use all the strength I have as I whip my body around toward him thrusting the piece of glass deep into his back.

I try running. I try one more chance at freedom as my weapon is now stuck in his back, but his grip tightens on my arm.

"You bitch," he says. I try to hit him, to do anything to get him to let me go, but instead, my hand freezes mid-air as I catch a glimpse of dark black eyes peering through his black mask covering his face. The same black eyes that raped me. The same black eyes from the car attack. They are the same black eyes as the ones I'm peering at now. How ... how is that possible? My rapist is in jail. The men who attacked Ethan and me are in jail. Yet the same eyes are staring at me.

It's the last thing I see as I'm hit hard in the head again. This time hard enough that I pass out.

Black eyes. Dark black eyes. I will find you. And I will kill you. I will not let you hurt me again. I will not let anything worse happen. I can't. I won't.

I'll survive this. I always do. First, I need sleep. Much more sleep. Then I'll come after you.

Chapter Twenty-Six

LANDON

I watch you as you lay in the bed.
I watch you gasping
Barely breathing
And I have trouble
Catching my own breath.

I'm a horrible fucking person. Worse than horrible. Caroline's face, when I left, was an image I will never get out of my head. I know because I saw the same image after I destroyed Caroline's life months earlier. Her cheeks burned red, her nostrils flared wide, but her eyes are what will haunt me forever. Eyes wide showing the whites along with her hatred for me.

I couldn't stay, though. I had to go to Alex. To make sure she survives. Even as I sit here on the plane for the next five hours, I have no idea if I'll make it. I have no idea if she'll survive, but I have to go. I have to be there for her. I don't have a choice. My heart beats for her. Her strength at surviving everything she has been through amazes me. I don't know how it's possible to survive everything she has. I'm drawn to her like no person I ever have been before. I don't want to live without her. I don't want to live without her strength by my side, without her need for a sweet mixture of pleasure and pain. She alone understands that life without pain isn't a life worth living. You can only find the pleasure in the pain.

But I'm giving up a lot to be with Alex. I'm giving up a friendship with Caroline that I've had since I was five years old. I'm giving up more money to Caroline than I ever thought possible. I'm giving up my right to destroy the videos that contain my darkest secret. I'm accepting almost certain retaliation from Caroline. I'm accepting untold media criticism. I'm accepting possibly going to jail for the rest of my life.

And I'm doing it all for what? To get a chance to say good-bye to Alex. For a chance to see Alex healthy, only for her to turn me away for another man. I'm giving up everything I have worked my entire life for a future with Alex that may never happen. I have to do this, though. I have to try. I know now it was wrong to accept my fate with Caroline. I should never just accept my own fate. I never have before. If I did, I should be broke, living as a drunk on the streets. Not a millionaire living my dream as a musician. I don't accept that fate brought this amazing woman in my life only to tear her away in a second by another man. I don't accept it.

I pull out my phone trying to find any distraction to get me through these next five hours on this flight. My hands shake as I fumble with the device. I scroll through my books, my music, games, anything that could distract me, but nothing holds my attention for more than a few seconds.

I feel like pacing up and down the small aisle in the center of the plane, but the fasten seat belt sign is lit. And if I did, everyone on the plane would think I was some sort of psycho. I have an uneasy feeling in my stomach. A feeling that no food, drink, or drugs can calm. Only seeing her alive will bring me any comfort.

I glance back at the time on my phone. Two minutes have passed since the last time I looked at my phone, leaving four hours and fifty-eight minutes until we land. Plus another twenty minutes until we pull up to a gate and I can run through the airport to catch a taxi. Plus at least an hour drive to the hospital. Then I have to convince a nurse to let me see her. So I estimate close to seven hours before I'll see her. Seven hours until I'll know if she'll live or die.

That's too long to sit here and do nothing. I have to do something, anything to help her. I've never been a religious person. I've seen too much shit happen to good people in my life to believe that a god is out there watching over me. But it's the only way I know how to help her. The only way I can protect her. So I bow my head, fold my hands in my lap, close my eyes, and pray. I pray so fucking hard that she will live.

Chapter Twenty-Seven

ETHAN

That night was the last time I expected to see her. It was a short, simple night. It should have been the last night I saw her. I should have never gone after her after that night.

THE PARAMEDICS TAKE FOREVER to get here. Longer than the five minutes the operator promised. In that time, Alexa's breath has grown slow and uneven. Her pulse so weak I can barely feel it at all.

The operator told me not to administer CPR if she still had a pulse and if she was still breathing on her own, so I don't administer CPR. I can do nothing to help her. She has to keep breathing on her own. Blood is oozing from her body although I can't tell from where exactly. I'm told not to move her, to apply pressure to any wounds I see, and to wait for the paramedics. Except all of her wounds must be on her back.

I cover my face with my hands trying to make this all go away. When I remove my hands, Alexa is going to be fine. She just tripped and fell. She's going to get back up and everything will go back to how it was before, but when I remove my hands from my face, Alexa is still lying on the floor unconscious with blood oozing out all around her.

Tears begin staining my face. I never wanted this. I never wanted Alexa to have to deal with so much pain. I grab her hand and hold it tight. Squeezing it so hard I'm afraid I'll leave a bruise. I scream as more tears burst out of me. This shouldn't have happened. I should have protected her. Instead, I left her to a monster.

I hear a loud pounding on the door and I stand up and rush to open the door.

"She's in the kitchen on the floor," I shout at them even though they are standing less than a foot away from me.

Three paramedics rush past me to Alexa's side as they begin to work on her. One begins asking me questions as I stare at the paramedics hooking up all sorts of equipment to Alexa's body.

"What happened?"

"I ... I don't know. I came back home and found her like this. I think someone broke into the condo."

I watch the man write something down.

"What's her name?"

"Alexa Wolfe," I say staring wide-eyed as a woman stabs her arm with another needle.

"Age?"

"Twenty-eight."

"Is she allergic to anything?"

"I don't know."

"What's your relation to her?"

"I'm her husband."

I watch as the paramedics place her on a stretcher and begin carrying her out of her condo. They move quickly and efficiently. Not quite running but managing to move much faster than a walk. They are pumping oxygen into her lungs as they move her. Keeping her alive when I couldn't.

I walk quickly after them. I watch her chest rise and fall with each step we take. As long as her chest is still moving, she is still breathing. She's still alive for another second with each step. I hold out hope that she will make it. She has to. She's my only chance at redemption.

They push her into an ambulance. I climb in after them, not

waiting for them to invite me along. I have to keep watching her. I have to make sure her chest keeps rising and falling.

We live close to a hospital. Maybe ten minutes away. Just make it until then. If she does, she'll survive. I know it. Just keep breathing until then.

I hear a loud beeping sound from one of the machines.

"She's coding," one of the paramedics says calmly like this happens all the time. It probably does in her world but not mine. This never happens in my world.

I want to scream or cry. But I don't. I can't. Instead, I go speechless. My mind goes blank. I watch the paramedics move paddles over her chest just like they do in the movies. I watch them shock her heart. I watch them fail.

I open my mouth to scream for them to help her, but nothing comes out. They recharge the machine, prepping it to shock her again. It takes precious seconds to recharge. Seconds that they could be using to get her heart beating again. I watch them shock her heart again. This time, it seems to work. I watch her chest rising and falling weakly. The beeping goes away. She's still alive. For now.

The ambulance pulls up to an entrance of the hospital. The doors fly open. I'm pushed out of the ambulance. The paramedics push Alexa out of the ambulance on the gurney to the waiting nurses and doctors. They rush her inside. I follow.

I follow until a nurse tells me to stop.

"I'm her husband. I have to go with her," I say trying to get past her.

"You can't. Someone will come get you as soon as there is an update on her condition. Right now, you need to fill out insurance information. You need to talk to the police about what happened. You need to call her family to let them know what's happening."

I nod reluctantly. My gaze frozen on the doors Alexa was just pushed through.

"Come on. I'll show you to the waiting room and get you something to drink so you don't go into shock."

I nod again and follow the woman down the hallway away from the door. Away from Alexa. Away from my life.

Chapter Twenty-Eight

ALEXA

I can only trust myself.

I OPEN MY EYES. Ethan's dark brown eyes staring down at me immediately replace the dark black eyes that have been haunting my dreams.

"Alexa, honey, you're awake," Ethan says through tears falling from his cheeks.

I blink my dry eyes several times staring at him. I feel beat up from head to toe. I don't feel like moving or speaking.

"Alexa, can you understand me?" Ethan asks the tears still falling as he grips my hand hard with one hand. His other hand reaches up to tuck my hair behind my ears. The movement feels warms and comforting.

"Yes," I croak. My throat is dry and red. I remember the feeling from the last time I woke up from a coma. I immediately begin checking limbs. Two arms and my one leg remain. I gently move each arm and my leg until I'm assured no permanent damage has been done. I sigh when I realize they are all working properly. Ethan holds a glass of water to my lips, and I drink the water slowly through the straw as the burning feeling in my throat melts away.

"What happened?" I ask, although I already know. I just don't know who.

"You were attacked when you walked in on someone trying to rob you. At least, that's what the police think happened based on the evidence so far." Ethan sits back in his chair. His grip grows tighter on my hand and his face grows darker. "I think *they* did this to you. King's men. I think he wanted us dead so no one can speak against him at his trial."

I nod as my hands begin shaking as the fear threatens to consume me. He can still get to us from prison. We aren't safe. We were never safe. We will never be safe. The fear threatens to take hold of my entire body, but I don't let the fear come back in. Instead, I shut it out with the rage that has been boiling inside me. I want them to pay for this. I want them to hurt for this. I don't tell Ethan. He doesn't need to know. He will think it's too dangerous, but I have to put an end to this. The police won't be able to help us.

"How long have I been out for?"

"Just a few hours. The doctors were afraid of brain damage, but they seemed to think it could also just be a concussion. I should go get the doctor to examine you."

I nod and watch as Ethan leaves bringing in a nurse followed shortly by a doctor. I resign myself to spending the rest of the day going through a million tests to ensure I'm okay just like last time, but I already know I am. I feel more determined than I ever have before. I'm tired of living for Ethan, or Laura, or Landon, or anyone other than me. I'm tired of not putting myself first. I'm tired of not going after what I want. And what I want is to destroy the men who have attacked me over and over. I want to find a way to make a difference in the world with photography, not just snap photos of pretty models and famous people. I don't want to stop working and just have babies with Ethan. I want to be able to choose if I want Ethan or Landon or any other guy on the planet. I don't want to feel obliged to stay with Ethan just because I married him before I lost my memory. First, though, I want revenge.

"Thank God, you're all right," James says running over engulfing me in his arms. I see Ethan stiffen in his chair behind James. His eyes glaring menacingly at James in a way I don't understand. A hug is innocent enough.

"How are you feeling? Are you going to be okay?" James asks sitting on the edge of my bed with concern etched in his forehead.

"I feel okay. Just a little beaten and bruised, but all the tests so far indicate that I will make a full recovery."

"Alexa I'm ... I'm so sorry."

"For what?" My forehead scrunches in confusion at what James could be sorry for.

"I should have protected you. It's my job to protect you, and I failed. I'm so sorry. How can you ever forgive me?" I stare in disbelief as tears sting his eyes.

"This is not your fault," I say sternly, placing my hand on his, trying my best to reassure him. "We thought the danger was gone. They were in jail. We all let down our guard. It's nobody's fault."

"Maybe, but I should have been protecting you. I won't stop protecting you. I won't let my guard down again."

I smile, but inside, I'm dying. How am I supposed to go after the people who did this to me if James is always here? I will have to shake Ethan and James to hunt these people down. There is no way either of them will let me out of their sights now.

"Thank you," I say instead.

I hear a knock on the door before a petite nurse pokes her head in. "The police would like to speak with you. Are you up for it?"

"Of course," I say smiling back at the young woman. Although I've had enough of the police, since they haven't done anything to help and protect me.

Two gentlemen walk in. "Sorry to disturb you, ma'am, but we would like to speak with you about the robbery and attack."

"I understand."

"I'm Officer Nash and this is Officer Stiles." He walks over to Ethan. "And you are?"

"Ethan Wolfe, her husband."

James stands up and extends his hand to the officer. "I'm James Proc. I'm their friend and I run security for them. I'll wait outside but would be happy to answer any questions or help in the investigation in any way that I can."

"Wait, you're James Proc?"

"Yes sir," James says.

"James Proc, you are under arrest for the robbery and attempted murder of Alexa Wolfe. You may ..." The police officer begins cuffing James, who just stands there wide-eyed.

"Wait! James didn't try to kill me!" I scream sitting up in my hospital bed.

"Ma'am, please calm down. We will take your statement in a minute. We have probable cause that James was the person who attacked you," says the second police officer whose name escapes me while the other one begins escorting James out of my room.

"Wait! You have the wrong guy! It wasn't him!" I scream again. I begin climbing out of bed despite the pain, only stopping when my IV tugs me back into bed. I rip out the thin tube and move to the edge of the bed to put my feet on the floor when I realize I don't have my prosthetic leg on. I can't chase after him.

"Ethan, stop them!"

Ethan has jumped up from his chair but is coming toward me, not James.

"Let them take him. You need to get back into bed."

"But he didn't do it!" I scream, tears now falling down my face choking me.

"Baby, calm down. Get back into bed."

I watch the police officers take James out of the room. "We will be back later to question you," one of them says before leaving.

"No!" I scream again hysterically as Ethan holds my body in bed.

"Alexa, stop it," Ethan says forcing me back into bed.

"But they have the wrong man," I sob.

"No, they don't." Ethan lets go of my arms. A somber expression on his face.

"What do you mean they don't?"

"The police officers in NY told me they thought a member of my staff had leaked information to Alfie King. That's why I got rid of our security and wanted us to move out here. I thought if we started fresh, we would be safe. The only person I trusted was James. But I ... I saw the surveillance tape in the hallway following the attack. It was James."

My mouth drops as my world stops. James tried to kill me. Twice. He was my friend, and he did this to me. But it doesn't make sense.

"I don't believe you. The man who attacked me had dark black eyes. James' eyes are light brown, not black. I would have recognized if James attacked me. He had on a mask, but I would have recognized his voice. It wasn't him."

"Oh, sweetie." Ethan brushes his hand on my cheek trying to calm me. "You were under a lot of stress. That makes it hard to remember anything. Trust me. I have a hard time figuring out what really happened to me and what didn't. But I saw it with my own eyes. James did this to you. The evidence will support it; you need to accept that James was never our friend. He was working for King the whole time. The good thing is now we are finally safe."

I nod, trying to accept it, but I don't. I don't accept anything. He's said we were safe before. He's lied to me. We weren't safe then, and we aren't safe now. I try to think back to all the dreams I've had lately. They all had black eyes. The man who raped me, the man who targeted us in the car accident, and then kidnapped Ethan, and the man who attacked me all had the same dark, menacing eyes. Eyes I would recognize anywhere. The same man was behind all of the attacks. He's tried to kill me three times now. Three times. Now, I just need to figure out who he is and why he wants me dead. I need to go back to New York. I need to put my past together. That's the only way I'll be able to find out who is behind all of this.

Chapter Twenty-Nine

LANDON

Please just keep breathing.
Please keep your heart beating.
Please don't let me lose my love.
Please don't lose, love.
Most importantly
Please don't die, love.

I JUMP out of the cab and run into the hospital covering my face with the hood of my sweatshirt and large sunglasses. I know she's here. A huge group of paparazzi waits outside the hospital, and it's the closest one to her condo. She has to be here. I run into the lobby of the hospital, but now, I have no idea where to go or how I'm going to get to her.

I slow down as I walk through the lobby trying not to draw any attention to myself. I see a sign labeling the use of each floor in the hospital. I scan the list: cardiology, radiology, labor and delivery, pediatrics, surgery, emergency, and intensive care.

I don't know if I should head toward surgery, emergency, or intensive care. The only information I have is what I've read in the tabloid magazines that have already declared her dead despite no official statement from her husband. She's not dead. She can't be. I would feel it if she were gone. She's not gone.

Intensive care, tenth floor, is what I choose as I step into the elevator. If she isn't there already, she will end up there.

The doors open on the tenth floor, and I step out as I contemplate my next move. I don't know if she will be allowed visitors or not. Especially non-family visitors. I try to walk past the nurse's station, acting like I've been up to this floor hundreds of time. Unfortunately, the experienced nurse sees through me.

"Sir, you need to check in. You must wear a name tag on this floor before you can visit."

I reluctantly follow her back to the nurse's station.

"Your name and name of the patient you are visiting?" the woman says. I glance at her own nametag that reads Pamela, RN.

"Pamela. I really don't want to cause a commotion. I'm just here to visit my cousin, Alexa Wolfe. I was told they moved her to this floor." I lower my sunglasses. "My name is ..."

"Landon Davis," Pamela says her hands covering her mouth in exacerbation. I grin smugly. Thank God, she is a fan. This is going to be easy.

She gives me a nametag, which I write Drew Davis on. I'm told that Alexa is in room 1025. That she is allowed visitors. Thank fucking God she is alive. I just need to see with my own eyes that she is all right.

I reach the door. 1025. I don't know what she is going to do when she sees me. Kick me out, most likely. I don't know what I'll do if that husband of hers is here. Kick his ass, most likely, and then get thrown out of the hospital. I don't know what I'm doing here. I can't do anything that will change our fates. I just need to see her alive.

I knock softly on the door before pushing it open. Before I lose my nerve and back out.

"Wow, that was fast," Alex says flicking the TV off before looking up at me. Her eyes grow wide at the sight of me.

"You're alive," I say as relief fills me.

"Yes, why do people keep saying that? Like it's a surprise or something."

"Not a surprise." I walk closer to her. I watch her hand that could press the call button at any minute to kick me out. "It's never a surprise that you can survive the unsurvivable. You're amazingly strong like that, but it's still comforting to see with my own eyes."

A door slams down the hall, but Alex jumps slightly, her eyes going to the door of her hospital room instead of locked on mine like I want. She slowly turns her attention back to me.

"Why are you here, Landon? Aren't you supposed to be sweeping Caroline off her feet in front of the cameras somewhere?"

The rib stings. I don't want to think about Caroline, but she needs to know the truth. I'm tired of doing the right thing. I'm tired of living a life that I didn't choose.

"I'm supposed to be on my honeymoon right now."

Alex sucks in a breath as her gaze drifts down to my left hand, searching for a ring that isn't there. She bites her lip, trying to pretend I don't affect her. Like the thought of me marrying another doesn't destroy her, but she doesn't hide it well. It's destroying her.

"Then why aren't you?"

I move closer and sit on the edge of her bed. I do my best to inspect every inch of her body, to find out what damage was done. But she seems as strong as ever. Her strength makes her more beautiful than ever, despite the hospital gown trying to disguise her amazing figure. I grow hard just thinking about her naked body beneath the gown. It's been too long since I felt her beneath me as I drive deep inside her. Too long since I last tasted her feisty lips.

I try to clear the image from my head. I didn't come back here to fuck her.

"Because it would be weird to go on a honeymoon when I didn't attend my own wedding."

She blinks back tears as I tell her I didn't marry Caroline.

"Because I had to be here for you even if you didn't want me here."

Alex swallows hard but doesn't speak. I know her tears are coming. I move closer to her body needing to be as close to her as possible if this is the only chance I will ever get.

"Because I don't love Caroline."

A tiny droplet begins moving down her rosy cheeks.

"Because I never fucked Caroline when I was with you."

A second droplet follows the first. I reach my hand out, brush the tear away, and close my eyes when she gently nuzzles my hand with her face. She takes a deep breath, breathing in my scent as she does. I open my eyes to find hers before I speak again.

"Because I still love you, Alex. I always have and always will."

She moistens her lips, almost as if she is anticipating a move that I will probably regret, but I can't stop from happening. My lips crash into her. Her lips don't fight me as I expect. Instead, they welcome me, as if they've missed me just as much as I've missed them. Nothing else feels this good. Nothing. I could kiss this woman forever. I need to kiss this woman forever. My tears finally fall when I realize she is really alive. It takes kissing her soft lips, connecting our souls through our lips, for me to finally believe with all of my heart that she is going to be okay. Whatever happens, I don't care because my prayers were answered. She's alive.

Alex kisses me harder as our tongues dance with each other. In perfect synchrony, we claim each other. We beg and plead for the other to be ours. Until we both surrender, accepting to be owned by the other. She pulls my lip into her mouth, biting down until a drop of blood oozes from my wound. She laps up the blood with her tongue, fully claiming me as hers. I willingly give all of myself to her.

I let all thoughts of everything else drift away from my mind. I let go of Caroline, Drew, Ethan, the press, music, everything. I lose myself in this kiss that will last forever if it's up to me. A kiss that says so much. I'm sorry. I love you. I need you. You're mine. A kiss that tempts fate to take away everything in a moment.

A temptation that I realize fate has accepted as a challenge, as I feel my body flying off Alex and into a chair. It should hurt being thrown into a chair, but I don't feel it. My body is still filled with joy from the kiss that ended far too soon for my liking. I stand up and come face to face with Ethan.

"Ethan, leave him alone. I can explain," Alex pleads. Ethan doesn't listen, though. I don't think I've ever faced a more furious opponent, and I've been in my fair share of fights over the years. His face has turned dark with rage and fire. His eyes turn darker so I can no longer see any whites surrounding them. His nose flares, and I swear smoke emerges when he breathes. His mouth turns into a grimace, ready to do battle. And so battle we will.

I run straight at him putting all the force I have into his waist backing him into the corner of the hospital room, where I'll have the upper hand. His tank of a body doesn't move as easily as I would expect for someone smaller than I am, but eventually, he inches backward despite his legs and arms pushing against me.

I get one good punch into the side of his face before he retaliates with a kick to the waist knocking the air out of me. He had been waiting for me to attack, so he could get the kick in. This man has been in a fight or two himself, despite his slick city looking suit. He's lived a day or two on the streets. You don't learn the moves he's giving out from a typical boxing or wrestling coach.

I punch him hard in the ribs, trying to knock the breath out of him, but it doesn't slow him down. Not one bit. Instead, his head crashes into mine knocking me backward.

I hear Alex scream, and it distracts me enough for him to get another good punch in. I don't feel anything other than her pain, though. She's climbed out of bed now and is hopping on one leg. She reaches Ethan trying to pull him away from me. Trying to stop the fight. I throw my hands up in surrender, not able to bear seeing her in this much pain, when Ethan shoves her backward. I watch as she hits the floor hard. Anger spools out from her. I know she's not a fragile woman easily broken and that she can fight her own battles, but now, I can't see straight. Ethan hurt her. Now, he will pay.

I throw everything I have into the next punch and watch him get knocked off balance. I take the chance to punch him over and over. I don't see anything but his face. I don't care about anything but inflicting pain on another. I don't care about anything except killing this motherfucker. He deserves to die for laying a hand on Alex. I punch and kick, each one more deadly than the previous one. Ethan tries to fight back, but I avoid each feeble attempt. He won't be able to touch me. The fire he ignited when he touched Alex is too strong.

Ethan falls to the floor in a crumpled mess after a hard kick to the side. I don't think about right and wrong. I don't think about myself. I just think about Alex. What this bastard did to Alex. I ready myself to kick this bastard over and over until he stops breathing when I feel someone's arms grab hold of me holding me back.

Ethan looks up at me a smug expression creeps over his face as I realize security is taking me from the room. Most likely the hospital and into a waiting police car.

"Yes, get this fucking idiot out of here," Ethan says as he stands to his feet. I glance behind Ethan and see that Alex has made it back to her feet and is leaning against the bed.

"No. Take both of them," Alex says.

"Are you sure, ma'am? If we escort your husband out, he won't be allowed back in the hospital," one of the security guys says.

"Yes, I'm sure. Get them both out of my sight."

He nods and grabs hold of Ethan's arm and begins walking us out. I don't bother to look at Ethan as we are escorted down the hallways and to the entrance of the building where I know there are hundreds of photographers waiting to find out news about Alex. Waiting to get a picture of a mourning husband. Instead, they will get one better. Of a beat-up husband and the scorned lover. My image will be effectively ruined between walking out on my own wedding and now this. The label could drop me for this. Not that I give a damn anymore.

The security officers push us both out the doors of the hospital.

"Stay out or we will call the police and let them know they can press assault and battery charges against both of you."

The officer smiles as he glances up at the photographers who are beginning to take notice of our bloodied appearance.

"They are all yours," he shouts to the photographers before going back into the building. It's the last thing I see before the mob of flashes begins.

Chapter Thirty

ETHAN

Now, my life is spent searching for a damn key. A key she hid from me before the attack and kidnapping.

IT'S BEEN three fucking days since I last saw her. True to their word, the hospital wouldn't let either of us back in despite how much money I offered to pay them. Luckily, the press is much easier to persuade when given a large amount of money. I couldn't keep the pictures out of the tabloids, but I did persuade them to spin the story my way. That Landon Davis is nothing but a douchebag who thinks he can take whatever he wants, whenever he wants. He wanted Alexa despite her telling him no, and I defended her honor. I came out like her noble knight in shining armor in the media, while Landon Davis looks like the scum of the earth. He won't make another penny selling music if I have anything to do with it.

Today, Alexa is being released. I know only because Mother has been able to visit. So I wait at the back entrance of the hospital away from the paparazzi at the front. Thank God, Alexa agreed to let me drive her home.

I watch as the nurse wheels Alexa out in a wheelchair. She's wearing sweats and a t-shirt. She will never learn. Even going out the back entrance, there is a chance the paparazzi will get a photo of her. I need to hire a full-time stylist for her for the future.

Alexa smiles and thanks the nurse before climbing into the back of the large blacked-out windowed SUV. I climb in next to her, and her smile immediately fades.

"Take us home," I say to the driver I hired.

"No," Alexa says. "Drive us around for a little bit so we can talk and then take us to my condo."

"You can't stay there. It's still a crime scene."

"I know, but I need to see for myself. And then I'll get a hotel room. I'm not staying with you."

"Yes, you are. I got us the house. The house with the amazing view and five rooms that we can fill with children. That's still the plan."

"No, it isn't. I don't stay with someone who lies to me and then beats up someone I care about without giving me a chance to explain first. Someone who loves me, as you claim, doesn't hurt me like that. Someone who loves me is honest and treats me like a partner, not a like a child you have to control."

"I never lied to you."

"Yes, you did! You told me I was safe when I wasn't. You chose not to tell me you suspected James. You kept me in complete darkness!"

"I'm sorry. I was just trying to keep you from worrying. I was just trying to keep you safe."

"Yeah ... how did that work out for you?"

"That's not fair."

"Nothing ever is."

"I had every right to beat the living shit out of Landon. He was kissing you! And you want to talk about a liar. How about you? You've been lying to me this whole time. You were fucking him while I was fighting to get back to you! You should be the one apologizing."

"You were dead! I moved on. That's not a crime. I should have told you about him. I'm sorry for keeping that from you, but I had enough shit to get straightened out in my own head that I didn't need to deal with explaining him to you."

I stare at her incredulously, my anger and rage returning. Her eyes grow wide in recognition of something she didn't see before.

"You were fucking him, weren't you? This whole time we've been together, you've been cheating on me behind my back."

Her wide-eyed stare turns to anger. "No. I didn't. The second I found out you were alive, I chose you over him. I chose you, a man who was virtually a complete stranger to me, over a man I desperately loved. But right now, I don't know why I decided to choose either of you when you both lie to me."

I grab hold of her body to plant a kiss on her lips. One she will never forget full of hunger and desire and rage. A kiss that will show her why she chose me and not that arrogant prick. I just reach her lips before she pushes me off her. I glance up and realize we are parked in front of her condo building just like she asked. I move to get out when she puts her hand up.

"I've spent the last three days thinking about what I want instead of thinking about what I was obligated to do." She pauses and takes a deep breath with tears in her eyes. "I want a divorce."

"No."

"Ethan. It's not fair to either of us to stay married. I need to decide for myself if I want to be married to you or not. I can't make that decision when we are already married. I need some time and space to figure out what I want."

"No."

"Ethan, I'm not asking. I want a divorce."

I shake my head. "You just need some time and space to realize you are making a mistake. You don't want a divorce."

She sighs and climbs out of the car. The driver hands her her duffle bag of clothes that she slings over her shoulder. She turns to head into her condo building but pauses at the door. She takes the rings from her finger and walks them back to me and places them in my hand.

"I can't wear these. I need to choose my own future and not be forced into one that I chose before the attack. I'm a different person now. I get to choose my future." She pauses for just a second. "I'm sorry." She turns and quickly walks into her condo building leaving me sitting in the back of the SUV feeling like an idiot.

I tell the driver to drive to my new empty house that I just bought that was supposed to be for us, but now, I'm not so sure about our future together. We aren't getting divorced. We can't. That much I know for sure.

Chapter Thirty-One

ALEXA

It was him. My memory comes back faster and faster. Somehow, I think I always knew. It was him.

THE CRIME TAPE covering the door shocks me when I see it even though I was expecting it. Ethan even reminded me about it, but it's still shocking to see it strewn across my doorway. I touch the tape and run my hand over the words. Somehow, after everything, this is what makes it real for me. Not living through it. Not waking up in the hospital. Not the pain or the scars. This flimsy piece of tape is what makes it a reality for me.

I remove one end of the tape, ignoring the sign that says 'do not enter.' I take my key and put it into the lock, the same way I did that day. It unlocks and I push the door open the same way expecting the fear to overtake me once I open it and walk inside, but it doesn't. The need for revenge takes away any feelings of fear.

I glance around the condo that is still a complete disaster just like it was that day. Whoever was here was definitely searching for something. The question is did he find it? I start in the kitchen keeping the memories at bay as I look at the bloodstained floor. I see the broken glass from my dishes that had sunk into my back leaving more scars. I don't care anymore about the scars or my disfigurement. Not like I used to anyway. I used to feel slightly ashamed, especially when I laid naked in front of Ethan or Landon. Now, I know each scar made me stronger. Made me ready to fight a battle I never knew I was fighting.

So much blood remains on the floor. Blood that James supposedly caused. I told the police they were wrong. That is wasn't James. It was someone else. They wrote my description of the attacker down but said they had indisputable video evidence that it was James. I haven't seen the video yet. Maybe when I do, I will feel different, but I don't think so. I know it's not James. I don't know how, but I just do. I need to go talk to James. Hear his story. I don't know if I will be able to help him without giving the police a more likely suspect, but I need to at least try. James has done so much to help me remember the past. I can't just leave him alone without any help.

I look around the kitchen, trying to remember if I kept anything in here worthy of stealing, but I come up empty. I kept dishes and kitchen appliances in here. Nobody would break into my condo to steal that.

I walk into my completely destroyed living room. Everything of value is still here. The DVDs and TV are here. Other than the couch and chair, that's all that was in this room and it's all still here.

I move to the door leading to my bedroom. It's closed just as it was that day. I hesitate as if it's all going to happen again if I push the door open. I push those feelings aside, though, as I push the door open. My need to find answers is more important than my need to run away afraid.

I walk into my bedroom and find it in shambles just like the rest of my condo. I glance in the bathroom and find it is more of the same. I head into my bathroom as I remember I had some valuable jewelry in a box on the counter. The box is open. The jewelry scattered on the counter, but it looks to all be here. Nothing is missing, although he obviously found the expensive items. This wasn't a robbery. This was personal. Whatever he was looking for was something specific he thought I had. I just don't know what that is.

I go back to my bedroom. To the clothes covered floor. There is nothing here other than clothes. I glance over to my nightstand. The locked drawer holding my most prized possessions had been pried open. I run over to it and rummage through the newspaper clippings. The articles about Ethan and me. The articles about my mother. I find the painting of a sunset. The one my mother painted is still intact with just a small tear in the corner. The only piece of her I have left is still here. I sigh as I slump to the floor. Nothing is missing from here either. He didn't find whatever he was searching for, which means he will be back to find it.

I sit looking at the simple painting trying to figure out what I need to do next. I have nowhere to start. So I just sit and stare into nothing.

No, I do have somewhere to start. James. I need to talk to James. I have other people I can talk to too. They all sit in jail. Whoever I'm looking for worked with those who sit in jail. They might just be willing to help me out if it means I can help free them sooner. So that's where I will start.

I roll up the painting and place it carefully in my bag. I'm not taking any more chances of leaving it here to be destroyed. I look through my clothes and select a few before putting them in my bag since I don't know when I'll be back here.

I glance down at my hand where Ethan's large rings used to cover my finger. After wearing them for weeks now, it feels weird now that they are gone. I haven't changed my mind about divorcing Ethan. I will never be able to choose between Ethan and Landon if I'm married to one. I can't be tied to one or the other to make my decision about who I want to be with. Or if I want to be with anyone. I don't know what to do, but I feel myself being pulled upstairs. I feel myself being pulled to Landon even if it is just to yell at him more for lying to me.

Chapter Thirty-Two

LANDON

It can't be true.
I'm lost without you.
Barely surviving without you.
My strength is fading.
My heart is straining.
Please don't let me lose my love.

I HEAR the pounding on the door, but I don't answer it. It's probably Caroline coming to finish me off. Or someone from the label to say they have terminated my contract. There is no point in answering the door. Doing that always brings disaster into my life. It's not worth it.

I hear the knocking growing louder, more desperate, but I still don't get up from my spot on the couch in front of the TV. A baseball game is playing on the TV although I couldn't tell you who is playing or who is winning. It's just background noise to tune out my thoughts.

"Are you going to answer that?" Drew asks he walk out of his bedroom into the living room.

"No."

"You are useless." I hear Drew walk to the door, but I don't hear any exchange between him and whoever is at the door. Maybe someone was just dropping off a package. I turn my attention back to the teams in the red and blue jerseys but still don't really pay attention to what they are doing.

"Come to the door," Drew shouts over the noise of the TV.

I respond by turning the sound up louder. I'm not moving to answer the goddamn door.

"Landon," a sweet voice says. A voice I know I'm imagining, but it still warms my heart to think she might come see me. Even though I know she won't. That kiss was a good-bye kiss, not an I-want-more kiss. No matter how much I wanted it to be a new beginning kiss.

"Landon," the voice says again a little louder with a hint of annoyance. I turn my head slightly to see where the sound is coming from that is making me imagine things when I see her. I turn the TV off and jump up to give her my full attention as I realize she is really here and it's not just a figment of my imagination.

"Alex. You came."

"Yes. Can we talk?"

"Of course," I say even though nothing good ever follows those dreaded words. "Do you want to go out on the balcony where we can get some privacy?" I ask hoping that if I take her back to the spot I told her I loved her she would fall back in love with me again.

"Okay," she says hesitantly.

She follows me upstairs to the balcony. The whole time, I keep glancing back at her trying to read her body. Trying to figure out why she is here. Why she came back.

I hold the door to the balcony open for her and watch as she takes a seat in the exact same chair as last time. So I take my spot in the chair next to her.

"I don't know what I want anymore. One minute, I have everything. The next, everything I thought was true is a lie. I don't know what is going on with my past or why people keep trying to hurt me. I also don't know who I am supposed to love anymore."

"Me?" I ask hopeful.

She smiles. "Maybe you. Maybe Ethan. Or maybe some other guy who I have yet to meet."

I frown. I don't like where this is going.

"But what I need both you and Ethan to know is that I want to figure out who I'm supposed to love on my own. I want to choose. I don't want to feel obligated to be with either of you. I'm going to make that decision on my own."

I nod liking my chances a little more now.

"You have both lied to me. Both hidden things from me that have made it hard for me to want either one of you much at the moment. I'm giving you both a chance to come clean. To tell me the truth. I've given Ethan his chance. Now, it's your turn. Tell me the truth."

I hesitate before answering. "I already have. I love you. I never cheated on you with Caroline. Those were rumors Drew and I fabricated to make the pictures of you and me at the airport disappear. I only agreed to marry Caroline to make it easier on you to forget me. I thought if you hated me, it would make your decision to stay with Ethan easier. I knew you would be loyal to your marriage and I knew I couldn't do anything to change that, so I thought I would be chivalrous for once in my life. When I proposed to you, I meant it, although I shouldn't have sprung it on you like I did." I want to tell her about my past, about my secret. I truly consider telling her, but I don't. I'm not brave or strong enough to tell her. It would end whatever lingering love she has for me. She wouldn't trust me ever again.

She nods soaking it all in. Trying to see where the truth fits in with her feelings. I have one chance to make her remember why she loves me and not Ethan. I'm going to throw out all the stops even if I'm not playing fair.

"Can I play you something?"

"What?" Her eyebrows raise in surprise.

"I'm taking that as a yes." I run through the door and grab my guitar from my bedroom. I quickly take my seat and begin strumming before Alex has a chance to protest.

I play the song I've been writing for her. The song I finished these last couple of days not knowing if she would live or die or ever be mine.

I used to think love didn't exist
That it is purely just a myth.
Something that is visited in fairy tales
But never found in real life.

But now that I've lost you
I know it really exists.
I never thought I could feel
So empty without you in my arms
Without your strength surrounding me.

As I watch you, my heart bleeds
At the sight of you kissing him.
You were my love; I know that now
But it's too late; you're his now.
I've lost my love.

Please find me, love.
Please give me back my love.
Please don't give up now.
Please come back to me, love.

I don't want to wait anymore to make you mine
But I'll wait forever if you need
For you to come back to me.
Don't stay his.
Find me still.
Please find my love.

Please find me, love.
Please give me back my love.
Please don't give up now.
Please come back to me, love.

I watch you as you lay in the bed.
I watch you gasping
Barely breathing
And I have trouble
Catching my own breath.

Please just keep breathing.
Please keep your heart beating.
Please don't let me lose my love.
Please don't die, love.

It can't be true.
I'm lost without you.
Barely surviving without you.
My strength is fading.
My heart is straining.
Please don't let me lose my love.

But I'd lose it all
As long as you keep your heart beating.
Just keep breathing.
This is my prayer.
This is my plea.
Please don't give up.
Please ...

WHEN I FINISH, I just stare at her waiting to see a reaction that she has hidden well on her face. I don't want to rush her if she hates it or loves it. I just want to know how she feels about me and the best way for me to tell her how I feel is through music.

"You can't just write a song for me every time you fuck up, you know," she says a slow grin forming on her face.

"Yes, I can," I say grinning back. I take a chance. I grab her hand as we both stand and I kiss her.

Chapter Thirty-Three

ETHAN

A key that holds information that will keep us both safe.

"WHAT DO you mean she gave you back the rings? Are you getting divorced? That can't happen."

"No, Mother. We aren't getting divorced. She's just mad I didn't tell her about James. She just wants a say in her own life. She needs to feel like she chose me and wasn't forced into this. Don't worry, I already have a plan in place to get her back. She just needs some space."

"You had better be right. If not, I will deal with her."

"I know, Mother, but it hasn't gotten to that yet. Let me handle it."

"I will, for now."

The doorbell rings. I get up from the couch in my newly furnished living room. I walk down the gorgeous marble floor to get the door.

"Mother, I have to go. I'll talk to you later." I hang up before she has a chance to scold me further. As if I don't know what's at stake here.

"Come in, Franco," I say to the older man standing in the doorway. I close the door and lead him into the kitchen.

"Can I get you something to drink?"

"No, my visit is short."

I nod and we both take a seat in the living room.

"How did it go?"

Franco shifts in his chair uncomfortably before clearing his throat to speak. "We haven't found her yet."

I narrow my eyes. "What do you mean you haven't found her yet. I gave you her credit card information. She had to check into a hotel somewhere."

"Yes, but she hasn't used any credit cards."

I frown. "And you're sure she didn't stay at her condo?"

"Yes, we entered the property several times, and she wasn't there. I have a team looking for any leads to find her. We will find her. It will just take some time."

"That's unacceptable. I'm paying you to find her now." I stand and begin pacing the room. I need to apologize. I need to send her extravagant gifts of flowers, candy, and jewelry to show how sorry I am. She needs to come see her new home that I bought for her. If she doesn't come home soon, I won't be able to hold off Mother.

"We will find her, sir."

I pause when the realization hits me.

"Have you checked to see where Landon Davis lives?"

"No, sir. I can look into that for you."

"Yes, do that now. And find anything you can dig up about him."

Franco excuses himself to make the call to find out where Landon lives. If I know her at all, she went to see him. To make things right with one of us. And if she is smart, she will choose me.

If not, she can expect that boyfriend of her's life to get worse. Much worse. So much worse that he will give her up to me rather than face any more public humiliation.

I continue pacing while I wait for Franco to return. My mind races with all of the ways I can cause Landon pain. Ways I could destroy his life if given the chance.

"Sir, we found him," Franco says as he returns to the living room.

"Where?"

"He lives on the top floor of her condo building."

"That slimebag."

"It gets better, sir. He has a secret."

I smile. "Excellent."

Chapter Thirty-Four

ALEXA

I look at the evidence on my computer. It's not enough to put him away. I need more.

His lips hover over mine for just a second, giving me time to stop it if I want, but the anticipation just makes me want it more. When his lips finally collide with mine, I'm overcome with bliss. Everything else disappears. I don't think about Ethan or James or Caroline or Drew. Thoughts of revenge melt away. My thoughts are consumed with how Landon's lips feels against mine. His soft lips drive me wild with need. But instead of giving me the more I desire, Landon pulls away after the one kiss leaving my lips tingling for more.

"I'm sorry. I shouldn't have done that," he says.

My eyes are still closed taking in the kiss that lights every nerve in my body. It was just a kiss. But that kiss made me remember all of the kisses before. It reminded me of how I feel when his lips connect with mine. Home. I feel at home when his lips touch mine. It's the only time I've ever had that feeling. No house I walk into has given me that.

No place on Earth has. No other person has made me feel at peace. Just him.

I open my eyes that are sparkling with need to connect with him in the wildest way possible. The kiss wasn't enough to satisfy me. I don't know if I'll ever get enough of this man to satisfy me.

"I'm sorry you stopped," I say smirking at the man in front of me. A man who doesn't apologize to anyone else in his life but is willing to take back the most amazing kiss if I want him to.

I close the gap between us with my lips as Landon's hands hold me so close to him I can feel every hard muscle pressed up against me. I feel safe wrapped in his arms as I slip my tongue in his mouth begging him to fuck me like he used to. Like I've dreamed about every night since we have been apart.

My tongue is wild within his mouth, pleading him to bring me the pleasure I need, but he doesn't move any faster. Instead, his movements try to slow mine. I grab at the hem of his shirt, hinting at my need for more. He grabs my hands, instead kissing my palm slowly before taking a finger into his mouth. He sucks and licks it like it's a Popsicle he can't get enough of. My toes curl as I moan from the pleasure he brings.

"I want you to fuck me," I finally get out between moans.

"I know, but I've waited a long time to get you back. I'm going to take my time." He drops sweet, torturous kisses down my arched neck. His lips feel fantastic against my soft skin, but it's not what I want. It's not what I need. I've had soft, sweet sex with Ethan. It doesn't interest me. I prefer honest, raw passion. Passion that Landon is capable of bringing.

His lips return to my lips teasing me softly as his hand runs down my body. I don't let him continue his soft touches. I grab hold of his back thrusting our bodies together so that his erection presses hard into my belly as I dig my nails into his back.

"Fuck," he groans loudly at my touch. I watch his eyes grow wild as my nails move down his body. "Fine. We will do this your way."

In one movement, Landon lifts me from the ground and carries me fast to his bedroom. We fall to the bed in a tangled mess of arms and legs. My heart beats fast as I rip his shirt off his body exposing his perfect skin. I nibble my way up his toned abs before he throws me back on the bed. His lips find my exposed stomach and he kisses the soft flesh before his teeth find the hem of my t-shirt and begins to pull it up over my head. I didn't bother to put a bra on, so when the shirt flies over my head, I'm exposed for him to see. His eyes travel over my body taking in my hard nipples but also seeming to assess any new scars.

"I'm fine. Barely a new scratch on me."

He shakes his head as he pulls off my sweats and underwear in one swift motion.

"I don't believe that."

He stands and shakes his own pants and underwear to the floor. I gasp slightly seeing his naked body again. He looks better than I remember. Somehow, his body has found a way to make his muscles even harder and more defined in the weeks since I last saw him.

Landon grabs my legs spreading me wide to see the warm liquid that has spilled out of me in anticipation of Landon filling me. He locks his eyes with mine as his lips sink lower and lower until I can feel his warm breath between my legs. He kisses me so softly there that I'm not sure if he really did. Only my toes curl in response. He lets his tongue barely brush over my clit for a second before moving away and driving me wild.

"Fuck, Landon," I groan. "Stop teasing me." I push his head down holding it there, begging him to bring me more pleasure. He does but only slightly. His tongue lingers slightly longer over my aroused bud each time bringing me closer to what I want but still denying me. I notice Landon removing my prosthetic leg with one hand while his lips stay locked on my slit.

Finally, he brings me close to what I desire. I feel my body climbing higher and higher. I feel his teeth sink into the sensitive flesh.

"Oh, Landon." I scream in anticipation of an orgasm that doesn't come as he stops just before bringing me there.

He smirks at me as he pulls me into a sitting position.

"You aren't going to come until my cock is buried deep inside you."

I sigh grabbing hold of his hard cock and pressing it to my entrance. He settles there but doesn't enter me. I move my hips trying to take him in, but he holds me still as his eyes find mine.

"I need you to know something ..."

I groan. "I need you in me. We can talk later."

He shakes his head as a large smile fills his face. "So needy. Trust me, this is killing me to stop, but it might be my only chance. You need to know that I love you. Flying back to you was the worst seven hours of my life. Thinking that you might be dead, killed ..." Landon chokes up slightly as he tries to get the words out. Tears form behind my eyes.

"When I thought you were dead, I wanted to die too. I wanted to be wherever you were. I realized these last few weeks that you are what I need to survive. I don't know how to live without you. I don't know what this is. If it's just sexual need. If it means you love me. If it means you are choosing me over Ethan, but if it's not, I just want you to know I choose you forever. I can't be with anyone else if it's not you."

Tears threaten both of our eyes as I sink onto Landon's cock. I close my eyes at the pleasure that fills me when he's inside me. I feel safe when he's inside me. I feel at home.

He begins moving in me filling me further. I open my eyes and lock mine with his as we move together, slowly. Needing this to last forever if this is the last moment we will have together. Have I chosen who I want to be with? I tried to. I tried to choose Ethan over Landon because I thought that was what I was obligated to do, but it's not what I want. Shit, we are going to have a big mess to clean up. We've both made some really bad decisions these past few weeks. Not that there is an easy or right way to handle a situation like this, but after nearly dying again, I've realized I have to choose what's best for me. When I die, I want to die knowing that's how I lived my life. With passion, and honesty, and trust. With love. And I know the only way I will be able to get it.

My eyes stay focused on Landon as we continue rocking together. "I choose you." Our lips find each other, but our eyes don't close.

Neither of us is willing to break that connection. We change our rhythm building faster to the brink of orgasm. When we come, we come together. Our eyes spilling their contents at the same time our bodies release. I choose Landon. I choose Alex.

Chapter Thirty-Five

LANDON

But I'd lose it all
As long as you keep your heart beating.
Just keep breathing.
This is my prayer.
This is my plea.
Please don't give up.
Please ...

LAST NIGHT WAS AMAZING. Easily the best night of my life. We connected in a way I didn't think was possible, but when we woke up today, reality hit. We can't stay locked away in our bubble forever. It wouldn't be fair to everyone's lives we have ruined in the process. Today, we have to make amends for the people we have hurt. Today will hurt. This week will hurt. Because we will be apart. I have a concert in Chicago that I can't cancel, and Alex needs to collect her stuff from New York. I tried to convince her to go with me, but she wouldn't be convinced. She wants to lay low for a while and not cause a media storm. Which will eventually happen once the world finds out we are together. But for now, that can wait.

Right now, though, I have to deal with Caroline. She agreed to meet me in Chicago. She already had a ticket booked since we were supposed to fly here together after a short honeymoon in Hawaii. I just hope that after we talk, the money will be enough to buy her silence at least about my past. She can crucify me in the media for leaving her at the altar for another woman. She can even demand I give her more money than I had originally intended; as long as she keeps the past in the past, I don't care what she does.

I walk down the long hallway to the hotel room Caroline and I agreed to meet in. A hotel room that feels a little too intimate for this conversation now that we are broken up, but I agreed. I will do anything to keep from upsetting her more. And I didn't really want to have this conversation anywhere public anyway.

I put the card into the card reader and watch the light turn to green before pushing the door open.

"Caroline," I shout into the large room. She should be here. Her plane landed hours before mine.

"In here," I hear her shout back from the bathroom.

I take the time to look around the suite. It has a large living space with a large couch and two smaller chairs. There is a full kitchen and dining area connected. A bedroom and the bathroom connects to the main living space. I take a seat on the couch and open my phone to answer emails while I wait for Caroline. I wait for five minutes, then ten. Caroline is still in the bathroom. I stand and walk over to the bathroom door. I knock softly.

"Are you okay?"

She doesn't answer. I press my ear up to the door and that's when I hear her retching. I open the door, thankful she didn't bother to lock it, and run over to hold her hair back while she finishes. I pat her back softly in slow circles as she dry heaves trying to get more out that isn't there. Caroline and I may not be together and she may rip me to shreds when we are finished here, but I will always care for her. She was my first real friend other than Drew. I will always have a soft spot for her.

She falls back on my body when she is finished. She seems exhausted. I try to keep my legs in place for her to lean on while I lean over the sink nearby to wet a washcloth. I manage just barely to keep her upright while at least partially wetting it. I take the washcloth and bend down so I can wipe her face. She takes a deep breath as I do, welcoming the touch.

I throw the cloth back in the sink when I'm finished.

"I'm going to help you stand."

She nods and I hold her under her arms helping her to stand. Once standing, she seems a little more sure-footed, but I keep my hands on her until she lies down on the couch.

"Can I get you something? Water? Sprite? Crackers?"

"Sprite and crackers." Caroline closes her eyes as I head to the kitchen probably trying to stop the pounding that is killing her head. I've taken care of her enough to know the look. She's hungover and I'm to blame. I walked out on her at our wedding in front of the entire world. It's been plastered all over magazines and will be for weeks still. I find some Sprite and cheese crackers in the cabinet that will have to do for now.

"Here." I hand her the crackers and Sprite before helping her to sit up.

I take a seat in the chair closest to the couch. I watch as she takes a bite of the crackers. She lifts the soda to her mouth, her hand shaking slightly as she does.

I want to do something to break the awkward tension that's growing between us, but I can't. So I say the only thing I can say. Although it will do nothing to ease the tension and make this any better between us.

"I'm sorry."

She raises her eyebrows at me as she sips her drink. She doesn't say anything, so I continue.

"I'm sorry I walked out on our wedding. On our arrangement. I wanted so badly to make you happy. I knew I could never fall in love with you, but I could love you like a husband should. I could make you happy, but then I heard that Alex was dying or possibly already dead. I didn't think. I just went."

A pained expression freezes on Caroline's face, but I continue.

"I realized after I left that what we were doing wouldn't really make either of us happy. Not really. Because happiness includes falling in love and I would be robbing you of that. You deserve to find you own love one day, but that won't ever be me. Alex has already taken my heart. I'm so sorry it couldn't be you. We would have made quite a pair, you and me."

"You and I never made sense."

I smile, just thankful Caroline is talking to me. "No, I guess not. But we did make great friends. I don't know if we can ever get back to that. I don't know if you can ever forgive me."

Caroline shakes her head. "I don't think so, but we need to try."

I nod. Caroline is making it easier than I thought she would.

"Just so you know, I plan to keep to our contract. I'll pay you double for the rest of our lives. You deserve it."

"Yes, I do."

"I don't have any right to ask, but what are you going to do with the video? With my secret?" I ask nervously. I notice my legs shaking slightly as I wait for her answer, which takes too long for her to say. She sips slowly on her drink as she studies my body. She slowly puts the drink back on the end table before answering.

"It's gone."

"What do you mean it's gone? You're not going to give it to the media?" I ask in disbelief. That was Caroline's ticket to getting revenge. She could use that to blackmail me into giving her more money. She could sell it to any media outlet for millions.

"No, I'm not going to give it the media." Her eyes light up just a little thinking about it, though. A little too brightly for my comfort. I don't believe she destroyed the video. She's too smart for that, but maybe if I keep her happy and try to rebuild her friendship, she will keep it to herself.

"Thank you," I say sincerely.

Caroline sits up straighter in her chair now as she looks at me. Ready to tell her own story.

"I didn't agree to meet you here to listen to your pathetic apology or make sure you stick to our arrangement. That's what I hired lawyers for."

I stare at her in confusion.

"Why did you agree to meet me then?"

"Go get my purse." She points toward the bedroom. I stand slowly and walk into the bedroom looking for her purse. I find a slinky black bag I assume to be her purse sitting on the nightstand. I pick it up and carry it back to her. I have no idea what else she could want. More money is the only thing that comes to mind.

She reaches into the purse and begins digging around for the item she is looking for. I wait patiently for whatever item she is looking for. I notice as she digs in the purse that she's still wearing the diamond engagement ring I gave her on her finger. I smile looking at it. She deserves to have it, even if it is no longer a promise of marriage. My mind slips to Alex. To the ring I will give to her soon. Last time I proposed, she didn't even see the ring. Only the words. This time, though, it will be different. This time, when I propose, I know she will say yes. This time, it will last.

Caroline finally pulls out a thin plastic stick and hands it to me.

"What's this?"

"Flip it over."

I do.

I stop breathing.

My heart stops.

My world ends.

'Pregnant' the test reads.

My hands shake as I hold the test in my hands. I try to think. When was the last time Caroline and I had sex? It was months ago before Alex. I glance back at Caroline's flat stomach. She's not showing, she couldn't be months pregnant. I let out the breath I've been holding. It's not mine. I feel terrible for Caroline, and I will do anything to help her, but I'm not the father.

A hazy image though crops up in my mind. An image of Caroline and me naked in bed together after a night of too much drinking. A night that happened just over a month ago. I suck in more air, but there is not enough air in the room to allow me to get the words out that I need to. I feel dizzy, sick. It can't be mine. It's not mine.

I close my eyes praying silently. Please don't let this be mine. I'll do anything. I'll give up all the money I have. I'll give up music. Just don't let it be mine.

"Whose?" I finally ask when there is nothing left for me to do.

I meet Caroline's gaze who takes the pregnancy test back out of my hands. She stares at it when she answers me.

"It's yours ..."

Chapter Thirty-Six

ETHAN

Without the key, I can't keep Alexa safe. Without the key, I'll never get the redemption I seek.

I WATCH as Alexa pulls up in her silver Tesla. She wanted to meet me somewhere public. I told her I wouldn't; I wanted her to meet me here at our new home. She reluctantly agreed. I have everything planned perfectly for her. A romantic dinner as we watch the sunset from our deck. A tour of the home where all our children will grow up. An apology with flowers and jewelry followed by a passionate night of sex. I run back to the kitchen to make sure the chef I hired for the night is ready to go. Yes, tonight is going to be perfect.

I make it back to the door in time to open it before Alexa has a chance to knock. She looks beautiful in her jeans and tank top, although I would have preferred her in a dress for tonight's fancy dinner.

I welcome her with a soft kiss on the cheek. She freezes when I move in to kiss her, but I don't care. By the end of tonight, she will be begging me to touch her body.

I grab her hand and pull her through the house out to where I have a cozy table for two complete with rose petals set for our dinner.

"It's beautiful, but I wasn't planning to stay for dinner."

"I hired a chef and everything. It's part of my apology. You were right. I was a lying ass. I should have been honest with you. I shouldn't have bought this house without your consent, but everything I did is because I love you. I wanted to protect you and give you the best. I won't apologize for that."

I walk over to her chair and pull it out for her. I can see her contemplating how she can get out of this, but I'm not going to give her that chance. I know she's been to see Landon. Now, it's my turn to wine and dine her. To make her mine again.

"Sit," I say.

She reluctantly takes a seat in the chair. The waiting staff I have hired for the night brings out a bottle of red wine and begins pouring each of us a glass. Alexa takes her glass as soon as it has been poured and downs it. I grab the bottle of wine and pour her some more smiling.

"The chef prepared a beautiful lamb shank tonight. I hope you will like it."

"I'm sure it will be fine." She smiles weakly at me before turning her attention to the sunset.

"It really is beautiful here. I'm glad you bought it. I think you will be very happy here."

I reach over the table and grab her chin turning her to face me. "This is your home too. I got it for us."

She nods as she fights back tears. "Ethan, I'm so sorry. I didn't come here to reconcile our relationship. I came here ..."

"Shh," I say as I reach my hand up to her lips to keep her from talking. "Let's not talk about that right now. Let's just enjoy our evening and then we can make those decisions. You haven't even given me a chance to apologize properly yet."

"Ethan, I accept your apology. I know everything you did was because you love and care for me, but that's not enough anymore."

I stare at her. She is not going to make this easy, but that's not going to stop me.

"You love me, and I love you. We are married. That's already enough."

"Ethan, I'm sorry, but it's not enough for me. I need more. I need to fall in love with somebody, not just love you out of obligation. I still want a divorce."

"But you have fallen in love with me."

She shakes her head. She lets the tears stream down her face as she speaks through them. "No. I tried. I tried so hard to fall in love with you. To be the perfect wife for you. To remember you, or at least, learn to love you again. It didn't work."

"It's only been a few weeks, though. Give it more time. You'll fall back in love again."

"No ... I won't. And I think you know why."

My face grows dark with anger. Yes, I fucking know why. I try to keep the rage at bay. I try to bury it deep in my heart, but it explodes to the surface.

"Yes, because you have been fucking that asshole!"

Alexa trembles a little at my outburst as she continues to sob. "I'm so sorry. I'm a horrible person. I've hurt you so much, but I have to follow my heart. Life's too short."

"You're fucking right you hurt me. You slept with another man when you were still married to me!"

"I didn't know you were alive!"

"I'm not talking about then. I'm talking about last night!"

"What? What do you mean last night?"

"I had security follow you. I wanted to make sure you were safe since you wouldn't stay with me."

She shakes her head. "I'm sorry. I didn't go there with that intention, but it happened. I won't deny it. You have to understand I don't consider us married. I don't even really consider us a couple. I told you I wanted a divorce. I don't know what else you need to hear to understand I can't stay with you. I don't remember who we used to be. All I know is who we are now."

"It still doesn't take away the fact that you cheated."

She wipes the tears from her face. "You're right. I did. I'm sorry for that. I'm deeply, truly sorry for hurting you. You deserve so much better. You deserve a woman who loves you. A woman who would really appreciate this house with you. A woman who enjoys dressing up and going to fancy parties. A woman who will be happy to be your wife and bear you kids. You deserve to be happy, but that's not me."

I watch as she stands from the table.

"I want a divorce. I'm filing the papers today. I don't want your money or this house or anything really. But I do wish you a happy future filled with love. And I do hope that someday we can become friends again once the wounds stop hurting. We deserve to be able to honor the past that we both lived through together."

I laugh as she tries to walk out on me. It stops her in her tracks hearing me laugh at her words.

"You're not going to file for divorce."

"Yes, I am."

"No, you're not. Not after you see the video."

"What video?" she asks as she turns to face me again.

"The video that shows who Landon Davis really is."

"What?"

I stand from the table and walk past her into the house. I walk past the kitchen and living space to the office at the far side of the house. I walk to the desk and pull the keys out of my pocket. I unlock the desk, happy to see that she followed me the whole time. She never once took her eyes off me.

I open the drawer and pull the flash drive with a file on it. I hold it up as I walk over to her.

"This is the reason you aren't going to divorce me. Once you see what's on this file, you will come back to me. You'll realize you are in love with a monster. A monster who will destroy you. A monster I could squash like the little bug he is if I release this video to the public."

I hand her the flash drive.

"So go home and watch it. Then tell me if you still want a divorce." I walk closer to her so that I can smell the shampoo in her hair. Close enough that I could kiss her neck if I moved an inch closer. I breathe for a second and watch as chills run up and down her body. "Because if

I see that you filed for divorce, I will release this video to the world. So I suggest you don't."

Alexa turns and glares at me.

"There is nothing on this," she says holding up the flash drive, "that could make me stop loving Landon."

"We will see, but if you do love him, you'll make sure that video never goes public. Which means staying married to me."

"I can't believe it took me this long to realize you were the blackmailing asshole you are."

I smile widely. "You have no idea how much of an asshole I can be."

She turns and stomps out of the office and continues out of the house to her car. I don't stop smiling, though. She'll watch the video and then she will be back.

Chapter Thirty-Seven

ALEXA

Find the key and remember everything ...

THE PRISON GUARD hands me back my driver's license, which I place back into my wallet inside my purse.

"You will need to leave all of your belongings in the locker here," he says pointing to a small locker. I put my purse inside before closing it. I stare at the locker; maybe it will catch on fire while I'm gone destroying the flash drive Ethan gave me with it. I haven't looked at it yet. It's been three days since he gave it to me, but I can't bring myself to look at it. Whatever is on it isn't good.

I haven't asked Landon what could possibly be on the flash drive that would damage him. Or how Ethan could have gotten such video footage. Actually, I've barely spoken to Landon these last three days. Every time I've called, he's been rehearsing, or making an appearance, or performing at a concert. But I guess that's the life of a musician and something I will eventually get used to.

I follow the prison guard back and take a seat on the small stool indicated for me to sit on at the long stretch of table. Each section divides into little stalls in an attempt to make each conversation feel more private, but it doesn't feel private. You feel exposed as other visitors come in and take their seats waiting to speak with their loved ones. Except I'm not here to visit a loved one. I'm here to see my rapist.

I'm surprised he agreed to speak with me. I tried to set up a visit with Alfie King or any of his men, but they all refused to speak with me. Not my rapist, though. Maybe because his trial is over and he has accepted what happened to him. He's currently serving a twenty-five-year sentence, which seems like a long time for a first-time rape.

I look around the room as I wait. It's almost exactly the same as the room I visited James in. It has the same blue dividers. The white walls are beaten up and need a new coat of paint. I twist my stool slightly. The only difference is that my chair doesn't squeak. I let my mind drift back to James as I wait.

I pick up the black phone as James sits down on the opposite side of the glass from me. He picks up the phone on his side. He looks sad in his orange jumpsuit. He looks scared. I've never seen James scared. He's one of the bravest guys I know.

"How are you doing?" I ask feeling weird speaking into a phone when he is sitting right across from me.

"What are you doing here?" he asks not answering my question.

"I needed to see you. I've seen the video, but I don't believe it."

James shakes his head, but I see a hint of a smile forming. "Leave it to you to not believe what's right in front of your face."

"Sorry, I guess I just trust my gut more than the facts."

"And what does your gut tell you?" James asks, his eyebrows raised.

I meet James' eyes through the glass. "That you didn't hurt me. You could never hurt me."

James nods. "I could never hurt you, Alexa."

"I don't know how to help you."

"You already did, by believing me. You're the first person who has. Even my lawyer thinks I did it and should confess to get a lesser sentence."

"Do they have anything on you except for the surveillance tapes?"

"I don't think so."

"Don't confess. I'm going to try to figure out who did this to me," I say

staring at James' sad eyes. The dark circles beneath them make him look like he's aged ten years since the last time I saw him. "To us," I correct myself. "I'm going to find him and I'm ..."

"Alexa Blakely, don't do anything stupid. Let the police handle this. I don't want anything else happening to you."

"I won't and don't you mean Wolfe?"

"No, I meant Blakely. I don't think legally you ever had time to change your name to Wolfe, and even if you did, I would always think of you as Blakely. I'm not sure Wolfe fits you."

"It didn't. I broke up with Ethan."

"About fucking time!"

"Wait, what? I thought you two were best buddies."

"We were, but you and I were best buddies too. And I never thought you two seemed right for each other even before everything happened."

I nod contemplating telling James more, but I decide to keep it to myself instead. I don't tell James about Landon. He can put two and two together. I just hope James doesn't want anything more than just a friendship. I look up when I see the guards signaling that visiting hours are almost up.

"Do you have any idea who could have done this?" I ask.

James shakes his head. "No, I wish I did. I've been trying to go through the evidence, but there is only so much I can do while I'm inside."

"Will you make bail?"

"No," he says flatly. I'll have to look into his bail terms and see if I can get him out.

"I have to go now, but I'll be back to visit soon."

James smiles at my words. "Stay safe, Alexa, and trust your gut. It's gotten you this far."

I smile back. "I will."

The memory melts away as Daniel Wood, a young gentleman sits across from me in the same orange jumpsuit. I don't know what I'm expecting when I look at the man in front of me, but it wasn't this. In front of me sits a young man. He can't be much older than twenty with light blond hair and a baby face. He looks fragile with barely a muscle visible on his skeleton-like frame.

What I can't stop staring at are his eyes. They are a beautiful bright shade of blue. Not black or menacing. This man doesn't look like he could hurt a fly much less be my rapist. He definitely doesn't seem like the hardcore criminal who should be put away for twenty-five years of his life. That's longer than he's even been alive.

I reach for the black phone and put it to my ear.

"It's been a long time since you've visited. Did you find it?"

I stare at the man confused. I didn't know I had visited him before the accident took my memory from me. Ethan sure didn't mention him. Nor James.

"Wha ... Did I find what?" I look at this stranger with confusion. He must have me confused with someone else.

The man stares back at me equally as incredulously. He laughs then. "Did you find what you've been looking for?"

"I'm sorry, um ... I don't remember ever visiting here before. If I did visit before, I apologize. I lost my memory in the car accident." Maybe this man is a crazy person. He doesn't look like he has any mental disturbance, but maybe he does.

The man slumps in his chair at my words a defeated look covers his face. "I'm sorry to hear that. I read in the paper that you lost your leg, which I'm also sorry for, but it didn't say anything about memory loss. You used to visit me about once a month."

I nod although I'm not sure if I believe him.

"Why would I visit you monthly if I thought you were my rapist?"

He smiles. "Exactly. You didn't think I raped you."

"But in the trial, I testified against you."

"Ah, the trial. Yes, you did testify, but that was before you got any of your memories back. You just said what that dang boyfriend lawyer of yours told you to say."

"Why did I think you didn't rape me then?"

"You started remembering. You came back here to look into my eyes or something. One look at my eyes and you knew I hadn't done it."

I nod. It's the same reason now I don't think he raped me. His eyes could never transform into the dark black circles of rage I saw before, but the evidence points to him. Just like James. Trust your gut. His words repeat in my head.

"I believe you. So were we working to find evidence to free you?"

"Yes, ma'am."

"Did we find any?"

"Yes, ma'am."

"Did we find out who raped me?"

"Yes, ma'am."

I huff getting frustrated with his 'yes, ma'am' answers.

"So who did it?"

He shakes his head. "Can't say. These calls are recorded and we don't trust the police."

My eyes widen. "The police are in on it?"

"Yes, ma'am."

"The car accident wasn't a drunk driver. It was one of the people my husband locked away. It was Alfie King. He tried to kill us. Then a week or so ago, I was attacked again in my home. They are all linked, aren't they?"

His smile brightens as I understand more and more. "Yes, ma'am."

"Please, call me Alex ..." I say while thinking.

"Sorry, Alex." I smile as I try to understand. All of the attacks were linked. And with at least two of the attacks, other people were framed. That leaves the second attack. I don't know if King was framed or if King is behind them all.

"You said I have evidence. Where would I keep such evidence?"

He thinks for a minute on what to say before answering. "Tessie."

I SPEND the entire flight back thinking about what Daniel could have meant. "Tessie," he said. How did he know that I named my car that? Only Landon knew. Did I know Landon before the attack? Or did Landon go to visit Daniel after he met me? Or did I call my car Tessie before the accident and somehow remembered when I was with Landon? I shake my head. All that visiting Daniel did was give me more questions. Questions that I hope my car holds the answers to.

I feel the flash drive in my pocket. I still can't believe what Ethan said. He's trying to protect me or win me back. That's all it is. Most likely another lie, but still, I'll have to ask Landon about it when he returns to LA.

I lay my head against the window of the cab as we drive from the airport to my condo where my car sits. I try to sleep, but it never comes. The cab drops me off at the door to my building, but I don't bother to go in. Not even to drop off my bag. Instead, I head straight to my Tesla. To Tessie. I glance at my phone; only three hours until Landon lands. Three hours to figure this out.

I climb in my car, but I have no idea where to start. I remember weird dreams about secret compartments in my car, but I have no frame of reference of where in my car it's located. I begin with the obvious locations: the glove compartment, the trunk, and the hood, but I find nothing. I begin running my hand over fabric feeling my way over every piece of carpet and leather in the car. Still nothing.

I look at the stereo and navigational screen. Maybe? I begin pressing buttons on the stereo system and I run my hands over the system. I press another button that I expect to do nothing when finally the screen lifts up. I lift it the rest of the way and find a box bolted to the car with numbers to enter a password on the front. I try opening it, but it's no use. It doesn't budge.

I try my birthday. I try Ethan's birthday. I try my mother's birthday. I try the day she died. I try the day I was raped. I try every important date or number I can think of, but nothing happens. I slam my hand into the box in frustration.

"Ow," I moan as I rub my hand to relieve the pain. That's when I see it. My tattoo for my mother. A tattoo to remember her by. All it has is the word 'Mom' with a date under it. The date she died. I already tried that.

I sit tracing the letters 'M', 'o', 'm'. I trace them over and over and then I see it. Tiny numbers that are barely visible form the letters. I don't know what the numbers mean, but I enter them into the keypad and stop when I notice the numbers repeating. I take a deep breath and then press enter feeling like this is my last chance to get it to open because I'm all out of numbers to try. The door pops open.

I reach my hand inside and pull out a small flash drive. I sigh. Another flash drive. I take the small device and put it in my purse next to the other one I've already collected. I quickly lock up the car and head to my condo to find my laptop.

When I reach my condo door this time, the crime tape is gone. I unlock the door and go inside. The condo looks back to normal for the most part. The cleaning crew I hired cleaned up the blood and broken glass from the floor. The stuffing from my couches has been thrown away. I glance in my bedroom where the clothes have been hung back in my closet. The condo is back to being livable.

I grab my computer and sit on my bed with my purse containing the two flash drives. I pull out each and lay them on the bed. I grab the one Ethan gave me. I'm still not ready to look at that one yet. I grab the second I found in my Tesla and connect it to my computer.

My hands shake a little as the flash drive pops up on the screen. Memories begin flooding back. Giving me clues of what's on the flash drive. Clues as to who is on the flash drive. I think back to everything I've been through these last few months. Of everyone I've met. Who would want to hurt me like this? Ethan's mother and Caroline immediately pop into my head as prime suspects. Followed by Alfie King. All of them make sense.

But who is the monster?

Laura.

Caroline.

Alfie.

Daniel.

James.

Drew.

Ethan.

Landon.

My head spins as I think about each person in my life. I can't envision any of them as the monster who has tried to kill me. Maybe it's someone else? Maybe it's a complete stranger?

I shake my head. No, I think. My gut tells me it's not a stranger. It's someone I know. No stranger would try this hard to hurt me. To kill me.

I try to think of the eyes. The only real clue as to who it could be. I think through everyone trying to imagine whose eyes could turn that dark, that heinous. I think back to my time with each of them and only two names come to mind. Both of them have lied to me. Both of them have hurt me. Both of them have tired to manipulate me.

Ethan is the first. I've seen his eyes turn dark and angry, but it can't be him. He was attacked just as I was. He is just as scared as I am. My mind goes to the other ... Landon. I've also seen his eyes turn dark. So dark they look black.

I feel the tears falling down my cheeks. It can't be either of these men. Neither of them could hurt me like this, except I think one did. One hurt me and if it's true, I don't know how I'm going to keep living.

I click the icon quickly, just needing to know. I have to be wrong.

Documents pop up on the screen and I click the first one. I've typed everything I know in the document. The rest are pictures and other evidence I found. I begin reading the document.

I, Alexa Blakely, want whoever this may concern to know who I believe my killer is if I die. I have evidence in these files to prove that he has tried to kill me before and he will try again if given the chance. If I am dead, I believe ...

I don't have to read any further. I know in my gut who is behind the attacks. Tears fall onto my computer as my world falls apart. But I force my eyes to travel one word further anyway. Just far enough to confirm what I already know to be true. It's him.

ALIGNED: VOLUME 4

Chapter One

ETHAN

I TRIED to get rid of the monster. I thought we could escape the darkness by starting over. I thought we could put our pasts behind us.

The demons found me, though. The urges came back. There is no such thing as redemption. I can't be saved.

I tried to put my urges to rest. But the need to inflict pain is too strong to resist. I can't hold back any longer.

I can't be saved from the monster because I am the monster.

Chapter Two

ALEX

23-489-37562-30 ... The numbers from my tattoo play over and over in my head, but I don't know what they mean.

It was Ethan. I stare at the computer screen in disbelief. It can't be. He couldn't have done the horrible things to me. He's my husband. He's supposed to love me. I take a deep breath and get up from my bed, leaving the computer screen with the evidence behind.

I walk to my kitchen needing a glass of water. My hand shakes as I pour the glass of water and bring it to my lips. When the water is gone, I place the glass back on the counter surprised by how steady my hand has become after simply downing the water.

It was Ethan. He raped me. He lied to me. He had another man convicted for his crime, and then he had the balls to marry me.

I expect tears to fall. I expect sobbing. I expect untold sadness, but it never comes. I don't mourn the loss of my husband. I've mourned the loss long enough.

It was Ethan. He hired the people that tried to kill me in the car attack. He faked his own kidnapping. I don't have the evidence, but I know he was the one who did this. He wasn't trying to help me that night. He was trying to get rid of me because he knew I had figured out that he was my rapist.

I look down at the scars etched on my body. I look down at my leg that I can never get back. Ethan did this.

I scream as the anger overwhelms my body. I run to the couch and take off my prosthetic leg. I fumble with it instead of taking it off smoothly like I always do. When I finally get it off, I throw it and watch as it crashes into the far wall. I look down at my disfigured body. He took my memories from me. I will never remember my mother. I'll never remember my life before. All because of him. This pain. This ugliness. It's because of Ethan. He did this.

"I hate him. I hate him. I hate him," I scream over and over.

I pound my fists into the couch trying to get my anger out. Trying to prevent it from taking over every nerve in my body. The pounding doesn't prevent it, though. Instead, it drives the anger wild as it spreads through every fiber in my body until I'm shaking. I slowly bring my hand up to touch my face that is burning red. I take a deep breath trying to calm myself so that I can think rationally, but there is no thinking rational. Not today.

All I see is Ethan dying at my hands. That's all I want.

I lean back on the pillows that are now empty from all the stuffing being ripped out. It was Ethan. He attacked me in my own home. He made me think I was going to die, again. He hurt me. And then he blamed it all on James.

I throw the empty pillows to the floor. They float slowly to the floor not bringing me nearly enough satisfaction from the motion. I squeeze my hands into fists and then release them. I do this over and over. It's not enough, though.

I know Ethan did every horrible thing that has ever happened in my life. I close my eyes, and that's when I see it. His eyes. They are dark black and empty. His eyes change from the dark brown he normally wears to dark black every time he attacked me. It was him. I may not have the evidence to prove it. All of the evidence may point to

Daniel as my supposed rapist, to Alfie King as my supposed attacker, and to James as my supposed attacker and robber, but I know it was Ethan.

I hop back to my bedroom leaving my prosthetic leg on the floor of my living room. I climb back in bed, and I begin reading. I read everything.

I read all of my theories on who my rapist was. Each one was crossed off until I get to Ethan. Every time, I kept coming back to him. I searched everywhere in our old apartment looking for evidence. I searched in Laura's house for evidence. I found nothing. Not until I searched his office at the law firm did I find something. And even then, I only found one tiny thing. One piece of evidence that he could never get rid of. The video. Video proof of the rape.

He couldn't part with it; even though he knew if anybody ever found the video, it would destroy him. The video is on the file. I just don't know if I can watch it.

I hover the cursor over the file for a long time trying to decide what I should do. I click it. I watch it. And it just makes me angrier. I can't believe he did this to me. Except I can. I always felt a disconnect between Ethan and me. I didn't understand why we were married. I still don't understand why I married this monster. But I did.

My eyes stay glued to the video as Ethan pushes me into a closet at the bar. He's holding his phone out and using it to videotape us. I watch my expression change from happiness at thinking he was just coming on strong and wanting a make-out session to fear as I realize what he really wants.

I watch myself scream before he covers my mouth with his hand. I watch as he jabs a needle into my neck. I wince and grab my own neck as he does. I feel the pain just as the woman in the video does. It's as if I'm there in the moment, even though I'm not.

I watch as he sets his phone on a shelf in the closet so he can get everything on video to relive over and over. I watch my body go limp but not my eyes. I see every painful thing done to me. I see the pain in my eyes. I see the fear. He did this to me. When he's finished, I pass out. He injects me again before leaving. I'm sure that second dose is what left me without memories from that night. The only thing I ever remembered was his eyes.

I have proof. Proof that could send him to prison for a very long time, proof that could release the man currently serving his sentence, but it's not enough. Alfie is serving a sentence he may or may not deserve. But James ... he is definitely serving a sentence that he doesn't deserve. I don't have anything that could set him free. Daniel told me not to go to the police. We don't know who to trust. So I won't. I won't go to the police. I just don't know what to do. I don't know how to save James. I don't know how to make Ethan pay. I don't know how to save myself.

I watch the video again. It's just as painful the second time. I try to the match the video to my nightmares, but it doesn't quite match up and I don't know why. I finally resign to stop torturing myself with the video and save it to my computer before I pull the flash drive out and put it in my pocket. I won't go anywhere without this file ever again. I need to know it's safe.

That's when I see it. The other flash drive. I pick it up and look at it. The flash drive Ethan gave me. The flash drive that supposedly has something on it so horrible about Landon that I won't want to be with him. That I will do anything to protect Landon from this getting out.

I stare the flash drive. I don't believe Ethan. I don't believe anything on this flash drive would destroy Landon. I trust Landon. I love Landon. Nothing on this could ever change that.

I get up from my bed and hop to my closet where my suitcase is. I dig through it until I find my prosthetic leg made for running. I put it on and then walk to the bathroom. I toss the flash drive Ethan gave me in the trash. I don't need to look at it. Whatever is on it is just a lie. A lie to bring me back to Ethan. I will never go back to Ethan.

I make my way out of my condo building and down the beach. The sun is setting over the ocean as my feet touch the sand. It couldn't be a more beautiful night. How can the world be so beautiful when I'm going through so much pain? So much anger.

Landon is supposed to land in two hours. That's all the time I have to figure out a plan.

I begin running across the sand. I try to let the beauty of the night heal me, but I soon realize I don't need healing. I've already healed. Scars have formed, and I've accepted my body for what it is. Landon helped me do that. I made the right choice when I chose Landon over Ethan. What I do need is to let the anger go so that I can do what needs to be done.

I run faster and faster until I can barely breathe. Until my feet can't move me any faster. Until each step becomes painful again.

I need evidence. I need evidence that Ethan tried to kill me. Twice. I got the evidence before. I reach into my pocket, feeling the flash drive there. I got it before, so I can get it again. Then when I have enough to nail him for all three crimes, I will go to the police. I'll find the police officer that Ethan doesn't have in his corner. But not until then.

I can't tell Landon my plan. He would never be okay with me putting myself at risk. Even though my life has been at risk every day since I met Ethan. I just didn't know it. He would hire untold amounts of security to keep me safe. He would move us across the country to keep me away from him. He might even go after Ethan. He might kill him. None of those options are good. I don't want protection. I don't want to run. And I don't want Landon to ruin his life.

No, I have to do this myself. But is Ethan spending the rest of his life in jail going to be enough to satisfy my revenge? What if he doesn't get life? What if he gets out on bail? What if he gets out after ten, twenty, thirty years? He'll come after me. He'll come after Landon. He'll come after any family I have.

I force my legs to move farther even though they are tired. Far too tired. I need to keep running until I get all of the anger out of my body. I soon realize that may mean I have to keep running every second for the rest of my life. I finally let my legs slow until I am just walking. Until I can breathe again. Until the pain is gone.

I exhale deeply. He only raped me once. Although now it feels like he raped me over and over again. He raped me every time since. I didn't know who I was fucking when I was saying yes. He was taking my freedom each time.

He tried to kill me twice. Both times to keep his secret. To keep the world from knowing that he raped me.

I smile. He failed. He failed twice at killing me. But I know what I'll do now. I'll get the evidence to free the men who don't deserve to pay, and then I'll kill him. And unlike Ethan, when I try to kill him, I won't fail. He'll be dead.

Chapter Three

LANDON

At three years old
I lost my faith.
I remember it
Like it was yesterday.

"IT'S YOURS," Caroline says.

My heart stops. My world stops. I had everything that I could ever want. I had Alex. I had an amazing career. I had money. I had Drew. Now, I have nothing.

Drew will hate me.

My career will be ruined.

All of my money will go to this kid. Caroline will make sure of that.

And Alex ... She'll never forgive me. I'll lose her. Again. And this time, I don't think I will ever get her back.

I look at Caroline whose eyes have just now met mine. I see the fear. I see the regret. I see the lie.

"You're lying," I say.

She just shakes her head like she was expecting it.

"I'm not lying. I'm pregnant, and the baby is yours."

"I don't believe you. We only slept together that one night. You've probably had sex with other men since then. How would I even know it's mine?"

I watch as the words cut through her causing her pain, but I can't stop myself. I hate her. I hate that she's lying to me. I hate that she is trying to ruin my life.

"You're just trying to keep me away from Alex. You're just trying to ruin everything. You're just trying to get payback for me leaving you at the altar."

I watch a tear fall from her eye. Shit, I wasn't expecting that. I wasn't expecting my words to hurt her. I was expecting her to deny it. I was expecting her to throw the hurt right back in my face.

I get up from my chair and sit next to her. I hesitantly place my hand on her shoulder expecting her to wince away from me. I expect her to hit me. I don't expect my hand to calm her, but it does. I see her shoulders visibly relax at my touch. So I keep my hand there. I keep holding her. I keep comforting her.

"I'm sorry," I say. "I shouldn't have said that. This is just unreal. And I'm not sure I believe you're pregnant. And I'm really not as sure as you are that the baby is mine."

She nods as she wipes her tears before turning to look at me.

"I'm pregnant. And it's yours. You're the only one I didn't use protection with."

I close my eyes at her words. If she is telling the truth, then it means the odds are in my favor that this child is mine. I just don't trust a word out of Caroline's mouth. How could I have been so stupid not to use protection? How could I have been so stupid to fuck Caroline in the first place when there was even a chance of getting Alex back? Alcohol.

I exhale deeply, thrusting all of the air out of my lungs and hoping that it will be enough to calm me so I can talk rationally with Caroline instead of throwing things like I really want to.

"I need proof," I say.

She nods and smiles slightly.

"I scheduled an appointment with a doctor here to do an ultrasound and start the process for a paternity test."

When she speaks, her voice is unwavering. It's confident. She's sure that this baby is mine. She's not lying. I just hope she's wrong.

Fuck!

"Okay. Let's do that. What time is the appointment?"

"Three."

I nod. I can do that and still make it to rehearsals for the show tonight.

———

I'M WEARING dark sunglasses and a hat when I enter the clinic with Caroline. Thank god, Caroline isn't a well-known movie star. I let her check in by herself, and I take a seat in one of the chairs of the waiting room. The chair creaks like it has been used far past its time and is liable to break from just me sitting on it. I'm surprised when it doesn't. I pick up a car magazine and begin flipping though it trying to hide my face from the other people in the waiting room.

I notice a very pregnant woman sitting across from me, and it makes me uneasy. I've never even really thought about if I wanted kids or not. Even with Alex. I've never had that conversation. I'm sure Alex wants kids, like all women do, but do I? I didn't have the best upbringing. My mother was dead. And my father was a deadbeat drunken father who never paid Drew or me any attention. We never had money. We hardly ever had food. We sure as hell never did anything fun. I don't want a child if it means that's all I can give them. But I know I can give them more. I can give a child all of the physical things that I never had. I just don't know how to be a father. I don't know how a father is supposed to act. I don't know how a father is supposed to teach his child to be a good person. I have no clue.

Caroline walks over and takes a seat next to me. I watch as her knee bounces lightly in her chair. The same movement Alex does when she's nervous. I try to push Alex out of my head. I can't think about her right now. I need to find out the truth, and then I can move on.

Then I can do my best to help Caroline as a friend. Then I can figure out my future with Alex.

I place my hand on her leg trying to calm her, but instead, her nervous energy just passes into my body. My hands shake and then my whole body until we are both trembling messes.

"Caroline Parker," says an older woman dressed in nurse clothing.

Caroline stands, and I follow her. The nurse introduces herself although I don't pay attention to her name. I don't pay much attention until Caroline is lying on the table with a drape over her stomach as she waits for the doctor to enter.

We wait, with her on the table and me in the chair next to her head, for what seems like hours although I know it isn't that long. It might as well be as my nerves have now taken over my body.

We both jump when we hear a knock on the door followed by a doctor.

"So you are definitely pregnant," the doctor says staring at the chart. "Congratulations," she says as she shakes Caroline's hand followed by mine. I glare at the doctor. Congratulations are not in order. She ignores my glare as if she is used to getting it from the fathers. She probably is.

"I'm going to examine you, and then I'll do an ultrasound to give you an approximate age of the child and due date."

The doctor begins to examine Caroline, and I do my best to keep my eyes on Caroline's face.

"So how long have the two of you been together?" the doctor asks while examining Caroline.

I look at Caroline. I am not going to be the one who answers questions. I can barely concentrate on breathing. I can't handle more than that right now.

"We've known each other since we were kids," Caroline says.

"Aw. That's nice."

She continues examining for a moment longer. "Everything looks healthy and as it should be. Are we ready for the ultrasound?"

"Yes," Caroline says.

I watch the screen as the doctor performs the ultrasound, but I can't make out anything that looks like a baby. I don't know what's on the screen. It just looks like a blur of black and gray to me.

"There," she says, pointing at the screen, "is your baby. It looks healthy so far."

We both nod but neither of us take our eyes from the screen.

"It looks like to me that you are about eight weeks along. That would put conception at about six weeks ago."

My eyes find Caroline. That's exactly when we were together. I can't breathe. This baby could really be mine. That little blur on the screen could really be mine.

"I'll print off some pictures for you to take home."

Neither of our eyes move from one another as the doctor gets the pictures and hands them to us. My eyes tell her I believe her. My eyes tell her that I know I'm the father while her eyes tell me she's sorry.

"Do you have any questions for me before I go? I know I won't be your regular doctor, but if you have any questions about what you should or shouldn't eat, things of that nature, now is the time to ask."

Now, Caroline is frozen. She doesn't move. So I speak. "We were wondering about a paternity test. We are pretty sure I am the father, but we just want to be sure."

The doctor nods. "Well, you have a couple of options for a paternity test. The least invasive and most accurate option is a DNA test. A blood sample would be taken with DNA from both of you and then we could run an analysis to see the odds of you being the father. I would also recommend blood being taken from any other possible fathers."

I nod. "When can that test be done?"

"Nine weeks. So you will have to wait another week before the test is done."

I watch as she reaches behind her desk and pulls out some pamphlets.

"Here is some information on paternal testing and some pamphlets on what she needs to be doing to remain healthy."

"Thanks," I say taking the papers from her hands.

We walk out of the clinic and find the car that I have rented. We both climb in without saying a word. I drive us to the nearest park without saying a word. I turn the key switching the engine off. I climb out of the car, and Caroline does the same. I walk until I find a picnic table to sit on. I sit down and watch her do the same.

I take a deep breath. "I'm sorry I didn't believe you. I should have trusted you."

She shakes her head while she fidgets with something in her hands. It's her ring, I realize. The ring I gave her when I proposed. "It's okay. I'm not sure I believed myself either. Not until I saw the baby on that screen. Not until I heard the date was when we were together."

"I know. That's when I realized that it was true too. I still want a paternity test to be one-hundred percent sure, but I can feel it. This baby is mine."

She nods agreeing.

"What do you want to do?"

I don't know what I want her to do. Abortion? That would make our lives so much easier, but I don't know if either of us could go through that. Adoption? No way in hell. That leaves having it. I just don't know how we would balance that together.

She wipes another tear that has fallen. "I don't know, Landon. I never wanted kids, but I don't know ..."

I reach across the table and grab hold of her hands. "I know. I don't think I could either."

She exhales a deep breath. "I just don't see how we are going to make this work. We don't love each other. We fight. We are horrible together. And you are with *her*. How are we going to make that work?"

I have no idea. Although I'm afraid as soon as I tell Alex, she will no longer be a problem because she will no longer be mine. She will want nothing to do with me.

"I don't know exactly, but we can figure it out together. I want to be part of this baby's and your life. In whatever capacity you will have me."

Another tear falls as she fidgets again with the ring. "I should give this back to you." She holds up the ring to me.

I narrow my eyes. "Why?"

"Because it's not real. We will never be husband and wife. I don't want it. I want to find a real husband. I want to find someone who loves me."

I take the ring from her and hold onto her hand. "You're wrong. This is real." I reach out and touch her stomach. "This baby is real. We love each other whether it is in a husband and wife relationship or not. That's what this ring represents. A friendship and love that will last no matter what. Even if it doesn't turn into marriage."

A soft sob escapes her lips. "But I want marriage. That will never happen."

I bite my lip to keep the words from coming out of my mouth. But it doesn't help. She needs to hear them because they are true.

"Never say never."

She sucks in a breath as she realizes the words are true. Painfully true. We could still end up married. If Alex wants nothing to with me and Caroline gives up looking for a future filled with romantic love, then we could. If we both fall hard for this baby, as I'm afraid we will, then we will end up together. It's inevitable. I slip the ring back on her finger. Back where it belongs. I just don't know what the ring means anymore.

Chapter Four

DREW

Caroline looks at me, and it's all it takes. I devour her with my lips, catching her breath between my lips.

"DAMMIT, Landon! You're late to your own rehearsal. We only have twenty minutes now to go through a two-hour show. All we have time to do now is a sound check."

I'm going to kill him. He can't keep pulling this shit. I don't care how much he loves spending time with Alex. He has to get his head into his music career before the label drops him. Before he loses it all.

"Sorry," is all I get before he hops onto the stage.

When he moves, that's when I see her. Caroline. She's standing next to the stage with her arms wrapped around her stomach. She looks sad — incredibly sad — and I can't help but think I might be part of the reason for her sadness.

We've been friends a long time. It was always the three of us. Landon, Caroline, and me. We were inseparable. But life has drifted us all apart and then twisted us together in ways none of us understands.

I screwed up. I'm the reason Landon walked out of his wedding.

I'm the reason that he didn't say I do. I'm the reason Caroline and Landon aren't married right now.

I could have kept my mouth shut. I didn't have to tell Landon that Alex was in the hospital. I couldn't, though. I had to tell him. I had to stop him from making a huge mistake. I had to stop Caroline from making an even bigger mistake. She deserves better than Landon. He doesn't love her. Not like he should.

I've made other mistakes when it comes to Caroline, though. Mistakes she will never forgive me for. A mistake that I don't regret, though. I may live with this ache in my chest for the rest of my life, but the pain is well worth the one night.

I walk over to Caroline curious as to what she is doing here. I expected Landon to have given her the cold shoulder after their meeting today. I expected her to be on a flight headed home. I expected her to be glaring mad at Landon if she did show up here. Instead, she is looking up at Landon with hope.

My heart flutters hard in my chest with every step I take closer to her. Nobody makes me feel this nervous. Nobody makes me feel this way. Just her.

"What are you doing here?" I ask and then hate myself for the words that come out of my mouth. I haven't spoken with Caroline since the wedding. I didn't want those to be the first words out of my mouth when I saw her again.

She looks at me in disgust. "I'm here to see Landon."

I put my hands in my suit jacket pockets as I stand awkwardly next to her. I have no idea what to say. There are no words to make this better. There are no words.

But I find words anyway. "I'm sorry."

She wipes under her eye trying to pretend she is just getting something out of it. But I know. She was wiping away a tear. Because of me.

Landon may have treated Caroline poorly, but I'm the one who destroyed her. I'm the one who ruined everything.

"Shouldn't you be barking orders or on your phone or something," she snaps.

My hand reaches out to her of its own accord, but I stop it short of touching her. "No."

She narrows her eyes at me. "Leave me alone, Drew."

"I can't."

She just shakes her head while keeping her eyes on Landon. So I just stand next to her while watching my twin brother sing on stage.

I will never understand what she sees in Landon. Sure, he's good looking. Landon and I look practically the same. I guess being identical twins will do that. Other than a different hairstyle and slightly different muscular build, you couldn't tell the two of us apart. Our looks are where the similarities end, though. Landon is outgoing, arrogant, and a typical bad boy while I'm loyal, honest, and responsible. Why would anybody want Landon? Why would she want somebody obviously hung up on another woman? I love my brother, but I will never understand why she thinks he is so amazing. Not after what he did.

Darren signals that the rehearsal is over, and Landon immediately jumps off the stage and walks over to us. I expect he is going to want to know how much time he has before he needs to be in wardrobe so that he can call Alex. Or to ask me to send her flowers or something. He isn't running over to me, though. He's running over to Caroline.

My eyes widen when I see him grab her hand. I try to get his attention to give him a quizzical look, but his eyes stay on Caroline. Both are filled with worry. Both are speaking to each other without speaking. I just have no idea what their eyes are saying.

"Caroline and I are going to go to my dressing room. Make sure nobody disturbs us unless absolutely necessary," Landon says. Still not glancing my way.

Instead of responding in my usual business manner, I freeze. Why the hell would Landon want Caroline alone in his dressing room? It doesn't make sense. The dancers and backstage crew will just start rumors. Eventually, one of them will leak the story to the media, and then Alex will find out. Why even chance it? Even if they aren't fucking. Why? After everything he did to get Alex back, he's just going to let it all go for something stupid.

"Earth to Drew," he says. His eyes have moved from Caroline's to mine, but just long enough to know that there is life behind my eyes.

"Okay," I say.

That's all Landon needs to hear. He grabs hold of Caroline's hand again and pulls her toward his dressing room. I don't follow despite how much I want to. I stay.

"God, please don't tell me he is back with that bitch," Nicole, one of the stage manager says.

"No. He's not." Fuck, it didn't take five seconds for people to notice Caroline here.

"That's a relief."

"She's not that bad," I say. She's just broken. Just like the rest of us.

"No, she's worse. I just hope he gets rid of her before the show."

"If she stays to watch the show. Be nice," I say narrowing my eyes at her.

She rolls her eyes at me as if I'm crazy. "Don't count on it. If she is here, I plan on staying as far away from her as possible."

I run my hand through my hair and grab the base of my neck. I have to push Caroline out of my head. I have to get back to work. I've done it my entire life, so I can do it again now. No matter how hard it is.

Chapter Five

ALEX

4. The number of items in my backpack. A spare item of clothing, an old camera, twenty bucks, and my mother's painting. That's all I have as I stand on the edge of the street at eighteen years old. I don't have a foster family to take care of me anymore. I'm on my own.

I PULL into the parking lot for the private airfield. I'm happy that Landon flew private instead of commercial. I don't think I could handle the paparazzi or crowds. I just want to be in his arms, where it's safe.

I park the car between two Audis and turn off the engine. I don't get out, though. I don't want to make a scene inside the terminal. So instead, I sit fidgeting in the car that used to be my safe haven, but now that I know it held secrets from me, I'm not sure how I feel about this car anymore. It doesn't feel safe anymore.

Landon isn't safe either. Not anymore. Not when he's with me. I need to convince Drew to hire some bodyguards especially when Landon is out in public. I don't want Ethan to hurt him. I don't want anyone to hurt him. But I can't tell him the truth. I can't tell him it was Ethan. He'd either kill Ethan or prevent me from doing what I need to do. Either way, I can't take the chance.

I glance up, and that's when I see him walking from the private terminal toward me. I smile automatically although there is nothing to smile about. Still, just seeing him makes me happy even when nothing else in my life should.

He climbs in the car, but his face isn't as bright as it should be. His smile is weak, forced. His flight must have been terrible. Seeing Caroline again must have been horrible.

Our arms go around each other on autopilot, and I exhale deeply. I feel safe, even when I know I'm not. I feel it.

We stay like this much longer than usual as the tension leaves both our bodies. This should be over. We should be able to live our lives now the way we want. But this is far from over. I don't know if he realizes it. I don't know if he senses it seeping out of my pores, but when he pulls away, his body is saying the same as mine. I love you, but...

But this fight isn't over.

But you're not mine yet.

But there is so much more yet to discover about ourselves. About our pasts.

But we can't just be happy.

But we might not ever really belong together.

I turn the ignition in Tessie back on and pull out of my parking spot. It's weird that he doesn't speak when he should have so much to say. It's weird that I don't speak either, I realize.

"How was your flight?" I finally ask.

"Fine," he says harshly. His hand goes to his head rubbing it as if he is trying to rub away every thought he has ever had.

"How was the concert?"

"Fine."

"How was Caroline?"

"Fine."

I stomp on the brakes harder than I intended to and the car screeches to a stop in the middle of the road. I hear a car honk behind us, but I don't care. I'm not moving until I have answers.

"What the hell, Alex?" Landon reaches over and tries to grab the steering wheel from me, but I push him back.

"Don't what the hell me. What is going on? You haven't answered one question since you got in this car, and you look like the walking dead. What the hell happened in Chicago?"

Landon glares at me, his face growing redder by the second.

"Nothing! Nothing fucking happened! I'm just not in a good mood. I'm entitled to not be a fucking smiling idiot every time I'm around you."

"What fucking happened? Why the hell are you so pissed off? Is it Caroline? Is she still upset with you?"

Landon turns away from me looking out the window as rain begins pouring down outside my car, mirroring how I feel inside.

"Get out of the goddamn street, Alex."

I lift my foot off the brake and ease on the gas. I drive up a couple of more blocks before I find a place to turn off in a dark alley where we won't be bothered.

I park Tessie and turn off the ignition. I wait trying to calm my anger. I need to give him a chance to tell me what happened. It's not as if I've been forthcoming with what is going on in my life. But my patience runs dry.

"What happened with you and Caroline?"

He runs his hand through his hair still not answering me.

I grab his arm trying to get him to look at me, but he just pushes me away. Why is it so hard for him to talk about somebody he hates? Did something happen to make him change his mind?

"You changed your mind," I say as I fall back into my chair.

"What?" His attention moves back to mine.

"You changed your mind. You want to be with her, not me."

Landon grabs my neck and pulls me to him, kissing me hard on the lips. His kiss is desperate. It's needy. It's everything a kiss should be. I feel empty when his lips move away, left panting hard in their absence. The kiss was just as good as his last kiss. Nothing has changed there. I rub my fingers over my lip as it tingles from where his lips just were.

"Then what?"

He shakes his head. "I love you, Alex. Just after seeing Caroline,

I'm frustrated. I'm frustrated that we will always have these attachments. These complications that we can never get rid of."

"What do you mean?"

"I mean I will always have Caroline. You will always have Ethan."

I shake my head angrily. "That's not true! Ethan will not always be a part of my life, and as far as Caroline is concerned, I thought you went to Chicago to end it with her."

"I did. Did you file for divorce while I was gone?"

I narrow my eyes at him trying to understand what's happening. He knows I will file for divorce as soon as I can. As soon as it's safe to do so.

"That's what I thought," he says when I don't answer. He turns his attention back to the raindrops pelting down on our car.

"That's not fair, though. You know I will file for divorce soon. I just need to talk with a lawyer and get it straightened out. It's not as easy as you think ending something that used to be such a big part of your life."

He turns back to me. "Exactly. Can you really ever end something that has been such a big part of your life for so long?"

I bite my lip trying to understand what Landon is talking about. I have no clue. Yes, moving on from Ethan and Caroline is going to be hard. But if we want to be together, isn't it worth it?

I close my eyes trying to calm myself. The only thing left that I thought was mine for sure is slipping away, and I have no idea why. He's hiding something from me. His words are far too cryptic. Something happened in Chicago. Something changed on that trip. I could talk to Drew. He might have an idea, but he could also just tip Landon off that I'm trying to find out what he's hiding.

Or I could dig the flash drive out the trash. I could see what's on that file. I could see if that is what Landon is hiding.

Chapter Six

LANDON

Father used the drink to wash away
The pain of losing her.
The pain that was just too much to bear.

She doesn't answer me, which just makes me even more crazy inside. She doesn't deny that it could be hard, if not impossible, to remove Ethan from our lives. I can't live like that. I can't be with her knowing that she is still thinking about that bastard from time to time. I can't live knowing that she probably plans to eventually be friends with him. I can't handle that.

She avoids eye contact with me as she thinks something over.

"What are you thinking about?"

She just shakes her head. She's hiding something. I know she is. I just don't know what it is. She smiled when she saw me, but it wasn't her genuine smile. Her embrace earlier was tense, scared. Even her kiss wasn't the same.

Something happened while I was gone. I just don't have time to figure out what it is. Not when I have my own secrets to hide to prevent her from worrying before I know the truth. Not when I should be pushing her away instead of bringing her closer. But I can't keep myself from wanting her. I can't keep my hands from touching her body. I can't.

I can't wait until we get back to our condos. That fight has left us both feeling even more distance between us. I grab and watch her eyes rise in surprise as I lock my lips with hers. She doesn't resist for long, though; she never can, even when she is obviously mad at me. Just one kiss brings her back to me. It's one of the reasons she is so amazing. It's one of the reasons I love her.

Our kisses aren't soft or reluctant. Instead, I kiss her roughly, showing her how desperate I am to have her right now. She attacks me right back. Her tongue thrusts inside my mouth as she lets out a loud groan.

My hands find her hips, and I pull her over onto my lap as our lips continue brutalizing each other, punishing each other for not telling the truth. Punishing each other for keeping secrets. How could this ever work when we keep these kind of secrets from each other?

Her hips thrust on top of me rubbing me until I'm hard, begging to be inside her.

Her lips move to my neck, and she sucks first before biting hard, showing me exactly how she needs it. Rough. Dirty. Passionate.

I growl my response as I lift her shirt and find her nipples, taking them roughly into my mouth. Her body convulses at the pleasure running through her body. Her legs dig into my sides as she squeezes my body underneath her. I feel the rough metal of her prosthetic, but it doesn't even faze me. It just feels like Alex.

I move to her other nipple sucking viciously as her hands tangle in my hair. I want her naked. I want her tied up. I want her screaming in pain as my cock moves inside her. I can't do everything I want, though, not here in her car. But I can't wait until later to have her. I have to have her now.

Her hands are fumbling at my jeans trying to get them undone. She feels the same. I help her undo the button and zipper, and her hand does the rest. Finding my hard cock, she releases it from the fabric keeping it from her. Her hand moves over me.

"Fuck, Alex!"

"That's the idea," she says smirking.

I push her back, and she squeals as I grab at her shorts pulling them down her legs. I'm tempted to rip them to shreds. She deserves it after her teasing, but then she would have to walk into the condo half naked and nobody gets to see her glorious pussy except me.

My hand finds her soaked pussy and begins moving over her and working her body into a frenzy. It doesn't take much at this point to bring her close. I can tell as her hips meet my hand with each movement that she is close. That she needs me inside her now. That she can't wait.

I position her pussy over my cock and drive her down on top of it. We both groan in unison as our bodies meld together. Even in the car where we hardly have room to move, it feels like heaven to be joined like this.

Everything feels better being inside her. Everything disappears. The sound of the rain. The dark sky. Caroline. Ethan. They are all just faint memories. All I can think about is Alex. Just Alex.

Our bodies move together faster and faster. With each movement, I try to get farther inside Alex. With each movement, she tries to pull me in farther. It's rough. It's carnal. It's just pure need. Need to know that we are both as connected as much as we can despite what we are hiding.

But even as we thrust in unison, I feel her slipping away from me. I know she feels it too. It's on her face. Her face is lost, barely even with me.

"Stay with me, Alex," I say not sure if she is having a panic attack or if her mind is just somewhere else.

Her lips find mine, and I bite down hard until I taste the blood that I need to fill my mouth. She moves away licking her lip.

"I'm with you, Landon."

I thrust again, and this time, her moan is carnal. It's animalistic. She no longer has control of her body, which is exactly what I want. I don't want her thinking; I just want her feeling. I need her to feel every drop of desperation and need that I pour into her.

My thumb finds her clit, rubbing fast, and I watch as her whole body changes as she grows close. I grab her hair, pulling hard to give her the pain she needs to send her over the edge, and it sends us both over at the same time.

Her body collapses on top of mine, and I feel her heart beating fast in her chest at the same speed as mine. I could stay like this forever. Despite how uncomfortable it is, I don't care. I want her on top of me like this forever. I want her to forget about secrets and pain and pasts. I want her to forget about what the future may or may not hold. I just want us to be in the now.

She doesn't get my silent plea, though. She pulls up her shorts and falls back into the driver's seat. I push myself back into my jeans and zip them up.

She is fussing with her hair as she stares out at the rain. That is so unlike her because she never fusses with her hair that much. When she glances back at me, I know I've already lost her. Again.

Her mind is on something else. Not on the amazing experience we just had together.

She starts the car back up in silence, and I grab hold of her hand needing her to be close to me. I need her to know I still love her. I need her to know I'm not letting her go. I need her to stay with me.

"I love you," I say.

She forces her lips into a tight smile. "I love you too."

The rest of the drive to the condo goes fast. Not because we enjoy our time together, but because I'm afraid the second we get back to our condos, she will want to stay in hers. Alone. And then I'll be alone.

I can't handle that. I need more. I need to fuck her all night until I knock whatever is going on in her brain out of her head. I need to fuck her until she can't think about anything but the pleasure between her legs. I need to show her that she is mine, not Ethan's. Not anyone else's.

We walk into our condo building side by side. We walk into the elevator together, and that's when we both freeze. Neither of us pushes a button. Neither one of us wants to have to make the decision of whose place we are staying at or if we should go our separate ways.

I take a deep breath and then step forward and push the button for my floor. My eyes stay glued to hers the whole time. I wait for her to push hers as well, but she doesn't. I sigh in relief when the elevator passes her floor.

When the doors open on my floor, though, she hesitates.

"Is this okay?"

I rush back to her and scoop her up in my arms. "Of course. I don't want you anywhere but with me."

She nods as I let her feet touch the ground again. I grab her hand and lead her into my condo.

"You hungry?"

She shakes her head.

"Thirsty?"

She shakes her head again.

"Tired?"

She shakes her head again.

I sigh. I don't know what to do with this woman. So I lead her up to my balcony overlooking the dark ocean. My favorite place. Our favorite place. The only place I have been able to win her back when I clearly don't deserve it.

I take a seat on one of the couches and pull her into my lap. I hold her and kiss the back of her hair. It feels good to have her in my arms. Almost too good. So good that I'm afraid to lose it again. It's what prompts me to say the only thing that I think will help keep her with me.

"Move in with me."

I feel her body tense when I say the words, but she had to have been expecting that. I've already fucking proposed. It's only natural to backtrack a little, and this is the obvious next step. We shouldn't move in together, at least not until I can be honest with her, but I just can't help it. That would also mean publicly living together. She may feel it's too soon to move in with me when she hasn't even filed for divorce from Ethan. When those wounds are still fresh.

I wrap my hands tighter around her body like that is going to prevent her from deciding to go elsewhere. Like that will convince her to move in with me. I listen to her chest rise and fall too many times before words escape her lips.

"Okay."

"Really?" I say spinning her body around so that she is looking at me. I need to see her face. I need to see that she is serious. Her face shows nothing but seriousness. I smile. I don't know what I was expecting, but it wasn't that. I was expecting a fight. I was expecting all the reasons we shouldn't.

"Not here, though," she says.

I cock my head to the side. "Why not?"

She smiles looking out over the ocean. "This place is beautiful, but you share it with Drew. I want a place that we buy together. I want a place that is ours."

I nod before I kiss her deeply. I'll give her whatever she wants as long as she stays with me. I'll do anything to keep her from slipping away including keeping another secret that will destroy her.

Chapter Seven

CAROLINE

I stumble backward until I'm pressed against a wall. I pant hard at Drew's controlling, possessive touch that makes me want him even more.

"WAIT," I hear him say as I climb into the limo that was provided for me. I don't wait I climb into the limo. The concert was long. Far too long. And now, I'm exhausted. I shouldn't have stayed, but I did. I needed to be with him as long as possible. I needed to see what my future life would be like. I needed to see how my child would grow up. My child will spend a lot of time on the road. I know that. Landon won't ever slow his life down, but he will give everything to my child. He will give my child money, and love, and everything that neither of us had growing up. He'll be the perfect father. The father any child deserves.

A hand catches the door as the driver attempts to swing it shut. A hand I recognize. A hand I don't want to see. I'm not ready for this fight. I'm still mad at him for breaking up my wedding. I'm still mad at him for all the rest too. I just need to get to my hotel.

Contrary to what everyone thinks, I did not fly to Chicago just to meet with Landon. I have an early morning meeting here before flying back to LA.

The door slowly opens, and I see Drew's intense dark brown eyes staring at me.

"We need to talk," he says.

I shake my head. "It's late. We can talk later."

"No. Now."

I sigh. I've known Drew my entire life, and there is no arguing with him. He's more stubborn than Landon is. More serious. He would make a terrible father. Too serious, too stern. Never allowing our children to have any fun. I don't envy the woman and children who end up with him. Not that he will have any children. That's not possible when you don't even date.

I slide over in the limo, and Drew slides in next to me before slamming the door shut and effectively shutting out everything except us. I let my eyes travel over Drew's body. His fitted suit looks just as clean and perfect as it did when I first saw him when we first arrived at the concert. I try to think back to our childhood, but I can't remember a time Drew didn't dress nice, formal. Even when we didn't have enough money to buy nice things, somehow, Drew always looked nice.

I feel his eyes on me taking in my lifted boobs exposed in this skintight dress. I smile. I love the attention. Even if it's his attention and not Landon's.

The driver begins driving, taking me to the hotel that Landon got for me. I assume Drew is staying there as well. Although, I am surprised he didn't take the private jet back with Landon.

"Why didn't you ride back with Landon?"

His glare intensifies as he studies my face. "I need to talk to you."

"So you are going to wait, be forced to spend a night in the hotel, and fly commercial tomorrow all so you can talk to me? I hate to tell you, but you're going to be disappointed because I have nothing to tell you. You should have gone back with Landon. I'm still mad at you."

He smirks in his cocky manner. "I should be right here. My job is to protect Landon. To protect his career from predators like you. I know you both too well not to know something is up. Landon will tell me whatever it is. He's too busy worrying about getting back to Alex to tell me now, but he will. I thought I would give you a chance to hear your side of the story first, though."

I wince when he says Landon flew back to see Alexa. It hurts. It hurts that even after finding out that I am carrying his child, he would still run back to another woman. Not for long, though. As soon as this baby is born, he'll be mine. As soon as Alexa finds out the truth, he'll have no option but me and this child.

"Why would you want to hear my side anyway? You'll just think I'm lying. You never liked me. You always thought I was bad for Landon. You always encouraged him to stay as far away from me as possible. You hate me. And I hate you."

Now, Drew's face shows hurt. I narrow my eyes at him not understanding why in the hell my words would hurt him. He doesn't care about me. He never has. He was happy when Landon walked away from my marriage.

"Try me," he says softening his voice.

I shake my head before staring down at my lap. I'm not going to tell him. He's right, though; Landon will tell him. They are twins. They tell each other everything. I just can't. He needs to hear everything from Landon. He'll believe him. He won't believe a word out of my mouth.

Drew takes my hand from my lap and rubs it gently like he used to when we were children. The touch is soft. It's sweet. It's comforting. I close my eyes as a peace comes over me that I haven't felt in years. He hasn't done that since high school. I forgot how centering his touch could be.

He stops when I open my eyes, and he can see the calmness in my eyes.

"Thank you," I say.

He nods before glancing at my other hand where I still wear the engagement ring Landon gave me.

He smiles at it. "I'm glad you kept the ring."

I nod suspiciously at him. Why would he be happy I kept a ring? Wouldn't he prefer I returned it so that Landon could get his money back?

"I was with Landon that day. The day he bought the ring." He pauses. “I thought it was the wrong decision. I didn’t think he was good enough for you.”

My mouth falls open slightly. “I always thought I was the one who wasn’t good enough for him.”

He shakes his head as his eyes meet mine. “No, he was never good enough for you. Especially after what he did. He didn’t deserve you, and he still doesn’t.” He glances down at my hand. “Still, I’m glad he gave you this ring. I’m glad you kept the ring. You deserve it. It’s just like your mother’s.”

I feel tears welling up in my eyes. I didn’t know that he was with Landon when he bought this ring. I didn’t know he even remembered that my mother had a ring like this.

I open my mouth and then close it before opening it again. “Who do you think I deserve to be with if not Landon?”

His eyes lock with mine for far too long before he shakes his head. “I don’t know. Anybody would be better than he would.”

I look out the dark window as we drive closer to our hotel. I don’t know why, but I feel disappointed.

Drew reaches out and touches my chin until I’m facing him again.

“Why did you come back? What is going on with you and Landon?” His hand goes back to mine, rubbing it calmly.

I take a deep breath. I don’t why I want to answer him, but I do. I don’t know if it’s the look on his face or the story about my ring or the comforting touch on my hand. He just makes me feel safe.

“I’m pregnant.”

His eyes grow wide, but his hand stays on mine soothing me even when he’s trying to soothe himself.

“Whose?”

I study his face, but he already knows the answer.

“His.” I nod.

“Are you sure?”

I nod again. “Pretty sure. The timing is right, and he’s the only one I didn’t use protection with. We are getting a paternity test to be sure.”

He sucks in a breath and nods. His hand moves a little faster over my hand now, but it still keeps me calm.

“How are you doing?”

I raise my eyebrows at him. I was not expecting that. I was expecting him to be worried about how this would affect Landon. About how it would affect his career and Alexa. I'm glad to have someone on my side. He might be useful in making sure Landon fulfills his responsibilities to me.

I smile. "I'm doing better now."

Chapter Eight

ALEX

263. The number of days I spent living on the streets.

I LOOK around the grand house. The fifth one we have toured. It's beautiful. It's everything anybody could ever want. We have the money for it, but it's not what I want.

Our realtor is busy explaining the craftsmanship of the house to Landon while I trail behind. I look up at the grand staircase in the foyer of the home that has seven bedrooms and eight bathrooms. It's too big. It's not safe here. There are too many large windows. Too many ways Ethan could see into our house to plan an attack. And it reminds me of the house Ethan bought.

I thought that house was equally as beautiful, and even though its beautiful views drew me in, it never felt like home.

Now, though, all I want is revenge. And to set everyone free who has been hurt by Ethan's crimes. I can't look past that. I can't envision a future with Landon and kids. All I can picture are my hands tightening around Ethan's neck. Or firing a gun at his head as a bullet sinks into his brain. Or stabbing him in the back. I can't see past my hatred.

I look up to see Landon glance back with a tight smile before turning his attention back to the realtor. He's been distant, far too distant, since he got back a week ago.

I reach into my pocket and feel both of the flash drives there. I went back to my condo to get the one I threw away. The one I still haven't decided if I should look at or not.

Landon and our realtor walk back to me.

"So what do you think?" Landon asks.

I shake my head. "I don't like it."

He tries to hide his sigh with a smile, but I still see it. He's frustrated, as he probably should be, after looking at houses for three days straight. He has another concert to go to this weekend, so today is the last day we can look together until next week.

I glance over at our realtor who is frowning. She expected after we said we wanted to find something quick that it would be quick. I suspect she is ready to get her million-dollar commission. I suspect she thought this would be an easy payday. It's not been, though.

"What about something smaller and cozier? What about something more secluded?"

The realtor looks at Landon, who nods in agreement. He doesn't seem to have an opinion about where we live, or if he does, he is keeping it to himself. So far, he has gone along with whatever I say.

The realtor pulls out her phone. "Just give me a few minutes to see if I can find something more *cozy*. Are we still looking at the same budget?"

Landon glances at me before answering. "Yes."

We both watch as she hurries outside to go find us something that better fits what I want. Although, I'm still not sure I know what I want.

"Is something going on?" he asks.

"No."

He moistens his lips as he moves closer to me until he is holding me in his arms. "It just seems to me like you don't want to move in together. Have you changed your mind?"

I shake my head. "No. I just realized I don't want this big of a house. I don't want maids to help me clean it and take care of it. I don't want guards to protect all of our expensive things. I just want something simple something that is just the two of us. I might change my mind later. If we take our relationship to the next level, maybe, but I don't want that right now. It feels too much like ..."

He narrows his eyes. "Like the house Ethan bought you."

I nod.

"But we can buy something better than what Ethan bought you. We can get something even grander. We have the money. We could buy a house with twenty bedrooms and thirty something bathrooms."

I raise my eyebrows at him as I lean back to look in his eyes. "And what will we do with all of these bedrooms?"

He shrugs innocently as he smiles cockily. His lips crash with mine as his tongue slips into my mouth for just a second, teasing me with what he wants before pulling away. "We could fill them."

My mouth drops. I had no idea Landon wanted children. I imagined the forever bachelor would never want such a thing. I'm not sure if I share the same vision.

"You really want children?"

He smiles wickedly. "Maybe. I haven't really thought much about it yet. But I want everything with you. And we could have fun trying in all of those bedrooms."

I blush as I stare up at a man who loves me. A man I love in return. How did I get so lucky to find someone like him despite all of my troubles?

"Someday, then. Now, though, I want somewhere for just the two of us. Somewhere cozy that we can grow closer instead of further apart."

"Cozy it is, then."

He pulls me against his chest as his lips find mine again. It's heavenly. Every single time his lips touch mine, I get lost in it. His tongue caresses mine making me moan in a not so innocent manner.

I hear our realtor clear her throat, and I pull away from Landon slightly embarrassed. He glares at the realtor, though, for interrupting what I can only imagine he thought was going to be a quick fuck in one of the house's seven bedrooms.

"I found something," she says.

I nod and pull Landon out of the house to his Porsche parked outside the house next to the realtor's SUV. She offered to drive us, but Landon wouldn't hear of it.

As we climb in his car, I'm glad he drove. It gives me time to think about what I want. It gives me time to hold Landon's hand while thinking about my plan. I need to start surveilling Ethan. I need to find evidence to free everyone, and then I need to find a way to kill him. I don't trust the police to keep him locked away. Not after I found out I've tried going to the police before and they just dismissed me as a crazy woman who was mad at her husband. I won't do that again. I will fix this myself.

Our cars climb higher and higher into the mountains. Each curve getting more and more secluded. I relax. This is what I want. Seclusion. Somewhere it would be hard for Ethan to plan an attack. Somewhere it would be hard for others to reach him if I killed him here.

We round the last curve, and that's when I see the house. It looks magical. There are old stone walls going around the house with green vines growing over them. A large, arched wooded door is at the entrance of the stone walls, keeping everyone out while still looking friendly. The house looks much the same. It's built of stone and brick and looks like something out of a storybook instead of a modern home. Landon parks the car and takes my hand this time as we walk to the wooden door. He feels it too. This is our home. This is what I want.

We push the door open, and I smile when I see the garden that goes all around the house. There are flowers that I don't know the names of. Green plants and large trees. It's paradise in here.

I glance at Landon, who is smiling as he takes it all in. We wait for the realtor to open the door before we walk into the home. Instead of the grand staircase entrance like all of the rest of the homes we have toured, the entrance of this one is small. Yes, there is a staircase, but it is tucked away to the side; instead, the front entrance of the house gives a view to the back of the house where a beautiful stone fireplace and cozy living room sits next to an expansive kitchen. I hear our realtor talking. Something about three bedrooms and three baths. And only one living room and kitchen compared to the other houses' two or three. I don't hear her, though. I'm too busy falling in love.

I glance up at Landon who, to my surprise, seems to be falling in love with it too. I thought he would want something modern. Something more manly. Something closer to his condo, but he seems to be falling for the charm of this place just like I am. I glance out the window to a large yard in the back. I see a small tire swing hanging from one of the large oak trees.

I try to imagine Landon pushing a kid on that swing while I read a book on the bench, occasionally glancing up to see them smiling and laughing together. I could imagine it. I could imagine a life without pain. A life without my past. A life that is just about us.

Chapter Nine

LANDON

He left me alone in the dark.
He left me on my own to deal
With my own pain, hurt, and loss.

I HATED LEAVING ALEX, but I had to. I have another concert in Dallas that was already booked. While Alex has to stay and move us into our new home.

I smile thinking about it. I didn't think I would like the home. I thought I wanted something big and grand. Something that showed off how hard we both worked for our money. Something that proved that I was never going back to living the way that both of us grew up. With nothing. But something about that cottage just felt right. It felt like a home instead of just a mansion. I'm happy she convinced me to try it out and not just because she loves it. I love it too.

I glance at Drew riding in the back of the SUV with me. He hasn't said a word. Not one fucking word to me since we got on our flight out of here. He hasn't even been on his phone like usual. Instead, he just stares out his window in a trance. I know I haven't been the best brother lately. I've been focused on Alex, then Caroline, then Alex, then Caroline again. I have no idea what's going on with Drew's life. I have no idea.

We used to spend a lot of time together, but other than our business trips, we haven't spent any time together since I met Alex. I should really make more of an effort, but I can't. Not while I'm still trying to figure out what I'm going to do about Caroline. Or what I'm going to tell Alex.

Dallas is hard, though. It's hard on both of us. It's where we grew up. It's where our father is.

"How are you holding up?"

"Fine," Drew says without looking at me.

"Are you going to see him?"

That gets his attention.

"I don't know. Are you?"

I shrug. "I've been thinking about it. It's been almost ten years. I think it's time."

"Yeah, maybe."

I sit back in my seat and stare out at the buildings as the Dallas skyline comes into view.

"I know," he says after a long break in the conversation.

"You know what?"

"I know why Caroline was at your concert in Chicago."

I glance up at our driver, and Drew follows my gaze. He won't say anything, not with the driver here. It doesn't matter how many non-disclosure agreements we have our employees sign. Things this dirty always get out. Always.

We can't take that chance. I know Drew won't rat me out.

"It's true."

"I know it is. What are you going to do?"

I rub my hand on the back of my neck. "I'm not sure, Drew. I really fucked up this time. I don't know what to do."

He sighs. "Yeah, you fucked up ... Just don't hurt her."

"Which one?"

"Both, I guess."

I turn my attention from Drew and back to the window. I don't know how that is possible. I don't know how to keep from hurting Alex or Caroline. I just hope I don't end up hurting them both.

Chapter Ten

DREW

When I let her come up for air, I expect her to tell me this is wrong. That this is a mistake. Instead, she licks her lips, begging for more.

I PICK up the blue phone at the same time my father does on the other side of the visitor's glass in the jail. He looks old. Much older than the last time I saw him. He looks worn down. He looks empty. At least, he's sober. If it weren't for him being arrested and thrown in prison, he would be dead. I have no doubt about that.

"Wow, both of my sons visit in one day. Ain't I a lucky man." His voice is crass as he speaks into the phone.

My lips remain in a firm grimace as I stare at the man who fathered me. Not that he did much to take care of us since the day we were born.

"What are you doing here, son? Come here to yell at me like your brother did?"

I flinch when he says the word son. I hate that I am his son. I'm surprised Landon came to see him. Even though he said he would, I doubted it. I guess the need to yell at Father for his fucked-up life was strong enough.

"You deserve to be yelled at, though," I say even though I'm still mad at Landon.

"Like hell, I do! I'm still your father, you ungrateful little shit. I deserved to be visited more than once every ten years."

I glare at my father. "This was a mistake coming here. I don't know what coming here was supposed to solve. I just thought..."

"You thought coming to see your old man would make you feel better about yourself. You thought seeing me like this would make your troubles seem small in comparison to me."

He spits on the ground. "I won't give you the satisfaction. See, I got fifteen months left, maybe half with good behavior, and then I'm out of here. I can start my life over again. I'll leave my troubles behind. My troubles are here in prison, but out there, I have no troubles. You, though. Your troubles will follow you wherever you go. Just like Landon's."

I frown. I forgot that his sentence is almost up. It makes no difference, though. This will be the last time I see him. The last time. I don't need to go through this again. He's the reason Landon and I had no childhood. He's the reason we fought for everything we have. His genes are the reason Landon destroyed everything. His genes are the reason we can never drink or end up like him. A monster. He's the reason Landon is a monster.

"I know about Landon's secret."

"What?"

"I know what he did to that man." He smirks as my eyes grow wide with fear. Fear for my brother.

"It's a wonder he didn't end up in the jail cell right next to me."

"You don't know what you're talking about."

He smiles. "Sure, I do. Don't worry. I won't talk. I'm not that much of a monster, no matter what you think. What I want to know, though, is how can you forgive him for what he did, but not me?"

"Because Landon has always been there for me. He's made mistakes, but he was always a good brother. Unlike you."

"I was a better father than either of you deserved." He shakes his head. "But that's not why Landon came here. He made a second mistake. A much bigger mistake in his eyes, and he blames me for it."

"Except he can't blame me for it. See, I haven't been a part of your lives for over ten years."

"But what I don't know is why *you* came here?"

I raise my eyes to meet my father's for the last time. I've carried the pain and guilt with me long enough. I thought I was never a good enough son. I thought that's why he didn't love me. I thought if only I could be better. If only we were able to make something of ourselves, then he would love us.

But that isn't the case. He's a monster. Whether he turned that way after my mother's death or before, I will never know. But my father is gone.

"I came here to say good-bye. I don't need you hanging over my head anymore. I won't come see you again. I don't want you to come asking for money after you get out. You are nothing to me. You are nothing to Landon. Good-bye, Father."

I hesitate a second before hanging up the phone and watch as his lips slowly curl up.

"You are just like your brother." He shakes his head. "This isn't good-bye. You'll be back. Just like Landon. You'll both be back. I'm the only family you've got."

I smirk. "You're wrong. I have more family than you know."

I hang up the phone before he can respond. I have plenty of family. I have Landon even when he pisses me off. I know nothing will ever change our relationship. Not like my relationship with my father. And I have a niece or nephew on the way. What more could I need?

Chapter Eleven

ALEX

65. The number of days it took to find a waitressing job.

I SPENT the weekend moving new furniture into the house. We both decided that neither of our furniture would feel right in our home that we share together. So I bought new, cozy furniture for the house.

The only things we moved from our condos were personal things. Clothes and pictures mainly. My camera. And a couple of Landon's guitars.

He's keeping his condo with Drew for now until Drew decides where he wants to live. He'll eventually move his studio from the condo into one of the bedrooms leaving only one left to be filled with …

I'm not going there. I can't. Not again. Not until my past has been reconciled can I think about the future.

I glance out the front window to see if Landon has made it back yet. He hasn't. All I see is Tessie sitting on the dirt driveway. I smile. Landon is going to hate having Silvia sit outside in the dirt when he is used to parking her in grand parking garages. If we stay here, we will have to build a garage. There is enough land for it, but in the meantime, Landon will squirm every time there is a little rain getting Silvia wet. I don't think he was thinking about that when we bought this house.

I walk back to the living room feeling the flash drives in my pocket as I do. I'm surprised I haven't heard from Ethan yet. I figured he would be impatient. I figured he would want an answer immediately or threaten to release whatever was on the flash drive. He hasn't. He hasn't tried to contact me, not once, but I know my time is running out. I know he will. I just don't know when. And I don't know what he is doing in the meantime, which makes him all the more dangerous.

My first step isn't to deal with him, though. My first step is to find the evidence that will free James. That's going to be tough. Ethan has video evidence, even though it isn't real. I need to talk to Curt and Nick, the other security Ethan hired. They might know more. They might be willing to testify on James' behalf.

I hear the engine of Landon's car roar as it makes its way up to our house. My heart rate picks up in anticipation of Landon coming home. To *our* home for the first time.

I meet Landon at the door just as he opens the door. My breath catches at the sight of him. His face is drained of all color. He looks tired and run down. He runs his hand through his hair as his eyes drift up to meet mine. He smiles when he sees me, but the smile wavers. What happened in Dallas?

He drops his suitcase at the door before moving deliberately toward me. His eyes stay firmly on mine and mine never leave his. Neither of us speaks. Neither of us is ready to spill our secrets. Instead, our bodies collide as Landon's lips land on mine with the same desperation as before he left for Dallas. The kiss overwhelms my body as shivers alight every nerve in my body. My hands find his neck as I hang on for dear life, the kiss getting more desperate.

His hands are urgent as they travel over my body. Before landing on my hips. He lifts me and I wrap one leg around him as he carries me to the living room never releasing my lips as he moves.

We fall onto the new couch I bought, but his eyes don't look around to see how the place looks now. His hungry eyes instead travel down my body to my breasts that are begging to be touched beneath my plain white t-shirt. His eyes travel further down my body to my jean shorts, to my leg. When his eyes meet mine again, I see even more hunger. I see even more need. And I need it just as much. I need to feel loved. And I need to feel the pain. I need to feel it all. I need to feel everything that he will give me.

I tug at his t-shirt and pull it up his back and then over his head. I dig my nails into his back as I do. He retaliates by biting my neck until I'm sure a small mark will form there. Harder than he ever has before, but it's not enough for me. I need more pain.

"Fuck, Landon. More," I say as I hold his head on my neck waiting for him to bite me again. He doesn't, though. Instead, he grabs my ass and slaps it hard. Harder than he has before and I cry out in pain and pleasure. I force my eyes shut to keep a tear at bay that formed from the sting of the pain. I don't want him to see because I don't want him to stop.

"More," I say when my breathing has slowed.

I feel his hips press hard into me until I can feel his cock pushing against me through our layers of clothes. I see his face darken as he grabs my shirt and rips it in two.

"You want more?"

"Yes," I breathe.

"You want me to fuck you and mark you so that everyone will know you are mine."

"Yes."

His hand finds my breasts squeezing them hard. Harder than any limits we have crossed before.

"You want me to slap you, and torture you, and own you."

"Yes."

I watch as his face grows darker and more controlling than I have ever seen. It's the last thing I see before he flips me over and my body crashes into the couch.

He has my hands behind my back and immediately ties something around them to keep them in place. I test the strength, trying to wiggle out of it, but I can't. I feel the fabric cut in slightly at my wrists as I try to move.

His body rises off mine, and I feel lost. Weird how one second of his body off mine will do that to me. And then his hand is ripping my shorts from my body just before his hand slaps my ass again hard. So hard, I cry out again.

"I'm going to fuck you so hard," he says hitting me again.

"Oh fuck," I moan as wetness drips down between my legs. Landon notices too and his hand immediately moves from my ass to my slick folds. He pulls the liquid up to my ass coating it before his hand slaps me again. The sting makes me come alive even more as a wave of emotion washes over me that I've never gotten from just the pain alone.

His fingers slip back in my seam before moving back to my ass. I moan at his every touch. I moan at every pain.

"You like that, baby," Landon says seductively in my ear as he slaps me again. I pant but can't catch my breath enough to respond. I feel his lips curl in a smile as he kisses my neck.

I feel his cock pushing at my ass. I feel him coating himself in the liquids he has spread there. But I don't expect him to thrust inside my ass.

"Fuck," I scream.

The pain though only makes me hotter. It only makes me want more and more.

"You're so tight," Landon moans as he begins moving inside me. I squirm beneath him as he moves. Each thrust gets me more and more excited. Each thrust drives me wild.

His balls hit my clit each time he moves sending warm pleasure up my body, but it's not enough to send me over the edge. The pain I felt from him initially entering me is gone. My ass is practically numb from the slaps he delivered. I need more pain to get off.

He senses this, and his thrusts grow more urgent and wild. His slaps get harder and spread around my ass, but it's still not enough. That's when I feel his hands pressing at my throat. He presses harder with each thrust. He presses, and I feel the pain. He thrusts, and I feel the pleasure.

"I love you, Alex," Landon screams as he pounds again putting more weight on my neck, causing just enough pain, and we both come.

It's not a beautiful come like we have experienced before. It's dirty and rough and wrong. So wrong.

As soon as Landon releases inside me, he removes the binding from around my hands. He doesn't collapse on top of me as he has before. Instead, he immediately picks me up and turns me to him so that I am sitting in his lap. He kisses me hard on the lips and it's one of the most intimate moments I've ever experienced. Sitting on his lap completely naked and exposed.

I can't believe I just enjoyed that. I can't believe that I enjoyed that amount of pain. *Instead of releasing me, he flips me onto my stomach and grabs my arms tying them together behind my back. I continue to scream and kick trying to get him off me.* The flashback of being raped comes on strong. I feel the tears welling in my eyes as Landon holds me, but this time, I can't keep them back. They fall hard and fast down my cheeks. I'm so fucked up. The rape. That's why I like pain during sex. It's because I was raped. It's because I had sex with my rapist over and over and over. He conditioned me to like this. He fucking conditioned me to like fucking rough sex.

"Oh god." I sob into Landon's shoulder as my body shakes.

"Baby. I'm so sorry. I shouldn't have done that. I don't know what came over me."

I can't respond to him. The tears fall faster. The terror at realizing Ethan did this to me is too strong. I can't even fuck like a normal person. He's ruined everything in my life.

Landon slowly moves me away from his shoulder so he can look at me. "You aren't having a panic attack, are you?"

I shake my head as more tears fall. The look on his face is of devastation. Complete devastation at what he just did. Except he didn't do anything. Ethan did.

I try to stop the sobbing to tell him that, but I can't. It's too much. The pain is too much.

Landon wraps his arms back around me squeezing me tighter than he ever has before. "I'm so sorry," he says over and over again while I face the fact that I'm sick. I'm twisted. I like sex that reminds me of my rape. How do I move on from that?

Landon rocks me back and forth until both of our tears have run dry. Until we are both shivering from the cold of being naked and wet with tears and cum stains. Landon spots a throw blanket on the end of the couch and wraps me in it. I immediately feel warmer.

"You have nothing to be sorry for," I say in a soft voice.

His thumb wipes away the last remaining tear. "I have everything to be sorry for. I shouldn't have hurt you. I don't know why I did that. I thought you wanted it. But no woman wants that ..." His face scrunches in disgust of what he did.

I grab his face with both hands until he is looking at me. Really looking at me because he needs to hear this. He needs to hear that he's not a monster. I am.

"I wanted that. I wanted the pain. I wanted you to hurt me."

He closes his eyes like my words are too painful for him to hear. I shake his head forcing his eyes open and back on me.

"That was the best sex of my life. I've never come so hard. I've never felt so connected to someone before. It's like you could read my every thought. You could understand what I wanted before I could. You did everything right."

"Then why are you crying?" His eyes look hesitantly into mine.

I tuck a loose strand behind my ear. I haven't told him. I can't tell him everything, but he needs to know something.

"I was raped."

"What? When?"

He moves to get up like he is going to go out right now and find my rapist. He moves with so much purpose and anger as he moves my body off him, and in seconds, he has his jeans and t-shirt back on. I am right in not telling him the complete truth. He can't handle the truth. Not now.

"Landon ..." I grab his hand, and he immediately comes back to me. His arms travel all over my body like they are checking for evidence of rape that he didn't see moments ago.

"It happened before. I don't really remember it." I see Landon's face turn a darker shade of red. His whole body tenses as I speak.

"He's in jail. He got like twenty to life or something."

Landon relaxes a little, but not enough to sit down next to me like I want him to.

"A lot of my panic attacks were about the rape. Although I've gotten past them."

Landon looks down. I grab his face again and force him to look at me. "You helped me get past the panic and fear. But now..."

"Shit, Alex. I brought them back, didn't I? When I hit you. When I hurt your neck. It brought back the panic and fear." Landon stands paces the living room. "Why did you let me fucking do that?"

I stand keeping the blanket wrapped around me. "It's not that. It didn't bring back the panic and fear."

"Then ..." I put my finger to his lips silencing him. I need to get this out, and I won't be able to if he keeps interrupting me. If he keeps guessing the wrong conclusions.

"I'm sick. I like it rough. I like it painful. I can't come without the pain. The rape must have done something to me. It must have made me like this. I'm sick."

A small smile forms on his lips as he looks down at me and tucks a strand of hair behind my ear. I close my eyes as he touches the spot where he bit me and then puts enough pressure on it that I flirted the line between alive and passing out.

"Alex, you're beautiful. You're strong. You're stubborn. Independent to a fault. You have a lot of demons, but you are not sick."

"Yes, I am."

He smirks. "No, you're not. You're stubborn. You're resilient. You're impossible. And you like dirty, rough sex. You like to fuck in a way that most people would find sinful. Just because you were raped doesn't mean anything. Many people like rough sex."

He presses his body against mine and then his lips tug at my lip hard until blood seeps in our mouths mixing together. "There is nothing wrong with us. There is nothing wrong with you."

"But I was raped. What if that triggered me to enjoy painful sex?"

He shakes his head. "Did these thoughts occur when we were having sex or after?"

"After, but I had panic attacks before when we tried to have sex."

"Yeah, but the pain is what took those feelings away. I don't think you enjoying rough sex has anything to do with the rape. And even if it did, you can't let it control you. You have to decide what you want for yourself now."

I nod. He might be right. Ethan raped me and then had normal sex with me after. He didn't seem to be into the rough stuff with me, or maybe he was afraid the rough sex would trigger memories of the rape.

But the pain didn't trigger the memories. It was Ethan. He brought back the panic attacks that Landon had helped heal.

"Now," he says grabbing my hand and shaking me from my thoughts. "Come to bed with me."

I smile, happy to be done talking. "Didn't get enough of me?"

He smiles. "Not nearly enough. And we need to christen our new bed."

I follow him but pause at the bottom of the stairs. "Are we going to have rough sex or normal?"

"Whatever you need."

I think for a moment, but then realize that thinking is going to do nothing for me. I try to listen to my heart instead.

"Dirty."

Chapter Twelve

LANDON

But light by light, you snuck into my world.
I thought I could never be a father after what mine did to me.
But you were born and you rescued me.

YESTERDAY WAS HARD. Alex told me she had been raped. I about exploded when she told me that. I so badly wanted to hunt the bastard down and strangle him with my bare hands. I've never been so angry sober. Never. I always suspected that that was what had happened, but we never had any proof that it did. Now, we do. Now, it becomes real.

She's known for far too long, though, without telling me. Just another secret we keep from each other. Just another lie by omission.

She won't tell me anything else, though. Just that the bastard is in jail. She won't tell me how or where or when. She says she doesn't remember, but I know she does. I won't force her, though. I don't need to know, but she will tell me eventually. I have faith that she will. In the meantime, I get to imagine all of the horrible ways he could have done it. I get to imagine all of the horrible things I want to do to him.

The sex last night, though. That's what I should really be focusing on. It was dark. It was dirty. It was rough. It was love. It was everything that either of us ever wanted.

But I can't think about any of it. Instead, all I can think about is three days ago just before I left for Dallas. It seems like such a short time ago and such a long time ago all at the same time. It was the day I went in to a clinic and had blood drawn. It was the day I submitted my blood for a paternity test. When I was sitting in the chair with a needle in my arm, all I kept thinking about was this day couldn't come soon enough. I kept thinking this couldn't be real. This couldn't be right. One night couldn't result in pregnancy. One night couldn't do that. Except one night did. I just don't know if it was my one night or another.

Today, I find out. Today, I find out if Caroline will forever taint my life. Today, I find out if I have a future with Alex. Today, I find out if I'm going to be a father.

I pull my car into the garage of Caroline's swanky Beverly Hills apartment and pull easily into a visitor's parking spot just as I have done hundreds of times before. Each time before was for a booty call when we were dating. And even after we were dating.

I deserve this, I think, as I climb out of my car. I've treated Caroline badly for years. I used her for sex. It's no wonder the gods decided that my punishment would be to have a child with the woman I scorned.

I enter the building but don't bother with the elevator. Instead, I take the stairs up to the fifth floor. It feels good to get my blood pumping a little as I climb the stairs. It shakes out some of the nerves so that by the time I reach her apartment door I'm not shaking as badly.

The door opens quickly as if she was waiting just on the other side for me to get here. I sneak in quickly, not wanting any of her neighbors to see me.

I don't speak when I see her; I just pull her into a hug instead. When I let her go, that's when I realize how much of a mess she is. Dark, baggy circles hang under her eyes. She's still in her pajamas and her hair is up in a messy bun. This isn't Caroline. She would never spend a day like this, not unless she was sick.

"Have you eaten anything?" I ask when I notice she somehow looks smaller instead of bigger despite being pregnant.

She shakes her head. I lead her into the kitchen and help her sit at one of the two barstools looking into her small kitchen.

I don't bother to ask her what she wants; I just open her fridge and search for something healthy. She doesn't have much food, though. Just eggs and milk and bread. I sigh as I take the eggs out and begin to make her scrambled eggs and toast.

"You have to start taking better care of yourself," I say not looking at her as I scramble the eggs in a skillet.

"I'm trying," she says weakly.

"You have to try harder. When is your next doctor's appointment?"

"Not for a few weeks."

"I'm going to hire you a chef and maid to help take care of things around here."

She doesn't object. She doesn't say anything. I'm going to have to start checking on her more or she's going to lose the baby, and as much as that would make my life easier, it's not what I want. She wouldn't ever forgive herself if she lost the baby.

When I finish making her breakfast, I place it in front of her and then I take a seat next to her.

She lifts the fork on autopilot and begins to eat but doesn't look at me.

"What are you thinking about?"

"That I'm going to make a terrible mother."

I grab her and force her to look at me. "You are going to make an amazing mother. You are not like your mother." *Just like I'm not like my father*, I think.

She shakes her head, and I understand. I understand that is too hard to believe. I understand because I feel the same way. I'm afraid I'll end up just like my father. And no child should be raised that way.

"I'm afraid you aren't the father, and then I'll have no one."

I take a deep breath when I realize her fears are the opposite of mine. She fears I'm not the father. I fear I am. "No matter what, I'm going to be in this baby's life. I'm not going to abandon you. I'll help financially. I'll help in every way you need."

She tries to turn her lips up in a smile, but her lips don't fully curl up. She still looks sad and worried.

"I'll go get it," she says getting up from the table despite only eating a couple of bites of her breakfast. I have to make her eat more when she gets back.

She comes back from her bedroom quickly with an envelope in her hand. I stand as she comes near me, and she hands me the envelope without looking at it. Instead, she stares at her feet as she wraps her arms around her stomach.

I turn the envelope over and am surprised to see it is still sealed. If it had been sent to me, I'm not sure I would have had enough strength to wait until she got here to open it.

"You ready?" I ask.

"Open it."

I keep my eyes on her as I slip my finger under the fold of the envelope and slice it open. I watch as she closes her eyes in fear as her arms wrap tighter around herself.

I pull the piece of paper out of the envelope with surprisingly steady hands. Probably because I already know what it will say. I already know that no matter what it says, it won't change how I feel about Caroline or Alex or this baby. It won't change my actions. It will just change my future.

I skim the paper with my name at the top and with several numbers that don't mean anything to me. I skim until I get to the bottom with the results. I skim until I see the number 99.998% probability.

I close my eyes and tip my head back just for a second. When I open my eyes again, Caroline is staring at me. She takes my actions as relief. And it is relief. Relief that I finally know the answer. That I don't need to guess about my future anymore.

"I'm going to be a father," I say handing her the paper and smiling at her the best I can, even though inside, my heart is breaking for Alex.

Chapter Thirteen

CAROLINE

I look at him with lust in my eyes. I don't know why I want him. He's not Landon. He's not what I want. Except he is.

I TAKE the piece of paper out his hands and stare down at it for myself. My eyes widen when I see the number 99.998% chance that Landon is the father. I'm not sure I believe it even still. I never thought it was really true. I just hoped because I know, despite what he thinks about his past, he will make the best father.

Better than any other man I have ever met.

A happy tear falls down my face as Landon pulls me into a hug. He's going to be in my life forever whether he marries that skank or me. He's mine forever.

When he finally pulls away from me, he is still smiling to my surprise.

"What are we going to do now?" I ask.

He sucks in a breath. "We are going to take care of you and our baby." He reaches out and touches my stomach. It feels amazing to have his hand touching me there, but it's not what I want an answer to.

"What about Alexa?"

A frown forms on his face at the mention of her. "I'm going to tell her the truth and then see what she wants to do."

I frown. I don't like it. It's not enough. She could forgive him for this. After all, they weren't together when it happened.

"I see," is all I say.

"Don't," he says lifting my chin to look up at him. "Don't feel like I don't care about you. Like I don't love you in your own way. I do. I just love her too. I'm just trying to do right by both of you."

"What if that isn't possible?"

He looks down at my stomach. "Then I'll do right by our baby."

I smile.

"I have to go, though. I have a meeting with my choreographer this afternoon. I'm going to call Drew, though. He can make sure you have whatever you need. You should probably start looking for a new place soon. He can help you do that. And I'll make sure he arranges to have a chef and maid to help take care of you when one of us can't be here."

"You aren't going to look for a house with me?"

He freezes as he looks at me. "No."

I nod in understanding because it's a hard line for him. He walks back to me and gives me a soft kiss on the cheek. "I'll call you soon. Call me if anything happens with the baby, and I'll send Drew over soon."

I nod again as he walks to the door. He pauses as he opens it and looks back at me. "It's all going to be okay."

I smile as he leaves. It is all going to be okay. It's going to be better than okay. I just need to make sure Alex is out of his life. I rub my stomach as I think about it. I'm such a bitch for ruining another woman's life, but I have to. I will do whatever to protect this baby inside me. I will not let the same fate come to this baby as what happened to me. I will be strong. I will be a mother.

"We need to stop for lunch," Drew says.

"But we have three more houses to look at."

He frowns as his eyes glares at me. "Lunch."

I sigh. "Fine, but I'm really excited to look at the next house. It might be the one."

"You said that about the last six. I don't know what you are looking for, Caroline, but any of them seem fine to me."

Drew parks his Mercedes in front of one of my favorite restaurants, despite the fact that I never go here. It has pasta and carbs and fat and everything an actress despises. I don't know if I will be able to turn it down today, though. I'm starving, and the baby is hungry.

I watch as Drew walks around to my side of the car; he opens my door and holds out his hand to help me climb out of the car in my teal dress and heels. I feel better after getting dressed properly. I'll feel even better after a good meal.

"Thank you," I say as I climb out. Drew smiles at me.

"You're welcome." His eyes dart to my dress taking in my still tight body despite the pregnancy. Although I doubt that will last much longer. His hand finds the small of my back as we walk to the restaurant.

"If I remember correctly, this was one of your favorites."

"Yes."

We take a seat at a small table opposite each other. The waiter comes over and asks us what we want to drink.

"White wine," I say on autopilot before I remember I can't.

Drew frowns at me, scolding me like the father figure he always was. He was always trying to keep Landon and me out of trouble. Except we didn't want to be kept out of trouble. Maybe we should have, though, and we wouldn't be in this situation. We wouldn't have so much baggage that we will never escape from.

"Water," I say quickly.

"Water," Drew says.

"Can we also go ahead and order our meals? I'm starving," I say as Drew beams at me, happy to hear that I will be eating something.

"Of course," the waiter says.

"I'll have the lasagna with a side salad dressing on the side. Can we also start with an appetizer of breadsticks and the Caprese salad."

The waiter writes everything down.

"Oh and a side of the fettuccine alfredo."

The waiter's eyes grow large as he turns to Drew.

"I'll just take a salad," he says handing the waiter our menus.

Drew just sits staring at me a huge smile on his face.

"What?"

"Nothing. Just happy to see you eating. You're far too skinny."

"I am not. Don't let my agent hear you say that. She won't let me out with you again. I'm already three pounds heavier than I was."

His smile just gets brighter. "You're beautiful."

I don't know why, but his words make me blush. His words never have before. I take a sip of the water the waiter brought us to cool my flushed cheeks.

"So what did you think about the last house we looked at?" I ask.

"It was nice."

"Just nice? It was grand and beautiful."

He nods. "It was. It also wasn't the house for you."

"What do you mean?"

He shrugs. "I don't know. It just didn't feel like the right house for you."

"Why not?"

"I expect you to find something that is completely unique and beautiful like you. That one didn't have enough ..."

"Enough what?"

"Enough strength in its beauty. It was just beautiful and fragile."

I stare at him wide-eyed. He's wrong if he thinks I'm anything but fragile.

The conversation ends, though, when our appetizers are brought out and I dig into the food. Loving the taste and how it feels as it slides down my throat.

"You know I'm going to be there, right?" Drew says suddenly out of nowhere.

I swallow my bite trying to understand what he's saying.

"I'll be there for you and the baby. No matter what happens between you and Landon."

The gesture is sweet. I know he means it, but I don't need Drew. I need Landon. And frankly, I'm still mad at Drew for ruining my best chance at happiness with Landon.

"I know, Drew, but I don't want you to. It's not your responsibility. It's Landon's. The test proved that."

He nods and then opens his mouth to say more but thinks better of it.

I return to eating. The test said it was Landon's. The test proved it, despite my reservations. There is no arguing with 99.998% accuracy. It's fact, not a theory. Landon's the father. It's Landon's.

Chapter Fourteen

ALEX

53. The number of days my mother had left to live when she got the cancer diagnosis.

I FIRE THE GUN, making me jump the first time the slick handgun backfires in my hand. I look at the paper with an outline of a man hanging opposite me. I hit the target right in the middle. Right in the heart.

I fire over and over, getting more precise with each shot. Each backfire seeming less and less extreme. Each shot making me feel more and more confident as I hit the target's heart over and over. Never missing.

I smile after I stop. I won't miss. When the time comes, I won't miss.

My phone buzzes in my pocket, and I answer it.

"Hello."

"I can meet you in ten minutes at the coffee shop on Fifth Street."

"See you then," I say hanging up the phone. I hate being secretive, but it's the only way. Nick agreed to meet me. He agreed not to speak of this to Ethan or Laura. I told him I was in trouble and needed him to come. I told him I thought somebody else might be after me, but I didn't want Ethan to worry. So he agreed to meet me and to keep it a secret. That's why we didn't agree on when or where until now.

I put the gun in my purse. I won't need it today, but soon. I know my time is running out, and I will have to use it soon to save my life. But I have to figure out how to save James first.

I get to the coffee shop five minutes late. I walk in and get a coffee, but I don't spot Nick anywhere. I take a seat at a table near the back and wait.

I wait for over an hour, but he never shows. I'm tempted to call him, but I'm afraid if he didn't show it's for a reason. Someone contacted and told him not to show. Ethan.

It just proves Ethan is tracking me or my phone or both. God, what the hell am I doing? I don't know how I'm going to do this. I don't have any skills. One day at a gun range doesn't suddenly make me a sharpshooter. I don't know how to protect myself. I don't know how to find the evidence. At this rate, he'll kill me before I even spot him, and then knowing him, he will blame my death on Landon or some other innocent person.

I can't do this. Not alone. I need to tell Landon. I need help. I need protection.

I look up deciding I've stayed here long enough when I see him walking straight to me. A frown on his face. Ethan.

I try to glance around the coffee shop for an exit, but the only exit is in front of me. Past Ethan. I'm fucked. I can't leave. I'm going to have to talk to him. I reach inside my purse and feel the gun there. I don't pull it out, but I leave my hand on the trigger all the same ready to use it if I have to.

When he reaches me, his frown turns to a smile as he takes a seat in front of me.

"I'm glad you haven't left yet."

"How did you know I would be here at all?"

"Nick told me."

Fucking asshole, I think. "What exactly did Nick tell you?"

"He said you were worried that James wasn't the only one after you. That you needed his help. You needed protection."

I take a deep breath, trying to remain calm. I didn't tell Nick anything. I didn't tell him that Ethan is the monster not James. I just told him I was scared. And I am.

"I'm scared," I say my voice shaky adding credibility to the lie. Except it isn't a lie. I am scared.

Ethan reaches his hand across the table and touches my hand. My gut reaction is to pull my hand away, but I don't. I let him touch me. I can't let him know he is the person I'm afraid of.

"I'm afraid James isn't the only one out there who wants me dead. So many people have targeted us. I must be missing some bigger picture. What if someone has been hiring all of these people to hurt me? To hurt us? What if he is still out there? What if he is hiring someone else right now to kill us?"

Ethan squeezes my hand harder. "That's why I want you home. So I can protect you. I can hire all sorts of protection to protect you."

"I can hire my own protection," I say. "But that's why I went to Nick. I want to know if you are keeping something from me that I should know. Do you know who is behind all of these attacks?"

"No. I don't. I've told you everything I know. I still wish you would come home. I miss you. And I really don't want to have to force you to come home."

I glare at him and remove my hand from his. "You can't force me."

He looks at me as if I'm a child. "I already told you I can. I can destroy Landon's career. I can send him to jail. I have evidence that will put him away for twenty years to life."

My eyes grow wider with fear. He framed Landon. The evidence is on the flash drive. I just don't know what evidence he claims to have. I add Landon to my mental list of the people I have to save.

"You have one week," he says getting up. "One week to come home or I turn the evidence over to the police."

I glare at him as I watch him leave, keeping my hand on the gun the whole time. I should just shoot the bastard in the back. It would be quick and easy, and then I would never have to worry about him again, but then I couldn't save any of us. We would all end up in jail.

As soon as I watch him walk out the door, I dig my phone out my purse to call Landon. I'm not going to be able to manage driving back by myself. I need him to come get me. And I need to tell him everything. All of my secrets.

"Baby, I'm so sorry. Please let me explain," Landon says as soon as he answers the phone. "I was going to tell you tonight, but it just broke first. I'm so, so sorry. Just let me come get you. Then I can explain."

"Slow down. What are you talking about?"

"You don't know."

"Know what?"

"Just let me come get you then I'll explain everything. Where are you?"

"Coffee shop on Fifth Street."

"Be there in twenty," he says hanging up the phone.

Twenty minutes is a long time to go without searching for answers, but I wait. I would want him to wait if it were me. So I wait.

"Hey, baby," Landon says sweetly as I climb in the front seat of his car.

I notice a bead of sweat dripping down his head and his hands grip the steering wheel much too hard.

I lean over and kiss him softly on the lips, but he doesn't let me get away with just a peck on the lips. He grabs my neck and sweeps his tongue in my mouth claiming me. Reminding me I'm his. He doesn't need to remind me, though. I know.

I lean back with a smile on my face feeling more relaxed than I have felt all day. When I glance at Landon, though, he looks more worried instead of relaxed after the kiss.

"Just tell me. Whatever it is, it can't be that bad. We will get through it."

He nods and begins driving us home.

"You know I love you," he starts.

"Yes, Landon. Just tell me."

"I didn't think I could fall in love again. I'd been so hurt in my past, and I was so focused on my career I didn't think it would ever happen for me."

I sigh. This isn't going to be good. Whatever it is, if he is this nervous and stalling this much, it isn't good.

"And then I met you. And I fell. I fell for your beauty, your strength, your drive to move on after so much tragedy. I fell for it all.

"And you helped heal me. You helped me learn that my past doesn't have to define me. That I can be a better person than I was in the past."

I nod hoping he will hurry and get to his point while also hoping he will never get there so I don't have to be disappointed in him.

"I was so lost before I met you. I didn't even know what I wanted."

I watch as he turns onto our street that leads up to our home.

"But then Ethan came back into your life and you let me go. You wanted to do what was right by your past. You chose your past over your future."

I nod. I know all of this. I know I chose wrong. I know with absolute certainty now that I chose wrong.

"So when you called me to accuse me of cheating on you, I did the same. I let you go. I chose my past over my future."

I nod. It hurts, but I made him choose Caroline over me. If I hadn't had chosen Ethan he wouldn't have chosen Caroline.

I watch as Landon pulls into our driveway and turns the car off.

"Just tell me," I say frustrated that he won't just get to his point.

He takes a deep breath and turns to me when he speaks. "When you were with Ethan, I was with Caroline."

I raise my eyebrows. "What do you mean with?"

"I slept with her."

I exhale deeply the breath that I was holding in. I feel a stabbing sensation go into my chest. It hurts. It hurts to know that he slept with Caroline. I can't be mad at him, though, when I slept with Ethan. We both messed up. I just wish he had told me sooner. I wish he had told me when I told him.

"Is that all?" I ask.

"No."

I hold onto the door handle bracing myself for what he says next. If sleeping with Caroline wasn't what is so bad, I'm not sure I can handle what he says next.

"She's pregnant. And the baby is mine."

"No." My eyes grow wide with fear. "It can't be. Caroline has slept with tons of men. I'm sure the media is speculating that it is yours right now, but the media does shit like this all the time. They report different celebs are pregnant all the time. It almost always turns out not to be true.

"And this is just the sort of thing Caroline would do it get attention. To try to steal you back from me. She probably isn't even pregnant. She probably made all of that up."

Landon places a hand on my shoulder.

"She is."

"How do you know?"

"I've seen the pregnancy test. I went with her to the doctor. I saw the ultrasound. She's pregnant."

I push the door open, needing air. I tumble out of the car as I take a deep breath of the fresh mountain air. I begin pacing around the garden. Landon is right behind me.

"It's not yours, though. It could be any number of people. It's not yours," I say as I cry and collapse to the dirt ground.

Landon squats next to me holding me closely as I sob. It's not fair. It can't be his. "It's not yours," I sob again.

I feel him take a deep breath as he pulls me out of his shoulder and holds my face so that I'm forced to look at him.

"It's mine. I took a paternity test. The baby's mine."

"It can't be," I say again.

"It is," he says more firmly trying to get me to accept it. But how can I accept that another woman is having his child? A woman I hate. A family I will destroy if I stay with him. A child who will grow up without a father that loves his mother. I can't do that. I already know I can't. I can't hurt a child like that.

"You couldn't have taken a paternity test and got the results back so soon, though. It just happened. You just found out. How is that possible?" I ask. The test must be flawed if he just took it today. There is no way the results can get back so fast.

He shakes his head though while I look at him curiously.

"I've known for a while. I took the paternity test earlier this week. I just found out for sure today, but I think I've known in my heart the whole time that it was mine."

He looks so sad, so distraught, but it must be nothing compared to how I look. I'm going to lose him again.

"When?" I ask angrily. "How fucking long have you known and not said anything to me?"

"Since Chicago."

I push Landon off me and storm into the house.

"Wait," he says running after me.

"Why the fuck should I? You have been lying to me for weeks!"

"I couldn't tell you. I didn't want to worry you. Not until I knew for sure."

"That's bullshit, and you know it! You didn't tell me because you knew I'd be mad as hell! You could have at least told me you slept with her. That would have been the right fucking thing to do. You didn't have to lie to me!"

"Like you have been so honest these past couple of weeks! You didn't tell me that you were fucking raped! You should have told me. I should have been there to help you go through that."

I snap my head in his direction. "You did not just compare me keeping the fact that I was raped from you to you keeping that you knocked up your ex-girlfriend from me!"

"I ... I didn't mean it like that. I just meant we have both kept secrets from each other. We both just need to stop. But it doesn't mean we don't still belong together. This can still work. I love you. I want to be with you."

"And what about Caroline? What about your baby?"

"I'll be there for them for everything, but my heart will always be here."

I shake my head. "It's not enough. It's not enough for any of us."

Landon drops his head. "I want you out," I say calmly.

He shakes his head, begging me not to kick him out, but I have to. I can't handle the fact that he lied to me. I can't handle it right now, not when I was about to trust him with my secret.

I can't trust him. I can't love him. He let me go once when he knew it was what was best for me. He let me go to give me a chance to find love with Ethan. To find love with my family. I have to do the same for him now.

"Just go."

Chapter Fifteen

LANDON

With your tiny fingers and cute smile.
You shined a light into my world and you ...
You saved me.

I WALK INTO MY CONDO, but it doesn't feel like home. It feels empty despite the fact that it looks exactly the same. Minus my clothes and my favorite guitar. I didn't bother grabbing any of my stuff when I left. I figured it would at least give me an excuse to go back over and see Alex again.

I see Drew on the phone in the kitchen. "We have no comment at this time," he says to another magazine before hanging up.

"You shouldn't even bother answering if the only answer you are going to give them is no comment."

He glares at me. "How many times are you going to fuck up your life? How many times are you going to put everything we have worked so hard to get on the line? Huh?"

I shake my head. "My career is going to be fine. In fact, we will probably see a spike in sales after all of this."

"I'm not talking about your career, asshole. Your career will be fucking fine. I just don't know what family you will have left."

I grab a beer out of the fridge before slumping in the chair in the kitchen. Drew grabs the beer out of my hand before I have a chance to drink it.

"She kicked you out, didn't she?"

I nod.

"You'll get her back. You always do," he says sarcastically.

I shake my head. "I don't think so. Not this time. This time, it felt final. This time, I feel more lost than I did the last time."

"Just don't get drunk like you did last time. You have more concerts this weekend, and we don't need any more mistakes."

"How is Caroline?"

"She's good, no thanks to you."

"She is the one who told the media."

"Yes," Drew says even though it wasn't a question. "Don't blame her, Landon. This isn't her fault."

"Stop protecting her, Drew. She is just as much at fault in all of this as I am."

"Maybe, but after you have hurt her, she doesn't deserve any of the blame."

"She's hurt me too. Time and time again."

He just shakes his head. "She doesn't deserve you. Neither of them do. They both deserve better."

I grab an empty vase that is usually filled with flowers but isn't because more important things have been going on around here lately and throw it at Drew. It misses and shatters on the floor.

I hate him, but he's right. Neither of them deserves the monster I have become.

Chapter Sixteen

DREW

I can't control myself when I'm with her. I have control of everything in my life except her. I grab her dress and rip it in half until I can see every inch of her body taunting me, begging me for more.

I HEAR the glass shatter on the floor as I walk from the kitchen to my bedroom. I slam the door shut as my anger overwhelms me. I have always lived in Landon's shadow. I'm used to it. I've never wanted to be in the spotlight. I never wanted to have every detail of my boring life on display and critiqued by every person in the world. I've never wanted Landon's life. I've never been jealous of his fame.

The only thing I've ever been jealous of is how Caroline looks at him. Just once, I wish she would look at me that way. But I've ruined any chance of that. And Landon finished it off by getting her pregnant.

"Dammit!" I scream as my phone goes off again. I take it from my pocket and stare at the number. Another member of the press. I throw the phone on my bed. I'm done covering for him. I'm done protecting him. He's on his own. Not that he needs protection from this. His latest single is climbing fast to the number one spot. His sales grow higher every time the media talks about him.

How did I end up here? How the hell did I end up alone with no friends and no relationship?

Landon. I've spent my whole life trying to protect him. I've been trying to look out for him. I've been living his dreams. But that didn't work out. I've failed two times now at protecting him. Two times now, he's ruined his life.

I can't protect him. I should just quit. I should follow my own dreams. I should move away, but I don't know if I can. I don't know if I can when I feel responsible for his mistakes. I don't know if I can leave when there is a chance I can be in Caroline's life, if only as the uncle to her unborn child.

Chapter Seventeen

ALEX

27. The number of nights I went to bed without food.

I FEEL SO LOST, so broken. I never realized what I wanted until I couldn't have it. I stare out at the tire swing hanging from the tree in the backyard. I never realized I wanted kids, not until I realized it wasn't a possibility.

I wipe a stray tear from my face. I'm tired of crying. I'm tired of crying over Landon. I'm tired of crying over children I will never have with him. I'm tired of crying over the loss of my body and mind. I'm tired of crying over the fear I have that at any second Ethan could come storming through that door and kill me without a second thought.

I thought I needed help to defend myself. I thought I needed Landon's help. I realize now that Landon can't help me. He is going to be a father. I can't have him risk his life for me.

I could still hire a bodyguard, though. I could still hire protection.

I shake my head. This is too personal. I don't trust anyone. I don't trust even hiring someone. Not after Ethan found out I was talking to

Nick. I would have no idea who to trust and who Ethan was paying. I thought I could trust Landon, but I was wrong. I can only trust myself.

I walk back to the living room and take my laptop in my lap as I sit down on the couch. A couch Landon and I fucked on only a few days earlier.

I reach into my pocket and pull out the two flash drives. I place the one that I have already looked at back in my pocket. It's the only ammunition I have against Ethan.

I take the other one in my hand and stare at it intently. I have to know. I have to know what Ethan has against Landon. I have to know what he is framing him for. I have to protect him. Just like I have to protect James and Daniel.

I put the flash drive into the computer. A video pops up. I push play without hesitation. I have to know.

It's a surveillance tape of a bar. It's crowded, but I can make out Landon and Drew immediately. They are both drunk, that much is obvious. They both seem to be celebrating as they knock down shot after shot.

I take a deep breath before I bite my lip as the video continues. I know Landon doesn't drink, and Drew has insinuated that when Landon does drink, it doesn't end well.

This video isn't going to end well. As happy as both men seem now, something happens. I just have no idea what could happen that is so horrible. What could happen that Ethan feels he could use as blackmail to get me back?

I continue watching for ten more minutes as Landon and Drew drink shot after shot after shot. I watch as they do shot after shot off women's stomachs. I watch as he lets women slobber over his neck as he grabs their asses.

I watch as Caroline and a man approach them. The man is tall and skinny with blond hair the same shade as Caroline's. He's older than she is, though. Much older, but if I had to guess, I would guess that they are related.

Neither of them looks happy as they approach the men. I watch as Caroline whispers something in Landon's ear that makes him frown.

The man with Caroline says something as well, and that's when Landon punches the man.

He doesn't stop at one punch. He punches the man over and over until the man's face is covered in blood. The man tries to protect himself but is no match for Landon.

Drew tries to tackle Landon to get him to stop, but the crowd around them has gone wild. Other people have started fighting while others just try to run out of the bar. Drew is pushed back with the crowd and unable to get to Landon.

I watch as Landon throws another punch to the man's jaw that sends the man tumbling to the floor. Landon doesn't stop, though, when the man falls to the floor. He kicks the man over and over. He kicks the man until the tape eventually runs black.

It takes me a long time to be able to breathe again after the tape ends. I don't understand what happened or what made Landon so angry. I know he and Caroline have a past. I know he hasn't always liked Caroline, but it doesn't excuse what he did.

That man might have deserved to be punched, but he didn't deserve to be knocked out. I'm not even sure if the man survived that attack.

I pull the flash drive out of my computer and stare at it. Ethan didn't frame Landon for this attack like he did James or Daniel. This video proves what Landon did. There is no way to manipulate this video. There is no way someone else attacked that man and then Ethan just simply put Landon's face on the image.

Landon did this. He attacked a man. He might have even killed the man. And I know from Ethan that Landon was never prosecuted for this crime. I know this video disappeared that night. I just don't know why.

God, are all the men I date monsters? Are they all evil, awful creatures that live off the destruction of others?

I don't know. The only problem is I still love one of them. Despite how my heart hurts again for being lied to. For falling for a man with demons in his past. Demons too great for me to forgive. I still love Landon.

I just can't *be* with Landon. I can't forgive him for lying. I can't forgive him for beating up that man and destroying both of their lives. I can't forgive him for sleeping with Caroline when he was still in love with me. I can't forgive him. I just can't convince my heart to stop loving him.

I was right all along. I knew I shouldn't have fallen in love again. I knew love wasn't worth the pain. I won't survive the pain of love this time.

I pick up my phone and find Ethan's number. I hesitate for just a second before I press send on the number. He picks up the second ring.

"Don't send the video to the police. I'm coming home ..."

Chapter Eighteen

LANDON

You saved me from the darkness.
You saved me from my worst self.

I KNOCK on the door to the house Alex and I bought together. A house I never imagined I would be knocking on the door of. I should be able to just walk into my own home. I should be able to walk in and give Alex a hug and kiss like lovers do.

I can't, though. I have to wait for her to answer the door and welcome me in because it is no longer our home. It's hers. I hate myself for everything that I have done. I hate myself for hurting her and Caroline. I hate myself.

The door creeps open as Alex stands stoically in the doorway. She doesn't look angry, or sad, or destroyed. I have no idea how she feels by looking at her. Maybe I didn't destroy her; maybe she's stronger than that. Strong enough not to let a man destroy her. She's survived a lot worse.

"Your stuff is in the living room," she says as she turns from the door leaving it open for me to follow.

I walk slowly behind her taking in her body as I do. She's beautiful, but her strength at this moment is what draws me to her. Her strength is amazing.

We reach the living room much too fast. I don't have time to remember every curve of her body or how my heart beats fast around her. I don't have time to remember how she pushes me. I don't have time to remember every detail I'm afraid I will forget if this is the last time I will ever see her. I don't have time.

She already has a suitcase with my stuff packed leaning against the couch that we made love on. My guitar is next to it as well. This is it. All of my stuff. The last excuse I have to come back here, but I need to come back here. I need to see her again and set things right. This is not how we are supposed to end. I can't let our pasts ruin this.

I turn to Alex. "I'm sorry," I say although I've said it too many times again.

She just shakes her head and backs away from just enough to hurt me. "Don't do this," she says, and I see the sting of tears burning in her eyes. "This would never work. Our pasts are too messy. We both lie to each other too much. You just need to leave."

I take a step forward to her, just needing to close the distance. If I could only close the distance, then I could make her remember why we are supposed to be together. Our love has defied so many odds and obstacles from her past. It can defy the obstacles in my past. It has to.

This time, when I take a step forward, she doesn't move. She doesn't have the strength to move. She still loves me. I know that much; she's just mad at me for lying to her. For being such an idiot.

I take another step forward until our bodies press together. Our breaths synchronize as my lips hover over hers.

"God, I need you," I say before I grab her neck and pull her lips the last inches to mine. I feel whole when my lips touch hers. Desire at the touch of her lips drives me wild.

I lose all control and all thoughts as her tongue slips into my mouth. I run my hands over her body as I forget everything but how her body feels pressed against mine. She moans as her hands travel over the muscles in my back.

We stumble backward together, desperate to find a couch or

anywhere that we can fall together. Instead of finding the couch, though, I trip over something hard, and we both tumble to the floor. Alex lands on me breaking her fall, but I land on a hard box.

The fall is enough. It was all it took to end the moment. Alex looks at me solemnly and then stands up. "That was a mistake."

I grab her hand to pull her back to me. If I can just get my lips back on hers, she will forget that this is a mistake.

Except she pulls her hand away from me and my plan is no longer attainable. I stand up slowly, shaking out my sore muscles as I do. That's when I see what I tripped over. A box. I glance around the room and see more boxes and suitcases that don't belong to me. They belong to her.

Is she moving back to the condo? Is she going to sell this house?

As much as I want her back at the condo near me, I don't want her to sell this house. Technically, the house is in her name, so she can do whatever she wants with it, but she bought it with the intention of us. This was supposed to be *our* home.

"Are you moving back to the condo?"

She avoids my eye contact as she picks up my guitar case and hands it to me. I reluctantly take it out of her hands.

"Alex?"

"It doesn't matter. We are over. You should go."

"Where are you going?"

I tilt her chin up to look at me. She closes her eyes as I do to block me out and not give me a response.

"Where are you moving to?" I ask again. I have to know. I have to know where to find her when I can no longer live without her. If I can't come back here then where?

I run my thumb across her cheek and feel the light moisture that has formed there from a stray tear.

"Where?"

Her breathing becomes slow and steady the longer we stay like this. Every time I ask, she seems to find a way to calm herself with her breathing. She's not going to tell me.

She would tell me if she was going back to the condo. I would find out soon enough anyway. She could be moving back to New York. Or she could be moving back with Ethan.

"No."

Her eyes open as the word leaves my lips.

"No, you can't go back with him."

She bites her lips to keep words that will start a fight away from her lips. She's calm, much too calm.

She moves from me and finds my suitcase and begins carrying it to the door. I run after her, grabbing the suitcase from her hand, and set it down on the floor.

"You don't love him."

She doesn't move as I say the words, but she doesn't deny them. She doesn't love him. She loves me. She chose me, and I failed her.

I force our lips together one last time. It's a desperate kiss. The most desperate kiss either of us have experienced. Our teeth clang and our tongues fight to get further into each other's mouths. When I pull away, we are both panting and empty. We both know that was the last one. The last kiss.

I grab my bag and guitar while she opens the door for me. *He probably is a better man than I am,* I think as I step out of the door.

I turn back to her at the last second. "Don't sell the house. Or let me buy it from you if you don't want it."

The tiniest of smiles forms on her sweet lips. "I could never sell it. It's too much a part of me."

I exchange my own small smile as I head to my car. I just wish she felt the same way about me.

Chapter Nineteen

CAROLINE

He takes no time in savoring me once he has me undressed. I guess he thinks the moment won't last if he does. He's right, of course, because even I know as my body begs him to fuck me my heart tells him no.

I HATE SITTING in the waiting room alone. I've never done well on my own. Perhaps that's why I chose a career as an actress. It involves being around many people.

I glance down at my phone. Five minutes until my appointment. Landon has always been there for me when I really needed it. Even when he almost destroyed my life. He has always been here for me. Through everything. I can't imagine him missing this.

"Miss Parker," the ultrasound tech says at the doorway.

I gather my purse and stand to follow the woman back. Except he is going to miss this.

I try to smile at the woman as I follow her back to the small room, but I can't smile. If he misses this, it will only mean one thing — that he doesn't care about this baby. Or me.

"You can lie down on the table," she says. I drop my purse off on the chair and then climb onto the table.

"How far along are you?"

"About thirteen weeks."

She smiles. "The doctor ordered an ultrasound just to check that the baby is forming correctly, and we don't anticipate any problems. I know you recently had one, but the doctor would prefer you have one done here."

I nod.

"Just give me a second to set everything up."

I nod again. I stare up at the wall trying to keep myself calm, but all I can think about is I'm alone.

"Lift you shirt, please."

I do and then I realize I'm not alone. I'll never be alone again.

"This is going to be cold."

I nod. I have nothing to say to the woman. I'm alone at an ultrasound, and it's embarrassing. I never wanted to end up just like my mother. I never wanted to be a single parent, but I guess that's what I am. I was wrong to depend on Landon. I was wrong.

She places the gel on my stomach, and I wince at the coldness covering my now curved stomach. I don't look pregnant yet. Not to most people. I just look thick around my midsection. I just look fat by my standards.

The door swings open without a knock stunning both the technician and myself. I smile as I stare at the man in the doorway.

"Sorry," is all he says as he walks into the small room and stands next to me. He smiles when he sees the smile on my face.

He's here, and the anger at him being late melts away.

The technician smiles at Landon. "You made it just in time, Father."

I watch as Landon's muscles tighten at the mention of being a father. When he catches me staring, he gives me tight smile.

"Okay, let's get started." She places the ultrasound machine on my stomach and begins moving the transducer around.

I turn my attention from Landon to the screen that looks hazy as the woman moves the cold gel around on my stomach.

"There." She points to the picture on the screen. A picture that looks very much like a baby.

"That's your baby."

I feel a rush of emotions I wasn't expecting. I haven't felt connected to this baby at all since I found out I was pregnant. And other than the morning sickness and bloating of my stomach, I haven't even felt pregnant. Not until I see that face does it become real.

I feel a tear slide down my face at the beautiful sight. I'm having a baby. I'm never going to be alone again.

My hand is being squeezed, and I glance away from the screen just long enough to see that Landon is holding my hand tightly. His eyes just as glued to the screen as mine just were. He isn't breathing or moving. He's just watching.

It feels like we are a family for the first time. Or at least that we can be a family.

"Do you want to know the sex of your baby?"

"You can find out this early?" Landon asks.

The woman smiles. "Not always, but in this case, yes. I'm pretty confident of the sex although you can confirm a little later in the pregnancy."

I look at Landon trying to read his eyes. His eyes say yes.

"Yes," we both say to the woman.

The woman smiles at us. "It's a girl."

Landon squeezes my hand tighter.

"I'll give you both a minute." The technician stands and walks out of the room.

"It's a girl," I squeal as I sit up on the table.

Landon pulls me into an embrace, and I can smell his cologne on his neck. Tears fall down my cheek as Landon grips me tighter.

"We are having a girl," he says his voice raspy like he has been crying.

I look up at him. He is. I reach for his neck to pull him into a kiss, but he anticipates my move and stops me. He pulls away, and I frown at the way he dismisses me.

"I thought ..."

"No."

He wipes a tear from my face.

"We need to talk first."

I look at him reluctantly.

"I want to be a good father. I will do whatever possible to take care of our daughter, but the rest ..." He holds out his hands to me. "The rest isn't possible. I tried being a good boyfriend. To both you and Alex." He pauses. "I failed both times. And as for a husband, I would make a horrible husband. All I know is I can try every day to be the best father to our daughter."

He smiles when he says the word daughter. I want more. I want more than just a good father for my unborn child. It doesn't have to be a husband. It just has to be him.

Chapter Twenty

ALEX

11. The number of foster parents I have had.

WALKING from my car up to the house Ethan bought for us is hard. It might be the hardest thing I have ever done. My legs tremble slightly as I move, and sweat beads down my face. I should run. I should run away and never look back. That's what I should do. That's the only way I know I will end up alive. If I walk through those doors, there is a good chance I will never walk out again.

I don't run, though. I'm done running. I have too many people to save to run. Even if I don't save myself, I have to walk through that door for Daniel, and James, and Landon. I have to walk through that door for all the people Ethan has yet to hurt but will if I don't stop him.

It doesn't make the walk from the driveway to the front door any easier, though. When I make it to the front door, I hesitate. I try to think of any other way to save them. I can't think of any, though. I have to play Ethan's game to keep Landon out of jail. And I have to get close to Ethan to find any evidence he is hiding.

I ring the doorbell and wait. Five seconds go by before Ethan answers the door with a smile on his face.

"Decided to come home."

I put a smile on my face. It's a fake smile, but I try my best to make it seem real.

"Yes." I walk closer to him until our bodies almost press together. I watch his breathing speed up just like I want. He's still attracted to me. He still wants me despite trying to kill me. Something has stopped him from finishing the job; my suspicion is that he is too attracted to me to be able to kill me.

I reach my hand out and touch his arm. His eyes instantly change to a look of lust at just the touch. It makes my smile grow bigger. This is definitely his weakness. I just have to learn to use it to my advantage.

"I was wrong. I chose wrong. I thought I was in love with Landon. I thought he was a good man. He's not. You showed me that."

"I'm glad you've finally seen who Landon really is. He should be in jail."

I nod. "He should be, but I don't want to talk about him. I don't want to have anything to do with him anymore." I turn my eyes into lust-filled orbs as I take in his tight button up shirt and jeans. I run my tongue over my lips when his eyes travel back to my face.

"I'm more interested in who you are." I force my body to move so my lips hover over his. "I'm more interested in falling back in love with my husband."

I force myself to kiss him. It's not a passionate, desperate kiss like the last one I experienced with Landon. I don't want him suspicious that I suddenly have strong feelings for him, but he does need to know I want that possibility. I want him to think I want him. Instead of just wanting him dead.

The kiss lasts too long for my liking, and the whole time, I'm thinking about Landon. How with this kiss I feel like I'm erasing that kiss, but I'm not. I'll take that kiss with me forever. Even though Landon betrayed me and lied to me, I still love him. I always will. That's why I'm here kissing a monster worse than Landon is.

I let Ethan be the first to pull away, and when he does, he wears a smug look on his face.

"I've missed you."

"I've missed you, too."

He takes my hand. My hand is moist with sweat. If he notices, he doesn't say anything. "Let me show you around. You need to see the changes I've made to the house since you were last here."

"I'd love to." I look longingly at Ethan.

The tour is long and exhausting. It seems Ethan has changed something in every room in the house. The house is beautiful, and when I first saw it, it felt right. That was before when I thought I could have a future with Ethan. Now, I know there is no future at all.

Each room he took me into was just another room where I'm going to have to spend time searching for evidence. We stop in the master bedroom. The room that we will share together until one of us ends up dead.

Chills run through my body at the thought of sleeping with this man, but I have to. I have to get close to him.

I watch as he walks into the closet and pulls out a gorgeous black dress. It's long and sleek and beautiful.

"I really wanted to take you to a nice dinner just the two of us on your first night back, but unfortunately, I already promised Mother I would take her out tonight."

He walks to me and hands me the dress. "I would cancel with Mother except today isn't a good day for her."

He looks solemn as he continues speaking. "It's the day my father died."

I put the dress on the edge of the bed and kiss him softly on the cheek. "I don't mind having dinner with you and your mother."

He smiles and looks at his watch. "Can you be ready in an hour?"

"Of course."

I HOLD onto Ethan's arm as we walk into the swanky restaurant. I'm nervous as I walk side by side with Ethan to our table. Laura has never liked me. And I'm afraid she is going to see right through my sudden loving façade. She is going to point out that I am an imposter just playing Ethan to try to save those he has hurt.

I can't flirt my way into Laura's good graces. I somehow need to make her like me. Or better yet, make Ethan not like her and trust me more than he does her.

Ethan holds out the chair for me, and I take a seat. He takes the chair next to me. I fidget nervously with my napkin in my lap.

"Are you okay?" Ethan asks.

I force a smile on my face. "Yes, just nervous to see your mother. I haven't exactly been in her good graces."

Ethan grabs hold of my hand trying to calm me, but his touch just makes my nerves worse.

"She likes you fine."

"Have you started working at the law firm here yet?" I ask changing the subject.

"I have. I'll be going in at least five days a week. Sometimes more. So you'll have to find something to keep you busy while I'm away. Maybe working with Mother on her fundraisers and charity events."

I take a drink of my water before I answer him. "Maybe."

I glance up and see Laura walking to our table. She looks beautiful and put together as always in a simple red dress.

When she gets to our table, Ethan stands to greet her and hug her. I do the same, and to my surprise, she hugs me with a smile on her face.

"It's good to see you back with Ethan, Alexandra."

My eyes widen at her. "It's good to see you too, Laura."

She takes a seat across from me at the table.

"It really is wonderful to see you two back together. You worried me for a second there, Alexandra, but it seems it all worked itself out in the end."

I look at her suspiciously. "I didn't know what I wanted. Now, I do." I lean over and kiss Ethan on the cheek to prove my point. He smiles at my gesture of love.

Chapter Twenty-One

LANDON

Daughter, you saved me
And showed me how to be a father.

"She went back with him." I run my hand through my hair as I pace back and forth in the living room as Drew eats his Chinese noodles.

"Maybe she likes him better than you," Drew mumbles between bites. I pick up a pillow and throw it at him, but he has already anticipated my move. He gets up before the pillow lands where he was just sitting.

Drew and I fight a lot, but despite it all, I would do anything to protect him.

Drew rolls his eyes at me. "Okay, maybe that's not why. Why then?"

I shake my head as I slump onto the sofa. "I don't know."

"I hate to tell you this, but it doesn't matter why she went back with him. Even if she wasn't with him, she wouldn't be with you. She's still mad at you, remember? And you're still having a baby with a woman who is sleeping in the guest bedroom right now."

I glance toward the guest bedroom that is opposite of Drew's. Caroline hasn't come out all afternoon. She's been asleep for the last two hours.

"Why is she here, anyway? Not that I'm complaining, but didn't she just buy a big house with your money."

"She doesn't like being alone. You know that. I think she still thinks I'll move into the house with her, and I might, but only for a little while to help take care of our daughter and not because I want to be with her."

"What?"

I sigh. "She doesn't like being alone."

"No, I mean you said daughter. Are you having a daughter?"

I grin. "Yes."

Drew stands so fast some of the juice from his bowl of noodles spills onto the sofa. I stand too as he races across the room to me and embraces me in a hug that is anything but manly.

"Congrats!" He lets me go but hits me on the back. I swear I see moisture in his eyes when he looks at me, but he turns his back before I get a chance to really see.

Caroline's phone rings. I know because my song "Please" plays when it rings. The lyrics play over and over.

I don't want to wait anymore to make you mine
But I'll wait forever if you need
For you to come back to me
Don't stay his
Find me still
Please find my love.

THE SONG WILL FOREVER HAUNT me because as much as Caroline might wish it were about her, it's not. It never will be.

The song stops, and I can breathe again. Drew has gone back to his noodles and is ignoring me. I let my mind drift to Alex when Caroline's phone rings again bringing me back to life.

Her phone is in her purse, which is sitting on the end table next to the couch. She must have left it here when she went and took a nap. I pick up her purse and pull her phone out. It stops ringing just as I pull it out.

I go to silence it so that it won't go off again when I see it. Two missed calls from an unknown number and then one text message from an Ethan.

I stare at the phone in disbelief. It can't be the same Ethan.

I click on the message and read it: I won't be turning over the video to the police. The plan worked perfectly. I owe you one.

I have no idea what the message means, but it doesn't feel good. I scroll through more.

Ethan: She hasn't come back yet. I'll release the video tomorrow if I don't hear from her.

Caroline: Give it more time. She will.

I scroll higher. I scroll higher until I find the video, and I hit play.

I watch the horrific video. A video of the worst day of my life. The day I became a monster as bad or worse than my father. The day I attacked Caroline's brother, Sean.

I've never seen the video, but I've played the scene over and over in my head. I've imagined how it must have happened. I never imagined it this bad, though. Seeing how it really happened is much worse.

"Landon?"

I can't take my eyes from the video.

"Man, you look whiter than a ghost." Drew gets up and walks to me. "What are you looking at?"

I hand him the phone. "The night I became a monster."

I leave him with the phone and walk out to my balcony. I need to breathe. I never thought I could feel this bad, but I do. I don't deserve to be a father. I don't deserve to have any sort of unconditional love. I can't believe Caroline ever forgave me for that. I don't think I ever could after watching the video. I don't think I ever could.

I lean over the edge of the balcony looking down at all the people below enjoying the sunny beach. It's always sunny here. It's too sunny right now for my mood. I should go back inside where it seems gloomy in comparison.

I hear the door open and close, and I know Drew is standing behind me. He walks next to me and leans against the balcony rail.

"What are you thinking?"

I don't look at him. "I'm thinking I should throw my body over the edge of this railing." My hands fidget with nothing as the silence consumes us both.

"What are you thinking?" I ask him.

"That I should throw your ass over this railing if you don't," Drew says it seriously like it isn't a joke, but I know it is. It's his way of lightening the mood when he can't say that everything is okay. When he can't say that I'm not a monster. He can't say any of those things because that's what I am.

I destroyed a man's life, just like my father. The only difference is Dad's mistake ended a man's life while mine only destroyed one. The difference is Dad is paying for his crimes while I live this life of luxury as long as I pay Caroline and her brother whatever she wants. I don't even know how Sean is doing now. I know he went to a hospital immediately after and then rehab to heal his wounds. I know that Caroline gives him the money for him to live off every month, but I have no idea if he has fully healed. Is he still in a wheelchair? Is he still in pain? I don't know.

"You know why she sent it to Ethan. To Alex's Ethan."

Drew stays silent. He doesn't nod. He doesn't move.

"She sent it to break Alex and me up. That's why Alex went back. Ethan blackmailed her to come back. She went back to protect me. To keep this out of the media. To keep me out of jail."

I turn to Drew, who is still looking out at the view. "What do you think? You must hate me after watching that video. You must hate me just like Alex. Just like Caroline. Just like Sean."

He doesn't look at me.

"Look at me, dammit!"

He closes his eyes and then opens them. "I can't. I can't look at you without seeing the worst of you. Alex has already forgiven you for this. She wouldn't be back with a man that she clearly doesn't want to be with if she wasn't. She wouldn't be saving your ass again. Caroline's brother has clearly forgiven you. All he wanted was money to be able to forgive you. And Caroline ... She's having your baby. She clearly forgives you." He pauses, and I watch his grip on the railing tighten. "I can't forgive you, though. Not yet. I can't believe you did what was on that video. I can't believe any brother of mine would do such a thing."

I turn back and look out at the ocean.

"It's a relief that you don't forgive me because I can't forgive myself."

We stay in silence, looking out over the ocean for a long time. Long enough that the sun begins to set over the ocean. I'm surprised Caroline hasn't woken up and come found us.

"You have to release it."

I feel his eyes burning into me. "No."

I chance a glance at him. "You have to. I need to set things right. I need to own what I did. Alex doesn't need to protect me. Caroline doesn't need to protect me. I have to face what I did."

"You can't. If you release that video, you could end up in jail just like our father. Your daughter will be raised without a father. You can't do that. Caroline didn't release the video. She just used it to get what she wanted. She just used it to protect your daughter. And Alex is a big girl who can decide for herself how to handle her husband."

"I have to."

"Think about your daughter. She could grow up without a father. You can't do that to her."

I turn back to look out at the ocean as a tear falls down my face. How can I raise a daughter when I did such a horrible thing to another man? How can I ever ask for her forgiveness if I never accepted my punishment for the crimes?

"I have to."

"You can't. Your daughter won't have a father."

I shake my head. "She never did."

Chapter Twenty-Two

CAROLINE

His tongue finds the spot that is my undoing. I scream my pleasure as he takes me in deeper.

"WHAT THE HELL WERE YOU THINKING?"

He won't look at me. He won't fucking look at me.

"What the fucking hell were you thinking?" I hit him hard on his chest like that is going to reverse time and change things. It won't. Nothing will. It's already been done.

It doesn't keep me from hitting him over and over. Until finally he grabs my wrists.

I look up at him as tears flow down my face.

"Why?"

"I had to. I hadn't seen the video before. I hadn't really understood what I had done. Even though I'd seen how badly your brother was hurt afterward. I didn't understand, not until I saw it. I had to make things right."

"You already did, though. You paid for his hospital bills. You did everything you could for him. You did everything you could for me. You can't do this now."

"I have to do this now. For her." He places his hand on my stomach after her releases my wrists.

"You can't do this because of her," I plead.

"I have to." He begins walking out the door, but I can't let him go. I can't let him turn himself into the police. I just can't. I cling to his arms trying to get him to stay.

"Drew," he says looking past me to his brother.

I grab hold of him harder until my nails are biting into his skin. Drew grabs hold of my arms as Landon slips out from beneath my grip until I am holding nothing and have nothing left to hold onto.

Landon walks quickly out of the condo and out of the baby's and my life.

I collapse unable to hold myself up any longer. Drew holds me and collapses just as I do until we are both blobs on the floor. We both hurt now that Landon is gone, most likely to jail for longer than I even want to imagine.

I feel Drew's pain the same as mine as he holds me on the floor of his condo. He doesn't try to console me. He doesn't make any of it better. He just hurts. Same as me.

I continue sobbing well into the night, and Drew doesn't do anything but hold me. And sobs along with me.

It takes forever for my sobs to calm to soft cries. I've never cried so hard in my life. Never. I'm cold. I don't cry. I don't show weakness, but losing him when I finally thought he was mine is unbearable.

Drew picks me up when he hears my sobs turn to soft cries. He carries me down the hallway toward my bedroom, but he doesn't turn right. He turns left to his bedroom. I'm too tired to argue or wonder why. I don't care where he takes me. I can't think about anything but the pain.

He kicks the door open and carries me to his bed. He untucks the covers before placing me in and then covers me up. I feel exhausted. My eyes are heavy, and I could fall asleep in an instance. He stands and watches me as I curl around a pillow as he takes off his shirt exposing his hard muscles. He walks out of view, and I find my eyes following him as he takes off his slacks and deposits them in a hamper in the corner. He climbs into the bed next to me all without a word.

Our eyes meet each other and say enough. Neither of us can be alone tonight. Landon never came home, which can only mean one thing. He's in jail.

I turn away from Drew, and he moves until he is up against my back. His hand reaches out hesitantly to find my hand. He starts the slow calming circles again that instantly relax me. It's not enough, though. I take his hand and wrap it around me until his hand is resting on my stomach making the same calming movements.

"I'm never going to leave you," he whispers in my ear.

"Never," he says again as I close my eyes and drift off to sleep.

Chapter Twenty-Three

ALEX

93. The number of times I almost gave up hope.

"WONDERFUL JOB WITH THE FOOD, ALEXANDRA," Laura says sweetly as the event runs to a close.

I try to force a smile, but I can't. I'm in too much shock that she has said something nice to me. The food is fine for a luncheon event like this, but I'm sure Laura could have done better. The Laura I knew would have found something wrong with the catering company I chose. Or she would have selected bruschetta over Caprese salad. Or white instead of cream napkins. She would have found something wrong with my planning even though she only gave me forty-eight hours to put this event together. She would have found more than enough things to criticize. She doesn't, which just makes me all the more suspicious.

"Thanks," I say hesitantly. I look up at her suspiciously, but she gives nothing away.

"Oh, Chantelle, darling. Let me introduce you to my wonderful daughter-in-law, Alexandra Wolfe."

I shake the woman's hand.

"I've heard so many good things about you from Laura."

My eyes dart to Laura's and back, checking to see if she is serious, and it seems she is. Her expression doesn't falter.

"That's good to hear."

"Has life gotten back to normal for you after all the horrible things that have happened to you and Ethan?"

"Yes."

"Wonderful to hear. I'd best be going. You two have thrown an exquisite event. I look forward to attending more of your events."

I smile and nod as the woman leaves and then I scowl at Laura.

"What was that?"

"What was what?" she says feigning innocence.

"Why are you being so nice to me?"

"I don't know what you mean, sweetie. I've always been nice to you."

I roll my eyes and walk away from Laura out of the ballroom and into the lobby of the hotel. I can't be with her another second, pretending that I like that woman. I can't. Not when she is being so fake in return.

I only agreed to work for her to try to earn Ethan's and her trust. Somehow, I've managed to do that in less than three days, and it doesn't make sense. Why would she be acting like this toward me? Did she help Ethan? Did she help him try to kill me? Did she help him cover it up?

Probably. Although I don't know if I'll ever be able to prove that. Ethan is too close to his mother to keep something like that from her. I just don't know why she is being nice now unless ...

I take a deep breath. Unless she is on to me. Unless she thinks I know, and she's trying to do the same thing I am. She's trying to gain my trust so that she can kill me. My time is running out. I've only been here three days, and I already know that I don't have much time left before Ethan, or Laura, or someone he hires tries to kill me again. I know too much to leave me free.

I just have to convince him I don't. That I don't know a goddamn thing. That I want him more than I want Landon. That I have truly changed my mind.

I glance up at the television in the lobby. I have to cover my mouth when I see the news to keep from screaming or crying or letting out any other awful noise.

I read the words as they cross the screen. "Landon Davis has turned himself in and has been arrested on charges of assault and battery and attempted murder. He is fully cooperating with the investigation. Bail has not yet been set."

A picture of Landon flashes on the screen with Caroline. "Landon is the alleged boyfriend of actress Caroline Parker, who is expecting his baby next spring."

The shock is too much. He turned himself in. Why would he do that?

I take out my phone to call Drew. To find out what the hell is going on. Landon could end up in jail for a very long time because of this. At the very least, his music label will definitely drop him because of this.

When I pull out my phone, though, I realize what I'm doing. I can't call Drew. I can't give Ethan any reason to doubt that I want him and not Landon. I put the phone back into my purse.

I let one tear fall for Landon. I let one tear fall for Caroline's baby that will grow up without a father. And then I let one tear fall for me. Because by turning himself in, he effectively ended any chance of a future for us, either.

I wipe the tear away. There wasn't a chance anyway. I wouldn't have changed my mind. He should be with Caroline. He should be with his child. Now, he never will.

It's too late to save Landon. He has to save himself. I try to put that pain aside so I can focus on what I have left to do. I have to save myself and exonerate everyone else.

I MAKE it back home before Ethan for the first time this week. He's beaten me home from work at the charity every day giving me no time alone. No time to search. It's six o'clock now. I might have an hour, maybe two, before he'll be home. That's all the time I have to search.

I run to his office as soon as I enter and realize he isn't here. I grab the handle of the door and am surprised when it turns without an issue. He left it unlocked, which just means there probably isn't anything in here worth hiding. Still, I have to start somewhere. I have to look.

I take a seat at his desk feeling my gun move in the waistband on my shorts as I do. I begin opening each of the drawers in his desk. Everything is so organized. So perfect that I have to move carefully not to disturb anything and give away that I was in here. I open another drawer that is files and files of papers.

I thumb through them quickly, but it looks mostly to be legal forms and tax information.

I move to his computer and turn it on. To my surprise, there isn't even a password to get on the computer.

I sigh in frustration but do my best to search through the files on the computer as quickly as possible. There are files and files of pictures of Ethan as a child. More files of pictures of us at our wedding. Pictures of us together. But no evidence of Ethan attacking me.

I click on more files, but nothing valuable is on this computer. There is no work information. There is no other personal information. There is no information leading me to think he is a dangerous killer. Just nothing.

I open the web browser and look through the search history. Nothing looks out of place. Not even a mention of a porn site. Nothing.

I lean back in the chair in frustration. Just because I can't find it doesn't mean it's not there. I just don't have a clue how to search for hidden things on a computer.

I get up from the chair and move to the filing cabinets. I open each drawer, but I don't find anything but forms for work in the cabinets.

I slam the drawer in frustration. I look around the office. Nothing else is in here. I try to find any hiding places, any hidden places where he could be hiding evidence, and I find none.

I glance at the large painting on the far wall. It's a detailed painting of soldiers fighting in war. Most likely painted by some famous person. I go over to the painting and lift it off the wall. Just like in the movies. I look to see if some hidden vault is behind the painting that might contain the evidence.

I close my eyes to keep the panic away when I realize nothing but a wall is behind the painting.

His office holds no evidence. Now, I'm all out of leads. Evidence could be anywhere in this house. It could be at his LA office. It could be at his mother's house. It could be in our NY apartment. It could be at his NY office. Or ...

It might not exist at all.

The only reason he kept the video of the rape was so he could watch the video over and over and relive that night. There is no video of the car attack. There is no video of my being attacked in my condo.

There was a surveillance video of James, though. Somehow. So a real video of Ethan sneaking into my condo must exist.

"Alexa, are you home?" I hear Ethan shout as he walks in the door of our house.

I quickly leave his office only glancing back to make sure everything is still in its perfect place. I hurry into the kitchen and find him standing there.

"I'm here," I say smiling at him.

He doesn't return my smile, though. Instead, he looks at me intensely.

"I thought you might have left after seeing the news today."

I walk over to him and kiss him softly on the lips. We haven't done anything other than kiss since I moved back, and I'm not planning to do more than that now. I just need him to know there is that chance again soon.

"What are you talking about?" I ask even though I know exactly what he is talking about.

He narrows his eyes. "You didn't hear?" He waits for me to reply, but I don't.

He runs his hand down my cheek stroking it softly before running his hand through my hair.

"You didn't hear that Landon was arrested today?" His body is so close to mine now that I swear he can hear my heart beating too fast in my chest. I can't lie. He'll know.

"I did." I look away from him just long enough to gather myself. When I look back at him, I feel calmer, stronger. "It just confirmed my decision even more." I reach up and touch his cheek much in the same way he just did to me. "You're the one I want. Not that monster."

He smirks at me. "You're not mad at me."

I squint my eyes at him. I walk over to the cabinet in the kitchen and get a glass. I begin filling it with water from the fridge trying to remain as calm as I can "What would I be mad at you for?"

He comes up behind me and puts his hands around my waist possessively. I try not to panic as his hands land just inches from where I've hidden the gun in the back of my waistband. "I just thought you might have thought I was the one who turned in the evidence to the police."

I turn to face him. "I wouldn't be mad at you if you did. He deserves to pay for what he did to that man."

"I didn't do it."

I smile. "I know."

"You don't miss him," he breathes on my neck just before he kisses me there.

"I miss you."

I feel his lips curl in a grin as he kisses me again on my neck. I try my best to moan in pleasure when all I'm really feeling is disgust. I hate that I have to let this man kiss me and touch me.

He pulls his lips from mine and waits until I look at him in the eye. "Prove it."

Chapter Twenty-Four

LANDON

At 28, I lost someone too.
I understood my father
And the pain he couldn't bear.

"I NEED A MOMENT WITH MY CLIENT," Allen, my lawyer, says.

I watch as the officers leave the room. And then, it's just Allen and me sitting on the metal chairs and table in the dank room.

He looks at me like I expect a father would after something like this happens. His face is sad.

I expected to have longer here to tell my story. I expected to already be in handcuffs and on my way to jail by now. Drew was fast, though. Faster than even I expected. He called our lawyer before I even had a chance to say a word other than showing the police the video.

I watch as he lays all sorts of papers onto the table.

"She wasn't legally able to turn over that video to the police. Don't worry, that video will be inadmissible in court."

"She didn't turn it over."

He narrows his eyes at me as he looks up from the papers in front of him. "Then who did?"

"Me."

He just shakes his head in disbelief. "Why would you do that?"

"Have you seen the video?"

"Yes, I saw it when I originally wrote up the terms of the contract between you and Ms. Parker the first time."

"I hadn't. Not until yesterday. I hadn't seen the video. I hadn't seen what I had really done. I couldn't live with myself without paying the consequences for what I had done. I couldn't pretend I was a good person to my daughter when I'm clearly not."

Allen just shakes his head at me. "You are a good person. That was one night that we don't even have enough evidence to really know what happened."

I shake my head. "We do. We have more than enough evidence. That surveillance video proves I'm a monster."

"Do you know what he said to you? What he said that caused you to hit him?"

"No. But no matter what he said, I shouldn't have lost my temper like that. I shouldn't have let it go that far. I could have killed him."

He grabs my shoulders forcing me to look at him. "But you didn't. You didn't kill him."

I shake him off. "It doesn't matter. I could have. I'm no better than my father is."

"Let's gather all of the evidence first before you sentence yourself to a life of punishment for a crime you didn't commit."

"I did ..."

Allen puts his hand up, stopping me.

"We need to talk to the police. They will most likely want to arrest you. I will be able to easily get you out on bail by the end of the day, though. Then we will gather all of the evidence. We will find out what really happened before we determine how we are going to plea. Do you understand me?"

I nod although I don't. I don't understand why he doesn't clearly see what I did. That I deserve to go to prison.

"I will most likely get them to take a plea deal and get you off on community service even if you really did this."

"No. I want to pay for what I did. I don't want to take a deal."

"You let me decide that. We need to call them back in. You don't say a word without speaking to me first. Not. A. Single. Goddamn. Word. Do you understand me?"

"Yes," I say harshly. It's just like every other time I've worked with him except this time when he looks at me, I see a hint of fear in his eyes. He's worried about me. He knows I did this. He knows I should pay for this, and he can't do anything to stop me from going to jail.

I watch as he gets up to let the police back in.

"We have enough evidence from the video alone to charge him," the officer says, looking at Allen and not me.

"I understand."

"It would be best if we hear from him what exactly happened."

Jim shakes his head. "We have nothing to say at this time. Not until we have had time to do our own investigation."

The officer nods and looks sad as he looks at me. He doesn't look angry or hostile like I would expect an officer to look at me like for what I did. He just looks sad.

"Landon Davis, you are under arrest ..."

I hear him, but I don't really hear him. His words are monotone. I don't think about anything other than I deserve this. I deserve worse.

Instead, they treat me kindly as he escorts me out of the building to a police car. He escorts me out the back so that there are no paparazzi or members of the media to take my picture.

The drive to the jail is quick. Quicker than I expected. And somehow, we manage not to be spotted.

He gets out and helps me out of the car because my hands are still handcuffed. He leads me up to the building and presses a code on the door that unlocks the door.

He pauses for just a second at the door. "Don't worry. Your lawyer will have you out of here in an hour, two max. This thing probably won't even go to trial."

I just shake my head at the officer that said things to me I'm sure he isn't supposed to say.

He takes me inside and a female officer working the desk looks up at me in surprise.

"This is ..."

"Landon Davis," the female officer finishes his sentence.

She looks up at me with bug eyes, and I know. I know I'll be getting the star treatment while I'm in here. At least until the video goes viral and they see who I really am.

True to his word, Allen has me out of here in an hour. They don't even bother moving me from a holding cell. When the female officer comes to let me out, she asks for my autograph. I reluctantly give it to her although I'm sure she will hate me soon. Just as much as I hate myself.

"Let's get you home," Allen says.

Chapter Twenty-Five

DREW

I smile as she pushes me away from her sensitive flesh, unable to handle my touch any further, but I've not had enough. I'll never get enough.

It was hard to pull myself from Caroline when the sun came up this morning. It was one of the hardest things I've ever done. It felt incredible to have her in my arms all night.

I didn't sleep a second. I was too afraid I would miss the sound of her breathing. Or the smell of her perfume. Or the feel of her smooth skin beneath my hand.

I was too afraid that something worse would happen. That Caroline would wake up crying or the morning sickness would get to her again.

I couldn't chance any of it. So I didn't sleep. Not one second, but when the sun began streaming through the window, I knew I had to get up.

So I did. I tore myself from her arms, and at the last second when my arm was almost free, she pulled me tighter to her, refusing to let me go.

The pain was almost unbearable in my heart as I pulled my arm away from her knowing that she will probably never hold me that tightly ever again. That she was only doing that because she was asleep and afraid, not because she wanted me.

Going back to her with breakfast is just as hard, though. It's hard because when I wake her up, I know she won't be dreaming of me. She'll be dreaming of him.

As I carry her breakfast back to my bedroom, I feel my phone buzz in my pocket. I pull it out and glance at it, but it is not Allen, our lawyer, who I tried calling as I made her breakfast. It's the music label. I hit ignore and slide the phone back in my pocket. That phone call is going to have to wait. I can't deal with the label right now.

I push the door open and carry the breakfast over and set it on the nightstand next to the bed. I stare at the beautiful woman in my bed who has been through so much. Who has fought for everything her entire life. She makes me feel at peace staring at her.

It does feel strange, though, to see a woman in my bed. Even a woman who I have dreamed about being there every night of my life.

I lean down and kiss her softly on the cheek.

"Wake up, beautiful," I whisper in her ear.

To my surprise, that's all it takes to stir her. The smile on her face, when she opens her eyes, is one of pure joy. Not something I would expect to see after yesterday's events.

"Good morning," she says still smiling at me.

"I made you breakfast." I point at the food sitting on the nightstand next to her.

She sits up in bed as I put the tray of food on her lap.

"Thanks, but I'm not really hungry." She holds her stomach as she speaks.

"I made your favorite, though."

"Oh, really. You made my favorite. I doubt you even remember what it is?" Her eyes finally leave mine long enough to look down at the food before her. And then her mouth falls open, but no words leave her mouth.

"Biscuits with chocolate gravy and strawberries. It's still your favorite, right?"

"How did you know? I don't think I've ever told anybody that. My grandma used to make this for me." She looks down at her plate with tears in her eyes. "It looked just like this. How?"

I shrug. "You talk in your sleep."

"Last night?"

I laugh. "No. You didn't say a word last night, but you did a lot when we were kids. Landon never heard you."

"He snores too loudly for that," we both say and laugh.

"But I was always a light enough sleeper. I heard every word you muttered."

"What else did I say?" Her cheeks flush bright pink as she says it, which just makes me smile brighter at her. I take a seat on the edge of the bed near her feet.

"Eat first then I'll tell you."

She begins digging into her breakfast, and when I feel she has eaten enough, that she is no longer starving herself or the baby, I speak. "Let me think. You used to talk a lot about Landon. How you had the hots for him."

"I did not," she mumbles between bites.

"Did too. You've been talking about how much you loved Landon since you were eight years old."

She blushes again but doesn't argue.

"You used to talk a lot about how much you wanted a horse."

She nods and takes another bite.

"You would talk about how you wanted at first to be a princess, and then a veterinarian, and then an actress."

She smiles at that.

"You used to talk about how scared you were."

I meet her gaze, and both of our eyes have turned serious. Her fork drops to her plate.

"You remember all of that?"

I nod. "I remember every word you've ever said. Whether you were awake or not."

She just stares at me for a while longer. Neither of us says a word. Maybe if things were different right now, I would throw the tray to the floor and kiss her. I would confess my undying love for her, but things aren't different. She's in love with my brother and carrying his child. I'm nothing more than a friend and manager to her.

I watch her face as the tears pick up and stream faster down her face. So fast that I'm afraid she is going to break down like she did last night.

I grab the tray and move it to the nightstand again. My hands immediately go to her face to wipe the tears and then I'm holding her again. I'm holding her so tight trying to take away all of the pain she is feeling because of my idiot brother.

She pushes me away, though, until I'm sitting inches from her with a stunned expression on my face.

She buries her face in her hands and continues to sob. I don't know what to do. So I just wait for her to decide what she needs.

"I've done something horrible," she finally says between sobs.

I wipe the tears from her cheeks smiling at her as I do. "You are not horrible. You're amazing. You're strong and beautiful and going to make an amazing mother to my niece."

My words only make her tears cry harder and her face turn even more distraught. I have no idea what has brought this on. What has brought on her feeling this way?

"I lied."

I take her hand in mine. "It's okay."

She shakes her head. "It's not. I lied. I said that Landon destroyed my brother's life because Landon hurt me so much when he broke up with me. I couldn't bear not to be with him."

"What are you talking about? The video is perfectly clear that Landon was the one who hurt your brother."

I watch her head move side to side, but I don't believe her. I don't believe that Landon isn't to blame for ruining her brother's life. I hate her brother. I've hated him since he was eight. I've hated him since he tried to hurt Caroline, but he didn't deserve what Landon did to him. Sean never physically hurt Caroline. He didn't deserve to live his life in a wheelchair.

"I lied. That video doesn't show what you think it does."

I stand from the bed. "What are you talking about? Are you saying you manipulated the video?"

She shakes her head. "No. The video is true. One-hundred percent true. You just are missing one thing when you look at that video. You didn't see the gun that my brother was holding in his hand when he approached Landon. You didn't see it pressed into my back as my own brother used me to try to blackmail Landon into giving him money for drugs."

She gets out of bed until she is face to face with me.

"Landon wasn't attacking my brother out of spite or because he drank too much. He was attacking him to protect me. To keep me safe. Just like he always does. Just like he has my entire life."

Caroline has never made me angry. Not one fucking time. Not even when we were children and she would make fun of me for being too serious. Not even when she would mimic everything Landon and I would say. It would drive Landon wild but not me.

Not until now has she ever truly made my blood boil. My face is red, and my nostrils flare as the words leave her mouth.

I never thought of Landon as a monster. I never thought he was as bad as my father was. But when I saw that video, my whole view of him changed. For just a second, I thought he was this horrible monster. I thought he might even deserve prison if it wasn't for the fact his unborn child would suffer like we did.

"Why?" I snap at her.

"After the attack, I took the surveillance tape. I convinced the owner to give it to me instead of the police. I needed it to protect him. But then, the next morning when you guys woke up and didn't remember anything, I saw my chance, and I took it. That's when I made the deal that kept my brother away from me by paying him the money he was so desperate for. The money that got him his drugs. That's how I got Landon to agree to be with me. I blackmailed him with a video that shows how horrible Sean is, not Landon."

I turn away from her not being able to look at her a moment longer. I've never been so angry or disappointed in someone. I can't believe I betrayed my own brother. I can't believe I thought he was capable of doing such horrible things.

I feel her grab my arm, but I force her to let me go.

"Please look at me."

I turn, and when I do, I see her wince away from the look of anger on my face. She's scared. *Good,* I think. She should be scared. She almost ruined my brother's life.

"Please don't hate me."

I close my eyes to keep from seeing the fear in her eyes, but it just brings out the pain in my heart.

I hated my own brother for probably one of the bravest moments of his life. And I lost the woman that I love to a lie.

I walk away from her. I walk out of the bedroom only stopping to grab my car keys and wallet.

"Where are you going?"

"To free my brother."

I head to the front door when I see him. Landon. My brother. My best friend. The only family I have ever had standing in the entryway. He looks tired and worn, but he's here, and that's all it takes for the anger to break and my heart to begin to heal.

Chapter Twenty-Six

ALEX

1,000. The number of pictures I took before I realized my purpose.

"PROVE IT," he says against my lips.

I hesitate, not sure what to do with his words. I need to prove to him that I came back for him. I need to keep him from growing suspicious. But I don't know if I can give him what he wants? Can I really have sex with this monster?

I run my tongue across my lip while I think of how to show him how much I want him. I have no choice, I realize. I have to.

"Gladly," I say as I grab his neck and pull his lips to mine. I thrust my tongue into his mouth before he has a chance to slip his tongue inside my mouth. I take control trying my best to show him my desperation. My need. My uncontrollable desire.

His hand travels up and down my body and lands on my ass. Just below where the gun hides in my shorts. A gun I would love nothing more than to remove and use to shoot him straight in the heart. I don't have the evidence, though, and when I kill him, I will not be going to jail.

I kiss him harder trying to focus on making him grow wild with lust and need so that he doesn't focus on the fact that I'm not exhibiting the same level of intensity that he is.

He moans as my tongue pulls out more desire in him. My hands begin moving hungrily over his body as my body pushes his back against the cabinets. Except it's not hunger for him that is making my hands move, it's anger and revenge. The need to make him feel as much pain as possible.

I kiss him again, but this time, my lip bites down hard on his, drawing far more blood than I ever did to Landon.

He pulls away with a wicked grin on his face.

"You want it rough, baby."

I nod.

And he attacks back. His body slams against mine shoving me hard against the cabinets opposite of where we just were. My back aches from where the knobs from the cabinets dig into my back. I don't cry out in pain, though. I don't give him that satisfaction.

Instead, I grab his neck and force his body against mine until I can feel his hard cock growing against my belly. I want to cry in disgust. I want to push him away, but instead, I pull him closer to me. I force his disgusting, vile lips to stay locked on mine. He tries to return the favor by biting my lip, but I don't let him. Instead, I claw at his back until I feel the skin rip exposing fresh blood.

He growls as I do. His eyes grow more with lust as he looks at me while my eyes grow darker with anger that I hope looks more like lust.

"You like that?"

He growls again as he sucks on my neck. "I love anything you do, baby."

I feel his teeth sink into my neck, and I can't hold back. I scream.

He takes my moment of weakness and lifts my body from the ground. I don't protest. I let him lift me and do my best to cling to him. He carries me quickly up the stairs. His hand on my ass as he does. At one moment, as he readjusts my body in his arms, I swear he feels the gun, but if he does, he doesn't say a word.

"Fuck, I want you," my voice slithers in his ear just before he shoves my body hard against the bedroom wall as his lips and tongue claim mine. The dresser vibrates against the wall as I feel the pain in my back again.

He grabs my shirt and rips it from my body. His hand palms my breasts, and I moan. Not because I'm supposed to but because it feels good. I immediately hate myself for letting him turn me on even for a second.

I try to regain control of my body, but he slips his hand in my shorts. His hand finds my pussy and pulls my juices up over my clit. He rubs, and I moan. I close my eyes and imagine Landon touching me. I imagine his fingers inside me. I imagine his soft lips touching mine just before he brings just the right amount of pain. That's what I imagine as I moan and pant. That's what I pretend I'm reacting to. Landon's touch. Not Ethan's. That's why my body is responding this way.

"Feels good doesn't it, baby."

I moan in response. It does feel good. He removes his hand just as I feel I'll explode if he goes any further. He puts his fingers in his mouth tasting me while his eyes intensify their need.

I need to respond to show him how much I need him, so I grab the hem of his shirt and yank it off over his head until I can see his fit body. I smile as I do, trying to show my appreciation of his physique.

He undoes the belt on his pants, and I watch as they fall to the ground. I watch his cock spring free hard as a rock. I feel his eyes locked on my face. I try to keep my face from showing disgust at the sight of what I'm going to have to do.

He throws my body to the floor until I'm kneeling in front of him. His cock presses against my lips.

"Suck it."

His cock presses harder against my mouth. I feel my lips turn down in disgust for less than a second; I close my eyes, and then I open my mouth to let him in. But his cock doesn't push inside like I expect.

Instead, he laughs. I open my eyes and look up at him quizzically. He grabs my hair hard. Too hard and I cry from the sting.

"You stupid bitch."

He throws me hard into the corner of the room. My head hits the edge of the nightstand as I fall. Hard enough that I'm sure I'm bleeding.

I look up at him with what I'm sure is terror on my face.

"You stupid fucking bitch. You thought you could lie to me. You thought you could trick me into giving you what you want."

"What? I never lied to you." I grab the side of my head to try to keep it from throbbing, but it doesn't help. The pain isn't going to leave. When I remove my hand, it's covered in blood. The room seems to spin, and Ethan shakes as he stands in front of me. I try to get up, but the dizziness keeps me down. My stomach churns. I can't move. Not without emptying the contents of my stomach or passing out from the pain in my head.

I stare at Ethan, who is still shaking side to side, but I don't miss the movement of him pointing a gun at my head. It's too clear, too focused for me not to notice.

I reach to my back trying to find my own gun, my own protection, but it's not there.

He just laughs when I realize that he is holding my gun. How he got it without me noticing, I'm not sure. But he did.

"You were very convincing. Even Mother thought you did a good job of pretending to love me. But I knew. I knew you still loved that bastard instead of me."

I curl up in the corner. He's going to shoot. He's going to shoot me right here. And I can't do anything. I can't save James or Daniel. I can't save Landon. I can't even save myself.

"It's the only reason you came back. To save him. It didn't matter, though. That bastard turned himself in." He chuckles. "He'll be in prison a long time now. And if he ever gets out, no one will ever buy his music ever again. He got what he deserves."

His eyes darken as he looks at me. "You, though, haven't gotten what you deserve yet."

I close my eyes as I watch the gun moving closer. This is it. The end. I hear him cock the gun. I hear him pull the trigger. Then nothing.

Chapter Twenty-Seven

LANDON

I thought I'd lose myself too
In the bottom of a bottle
I thought I'd get sucked into.

"THEY LET YOU GO," Drew says with a stunned expression on his face.

"Yeah, it seems that way." I brush past him to the kitchen. My stomach is growling. I need food. And then I need to find Caroline and make sure she is okay. And then call Alex and make sure she knows she can leave. That she doesn't need to protect me.

I walk until I reach the fridge. I open it and pull out a carton of eggs and bacon. I carry them to the counter and then glance up at Drew, who is walking into the kitchen with tears in his eyes. I cock my head in confusion. Drew doesn't cry. He's too rationale to cry.

His arms go around me as soon as he reaches me. He holds me in an embrace I'm not used to from him. It's awkward and loving at the same time. I pat him gently on the back until he lets go.

"It's going to be okay. My lawyer doesn't even think I'll spend any time in jail. Probably just get community service. Even though I feel like I should pay a lot more for what I have done."

He shakes his head. "You won't serve any jail time. You won't serve community service either."

I crack an egg over the stovetop. "Yeah, I will. They can't let me go scot-free; even as much as they want to, they can't."

"No, you won't."

I stare at him my eyebrows raised.

"You won't because you didn't do what you think you did."

God, what is it with everyone thinking better of me? "I did. I attacked him. I almost killed him."

"Yes. You did that. But he deserved it."

"No one deserves what I did."

"He did. He had a gun held to Caroline's back."

"What?"

"He was blackmailing you to get his drug money. He hadn't realized that you two had broken up. Not that it mattered. You would have reacted the same way whether you were together or not. He was using her to get money from you. Her own brother."

I slump to the floor with a spatula in my hand. I try to remember that night. I can't, though. I don't remember any of it because of the alcohol. I rest my head in my hands trying to remember because I'm afraid it's the only way I'll stop feeling like the horrible person that I am.

Drew comes over and sits beside me. He places his hand on my back. "You're not like our father. You're not a monster."

"Aren't I?"

"No. I'm sorry for ever thinking that you were. If anybody is a monster, it's Caroline's brother. And maybe, even to a lesser extent, Caroline."

I nod although I'm not sure I believe him. I still feel horrible. I still feel like a monster.

We sit in silence for a long time after that. Both apologizing without saying a word, even though neither of us has anything to apologize for.

"Can I talk to you?" Caroline's voice is meek and scared. I glance up to meet her tear-stained eyes as she stands hugging herself. I glance at her belly that is just starting to protrude — just enough that it reminds me what she carries. My child.

I nod but don't get up. I don't think I can.

Drew does stand, though. He walks past Caroline giving her an evil glare as he does. I watch him disappear back in his bedroom, giving us privacy.

She walks slowly to me, expecting me to stand and greet her. When I don't, she sighs before sliding to the ground next to me. She hugs her knees to her chest. She doesn't say anything. I guess speaking is too hard. I understand; speaking is too hard for me too. Moving is too hard. Even breathing is difficult.

Somehow, I find the strength, though. "Why?"

"Because I love you, and I couldn't live without you."

I suck in a deep breath and count to three before I speak, trying to let the anger subside. I can't be mad at the mother of my child. No matter what she has done.

"That's not a reason."

"It's true, though. I loved you and couldn't bear to be apart. I couldn't bear not to be yours. I still can't."

"Why, though? Sure, we've been friends since forever. But we tried dating, we tried the falling in love thing, and it didn't work. If you admit the truth to yourself, you never fell in love with me, either. Not truly. Not when we were dating. Yes, I love you, and you love me, but it's in the same sense that I love Drew. It doesn't mean we should be together."

She shakes her head. "You don't understand. I do love you in that way. We struggled when we dated because neither of us could give up any control. Neither of us was willing to relinquish our independence."

"Nothing's changed."

"Maybe not, but that doesn't change that I still love you. I have since we were eight."

I narrow my eyes at her. "What do you mean?"

"I fell in love with you when we were eight. I fell in love when you saved me."

"What are you talking about?" I don't remember saving her. Drew and I were just barely surviving. We didn't have enough strength or money to save anyone else.

"It was my eighth birthday."

I nod. I remember that day. I remember Drew and I saved all of our money to buy her a cupcake and a single candle to celebrate her birthday with. That can't be what she is talking about. She couldn't have fallen in love with me because I bought her a damn cupcake. And if she fell in love with me, she should have equally fallen in love with Drew. He was there. He did the same thing.

"You and Drew bought me a cupcake for me. You remember?"

"Of course, I remember."

She smiles, but I still don't remember what else she could be talking about.

"That day my father died. Mother turned into a pill popping mess. And my brother ..."

She closes her eyes unable to continue.

"Your brother ... What did he do?" I tilt her chin up to look at me. She looks so scared, so broken.

"He had been drinking. That was the first night I ever saw him drink. It's probably the night that started the years of abuse. Years of drug problems. It's what started it all."

I hold her hand and nod. She glances down at our hands when I touch her, but she doesn't smile. She's still too lost in the world. Still trapped in time when she was eight and something horrible happened that I somehow saved her from.

"He tried to molest me. My brother. He tried to molest me." She looks stoic as she says it. She doesn't cry. Doesn't show any sadness. Just calmness as if she has relived it long enough that it no longer affects her.

I cry for her, though. No child should go through that.

She looks into my eyes when she sees the tear fall. Her thumb caresses my cheek as she wipes the fallen tear. She smiles now when she looks at me.

"He didn't succeed, though, because you saved me." I take her into my arms and just hold her. I feel her body shake remembering that awful night, and I don't make her relive any more of it. I just hold her. Even though I don't remember how I saved her. Even though I have countless questions, I don't ask them.

"You saved me," she says again into my ear. "You saved me."

Chapter Twenty-Eight

CAROLINE

I push him back until he's standing, and I'm on my knees. I pull his thick cock from his pants and suck. His eyes intensify as I do showing me his pleasure, and I realize how much I want to bring him that pleasure.

"DO you have any evidence to back up your claims?" the officer asks. His voice isn't harsh like I expected. I didn't expect the police to so easily believe me, but they seem to be going along with every word that I say.

"Can I see the video?"

I watch as one officer smiles at me and walks out of the room. He enters again with a computer. He pulls the video up on the screen. I play the video and then wait. I wait until one of the worst nights of my life replays on the screen before me. Not because my brother threatened to kill me just so he could get enough money for drugs. Not because Landon almost killed my brother, but because I was sad when I found out he didn't. I turned into a monster that night desperate to do anything to get away from my brother. Desperate to do anything to keep him from hurting me. And the only escape I saw was Landon. I loved him. I thought he would save me again when I wasn't strong enough to save myself.

I click pause on the screen when we come on screen.

"There," I say pointing at my brother's hands. "Look closely at his hand. He's holding a gun." I watch as Landon's lawyer and the police officers lean in close to get a view of the picture. Now that I point it out, it's hard to miss. He's holding a gun.

One of the officers nods and then smiles at me. "Thank you for coming forward. If we have any more questions for you, we have your contact information."

I nod and stand as I've been dismissed.

"Wait. What will happen to my brother?"

The police officers exchange glances. "We will investigate the claims you have made, but he will most likely be charged with attempted murder and drug-related charges, depending on what we find in the investigation."

I nod and then walk out of the room. He may finally be gone. I may finally be safe. I know I should have turned him in a long time ago. The fear held me back, though. And the lack of trust in a justice system I've never seen do any justice. I did the only thing I could do. I held onto Landon and his money that would set me free.

I glance up as I walk out of the small room, and I see Drew. He has a frown on his face at the sight of me. Landon may have forgiven me, but Drew sure hasn't. I don't think he will ever forgive me.

"Can I wait with you?"

He doesn't answer. He just stares at me. I take a seat in the chair next to him. We watch as the officers and lawyer walk from the room I was just into where Landon is waiting to be told what they are going to do about the charges.

I can only assume they are going to be dropped, but I don't know. They could still charge Landon with something, even though he was trying to defend me.

"I'm sorry."

"I'm not the one you need to apologize to."

I sigh. "I already apologized to Landon, multiple times. He's forgiven me. Why can't you?"

He faces me now as his eyes burn into me. "Landon only forgave you because you are having his child. If it weren't for that, he would have already kicked you to the curb."

His words sting, but I try not to let them affect me. Because I know that's not true. He didn't forgive me because I'm having his child. He forgave me because I told him the truth from our childhood.

"You of all people should be able to grant forgiveness."

"Maybe, but right now, I can't. You made me hate my brother. You made me think he was a monster for what he did. You made me..."

"I didn't make you do or believe a damn thing. You chose to believe the lies. You chose to believe that your brother could do such a horrible thing without reason."

He looks down at his lap. His hands twist in anger before he glances back up. "I know. Some brother I am. That's why I didn't ask for forgiveness. I don't deserve it."

We both turn as the door opens. Landon and his lawyer walk out.

"Free of all charges," his lawyer says smiling.

I get up, run over to Landon, and wrap my arms around him. He smiles at me, but he holds back whatever emotion he is feeling.

I let go and glance back at Drew, who is frowning at me again.

I don't care if Drew likes me or not. All I care about is Landon. I just got him back, and I'm not going to let him go.

Chapter Twenty-Nine

ALEX

1. The number of people it took to believe in my pictures and to convince me I was good enough. I could make a difference.

THE ROOM IS FOGGY, and my head hurts. I blink several times trying to clear the fog, but it doesn't clear. So I just keep my eyes closed trying to remember what happened. I was lying on the floor, my head was bleeding, and Ethan was holding a gun in his hand. He pulled the trigger, and I thought I was dead. I thought that was the end. It wasn't.

He just used it to scare me. He didn't shoot me. At least not with a gun. He pushed a needle into my neck instead. The same needle he stuck into my neck the night he raped me. The same needle he stuck in my neck the night he faked a car accident.

This time, though, when I wake from the fog, it's different. This time, I remember. Everything.

I don't know why this time is different. I don't know why this mixture of drugs in my system cleared the chaos that floated around in my head, but it did. Everything aligns in place.

It's too late. I'm going to die before I get a chance to use my new memories. I'm going to die.

I wiggle my arms but feel the sharp metal from the handcuffs dig into my wrists. My arms hurt from being stretched over my head and attached to each corner of the bedpost.

I test my legs and realize they are both tied with some rope to the other end of the bedposts. I can't move.

"Comfortable," Ethan says.

I blink my eyes trying to stop them from seeing multiples of Ethan as he walks over to the side of the bed, but it doesn't work. The drugs are too strong, and I feel them trying to pull me back into a deep sleep. I fight it, though. I fight to keep my eyes open even though I can barely make him out. I will not let him see the drugs working on me.

He laughs. "The drugs are still drawing you under. Still pulling you back to that dark place. You shouldn't fight it."

I shiver as he touches my leg. Dragging his hand slowly up, he stops just short of my underwear. I keep shivering, and that's when I realize I'm naked except for my bra and panties. Now, my body is shaking uncontrollably.

"That's the drugs. You're going through withdrawal as it leaves your system. You'll feel worse before you feel better."

I groan, as the pain gets worse, as if it was responding to his words.

He walks closer to me until he is standing over me. He strokes my hair, and I do my best to shrink away from his touch. I see his wicked smile as I do.

"You probably don't even remember the last twenty-four hours."

I close my eyes forcing them to be clear when I open so that I can look him in the eye when I say it. When I open them, I see him clearly. Clearly enough to see his wicked grin as he stands above me.

"That's where you're wrong. I remember ... everything."

I see a second of fear cross his face, but then it's gone. "You think you remember everything. Huh?"

"Yes. I do."

He smiles and pets my face again. "Good. That will make these next few days more enjoyable. We will be able to have honest conversations while I torture you to within an inch of your life. Until you beg me to kill you."

I keep my face calm. I don't show the fear festering inside me. I won't give him that satisfaction. But I need to know the answer to one question. One question that will haunt me if I don't know before he kills me.

"Why?"

He shakes his head. "So eager."

He runs his hand down my body until he grabs my breast and squeezes it.

I close my eyes trying to block out his touch as he continues to massage my breast.

"I guess you deserve to know why you are going to die. But the answer is much simpler than you would probably like to hear. I like torturing, raping, and killing women. It's that simple. I've done it most of my adult life. It turns me on to watch women scream and cry and beg for me to kill them."

My eyes widen. "I'm not the only one you have done this to."

He moves his hand to my other breast, but I barely even feel it this time. "Yes, I've done this dozens of times to women who nobody wanted. To women who lived on the streets just like you did. I would seduce them. I'd drug them and rape them. And then I'd torture and kill them."

"Why me then? Why didn't you kill me right away?"

He looks at me, and I see the lust grow as he squeezes my breast too tightly. I don't make a sound in response to his touch.

"I would say that you intrigued me more than the others, but that's not true. The difference is that when you awoke from the drugs, you didn't remember. The drugs caused you to forget. So unlike the other women, I didn't have to kill you to keep my secret.

"I tried to keep my distance from you at first, but then I had an idea. Mother had been begging me to stop what I was doing. She thought I would get caught."

"Your mother knows what you have done?"

"Of course. She knows everything. She begged me to stop. But I couldn't. The animal inside me needed to rape, to torture, to kill. I needed to do it. I couldn't control it.

"So I came up with a plan. If I could form a relationship with you, I could use the drugs and rape you whenever I wanted. All I had to do was use the drugs, and you would forget that I raped you."

I close my eyes as I realize his words are completely true. Images of rape after rape, physical torture, all at the hands of this man fill my head.

"You're thinking about it now," he says. "You remember every time I hit you. Every time I fucked you against your will. Every time I injected you with drugs." He smirks. "You could say it was all for a good cause, though. Every time I had the urge, I raped you. So really, you were doing the world a favor because when I was raping you, I wasn't raping other women. I wasn't killing other women. You fulfilled that desire in me."

He rips my bra off and twists my nipple so hard I'm afraid it's going to come off. I can't hold back the cry that comes out of me. It's too painful for me to bear and keep inside. I have to scream to handle the pain. I squirm against the handcuffs and rope, but it just makes the pain in my arms worse.

"Don't act like you aren't enjoying this. You liked the pain. Even when I was torturing you and raping you, you enjoyed every minute of it. You couldn't keep it from appearing on your face.

"That's why you like the pain now. That's why even when Landon slept with you, you craved the pain that I conditioned you to like over and over again. I control you."

He slaps my breast hard when he stops. I try not to think about Landon, but I can't. This is why I like the pain. This is why I like it rough. It's because of Ethan. Now, I know for sure, and I hate myself even more.

"You were nothing. You still are nothing. I made your career. I made you into the photographer you are today. I made you. I made you live out your dreams. You should be grateful."

I remember, though. I fight through the tears to speak.

"You didn't make me. I'm not grateful that you found me on the street and proceeded to rape me and then tried to kill me when I found out what you were doing. I never wanted to be a fashion photographer. I never wanted the money or the fame. I was living on the streets for a reason; because every cent I made went to a cause I was fighting for.

"I wanted to photograph cancer survivors. And families of cancer victims. I wanted to honor my mother. I wanted to fight cancer, not photograph famous people."

I glance down at the numbers on the side of my chest. That's what the number on my side represents. It represents every part of me. The pain and the happiness. All of it together makes me whole. And all of the numbers put together equal me and everyone else who has ever suffered in pain alone. They equal the people I want to save. That's who I was fighting for. Those people on my chest.

"How honorable, but I think I've had enough of honorable. Enough talking. I think it's time to give you what we both want."

He stands and walks to his closet. When he returns, I expect to see some crazy torture device. I expect to see a gun or a whip or more rope. I expect to see another syringe. I don't expect him to be holding a belt. Just a belt. How could something so ordinary, so simple, bring about pain? He walks to the edge of the bed with it in his hand, and I know I'm about to find out.

I promised myself I wouldn't think about Landon. I promised I would let him go and be happy with Caroline and his child. I promised myself I wouldn't think about him. Not after he knocked up his ex-girlfriend and lied to me about being a monster. I don't think he's a monster, though. Not really. He may have an alcohol problem, and he may now have a jail problem, but I don't think he's a monster.

The real monster is moving closer to me with a belt in his hand. It doesn't matter if I think about Landon. Pining after a man I can never have isn't such a bad thing anymore because I won't be able to have Landon or any other man. I won't be able to hurt him. I won't survive this.

So I let my mind go to Landon. I let my love fill me and do its best to protect me. I'll pretend his lips are biting me each time the belt touches my body. I'll get through this.

I watch as his hand raises just before the belt comes down across my breast. When the belt touches my soft skin, though, I realize I'm wrong. I won't survive this. This is unsurvivable.

Chapter Thirty

LANDON

But you saved me.
Daughter, you saved me.

"We have to go home," I say to Drew, who is sitting on the plane right next to me.

He scrunches his nose. "What do you mean we need to go home? We just got to New York. You're going on *The Tonight Show* to explain everything. So the label will be happy with you again. Although I don't know why they care. Your sales have been sky high since people found out you were arrested. Everybody likes a real-life bad boy. Now, your reputation truly matches your appearance."

"We have to go home."

"Why?"

"It's just a feeling."

"Is it Caroline?"

"I don't know."

"Alex?"

"I don't know. I just know something is wrong."

"Call them then. Call them before we fly across the country to go check on them and you flake out on an appearance and get the label even more upset with you than they already are."

I nod. He's right. I take out my phone as the private jet taxis to a stop. I dial Caroline first. She picks up on the first ring.

"Is everything okay?"

"Other than I'm missing you."

"Caroline?"

"Yes. Everything is fine. I'm just lying here eating Ben and Jerry's and getting excited to watch you on the show tonight."

I sigh. Glad that nothing is wrong with her or the baby. "Okay. I have to go. I'll call you later. And Caroline, eat real food, not just ice cream all night."

I can feel her rolling her eyes at me as she hangs up the phone. That leaves Alex. I've tried calling her several times, and she never answered my call. I have to try again.

I call, and it rings and rings and rings. I try again with the same result. I try a third time and finally resolve to leave a voicemail asking her to call me.

Drew watches me the entire time. As soon as I'm done, he picks up his phone and dials a number.

"Who are you calling?"

"Alex."

I nod and wait. He tries again and again, and she doesn't answer. He leaves a voicemail and a text message. No answer to either.

"You still have that feeling?" he asks.

I close my eyes, and all I feel is pain. Incredible, unbearable pain.

"Yes."

He nods looking at me with scared eyes. "I'll be right back. He walks to the front of the plane and then is back within minutes. Just long enough for me to worry about what could be happening to Alex. She's prone to accident after accident. She's prone to attacks. I can only imagine what is happening to her right now that is causing her this much pain.

Whatever it is, I have to go find her. I have to put a stop to it. Even if she is still mad at me and never wants to see me again, I have to save her.

Drew won't understand. The label won't understand. And *The Tonight Show* definitely won't understand. But I have to go back to her. I have to.

Drew walks back and takes his seat. I watch him buckle his seat belt again.

"What are you doing?"

He smiles at me. "We are going home."

"You believe me?"

"I believe that you think something is wrong with Alex. And I'm done not doing everything I can to fight for my brother." He glances down at my lap. "Buckle your seat belt. We are going home."

I reach down, buckle my seat belt again, and watch as he makes several phone calls to cancel everything. I can hear the anger on the other side of the phone, but Drew doesn't falter. He defends me to the end.

He hangs up just as the plane begins taking off back across the country. I've only had one other flight that was this horrible. On that flight, I spent the entire time praying that she would survive. I expect I will do the same thing again on this flight. The only difference is I have Drew this time. And this time, I have no idea what Alex is facing.

Drew reaches out and puts his hand on my back trying to comfort me. He's a good brother.

Just hold on, Alex. I'm coming home.

Chapter Thirty-One

DREW

The look in her eyes when she sucks me is beautiful. This is right. She wants this, as much as I want this.

THE ENTIRE PLANE ride is silent. I know Landon's praying, despite not being religious. So I pray too.

I pray that whatever mess Alex is in, she'll be okay.

I pray that she'll take him back because they both deserve each other. They both deserve to be happy.

I pray that Landon's career survives this.

When I called to cancel the appearance, the label threatened me. They threatened to drop him if he didn't make the appearance and set the record straight for why he was arrested.

I said it didn't matter. This was more important. I just hope I made the right decision. For all of our sakes. Landon was too blind to make this decision rationally.

And I think they were bluffing to try to control him; if they weren't, his career could be over. Sure, a different label could pick him up. Or he could try to go it on his own. Or he could never write or sing another song again.

It doesn't matter right now. All that matters is getting Landon to Alex. That's it.

The tires of the plane skid across the runway, and I grab the armrests until the plane has come to a complete stop. I hate landings. I hate takeoffs. I just generally hate flying. If it were up to me, we would never go anywhere and keep our feet firmly on the ground where it's safe.

As soon as the plane stops, Landon jumps up from his seat and barrels down the aisle to get off the plane. I run after him.

"I called a driver to come pick us up. Should be waiting on the tarmac."

Landon runs down the stairs off the plane, and I follow and then I see her. Caroline standing on the tarmac with a frown on her face in front of her car. The driver I hired is parked behind her.

I don't know what she is doing here, but it can't be good.

I watch her stop Landon, and my anger overtakes me. I run to them and pull her off him.

"What did you do? The label called and told me to talk some sense into my boyfriend, or they were going to drop you. What did you do?" she pleads to Landon. She tries to grab hold of him again, but I hold her hands to keep her from him.

Landon looks at me curiously and raises an eyebrow. "Thank you," he says in response to finding out I told him to come here for Alex. To risk it all for her. I'm behind him one-hundred percent.

"What did you do?" Caroline asks again.

I hold onto Caroline to keep her from breaking down right here.

"Go," I say to Landon. "I got this."

He looks from me to Caroline for just a second longer and then he goes. He goes and doesn't look back.

Chapter Thirty-Two

ALEX

3,100. The number of pictures of happiness and pain showing equals side of the human condition I have taken over the years.

THE BELT COMES DOWN on my breasts, and I scream a blood-curdling scream. A scream I've never heard myself make.

My brain immediately proves me wrong. Replaying countless scenes of Ethan doing similar things to make me scream like this.

When I'm done screaming from the first hit, I open my eyes and see Ethan's reaction. His eyes are closed, and his mouth is open in the same way I've seen him come countless times before. He's getting off from hitting me. He's disgusting.

He opens his eyes and cracks his head from side to side, letting the release flow through his body.

He whips the belt across my stomach this time with no warning. I scream, and my body tries to move away from the pain, but I can't escape.

"I know you love it. Love the feel of your flesh being ripped from your body."

Tears and sweat burn my eyes forcing them closed. It's probably better this way. I can't see the painful welts forming with every whip. But now, I can't anticipate his next strike. I tense my body preparing for the belt to hit anywhere on my body.

He hits me again three times in quick succession across my stomach. Each one burns more than the next until, with the last one, I'm sure he's ripped the skin off my stomach.

I scream again louder until my voice hurts from the screaming. Maybe someone will hear me. If I can just yell loud enough, maybe I'll get the attention of a nosy neighbor.

We don't have neighbors, though. Not any close enough to hear me. He made sure of that.

"Your screams are music to my ears. Let's see if we can make you take it up a notch."

He moves back to my breast hitting me with one long stroke. He's right; I scream louder until my saliva and sweat are choking me preventing me from screaming any longer.

He strokes my cheek as I choke. I turn my head and spit on his hand. He laughs and then slaps me hard across my face forcing my head to turn.

The move makes me feel defeated. Even defiance won't work with him.

I try my original strategy of not making a sound and just focusing on Landon, but when he hits me again this time on my pussy, I can't hold back my cries.

"Please ..." I beg through the cries, and then I hate myself for begging. I bite my lip to keep my mouth from begging again.

I feel his thumb on my lip forcing me to let it go.

"You can't beg if you are doing that, and I love it when you beg. I won't stop until you beg me, until I believe you won't survive if I hit you again."

He hits me again on my pussy forcing another scream, but then his hand goes inside my panties. He rips them down and then starts massaging my soft bud. I feel my body coming alive at his disgusting touch. He hits me there with the belt and then immediately massages me with his hand. He's conditioning me. He's turning me on and making my body respond to the pain just like before. I won't let him.

Images of women that he did this to float in my head. Images of faceless women he raped and tortured like this and then killed scroll across my eyelids. I have to stop him for them and for all the women he will hurt after me if I don't.

He hits me again, but this time, I don't move. I don't scream or cry. I feel the women giving me power. I feel them giving me strength. I have to fight back.

The belt hits me again, and I laugh. I laugh in response to the pain. "Is that all you got?"

I open my eyes through the tears, and I see his face redden. He hits me harder. "You're such a pussy."

"You're a slut who likes to be raped and tortured."

He hits me again, and I smile.

"I don't believe you raped dozens of women."

He pauses for just a second and then hits me again.

"I don't believe you killed them either. You're just trying to scare me."

He pauses. "What makes you think that, when you're tied to my bed getting whipped within an inch of your life."

He hits, but this time, his heart isn't really in it. The pain is less. He didn't use his full force. I can do this. I can stop him.

"You tried to kill me, twice. But you failed. You failed because you aren't really a killer. You won't kill me. You're too weak for that."

"Stop."

I smirk. "You're a mamma's boy. Your father left you because you are such a weak pussy. You won't hurt me. You definitely won't kill me."

"Stop," he warns again as anger grows darker in his eyes until his eyes are completely black. I know it's coming. The unbearable pain that will break me. I just have to break him first.

"You won't kill me. I'm going to walk out of here alive. But first, I'm going to kill *you*."

He punches me hard in the ribs. So hard I can barely breathe. I struggle to breathe as I watch him run from the room. When I catch my breath, I'm relieved. He's gone. If only for a few minutes, I'm still safe. I can regroup. I can find my strength again.

He bursts through the door what seems like only seconds later. All I see are pictures, flash drives, and CDs. Several tumble to the floor. He takes the first and presses it to my face.

"This is Samantha. She was homeless. Just sixteen. She was my first. I raped and killed her. She's at the bottom of the ocean now."

"And this one." He thrusts a picture this time of a woman's body cut into pieces. I feel like vomiting after seeing the picture, but I don't let him see it. "I burned her body until she turned into ashes."

"This one. This one I kept for a week. She could handle pain like no woman I ever had. Other than you, of course."

He throws the loads of pictures of the women he raped and killed until they are floating around the room.

"Still don't believe I raped them? Still don't believe I killed them?"

"No," I spit out. Although I don't know why I'm still inciting him. I got what I want. I have the evidence. It's floating around the room. Now, I just need him dead.

That does it. He jumps on top of my body agitating the wounds he's caused, but that's not where the pain comes from. The pain comes from his hands choking me. I can't breathe. His hands are suffocating me. I pushed him too far. This is how I'm going to die.

His eyes watch mine. He watches the fear and watches the life drift out of my eyes.

"Still don't think I'm a killer?"

And with the last breath I breathe, I say, "No."

Chapter Thirty-Three

LANDON

You shined a light when no one else was there.
You saved me
And showed me how to be a father.

I PULL up in front of the house that Ethan bought for her. The house is amazing. Easily one of the grandest I've seen. This is obviously why she didn't want a big, expensive house. It reminded her of Ethan. Or she knew it could never compete with the house Ethan got for her.

I try calling her phone again, but this time, it doesn't even ring. It just goes straight to voicemail. The feeling of pain intensifies when I get out of my car. Something is wrong. I just don't know what.

The garage door is closed, so I don't know if her car is here or not, but I feel her. I know she's here.

I run to the door and ring the doorbell, but I can't wait for the doorbell to get someone's attention. I need the door open now. I try the doorknob, but it doesn't open. So I begin pounding on the door loudly. I pound, but no one answers.

"Alex! Ethan! Someone come answer the door."

No one comes, though. *Dammit!*

I walk off the porch through the landscaping in front of the house to look in the large windows. I don't see anyone. I know she is here, though, and I know something is wrong.

I should just leave. She's made it clear she wants nothing to do with me anymore, but I can't leave. I can't. Not until I know she's safe, and I know that she is happy with him.

I shouldn't do this. Not after I just got my charges dropped, but I don't have a choice. I continue down around the side of the house to the garage that's connected. I test the door on the side that leads to the garage. It's locked, but the knob is weak, much weaker than the front door.

I glance around to make sure no one is watching, and I pop the lock open. The door opens easily. I sneak into the garage without being seen and without setting off any alarms. I'm sure there are alarms, but no one ever seems to remember to put alarms on the garage doors. That's why Drew and I used to sneak into other people's houses through their garages. We never stole anything but food. I'm not proud of it, but it does come in handy now.

I glance around the garage. Alex's car Tessie sitting in the first spot. She's here.

I walk silently to the door that leads into the house. I test the door, but it's unlocked. I smile. No one ever thinks to lock this door. They think they are safe as long as their garage is locked. They aren't.

I just have to hope I don't trigger the alarm. Even if it does go off when I open the door, I don't care. I just need to make sure she is safe. I'd gladly go back to jail for breaking and entering.

I take a deep breath and push the door open as silently as possible. I poke my head in the house. It's silent, and I see no signs of people.

I close the door and begin moving as silently as possible through the house. I almost turn right, but my body forces me left. Almost like it's drawing me to her.

I find the stairs and creep up them. It's then that I realize I have nothing to protect myself with. If someone dangerous is here, I have no form of protection.

I round the corner at the top of the stairs. I glance down and notice a beam of light streaming from under a door. I glance in the other direction where there are several more doors. No signs of life in that direction, so I creep to the door. I force my legs to move slowly and silently, even though I want to move quickly. I want to run and crash through the door.

I make it to the door as my heart races in my chest. She's fine. She's survived everything. No matter what I face behind the door, I know she is going to be fine. She's a survivor.

I lean against the door, but I can't see through the crack in the door, and I can't hear a thing. I have to push it open.

I do quickly and silently, and then I see my worst nightmare. I gasp for air immediately sucked from my lungs at the sight of her tied to a bed bloody and beaten. Duct tape covers her mouth, and her eyes are closed. I force my eyes to look back to her chest despite how much pain it brings me to see the welts, lacerations, and blood covering them. I need to make sure she is breathing.

My first thought is I just interrupted a crazy sexual fantasy that she is playing out with Ethan. A fantasy that in my opinion has gone too far. She likes it darker than I ever imagined.

Her eyes shoot open at the sight of me. Her eyes don't say she wants this, though. Her eyes beg for help and beg me to run at the same time.

I run to her, my hands go to her face trying to comfort her.

"I'm going to get you out of here."

My hands move to the handcuffs. I try to force them open, but they don't budge. I can't open them.

I try to glance around the room for a key, but I don't see one. I move to the tape to get it off her lips. So she can tell me what the hell is going on.

"Freeze."

I look at Alex's eyes that have gone wild with fear. I can't get her out of here. I failed.

I turn slowly to face the direction of the voice. When I turn all the way around, I see him. Ethan standing in the doorway of the bathroom with a gun in his hand pointed at me.

He smirks when he sees me. "You got out of jail even faster than I imagined?"

My nostrils flare, and my face reddens as I glare at him. "Yeah, they tend to release you when you're innocent."

"Aw, but are you really innocent?"

"Yes," I say admitting it to Alex and myself for the first time. "I'm innocent. The truth came out. I was defending Caroline from her drug-addicted brother, just like I'm going to defend Alex against her psychopath husband."

He cocks his head sideways and takes a step closer still pointing the gun at my head. *Let him*, I think. As long as he's pointing the gun at me and talking to me, he can't hurt Alex.

"I'm a psychopath, huh?" One more step closer and then he smiles. "Yeah, I guess that would be about right."

"Let her go."

He shakes his head side to side. "I can't do that. She knows too much. And now, I'll get the honor of killing you too." He rolls his neck side to side as if the thought of killing me is almost too much joy for his body to handle.

"Just let her go and we will too. It was just rough sex gone too far."

He points the gun from me to her and then back at me. "You think that's what this is? You think this was just a one-time thing? This has been going on since the moment I met her. I raped her and then framed another. I hired the guys to kill her and fake a car crash. I attacked her and framed James."

He glances down, and I follow his gaze. It's the first time I see the pictures scattered on the floor. "All of the women in these pictures on the floor. I raped them. I tortured them. I killed them. And now, I'm going to do the same to her."

"You don't need to do that. We have money. Lots of money. We can pay you." I stay calm even though I want to run straight at him and pummel him to the ground. I want to hit him so hard that what I did to Caroline's brother is going to seem like a scratch in comparison. I can't, though. If I do, there is a good chance he'll shoot Alex. And I can't let that happen.

"I don't want your money." His eyes widen as the idea crosses his mind. "I have something better in mind. You coming is really a bonus, see. Because before I was just going to rape, torture, and kill Alex for the cameras. To relive over and over in my own brain, but now that you are here, you get to watch the love of your life being raped, tortured, and killed."

He grips the gun tighter.

"Put your hands up and move to the corner of the room."

I put my hands up but hesitate to move. If I do, my body will no longer be between him and Alex.

"Now!"

My body shudders at his words.

"I'm moving." I slowly walk away from Alex to the corner he indicated. I watch in disgust as he takes my place next to Alex. He strokes her cheek making her flinch. She keeps her eyes on me despite how hazy and tired they are. They stay on me. At least I will have her beautiful eyes to look into when we both die.

Ethan keeps the gun on me as he opens the nightstand drawer and pulls out a syringe. He fills the syringe and then tosses it to me.

It drops to the floor at my feet.

"Pick it up."

I bend down and slowly pick up the syringe. I keep my eyes on Alex the whole time. She's shaking and shivering.

"She needs a blanket."

He laughs. "You don't get to decide what she wants." He grabs her breasts and squeezes her nipple causing her to writhe and moan as he does. "I decide what she needs."

"Stop. Torture me, not her."

He twists one more time just to torment me and then stops.

"Oh, I plan to do both. Now inject yourself with the syringe."

I look down at the syringe in my hand with confusion.

"No."

He points the gun at my head now.

"Inject yourself with the syringe."

I take a deep breath. "I can't do that, Ethan."

He grabs Alex's hair twisting her head. Hard enough that a tear leaks from her eye. He points the gun at the side of her head. She winces for a second then opens her eyes and looks deep into my eyes. Her eyes are calmer now. Much calmer than I expected.

I take a step to her on instinct.

"Don't move," he says as he presses the gun hard against her head. I freeze.

"Okay, Ethan. Don't do anything crazy."

"Inject yourself with the fucking syringe!"

I glance down at Alex, who shakes her head gently side to side. I hold the syringe firmly in my hand. A syringe that I'm sure is going to knock me out. It might even kill me.

I keep my eyes locked on Alex's beautiful eyes.

"I love you," I say, and then I plunge the needle of the syringe into my arm.

Chapter Thirty-Four

CAROLINE

I feel his release building higher and higher. "Come for me," I hiss.

My hand flies through the air and slaps Drew on the face. He snaps his head back to look at me despite the sting I know he feels on his cheek. I'm so angry I can't think straight. Drew does nothing but ruin everything anytime Landon or I seem happy. I can't stay here. I need to go after Landon.

I turn and storm back to the driver's side of my Audi. Drew's faster, though. He runs ahead and puts his body between the door and me.

"You're not going to drive when you're angry. You're not going to get yourself and my niece killed."

I huff and try to push past him, but he stands strong. "Then I guess I won't be leaving this fucking tarmac then."

He holds out his hand. "Keys."

I throw them at his chest, but it doesn't give me the satisfaction I was hoping for because they bounce off his chest and into his hands. Drew opens the door and gets into the driver's side of the car while I climb into the passenger seat. I slam the door shut to make sure he knows I'm angry.

He begins driving us back to his and Landon's condo. And even though I have my own house now, I don't want to be alone. I haven't slept one night at my house. Instead, I've spent every night at the condo. I'm not about to start spending the night on my own tonight. Not when there's a chance Landon will be back tonight, and I can get to the bottom of this.

Tears burst from my body as the feelings of the day overwhelm me. I could blame it on pregnancy hormones, but that's not the cause. Not really.

The car stops at a stoplight, and that's when Drew decides to look at me. I expect some snide remark about how stupid I am for loving Landon. How wrong I am.

Instead, he says, "I'm sorry." He takes a deep breath. "When I made the decision to fly us back to check on Alex, I wasn't thinking about you. I wasn't thinking about what was best for Landon. He was a mess and unable to make a decision. I had to decide." He turns from me to look back out the window.

"If it makes you feel any better, I don't think the label will actually drop him. And even if they do, another label will pick him up."

I shake my head. "I'm not upset because of Landon."

He raises his eyebrows.

"I'm not."

"You're mad at me."

"No. I mean yes. Yes, I'm mad at you. All you have fucking done is ruin my life. You ruined my chance at marriage. You ruined my chance at love. You ruined Landon's career all so he could chase a girl who doesn't want him."

I burst into tears again. It's not just about Drew. Yes, I'm angry, but this emotion isn't all because of him.

It's because of a call I got earlier. A call that told me they had my brother and he was going to be going to jail. A call that told me he was still in a wheelchair, but not because he couldn't walk, but just because he never went to rehab to build up his strength again. A call that told me he was still using the money I sent him from Landon every month for drugs instead of taking care of himself. A call that told me I was safe, but it makes me hate myself for being happy. It makes me hate everything, and it makes me hate Drew even more.

Drew doesn't say another word until he parks the car in the garage. He turns the car off and then looks at me hesitantly. His face looks sad and is full of longing.

"Why do you want him?"

I frown and grab the door handle ready to get out of here. I don't want to hear him tell me I'm an idiot for wanting Landon. Or that I no longer deserve him because of my actions. He doesn't need to know why. I know he is who I'm supposed to be with. That's all that matters.

"Wait," he says and grabs my arms. He takes a deep breath before he continues. "I forgive you."

"What?"

"I forgive you. I was mad at you, and I thought I hated you, but I don't. I was more mad at myself for not believing better of my own brother than I was angry with you. You were just trying to survive. I forgive you."

I feel the tears falling again this time at his sincere words. I didn't expect them. Not from him.

"So when I ask you why, it's not out of hate. It's not because I don't want you to be happy. I do. I need you to be happy. You two just never made sense together. So other than this baby that is coming, what is keeping you holding on to him?"

My stomach growls, ruining the moment. We both smile. "Go cook me some food and I'll tell you."

Chapter Thirty-Five

ALEX

2. The number of people I want to find love with. A husband and child.

He's here. I can't believe Landon is actually here. I don't know how or why. I thought he was in jail, but he said they released him. He said he was innocent, and right now, I choose to believe him. I need him.

I don't know how he knew to come after me, but he did, and I know I just fell harder for him. But I wish he had stayed away because now, he's going to die. Just like I am.

His eyes stay locked on mine. Beautiful golden brown eyes that should have so much life left in them are now filled with fear. The same fear that reflects in my own eyes. He holds the syringe loosely in his hand.

I shake my head. If he injects himself with the syringe, he'll be as good as dead. I can't let him.

And then I watch in terror as Landon pushes the syringe into his arm. I scream and thrash against my restraints trying to break free. I can't move, though. I can't save Landon. I no longer feel the pain, though, when I move against the restraints. All I feel is fear at what Landon just did.

I watch as Landon collapses to the floor from the drugs now pulsing through his system. Drugs that paralyze and poison the body. Just keep breathing. Keep breathing. I can't watch him die.

I look back at Ethan who still has the gun pressed against my head. He's smiling as he watches Landon collapse to the floor. His eyes turn to me.

I try to speak to tell him he needs to go to Landon. To make sure he's still breathing. The duct tape covering my mouth prevents me, though, and my words just come out like pained groans.

I try pleading with my eyes. I try begging. I try moving my head back and forth between Ethan and Landon. I try anything to get him to check on Landon.

He strokes my cheek. "Don't worry, baby. He's not dead. Not yet. The drugs just knocked him out."

Ethan puts the gun on the nightstand and then walks over to where Landon lies on the ground. He kicks him hard in the side, and I watch as Landon's body jerks from the force of his kick. But Landon doesn't wake. He doesn't move. He doesn't fight back. The drugs have taken full effect.

I watch without being able to do a thing as Ethan walks out of the room and then comes back minutes later with more rope and duct tape.

Ethan lifts Landon's body and drops him in a chair. Landon's head flops side to side when he lands in the chair. Ethan stands in front of his body to keep him from sliding down.

"You know if it wasn't for this motherfucker, things might have turned out differently. You might both get to live."

I groan.

"You want to know why? Why things would have turned out differently?"

I groan again. I don't give a shit about hearing Ethan's side of the story. He's a fucking monster that deserves to die, but I don't get to tell him that. Instead, I watch as he begins to tie Landon's arms to the chair. Wrapping the rope so tightly around his arms, he makes sure there will be no hope for escape.

"I guess it's not Landon's fault. There have been so many times. Instances that could have caused your life to end sooner. I would have killed you the next morning after the rape. That was my plan, but when you saw me and didn't remember, I knew I could have you again. I knew I didn't have to kill you."

He begins tying Landon's other arm with the efficiency of someone who has done this countless times. I look around the room at the pictures of all the women I could never save.

"But then you had to do something stupid. You started remembering. You had to investigate. You found out, and I had to kill you, but it was too late for me to do it myself. We were getting married. I had to hire someone."

He moves to Landon's legs as he keeps speaking as if he is trying to justify each of his actions.

"I had to hire Alfie King's men to kill you. I promised him I'd help him escape from jail if he did. I have cops, and I have dirt on all of them. They would do whatever I say, but King's men fucked up. They didn't kill you like they were supposed to. So I made sure King is going to spend the rest of his life in jail."

He moves to his second leg. "I took some time on my own. To figure out what I wanted. Mother called me daily. She begged me to give up my obsession with killing and raping. She begged me to give up you."

He stands and unrolls the duct tape and rips some off before placing it over Landon's mouth.

"I couldn't, though. I couldn't give any of it up. I had to come back. I thought you could be my redemption. I thought you could save me from the monster inside me. We could live our lives like normal people. All I had to do was destroy the evidence that you had hidden. But I couldn't find it. So I had to kill you."

I watch him walk to me, his eyes lusting over my bleeding cuts all over my body. "Except I couldn't. Even then, I still thought you could save me. I thought if I just found a way to make you love me again. If we could have a child, then we could start over together. Find a way to move past our pasts."

He walks back to Landon. "But then this motherfucker came into your life and stole you from me. You were mine! He had no right."

I watch as he punches Landon in the jaw, and again, Landon doesn't awaken. It makes me fear that maybe he isn't really breathing. That he might already be dead. I study his body, though, and watch his chest rise and fall just slightly. He's still breathing.

"And then, to top it all off, you started remembering again."

He runs his hand through his hair. "I thought you could save me. I thought you could destroy the demons that lurked underneath my skin. You can't, though. You're just like the rest of them. I should have killed you that first morning."

He walks to the door and pauses there. "Maybe you can still save me. If you can last long enough. If you can make all the demons go away, then maybe you will be my last. The last one I kill." He smiles. "Or maybe not." I watch as his eyes drift to Landon indicating he will be the last one he kills. "Don't worry. It will take me a long time to get rid of my demons. I promised Mother you would be the last. The last one and so you shall. So I will have to savor every second of it and draw it out as long as you can last."

He glances over at Landon. "I'll be back. When he wakes up and can enjoy the fun."

Chapter Thirty-Six

LANDON

Daughter, I'm not proud of who I was.
I've been a monster more days than one.
I don't deserve your love.

I HEAR ETHAN TALKING. I hear Alex groaning, but I can't move. I'm frozen. I can't even open my eyes to see what's happening.

But I hear Ethan talking. I hear him threatening Alex, and I try to force my eyes open. It's no use, though. I'm trapped in a body unable to move.

I feel Ethan kick me, and I should gasp for air to try to reclaim the oxygen he knocked out of my body. But my body doesn't respond. Instead, I feel like I'm suffocating. It takes a long time for my body to receive enough oxygen to breathe properly again.

I feel Ethan tie ropes around my arms and legs. I feel him punch me in the jaw. I try not to focus on the pain my body feels, though, because whatever I feel, Alex feels worse. Much worse.

I try instead to focus my mind on what I need to do to save us, but my mind spins. I can't focus on one thought at a time. Everything swirls around in my head causing more confusion; the only thing I can focus on is the pain.

And then I hear silence. I don't know if it's from me losing my hearing as well as my sight and mind, but I hear nothing for a long time. It scares me; the silence worse than when Ethan was talking because I have no idea what is happening. I have no idea if I'm still alive or already dead.

But slowly, I feel my mind clearing. I can feel enough to move a finger and then another. And then, finally, I open my eyes.

I look straight to her. Straight in her eyes that are staring at me. I see relief fill them when she sees me open my eyes. Mine fill with relief too seeing that she is still alive and no other damage has been done.

I try to speak. To tell her it's going to be okay. That we will find a way out of this and not to give up hope. But the duct tape prevents me from speaking, and it all comes out in grunts and groans.

She nods her head at me, though. She understands.

I begin looking around the room, knowing that I can't waste my time looking into Alex's eyes as much as I want to. We need a plan to get out of this.

I can't believe I never saw it before. I can't believe I never realized what Ethan was. I can't believe that Alex hid this from me. This was her secret. She went back to stop him. She didn't trust me with this secret. If we do ever get out of this, I'm never leaving her alone again. Even if she won't be with me, I will never let her hurt again.

I test the bindings at my wrists and ankles. I can't break free. I try moving the chair. I can move just an inch by rocking the chair back and forth, but it's slow and exhausting. I don't have the energy to move far enough to do anything. Not until the drugs are completely out of my system, but I can move I just have to figure out where. I glance around the room trying to find something useful — something to break our bindings or defend ourselves with — but I see nothing.

I glance back at Alex. Just for a second, just needing to see that she's still okay. Her eyes smile at me and then she tilts her head to the nightstand and grunts.

I tear my eyes from her to the nightstand and see the gun. He left the gun on the nightstand. I just have to find a way to get there.

I begin moving again. Inch by inch. Until I've moved three inches, then five, then seven. Each move gets me closer, but each move drains me even further. I have to make it, though. It's our only chance.

I hear the door swing open. "Going somewhere," Ethan says smirking at me.

I try to yell at him, but it comes out in a groan. He walks to me, grabs my chair, and drags me back to the corner until I've lost all of the inches I have gained.

"Glad to see you are finally awake."

I glare at him with my eyes. *I am going to kill you*, I moan.

He just smirks at me. "I've been thinking while you were out what I should do to torture you first. What would bring me the most pleasure?"

He walks to Alex stroking her leg. "And I think I've finally decided."

My eyes widen in fear as I watch his hand inch higher between her legs. I turn my face away for just a second as his hand travels between her legs.

"Ah ... I guessed right. Watching her struggle through pain isn't what would torture you the most. Seeing her being fucked by another man is your worst nightmare."

I don't look at him. I don't give him the pleasure of knowing that he's right. That I can't stand to look at what he will do to her.

"Look at me!" he shouts as he grabs my chair jerking me until I face him. He watches my eyes until he's content that he's guessed right. That seeing him fuck her will be more torturous than watching him beat her. The only thing worse would be watching her die.

He grins as he walks back to her.

"We'll take it slow," he says keeping his eyes on me reading my reaction. So I give him none.

"This first time, I'll just taste her. I'll taste her and make her squirm in pleasure beneath my lips. Next time, I'll claim her pussy. Then, I'll claim her ass."

I watch as he walks over to the edge of the bed. I watch him crawl up between her legs and place his hand on her pussy.

I watch until he sinks a finger into her and her body tries to squirm and she groans in pain. Then I close my eyes. I can't be here. I can't watch this.

I hear him laugh. "I don't know what you saw in him, Alexa. He's not even strong enough to watch the love of his life being fucked by another man."

I open my eyes to glare at him again, but he's not looking at me; he's watching Alex. I turn my gaze to her and find her watching me. She isn't watching him. She isn't focused on what he is doing to her. She's worried about me.

I have to do the same for her. I have to be strong for her. So I don't look at Ethan anymore. I keep my eyes on hers. I let her know I'm okay. I tell her that I'm going to get her through this.

I see her eyes brighten just a little as I look at her and she realizes what I'm saying. We are going to get through this together.

Ethan moves his hands again, and I watch her face squirm in pain.

I try to catch her attention with my eyes, and after a few seconds, she stops squirming and moaning and calms.

"You like that, baby," Ethan says as he must intensify whatever he is doing because her eyes widen and she lets out a soft moan.

I glance back at Ethan for just a second to see him untie her legs from the posts. I watch his head disappear between her legs as he pushes her legs back causing her to moan.

I try to push the image out of my head, but my anger at what he is doing is almost too much. I groan and thrash in my chair trying to get him to stop.

"Do you hear her moans? Do you hear what I do to her?"

He does something that makes her moan again, but when I catch her eye, there is fear. Fear because I know she is enjoying whatever he is doing to her and she can't stop her body from responding.

"She's mine. Her pussy is mine."

He disappears between her legs again, but this time I know how to help Alex. I know how to win this fight.

This time, when she looks at me, I implore her to keep her eyes on me. I try to make my eyes as lust-filled as possible. I try to show her how turned on I am by her moaning. If she can just imagine it's me licking her. It's my fingers thrusting inside her. It's my tongue swirling over her clit. Then she can get through this. Then she can carry the weight of this moment with her forever because she wasn't strong enough to hold back her pleasure at the hands of a monster.

She keeps fighting him. Fighting the pleasure as she looks at me quizzically not understanding. But when a pleasurable moan escapes her lips, I nod my head as my lust grows stronger. It takes me a second to realize, though, that my lust for her is growing stronger at the moment instead of just pretending.

When she realizes what I'm doing, what I want, she moans loudly as her eyes stay on mine. My eyes intensify seeing the pleasure on her face.

"Your pleasure is mine ..." Ethan continues speaking thinking he's winning. That Alex is enjoying herself because of him. That he is torturing us both by what he is doing.

He's not, though. Somehow, instead of torturing us or tearing us apart, he's bringing us together. With every touch of pleasure he brings her, it brings us closer together.

Our eyes connect in a way that I don't understand. Our hearts connect as Alex moans louder. Our souls connect as she screams her orgasm.

He may claim that she is his. But no matter what he does to her. Or what he does to me. Or what the world brings. She is mine. And I am hers.

Despite it all, our worlds are perfect. At this one moment, we both find pleasure together.

And then in a second moment, our worlds come tumbling down again.

"You fucking bitch! You did that on purpose."

Alex's eyes leave mine, and I follow to see what happened. I see Ethan holding his face that looks like he just got hit by her prosthetic leg. I know the feeling.

He grabs her leg, though, and rips it off her leg. He stands holding the leg like he did her the honor of removing it from her body.

I watch as he holds it in his hand with disgust on his face.

He looks at me. "I fell for her when she was still whole. I don't know how you could fall for her now that she's a disgusting cripple."

The last bit of drugs in my body holding me captive leaves my body at his words. I find the strength to push forward more than an inch this time. I'm going to kill him.

Chapter Thirty-Seven

DREW

She pulls me out of her mouth just as I come. I come all over her perfect breasts.

I PLACE the grilled cheese I made in front of her and add an apple and banana. She smiles at my addition of something healthy to her lunch, even though she only asked for the grilled cheese.

She takes a bite of the grilled cheese and then a bite of the apple. It makes me smile to see her eating something healthy.

"This is the spot," she says between bites.

I look at her quizzically, trying my best to be patient but not understanding.

"This is the spot where Landon asked me to marry him."

I suck in a breath and then slowly exhale. I'm not sure why I asked why she is in love with Landon and why she wants him. I thought hearing her explanation might somehow bring me closure. It might help me move on, but I'm afraid it's just going to rip out my heart.

"I thought my life was going to be perfect from that day on. But nothing is ever perfect, is it?"

I shake my head. "No, nothing ever is."

She eats the first half of her sandwich without another word.

"I want Landon because he was the only one who ever protected me. He was the first person to ever care about me or tell me he loved me who wasn't my father."

I narrow my eyes at her. She's wrong if she thinks he's the only one who has ever protected her or loved her.

She closes her eyes as she imagines it, and she starts talking, telling the story in exact detail as if she was reliving it.

I smile as the sun shines in through my window waking me. I smile because today is my favorite day of the year. Today is my eighth birthday.

I roll over, but I don't see the candy my father usually puts on my pillow. I frown. He must have forgotten. I guess it will have to wait until after school. Until after he gets home from work.

I put on my favorite pink dress with butterflies on it. And then comb my hair into pigtails like Mama taught me. I frown when I see them in the mirror. They are lopsided, but I don't know how to fix them.

"Caroline! We have to go!" my brother, Sean, shouts.

My body startles at his loud voice as he bursts into my bathroom. He grabs my hand a little too hard as he pulls me out of the bathroom and to the car. It hurts, but I don't tell him. He's just taking care of me like an older brother should.

I walk into my classroom with excitement on my face. My teacher always does something special for each of her students' birthdays, and I can't wait to see what she has done for me.

"Good morning, Mrs. Franklin." My smile is bright on my face as I look up at hers. She doesn't return my smile, though. She doesn't say a word. Her tears say it all, though, as she reaches out and takes my hand to tell me why my father didn't leave chocolates on my pillowcase this morning.

The walk to the principal's office is long and quiet. I know something is wrong, but Mrs. Franklin won't tell me. She just walks me to the office. She holds my hand as we step inside. I see my mother with tears in her eyes. I see my brother sitting next to her stoned face. I don't see my father, though.

"What's wrong?" I ask looking at my mother, but she doesn't say anything.

I look at my brother, but he just stares straight ahead and doesn't answer me either. I look at the third person in the room. A police officer. He looks sad as he kneels down in front of me.

"Caroline. I'm so sorry to tell you this, but your father passed away this morning," the officer says.

"No. He can't be. Today's my birthday. He always gives me chocolates on my birthday."

"You stupid brat. Your father didn't care about you. He chose to kill himself on your birthday. What do you think that made him think about you?" Mother says.

I squeeze my eyes shut to try to block out the pain, but it doesn't work. My mother's words hurt anyway. They tell the truth, though. What loving father would kill himself on his daughter's birthday?

I climb into the back of the car. Sean gets into the driver's seat while Mom sits next to him. Sean drives us home in silence. His hands are steady on the wheel as he drives while Mom's hands shake as she pulls some pills out of her purse. I don't know what the pills are for. I didn't think she was sick, but she takes ten, so she must be.

My eyes travel back to my brother. He's so brave and strong. I try to hold back my tears. I try to be like him.

I don't know what I expect when we get home, but it isn't what happens. Mother doesn't say a word to me. She just goes to her bedroom and locks the door.

I turn to Sean. I don't know what we are supposed to do now. It doesn't feel real yet. I don't believe Dad is really gone.

I watch as Sean walks to the fridge and pulls out one of Dad's beers.

"You aren't supposed to drink that. Dad wouldn't like it."

Sean looks at me with empty eyes. "Dad's not here." He plops into Dad's recliner with Dad's beer.

I walk to my room alone. And I cry. I cry because today is my birthday, and not one person has told me happy birthday. I cry because something is wrong with my mother and brother. I cry because my father is gone. He didn't even love me enough to stay one more day. He didn't love me enough to last through his pain to tell me happy birthday.

I wait for someone to tuck me into bed, but then I realize no one is coming. Dad was the one who always tucked me in and kissed me good night, and now, he's gone. I'm on my own, I realize.

I don't bother changing out of my dress or brushing my teeth like I'm supposed to. Instead, I just climb into bed. I pull the covers over my head when I hear my door crack open. I pull the covers down hoping that it was just a terrible nightmare and that Dad is going to walk through the door to tuck me in like he always does.

When I look at the door, though, it's not Dad, it's Sean. I smile as he walks over to me, but instead of tucking me in like I expect, he climbs into bed next to me.

My brother and I aren't close. He usually steers clear of me and thinks of me as an annoying little girl who tries to tag along with him. He never lets me, though.

I feel tears pouring down my cheeks out of nowhere, but this time, it's out of happiness instead of sorrow.

"Shh," he says as he wraps his arms around me.

I cry into his arms for a minute as he holds me close to him. So close that I smell his beer on his breath.

I close my eyes that I've been fighting to keep open. I just want to sleep and then maybe tomorrow will be better.

I feel Sean's arms move, and I think he's going to back to his bedroom, but he slips his hand under my dress. He rubs my stomach, and I begin to feel uncomfortable although I don't know why. He's rubbing my stomach slowly as if he's trying to comfort me.

I try to move his hand slowly to my back. I know I would feel more comfortable if he rubbed my back just like Dad did.

Instead, he moves his hand back and begins moving it down to my panties. I jump out of bed. I don't know why his move bothers me so much, but it does.

"Come here, Caroline. I just want to make you feel better."

I feel my body shake. "No."

He climbs out of bed and begins walking to me. That's when I see he isn't well. He sways as he walks.

He staggers to me, reaching his arm out like he's going to grab me or hit me. I slink back into the corner of the room, not understanding what he's doing.

"Stop," I say. "Sean, stop."

He doesn't stop, though. He keeps walking forward. I close my eyes preparing myself for whatever he's going to do.

But he doesn't do anything. When I open my eyes, I see him on the floor and Landon holding a baseball bat. He runs over to me and grabs my hand. He pulls me out of my bedroom and out of the house. When we are outside, he holds me while I whisper over and over in his ear, "You saved me."

When she's done telling the story, she looks at me with tears in her eyes. "He stayed with me all night. We slept in my mother's car." She stops and thinks. "He was the only one who wished me happy birthday that day. He gave me a smushed cupcake and clips for my hair."

She looks at me. "That's the day I fell in love with him. I knew that day I wanted to be with him forever. He protected me. He saved me."

I close my eyes as my own tears sting my eyes.

"So you can understand now. Every day since then, he's been protecting me. I'm not sure what my brother would have done that night, but I know enough of my brother that night to know he would have destroyed me."

I reach out, touch Caroline's hand, and rub it as I have so many times before. I did it that night as she fell asleep. I smile at the misunderstanding. That is my luck. A simple misunderstanding is the only thing that has kept her from loving me instead of Landon.

"Landon wasn't the one who saved you that night."

She raises her eyebrows at me like I'm crazy.

"It was me."

Chapter Thirty-Eight

ALEX

2. The number of people it took to save me.

I SHUDDER FEELING the aftermath of my orgasm. It was one of the most intense orgasms of my life and not because of what Ethan was doing to me. It was because of Landon. The way he looked at me.

His eyes alone made me come.

But now, all I see is Landon still attached to a chair tackling Ethan to the ground. And I can't do anything to help him. I can't save him like he saved me from losing myself when Ethan touched me. He saved me from being raped again. Because what happened felt like anything but rape.

I scream trying to get Ethan's attention. But it doesn't stop the fight. My eyes grow wide when Ethan stands to leave Landon still attached to the chair on the ground. I watch as Ethan grabs the gun and points it at Landon.

"I was going to wait to do this. I was going to let him watch every torturous thing I do to you, but I can't keep him alive. Not now that he's attacked me. He would just interfere with our fun."

He looks at me and rips the tape off my mouth.

"I want to hear you scream when I do this."

"Please," I plead with tears already in my eyes. "Please."

He smirks at me and then pulls the trigger. My eyes travel as fast as the bullet from Ethan to Landon's eyes. Eyes that tell me he loves me before they close.

Ethan's right. I scream, but it doesn't make the pain any easier to bear. I thought I had felt pain before, but I was wrong. The pain at seeing Landon shot lying on the floor while I can't do anything is the worst pain I've ever felt.

Love isn't worth the pain. That's been what I thought all along. I thought loving again would destroy me, and it has. At this single moment, it has. But knowing the pain, feeling it, isn't enough to give up all the love I've experienced with Landon.

Ethan tosses the gun to the floor with a smirk on his face. He glances at his watch as he kicks Landon, and a low moan escapes his lips. He's still alive.

"I have to go, sweetheart," Ethan says leaning down and slobbering on my lips.

"Get away from me."

"Enjoy watching Landon bleed out slowly. He'll die from the blood loss before I get back." He sighs. "I really wish I didn't have to go. I would have loved to watch that with you. Don't worry, though. The cameras will capture it." He points at the corner of the room where a camera must be, but I don't see one. "We will watch it together later. I have to go make sure James takes a deal that will keep him in jail for most of his life."

"You won't get away with this. You picked someone too public this time. The world loves Landon. You can't just make him disappear."

He smiles as he stands at the door. "Don't worry about it. I already have it all planned out. See, I think that girlfriend of his who is having his baby would be shocked when she found out he was still sleeping with you. I think she would gladly kill you and Landon when she found out that depth of his deception."

I suck in a breath. I hate Caroline, but she doesn't deserve to go to jail for this. Her baby doesn't deserve to grow up without either of its parents.

"No. Please don't ..."

"I have to go." I watch as he disappears out the door and then I'm alone. Naked and beaten with my arms still tied to the frame of the bed. I'm not worried about me, though.

"Landon!" I scream as soon as Ethan leaves the room. "Landon!"

I hear him groan, but he doesn't say anything else. He doesn't move. I can't see where Ethan shot him, but it looked like his chest or stomach. I can't even tell if Landon is breathing.

"Landon, please talk to me! Tell me you're going to be okay."

I wait, but all I get is another soft moan. It scares me how soft and quiet it is. He's dying; I know that.

"Just keep breathing, Landon. I'm going to get us out here. I'm going to save us. Just don't you dare stop breathing on me, Landon."

I pull on my wrists that are still handcuffed over my head. They don't move just like every other time I've tried them. I don't know what to do. I don't know how to save him.

Another pained moan comes from Landon making me fight harder against the handcuffs to try to get to him. I can't, though, which only feeds my panic. I take a deep breath remembering all of the times Landon had calmed my panic attacks. How, just moments earlier, he kept me calm through one of the worst experiences of my life. Now, it's my turn to return the favor.

"Don't you dare stop breathing, Landon." I glance around the room trying to find anything that could save us. Anything that could help. "You're going to be a father, Landon. You're going to be a father. You can't give up."

I look to my left, but nothing useful is on the nightstand.

"You never told me if you were having a boy or a girl. Either way, you're going to be an amazing father, Landon. I imagine you having a girl, though. A daughter who you can protect and love with everything that you have." I glance back at Landon. His shoulders move, thank god.

"You're going to be a father. You're going to have a daughter who you're going to name something beautiful like Isabella. She's going to be the love of your life. You'll love her even more than you love your car."

I glance from Landon to the gun lying next to him. If he could only move, he could grab the gun. He could kill Ethan the next time he comes back, but by then, Landon could be dead.

"I know you don't think it's possible to love something more than you love your car. Or to love someone more than you love me or Caroline or any of us. But just keep thinking about your daughter. You have to keep breathing. For her. She can't grow up without you."

I look to my right and see my prosthetic leg that Ethan ripped from my body. That he threw at me like it was a disgusting piece of trash. A tear falls down my face. Landon is going to die and I can't do anything about it. And then I'm going to die.

I try to grab my prosthetic leg. Maybe I could whack Ethan with it when he gets back, but that's all I would be able to do. Get one strike in and then he'd have control again.

Still, I grab it, and then I don't know what to do. I have to find a way, though, to use it to save him. He deserves to be saved. He has to be saved for his daughter.

I slide my hand up my prosthetic leg that I never got fixed. I'm surprised it held up as well as it did when Ethan threw it.

The loose pin. If I can get it out, I might be able to pick the lock on the handcuffs and get free.

I quickly slide the prosthetic up until my fingers grasp the pin and pull it free.

"Just hold on a little longer, Landon. I'm going to save us."

Chapter Thirty-Nine

LANDON

But somehow, you found the light that was still hidden in me.
You saved me.

I DON'T KNOW whether I'm living or dying. I don't feel a thing. I don't hear a thing. I'm just trapped and unable to move. Unable to die and unable to live.

And then I see a light, a beautiful light shining brightly. The light moves closer, getting brighter. I'm going to die. It's here to take me away.

It takes me a second, but I realize it's not a light walking to me. It's a girl. The most beautiful little girl is skipping to me in a pink dress.

She reaches out and grabs my hand, and I melt. "Come on, Daddy."

I smile down at her. "I'm coming, Isabella." The name just falls from my lips as if I already know her name. I follow her as she drags me away and pulls me into her bedroom.

The whole room is different shades of pink. She pulls me until we get to a small table. She takes a seat, and I take a seat in the chair opposite her. It is much too small to sit comfortably in, but I don't care. I could sit here all day as long as I'm with her.

She pours me some fake tea and hands me a cup. I take it from her small hands and pretend to sip from it just as she does. She giggles, and it's the most beautiful sound I have ever heard.

Isabella stops when she hears something. She smiles at me and then turns to the door. "We are coming, Mom," she says in a sweet voice.

She stands from the table, and I do the same. She grabs my hand again, and we start walking down a hallway that turns darker with each step. We take another step and an unbearable pain forms in my chest. I stop walking, and she looks up at me curiously.

"Come on, Daddy." She tugs at my hand again.

I shake my head. "I'm sorry. I can't. It hurts too much."

She smiles at me in her sweet way. "We have to go. We have to find Mommy."

She tugs at my hand again, and the pain returns when I take another step into the darkness. "Come on, Daddy. You can do it. I'll protect you."

She looks at me with her eyes. Beautiful eyes that are just like her mother's, and it's all I need to see to get through the pain. I push through it and follow her. I follow her through the pain.

Chapter Forty

CAROLINE

I stand as soon as he comes. I can't let this go any farther. Not when Landon is passed out in the next room. Not when I still have a chance with him.

"WHAT? What do you mean it was you?"

Drew shakes his head as if he can't believe his life. "I mean it was me that night, not Landon."

I replay the memory over in my head. He's wrong. It was Landon. I would know. I was there. It was the most memorable night of my life. I try to draw my hand back from Drew's, but he doesn't let go. He just keeps holding it and rubbing his thumb across my palm.

I look out at the ocean as I take another bite of my grilled cheese that has gone slightly cold. Drew's lost it, is all I think.

"It was me, Caroline. I was the one who came back that night, not Landon. I hit your brother with a baseball bat. I broke into your mother's car and held you all night in the backseat. I gave you the smushed cupcake that I smushed when I dropped it as we were running out of the trailer. I saved for months to get you the perfect pink and purple butterfly clips that I knew would match your dress. Your favorite dress that you wore at least once a week, and I knew you'd be wearing that day."

My mouth falls open when he tells specific details that only the person who saved me that night would know. I turn to look at him with tears in my eyes that match the ones in his eyes. "It was me."

"How? How did I not know?"

He smiles at me and wipes the tears from my cheek. "You used to always get Landon and me mixed up. Back then, we dressed alike, and no one could tell us apart. We never corrected you. We thought it was funny. The best part of being a twin." He pauses. "That night, you only said Landon's name once right before you fell asleep in my arms. I didn't bother correcting you because it didn't matter. It didn't matter if you knew it was Landon or me because if Landon had been there, he would have done the same thing. He just got the short end of the straw that night. He had to go home to take care of Dad while I got to take care of you."

More tears fall. Everything I thought my whole life about Landon is wrong. He didn't save me that night. Drew did.

I watch Drew take a deep breath before he smiles at me. "It doesn't change anything. I just needed to know. Now, I do. I saved you that night. He saved you another night. That's how it always was. We all protected each other, but fate knew that you belonged with Landon, not me."

His hand moves from my hand to my stomach, and then he quickly removes his hand leaving me empty as he gets up and walks back inside.

"Drew," I beg as I follow him. He stops but doesn't look at me.

"I didn't know. If I had known ..."

"It wouldn't have changed anything. This is what was supposed to happen. You're supposed to have Landon's baby. We had our one night. A night I will never forget. A night when I told you how I feel."

He touches my cheek gently with his hand. "I love you, Caroline. I always have. I fell in love with you that night. You fell in love too. You just fell in love with him."

He removes his hand from my cheek and walks away again. And I know if I let him go, he won't ever pursue me again. He's letting me go.

He's letting me go to be with Landon. If I let him go, he'll just be an uncle and a friend but never anything more.

I don't know what I want anymore. My whole life, since that night, I thought I did. I wanted the boy who saved me when I was eight. I just thought that boy was Landon.

Now, I don't know what I want. Except I feel my heart beating rapidly in my chest. I feel my breath catch. My heart still knows what it wants. It wants the boy who saved me when I was eight.

Chapter Forty-One

ALEX

Infinity. The number of people I will help heal.

It only takes me a couple of seconds to get the pin out of my prosthetic leg, but it takes me what seems like hours to get the pin to unlock the handcuffs. Each second that I don't get it to unlock is another second that Landon has to hold on. Each second might be one second too long. It might be the second when Landon can no longer be saved.

I wish Landon were awake. He's broken into my condo before. He knows how to pick a lock. I don't. I just know I have to. It's the only way to save him.

I don't know what's different this time when I push the pin into the lock, but I feel it spring free, releasing one of my hands.

"Just hold on, Landon. I'm coming. Just one more." I begin picking the second lock, and this time, it unlocks much faster now that I can see. When it springs free, I jump off the bed and go to Landon.

"I'm here. Everything's going to be okay." I'm practically crying as I say it. I put my hand on his wound in the center of his stomach. There is blood, too much blood, soaking his stomach and chest. I crawl the foot or two to grab some clothes out of the dresser drawer and press it to his wound, but I'm not sure if it really helps.

"You're going to be okay. Just keep breathing." I watch his chest barely move at all as he breathes. I remove the tape from his mouth hoping it will help him breathe, and it seems to help as he gasps when it's removed, but he doesn't wake up.

I want to remove the rest of the duct tape, but first, I have to call for help. Landon needs an ambulance. Now. I don't know where my phone is, so I search Landon's pockets and find his phone. I dial 911 and tell them the address. I'm instructed to hold pressure on the wound until they get there so that's what I do while I begin removing the duct tape.

"They are coming, Landon," I say as I fumble with the tape. "They are coming. Just hold on a little longer. You're going to make it."

I hear the garage door open and close which makes me jump. There is no way that an ambulance or police got here so fast. It's Ethan.

My heart races as I try to form a plan. All I care about is that he doesn't hurt Landon. He has to survive. He has a child he has to protect. Landon has to live.

I grab my prosthetic limb and slip it on quickly. I grab one of the shirts and shorts and the gun that's lying on the floor.

Then I lean down and kiss Landon on the lips. "I love you. Hold on for her."

I have to draw Ethan away. I have to protect Landon for just a few more minutes. Ethan will come after me, not Landon. So I get up and I run, and I hope like hell that Ethan runs after me.

I RUN down the stairs as fast as I can despite the fact that my leg is missing a pin, and the prosthetic could fall apart at any second. I throw a t-shirt and shorts on the best I can as I tumble down the stairs.

I run to the front door, but I don't see Ethan. He has to see me leave. He has to come after me. It's the only way to keep him away from Landon. I open the front door trying to be as loud as possible. "Ethan!"

I see him round the corner from the kitchen. His face shows a look of disbelief for just a second, and then he cocks his head and smirks at me. Our eyes lock for a just a second longer and then I run.

I run for my life.

I run for Landon.

I run for James and Daniel.

I run for all of the girls who were never given a chance to run.

I feel Ethan running behind me, but I don't look back. I just run. I have to get him as far away from the house as possible. As long as he's running, he won't stop to go after Landon. That's the only person left who needs saving.

I run faster than I've ever run before. I run past houses, but no one bothers to look out their window to see me. To save me. I no longer care about surviving; I just care about running.

My breathing is hard and fast as my legs take me farther up the road. I hear him panting behind me, but I won't let him catch me not as long as my feet keep moving.

I reach the hill that leads to a main street. If I can just make it up the hill without him catching me, I'll be safe. All of us will be safe. I pick up speed as I begin running up the hill. I run fast. Faster than I ever have before.

I make it halfway up the hill when I hear his panting and footsteps stop. He's given up. Or he's going back to the house to get Landon.

I turn my head for just a second to see what he's doing. That second is just long enough for me to make a mistake. I feel myself tumbling to the ground as my prosthetic gets caught on something. A rock most likely that makes the remaining pin come loose rendering the prosthetic useless. The side of my face lands on the hard cement.

I immediately roll over to look at Ethan. I point my gun in his direction and watch him smile at me as he walks closer until he's less than a foot away.

"Don't move," I say gripping the gun tighter so close to pulling the trigger.

"Or you'll shoot?" He raises his eyebrows at me. "You won't shoot me."

"Yes, I will."

He shakes his head and then pulls out bullets from his pocket. "You don't think I'm crazy enough to leave you alone with a loaded gun."

My eyes widen. It can't be. I pull the trigger begging a bullet to fly out and hit him, but none does. It's empty. The gun is empty. I toss it to the side and begin crawling backward up the hill while keeping my eye on Ethan.

He just walks calmly toward me each time I move back. He pulls a large knife out of his pocket and holds it casually in his hands.

I hear sirens in the distance, which causes Ethan to pause for just a second.

"What did you do?"

Now, it's my turn to smile. My heart calms, and my breathing returns to normal.

"I saved Landon," I say. "I might die, but he's not going to die." I smile as the sirens get louder. The sound of a car engine coming up the road is music to my ears. "But you are."

Chapter Forty-Two

LANDON

When the pain was too much to bear
You saved me.

THE SECOND SHE LEFT, my eyes open. I tried so hard when she was holding me and keeping me alive, but no matter how hard I tried, I couldn't do it. I couldn't show her that I was alive.

But feeling her leave knowing that she was doing it to protect me gave me enough strength to fight through the fog and the pain to open my eyes. Just opening my eyes is painful physically and emotionally. Physically because it fucking hurts to be shot in the stomach, and it doesn't just hurt where the bullet entered my body. It fucking hurts everywhere.

And emotionally it kills me to be away from her. I know I need to stay alive for my daughter who has yet to be born, just as she said. But I don't want to live in a world where she's not breathing. I won't do it.

So I move. So slowly that I'm not even sure I am moving. But I do. Every fucking centimeter it takes for me to sit up. I put one hand on my stomach trying to keep myself from losing any more blood while the other removes the last piece of tape from my leg that Alex hadn't removed.

I somehow stand. I don't know how. I don't know if it's the fucking adrenaline they say you get when going through a life-or-death situation or if it's something else. Like love. I don't care what it is, but whatever force greater than me keeps me moving. I move down the hall. I tumble down the stairs. I move through the house to the garage. And then I climb into the first car I see. Her car. Tessie.

I put the car in reverse and pull the car out of the garage. It screeches as I turn it. She could have gone one of two directions. Down the hill would have been easier, but there is nothing there but woods. Up the street is harder, but she could have made it to civilization. A chance she could have made it to somewhere safe.

I turn the car up the hill as I hear sirens in the distance. I should wait here for the ambulance. I feel lightheaded from the blood loss, and the pain grows worse with each second, but I can't wait for help.

I step on the gas and drive up the street. I drive until I see her lying on the ground while Ethan has a knife in his hand threatening her. She doesn't look scared, though, as she looks death in the face. She looks calm, content, as if she has already lived what she was brought on this earth to do and is content even if he ends her life.

I won't let that happen, though. Her eyes light up just a second when she sees me in the car. "I love you," I mouth to her. "I know," she mouths back.

I turn my attention from her to Ethan. *She's going to hate what I do to her car*, I think, but it's the only way I can save her. She'll get over it.

I watch as Ethan turns as he hears the car approach. I get to see the terror on his face as the car picks up speed. I watch as he makes a split-second decision to take out Alex with him instead of trying to run away. *Wrong move*, I think.

Because I look back at Alex, who is already a step ahead of him and has rolled too far out of his reach for him to take her out with him. The fucking bastard looks back just in time for me to see the light leave his eyes as I hit him with Alex's car. I don't stop when I hit him, though. His body lands on the hood of the car, and I don't stop until his body is obliterated between the hood of the car and a tree.

I take a deep breath when the car comes to a stop. It's over. And she's alive.

Chapter Forty-Three

DREW

I grab her hand. "We aren't done yet."
She looks at me with sad eyes. "Yes, we are."
She tugs her hand free, and I grab her, forcing her to look at me. "I love you."
She shakes her head. "You can't love me."

HOW HAS my entire life gone to hell because of a mix-up? My life could be completely different if I had corrected her that night when I was holding her in my arms, and she said Landon assuming my usually more outgoing brother was the one who came to her rescue instead of me. The rule follower. The boring one. It made sense for her to think it was Landon. And I never corrected her. It didn't seem to matter at the time. Not when so many more important things were going through her head at the time than which brother was holding her and protecting her.

After that night, we never spoke of it again. Her brother dropped out of high school the next day. He ran away to join a gang, and for a long time, we never had to deal with him. Not until the next time he almost destroyed our lives. I shake my head. I'm not going to think about it. I'm done thinking about all of it. I lost.

I told her it wouldn't have mattered. That even if I'd told her, she would be destined to be with Landon, but I don't believe that. That night affected us both. If I had told her, she would be mine right now. The baby growing in her stomach would be mine, not his.

"Wait," Caroline says.

I freeze even though my heart has already closed to her. It had to to be able to let her go.

I feel her soft hand touch my arm, and I turn to her. The tears have multiplied in her eyes as she looks at me so tenderly like I'm a piece of glass she could break with just a tap. She can't, though, because I'm already broken. I've been broken for months now. Since she told me she could never love me. That the only reason she sucked me off was because I looked like Landon. Since the night he got her pregnant.

Her eyes search mine for something, but there is nothing left to see. She steps closer, but there is still nothing for her to find. I have nothing left.

I think she is going to tell me how sorry she is. How wrong she was. I think she is going to tell me some other amazing woman is out there for me, and I just have to be brave enough to go out and find it.

Instead, she tells me so much more. And not one of them is with words. She grabs my neck, and our lips collide. Not like before. Before when I kissed her, it was hungry and needy. This kiss is more. I will compare all kisses to this kiss. I wanted this kiss when I kissed her the first time.

She gives me everything as her tongue explores my mouth. Telling me how much she loves me with just her tongue. I push back against her tongue showing her that I love her just as much.

My hands find her long locks of hair and tangle themselves there. Just needing to have her surrounding me in any way possible. She grabs hold of my shirt and forces us closer together until we press together. Chest to chest. Stomach to stomach. Baby ...

Her stomach presses against mine, and I can feel the life growing within her. Landon's child. I gently back away, forcing our lips apart. Her eyes stay closed as I force us apart.

“Landon,” is all I say. I can only force that one word out of my lips. I’m not strong enough to say more or to convince her why we can’t do this. She already knows.

She opens her eyes with her hands still grasping my shirt. I suck in a breath as I stare at her gorgeous soft eyes.

“Drew, I have to tell you ...”

And then she’s falling, collapsing to the floor in a pile of pain. Pain that I don’t understand where it’s coming from. I collapse with her.

“Caroline, what’s wrong?”

“I don’t know ... stomach ... head ... dizzy.”

She’s on the floor holding her stomach in obvious pain, and I don’t know how to help. I’ve never been this scared in my life. She can’t lose the baby. She can’t.

“Come on; let’s get you to the hospital.”

Chapter Forty-Four

ALEX

548798879432 ... Every part of me. Stubborn. Strong. Happy. Sad. Pain. Pleasure ...

I SCREAM as I watch Landon crash into the tree. I see the car smoking but no movement from inside. I know Ethan's dead. There is no way he survived that, but I don't know about Landon.

I pull myself up. I grab my prosthetic and then hop on one leg as fast as I can to the car.

"Landon!"

He doesn't answer or move. I get to the door and yank it open to find Landon slumped over the steering wheel.

"Don't you dare die on me now, Landon." I pull him off the steering wheel trying to see if he's still breathing. I put my head to his chest, but I can't hear or feel anything. He's dead...

"He can't be dead! It was supposed to be me. It was supposed to be me ... I'm the one who is supposed to be dead," I yell to a god I don't think exists. If he did, he wouldn't allow this to happen. He wouldn't allow a daughter to grow up without her father.

I collapse on his chest as the tears fall. "You can't die, Landon. You just can't."

I feel his chest move just enough to force me to sit up and look at him. He coughs, and I notice blood spews from his mouth.

"I wouldn't dream of it," he barely gets out.

"Oh, my god! You're alive!"

"I could never leave you."

I sob and wrap my arms around him. "How are you alive? Just... how did you make it to the car? You were barely breathing when I left you."

He strokes my hair gently. "You saved me. I had to save you too."

We both hear the ambulance sirens getting louder as they come toward us. We both are running out of time together before we spend the next days or weeks getting poked and prodded while trying to heal. We are running out of time until we will be questioned about everything that happened and why Ethan is dead on the hood of my car.

I look into Landon's eyes. There is so much to say and no time to say it. So I say the only words that matter. "I love you."

He sucks in a deep breath. "I love you too."

THEY WANTED me to ride in a separate ambulance. They said they needed to work on us both, and they could do that the best if they separated us. I said no. I wasn't leaving him again.

They reluctantly let me ride along with Landon. One tried to fuss with my wounds while the ambulance sped off. I wouldn't let them, though. I wouldn't let them focus on me when Landon clearly needed the most attention.

Instead, I held his hand while they stuck him with IVs and loaded him with drugs. I watch as they pushed oxygen through his lungs. I watch as they cut off his clothes and begin working on his wound.

I hold his hand and watch his eyes. I hold his gaze until the drugs pull him under, and even then, I don't let go of his hand. I watch as we turn down the road to the hospital, and I know if he's made it this long and is still breathing, he's going to live.

I sigh in relief as we pull up to the emergency entrance. I release his hand for just a second as I climb out of the ambulance. They move Landon quickly out, and I grab hold of his hand again as they rush him inside. When we get inside, I hear the paramedics talking to the doctors and nurses that meet us. Surgery, I hear, but I guess I was expecting that.

I feel a woman's arms touch me and pull me gently from Landon. "He's going to be okay. He needs to go to surgery now. You have to let him go."

I slowly let go of his hand. "I love you. You're going to live," I whisper into his ear before kissing him softly on the cheek. I let him go and watch him quickly rolled past a door to surgery.

"Miss, will you let me check you out?" the young nurse asks.

I nod and follow her when I no longer have sight of Landon. We walk back to the emergency room.

"I need a doctor," a familiar voice says as he bursts into the emergency room. I stop following the woman and turn in time to see Drew escorting a hurting Caroline into the emergency room.

My eyes meet hers. I see her pain. I feel her pain. I glance down at her growing stomach. At her baby that has to survive because I know deep down that I didn't save Landon. His daughter did.

I nod in her direction telling her that she has won. I won't fight for him any longer. No child deserves to grow up without a father.

Chapter Forty-Five

LANDON

When I was truly scared
You saved me.
When I was crying on my knees
You saved me.
When the darkness was controlling me
You saved me.

I OPEN my eyes and expect Alex to be there. Just like she was the entire ride back to the hospital. I don't see her eyes, though. Instead, a tired Drew stares back at me.

He smiles in relief when he sees me open my eyes.

"How are you feeling?"

"Like hell. Where's Alex?"

He looks at the ground uncomfortably, and I sit up too fast, causing incredible pain in my stomach and chest. "She can't be dead."

Drew puts his hand on my shoulder guiding me back. "No, I didn't mean that. She's fine. They released her a couple of days ago."

"Then what's wrong?"

"Nothing's wrong with Alex. She's in with Caroline actually."

"What?"

"Caroline had a complication with her pregnancy while you were …"

"Killing Ethan," I finish for him.

He smiles. "Yes. While you were killing Ethan."

"Is she okay? Is the baby …" My voice trembles as I say it.

"The baby is fine for now. She has something called preeclampsia. It's serious. She could have to have the baby early if they can't get it under control. But she's in the best doctor's care possible. They are both going to be fine."

I suck in a deep breath. I'm not sure I can survive if anything happens to them. "Why is Alex with Caroline?"

"Because someone needs to and I can't be in two places at once."

"But why isn't she here with me and you with her?"

Drew looks down at his hands and then back to me. "Because Alex thinks you should be with Caroline and I agree. You three need to be a family."

I shake my head. "I get to decide what I want. And that's not …"

Drew puts a hand up. "Calm down, Landon. No one is telling you what to do. We just didn't want to complicate things further while you were unconscious."

"Complicate things …"

"Landon, I've been a horrible brother. The night you and Caroline were together. The night you conceived your daughter. Caroline and I …"

"Had sex?"

"No! No, no. We made out and other things. It never went that far, but I should have told you. I shouldn't have kept it from you."

I smile. "Drew, it doesn't matter. Not after everything we have put each other through. I don't care what you and Caroline did."

He nods, but I don't think he will forgive himself so easily. I can see that he won't talk much more about Alex or Caroline or the baby. "What happened after they brought me to the hospital?"

"Alex explained everything. They found the evidence to free James and her convicted rapist, Daniel. The rest of the men are still in jail.

The police believe Ethan hired them. Ethan's dead, but I guess you already knew that."

I smile. I did. I knew the second I drove the car into his heart that he was dead.

"And his mother is in jail, but no one thinks she will serve much time."

"So what do I do now?"

"You heal. And then you become the best father you can be to your daughter."

"What about Caroline and Alex?"

He looks sadly at me. "I don't know."

Chapter Forty-Six

CAROLINE

I run to the bathroom and immediately sink to the ground as I cry. I watch as Drew's cum sinks down my breasts to my stomach and lower ... And now I know what to do. Landon will never be mine, not really. Even if he marries me, he's doing it to protect her. There is only one way he will ever be mine, and Drew can help me with that. When all the tears are gone, I clean myself of my sins and climb into bed with him. I climb in bed with Landon.

I've been in the hospital on bedrest since Drew brought me in weeks ago. And I'll be in here until the baby is born. They won't let me leave. My blood pressure is too high. I could endanger my life and the baby's life. Still, it hasn't been easy to lie in bed all day.

My only visitor since I arrived has been Alex. Drew never came back. I think he thinks if he avoids me, he can push his feelings away and keep from getting hurt, and Landon has been in a different wing of the hospital healing. They wouldn't let either of us go to the other.

That changes today. Today, Landon is being released, but Alex says he will just go from sleeping in his room to the recliner in mine. He won't leave as long as I'm here. I don't want him here, though.

I've made enough mistakes in my past that I need to set right.

Alex has come to my room every day since I've been here. She keeps me updated on Drew and Landon. She brings me food and clothes and entertainment, but what has surprised me is how she can be so nice to me when she must feel I ruined everything. Even if Landon does choose her. She should hate me, but I haven't found the strength to ask her why she stays and tries to befriend me.

I look over at her sitting in the recliner as she does every day. She looks strong despite the wounds that mark her body and will never go away.

"Why? Why do you come here every day? Why are you so nice to me when I've been nothing but horrible to you?"

She glances up from her phone. "For the same reason you let me. We both love him and will do anything for him. Even if that means I have to give him up, I will."

"Why don't you visit him, though?"

"Because I'm afraid he'll choose me when he should choose you and your daughter." She takes a deep breath. "I'm also afraid he won't. That he'll choose you instead. You see, either way, I lose. But here, at least I can still love him from here. I can love his daughter and take care of her mother. That I can do."

I close my eyes feeling the pain I've caused her. That's all my life has been. I know pain. I felt pain when I lost my father. Pain every time my mother turned to pills. I felt pain caused by my brother.

But the pain I've caused Landon, Drew, and Alex is much worse. I don't deserve any of them.

I let the tears fall down my cheeks. I let tears fall for all of their pain and mine.

"Caroline, are you okay? Should I get a nurse?" Alex asks when she sees my tears.

I shake my head and wipe them quickly. "You're wrong, Alex. He will never choose me. It's always been you. He was always yours, even now." I touch my stomach. "He's still yours if you want him."

"I could never do that ..."

"See, that's the thing, Alex. You wouldn't be hurting my baby or me. I've realized that I was wrong. I don't love Landon. I love someone else. Someone who will probably never forgive me for what I've done.

"But you, you still have a chance at real love."

I take a deep breath, saying the words that are so hard for me to say but have to be said. I can't keep pretending. I have to make things right. They deserve to have a chance at love even if I will never have a chance with Drew.

"I lied ..."

Chapter Forty-Seven

ALEX

3. The only pieces of me that matter.

CAROLINE TOLD ME EVERYTHING. She told me the truth. She may be a lying slut most days, but after what she told me, I understand her better. Even though her words hurt, even though the truth hurt, it set me free. It set us both free.

Now, I sit outside Landon's hospital door listening to him play the most beautiful song for his daughter. I sit memorizing the beautiful melody while I wait for him to be discharged.

I wait over an hour, but I don't care. I could sit out here and listen to him all day as long as he keeps playing like that. I hear the door crack open, and I watch as Drew pushes Landon in a wheelchair out of his room. Both men have a shocked expression on their face as they see me sitting against the wall opposite his hospital room.

I stand slowly as my eyes travel over Landon's body. A body that looks healed in comparison to the last time I saw him, although I can tell he has a long way to go until he gets his strength back. I keep my eyes on Landon's and watch as he studies me with anger in his eyes.

Anger I probably deserve since I haven't visited him even though he's been in the hospital for about a month.

"Drew, go see Caroline. I got him from here."

Drew doesn't let go of Landon's wheelchair. In fact, he holds it tighter. I force my eyes away from Landon's daggers to Drew's heart-broken eyes. I look at him sternly. "Go see Caroline. Tell her the truth. That you love her and then listen to her. Listen to every fucking word she says. And then forgive her."

Drew looks at me with a confused expression. I don't think anyone expected Caroline and me to be friends. No, I wouldn't call us friends. Not yet, but our lives will forever be intertwined.

"Go," I say again. Drew reluctantly lets go of Landon and walks slowly toward Caroline's room without saying a word to either of us.

I take his place behind Landon's wheelchair. I push him out of his hospital room and down to where his car, Silvia, is parked. The nurse follows us with his guitar and a bag of clothes.

She helps Landon into the car along with his stuff. I climb into the driver's seat.

"I need to go see Caroline."

"You will, but you need to give her some time with Drew first. You can go see her tomorrow."

"I need to see her today."

I shake my head. "No. They need time to work things out first."

"Drew loves her."

I nod.

"God, this is so fucking messed up," he says running his hand through his hair exposing the scar that has healed on his forehead from when he hit the tree.

I want to tell him. I want to tell him everything right now, but I wait. When we get to the condo, I help him out. He can walk, but his movements are slow and painful. He leans on me all the way up. We make it to his condo both sweaty and exhausted from the journey. He should probably climb into bed to sleep, but I need to do something first. So I lead him out onto the balcony. When he is finally seated, I see the anger return to his eyes.

"Why didn't you come visit me? I worried about you every day. After what we went through, how could you just leave?"

I suck back the tears to keep them from falling. I can't let them fall, not until I get through this. "I couldn't. I couldn't because I wasn't ready to hear your answer. I didn't want to know who you chose."

"But you made me suffer everyday instead. The physical pain I felt was nothing compared to the emotional pain I felt at not being near you. I felt abandoned. I felt like you and Caroline were choosing for me. And now, I don't know if I want either one of you. All I want is my daughter."

I close my eyes at his words. They hurt, but they are true. Neither of us deserves his love. But I'm going to try. Just like Caroline will have to do her best to earn Drew's.

I walk back inside and find his guitar. When I walk back outside, I hand it to him. He looks at me curiously.

"Play the song. The song you wrote for your daughter."

His eyes widen. "How did you know I wrote a song for my daughter?"

"I sat outside your room most of the day just listening to you play."

He reluctantly begins strumming the strings on the guitar. He closes his eyes as he plays, blocking the whole world out. The song is beautiful, easily the best song he has ever written.

I wait my body shaking as he strums the beginning of the song. My palms grow sweaty, and I have to wipe them off on my shirt. I swallow hard preparing for when he is going to start singing the lyrics.

Instead, when he opens his mouth to sing the first lyric, I open mine instead ...

"I was stuck in a bed

And I thought I was surely dead."

Landon stops playing the guitar as soon as I start singing; his mouth has fallen open in what is most likely shock.

"Please," I say.

Landon begins strumming again, but this time, he keeps his eyes open and locked on mine.

I start again ...

I was stuck in a bed
And thought I was surely dead.
Then you burst in
And you saved me.

When I thought all was lost your eyes held me close.
You wouldn't let me go
Even when I thought
I wasn't worth saving.
You saved me.

When the pain was too much to bear
You saved me.
When I was truly scared
You saved me.
When I was crying on my knees
You saved me.
When I had nothing left in me
You saved me.
When the darkness was controlling me
You saved me.

LANDON STOPS PLAYING as we are both in tears. We both went back to that night as I sang different lyrics to his song. I know the thought of his daughter is what kept him alive that night, but he kept me alive. We are all interconnected. I can't live without him. He can't live without her.

I need to finish the song, though. He needs to know the rest, but he doesn't let me finish. He puts the guitar down and tries to stand. I don't let him stand, though. I jump from my seat and walk to him taking a chance and kissing him firmly on his lips while I climb into his lap.

The kiss is sweet, tender, and perfect. But as soon as I think that's all it will be, Landon thrusts his tongue into my mouth begging me for more. I moan into his mouth as I give him all the passion that I can. I give him all of me and hope I can get as much of him as possible in return.

He pulls away just slightly with a smile on his face, and he says against my lips, "You can't just write a song for me every time you fuck up, you know."

I smile at the words I said to him the last time we were on this balcony saying the words. "Sure, I can."

He pulls me back to his lips not able to get enough of me, but I'm not sure what the kisses mean. I'm not sure if he is choosing to be with me over Caroline just as I chose him over Ethan. I just don't know. So I force our lips apart.

I open my lips to ask what he wants, but he beats me to it...

With the largest grin I've ever seen on his face, he says, "I choose you."

My face lights up at his perfect words, and I wrap my hands around him tightly as I kiss him again. He moans in pain when I do.

"I'm sorry." I loosen my grip on his body realizing that I can't be as rough with him as I want.

"Don't ever be sorry. We've both made mistakes, but I don't want us to apologize for them. I just want us to accept each other for who we are and move forward."

I take his hand that is rubbing gently against my cheek into mine. "I agree."

He chuckles. "You have nothing to apologize for except for your terrible singing."

I smack him on the shoulder, which just makes him laugh harder. "It wasn't that bad."

He just smiles at me. I hear the buzz of Landon's phone. A phone call I was expecting. I guess now is as good of timing as any.

Landon glances at his phone. "It's Caroline."

"Answer it," I say getting up, but he holds me firmly on his lap.

"Hello."

I lean against his chest so I can hear what Caroline is going to say although I already know and I'm afraid I'll be able to hear his heart breaking.

"Have you gotten back together with Alex?" Caroline asks.

Landon squeezes me tighter and answers honestly. "We never fell apart. We have always been in this together."

"Good, I'm happy for you."

"Are you really?"

"Yes, you two should be together."

"Is everything okay? Is everything okay with the baby?"

I feel Landon's heart rate speed up as he thinks about his daughter.

"Yes. I'm fine; the baby is fine. But I need to tell you something. Something I should tell you in person, but I don't want to tear you any further away from Alex."

"It can wait. We will be coming to check on you in a couple of hours."

"No, it can't wait, and no, you are not." I hear Caroline take a deep breath, and I brace myself for the pain she is going to cause Landon. "Landon, I lied to you. You are not the father of my baby."

Landon's heart stops. It literally stops, and I have to rub his chest gently to get it to beat again. He looks at me with wide eyes, and I nod my head begging him to listen.

"How? The paternity test proved that I am."

"Yes, but it also proved that someone else is too."

I watch as his face curls in confusion. "That night that I told you we slept together. It never happened. You didn't have sex with me. You just passed out as soon as we got you back to your room."

"Drew," he says. "He told me he didn't fuck you!" His voice rises in anger.

"He didn't. He came on my breasts. I was the one that took it further. I went to the bathroom right after to clean myself up. But instead of cleaning myself off, I used it to get pregnant. I knew I could convince you the baby was yours. That the tests would prove it too."

I feel Landon's heart break as he finds out it was true.

"You're not going to be a father. Drew is."

I hear Caroline crying on the other end of the phone. "I'm so sorry for hurting you, Landon. For tricking you and Drew, but Drew and I are happy. We are supposed to be together."

"I love her, Landon," Drew says into the phone making me smile. I wasn't sure if Drew would forgive her so soon, but he did.

"Landon, are you still there ..."

I run my hand on Landon's chest gently encouraging him.

"Don't be sorry, Caroline. Your daughter saved me when I thought I was dead. She saved me. And I'll still love her like a daughter. Like a niece."

Landon ends the call, and I see the tears falling down his cheek.

"I don't understand how it could be true. When I was surely dead lying on the ground with a gunshot wound to my chest, I shouldn't have made it, but my daughter kept me alive. How could she not exist?"

I smile and push myself off Landon's chest until I look him eye to eye. Tears are already falling in my eyes matching his.

"You feel that way because she does exist."

"What do you mean?"

I touch my stomach. "I'm pregnant, Landon."

His eyes grow wide. "He never touched me, Landon. Not in that way. The baby's yours."

He jumps from the chair lifting me and twirling us around despite his still healing wounds that should prevent him from doing so. We both laugh. We cry.

Landon finally puts me down so that my feet are touching the ground. "I'm going to be a father."

"I'm going to be a mother."

"I love you," we both say at the same time before our lips collide in a passionate kiss. When we pull away Landon begins singing ...

At three years old
I lost my faith.
I remember it
Like it was yesterday.

Father used the drink to wash away
The pain of losing her

Was just too much to bear.

He left me alone in the dark.
He left me on my own to deal
With my own pain, hurt, and loss.

But light by light, you snuck into my world.
I thought I could never be a father after what mine did to me.
But you were born, and you rescued me
With your tiny fingers and cute smile.
You shined a light into my world and you ...
You saved me.

You saved me from the darkness.
You saved me from my worst self.
Daughter, you saved me
And showed me how to be a father.

At twenty-eight, I lost someone too.
I understood my father
And the pain he couldn't bear.
I thought I'd lose myself too
In the bottom of a bottle
I thought I'd get sucked into.

But you saved me.
Daughter, you saved me.
You shined a light when no one else was there.
You saved me
And showed me how to be a father.

Daughter, I'm not proud of who I was.
I've been a monster more days than one.
I don't deserve your love.

But somehow, you found the light that was still hidden in me.

You saved me.

When the pain was too much to bear
You saved me.
When I was truly scared
You saved me.
When I was crying on my knees
You saved me.
When I had nothing left in me
You saved me.
When the darkness was controlling me
You saved me.

Daughter, you saved me ...

I JOIN Landon on the last words of the song while he sings 'and taught me how to be a father,' I sing 'and taught me how to be a mother.'

I smile because I know I've finally put my past behind me. Landon is my past and my future. This child is my future. Their love at this moment was worth all of the pain. I link my hands with Landon, finally feeling at peace. Finally feeling our paths aligning. And I know how we will live our future. As one.

Epilogue

LANDON

"I CAN'T BELIEVE we are going to miss your brother's wedding."

I roll my eyes at Alex, the most amazing, selfless woman. Only she would be in labor and still thinking about someone else.

"I'm not. It's his own fucking fault he planned a wedding three weeks before our daughter was supposed to be born. He knew the chance he was taking."

"Ow," Alex moans in pain again as she squeezes my hand tightly. Her engagement ring digs into my hand just a little as she tightens her grip further. A ring I gave to her properly in the backyard of our new home with nothing but the stars overhead lighting the proposal.

"Just breathe," I say. "You got this."

She breathes through another contraction and then returns almost immediately to her calm self. "I just hate that we are going to miss it. I understand why they chose today when it means so much to them. I guess now this day is going to mean a lot to us too."

I smile at her and tuck her hair behind her ear. Today is Caroline's birthday. The day she fell in love with Drew so long ago when she thought it was me. Now, I guess our daughter is going to share a birthday with her, as well. We will always be connected — all of us — and I wouldn't have it any other way.

"Shit, I'm supposed to be meeting a survivor today to do a shoot."

I smile as I think about the amazing business Alex started. The business she always wanted to start. 'Aligning the broken pieces ...' is the perfect title for the company. She photographs survivors. Survivors of cancer. Of sexual violence. Of most anything. She finds all the pieces that broke after the experience and helps them align them all. Each picture she takes tells a story of pain and pleasure. Past and future. Happiness and sadness. They all make a part of each person's story. She just puts them together and helps them heal. She doesn't get paid for what she does. All the money goes to helping the survivors and helping prevent future survivors. Instead, she heals a little more each day from helping others heal.

And I heal a little more each day watching her and our baby grow.

"You know, we are both going to have to learn to curse a little less when our daughter arrives."

She smiles, but it fades when another contraction prevents her from speaking. "I." Breath. "Guess I had better." Breath. "Get it all out ... Fuck!"

I watch as her face turns a brighter shade of red as her body tenses with another contraction. "You got this, baby."

"Fuck!" she screams again.

I laugh. "That's not the breathing we were taught in your birthing classes."

She just glares at me as her contraction ends.

The door bursts open and three of my favorite people in the world stumble in the door. Drew, Caroline, and sweet Amelia.

"What are you doing here?" I take Amelia from Caroline's arms as she smiles at me. She coos at me as I hold her.

"We couldn't miss the birth of our new niece," Drew says.

"But what about your wedding?" Alex asks.

"We couldn't go through with it, not without the people who brought us together there. We don't care about our wedding. We care about our family. It could be better this way. We could have a double wedding with both of our daughters there now," Caroline says.

I smile at her as she goes over to check on Alex. I would have never imagined that the two of them would have wound up friends. I never imagined that they would get along like sisters, but somehow, they have made it work.

"Fuck!" Alex groans again, and I quickly cover Amelia's ears as I turn to glare at Alex. Caroline just laughs and takes Amelia from my arms.

"Don't you dare tell her she is in the wrong. Not today. Amelia will survive hearing a couple of cuss words," Caroline says.

Alex's nurse bursts through the door, and after taking one look at Alex, she rushes everyone out.

"It's time," the nurse says.

I take my place beside Alex as she begins pushing. I hold her hand as each contraction takes over her body.

"I can't do this!" she shouts exhausted after an hour of pushing.

I don't fear it, though, because I know she can. She has done incredibly wonderful things. She can do this. "Yes, you can," I whisper in her ear.

She gathers her strength and pushes our daughter into the world. I watch as the nurse places our daughter on her stomach.

"She's beautiful."

Alex smiles as she holds our daughter on her chest. She holds her for a long time before she hands her to me. "You're not going to drop her," Alex says when she sees how nervous I am to hold her. Despite all the practice I've had with Amelia, this moment still makes me nervous. I still feel deep down like I don't deserve her. I still am afraid I'm not going to be a good father, just like my father.

Alex sighs when she sees me holding our daughter. "We still have to pick out a name."

I begin rocking our daughter on instinct, back and forth, as I walk around the room.

"I still like Hailey," Alex says.

I shake my head as I look at our daughter. The name doesn't fit.

"Emma?"

"No."

"Ashley?"

"No."

"Sydney?"

"No."

I hear Alex sigh. I continue rocking our daughter in my arms. She seems to relax with every movement, seeming to fall asleep. But just before she does, she opens her eyes for me and for the first time I see her eyes. Emerald eyes. Just like her mother's. Just like my daughter from the dream that saved me. It wasn't Amelia in my dream. It wasn't some figment of my imagination that didn't really exist. It was my daughter who I'm holding in my arms. She saved me.

It was ... "Isabella. Her name is Isabella."

ALIGNED: EVER AFTER

Chapter One

LANDON

I FEEL her soft lips touch mine enticing me to wake up as her tongue licks over my bottom lip.

"Wake up," she says, as her lips hover over mine.

I grin, but have no intention of waking up. I have intentions of doing other, more sinful things that involve her naked and tied to my bed first. I grab the back of her neck pulling her lips back to mine. I know her well enough to know that two more kisses will be all it takes for her to give in. Two more kisses and she will submit to anything I ask. Two more kisses and she will be mine.

But, she doesn't give me the chance to kiss her on the lips. Instead, she pulls away and giggles as my kiss lands somewhere in her hair. I groan my frustration.

"Come here woman and let me kiss you."

I still don't open my eyes, but I can see her smile as she laughs at me. Her body is sitting just above my hard cock that is begging her to move just a few inches lower so that I can take her like I want to.

"No," she says, laughing again.

I frown. "What do you mean no?"

She leans down so that I can feel her soft hair brush my chest before landing on each side of my face again as her lips land on mine for the briefest of kisses. I grab her neck to try and deepen the kiss, but she's too fast for me. She's probably already been awake for at least an hour now feeding Isabella. I, on the other hand, am barely awake; my reflexes can't match hers — yet.

"I'm not letting you fuck me until *after* you marry me," she says.

"Oh, come on." I feel her begin to climb off of me, but this time I grab her wrist before she is able to get off of me. I pull her down hard to my chest as a gasp escapes her lips. I grin before landing a kiss on her plump lips. She moans a little as I do, which makes my cock twitch for her.

Her determination is stronger than I imagined as she tries to wiggle out of my grasp. "Nope. You can wait a few hours until *after* we are married."

"Fine," I sigh, but have no intention of giving up that quickly. When she spoke, it was with panted breath. She wants me now. Not in twelve hours after we are married. I can't wait and neither can she.

I reach up sweetly to her until I feel the side of her face. She leans into me just a little as I stroke her cheek letting her defenses down. I tuck her hair behind her ear and slowly let my hand trace the ridges of her neck. I still don't bother opening my eyes. I know her body without having to open them. I know what I am doing is driving her wild with need. I know that even though my touch is sweet, it isn't meant to feel sweet. It's meant to start a fire that is slowly building inside of her. One that I know once ignited, isn't easily extinguished. A fire that only takes a single spark to ignite.

I feel her shiver as my hand moves lower. It's now or never. I grab her neck tightening my grasp around her neck as I sit up quickly to plant the softest of kisses on her lips. The tenderness combined with the pain is her undoing. I feel it the second her body gives in to me, but my words are what clinch the deal.

"I'll wait to fuck you until tonight, but just know that when I claim you as my wife, it's not going to be magic and rainbows. It's not going to be just making love to the woman I vowed to spend the rest of my life with. It will be fucking the most beautiful woman, a woman that is my life now, until you never want to tell me no again."

I release my grasp on her neck and listen to her pant. I lie back down and wait. One... two... three...

"Fuck it," she groans as her body attacks mine.

I smirk. "That is my plan."

Her lips land on mine, wiping the smirk from my lips. Her hands claw my body begging me to give her what she said she didn't want. Begging me to fuck her. Begging me not to wait. Begging me to give her everything.

I feel her pussy slide down on top of my hard cock that has been begging for her touch since I woke up this morning. Her hips immediately begin moving up and down thrusting harder and harder showing me how desperately she needs me. I meet her thrusts, happy to oblige.

She moans loudly with each thrust. I want to open my eyes to see her thrusting on top of me and to see her beautiful face as she takes control and makes us both come. But before I can open my eyes and see her face, soft silk fabric is thrown over my face blocking my view of the beautiful woman riding me. I move my hand to remove the fabric blocking my view, but Alex's hands grab hold of my wrists stopping me.

"I don't want you to see me. I want to pretend that we are strangers. I want to pretend that this is the first time we met and we are hooking up for the first time. I want to pretend that this is the last time we will ever get to fuck a stranger. That way when you fuck me tonight it will make it all the more special," Alex says.

I smile happy to play along with her games. I leave the fabric where it is, covering my eyes as her hands intertwine with mine. Her movements become more frantic, her breathing becomes faster, and her moans become louder. Everything about her shows me that she won't last long. Her hands release mine and move to my chest, needing better leverage to move faster, harder.

I reach down between her legs and find her clit with my thumb trying to take her over the edge of the cliff that she is so desperate to climb. She moans loudly as I do. I rub faster as she continues to move up and down on my cock, until I can't last much longer. I try to slow her movements, worried that I will come before her, but I should know my almost wife better than that...

"Landon!" She screams as she comes and I follow right after her.

Her body collapses on top of mine. Her head next to my head and our chests lined up so that our hearts are beating fast on top of each other. Our breathing keeps pace with one another, both trying to slow down from the intensity that just happened between us.

"I can't believe we are getting married today," she says.

Panic rises in my chest as I remember my last dream before a wedding. When I thought I was having sex with Alex, when I thought I was marrying Alex. When in reality I wasn't getting married to Alex, I was getting married to Caroline.

I throw the silky fabric off my face terrified that my nightmare is about to come true. That I'm not marrying Alex tonight. That this is some cruel joke. That instead of Alex I'll come face-to-face with Caroline again.

I thrust the woman off my chest trying to get a good look at her. Hoping that I see red locks instead of blonde. Hoping I see Alex's strong body instead of Caroline's soft one. Hoping to God I see a missing leg instead of a whole one.

"What are you doing?" Alex says.

I exhale deeply as my eyes focus on Alex's green eyes and red hair. I flop back on the bed and close my eyes able to relax again now that I know my nightmare isn't about to come true.

I feel a little nudge on my shoulder and I open my eyes. "What was that?" Alex asks.

"Nothing," I say.

"That wasn't nothing," she says, eyeing me suspiciously.

"Trust me, that was nothing," I say.

"Really? You're going to start our married life telling me a lie?"

"Technically, we're not married yet. And even if we were, it's not a lie, it was nothing."

Isabella cries and I watch as Alex turns her attention from me to our six-month-old daughter. I smile, our daughter really does have perfect timing. Never once has she cried when I've made love to Alex. Never once has she cried when I'm playing a song. Never once has she cried when I'm on an important call. Yet, she cries right on cue anytime Alex gives the slightest hint that she is upset with me. It's almost like my daughter is still protecting me. Still doing everything she can to keep me out of harm's way. Even if harm's way is just Alex yelling at me and rightfully so.

Alex quickly climbs out of bed throwing a robe around her shoulders before moving to the crib in the corner of the room. I watch in awe as she picks up our daughter and holds her in her arms rocking her gently back and forth. Isabella quickly quiets just being in Alex's arms.

"Shh, Izzy. It's okay, Momma's got you. I'm not going to yell at your father even though he deserves it." Alex gives me a dirty look from across the room.

I flash her a crooked grin and watch as Alex's face lightens just a little. She can't help but love me even when she's annoyed with me.

"You hungry, Izzy?" Alex asks.

Izzy coos as Alex speaks to her.

I hear a knock at the door to our hotel room followed quickly by the door being pushed open. I watch as Caroline pushes her way into the room. I grab the covers covering my naked body as she enters the room. Caroline looks at me and smirks "No need to cover up. Nothing I haven't seen before."

I frown.

Caroline smiles as she looks from me to Alex who is also frowning.

"Sorry," Caroline says not in the least bit apologetic voice.

"You're forgiven," Alex says though, as Caroline scoops up her favorite niece into her arms. Izzy coos and laughs with excitement as her favorite aunt picks her up into her arms.

"I'm stealing you," Caroline says to Izzy. Izzy just smiles brighter as Caroline speaks to her and twirls her around in her arms.

"I really don't think I can be apart from her, not today. You can steal her tomorrow," Alex says her voice unsteady.

"Don't worry, I'm stealing you too," Caroline says smiling.

"What?" Alex asks.

Caroline doesn't give her an explanation, just grabs Alex's arm and begins pulling her out of the hotel room while still carrying Izzy in her other arm. Alex quickly grabs Izzy's diaper bag as she is being pulled from the room.

"Wait," I say.

Caroline doesn't hesitate for a second, she just continues to take the two loves of my life out of my room.

"Shower. Drew will be over in an hour. No drinking," Caroline says to me.

I roll my eyes at her. I think I've learned my lesson when it comes to drinking. Alex flashes one last grin before Caroline pulls her out the door, happy to have found a family at last. A family that she can connect with. Something that she has desperately wanted ever since her family left her.

I'm happy that she has finally found what she is looking for, I just wish it wasn't with Caroline. I will never understand how Alex was able to so easily forgive Caroline for what she did. Even I wasn't so quick to forgive her. Forgiveness only came after I realized that Alex could finally be mine. For Alex though, she continues to see the best in people even after everything that has happened. Even if it means she could be risking her life...

Chapter Two

CAROLINE

I CARRY Izzy to the elevators as Alex follows closely behind me. I can't believe she shared the same hotel room with Landon the night before her wedding today. Doesn't she know it is bad luck to sleep with your future husband the night before the wedding? I sigh as I stop at the base of the elevators waiting for the door to open.

That's why I came over first thing this morning to steal Izzy and Alex. They need at least some time away from each other before the wedding. Alex didn't have anything fun planned before the wedding. She just wanted a simple wedding where she did her own hair and makeup. She didn't want to make a "fuss" she said. She isn't planning a big wedding either. Just a simple wedding on a beach here in Mexico with only ten or so people invited. Followed by a week-long honeymoon just spent relaxing on the beach.

But after everything I have done for her and everything she did to prepare for my wedding, I can't let her just have a simple wedding. She deserves to have the wedding of her dreams just like I had. She deserves everything. And I know she will regret that decision if she didn't go all out for her own wedding.

The elevator doors open and I carry Izzy into the elevator followed by Alex. The doors close and I press the button for the ground floor.

"Where are we going?" Alex asks. A large smile is plastered on her face confirming that she is going to be happy with my plans for the day.

"You'll see," I say.

Izzy grabs my hair that is hanging down in waves on my shoulder. I smile at her, not minding at all that she is pulling hard enough to cause a sting in my scalp. I love Izzy almost as much as I love my own daughter that is just a couple months older than her. Both are growing up too fast, so I will do anything to cherish these moments together.

"Does Drew have Millie for today?" Alex asks.

"Our nanny, Beth, is watching her at the moment. Drew is in charge of Landon today," I say to Alex who raises her eyebrows at me but doesn't protest. They will be fine together.

I turn my attention to Izzy, "But don't worry, you will get plenty of time to play with cousin Millie."

The doors to the elevator open and we step out into the lobby of the hotel. I stride forward through the lobby with purpose and out into the warm Mexico air where a limo is waiting just outside for us. I nod to the driver and then turn to Alex, "Get in."

Her smile brightens just a little more as she climbs into the limo. I hand her Izzy and then climb in after her. A few moments later the driver begins driving without a word of where we are going just like I asked of him.

"Is Millie meeting us to get our hair and makeup done?" Alex asks, already trying to guess where we are going.

I smirk, hiding the secret. We aren't going to just get our hair and makeup done. That would be too simple of a surprise. It's her wedding day. I wouldn't be a worthy maid of honor if that is all I arranged for today.

"Millie is meeting us," is all I say.

I pull the champagne out of the cooler along with two flutes. I pour the champagne and hand one to Alex. I lift mine as she does the same, "To you and Landon. May your wedding day be everything you have ever dreamed about and just as special as my wedding day was." We clink our glasses together and then both take a sip. I watch as Izzy snuggles into Alex's side. Everything is going to be perfect today just like my wedding day was, I think, as we drive off to the first surprise.

"You look beautiful. Drew is going to die when he sees you," Alex says to me. Millie and Izzy coo their agreeance in their cribs next to us.

"I can't believe you were brave enough to wear a see-through dress, but if anybody can pull it off it is you. You look hot!" Abby, Alex's assistant says.

"Thanks," I say smiling at myself in the mirror. I do look hot. This dress is everything I ever wanted. It's fitted and see-through in the midriff before flaring out in a beautiful lace train at the bottom.

I pick up Millie, who is smiling at me in her pink frilly dress. "You ready for mommy and daddy to make it official?" I ask.

She smiles up at me as drool slips from her adorable mouth. I wipe it off with my hand not caring that it is my wedding day and I risk getting drool on my dress.

I hear a knock at the door, followed by Tiffany, the wedding planner I hired. "We are ready for you when you are," Tiffany says.

I look around at the room filled with my bridesmaids and flower girls. "Ready?" I ask them.

Everyone smiles and nods at me.

"We're ready," I say to Tiffany.

"Then I need all of the bridesmaids except Alex, who is still planning on pulling the girls out right before you walk out, correct?" Tiffany asks.

"Yes," I say looking at Alex for confirmation.

"Great, I will be back to get Alex and then you," Tiffany says.

When my bridesmaids leave my heart begins to race. I wasn't nervous before. I know I'm marrying the man of my dreams. I'm getting the wedding of my dreams. I already have the ring of my dreams even if Landon was the one that initially gave it to me. And I already have the daughter of my dreams, but it still doesn't calm my nerves at the thought of walking down the aisle to Drew by myself. I thought I was strong enough since I don't have a father or brother that is worthy of walking me down the aisle like I should have. I don't have any other family that could walk me down the aisle. I have to do it by myself.

"You okay?" Alex asks.

"Yes," I say. "Just need water." I pace the room looking for water as I place Millie down in the wagon that Alex will be pulling her and Izzy in.

"Here," Alex says handing me a bottle of water.

I put the bottle to my lips and pour the cold liquid down my throat quickly emptying the bottle.

"Better?" Alex asks.

I nod although I don't really feel any better. I feel nauseous. I feel like I'm going to trip and fall as I walk down the beach with hundreds of people looking on.

Why did I plan a big huge wedding again? I always said I wanted something small and intimate, but Drew knew me better. I said we should do a joint wedding with Alex and Landon, but Drew knew better. He knew I would want all of the spotlight on me on my wedding day. At the time it made me fall even more in love with him. But now, I think it was the stupidest idea ever, because now I will have to walk down the long aisle alone.

Alex looks at me with sympathy in her eyes. "I have a surprise for you and I think this is the perfect time to give it to you."

I suck in a deep breath trying to keep myself from vomiting. "I appreciate it Alex, but I don't think I can take any surprises right now."

She smiles, "I understand, but I think this one will fix what you are nervous about."

Alex walks out of the room while I continue pacing as my anxiety increases with each step I take. She's gone, what seems like hours, even though I know it's only a matter of seconds before she returns.

"Alex I —."

"I thought I would walk you down the aisle. If that's okay with you?"

I look up to see Landon standing in front of me with his goofy grin on his face.

I take a deep breath and look over at Alex who is standing just behind Landon. She's smiling and nodding at me as if she knows I need reassurance before I say yes to Landon. I don't know why she's being so nice to me, I know I don't deserve it. But at this point I can't think about that, all I can think about is that I can't walk down the aisle alone.

"Yes, thank God, yes. I didn't realize how hard it would be for me to walk down the aisle alone until now. So thank you! Thank you," I say.

Alex and Landon both smile at me and say at the same time, "You're welcome."

Tiffany peaks in through the door and says, "I'm ready for Alex and the flower girls."

Alex comes over and gives me one last hug, "Relax, you're getting married today. Everything's going to be perfect."

I watch as Alex adjusts the girls in the wagon, and then I kiss each one on the cheek. She then pulls them out of the room in the wagon, both of the girls clueless as to what is going on. In just a few moments she will be pulling them down the aisle and a few moments later I'll be walking with Landon, a man I almost married, but instead will be marrying his brother.

"If it makes you feel any better, you look better than Drew does. He is a nervous wreck. He thinks you're going to back out at the last minute and leave him standing all alone like I did to you," Landon says.

"It doesn't make me feel any better, but thanks for trying." I glance down at my nails while nervously picking at the polish on my perfectly French manicured hands. "Are you sure Alex is okay with this? I know she forgave me for everything that I did, but still this is more than I deserve."

Landon smirks, "It is more than you deserve, but Alex is willing to put the past behind us and so am I."

A second later, Tiffany pushes the door open to our hotel room again, "It's time."

I suck in one last breath, doing my best to calm my nerves. I can't do this, I keep thinking over and over in my head. I can't do this.

But then Landon is holding out his arm for me and I take it. He pats my hand that is holding onto his arm and I immediately relax. Everything is going to be perfect.

We began walking out of the room and through the hotel lobby to the back of the building where more than a hundred chairs and thousands of flowers make a beautiful beach oasis- the perfect place to get married.

I watch Tiffany and her assistant grab hold of the two French doors leading outside to the wedding venue. "On the count of three," Tiffany says to her assistant.

"One...two...three..." the doors swing open giving me an all-encompassing view of where I'm going to get married.

Landon pats my hand one more time in a comforting manner, similar to Drew, but still somehow different and then we are walking. We walk past hundreds of strangers that I still don't know why I invited to our wedding. Music is playing, but I can't tell you what I even picked out. Flowers surround me, but I can't recall the names. All of the attention is on me just like I wanted, but at the moment I can't remember why I wanted it.

We take another step forward and then another, but I don't really know how I'm walking. It must be Landon that is pushing us forward.

"Look up," Landon says.

I look up even though I don't really know what I'm looking at and then I see him. Drew stands at the end of the aisle in a tuxedo looking handsomer than I've ever seen him, but that's not what soothes my nerves. What soothes me is his unwavering smile as he looks at me, and the intensity in his eyes telling me he loves me; reassuring me that today is going to be perfect.

The limo comes to a stop just outside the entrance to the airport.

"What are we..." Alex says.

"I'm giving you the perfect wedding day just like you gave me."

Chapter Three

ALEX

I DON'T KNOW what I did to deserve this. I don't recall doing anything for Caroline's wedding except allowing Landon to walk her down the aisle. That was nothing compared to this. What she did for me is over the top.

Caroline basically planned a whole new wedding for me. From location, to photographer, to decorations, and even cake. Everything that I originally planned, she re-did except better. I thought I was going to have a simple, quiet beach wedding in Mexico; I was wrong.

The paparazzi found out our location as soon as we started planning it. Caroline realized that our simple, quiet wedding was going to be overtaken with helicopters and paparazzi, but instead of telling me and allowing me to worry about it, she fixed the problem.

She planned a wedding beyond my wildest dreams and somehow kept it all a secret from everybody, including me and Landon. She had multiple private jets to fly our entire wedding party from Mexico to private islands in the Bahamas. From there she found a private location buried within the island that is so remote that even if the paparazzi found out about our location, it would be too hard for them to get a good picture or interrupt the wedding.

The location is beautiful, complete with a waterfall and a jungle filled with exotic flowers and plants. She had the best photographer. The best minister. The best hair and makeup artist. The best everything.

She spent the day getting me and the babies pampered and massaged so that there is no way for me to be nervous about what comes next. The only thing she didn't change was my wedding dress. The wedding dress I found among my mother's belongings. It is the only thing that ties me to my past besides my scars and missing leg that I will never get back.

"You look beautiful," Caroline says looking at me in my wedding dress. "Landon is one lucky guy. He's going to die when he sees you," she says repeating the same words I spoke to her.

I smile. "Thank you." I walk over to her and embrace her in a tight hug. "Thank you so much, really, for everything."

I release her as a tear drops from my eye. Caroline hands me a Kleenex and I quickly wipe the tear way. "I never thought I would ever experience what it is like to have a sister, but thanks to you, now I know."

I watch as Caroline's own tear rolls down her cheek. She grabs another Kleenex and wipes it away. She smiles, but neither of us says anything more. We both glance down at our daughters, who are laughing and playing with each other in their pretty dresses on the floor of the hotel room. Both already great friends, ensuring that we will always be connected.

"I need to go find Drew and the minister and then it will be time to start your wedding," Caroline says.

I nod and then watch Caroline leave before sitting down on the floor where Millie and Izzy are playing. Not caring if I wrinkle the simple lace trumpet dress that I'm wearing. I immediately feel calm even though I don't really know what awaits me outside of this room. I've seen the venue for the wedding. I've seen the gorgeous waterfall and beautiful flowers and white chairs outlining the aisle. But, what I haven't seen is who she invited beyond the ten people I originally invited. What I haven't seen is the reception room. What I haven't seen is Landon in almost twelve hours.

But, none of that matters because I trust Caroline with my life and my wedding. And sitting here with both of our daughters, about to marry the man of my dreams, I couldn't be happier than at any point in my life. It doesn't really matter what the decorations look like, or what the minister is going to say, or who is going to be sitting in the white chairs. All that matters is that today I get to marry Landon.

The door swings open, and Caroline rushes in followed by Drew. "You're going to ruin your wedding dress!" Caroline screams as she rushes to my side. I laugh at Caroline's frenzied state along with both of the babies sitting in front of me seeing their mother and aunt in such a crazy state.

I slowly get up, and pat out the wrinkles in my dress not really caring if they are there or not, but trying to appease Caroline. She glares at me for a moment, which somehow just makes me laugh harder.

Drew walks over between me and Caroline and gives me a tight hug. "You look great, wrinkles and all," Drew says.

I hug him tightly. "Thanks, you don't look so bad yourself." I release Drew. "How's my almost hubby doing?"

"He's mad."

"Mad?"

Drew nods. "He's mad that Caroline and I made all the changes to your wedding without talking to him first."

I smile, relieved that he is not mad at me. "He'll get over it," I say.

"You're not mad?" Drew asks.

"Hell no, I'm not mad. From what I've seen this is everything and more."

"Okay you two, enough talking about my brother-in-law, it's time to get Alex married," Caroline says.

I WATCH as Caroline pulls Izzy and Millie in a beautiful carriage-like wagon through the white silk that blocks my view of where I'm going to get married. Even the wagon is more extravagant than what I had originally planned on using. I was going to just use the same wagon that Caroline did at her wedding, but evidently that wasn't good enough, because Caroline picked out a new wagon for my wedding. Along with everything else new for my wedding.

"Ready?" Drew asks.

I nod, suddenly unable to speak.

Drew smiles widely at me. I take his arm that is extended up to me and take a deep breath as excitement pulses through my body. The music changes, giving us our cue that it is time for us to walk down the aisle. Drew gives me one last reassuring smile, and then we begin walking through the white fabric that leads to the beautiful oasis where I'm getting married.

My mouth drops when I see all the people filling the white chairs. There must be hundreds of people that all came out for *my* wedding. I glance around nervously hoping that they are people I actually know and not strangers Caroline has invited to make my wedding grander. When I do, I see hundreds of familiar faces smiling back at me. I see celebrities I photographed, along with inspirational people I photographed. I see people I work with at the magazine. I see people that work on Landon's tour. What I really see when I look around the room is family that I didn't even realize that I had.

I turn my attention toward the end of aisle, and that's when I see him. The man I've fallen in love with time and time again. The man that I almost had to stop loving. The man that saved me. The man that taught me how to breathe. The man that taught me that love does really exist.

Landon's eyes still lock on mine as we walk down the aisle. I beg Drew to walk faster so that I can reach Landon; not able to stand being apart from Landon any longer now that I've seen him. Drew doesn't let me, instead he keeps our steady pace, which drives me crazy with need for my almost husband.

Landon seems to read my thoughts and meets Drew halfway down the aisle.

"I can take it from here," Landon says.

Drew laughs, "Of course you can." Drew hugs his brother and then walks past us to take his place as best man.

Landon holds up his arm for me, and I take it, feeling suddenly calm now that we are back together again. We begin walking both at a rapid pace, both desperately needing to get married as soon as possible, and put behind any lingering thoughts that we won't be able to live happily ever after.

Landon leans over as we walk, "You look beautiful."

I nod and smile, but no words come out. Landon laughs, "Speechless, that's a first."

I smile wider, but still no words come out. It makes me nervous that I'm not going to be able to read my vows when the time comes. I swallow hard as we come to a stop in front of the minister, under the beautiful arch, filled with bright exotic flowers overhead. I can hear the waterfall trickling down just behind where the minister stands, but I don't glance away from Landon to see its beauty. Right now in this moment I don't care where we are getting married, just that we are.

The minister begins talking, but I don't hear him over my beating heart and my heavy breathing. I don't see him out of the corner my eye. I barely register his presence at all. All I see or hear or feel is Landon.

Landon must hear what the minster says though, because he takes my flowers from me and hands them to Caroline. He takes both my hands and then begins singing me his vows:

You are my everything.
Lover.
Friend.
Savior.
Fighter.

You are my everything.
Daughter.
Strength.
Courage.
Desire.

Music begins as Landon continues to sing...

I vow to give you my everything and more.
This I promise.
I promise to sing you a song whenever I make a mistake.
I promise to care for you no matter how you are breaking inside.
I promise to stand by you no matter how bad the times.
I promise to teach our daughter to find her own strength inside.
I promise to be your legs when you need to fly.
I promise never to give up on love because love is what has seen us through everything.

I promise to be everything and be your counter in life.
Laughter.
Need.
Calmer.
Husband.
Father of our child.

I promise to give you the darkness that you seek.
I promise to be the darkness to your light and your light when you see nothing but darkness.
I promise to be a miracle when there's nothing but despair.
I promise to be your forever.
I promise we will live happily ever.
I promise to be your fairytale.
I promise to give you all of myself.
I promise to always be yours.

The music ends as Landon sings the last lines of his vows.

I wipe the tear, that has somehow found its way down my cheek, off my face as I smile at Landon who is almost in tears himself. I hear our daughter Izzy cooing and crying softly in the background like she does every time her father sings.

"Alex, you can now read your vows to Landon," the minister says.

I take a deep breath, "I don't know how I'm supposed to follow that," I say, laughing nervously as the crowd laughs along with me reminding me that they are there.

Somehow I find the words anyway...

You are the forever that I seek.
You are the love I didn't believe existed.
You are the strength that I needed.
You are the father our daughter deserves.
You are the dark lover my heart desires.
You are my forever.
I vow to be yours forever.
I vow to be more connected still.
I vow to never sing unless you need a laugh.
I vow to be your patience when you have none.
I vow to be the love you seek.
I vow to be a mother to any child that may come our way.
I vow to ask for your help when I need and never take on the world alone again.

I vow to love you forever.
I vow to be your forever, forever.

LANDON STANDS frozen looking at me, and I can't tell from the expression on his face if he liked my vows or not. "Sorry, that's the best I got," I say quietly to him.

His eyes widened as he looks at me, "You have nothing to be sorry for, your vows were beautiful. You should help me write songs in the future."

I smile. "I think I'll stick to just writing my vows now."

"Who has the rings?" The minister asks.

"I do," Drew says. Drew hands the minister our wedding rings.

"Landon, do you take Alex as your lawfully wedded wife?" The minister asks.

"I do," Landon says taking the ring from the minister's hand and placing it on my ring finger as he says the words.

"And do you Alex take Landon as your lawfully wedded husband?"

"I do," I say taking the last ring on the minister's hand and placing it on Landon's finger.

The minister continues speaking. I'm sure he's saying some things about what it means to be a husband and wife or what it means to be married or something about true love, but I don't care about his words. All I care about is that I'm married to Landon. Something that a year ago, I thought could never happen.

I feel the excitement build as it shoots back and forth between our hands, and I know neither of us can wait to make it official, so we make it official. Landon grabs hold of my face as I grab his neck and our lips meet and we kiss for the first time of our married lives. I hear laughter in the crowd followed by applause, but I don't care. I'm married to Landon.

Landon breaks away first as the music sounds giving us our cue that we can leave as husband and wife. Landon takes my hand as we run down the aisle and don't stop until we find a secluded space just outside of the hotel where we can have a few moments alone. Landon picks me up and twirls me around as our lips connect again and again, never getting enough of each other. Not believing that we are married. Not believing that *anything* has changed when *everything* has changed.

"Can you believe we're finally married?" I ask.

"No! I can't, but it's true and I wouldn't have it any other way."

"We should get back to Izzy," I say feeling anxious all of a sudden.

Landed kisses me again and again not focusing on the words that I just said. I pull away.

Landon sighs. "Izzy will be fine. Caroline hired a nanny to watch both of the girls for tonight. We will make plenty of time to see her at the reception before she falls asleep."

I nod. Not sure why I feel anxious at the thought of leaving Izzy with the nanny. We begin to hear voices as the crowd that came to watch us get married, begins to move from the ceremony area to the reception venue.

I grab Landon's hand, "Come on, we need to get back or people will be wondering where we are."

"I have a better idea," Landon says, pulling me back toward the hotel suite that I used to get ready earlier today. As we round the corner though, we see Drew and Caroline sneaking into the suite.

We both laugh. "Dirty minds think alike," I say.

Landon laughs, "I guess you're right. We will sneak away later." Landon winks at me as we make our way to the reception.

Chapter Four

DREW

CAROLINE LAUGHS as I push her inside the suite that Caroline and Alex got ready for the wedding in.

"What are you doing?" she asks as I push her inside like a horny teenager that can't wait until school gets out to fuck her.

I push her against the wall of the hotel suite. Kissing her hard and long before I back away an inch to remove my tuxedo jacket.

"I'm fucking you," I say as I kiss her again.

Caroline moans as I kiss her again and again. Not able to resist being kissed, being used, being loved.

I move to her neck, loving that her blonde locks are piled on top of her head giving me better access to her smooth neck. She moans again.

I grin against her neck loving the little sounds she makes each time I touch her. I drop my kisses lower, loving the strapless neckline of her champagne colored bridesmaid dress that gives me access to her plump breasts. I kiss to the top of her mounds ready to dive deeper.

"We can't," Caroline says suddenly stopping me.

"We can't?" I ask in confusion. Caroline has never turned me down before. She loves the thrill and excitement of being fucked in a public place, even when we shouldn't. And as far as public places go, this is about as tame of a place as we have fucked; front seat of cars, parks, coat closets, restrooms, alleyways, the list goes on and on.

Maybe this isn't exciting enough for her? Maybe she wanted something more exciting? Should I have pulled her behind the waterfall and fucked her so that everyone could see the outlines of our bodies as we joined together? So that they could just make out her moans over the sound of the waterfall?

"We don't have to do this here if it's not exciting enough for you..." I say.

Caroline laughs. "That's not why. Sex with you is always exciting no matter where it is. And honestly I would be happy to just do it in a bed for once."

I sigh in relief. "I would really like to fuck you in a bed too. So what is the problem then?"

Her eyes narrow as she looks at me. Her cheeks flush a shade of pink like whatever she is going to say is embarrassing. She scrunches her nose, "I don't know exactly. It's just a feeling that we shouldn't be doing this. That we should go check on Millie."

I smile at my wife; so beautiful even as she worries about our daughter who is perfectly fine. I tuck one of the loose curls that frame her face behind her ear. "Millie is fine. She's with Beth who has always done an amazing job." I can see from the concerned look on her face that my words aren't comforting enough for her. I pull my phone out of my tuxedo pocket, "But, if it makes you feel better, call Beth and make sure everything is okay."

Caroline smiles at me, but doesn't take the phone. "I'm sure Millie is fine. I'm worrying about nothing."

"You sure?" I take her hand in mine and rub it softly in a way that I know is both calming to her, yet turns her on at the same time.

She nods as desire returns to her eyes.

"This is going to be hard and fast, I don't want you to worry about Millie any longer then you have to. And we both have speeches that we have to give. Don't want Landon yelling at us for missing our speeches."

Caroline laughs. "I don't think Landon will care. He's probably off doing the same thing to Alex right now. You twins think too much alike."

I grin, but don't want to think about my brother right now. All I want to think about is taking my wife.

I grab her legs, lifting her as her arms immediately go around my neck like they have hundreds of times before. Her lips attack mine with hard aggressive kisses, showing me that she agrees that she wants this hard and fast.

I drop her hard on the bed before I undo the button and zipper on my tuxedo pants setting my cock free. She bites her lip at the sight of my cock and I can't wait any longer to be inside of her. I grab her legs throwing her cream colored stiletto heels over my shoulders as I push her dress up exposing her naked pussy.

I groan at the realization that she hasn't been wearing any underwear all day. She anticipated this. She wanted this as badly as I did.

"You're beautiful," I say as I slide my cock into her.

I don't give her a chance to get used to me stretching her before I pound into her, needing to show her that I can't wait. That even after being married a couple of months now, I will never get enough of her. She will never satisfy me enough. I will never fuck her enough.

Her heels dig into my back making her mark on me as I fuck her over and over. I feel her body tensing as I bring her closer and closer. Until we are both screaming each other's names as we both come.

"I love you beautiful."

"I love you too husband." She sits up quickly forcing me out of her and I immediately miss being inside of her.

"Now, help me clean up so we don't miss any more of the reception that I planned."

I raise my eyebrows at her as I begin cleaning myself off, "What else did you plan?" I feel anxiety creeping up my chest. Caroline had done a fantastic job of planning everything so far, but I know her. I know she likes things over the top, and I'm afraid that what she might have planned will make Alex and Landon angry and they will never forgive us.

"You'll see," she says, kissing me softly on the cheek, as she begins tucking the loose pins back up that have fallen out of her up do. But the kiss does nothing to ease my anxiety. I just have to hope that whatever she has planned will be just as amazing as the wedding.

Chapter Five

LANDON

Alex drags me through the hotel lobby. We follow the signs showing our guests where to go to get cocktail drinks before the reception begins. Alex pulls me past the cocktail room where many of our guests have begun to gather. She pulls me to the reception area constantly searching to find our daughter.

I let Alex pull me, but I'm not really worried. Our daughter is in good hands and for once Alex needs to enjoy herself and not worry about protecting everyone else. Today is about celebrating how far we have come. It's about celebrating the fact that we have defeated all of our pasts, our monsters, our demons. It's about celebrating the fact that we won and now can live a life filled with happiness. She needs to stop focusing on the negative things that could happen and focus on the positive because there is no way life is going to throw anything else negative our way. We have already faced more than our fair share of bad things. Life won't touch us again.

Still, I let Alex pull us knowing that she won't relax until she sees our daughter. Until she knows that she is safe and her mommy instincts are wrong.

Alex stops in her tracks when she hears a soft cry. We both turn around and see Izzy crying softly in the arms of the nanny that Caroline hired. The older woman smiles at us as Alex runs over to take Izzy out of her arms. Izzy quiets immediately as soon as she is in her mother's arms.

I smile and walk over slowly giving Alex some time with Izzy before Izzy sees me. I know Alex needs some time to relax and see that nothing is wrong with our daughter.

When I walk over Izzy sticks her hands out to me and Alex hands her over to me. I immediately spin her around and then toss her in the air and watch as she squeals. My heart melts seeing my daughter so happy. When she lands safely in my arms I go to hand her back to Alex, but Izzy squeals again wanting me to toss her again. I can't say no to my daughter, which may become a problem in the future, but right now I don't care. I just want to make her happy. So, I toss her two more times before handing her to Alex who spins her around trying her best to continue the fun so Izzy will want to stay in her arms.

"See Alex, Izzy is fine."

Alex nods as she kisses Izzy on the cheek. "I know you're right. She just missed her parents."

"She has been an angel though since Caroline gave her to me when the wedding was over. She just cried when she saw you two. I will take good care of her," the nanny says.

"Thank you for taking care of her..." I say.

"Beth," the woman says.

"Thank you for taking care of her, Beth. I'm sure you will do a great job the rest of the evening."

"I will take care of her like she is my own. I have been nanny to little Millie here for three months now," Beth says before picking up Millie from the wagon. Millie smiles at Beth and any worries that Beth isn't the woman for the job disappears.

Suddenly though Millie is crying. Beth begins bouncing her up and down, but it does nothing to soothe her cries. Millie reaches out and squirms to get out of Beth's arms. Beth resigns and puts Millie on the ground on her feet despite Millie just barely being able to walk. Millie takes a couple steps forward and I turn to see Caroline and Drew running toward their daughter; Caroline at a much faster pace than

Drew who walks leisurely behind his wife. Caroline scoops Millie up in much the same way that Alex did to Izzy.

When Drew reaches me, we both exchange a knowing glance that both of our wives may be a tad bit crazy, but we don't dare tell them that. When Caroline has had her fill of snuggles, she passes her daughter to Drew who roughly tosses his daughter around in much the same way that I did Izzy until she is smiling and laughing.

"What time is it?" Caroline asks Beth.

"Five 'til eight," Beth answers.

Caroline takes Millie back from Drew and kisses her on the forehead before handing her back to Beth.

"The organizers will be moving everyone from the cocktail hour into the reception. We need to leave so they can do that and then we can announce your entrance," Caroline says.

Alex nods and kisses Izzy one last time before placing her in the wagon. She seems calmer now that she knows her worries were for nothing. We follow Caroline out of the tented area and back to the hotel. As we do, I look around the tented space for the first time and get a chance to see how beautiful it really is. Beautiful doesn't even really do the space justice. White tents are scattered around the area. Lights hang from the ceiling and are coming to life as the sun begins to set. Candles and beautiful colorful flowers fill every table. A large dance floor has been erected in the center tent with a band set up just behind it. All of the other tents surround the dance floor. All around the outside tents is more jungle, more beauty, except for one open space that leads to the ocean and open sky. It's perfect. This alone has made me forgive Caroline for all of the trouble she caused us earlier.

I grab Alex's hand as we walk back inside and wait to make our grand entrance back into the reception room. Alex isn't focused on me though. "Where will the girls be all night?" Alex asks Caroline.

"They will be in the tent closest to the hotel. That way when they start getting tired Beth can bring them into the hotel suite I have for her and the girls and can let them sleep in beds," Caroline answers.

Alex nods. "Sounds good."

When we are back in the hotel lobby, I grab Alex's face and force her to look at me. "Izzy is fine. We only get one wedding, one reception, and one wedding night. Let's enjoy this."

Alex smiles. "You're right. I will stop worrying about Izzy. Let's enjoy this."

Alex kisses me and I forget about everything. I forget that we are standing in a lobby and not in our hotel suite already. I grab her ass and pull her tightly against my body. I tangle my hand in her long hair that sweeps in beautiful curls down her body. She begins to pull away, but I bite her bottom lip sucking her back in and not letting her go.

Someone clears their throat, and I reluctantly come back to the real world and let go of her lip.

"I know you just got married and all, but can you at least wait until you get to your room to do that," Abby says.

I glare at her, but Alex just laughs at her crazy friend and bridesmaid. I thought Alex would have chosen Abby to be her maid of honor, but to my surprise she chose Caroline just as Caroline had chosen her. I shake my head; I really don't understand her.

I walk over and shake my bandmates' hands that served as my groomsmen, while I watch Alex hug Abby and the rest of her bridesmaids that work with her at the magazine.

"Okay, everyone. They will begin announcing everyone to enter the reception, so line up with the groomsman you walked down the aisle with," Caroline says as she begins getting everyone lined up to enter the reception.

Two staff members hold onto the door and begin opening it to let each couple enter the reception when their names are announced by the DJ. Alex and I wait at the back until we are the only ones left. I glance at her and again I'm in awe.

"I still can't believe we are married," we both say at the same time to each other and then laugh.

I tilt her chin up so that I can kiss her, but she only lets me get a peck in before she turns away.

"Don't start that again. We have to go do our married duties and thank everyone that came all this way for our wedding."

I narrow my eyes at her in frustration. "Fine," I sigh.

She grabs my hand as the doors swing open and then we are

walking down an aisle of flower petals to the center tent where our bridal party is waiting, cheering us on. The ground is uneven, and I notice for the first time that Alex chose to wear heels, despite how hard it is for her to walk in them, especially on this uneven ground. I'm surprised I didn't notice her having difficulty when she walked down the aisle toward me earlier.

I can see a twinge of pain on her face with every step and although I know she would never ask for help, despite her vows promising otherwise, I scoop her up in my arms under the pretense that I can't keep my hands off of her instead of me trying to help my wife that needs help. I smile and run to the dance floor tent and spin her around in my arms. She smiles at me knowing what she needs even though she doesn't ask.

"And now for the first time ever, Mr. And Mrs. Landon Davis will dance their first dance as husband and wife," the DJ says.

"You okay to dance if I put you down?" I whisper in Alex's ear.

"Yes," Alex says.

I place her gently on the ground, as another song I wrote for her plays in the background. I sing along in her ear as we dance our first dance in perfect synchrony. She moves as if she still has both of her legs.

The music plays, but doesn't give the whole song away, only the first part, but not the why. So, I sing the second part of each line in her ear that only she can hear. We will decide later which version of the song we will release for the public, but for now, half of the song is just for her.

Ours is not a love at first sight.
It isn't a quiet melody that just played along until two hearts beat as one.
It isn't about second chances or forbidden love.
It isn't about best friends falling in love or even tragic pasts.

Our story is about something more.
It's about the way we fell.

It's about something (in your eyes when you look at me).
It's about something (like your dirty mouth scolding me).
It's about something (in the way only you walk that makes my heart skip).
It's about something (like the tattoos that might as well be carved in my own skin).

Our love isn't a long distance romance.
It's not a tale of lovers in denial.
It's not about how opposites attract.

It's about something more.
It's something (in the way our daughter shares your eyes).
It's something (in the strength that you destroyed our pasts).
It's something (about how you rebuilt our whole world).
It's something (about you that inspires my every song).
It's something (about the home we share).
It's something (about our new quiet world).
It's something (about you that fits so perfectly with me).

It's something about you that makes me love you.
It's something about you that makes you my most precious thing.
It's something about you that makes me love you.
It's something about you...

I KISS the tears that are falling down Alex's face. And then she kisses the tears away that are also staining my cheeks.

The rest of the wedding, I'm sure, will go by perfectly just like Caroline planned. There will be wonderful food, beauty at every turn, a gorgeous cake that I'm sure Alex is going to throw in my face, and lots of dancing. But, this moment that I was able to plan for Alex is perfect, and I'm not sure that any other moment tonight will be able to top this moment.

THREE HOURS later I was almost right. No other moment topped that moment with Alex. No other dance was better or more memorable with her than that first one, despite dancing for more than two hours straight. The steak dinner Caroline ordered was delicious. The cake was ten layers of gorgeous and delicious cake of everything from vanilla to red velvet to something called chocolate death. I thought the name was a little inappropriate for a wedding, until I tasted the flavor and then I understood; more than one bite of that one would have been death by chocolate. Not that I tasted more than that because, like I suspected, Alex smeared more cake on my face than in my mouth. Everything was perfect. But, I was wrong about one thing. One dance came close to topping the first one and as far as I'm concerned is a tie with the first one; it was one Alex surprised me with.

It was a father daughter dance with the song I wrote for our daughter mixed in. It turned into a dance with my entire family: Izzy, Alex, Caroline, Drew, and Millie. Everyone I ever cared about. It was a dance filled with love and then finally tears when Alex surprised me with a couple of lyric changes:

At three years old
I lost my faith.
I remember it
Like it was yesterday.

Father used the drink to wash away
The pain of losing her
Was just too much to bear.

He left me alone in the dark.
He left me on my own to deal
With my own pain, hurt, and loss.

But light by light, you snuck into my world.

I thought I could never be a father after what mine did to me.
But you were born, and you rescued me
With your tiny fingers and cute smile.
You shined a light into my world and you ...
You saved me.

You saved me from the darkness.
You saved me from my worst self.
Daughter, you saved me
And showed me how to be a father.

At twenty-eight, I lost someone too.
I understood my father
And the pain he couldn't bear.
I thought I'd lose myself too
In the bottom of a bottle
I thought I'd get sucked into.

But you saved me.
Daughter, you saved me.
You shined a light when no one else was there.
You saved me
And showed me how to be a father.

Daughter, I'm not proud of who I was.
I've been a monster more days than one.
I don't deserve your love.

But somehow, you found the light that was still hidden in me.
You saved me.

When the pain was too much to bear
You saved me.
When I was truly scared
You saved me.
When I was crying on my knees

You saved me.
When I had nothing left in me
You saved me.
When the darkness was controlling me
You saved me.

Daughter, you saved me ...

AND THEN MY daughter's voice comes over the system and rocks my world: Dada.

ONE WORD, "DADA", brings me to my knees. One word that I have never heard my daughter say before. I look to Alex trying to understand what just happened. That wasn't really my daughter that just said my name.

She nods and smiles though confirming that yes that was my daughter's voice. When the song is over and I finally stop crying Alex explains, "About a week ago this song came on the radio when I was driving in the car with Izzy. She said "Dada" when the song was over. Her first words. I couldn't believe she had said her first word, but I knew you'd be so sad that you weren't there to hear it. So I pulled the car over and pulled the song up on the phone to play again for her. This time when the song was over I hit record and to my surprise she said "Dada" again.

"For the last week I've been trying to keep her from hearing that song around you so she wouldn't say "Dada" and I could surprise you tonight."

I look at my daughter, who is smiling happily at me, even though she is completely exhausted and should be in bed. I hug her tightly, "That's my girl."

She smiles and coos and then says, "Dada," in her high pitched little voice.

"Oh my God! She just...she just said..." I say.

Alex smiles and nods. "She's quite the littler chatter box lately. I wasn't sure I could keep her from saying that until tonight."

"Dada...Dada...Dadadadada," Izzy says.

I laugh and smile each time encouraging her to say it over and over until it becomes less "Dada" and more like a repetitive dadadaaa sound.

Caroline walks over with a passed out Millie in her arms. "I have one last surprise for you and then we can spend the rest of the night dancing or call it a night and head to your suite. It's up to you."

"Definitely heading up to our suite after the last surprise. I've waited long enough to fuck my wife," I say.

Alex blushes and Caroline says, "Eww, didn't need to hear that Landon."

"Sorry," I say as I wink at Alex even though I'm not the least bit sorry. I want Alex to know how much I want her right now. I take Alex's hand as I bounce Izzy in my arms trying to keep her from screaming out of exhaustion.

"Beth," Caroline shouts over to the side of the tent. Beth walks over and Caroline begins handing Millie off to her. "I think it's time for the girls to go to bed. There is only one last surprise and I don't think they would like it too much anyway," Caroline says to Beth.

"I can carry Izzy back and put her to bed for you," I say to Beth.

"My daughter, Courtney, can take her," Beth says pointing to her daughter that is now by her side at the mention of her name. She looks like a sweet girl. I'm guessing middle school maybe early high school age. Courtney holds out her arms to Izzy who takes to the girl immediately and crawls into her arms.

Beth and Courtney begin walking back to the hotel as Caroline excitedly tells us to follow her. Alex winks at me as we walk down the beach to the ocean, our guests following closely behind.

"So I thought you would want to go to bed tonight as soon as possible, but I knew if you were in the same hotel as Izzy you wouldn't be able to enjoy the night without worrying about checking on her and I wanted tonight to be as special as possible so..." Caroline says.

I look to Drew hoping he knows what Caroline is rambling about, but he just holds onto his wife's hand and shrugs his shoulders. He's no help. Alex on the other hand doesn't seem worried at all by whatever

Caroline has cooked up. We continue walking down the beach and when we near the water's edge, that's when Caroline's intentions become known. At the edge of the water is a beautiful yacht.

"I thought you should have your own private yacht for tonight. The only other person on it will be the captain that can take you wherever you want to go and in the morning a chef will meet you to cook you breakfast. I want tonight to be perfect for you," Caroline says.

"Thank you," I say, trying to sound excited that we have a whole boat to ourselves that I can fuck Alex on without any interruptions. I hug Caroline and then Drew before turning back to Alex. The DJ shouts over the crowd to make way for Mr. and Mrs. Landon Davis. Something that causes shivers every time I hear Alex referred to in that manner. She's mine now and nothing will take her away from me ever again.

We begin running down the beach hand in hand. Alex doesn't stumble this time; I convinced her early on to ditch the heels, which she did gladly. I don't know when the guests got sparklers, but suddenly everyone has sparklers that are being waved overhead as we run down the beach between our guests to our yacht for the evening.

Alex tries to stop at the end to hug Drew and Caroline again, but I don't let her. We've hugged them enough. I need her now. It. Can't. Wait.

She laughs and rolls her eyes at Caroline who just laughs back as I pull her onto the yacht.

"We didn't even get to tell them goodbye," Alex says.

"They understand. We will tell them good-bye tomorrow before we leave for our honeymoon. They already had sex tonight, we haven't. They get it."

Alex just laughs.

"Hi, Mr. and Mrs. Davis. I'm Kurt, I'll be your captain," a good looking man not much younger than I am says and extends his hand to us. I shake it followed by Alex and glare at the man the whole time as he touches Alex. I hate that he is good looking and our age. I figured our captain would be an old man that had been doing this for years. Not someone that I would have to worry about trying to seduce my wife.

Alex gives me a dirty look when she sees me glaring at Kurt. But I don't care. I don't trust men. No man, even a good man, has innocent thoughts.

"We are going to go out to the bay where we will stop for a minute. Mrs. Davis," Kurt stops and looks at Alex. "I mean Mrs. Caroline Davis requested that the two of you move up to the top deck for the next half hour where you will get one final surprise and that I am not to disturb you the rest of the evening, unless called upon. I will stay in the bridge unless you call upon me."

I grin, thankful that Caroline knew I would want to fuck Alex on every nook and cranny on this yacht. And that I wouldn't want to have to deal with this motherfucker any longer than I had to.

"So, after the surprise is over, I will just drive the yacht around for the night trying to give you the best views of the island unless you have a specific plan in mind. Then we will meet Theresa, your chef, near port here in the morning before pulling back into port so you can go on your honeymoon," Kurt says.

"Sounds fantastic," Alex says. "Thank you again for doing this."

"My pleasure, Mrs. Davis," Kurt says.

I smile when I hear him call her Mrs. Davis. At least he acknowledges that she is *mine*. Not *his*.

"I will leave you to it then," Kurt says, but then grimaces when he realizes that what he just said could be seen as dirty. He shakes it off quickly, "If you would just head up to those stairs there we will make our way out to the bay." He points to the stairs just behind him.

I grab Alex's hand and pull her toward the stairs happy to not have to deal with him any longer. Alex follows me and then we climb the stairs to the top deck just as the yacht begins moving. Alex moves to the railing to look out over the ocean with nothing but stars in the distance. I come up behind her and wrap my arms around her.

"It's so beautiful up here," she says.

I nod. "It is, but I can think of something a lot more beautiful that I would like to see right now," I say into her ear before I begin kissing her neck. She shivers when I do.

"Wait, we need to see whatever Caroline's last surprise is before we do that." Alex begins looking around the deck for whatever Caroline's surprise is.

I turn her toward me and plant a kiss on her lips begging her to give me what I want. "Whatever her surprise is can't be as good as me fucking you," I say against her lips.

"We have all night; we owe Caroline to see whatever last surprise this is after she planned such an amazing wedding for us."

I sigh, realizing that I won't win this fight and help Alex look around for whatever surprise Caroline planned for us. We find a bottle of champagne that I pop and pour us two glasses along with chocolate covered strawberries and a couple extra slices of our wedding cake. Not that I can think about food at a time like this, but I know Alex won't be content until we enjoy Caroline's last gift.

I take Alex's hand and walk to the railing again.

"To us living happily ever after," I say, raising my glass.

She does the same and then we clink together and then sip our drinks. As we do, a loud popping sound makes us jump behind us. We turn and that's when I see fireworks shoot up from the island. I see our guests gathered on the edge of the beach looking up at the beauty of the fireworks that are just for us. But, I'm not sure fireworks are what Alex is going to want to see on her wedding night. Not when fireworks were what Ethan used to propose to her with.

I look at her, but just wrap my arms around her tightly with her eyes focused on the sky above us.

"I'm sorry. I never told Caroline about your past with fireworks. I'm sure she meant well. We can just go below the deck until they are over. Caroline won't know whether we watched them or not—"

"No," Alex says.

"No?"

"No. We can stay right here. Erase the past with this moment. I don't want to avoid fireworks the rest of my life or anything else that could make me think of my past. I want to start new right here tonight on our wedding night. I want to build a new life without fear. And what better way to start than right now."

I smile and couldn't agree more. Tonight isn't about sex or fears or anything else. Tonight is about us starting our lives together without the fear of our pasts. Tonight is about love. And I plan on making a lot of that tonight.

A LOUD KNOCK rattles on the door over and over again. "Wake up! Wake up!" I hear Caroline's terrified voice screaming against my door.

Alex and I both pop up in our bed. I glance at the clock that reads just after six in the morning. I have no idea why Caroline is screaming on the other side of the door. If she planned a surprise this early in the morning for us I'm going to be pissed. Especially, since we have only been asleep for about two hours at this point. I get out of bed and throw underwear and a t-shirt on before opening the door. Alex stays in bed covering her naked body with a blanket.

"What?" I say in an annoyed voice as I look groggily at Caroline.

"The girls are missing," she says looking from me to Alex.

"What?" I ask again, not sure I understand what she is saying. Alex pops out of bed, puts her prosthetic leg on, and is by my side even though she is completely naked. I begin taking my shirt off and hand it to her as she automatically pulls it over her head.

Tears squirt from Caroline's eyes. "The girls have been missing for almost five hours. Beth doesn't know what happened. She was sleeping and woke up to go to the bathroom and then girls were just gone. The police have been looking all night, but no one has found them yet. They are missing."

"Why weren't we told earlier?" I ask.

"We tried to contact you but the reception on Kurt's phone was bad and all of your phones were turned off. This is the first we could get ahold of you."

Alex gives me a dirty look. I was the one that convinced her to turn our phones off last night. I was tired of the endless text messages wishing us a "happy wedding."

"I need to talk to the police now," Alex says and Caroline nods. They begin walking even though Alex is only half dressed. I grab me a shirt and shorts and some pants for Alex and then hurry after them. We reach the main deck and that's when I see Kurt staring down at

Alex's naked legs. Her body is just barely covered by my t-shirt that she is wearing. But, then he stares at her prosthetic leg and a look of disgust covers his face. I hand Alex some pants, as I begin dressing myself, even though what I really want to do is pummel the guy for thinking Alex is anything but beautiful.

We follow Caroline off the boat where the police are waiting to explain the situation. The night sky is still dark with just the tiniest bit of sunlight beginning to rise over the horizon just like the amount of hope that is left inside me. Just the tiniest bit of hope that something horrible didn't happen to our daughter, when I know even before the police tell me that our daughters have been missing for five hours. That they have been searching all night without finding a clue to where they are. That the security cameras have been turned off intentionally indicating that they think someone intentionally took them. That the girls aren't the only things missing; several of our wedding gifts are also missing. I already know something horrible happened before they ask us if we know of anyone that might have done this. I already know.

"Do you have any idea who would have had motive to kidnap your girls?" one of the officers asks.

It was a man that was recently released from prison. A man that has killed before. A man that was angry that he wasn't invited to our wedding. Or back into our lives. It was my father.

I'm going to kill him when I find him. I'm going to kill him before he hurts Izzy. She saved me, now it's my turn to save her.

I know in my heart that my father kidnapped my daughter.

Chapter Six

CAROLINE

It was my brother. He hates me for ruining his life. For not giving him the money he needs. For sending him to jail.

It was my brother. He kidnapped the girls. I can just pray that he is just using them to get money out of us. He wouldn't hurt them would he?

It was my brother...

Chapter Seven

ALEX

It was Laura.

Ethan's mother hates me for killing Ethan. For destroying her life. I shake in terror at the thought that Laura has my daughter. She won't want money. She won't want anything but revenge. She will kill Izzy to inflict the same pain on me that I inflicted on her.

It was Laura...

Chapter Eight

DREW

It was my father.

I know it was him. He hates us for not letting him back into our lives. For not letting him meet his granddaughters. He took them. He will rot in prison for this.

It was my father...

Chapter Nine

LANDON

My world is over, keeps repeating in my head after we finish speaking with the police. My whole world is over. If I thought losing Alex was going to be hard, losing Isabella will be a million times harder. I can't lose her. Even if I still have Alex, I will never be the same. A large piece of me will always be missing. I will have failed the woman I love. I will have failed to keep the one person she cared about more than me safe. Losing Izzy will destroy Alex. We won't survive it. Our happily ever after came crashing down in only a matter of hours after our wedding. Maybe we weren't meant to be together after all. This is the end. The end of my world.

My body doesn't believe my words though. My body runs through the hotel like the girls are simply playing a game of hide and seek and the police are too stupid to know where two little girls might hide. The only problem is Izzy and Millie are too little to play hide and seek. Even at their most mobile, they wouldn't have crawled or walked far. Not after the night they had draining most of their energy.

Still, I run around the hotel, opening doors I'm probably not supposed to be opening. Asking every stranger I see if they have seen two babies or a man with two babies. Every person says no. Every person looks like they are about to cry as they have to tell me no that they haven't seen my daughter. Every time I speak to someone or poke my head into another empty room, my heart drops, but my body continues on as if unfazed. As if my world hasn't already ended.

I don't know where Alex is. As soon as we were done talking to the police, I took off to the hotel not waiting for Alex, who although is fast, can't really outrun me, not on the sand. It should be a bad sign that I don't want to be with the woman I love when faced with this bad of a crisis. But I can't face her. I can't look at her when I know that our daughter is gone and neither of us can bring her back.

"Landon!" I hear Alex shout. "Landon!"

I turn slowly, hating that I have to face her. Hating that she will probably bring more bad news or hate me for not being able to protect our daughter. When I finally turn all the way around I see her running toward me with a weak smile on her face, but the smile is there. I see it and my heart melts just a little. It's good news I pray. It has to be good news. Except, she isn't holding Izzy, so it can't be good news. I frown as she nears, just doing everything I can to not break down completely and show her how scared I really am. Because, I'm terrified that my father took Izzy and I don't trust that he will keep her safe.

"Landon!" Alex says again before she is completely out of breath when she stops in front of me. I should reach out and hold her. I should comfort her, but I can't. I just can't. If I hold her, if I just touch her, I will lose it. I will cry and not be able to be her strength. I will not have the strength to find my daughter.

Alex sucks in a breath and then another, wheezing a little as she does, obviously in pain from running so fast to get to me. I try to keep from touching her as she catches her breath, but as several seconds go by I can't. I reach out and touch her shoulder just trying to comfort her. I lose it. Tears overwhelm me as my body shakes in fear. I remove my hand from her shoulder trying to regroup, but instead I fall to my knees in pain. Unbearable pain at not having my daughter.

"I'm sorry..." I say and then repeat through sobs. "Sorry..."

"Landon," Alex says. "They found her."

I don't believe her words though. I don't believe they found her. I'm dreaming. I have to be. If they found her, Alex would be with our daughter, not here with me.

"They found Izzy. They found our daughter."

"Why aren't you with her?"

"I had to have you with me. I couldn't let you suffer in pain anymore. Come on," Alex says grabbing my hand and pulling me back up just like she always does. She's always my strength and I'm her weakness.

We run through the hotel, hand in hand this time, never letting go of each other. Even though I can outrun her, I don't dare leave her, not now. Even when I'm desperate to see my daughter; desperate to feel whole again.

We make it back to the lobby when I see her. Our daughter. I try not to be selfish. I try to hold back to let Alex grab Izzy before me, but I can't. I'm selfish. I grab Izzy first and then hold her to Alex so that we hold her tightly between us.

I can finally breathe again having her back in my arms, but I won't feel the pain completely disappear until I ensure that Izzy is safe and that whoever took her is caught and punished. But, right now all I can do is hold my daughter between me and my wife.

Alex is the sensible one that breaks first and begins looking our daughter over for any signs of injury. When she is satisfied, she looks to Caroline who is holding Millie tightly between her and Drew. Both wearing the same face of desperation, relief, and love on their faces.

I look to Drew and I see the anger there. The same anger on my face. He thinks it was our father too. And he confirms that when he beats me to being able to speak to the police officers standing and watching us hold our daughters. "Do you have him in custody?" Drew asks.

"Who?" one of the officers asks.

"Our father?" Drew asks.

The officer shakes his head no. Drew and I exchange glances and then both let go of our daughters leaving them with our wives. "I'll be right back," I say to Alex who nods and snuggles our daughter.

Drew and I walk with the officers away from our daughters and wives. I want to hear the truth about what happened to my daughter and I want to do all I can to protect Alex from that truth if my father was the one involved in this.

"What happened? What do you know?" I ask the two officers standing in front of me and Drew.

The officers exchange glances and I know it isn't good.

"We don't know much. The security cameras haven't been working for the past two weeks, so we don't have any footage. The girls were found safe and sound back in the hotel suite they went missing from, but we don't know how they ended up back there. We are looking over the room trying to find any evidence of what happened, but so far have found nothing. The gifts are still missing."

"So basically you have nothing," Drew says a deep frown on his face.

"Yes," the officer says.

"So what do we do now?" I ask.

"We keep investigating and, trust me, we won't stop until we figure out who took your babies. We don't mess around when children are involved. We will figure it out. In the meantime, I would hire every person under the sun to keep your family safe. Whoever did this may not be done. This may be a warning. Just do whatever you can to keep your family close and safe."

I nod and look at Drew and we both know what we have to do. We will hire every body and security guard we can afford. And we have to keep our families close, no matter what our wives say: No tours. No work. No honeymooning, until our father is caught.

Chapter Ten

CAROLINE

It's been ten days since Alex and Landon's wedding. Ten days since our daughter went missing only to be returned hours later without any clue to what happened to her. I know though. As much as Drew thinks it was his father, I think it was my brother.

For the ten days since we have lived in fear that it could happen again, we have lived our life within the walls of our LA house with security guards watching our every move. For ten days we have kept our daughter close. We haven't even left her alone to sleep in her own room. Instead, she sleeps in her crib that we have moved next to our bed, while we take turns watching her sleep unable to sleep ourselves for fear that if we do, she will be taken from us again. We haven't let Beth watch her and we probably never will again or any other nanny. Even though it wasn't her fault, it would be too much to leave Millie with anyone that isn't family ever again. At least not until our wounds heal.

Today though, we have to take steps to ending our fear. We have to take steps to living again. If not, then my brother has won. I can't let that happen.

I have a small part in a TV show that I am supposed to do today.

I'm only booked to shoot for three hours, with two hours of makeup, before the shoot. It is a simple day really and I plan on going.

I've already arranged with security to make sure they get me and Millie there and back safely, as well as Drew, if he wants to go. I've talked with the producers of the show to let them know the situation and that I will be bringing my daughter. They have increased their security and assured me that I could have my daughter with me all through makeup and hair. And that my daughter could hang out in plain sight while I'm shooting. I'll either have one of the security guards hold her or Drew hold her in between takes. It is the best step I can think of in taking back our lives. I just don't want to hear what Drew says.

I step out of the shower and quickly dry off before putting on a pair of jeans and tank top. I leave my hair wet to dry on my way to the shoot. There is no reason to style it when the stylists at the shoot will do it however they want.

I run downstairs to grab breakfast and meet with our head of security to make sure nothing has happened over night and to change our plans to ensure our safety, when I see Drew standing in the kitchen with a frown on his face.

"Good morning," I say before I kiss him softly on the cheek. I walk past him like I would any morning to grab what I need to make a quick smoothie for breakfast. I grab the items out and put them into the blender and then walk over to Millie who is in her high chair with cereal and fruit that she is feeding herself.

"Good morning Millie," I say to her before kissing her on the only clean spot on her cheek that isn't covered in banana and cereal.

"Mama," she says back and then squeals with happiness.

I turn back to the blender and pour my smoothie into a glass, but before I can take a sip, Drew grabs my glass out of my hand and places it on the counter.

"What are you doing?" he asks.

"I was going to drink my smoothie, but I guess I'm not allowed to have breakfast now," I say raising my eyebrows at him.

"That's not what I'm talking about."

"What are you talking about then?" I ask picking up my smoothie glass and sipping on it in defiance.

"You are not going to the TV shoot today."

I frown. "You don't get to tell me what I can and can't do. You aren't my father. I can make my own decisions."

"Like hell you can! You are not going. It is not safe! And you sure as hell aren't taking my daughter anywhere!"

"I am too! I signed a contract and gave them my word. I'm going!"

"No, you aren't. We don't need the money. We are fine."

"It's not about the money. It's about me! I want a career. I want to be more than just a mother and a gold digger. And we have to get on with our lives."

"I said no. It's not safe. Now drop it!"

Millie cries as we yell at each other. I stop and go pick up our daughter. She doesn't soothe like she usually does. I hand her to Drew who tries, but she still cries.

"If you won't listen to me, listen to your daughter. Don't go."

I sigh. Drew's wrong. There aren't many things that Drew and I have disagreed on. We've only had a handful of arguments in our short time together. This might be one of the worse. I want to argue more. I want to fight, because I know Drew is wrong. We have to keep living.

I don't fight though. When I look at my daughter crying in her father's arms, I know today isn't the day. Soon, I will fight to move on with our lives; just not today.

Chapter Eleven

ALEX

It's been fifteen days since our wedding. Fifteen days since we were able to wake up without worrying about what dangers lurk behind every corner. Fifteen days since we were able to go to bed and actually sleep instead of worrying if someone was going to take Izzy while we slept. So, it's been fifteen days since we actually slept. It's been fifteen days since either of us left the house. Fifteen days of silence and unspoken words.

We both have our suspicions over who could have taken Izzy. I think it was Laura, Landon thinks it was his father. And I'm sure Caroline and Drew have their own theories. The only ones that don't have any theories yet are the police. We have had weekly meetings with the police to discuss our case, but each time we do they have no suspects, no theories. Each time we do, we leave feeling more empty and depressed than before, because there is no end in sight to us feeling safe again.

Fifteen days. It's been too long. Too long to go without sunshine. Landon won't even let us go in our own backyard. Too long without feeling comfort from my husband. Too long without sex. We haven't slept together since our wedding night. We should be on our honeymoon right now. This should be one of the best weeks of our lives.

Instead, Landon is too focused on protecting Izzy and I to think of sex.

It's made me have doubts. Doubts about his attraction to me, about my beauty, my intelligence, my strength. Doubts that maybe we made a mistake. That maybe we shouldn't have gotten married.

Today, things are going to change though. Today, I'm going to take Izzy to the park. We need sunshine, we need air. We need to be able to breathe again. We need to have one hour of just feeling like ourselves. I know that there is danger out there that could be after my family, but I have never run from danger before. If I give in to the fear, I will lose myself again. I will lose everything I have gained over these past few months. I will lose all of my strength. I will not teach my daughter that it is okay to live your life afraid.

"You going to be okay here by yourself today?" Landon asks, bringing me away from my thoughts and back to reality. Now is the time. I have to tell him now what we are doing. That I am taking Izzy to the park today. And he can come or not.

I hear the doorbell. "That will be Drew and Caroline and the security team," Landon says.

"What?" I ask confused.

"Sorry baby," Landon says kissing me softly on the cheek. "I wasn't sure if you heard me when you were in the shower, but Drew and I have to go meet with the label today. They won't let us put it off any longer. We have to set the release date for the new album I'm working on and sign some contracts. We tried to get out of it, but there is no getting out of this. We have had it planned for weeks, as soon as we got back from our honeymoon."

I nod and smile. Happy that we are getting out of the house. "So, we are all going to the office today?" I ask, my smile getting larger at the thought of just getting out of the house.

Landon frowns. "No, Drew and I are going. You, Caroline, and the babies are staying here. I had Caroline come over so that she could bring her security team here to watch you guys as well, so if we take a couple of our men with us there will still be plenty of security here."

"But..."

Landon kisses me firmly on the lips shutting me up. After not getting any physical attention for two weeks this kiss feels like everything I have been missing. Even though in reality the kiss was nothing more than a quick peck on the lips. There was no heat, no emotion behind the kiss. It was just a kiss. But I'm going crazy needing more. Needing sex. Needing love.

I watch from the living room as one of our security members lets Drew, Caroline, and Millie in. As soon as they enter, Landon gives them his attention instead of me. He and Drew begin talking and then leave without telling me goodbye. Without even acknowledging that I am here. I know Landon is under a lot of stress, we both are, but I'm tired of feeling unloved. I'm tired of feeling like an afterthought. I'm tired of feeling alone.

Caroline walks into the living room carrying Millie and places her on the floor next to Izzy who is playing quietly on the rug. Caroline plops down on the couch next to me. She looks just as tired and exhausted as I am.

"Want to take the girls to the park with me?" I ask.

Caroline smiles, "Hell yeah! I would do anything to not feel like a locked up prisoner."

I smile. I don't know why I ever hated her.

THE PARK IS AMAZING. We brought our entire security team so we feel completely safe if not a little weird to have a dozen men with us at the park, but we are safe. And Landon and Drew have no reason to be mad at us when they get back. They didn't ever tell us we couldn't take the girls to the park, because they never gave us the opportunity to ask. And we took the entire security team. We are safe.

We push both of the girls on the swings as they both laugh. It's been almost two weeks since I have seen Izzy this happy. She's picked up on Landon's and I's anxious energy and in turn has become a fussy, crying baby like she never has before. But, now she seems back to her happy self. If only for an hour or so.

I glance over at Caroline and Millie who both look happy as well.

Even though I'm happy now I don't want to go back to the fear of the last fifteen days. I don't want to go back to being unhappy.

"What are you thinking about?" Caroline asks.

I sigh. "Nothing."

"Come on tell me. We both need some girl gossip to get us through these next few days with our husbands."

I bite my bottom lip. Caroline and I have grown close over the last few months. Raising our girls together and being married to twin brothers has helped, but it is still hard for me to talk much about Landon with her. Knowing that they used to date, that she used to be in love with him, that he almost married her is hard. It still hurts and no matter how amazing she has been to me since, it still doesn't erase what she did in the past. It still doesn't take away the pain. It still hurts. "I don't think I can."

Caroline frowns. "I'm sorry. I was hoping that giving you this fantastic wedding would go a long way toward you trusting me. For you realizing that I don't have any feelings for Landon and that Landon and I were the worst for each other. That you and Landon make sense and always have. He never loved me like he loves you."

I nod. "I'm sorry. I have forgiven you. I have moved past it. It's just hard for me to talk about Landon much with you. I want to though. I don't have many girlfriends that I can talk honestly with."

"Then let me start and see if that helps. Drew is driving me crazy! I feel like he is suffocating me. I feel trapped. He won't let me go anywhere. He won't let me do anything. We haven't had sex since your wedding! I'm going crazy over here.

"I never thought I would be the one begging him for sex. His appetite for sex has always been good. But, in the last two weeks it's like we have gone from being husband and wife to just two roommates that live together. I know he wants to protect Millie and I from whomever did this to us, but this is ridiculous. I'm losing my mind!"

I laugh. "Me too. Landon is driving me crazy too! We are supposed to be just getting back from our honeymoon. We aren't supposed to be going through a dry spell right now. It's like it hasn't even crossed his mind that I have needs that need to be met."

"Davis men are clueless," Caroline says.

And we both laugh in agreement over our silly husbands' behaviors.

"I think we should change that tonight. We are both hot, sexy women that have needs. We both have plenty of sexy lingerie, that I don't know about you, but when I wear mine I have a hundred percent success rate when worn. I say we take back our lives and start in the bedroom."

I smile. Her plan is so simple I don't know why I didn't think of it before, but of course that would work. Except, an uneasy feeling in my stomach creeps up at the thought. A feeling that tells me why I haven't tried it. I have doubts that it will work. I have doubts that Landon still finds me attractive.

"Excuse me, Mrs. Davis and Mrs. Davis," Jackson, head of our security, says causing Caroline and I to both laugh at how ridiculous it is that they refer to both of us as Mrs. Davis. "But I think we should leave now."

"Why?" I ask.

"Because we believe that man over there is a threat," Jackson nods in the direction of the far side of the park where an older man in his late fifties or early sixties sits on a bench staring straight at us.

I glance over at Caroline who is frozen in fear as she stares at the man. She knows who it is and is terrified.

"Okay, I agree," I say to Jackson.

"We brought the car around to this side so you don't have to walk past him," Jackson says.

I nod. I grab Millie first and thrust her into Caroline's arms. Millie immediately begins to cry when her mother's anxious arms tighten around her.

"Caroline," I say trying to snap her out of her frozen state so that she can take care of her daughter. But Caroline remains frozen.

"Caroline!" I say louder slapping her softly on the cheek.

Caroline turns to look at me and I see the pale whiteness on her face. She's scared.

"Take Millie to the car. Now," I say.

Caroline doesn't acknowledge that I spoke or slapped her, but she does begin walking toward the direction of our car.

I pick Izzy up out of the swing calmly trying not to scare my child and evoke fear like Caroline did to Millie.

"Who is he?" I ask Jackson.

Jackson clears his throat buying time to decide if he should tell me who the man is or not. "We believe it is Mr. Davis' father."

I nod and chance a glance over at the man again who is now surrounded by at least three members of our security team from what I can tell. He doesn't look threatening. And this might be my only chance to put a stop to this if he is really behind all of this.

"Jackson follow me," I say holding my daughter tightly in my arms. Hoping that if I bring Izzy with me I will be able to read what his intentions are. If he really wants to hurt her or if he just sees her as a child.

"I don't think that is a good idea, Mrs. Davis," Jackson says.

"I understand. You are not responsible for what happens when I don't follow your orders, but please follow me and give me the best protection that you can," I say and begin walking toward Landon's father.

I'm tired of being told what to do. I'm tired of living in fear. It ends. Today.

I walk over to Landon's father with a fierce look on my face. I will not show him that I'm afraid because I'm not. I don't feel danger coming from this man. I don't feel scared that I'm not going to be able to hold my own with him. I know I'm strong enough. That was the only thing Ethan taught me. I am strong. I am fierce. I can face anything. And holding my daughter in my arms only makes me that much more protective to ensure that nothing happens to her.

"Hello, Alex. Thank you for meeting me. As your security team has probably already told you, I'm Landon's father, Neal," he says.

I nod. "Don't thank me for meeting you. If you wanted to meet with me, you should have called and arranged a time like any normal person would. Not kidnapped my daughter to get my attention."

Neal looks at Izzy who is smiling at him. He smiles back. "I didn't kidnap your daughter. I would never do anything to jeopardize getting a chance to be in her life. And I have tried calling several times. Your husband won't take my calls."

I frown. "Do you blame him? You haven't exactly been a good father to him. You've been in jail most of his adult life. Why would he want to talk to you?"

"Because I'm his father and I've changed," he says.

"I don't believe you."

Disappointment covers his face. He looks from me to Izzy. "What's her name?" he asks with softness in his eyes.

I hesitate, but then answer. There is no harm in telling him her name. "Isabella, but we call her Izzy."

"Izzy," he says smiling at my daughter.

Izzy smiles back to the man and reaches out to him wanting him to hold her.

Neal's eyes widen like he wasn't expecting that. He probably hasn't felt love in a very long time. He probably hasn't been hugged or shown love from anyone since his wife died. A wife that, from what Landon has told me, his father desperately loved. I could see how after losing someone that you desperately love you could turn into a completely different person.

Without thinking, I place Izzy into his arms. He freezes obviously not sure if he should be holding her. My security team practically runs to his side to remove her from his arms.

"It's okay," I say to my security team.

"What do you think of your granddaughter?" I ask him.

"She's beautiful," he says as he begins to hold her like someone experienced with dealing with children.

I smile. It would be nice to have one grandparent in her life. He's the only one Izzy has. It would be nice to try to rebuild a relationship with him. If not for Landon's sake, then for Izzy's. She doesn't deserve to grow up without grandparents simply because Landon and him don't get along.

I watch as Izzy gives one of her wet open kisses to him. I smile as he looks on lovingly at my daughter. He may have made mistakes in the past, but I'm happy to forgive him. Happy to give him another shot even if it means we have to bring our entire security team with us every time he meets with Izzy for a while.

I glance over at Jackson who is obviously getting anxious the longer we stay here.

"We need to get going," I say.

He nods and hands me Izzy back.

"Thank you," he says with what seems genuine affection.

"I'll talk to Landon for you. I can't promise anything though. Understand?

"Yes, you don't need to do that. I don't want to come between you two, but I'm not going to tell you not to. It might be my only chance to regain a relationship with my sons and grandchildren. So, thank you."

I nod and then turn and walk out back to our car. Caroline is silent as I climb into the car. I doubt she is happy with what I just did. And maybe she is right. She knows his past more than I do. She lived it. I didn't. But, if anybody knows anything about asking for forgiveness it's her.

Jackson climbs in and then begins driving. He doesn't speak to me either.

I sigh. I may have just made a really stupid mistake. I may have just put my entire family in danger. Or I may have laid the foundation for starting to heal wounds that could lead to our family becoming one again. Either way, I know I changed the dynamics in our family. I just hope I did the right thing.

Chapter Twelve

DREW

I WATCH Landon pace back and forth in the living room of his house. Desperate for Alex and Izzy to come home. We heard from Jackson that they went to the park and are on their way home now. It's not a very comforting feeling knowing that they left without speaking to us first. Knowing that they could be putting themselves in unnecessary danger. But, I'm holding myself together better than Landon.

Maybe it's because of what Landon has gone through almost losing Alex countless times that makes it harder for him to be without her. Maybe he loves her more then I love Caroline, I shake my head though knowing that's not true. My heart aches not having her with me. Maybe I just don't understand the danger like he does. Whatever the reason, it hurts to watch him in so much pain and anguish.

"They will be here soon," I say trying to get Landon to calm down. If not, I'm afraid he is going to say something he doesn't mean to Alex when she returns, and the last thing we need is them fighting.

"Don't," is all he says.

I sigh and wait. And wait. And wait...

I stand immediately when I hear the back door open. Landon is already running to the door and I follow only a step behind him. I exhale when I see all four of them safe and sound. I push past Landon, who is grabbing Izzy from Alex's arms, to Caroline and Millie. I embrace them both in my arms and that is when I see Caroline. Her face whiter than a ghost, without any emotion on her face.

"What's wrong? Are you hurt?" I ask.

Caroline doesn't answer.

"What the fuck were you thinking?" I hear Landon shout.

So much for remaining calm when the girls returned.

"Landon, enough. That's not helpful," I say.

But, it doesn't stop the two of them from continuing to shout at each other.

"I was thinking I didn't want to be treated like a god damn prisoner in my own home!" Alex says.

"You could have gotten Izzy fucking killed!" Landon says.

"Oh, I see! All you fucking care about anymore is Izzy! What about my safety? What about me?" Alex screams.

"You're a fucking grown up. Or at least claim to be. You obviously think you can make your own decisions as far as your safety goes."

"Hey!" I yell interrupting them. "Stop and tell me why my wife is frozen in fear, then you can go back to tearing each other apart."

"Because, we saw your father," Alex says angrily.

"What?" I grab hold of Caroline realizing now that Landon has every right to be angry. That they really were in danger. That Alex put them in danger.

"We saw your father. I talked to him. I don't think he was the one that took the babies," Alex says.

Caroline stirs at Alex's words. "You put us in danger. You don't know what he has done. You don't know the type of man that he is. You don't know..." Caroline trails off.

Alex looks at Caroline and I expect to see anger coming from her toward Caroline for not taking her side, but there is none there.

"I think you should take Caroline and Millie home. It's been a long day," Alex says.

I nod and begin moving Caroline and Millie back to our car. Our security team follows. I shake with fear as we climb into the back of the car. Millie in the car seat, Caroline in the middle, and me on the other end. I hold onto my wife desperately with both hands as

Jonathan begins driving us back to our house. I could have lost them both. In that moment I realize how desperate I am for her. I have to have her. Now. I have to feel close to her. I don't care that Millie is right next to us. I don't care that Jonathan is in the front seat. I need her. Now.

I turn her head toward me and kiss her firmly on the lips. She moans like I haven't touched her in weeks and that's when I realize I haven't. I haven't kissed her since their wedding. No wonder she is so wound up.

She slips her tongue into my mouth begging me for more. I massage her tongue with mine as I grab hold of her hair showing her that as soon as we get back to our house I will have her. I will make all of the pain and fear go away. I will fuck her and make love to her. I will erase everything except us.

I expect it to be enough. We live twenty minutes away. We can make it twenty minutes, but her moans grow more desperate. Her hand grabs at my crotch trying to find my cock beneath my jeans but coming up empty. It drives me wild, but I know I'm not the one that needs comfort right now. I didn't have to face my father, she did. She wasn't the one that shut me out of her life for the last couple of weeks, I was.

I continue kissing her, but open my eyes to look around the car to find anything that I could use. I glance in the back and find an old jacket of mine. I drape it over Caroline's lap thankful that she almost always wears a dress or skirt and that today is no different. She's wearing a short skirt giving me easy access.

I glance up at Jonathan who either doesn't know what is happening or is doing his best to not look. I glance over at Millie who has fallen asleep in her car seat. And then I give my wife the pleasure that she is so desperate for that I have denied her for too long. I slip my hand between the jacket and reach up her skirt. I move her panties that are covering her entrance. They are soaked with wetness that I caused with just a couple kisses.

I don't make her wait any longer. I slip my one finger inside her and then another. She moans louder and I do my best to smother her moans with my lips, but I know Jonathan knows exactly what is happening. I don't care though. All I care about is bringing my wife pleasure.

I rub my thumb over her soft bud as my fingers slip in and out of her slit. Each time I do, her moans get louder, her body tightens showing me that she is close. I rub faster even though my cock twitches in pain at not getting the attention it needs. I rub and thrust my fingers faster, harder until I feel her tighten around my fingers. With my other hand I cover her mouth as she comes doing my best to muffle her screams.

When she stops convulsing, I remove my fingers and lick them clean. Her bright eyes stay locked on mine as I do promising more the second we get home. I lick my lips and then pull her close. We have at least ten more minutes to go until we get home and if she so much as looks at me again, I'm going to fuck her right here in the car and not care that Jonathan can see. I need my wife and can't believe I have been so stupid these last few weeks to not have had her every night. It's the only way to keep us calm. It's the only way to stay connected. It's the only way to survive together.

I just hope Landon and Alex learn the same lesson.

Chapter Thirteen

LANDON

"WHY? Give me one good reason that you would have been talking to my father. He killed someone. He's a dangerous man. He kidnapped Izzy and Millie. Why just why?" I ask, hoping that Alex is going to say that he forced her to. That my father had a gun on her and that was why she talked to him. That she didn't have a choice.

"Because he's family and deserves a chance at our forgiveness," is what she says instead.

"Fuck that! He doesn't deserve anything from us. He deserves to rot in prison for the rest of his life."

Alex just shakes her head. "Landon, just listen to me. I think your father has changed. I think— "

"I don't want to hear what you think. You're wrong! Don't fucking leave this house again, do you hear me?"

"You can't just order me around like I'm your slave. We have to be able to have discussions and decide what is best for both of us."

"No, you fucked up! You put my daughter's life at risk. You don't get to have any say— "

"She's my daughter too."

"Like hell she is! She isn't when you make stupid fucking mistakes!"

"Please Landon. Just stop and listen. I may have made a mistake, but I might not have. We still don't know it was your father— "

"I do. I know it was my father!"

Alex collapses on the couch. We have been yelling at each other and pacing back and forth in the living room for over an hour now. Izzy is in her room with Jackson. I didn't want her to hear us screaming, but I thought we would be done by now. I was wrong.

I don't sit down. I'm too upset at Alex to sit. I can't believe she put Izzy's life at risk like that. Or her own. How stupid can she be?

I continue pacing and Alex continues sitting, both fuming. Both stubborn and unwilling to give in. Both exhausted and terrified. Until...

"Fuck me," Alex says.

"Huh?" I ask frozen in my tracks. Not believing what she just said.

"Fuck me," Alex says again.

I pace, my face getting redder with anger. "You don't want me to fuck you right now. I'm so mad at you I would hurt you. And then you would be asking me for a divorce instead of just asking me to listen to you."

"You won't hurt me. Fuck me."

"No," I say shaking my head.

"Please."

"No."

Alex gets up suddenly and I think maybe she is going to apologize for what she did. That she will say she was wrong and will listen to me now, but when I see the look of defiance on her face I know that she hasn't give in. I know that I haven't won.

She storms past me and heads toward the garage. I run after her grabbing her hand and jerking her back before she can get to the door.

"You aren't going anywhere!"

"Yes. I. Am. I can't stay here. I can't stay with you when you are like this."

"You aren't going. It's not safe!"

"I can't be with you right now."

"Fine. You stay, I'll go!"

"Fine." Alex storms toward our bedroom while I head outside. I call Jackson and tell him to not let Alex leave no matter what. I tell one of the security guards to follow me and then I climb into Silvia and begin driving away hoping that just driving and giving Alex some space will calm me down.

Instead, all I think about is why the hell did I turn down sex with Alex? What the fuck was I thinking?

It's been fifteen long days since the last time I had her. I've kept my distance because I can't stand that I let her down. I can't stand that I risked our child's life. I don't deserve her love.

But, right now I feel like an idiot for not showing her that I love her. I consider turning the car around and telling her I need her, but I can't. I'm too afraid that I will hurt her and she will hate me. I can't.

Instead, I relive the night of our wedding over and over in my head.

A perfect starry night overhead.

Alex naked in the moonlight.

Her screaming my name almost as if it was her first time.

The cool salty air mixing with our own sweat.

Her tight body on mine.

Wax.

Crops.

Rope.

None of that was needed.

It was just us.

Just love for the first time without pain.

That night was everything.

And in an instance I lost everything.

Chapter Fourteen

CAROLINE

"THANK you for coming in and telling us about your experience with Neal at the park. We will definitely be bringing him in for questioning," the officer says.

I nod.

"We will bring in your nanny to see if she recognizes Neal along with Alex and Landon," the officer says.

Drew stands and shakes the officer's hand and I do the same before following Drew out of the office. We walk past Landon who is waiting for his turn to speak with the police with Izzy in his arms. Drew nods, but we don't stop and talk. There is nothing to say anyway.

I spot Alex speaking with Neal over in the corner and my heart hardens. I shouldn't be mad at Alex for speaking with Drew's father. She didn't know better. She didn't know what he had done, not really. But, I'm mad. Angry. Furious.

I shouldn't be so easy to anger. I should be able to forgive Alex easily after she has forgiven me so easily, but I can't. I'm too angry.

I take Millie out of Jonathan's hands and then walk to the car. Drew follows. I quickly buckle Millie in and climb in followed by Drew. I think back to the last time we were in the car. How Drew gave me everything I wanted. How amazing that felt. Now I'm so angry that I wouldn't let him touch me there or anywhere.

Drew reads me well keeping his distance as Jonathan begins driving us back home. A few minutes pass though, and I find Drew gently rubbing my hand. I pull away, but he grabs it back and starts holding my hand tightly and rubbing it until I begin to relax.

"I know. I'm scared too," he says.

That's when I realize what the emotion I feel is. It's not anger at Alex that is making me crazy. It's fear.

Chapter Fifteen

ALEX

I KNOW THE TRUTH. We aren't in danger at all. We've just all been through so much that as soon as something happens we all assume we are in danger.

I get it. I felt it too, but we were all wrong.

We aren't in danger.

It is all just a simple misunderstanding.

That isn't what I'm going to have a hard time convincing everyone of though. What I'm going to have a hard time convincing everyone to do is to forgive when forgiveness might not have been fully earned. I did it for Caroline and it has made us grow closer than ever. I forgave Landon and Landon forgave me. When it comes to family, forgiveness can be found. There is one last wound left to heal.

"Go to Drew and Caroline's place," I say.

"Yes. Mrs. Davis," Jackson says turning toward their house.

"Why?" Landon asks.

"Just trust me."

Chapter Sixteen

DREW

THE DOORBELL RINGS, but I don't bother getting up from the couch. I'm too drained to be able to move. Fear exhausts you and then gives nothing back.

Jonathan goes to open the door and lets in Alex, Landon, and Izzy. I sigh. I don't have the energy to yell or argue or discuss what is happening to us. I barely had the energy to carry Millie inside and make sure Caroline wasn't going to completely break down.

"Unless you are here to tell me something new, like they have evidence to put my father behind bars again, I don't have the energy to talk," I say.

"I do," Alex says.

I jump up along with Caroline who was half asleep on the couch next to me. I look to Landon who seems to have no idea what is wife is talking about. I sit down hesitantly on the couch when I see Landon. I see that he doesn't seem to think that they should be here. Caroline sits back down next to me. Both of us only holding on to the tiniest bit of hope that Alex is going to say anything to calm our fears. To make us feel safe again.

Alex walks over and takes a seat on our love seat. Landon puts Izzy on the floor and then sits in the chair opposite her. It's obvious the two still haven't made up.

"So...? Is he in jail?" I ask unable to wait for Alex to speak.

"No," Alex says. "I didn't come here to tell you that your father has been arrested. I did come here to tell you the truth."

I sit forward in my seat along with Caroline. Landon doesn't move, but I see him out of the corner of my eye and he is just as tense as the rest of us.

"Courtney was the one that took the girls," Alex says.

"No way. Courtney is a sweetheart. She wouldn't kidnap the girls," Caroline says.

Alex smiles. "Exactly, Courtney didn't kidnap them. What Beth didn't tell us is that she has been battling breast cancer. She's been on chemo for the last couple of months and is completely exhausted. The girls were fussy and Courtney wanted to make sure her mom got good sleep. So, when the girls began crying she took them out of the room to her room just around the corner. She got the girls back to sleep and then fell asleep herself. By the time she brought them back, she realized the police thought someone had kidnapped the girls and was scared she did something wrong so she didn't say anything and thought things would just blow over."

I close my eyes realizing for the first time that we are safe. That we were stupid and jumped to conclusions.

"What about the gifts that were missing?" I ask.

"A couple teenage kids of the guests took some of the electronic gifts, but they later returned the gifts. No harm done."

"So my father was innocent?" I ask.

Alex nods.

"Our father is not innocent. Just because he wasn't there doesn't me he is innocent," Landon says.

Alex frowns, "I need to show you something." Alex gets up and goes to the car then returns with a bag. She opens the bag and begins to pull paper after paper out and begins handing them to us. "This is every lead your father looked into when he found out the girls had been missing. He was worried about them. He tried to do everything he could to help. He was the one that came to the conclusion that he thought Courtney had taken the girls. He told me and I went and talked to Courtney and found out the truth."

She pauses and waits for it all to sink in. "He's messed up maybe more than any of us, but he's trying now. He's trying to be the grandfather when he couldn't be a father. He is asking for forgiveness and a chance to be in our daughters' lives. He's asking for a chance to love someone again. You of everyone should know what it feels like to lose someone you desperately love. You can't blame him for screwing up when he lost the love of his life."

"I'm not going to make this decision alone. I've learned my lesson there. We either all agree he can be back in our lives or he doesn't enter back into any of our lives."

Alex stands and walks to the door putting her hand on the handle. "I just want us to give him a chance."

She opens the door and my father hesitantly walks in. He looks so different from the last time I saw him in prison. He cut his hair shorter. He's shaved. He's wearing nice clothing. He looks better than I've seen him since I was a young child.

His eyes immediately go to Izzy and Millie and he smiles sweetly at them. He doesn't take a seat, instead he stands hesitantly at the edge of the living room. He looks to Landon and then me, "I'm not here to ask for forgiveness. I don't deserve it. I'm just here to tell you how sorry I am. That I have done my best to change since I got out of jail. I realized after you came to visit that I was wrong. I got clean. I've been clean three months now. I got a job working with waste management. It's not a glamorous job, but it pays the bills and keeps me out of trouble. I would love a chance to have a relationship with my granddaughters in any capacity that you will let me, but I'm not sure it is deserved. And, no matter what I will understand your decision. I will continue to try to make amends for what I did no matter what your decision."

I look into my father's eyes and for the first time since I was little, I see him. Not the alcohol or drugs or abuse. I see a man that has fucked up too many times. A man that is finally broken enough that he is now trying to pick up the pieces. I can't forgive him for what he has done to me, to Landon, to the man he killed, to my mother. I can't forgive him for any of that.

But, I can give him a chance to have a relationship with my daughter and to not live in fear that something bad is going to happen. I can give him a chance.

"I don't forgive you, but I want you to have a chance to form a relationship with my daughter. But, only if Landon agrees," I say.

Chapter Seventeen

LANDON

I LOOK at Drew shocked at what he is saying. That he is giving our father another chance. I look at Alex and see that she agrees. That she was right, I was wrong. That she has done more to protect our family than I ever have.

I look to my daughter who is smiling at my father like she has known him her whole life. Can I really prevent her from having a relationship with her grandfather?

I look to Caroline. Alex forgave her even when she had no reason to. She forgave Caroline, and it was one of the best things that happened to either of them. It gave Caroline a chance to right her wrongs and become a better person. I know what Alex would do, so that's what I will do.

"I will give you a chance to get to know my daughter. It will be supervised since you have not gained my trust yet. But, I will give you a chance to be saved by my daughter just like I was."

My father smiles at me, although I can't smile back. I have more to say and this is hard, but it is the right thing.

"One more thing. Father, I forgive you. You don't deserve it and we will probably never mend our relationship, but I forgive you."

Tears stream out of my father's eyes. "Thank you," he finally says.

I nod. Alex was right. She's always right. We have to stop fearing just because bad shit happened to us in our pasts. Our past experiences don't affect our future. I walk over to my wife and kiss her hard. I need her now. I need her to know that I still love her and always will. I need her to know that we can live happily ever after and our pasts don't define us.

When I release her, she winks at me and then whispers in my ear, "Meet me in the bathroom in five minutes."

I smile. God I love my wife. She's perfect for me and I can't wait to spend the rest of our lives together without constant fear. Just love, a little forgiveness, and family.

Epilogue

ALEX

One Year Later

"Come on Alex, we are going to miss our flight!" Landon shouts, as he enters Izzy's bedroom.

"I know, I know. I'm just not ready to leave her yet."

Landon holds us both tightly before pulling Izzy from my arms and swings her around. She laughs as he does.

"My dad is going to do a great job watching her and Caroline and Millie will be here to help out," Landon says.

"I know; I'll just miss her."

Landon sighs. "We are only going to be gone ten days."

"Ten days is a long time," I whine.

Landon grabs me pulling me tightly to his body so that I can feel his erection pushing into my stomach. "My cock disagrees with you. Ten days will feel like nothing to it. We need this honeymoon."

"Watch your mouth around my granddaughter," Neal says as he enters the bedroom and steals Izzy from Landon.

Landon smiles at his father, not caring in the least that he was just scolded like a teenager. I think after missing that part as a teenager his father has done a lot to make it up to him since. It's surprising how fast relationships can heal after forgiveness is finally granted.

"Hurry up you two or you are going to miss your flight," Neal says as he carries Izzy out of the room.

Landon grabs my ass pulling me back to him as his lips land on mine. He pulls my lip into his mouth biting hard like he always does when he really wants me and can't wait any longer. The mix of pain and pleasure is usually my undoing. But, I plan on making him suffer a little for making me leave my daughter for ten days when I'm this emotional.

I pull away and a frown forms over Landon's face. "Oh, come on we have time for a quickie..."

I laugh. "We do not. You just said we had to go or we would miss our flight. Plus, I'm going to have to stop at least twice on the way to the airport, because I'll have to pee or throw up or— "

"Wait, what? Why? Are you sick? Please, tell me you aren't sick. I need this honeymoon," Landon begs completely clueless.

I smile. "No, I'm not sick."

"Then what?"

Landon loses himself in thought for a second while I give him one last hint and rub my already beginning to swell belly despite being maybe eight weeks along, at most. This time around I'm afraid I will gain more weight than the last.

"You're pregnant!"

I nod and smile and then he is lifting and spinning me in almost the same way he did to Izzy. He kisses all over my body and down to my belly and plants several kisses there. He stands suddenly, "But traveling can't be good for the baby."

I laugh. "I already talked with a doctor, it's fine. And, after what happened when I was pregnant with Izzy, I'm sure this baby will be just fine with ten days of relaxation."

Landon relaxes just a little, but I know deep down he is going to worry this entire trip. Doing everything possible to protect me and this unborn baby even though there is nothing to fear. There is nothing to worry about.

"What do you think? Is this one a boy or girl?" he asks excitedly.

"No clue, we still have a few weeks before we will know for sure."

He sighs. "We should think of names..."

I shake my head at my silly husband but happy to see he is just as excited about this one. I begin walking downstairs so that we don't miss our flight as Landon follows.

"How about Aiden?"

"Maybe."

"Or Logan?"

"Maybe."

"Or Mason?"

"Maybe."

"Or Eli?"

"How come these are all boy names?"

"Because, I'm pretty sure you're having a boy."

I smile, knowing that either way boy or girl, Landon will treat the baby like a prince or princess, just like he has done to Izzy. And, that either way this baby will grow up with an entire family worth of love.

Landon stops dead in his tracks. "Yes!"

I turn and look at him. "What?"

"I beat Drew to having the second child first."

I laugh again at my husband and then pull him into a kiss. It's silly how he and Drew are together. Loving one another, but always competing for the best career. The girl. And now the first to have more children. Still they love each other just like families should. And I don't have the heart to tell him that Caroline is almost three months pregnant. He doesn't need to know that yet.

Landon pulls away. "So, this is what happy feels like?"

"Yes, this is what happy feels like without fear. It feels like love."

The End

Thank you so much for reading Aligned: The Complete Series!

JOIN ELLA's NEWSLETTER & NEVER MISS A SALE OR NEW RELEASE → ellamiles.com/freebooks

Love swag boxes & signed books?
SHOP MY STORE → store.ellamiles.com

Also by Ella Miles

LIES SERIES:

Lies We Share: A Prologue

Vicious Lies

Desperate Lies

Fated Lies

Cruel Lies

Dangerous Lies

Endless Lies

SINFUL TRUTHS:

Sinful Truth #1

Twisted Vow #2

Reckless Fall #3

Tangled Promise #4

Fallen Love #5

Broken Anchor #6

TRUTH OR LIES:

Taken by Lies #1

Betrayed by Truths #2

Trapped by Lies #3

Stolen by Truths #4

Possessed by Lies #5

Consumed by Truths #6

DIRTY SERIES:

Dirty Obsession

Dirty Addiction

Dirty Revenge

Dirty: The Complete Series

ALIGNED SERIES:

Aligned: Volume 1 (Free Series Starter)

Aligned: Volume 2

Aligned: Volume 3

Aligned: Volume 4

Aligned: The Complete Series Boxset

UNFORGIVABLE SERIES:

Heart of a Thief

Heart of a Liar

Heart of a Prick

Unforgivable: The Complete Series Boxset

MAYBE, DEFINITELY SERIES:

Maybe Yes

Maybe Never

Maybe Always

Definitely Yes

Definitely No

Definitely Forever

STANDALONES:

Pretend I'm Yours

Pretend We're Over

Finding Perfect

Savage Love

Too Much

Not Sorry

Hate Me or Love Me: An Enemies to Lovers Romance Collection

About the Author

Ella Miles writes steamy romance, including everything from dark suspense romance that will leave you on the edge of your seat to contemporary romance that will leave you laughing out loud or crying. Most importantly, she wants you to feel everything her characters feel as you read.

Ella is currently living her own happily ever after near the Rocky Mountains with her high school sweetheart husband. Her heart is also taken by her goofy five year old black lab who is scared of everything, including her own shadow.

Ella is a USA Today Bestselling Author & Top 50 Bestselling Author.

Stalk Ella at:
www.ellamiles.com
ella@ellamiles.com

Lightning Source UK Ltd.
Milton Keynes UK
UKHW010108100223
416720UK00001B/6